W9-BKW-646

DAVID BALL

EMPIRES
_of_ SAND

A DELL BOOK

Published by
Dell Publishing
a division of
Random House, Inc.
1540 Broadway
New York, New York 10036

Copyright © 1999 by David W. Ball
Cover art © by Redstone Studios
Map Illustrations by David Cain

Book design by Glen M. Edelstein

Library of Congress Catalog Card Number: 99-24798

ISBN: 0-440-23668-1

Reprinted by arrangement with Bantam Books

Printed in the United States of America

Published simultaneously in Canada

March 2001

10 9 8 7 6 5 4 3 2 1

OPM

*Please turn the page for more
extraordinary acclaim. . . .*

For Melinda, Ben, and Li
Without whom there would be no light

And for Carol and Jack
Without whom there would have been no beginning

ACKNOWLEDGMENTS

As a reader I never knew the importance of a book's editor. As a writer I have learned the truth of it. I cannot adequately express my thanks to Beverly Lewis, the wizard at Bantam whose vision so dramatically helped this novel and whose keen insights saved me from myself more than once. Assistant editor Christine Brooks always kept the wheels turning, once even helping me to find the manuscript in a snowdrift.

My agent, Jean Naggar, has been marvelous throughout a long process, lighting the way with patience and grace. She is surrounded with talented colleagues: Frances Kuffel, Jennifer Weltz, Alice Tasman, Joan Lilly, and Russell Weinberger. I am fortunate indeed to know such a group.

Friends and family suffered without complaint through the endless travails of the manuscript, offering suggestions and support, or sometimes bringing brownies just in the nick of time. To these wonderful people—Carol Ball, Sue Ruhl, Barbara Burton, Susie Cardin, Erin McIntire, Linzie Burton, Chuck and Denise Elliott, Laura Uhls, Isa Ploehn, Ron Peterson, Allen Lane, Jody Wheeler, Renée and Peter Berglund, Joseph Rossa McGrail, Alma Markoff, Cathy Fleury, Carol and Martha Rasmussen—I am forever indebted. And there are no words to express my gratitude to my wife, Melinda, whose book this is as much as my own.

Special thanks are due to Dr. Jeff Pickard, for assistance on medical questions; to Rhoda Miller, for translations; to Yusuf Fukui, for help with Tamashek; to Rose-Ann Movsovic at the library of the University of

Reading; and especially to Thom Barnard, who not only traveled with me to many of the locations in the book but saved my life in the bargain. And without the help and encouragement of King Harris, Jim Kirtland, and Bob Kawano, this book would never have been written.

Thanks also to the staffs of the British Library in London, Norlin Library at the University of Colorado, and the Boulder and Denver Public Libraries, where I passed so many wonderful hours in reading rooms and among the stacks.

A number of scholars provided specific help, especially Karl-G. Prasse of Copenhagen University, and Professor Douglas Porch, whose book *The Conquest of the Sahara* is a marvelous work of history.

All of these people steered me toward the truth. Where I have failed to find it, I alone am responsible.

Finally, my profound thanks to the marvelous Tuareg living near Tamanrasset, Algeria, whose hospitality was always so gracious and whose story I have tried to tell.

PRINCIPAL CHARACTERS

Count Henri deVries, a wealthy explorer.
Serena, a noblewoman of the Tuareg; married to Count Henri deVries; sister of El Hadj Akhmed.
Jules deVries, a colonel in the Imperial Guard; brother of Count Henri deVries.
Elisabeth deVries, wife of Jules deVries.
Moussa Michel Kella deVries, son of Count Henri deVries and Serena.
Paul deVries, cousin of Moussa deVries.
Mahdi, son of El Hadj Akhmed; nephew of Serena; cousin of Moussa.
Daia, a young woman of the Tuareg.

OTHER CHARACTERS

IN FRANCE

Delescluze, officer of the guerilla *Francs-tireurs*.
Gascon Villiers, retainer of Count Henri deVries.
Sister Godrick, teacher of Moussa and Paul deVries at St. Paul's.
Marius Murat, the bishop of Boulogne-Billancourt.

IN THE SAHARA

Abdulahi, prisoner of Jubar Pasha; friend to Moussa deVries.

Ahitagel, amenokal of the Tuareg at the time of the Flatters expedition.

Attici, Tuareg nobleman, in line to be amenokal.

Lieutenant Colonel Paul Flatters, leader of the French railroad survey expedition.

El Hadj Akhmed (Abba), the amenokal of the Tuareg.

El Hussein, ambassador to the sultan of Morocco; brother-in-law of Jubar Pasha.

Hakeem, aide to Paul deVries.

Jubar Pasha, ruler of Timimoun.

Lufti, slave of Moussa deVries; husband of Chaddy.

Melika, nurse at the mission of the White Fathers.

Tamrit, suitor of Serena; organizer of the Senussi.

PART 1

FRANCE

1866

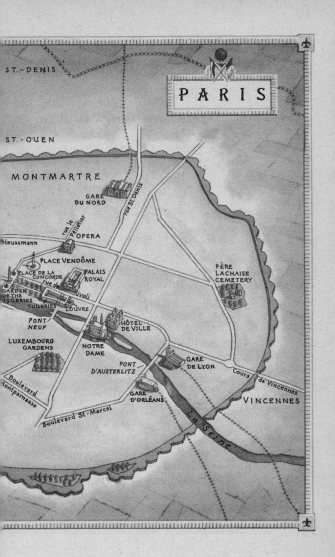

CHAPTER 1

"THE CHILDREN! HOLD FIRE!"

It was too late. The gun roared and kicked back against the huntsman's shoulder. It was a long shot, a hundred and fifty meters or more. He had almost not seen the boar, nearly swallowed as it was by the shadows and the sunlight dancing on the leaves of a distant thicket. Everyone else's eyes had been on the sky, on the count's hawk, but the huntsman had seen a movement, and there it was, scrounging for acorns: a huge boar, a prize boar, a malevolent devil of a boar. Rare in this forest. He decided at once to take it.

Another man would have advanced for a better shot, to avoid the possibility of missing or, worse, merely wounding the animal. The extreme distance made the difference between a good shot and a spectacular shot, a shot all the more exciting because of its uncertainty, a shot to ensure tavern bragging rights for months. He knew he could do it because he knew his weapon. It was new, a bolt-action military rifle. The long barrel gave it a degree of accuracy never before known. He'd honed the sights to perfection through a thousand rounds of practice.

He raised the weapon and found his mark. The shout from the count startled him, but only for an instant. He steadied his aim and fired. Even then, even before the bullet left the gun, he knew he'd done it. He didn't need to see or to hear the impact, he just *knew*. A second later his certainty was justified as he heard a smack and a mad squeal of pain. There was a flurry of motion, and the animal disappeared into the brush.

The huntsman whooped in excitement. To hell with the count! By God, he'd bagged it! A boar! He would have his trophy, and it would not be some piddling grouse. Without turning to see the others, and particularly not wanting to face the count, he raced forward through the clearing.

COUNT HENRI DEVRIES WAS HOSTING A GROUP from the Société Géographique, there to observe the ancient art of falconry. The count's family had kept hawks for generations. They were hunting on land adjoining his estate.

Henri had seen the boar even before the huntsman did. He had reacted with disbelief as he watched the man raise his rifle. Didn't the fool realize the children played nearby? When he heard the pig squeal and saw it move, his worst fears were realized.

Now there was death on the run.

Without a word he left the hunting party—and his own hawk in the air—and dashed for his horse. A wild boar was always dangerous, but a wounded one was unpredictable, lethal. No one was safe, not even an armed man on horseback. Not while a boar was alive and hurt.

He swung up onto his horse, which knew its rider and felt the danger and surged forward even before the count was fully mounted. They took off at a right angle to where the boar had disappeared and raced for a distant clearing. Rider and horse thundered through the forest, under the golden oaks and elms of the great Bois de Boulogne that had once been the hunting grounds of the Valois kings.

HENRI'S WIFE, SERENA, SAT IN THE SHADE OF A large tree. She had been paying no attention to her surroundings, none at all. Normally she would have been hunting with Henri. But she was Tuareg, a woman of the desert, and had secretly begun learning to read

French, her husband's native tongue. She had not yet told him. On her own she had found a tutor, a teacher at the Lycée in Paris, with whom she had spent long secret hours, followed by more hours of practice alone. Gradually, a newfound love had awakened inside her. Each story had increased her enchantment. The subjects didn't matter. Henri's library was rich with scientific journals. The words and meanings in most of those eluded her, but there were also novels and articles and essays. The words were music and brought her an almost mystical pleasure as new worlds opened to her.

She had an inspiration. Henri would have a birthday soon. The two of them would leave Moussa at home and together they would ride into the forest to a secluded waterfall on the edge of the estate. She would bring a picnic lunch, pick a soft sunny spot, spread a blanket on the ground—no, *lots* of blankets in case it was cold—and pour him a glass of wine. He would lie back on her lap and then she would read to him, treasuring the surprise and delight she knew she would find in his eyes. Later they would make love. She took great pleasure in working out the tiniest details of that day. She had redoubled her studies to be ready, and so it was that this day she had been captivated, reading Victor Hugo.

The count's abrupt approach shocked her from her reverie.

"The boys!" he shouted as he drew near. "Where are the boys?"

She had no idea what had happened, but there was no mistaking the urgency in his voice. She looked around desperately. She had last noticed them playing nearby . . . when? A quarter of an hour ago? More? She couldn't be sure. It was a quiet fall day. They'd been just there, by the fallen log, and there was no reason to have been particularly concerned for their safety. They played in the woods all the time. But in a moment of awful panic and guilt she realized that she had no idea when she'd last seen them, or where they might have gone.

THE GREAT WILD PIG CRASHED MADLY THROUGH A thicket of scrub oak. The bullet had broken a rib and punctured a lung. Somehow it had missed vital arteries, but the lung was filling with blood. The animal's breathing was hot and labored, and the exertions of flight would bring the end more quickly. But the end would not come now—not for a long while yet. The boar gathered itself and trotted forward, crazily forward in a zigzag, away from its pursuer.

After a few moments it came to a stop, chest heaving, heart racing. It was a massive and hideous animal. Even in its agony its senses were still alert. It listened, sniffed, and watched, its posture full of menace. Its ears lay flat against its head and its snout was down, close to the ground. Through long habit and reflex it clashed its top and bottom tusks together, to sharpen them. No man could tell what a boar in these circumstances might do. It might lay in wait for its pursuer and force a deadly duel. If there were no dogs or horses it might run. Or, badly wounded and deranged by pain, it might do the unpredictable—turn on another boar or anything else in its path.

The hunted listened, and heard the hunter. The man rushed headlong through the woods, footfalls heavy on the pad of leaves lining the forest floor in autumn. He picked up the bloody trail, his excitement high, his gun at the ready. On a dead run he broke through a low hedge. A bit of brush caught his boot and he stumbled. A tremendous effort kept him from falling, but just as he reached that critical point between fall and recovery he saw the boar. He'd known it was close, very close. And in that one instant he knew he had lost, for his gun was down and extended out from his body, where he'd swung it to recover his balance.

The boar rushed to meet him. The huntsman brought his gun up and fired without aiming. It was a fraction of a second too soon. The bullet caught the boar in the shoulder but the beast kept coming. With a single mighty stroke it ripped the man open from navel to neck. He was dead before he hit the ground.

Out of breath, the boar stopped to recover. The new wound pounded and bled. The animal panted, moving its head up and down as it sought to still the fires inside. After a few moments it began to run again, to get away, anywhere. It stepped on the steel barrel of the rifle, which bent under its weight. Favoring its wounds, the boar ran haltingly but still with power.

In a clearing it stopped again. It heard something new, something troubling. Through mad red eyes it glared in the direction of the noise. Its sight was poor, unlike its hearing or smell, but through the haze and the pain and the torment of dying the boar made out the figures of two boys, playing at the base of a tree. The animal lowered its head and charged.

To THE VAST AMUSEMENT OF HIS COUSIN PAUL, Moussa was peeing on an anthill. A mass of black ants scurried to avoid the stream, disappearing down holes or hiding under leaves, running away as fast as they could. Quickly Paul joined in and together they scattered an entire army, watching in delight as order and purpose turned to muddy chaos. Some, Paul noted with glee, were not nearly fast enough.

"The lout!" he cried, trying his best to drown one. "He should learn to swim!"

Moussa laughed. "He should get a parasol!"

"Or a boat!" They giggled and aimed and peed until they ran dry.

The boys were six years old and had sneaked away from Moussa's mother. They knew these woods well and had come to their private kingdom. No adult knew about it except Gascon, the count's retainer. A massive oak held their secret tree house. It wasn't a tree house, actually, but a fine castle with lookouts and windows and parapets where they could spy on carriages passing by on the road across the lake. Sometimes the emperor himself could be seen, the mighty Napoléon III, coming so close they could make out the fine waxed points of his mustache. He would be surrounded by a grand escort of Cent Gardes in blue tunics and plumed helmets and flashing jackboots, everyone in fine carriages or riding magnificent horses. Or they might see Empress Eugénie, with her equerries and lords and ladies of the court, an elegant procession of tassels and feathers and velvet and lace.

It was all quite exalted. In this, their sovereign land, the boys looked down upon emperors and ruled the known world.

Gascon had built the castle for them with bits and pieces of wood scavenged from the estate. The boys decorated the interior with velvet draperies they'd found hanging in the bedroom of Paul's mother, Elisabeth. She never knew what happened to them and Gascon wasn't saying, which was just as well because by the time the boys and the squirrels had finished, the draperies were no longer suitable for domestic use. Paul and Moussa improved upon things with a chair, then two chairs, and then an end table, and a brass lamp from the count's library that Gascon wouldn't let them light. They were struggling up the tree with a box of the count's books when Gascon drew the line. He knew the count's limits.

There was no ladder up to the castle, only hidden handholds and footholds that you just had to *know* about. Moussa and Paul knew as, of course, did Gascon; and together they made up the entire membership of the Club des Grande Armée. They had clandestine meetings and secret codes and their fortress was well armed. Gascon had spent fifteen years fighting in the First Regiment of Lancers in Algeria. He knew all the weapons and how to use them, and had seen to the provisioning of the castle arsenal, a fine collection of wooden swords and bark-covered shields, and daggers made of oak. He showed them how to wrap the sword handles in twine for a good grip, and how to layer the bark so that blows from the mightiest sword would fall harmlessly to one side. They had pouches for their daggers and helmets made from milk cans.

He told them stories while they worked on the castle, stories of olden days, of knights and dragons and far-off places and great battles of kings and popes and emperors. They sat hushed and wide-eyed as he told of the

Sahara, of dervishes and devils and genies. They laughed at his magic tricks. He could make shiny coins appear from behind their ears, or grasshoppers from their belly buttons.

Gascon taught them how to climb and how to swim. He spent hours with them digging a moat around the castle. The boys helped; and over the summer the moat became ever more elaborate, winding in a grand circle around the tree, with bridges made of branches where one had to give the password. And on the bottom of the moat were carefully arranged patches of rocks that—if you looked just the right way at them—became crocodiles that ate trespassers, tax collectors, and knights of the evil kingdom. Sometimes they covered the moat with branches and leaves and dirt until it was transformed into the castle maze, a series of tunnels with secret escape hatches and passages leading off this way and that. From the surface it was all but invisible. Just last week Gascon had given them a new prize: a rope hanging from a branch of the tree. The rope had a stirrup that allowed them to swing out over the lake and scout for pirates. Gascon said that one day soon they'd be able to swing out and let go, and fall all the way to the water.

It wasn't all as casual as it might have seemed. There was method to the games and the make-believe, a plan behind the dungeons and the rogues. The count had carefully laid out his objectives for this phase of the boys' education with Gascon, who was only too pleased to oblige his lord, for he loved the boys and enjoyed himself immensely as they played. He skillfully inter-wove forest lore with the magic, and during a hundred dangerous missions scouting for monsters and thieves worked at developing the boys' agility and sense of re-sponsibility. Perhaps Gascon enjoyed it most of all, for it stirred memories of his own boyhood in the south-west of France, where he had not been so fortunate as to have a father like the count or an estate like this.

All in all, agreed the initiates of the Club des Grande Armée, the world was perfect, and their kingdom was better.

———————

MOUSSA AND PAUL FINISHED BLASTING THE ANTS and turned to cross the moat and scale the castle wall.

Paul heard it first, a low distant rumble like thunder. He turned and saw it, hair and hooves and tusks, grunting and shuffling through the leaves. It was headed directly at Moussa. Paul thought it was a dragon. In his imagination he saw it flying and saw the fire in its eyes and the murder in its mind. He shrieked and shrieked. It *was* a dragon.

Moussa was between Paul and the boar. He saw Paul pointing, a look of horror in his eyes. And then Moussa looked too, and froze.

Full-grown men could train for years to hunt boar, learning lessons that came at a terrible price. They could prepare themselves with weapons and surround themselves with comrades and horses and all the defenses that man could muster against beast. And at long last, when the moment came, when all the preparation and training was finally put to the test, even the best man could feel his guts turn to jelly as the boar came to settle up. More than one man had died at that instant when fear and training came together in a test of the ability to act.

It was too much to expect two boys to do anything but stop and stare in dread at the animal rushing down upon them and wait for whatever was coming. They had never imagined such a creature except in the wildest stories told them by Gascon, and even he had never described a vision so horrible as this.

So it was with extraordinary presence of mind that Paul did what he did.

"Run!" he shouted.

Moussa stood there, dumbstruck.

"Run!" Paul shouted again, but to no avail. And as the beast bore down upon his cousin, Paul sprang forward and pushed Moussa as hard as he could, to knock him toward their moat, into which Paul himself then jumped.

The push saved Moussa's life. Without it the boar

would have hit him head-on, goring him full in the stomach. Instead it ripped him in the side with a glancing blow. There was still enough force to propel Moussa through the air, completely over the moat. The boy landed in a heap, unconscious and bleeding.

Abruptly the boar stopped its charge, having come to the edge of the ditch. At the bottom lay Paul. The boy looked up and saw the terrible jaw and teeth and tusks. He'd run out of courage. All he could do was curl up in a ball and whimper.

The boar's injuries grew steadily worse, yet a formidable animal remained, with deep reserves of strength bolstered by adrenaline. It would not die, not yet. Frustrated by the moat and unable to continue its attack, the boar ran frantically back and forth, its eyes narrow and angry, looking for a way to get into the moat to Paul, or around it, to Moussa.

On the far side of the tree the pig saw solid ground, a path that led straight to the focus of its rage.

It lowered its head and began to run.

At that very moment across the lake, Monseigneur Murat, the bishop of Boulogne-Billancourt, was returning to his palace after an audience with Empress Eugénie. He was well pleased. The audience had gone brilliantly. Of all the troubled souls in the Tuileries, hers was the most malleable, the most Catholic and God fearing, the most susceptible to his persuasions. Now his influence with her had reached a new and sublime level. She had entrusted him with an international fund being raised for the reconstruction of the Church of the Holy Sepulchre. He could barely contain his glee. She had done it in front of countless observers, whose impressions would elevate his stature in every salon of Paris. Her trust in him would make the sale of influence and the granting of favors all the easier for a man who was already a master at such things. He had left the Tuileries Palace far taller than he had entered it.

It was a beautiful day, sunny and crisp and blessed of

autumn color. To celebrate he instructed his coachman to take the new road through the Bois de Boulogne, the forest-park so cherished by the emperor, who had personally spent hours in its planning and attended to the tiniest details in its execution. The park would not be complete for several years, but already all Paris loved it, and none more than the bishop, whose diocese it bordered.

His carriage was magnificent. In all France few could match it, and this was only his fair-weather transport. For inclement weather he had another just like it but with a top, and in his carriage houses there were six others. The coach rode on gilded wheels whose spokes were sculpted like the wings of angels. It was pulled by four horses with ostrich plumes dancing from their harnesses and silk pads on their backs. The carriage was made of brass and rosewood inlaid with mother-of-pearl. In the rear was a golden likeness of the bishop's coat of arms. On the sides above each wheel and well protected under eight layers of burnished lacquer were miniature oil paintings depicting various scenes: the Last Supper, the Sermon on the Mount, St. Anthony being tormented by demons, and St. Peter receiving the keys to the Kingdom of Heaven. Fourteen of the region's finest artists and craftsmen had worked more than a year to build it, at a cost to the diocese of a hundred thousand francs. It was rare that any expense was spared for the bishop of Boulogne-Billancourt, whether in his carriages, his vestments, his personal quarters, or the amusements he so lavishly showered upon himself and the more deserving of his guests.

The carriage was merely a small reflection of the prelate's appetites, which were as huge as the man himself. He was immense, and wore flowing violet robes that did little to hide his dimensions. Around his neck hung a golden bishop's cross. His pudgy hands were adorned with fabulous rings: opals and diamonds and rubies.

On this day the bishop rode alone in the rear, settled deeply into the luxurious crimson velvet cushions built specially for his bulk. He snacked on roast chicken from a wicker hamper and poured himself wine from a bottle riding in a specially made case. He licked his fingers noisily and ignored travelers who sought his eye or some small acknowledgment as he passed.

The bishop's coachman pulled abruptly to a stop. He'd seen the boar, and then the boys, as the terrible scene unfolded across the water. At first he couldn't believe it, thinking he'd seen a mirage. But there it was.

"What is it?" The bishop was irritated. Wine had spilled on his cloak.

"It is . . . it is a boar, Your Grace, a wild boar!" The coachman was agitated. He pointed. With indifference the bishop looked and saw the beast, not fifty meters away.

"So it is," he said. "A boar, indeed. Now carry on."

The coachman pulled a rifle from its mount on the carriage floorboards. He was always armed, for the bishop's security could never be taken for granted. The diocese spanned forty-two parishes and fifty-seven curacies in wild hill country where rogues showed no respect for high office or mighty persons.

"What are you doing?" The bishop saw the man take up the weapon. "I told you to move on."

"But Your Grace! Children!" The coachman dropped the reins and moved quickly. He had just enough time to get off a shot, maybe two. He had to try.

The bishop looked across the lake and saw Paul and Moussa. He recognized them immediately, for Moussa's clothing was unlike that of other children. Everything about Moussa was unlike other children. Everything about his whole family was unlike every other family. Everything about the deVrieses angered the bishop. Especially the mother, that godless woman who brought his blood to the boil: the she-devil who prayed to false gods and would not convert and whose marriage could not be sanctified so long as she kept to her pagan ways. A bitch was she, a bitch who mocked him, yes, mocked him in his own diocese, mocked him before the priests and the curés and even the sous-curés, mocked him before God with those foreign eyes and that prim smirking mouth, mocked him with her refusal to yield, to repent, to abandon her sinful ways and accept the Lord Jesus Christ. She mocked him with indifference and mocked him with glee. His hands shook and his face flushed every time he saw her, or any of them.

Yes, thought the bishop. *I know that boy well*.

The coachman shouldered his weapon and took aim.

"Put that gun down."

"Your Grace?" He was certain he hadn't heard correctly. He drew himself straight in his seat and squinted as he found the boar through the sight. It would be a difficult shot, but not impossible.

"I said put down the gun. Don't shoot. You'll frighten the horses."

The coachman, his panic growing, thought he must be dreaming. The boar would be on them in a moment.

"The *horses?*" He was dumbfounded. "Your Grace, they'll be killed! There's no time!"

"God's will be done," said the bishop.

"But they are children!" The coachman was pleading. His gun was to his shoulder and he could still fire, but his finger eased for he knew the bishop's tone. Debate had ended.

"Yes, they are children. The Lord most especially watches out for His children." The bishop gazed impassively upon the scene unfolding across the lake. His voice dropped to a murmur. "But mistake not, there is only one child of God before you. Only one. God will save that one. The other is a bastard, the half-breed son of sin. And now the devil has come for him."

In the distance the boar hit Moussa, who flew through the air like the stuffing from one of the bishop's cushions. There was no sound, only the sight. The coachman moaned and crossed himself. His gun came down.

The bishop reached into the hamper for another piece of chicken.

It was a sign. A boar had come. A big one, with horns and cloven hooves.

THE COUNT WAS AT THE FAR END OF THE LAKE, storming along the shore and calling out for the boys when he heard a shriek. Instantly he turned and raced forward, drawing his pistol, furious with himself for not having brought a rifle. This was his own land and he knew it well. No one had seen a boar this close to Paris in years. Yet he cursed himself, his lack of preparedness and caution. Paris or not, he knew better. This was still the forest, alive with surprises that could kill the unwary. He'd spent a lifetime learning not to drop his guard and burying people who had. And now it was Moussa who might pay for his stupidity.

Mon Dieu, not my son!

Ahead through the trees he saw the clearing and the boar and the great oak, but not the boys. The boar had started to run around the tree. As Henri drew near he made out the still form of Moussa on the ground. The terror rose in his throat as he pushed on, harder, faster, and then a great deep cry welled up from inside as he delivered a hoarse scream to divert the boar, which was again bearing down upon Moussa.

There was no time to aim the pistol, no time to fire, not one second to spare. Over the ditch soared horse and rider. The pig turned away from Moussa and raised its head to meet the horse; and in a great kaleidoscope of legs and tusks and noise and arms and dust, all three—horse, rider, and boar—came crashing down.

There was a moment of quiet. The combatants lay stunned. The horse had taken a horn full in the chest and lay dying. The boar had been bowled over backward by the impact and landed flat on its back. It lay dazed, panting heavily. The count barely escaped being crushed under his horse. His right leg had snapped and the wind had been knocked from him. Sheer force of will had kept his fingers wrapped tightly around his pistol. Now, as the dust settled, sheer force of will kept him in the race with the boar for equilibrium and advantage. He tried to pull himself up but his leg was trapped by the horse. He gasped in pain and sat up as far as he could. Through the blur and the shock he sought his target, hidden from view by the side of his horse. He could hear the boar stirring and struggling and saw Moussa's quiet form not three meters away. Again he desperately tried to free himself. A wave of dizziness and nausea overcame him. His hand went limp. He closed his eyes and slumped to the ground, unconscious.

The boar struggled up and shook itself. It was no longer the hunted, but the hunter. There was no malice, simply the desire to survive, to destroy that which must be destroyed to permit survival. It heard a noise and turned to face a new threat.

From point-blank range Serena fired.

She too had heard a scream, and as she raced across the open field on her horse she watched the dreadful scene unfolding. She had never seen such ferocity, such determination. And now she stood over it, this animal that would not die, and aimed at its head and fired. Its legs buckled and it sagged to its knees. It rested. There was a moment of quiet when it was not clear whether it might fall or try again. Then once more it struggled upward, hooves scrabbling at the dirt, its breath grating, rasping like a storm in a bellows, head swaying from side to side. Its tusks stabbed at nothing, at everything, at the air. It was not ready to quit.

Serena fired again, and again. Her hand was steady. She was not afraid.

The animal looked up at her almost quizzically, as if to say, *You cannot beat me. I will not let you beat me.*

But at long last the great creature gave out a groan. It closed its eyes and sank to its belly, and died.

IN THE LATE AFTERNOON, SOME OF THE HUNTING party fetched a wagon and went off to the field to collect the bodies of the huntsman and the boar. It took six men to get the boar into the wagon. It lay outside the stable where Gascon had to cover it with a tarpaulin to keep the dogs away. A stream of visitors came by, raising the tarp to regard the animal with hushed awe. They measured its tusks and counted its wounds. Afterward they went into the kitchen to inquire after the well-being of the count and his son. Madame LeHavre, the cook, saw to it they all had something to eat and then shooed them away.

Dr. Fauss arrived late. He was an old man whose age was impossible to discern. He had tended the deVries family for more years than anyone could remember. He'd had a long day. He spent a busy morning in the city treating coughs and vapors and bumps and scrapes, and then came word of the boar. Gascon had come for him in the count's coach. The doctor disappeared into the house just at twilight.

The main part of the mansion was two hundred years old. It was two stories, made of stone and brick, and had been added on to a much smaller structure built in 1272 by the Comte Auguste deVries on land granted him by Louis IX. The walls were thick and covered with ivy. It was a comfortable country estate in which both Henri and his brother, Jules, had grown up, and in which both their families now lived. Upon the death of their father, the house, the land, the noble rank, and all the money had passed formally to Henri, the elder brother.

It was a wonderful house which seemed to have been built solely for the pleasure and entertainment of children. It was filled with corridors and staircases and places to hide. There was a hidden passage on the second floor between the walls and the outside slope of the roof. It ran all the way from one end of the house to the other, connecting the bedchambers with trapdoors hidden behind panels inside massive wardrobes. The count's father had shown him the passage and the count had shown it to Moussa. Even now Henri took great delight when he heard excited whispers and muffled giggles as someone sneaked from one end of the passage to the other.

The rooms were large and informal. The kitchen was the center of the house, always comfortable, warmed by an iron cookstove that never went out. Every room had a fireplace. When he was not away, the count spent most of his time in the library, which contained one of the finest collections of books in France. The library had nearly been destroyed during the days of darkness after the Revolution, when angry crowds stormed estates and burned books, and chopped off the heads of those who read them. But while books had been lost, the house and its occupants happily had not. The intervening years had seen the collection grow once again, until under Henri it far surpassed its former glory. Now the shelves were filled with papers and leather-bound volumes and mementos of a lifetime spent traveling in places most people had never heard of. There were carvings and masks and amulets and ivory figurines, and at the center of the room the count's only extravagance: a large globe, handmade in London by the world's finest cartographers. It was nearly a meter in diameter, the oceans and continents and poles richly colored. Henri took great pleasure in pointing to spots in Africa and Asia that were ill-defined or entirely blank, and describing exactly what was there. Serena was also knowledgeable, even more so than he where the Sahara was concerned, as it was from the Sahara that she came.

DR. FAUSS EMERGED FROM THE MASTER BEDROOM, quietly closing the door behind him. He was ready to leave.

He rapped lightly on the door to the boys' room.

"Come in," said the quiet voice.

There were two beds in the room. Serena sat in a chair next to one, holding Moussa's small hand. In the next bed lay Paul. Both boys were asleep.

"*Ah, bon, madame la comtesse,* I found you."

Serena gave him a wan smile, anxious for news of Henri.

"Your husband is as lucky as he is strong. I set the leg and splinted it. He'll have to sit still for a month while it heals. I suppose that will trouble him more than the break itself. I'll leave you a medication before I go. Give him brandy for the pain."

She nodded. "And Moussa?"

The doctor drew up a chair next to the bed. He felt the boy's forehead. "Countess, I must confess to amazement." He pulled back the covers. The boy's tiny form was a mass of trauma. A long gash just below his rib cage bore rough black stitches. "He should be dead. The horn grazed him there. A miracle it did not penetrate more deeply." He indicated a bruise that ran from his shoulder to his groin. "Tomorrow that will be worse. It will swell badly. You must keep it cool." He covered the boy again and sat back in his chair, exhausted by his labors. "His collarbone is broken, and three ribs, and a finger. And he has a skull fracture. A concussion."

"A—?" Serena did not know the word.

The doctor tapped his temple with a finger. "His head. It is broken too." He smiled to reassure her. "Do not worry, Countess. It is a strong head. A stubborn one, like his father's."

At that moment Paul's mother, Elisabeth, burst into the room. As always her entry was melodrama in motion, a breathless explosion of curls and color and perfume. She had just returned from the city and heard the news. She was frantic.

"Paul!" she shouted. "What happened to my little Paul?"

"Calm yourself, madame," said the doctor, accustomed to her outbursts. "You'll wake the boys. Paul was not hurt. He is fine. A hero."

She rushed to his bed, fussing and cooing and smothering him in kisses. Paul woke up and wriggled away, struggling to maintain his six-year-old dignity. As soon as his mother let up a bit he smiled. "*Maman!*" He sat up brightly. "Know what happened?"

"*Oui, mon petit,* I heard of the boar. You were *magnificent!*"

Paul grimaced. Mothers didn't know anything. That wasn't it at all.

"No! We pissed on an ant pile!"

Elisabeth rolled her eyes.

BY THE LIGHT OF A CANDLE SERENA SAT WITH
Moussa. The house was quiet now, the visitors gone
home, everyone asleep. She had checked on Henri and
then settled next to her son. She traced a finger on his
forehead, touching him in that way only a mother can, a
touch of joy for his life and wonder at his luck, a touch
of fear for the little body so broken and bruised. She
was exhausted, but sleep would not come. Waves of
emotion rose within her through a long night of reflection, alternately flooding her with guilt and relief and
the dread of what might have been.

This is my son: her flesh and blood, a small child.
Today death had come calling, and death had been denied. How easily it might have been different, she
thought. How quickly a son gone, or a husband. Even
though he was safe now, the terror kept coming back:
terror that rose in a lump in her throat until she wanted
to scream; terror that made her chest pound; terror that
forced tears from her eyes. Her emotions were wild and
physical, sweeping back and forth between nausea and
euphoria. How fragile was life! How innocent the boy!
How lucky she was!

This is my son: so small, so helpless, so dependent.
She had often faced death in the desert, where existence
was fickle. A father lost to treachery, a mother to disease, brothers and a sister to accidents and war. Life
there was neither easy nor kind. If death was never welcome, it was never a stranger. It came when it would.
But this was a completely new feeling for her, terrifying
and different.

This is my son. She had carried him in her womb.
She had nursed him and watched him grow. She saw
Henri in his deep blue eyes and herself in his high cheek-
bones and smile. His laugh came easily and brought joy
to her heart. She had pushed him for hours in a swing
and emptied rocks from his pockets and helped catch
insects for his collection. She had tended torn knees and
elbows and watched him learn to walk and to eat by
himself. She taught him to speak Tamashek, her native
tongue. She had sung him nursery rhymes, and com-

forted him when the other children made fun of him. He was only five the first time it had happened. She had never dreamed it would begin so soon.

"Maman, what's a half-breed?" His eyes had been so puzzled, so wide, so hurt. Of course none of the children had the slightest idea what a half-breed might be: just words picked up from parents. But in the manner of children they could use words cruelly, playing happily with him one moment, making him feel isolated and alone the next. This had been a double insult, for the child had called him *demi-sang,* a term reserved for horses, not men. One of the children discovered that he could make a rhyme of it, and the rhyme caught on and all the children except Paul joined in.

Moussa burst into tears and ran away.

Later he climbed into Serena's lap where she stroked his hair and searched her mind for words of comfort, but the words would not come. She knew it would not be the last time he would feel the sting of disapproval, the agony of being different. She felt it herself every day, had felt it ever since coming to France with Henri. People stared at her and laughed and whispered and pointed. They made fun of her accent and touched the long locks of her hair as though she had crawled from under a rock. She was strong, stronger than they, strong enough to stand straight and stare back, and so could only tell her son that which she knew: "It doesn't matter what they say. You must ignore them. You must be strong." Her words fell on the uncomprehending ears of a five-year-old. He was not consoled.

"I don't *want* to be strong, Maman," he sobbed bitterly. "I want to be like *them.*"

This is my son: her firstborn and only child. Born so high and yet so low. A noble half-breed, indeed. In the Sahara he would be a prince among his people, for among the Tuareg nobility passed through mother to son. The amenokal was the leader of the Tuareg, and he was her brother. One day Moussa might be the amenokal, in spite of the French blood flowing in his veins. And in France he would one day be count and inherit his father's mantle in spite of the Tuareg blood flowing in his veins. She closed her eyes and tried to imagine what his life might be. She saw darkness and turmoil and pain. Emotions ran deep where blood was concerned.

This is my son. He wore an amulet around his neck. A present from the amenokal, a leather pouch whose contents were secret. A verse from the Koran, perhaps, or a fragment of bone, or a piece of paper covered with magic squares. The amenokal would nod and say it was the amulet that thwarted the boar. Serena didn't know. Perhaps it was. Perhaps it held the luck of generations and the power to promote and heal and protect. Moussa had worn it and survived a childhood fever that killed scores of children his age. Today he had worn it and survived the boar. The doctor had started to remove it as he had bound Moussa's broken collarbone with a cloth that wound round his shoulders and under his arms.

"You must leave it be," she had told him, covering his hand with her own. She was not religious or superstitious, so the firmness with which she stopped him surprised her, but she did it anyway. Maybe it was just because the charm was from the amenokal and reminded her of home. Maybe it was because Moussa had worn it from the day he was born. It belonged on that little chest. It fit. It was comfortable and right, something she was used to. And maybe, she allowed herself to think, maybe this day it had made a difference. It would not be disturbed.

This is my son. He stirred in the candlelight and whimpered in pain. She hushed him, and brushed the hair from his forehead. The hours passed and the candle burned out and the night became dawn. At last she slept, to dreams of the desert.

CHAPTER 2

HE FELL TO HER FROM THE SKY.

Henri had launched the balloon from the village of Bou Saada, intending to follow the winds that blew along the high plateau skirting the range of Atlas Mountains that ran parallel to the coastline of northern Africa, winds that would carry him, he hoped, to Morocco. He and Gascon had waited weeks for the right conditions, each day watching the sky, each day turning away disappointed. There had been no wind, only utter stillness. Patiently they tended their supplies and tested their gear, checking and rechecking to make certain that all remained ready. Even though Henri expected to be aloft only a few days, the balloon was loaded with water and food enough for two weeks. He was an adventurer, but he was never casual or careless.

And then at last one morning he walked outside and a strong breeze ruffled his hair and he knew it was time. He and Gascon hurried to the compound where their airship lay waiting. They inflated the balloon to the delight of the astonished swarms of curious Arabs who had come to watch them each day and who squatted in circles and drank tea and chattered noisily as the fabric billowed up and out, straining against the tethers that held it to the ground. Finally the great contrivance was ready. Henri and Gascon clambered into the basket, much to the consternation of the French prefect of the district, who had reminded Henri a dozen times over the weeks—politely, of course, for after all the man *was* a noble of the empire—that he was a perfect fool. The prefect was beside himself with worry that the count should be lost in Algeria from *his* prefecture. It was madness! No European had ever tried such a thing. The inquiries from Paris would be never-ending. So he had implored the count: Could he not begin his voyage from Algiers? From Aïn Sefra? Would a journey by camel to Morocco not satisfy his needs? But the count would not listen, and the prefect was miserable and drank too much absinthe and imagined his career soaring away with the balloon. He looked beseechingly at Henri one last time as he cast off the land lines.

"You will die!" he predicted with grave certainty as the balloon lifted away from its moorings.

"Not today!" Henri shouted back cheerfully, and he waved good-bye and was gone.

They gained altitude quickly, soaring away from the throngs of Arabs below. As the magical ascent began, the crowd gave out a great roar of approval and delight. The balloon moved silently to the west. Henri and Gascon watched as the forms of people in the fields grew tiny and their donkeys became toys and their houses little boxes. When the shadow of the balloon passed overhead the people on the ground looked up and saw it, and a commotion would inevitably occur. A great cry would follow—sometimes of alarm, sometimes of wonder—and the balloon was too high for Henri and Gascon to hear but they could see as the little people bound to the earth gesticulated and waved and raced in circles on their donkeys and pointed to the sky. Some damned the apparition and some danced with joy, and some fell to their knees in prayer.

For several hours everything went perfectly. They saw Djelfa, then Aflou and Aïn Madhi, checking off each on the map as they passed. They settled into the quiet business of flight, gazing in awe at the earth passing beneath them, marking the lakes and streams they saw on the maps they carried, identifying animals and birds and trees, tending to the drag lines and rigging and other equipment of the balloon. The count meticulously recorded atmospheric conditions, wind speeds and currents, and variations in temperature and pressure as they flew. The sky was cloudless as far as they could see, perfect and deep blue. But late in the afternoon the wind shifted its direction and began blowing from the north. The change was subtle at first, then grew stronger as the wind thrust them toward the mountains. It would soon carry them over.

"We need to make a decision, Gascon," Henri said. "We can keep going that way"—he pointed to the south, toward the unknown—"or we can set it down on this side and wait for a safer wind."

Gascon looked out over the mountains. He had been with the count for years and knew without asking what the count wanted to do. He liked it that his master asked his opinion, and treated him more as an equal than a servant. That was what made the count so special, so different. Others of rank would simply command or demand. The count always asked, even though he didn't have to.

On that day high above the Atlas Mountains, it was not a difficult decision. He shared the count's love of adventure, and they were well prepared. Gascon had no family, nothing to hold him back.

"We never learned anything setting it down, sire," he replied.

Henri smiled. "I was hoping you'd say that."

"Yes, sire. I know that."

"*Alors,* we'll need more altitude."

Gascon dropped ballast and the balloon soared upward, to where the obliging winds increased in speed and carried them across the Atlas Mountains, over the Djebel Amour and into the unknown beyond. There was a transition startling in its intensity, as though a great line had been drawn between the green, fertile northern slopes of the mountains and the reddish brown rocks and barren hillsides of the southern side. The mountains melted away to a plateau, the plateau to a sudden and brilliant golden range of dunes. They floated between heaven and earth, the wind at their backs, the great expanse of the Sahara before them. They ate dried meat and sipped from their water flasks and watched the world pass silently beneath them. The maps they carried were reasonably accurate up to the mountains, for thousands of Frenchmen had explored and settled there. But few Europeans had ventured to the south of the mountains, and fewer still had returned. There were a thousand legends but little reliable information about what lay in that vast region, which the Arabs of the fertile north called the Land of Thirst and Fear. It was a much-storied region to which they floated, inhabited by a mysterious race of men who were said to be giants. The Arabs called them the Tuareg, the abandoned of God, the people of the veil, and when they spoke of them it was with a mixture of fear and dread and respect. They were known to be superb fighters who were masters of the desert and ruled the great caravan routes along which flowed steady streams of salt and slaves and gold.

Onward they flew toward the legends before them; and as the sun dipped to the horizon they saw a simultaneous sunset and moonrise, and it took their breath away, the moon coming up gold and full and glorious, the sun blazing red as it dipped through the sand haze of the horizon. They stood spellbound in their basket, looking from east to west and back again so as not to miss a moment of the heavenly display.

Henri had a brass sextant made in London that he carried in a worn leather case. He used it to plot their position, sighting carefully on the stars as the dusk turned to night. He marked his estimates on the special paper he had brought to make maps. The moon was so bright he barely needed the light of the small gas lantern that sat on the floor of the basket. They could see the desert below almost as clearly as during the day. "We're here," he said to Gascon as he marked their coordinates with a small X on the paper. "Wherever 'here' is."

When he had finished with his work Henri pulled a small recorder from his pocket, a wooden flutelike instrument he'd found in a market somewhere. He wasn't formally trained at music, but had a good ear for copying what he heard. Sometimes he would make up a melody to suit his mood. That evening he found the notes to float in the air with the balloon, velvet notes that captured the freedom and tranquillity of their passage and settled over the sleeping desert below. Gascon propped himself contentedly against the ropes and listened with his eyes closed.

They spelled each other through the night, one napping while the other kept a watchful eye on their progress. It was a night of peace and awe as the moonlit earth passed beneath them. The air was cold and crisp and they huddled under heavy robes. The morning sun rose over dunes as rich and golden as the moon had been. The slopes of the dunes that faced away from the sun were covered with a silver layer of frost, and looked like snowdrifts glistening in the soft light of dawn.

Henri peered intently at the map. "We're over the Grand Erg Occidental," he said. The Erg was one of the few sand oceans in a desert that had a thousand faces. Henri was aware of its existence and general location, but not its extent. The map was useless. An Arab trader in Bou Saada had told him that beyond the Erg lay a busy trading route. They could not set down until they were past the Erg, as they would never be able to escape on foot from the dunes. It was better to keep flying and hope that the wind would shift direction again and carry them to the west, for the Atlas Mountains swung in an arc in a southerly direction. With the right winds they would then cross the mountains once again, to Morocco. But the wind had its own plan and blew strongly all that day and night—to the south.

The dunes were undulating and endless and ran away into the distance as far as the eye could see. The heaps were laid out in great rows, one after the other, methodically, as though by some gigantic shovel of the gods. They were smooth and feminine and looked gossamer soft and pure. Sometimes gusts of wind would carry away gentle wisps of sand from their summits, like snow from the tops of mountain peaks. One range was gold, another reddish brown, the next yellow, the sand ever-changing in the light and shadows. The dunes had dimples and swirls and graceful long lines. Between them the land was flat but not always barren, occasionally sprouting scrub and bushes that clung to life.

Sometimes between the rows of dunes they could see

small herds of gazelle grazing on the sparse tufts of grasses and weeds. A lone jackal ranged along the base of the dunes in search of mice. In the afternoon, Gascon spotted two ostriches, whose gangly legs were much exaggerated by the long shadows of the sun until they looked twenty feet tall, strutting and bouncing along like animated giants. The animals were oblivious to the silent passage of the balloon overhead.

Henri took careful notes, marking the features of the land. The balloon drew farther away from the Atlas, until with field glasses they could just make out the faint outline of mountains against the horizon. In his stomach, deep down inside, he felt an old familiar tingling sensation of fear mixed with anticipation as he watched the world he knew disappear.

And he loved it.

It was what he had always done. He had been born to a life of privilege. He had disappointed those, including his father, who had expected him to go into the military as countless generations of deVries men had done since the time of Louis IX. He left the military to his brother, Jules, whose temperament was vastly more suited to it than his own, and spurned the easy life to which his wealth and position would have entitled him. Instead he traveled, going places and doing things other men could not or dared not. He explored the wondrous caves of Cappadocia in central Turkey and the deserts of Arabia and the mountains of the Hindu Kush in Afghanistan. He wandered the markets of Macau and the streets of Tashkent. He had been shipwrecked in the Celebes Sea off the coast of Borneo and had seen whirling dervishes in Sudan. In order to travel to Marrakesh, where it was forbidden for Christians to enter, he had masqueraded as a Jew from Damascus, wearing a red skullcap and turban. He relished his life and cherished his freedom and wrote of his travels for the Société Géographique in Paris, where his journals were eagerly awaited by readers from Paris to London to New York.

So it was that floating into the unknown reaches of the Sahara did not strike terror into his heart, but rather gave him a familiar surge of adrenaline that gnawed at his belly and enlivened his senses and made colors brighter and smells sharper—made him want to laugh out loud with the delight of it all. He needed the feeling and fed it with his travels. It was a sort of ecstatic fear that dwelled near his sternum and radiated outward in a dull, hot rush. It was an almost mystical obsession, the passion of adventurers to penetrate the mysteries of the world, to see places never seen, to do things never done. It was a longing that would never be fulfilled, for as quickly as one horizon was reached another beckoned, and he was off again. Many years earlier, a soothsayer in a Delhi market had read his palms and told him he would die an old man. He laughed with all the self-assured conviction of a skeptic with a scientific mind. But he believed her and had spent his life since in a gray area somewhere between folly and inspiration.

On the morning of the third day the wind died at dawn. Seeing only more sand, they decided to increase their altitude so that they could look farther. Gascon dumped ballast, and they rose until they could see past the dunes to a great plateau that lay beyond. Henri peered through the field glasses. Between the dunes and the plateau there was a vast depression filled with wadis and deep canyons. Beyond that were more dunes, an infinite expanse of gold stretching away to the southwest. To the northwest, at the upper end of the depression, he could see the outline of a lake bed. It looked dry, but from the distance he couldn't tell for certain. If it was a *sebkha*, a seasonal lake, it would suggest the presence of wells and people.

"We've come far enough south," he said, not wishing to unduly tempt fate. "I think we'd better land and wait for favorable winds."

Gascon nodded. "I agree, but we may be waiting a few days." There was a gentle sloping riverbed that was lined on both sides by bushes and large boulders. "The rocks in that wadi will give us shelter. If the winds don't come we can leave the balloon there and make our way out on foot back to the northwest."

Henri pulled on the rope that opened a vent in the

top of the balloon, and they began their descent to the valley below.

The balloon floated just above a ridge that ran along one side of the valley. They could see no one, no animals or sign of any life, but there were trails in the hard sand bed that suggested people occasionally passed this way. Such trails could be misleading, for in the desert they could exist for an eternity, and one could never tell how old they might be.

They neared the ground and passed over the canyon wall, expecting to settle their craft gently to the floor of the wadi. Suddenly the balloon was caught by a violent updraft that flung them quickly aloft. Before they could react a downdraft hurled them precipitously toward the rocks below.

"Ballast!" shouted Henri, even as Gascon was cutting the ropes holding the sandbags to the outside of the basket, but it was too late. The wicker basket slammed into a ridge of jagged rocks that ripped out the side. There was pandemonium aboard the craft as bodies and provisions flew about. Henri grabbed for some of the supplies as they disappeared over the side, but just as he reached out he was dashed to the bottom of the basket. The wind tore at them, dragging them along. The rocks caught the basket a second time, and the envelope of the balloon became a windsail that dipped down at an angle, the ropes straining to hold against the terrific force. One of the ropes caught on the sharp rocks and broke, then another, and at last the balloon ripped away free. Having lost most of its buoyancy by tilting at such an extreme angle, it quickly collapsed and fluttered emptily to the ground. As the ropes gave way, the basket plummeted the last few feet to the wadi floor. Both men fell hard and lay dazed and panting.

During the last moments of the balloon's flight, seven riders atop their camels had emerged from around a bend in the wadi. Transfixed, they stopped dead still and watched as the balloon appeared over the ridge, its basket hugging the ground, the men inside struggling to maintain control. At first the fabric of the balloon billowed gently against the wind, then rose before them like some mighty celestial apparition, a silent flying ball of magnificent white cloth set against the deep blue sky.

"*Hamdullilah!* It is the *djenoum!*" said one rider in an urgent whisper, referring to the genies known to inhabit the rocks and the dark places in between. He drew his sword, a large double-edged blade, and held it at the ready by his side.

"Comes Allah!" said another.

"It is the moon, fallen from the sky!"

"Flying men of the clouds!"

Awed but unafraid, the group moved forward, watching as the mysterious craft rose and then fell, bouncing and flopping and finally dumping its cargo of flying men of the clouds unceremoniously onto the ground.

Momentarily stunned, Henri lay still. He heard the voices and did not recognize the language. Since it was not Arabic, he guessed it must be the language of the Tuareg.

Henri got to his knees and helped Gascon, who still lay gasping. The riders had drawn forward into a semicircle around the two men, and Henri had to look nearly straight upward to see them. From his position they looked twelve feet tall astride their camels, their silhouettes forbidding and yet magnificent against the sky. He was as awed by their appearance on the camels as they had been by his in the balloon, and for a moment the French count and the seven riders regarded each other silently, warily. The Tuareg were resplendent atop their mounts, cloaked from head to toe in rich indigo and dazzling white cloth, which covered their heads and bodies completely except for a slit for their eyes, eyes which were shadowed and dark and unrevealing. The cloth of their turbans was drawn numerous times around their heads, heaped high and tight, helmet-like, adding to the sensation of towering height and imposing presence. They were armed with lances. Heavy striking swords in well-tooled red leather scabbards were suspended from cotton bands slung over their shoulders. They carried shields of antelope hide upon which a series of small cuts formed the image of a Latin cross. They sat in high-backed riding saddles whose pommels also formed the likeness of a cross. To Henri they looked like the medieval crusaders whose portraits could be found among those of his ancestors at the Château deVries. They looked like kings.

The lead rider was an elegant man, tall and aloof, who looked down upon the two aeronauts as though he were the lord of creation, the master of all men. Behind him, Henri was astonished to see that the only one of them whose face was not obscured was a woman. She nudged her camel forward through the group and stopped to regard him silently. Whenever Henri looked at a woman he invariably noticed her eyes first. Before her clothes, before her hair, before her face or figure, before anything else he looked in her eyes, for there, he knew, he would always find the woman. This woman's eyes captivated him. They were deep brown, shining with humor and intelligence, enchanted pools alight with character and life, and for a long wonderful moment her eyes held his. She wore robes like the others; but, extraordinarily for a North African woman, her head and face were bare. She was beautiful, her features as unfamiliar to Henri as her language. She looked neither Arabic nor African nor European. Her cheeks were high and her skin was light, shining and smooth. *Perhaps Berber,* he thought. Her neck was slender, and she smiled through perfect, even white teeth. She had long dark brown hair that she wore in tight braids. There was great dignity in her carriage. Like the others she sat tall in her saddle, imperious and erect. She regarded the balloon with delight and Henri with faint amusement as he dusted himself off. He helped Gascon to his feet, but didn't take his eyes off her. She was an exquisite mystery to him.

When she spoke he heard authority and certainty in her voice. He listened hard, as though he might be able to understand her words even though the language was unfamiliar.

"It is called a *ballon*," she explained to the others, who were still debating among themselves about what manner of sorcery lay before them. "I have seen one like it in Algiers."

"What is a '*ballon*'?" asked one of the veiled men.

"It is a flying machine," Serena answered over her shoulder, "only this one does not seem to fly so well."

"If they are not *djenoum* we should kill them now and take their bags," said another. The crash had strewn luggage everywhere across the sand, including Henri's sextant and a barometer that gleamed bronze in the light. There were several leather boxes, a valise, fine cloaks, and water flasks. It was clear to the Tuareg that these were men of means who carried vast wealth and mysterious devices, no doubt employing evil spirits to accomplish their ends.

"We should kill them and burn what they carry," said another. "They are vile, they are *ikufar*." It was the word for "heathen," used to describe the primitive people of Europe. Several of the others murmured assent.

Gascon eyed the Tuareg suspiciously. Their language was nothing more than gibberish to his ear, but he knew menace well enough when he heard it. He studied the group as he instinctively calculated his battle strategies, looking for any weaknesses to exploit. There weren't many. They were armed and mounted well above him, and had tightened the semicircle they formed around him and the count. His eyes moved among them, noting the lances and swords and the well-worn silver hilts of knives he could see. There would be other weapons that he could not see, blades hidden beneath the folds of cloth. These men were fighters, of that he was certain; and without better weapons he and the count would be no match against their number. Gascon wore only his knife, and knew the count had no weapon at all. He glanced around at the wreckage, wondering where he might find one of the rifles. There had been no reason to keep them at the ready during the flight, and now they were nowhere to be seen.

The worst of it was that he couldn't see their faces,

couldn't read their expressions. He knew these were no more than mortal men, that it was nothing but the cloth over their faces that so unsettled him. Yet he felt naked before them.

"I don't like the looks of them, sire," he said in a low voice.

"The man eating sand doesn't like the looks of *us?*" The woman spoke sharply in French, so startling Gascon that he almost jumped. And then she laughed, and it was a warm and genuine laugh that echoed delightfully off the sides of the boulders nearby and helped to shatter the tension; and in spite of himself, Henri laughed too. Gascon did not share in their enjoyment of his appearance, but wiped a hand across his face, which was smeared with the grit of the wadi floor. The rest of the Tuareg had not understood the exchange, for among them only Serena spoke French. Henri spoke immediately.

"Mademoiselle, I am Henri deVries of France. My companion here who eats sand is Gascon." He gave a slight bow. "I am surprised to find you here and very pleased that you speak French."

"That was quite a crash, Henri deVries."

"That wasn't a crash," he responded, much too quickly and a bit defensively. "It was a hard landing."

She laughed again. "Had you been on a camel and done that, I would call it a crash, and afterward the camel would have bitten you for the ride."

"Then it is well I was not riding a camel," Henri said, grinning. He enjoyed this woman.

"Serena! What does he say?" Tamrit ag Amellal, the lead rider, was annoyed by her laughter and uncomfortable that he didn't understand what was being said. He was accustomed to being in charge. She ignored him.

"From where have you come with your balloon?"

"From Bou Saada."

"Bou Saada! That is across the Grand Erg!"

"Yes. We have been two nights in the air."

"And where were you going?"

Henri shrugged. "Morocco."

Serena looked at him in astonishment. "Morocco!

Monsieur, you have crashed three weeks' ride from Morocco!"

"Yes, I know. The wind was wrong."

"How can the wind be wrong?"

"It did not go where I hoped it would go."

"You fly your machine with hope?"

"No—yes, I suppose so." The desert woman was tangling him up.

"Then you would do better with a camel." She looked at the sky. "Even the camel knows this wind will take you to the Tanezrouft." She waved to the southwest. "But for your crash, your hope would have taken you there, and there you would have perished. Nothing lives in the Tanezrouft," she said matter-of-factly. "Nothing at all."

"I would have been all right," Henri insisted.

"Yes, you would have been all right, and then when your water ran out you would have been dead. It is lucky for you we have passed this way."

"Where are you going?"

"Arak," she said, pointing to the southeast, "at the foot of the Atakor."

Serena turned to Tamrit and rapidly explained in Tamashek what she had learned. Excited murmurs of disbelief arose among the Tuareg. Bou Saada! None of them had been there, but each knew of the village that lay on the other side of the great mountains. The great sand Erg was impassable, a field of death. To go around it took weeks of hard riding by camel. They had seen for themselves how the balloon had flown, but the thought of it having come directly over the Erg was inconceivable, preposterous!

"They lie!" said one. "It is clearly the work of the *djenoum!* We should kill them now!"

"*Djenoum* or not, we must kill them!"

"*Eoualla,* I say yes!"

"It is agreed!"

"No!" Serena spoke sharply. "We will take them and their flying machine to the amenokal. He will be amused by it. He can decide what is to become of them!"

"Bah! Their flying machine! It crashes better than it flies! Behold, it lies in ruin among the rocks! No sane man would venture in it!"

"They did!"

"They are not sane, they are French!"

"Where the French go, horror follows. They are thieves and killers. The Arabs of the northern country have suffered at their hands. They must die!"

"The Arabs of the north deserve the French!"

As the discussion among them grew more heated, Henri spoke quietly to Gascon. "Do you know where the rifles fell?"

"I cannot see them, sire. I'll have to look more closely. There is wreckage everywhere."

"Then do it now, quickly, while they argue. If you find them be ready to throw me one, but don't take it up yet. If you don't see them I have a pistol in the valise there. Be ready, look sharp. I think they are discussing whether to use swords or lances on us. If anything happens make for those rocks." He indicated two large boulders sitting close to each other, backed by a sandstone wall. They gave scant sanctuary, but were better than nothing.

"*Oui, mon comte.*"

Gascon moved toward the ruins of the basket. As he did so, Tamrit shouted. "That one! He goes for weapons! They will have rifles! Stop him!" He raised his lance. Others drew swords and produced knives from among the folds of their robes. Gascon's hand went to the knife at his belt while Henri, unarmed, could do nothing but step back.

"Hold!" Serena's voice lashed out. She saw the situation getting out of hand and knew she had to act. She surprised herself with what she did next, with her lie. "Leave them, Tamrit. It is too late. I have already given them my protection. I have granted them the *Amán* of safe passage."

Tamrit exploded at her.

"By what right have you done this?"

"I have the right, Tamrit, you know it well. They

may pack their flying machine on camels and ride with us to Arak."

"No, Serena! I lead!"

She snorted. "It is done! I have done it!"

Tamrit was furious. He stamped his lance into the ground. "I will not honor this!"

"Then you will dishonor us all, and answer to the amenokal!"

Tamrit swore. This woman was too independent, too strong-headed. He was hopelessly in love with her. He had courted her for two years, brought her gifts of camel meat and fine cloth, written poems to her, done everything a man could do. But she was impossible, and now she bullied him and humiliated him before the others. Cursed woman! She was right, of course. Whether he liked it or not, if she had granted safe passage he had no choice but to honor it. At least, he thought, until the proper opportunity arose.

Serena saw his hesitation and knew the momentum was hers. She had to finish it. She moved her camel forward to Henri. She spoke quickly, with authority.

"They thought you looked for weapons. I assured them that was not the case, but if you have weapons and attempt to use them against us you will die quickly, Henri deVries. I will kill you myself. You have the offer of safe passage if you wish it. You may ride with us to Arak, where you will show your flying machine to our leader. From there you may find transport among traders returning to the north."

Henri hesitated. He considered his options, which at the moment were limited. He didn't know whether he could trust the word of this woman. She fascinated him and seemed influential among the others. Clearly her words carried much weight. It was extraordinary, that she seemed to so dominate the men. What African woman—or European woman, for that matter—had he ever seen do that? He had wandered the souks and medinas of the northern towns and villages where the women were timid chattel, veiled nonentities kept under lock and key by fathers and husbands who subjugated them and punished them like mules. This woman was certainly no chattel, and here it was the men who wore the veils. What manner of people were these? Tales of Tuareg treachery abounded in the north, reports of scores of murdered travelers. Yet they had offered safe passage. If the fabric of the balloon was too badly damaged he knew they might not be able to repair it. And if what the woman said about the wind was true, the right wind might never arrive anyway. To walk out alone might be impossible. Even if they attempted it, he and Gascon might then encounter a different party that would kill them on sight.

Serena heard more murmurs behind her and knew that further delay was dangerous, that she could lose control of the situation at any moment. "You must answer quickly," she urged him. "Your life depends on it."

Henri glanced at Gascon, who had weighed their chances and thought it prudent to accept. Gascon nodded.

"Your offer is accepted with thanks," Henri said. "We are honored to accompany you."

"Then it is done," Serena said.

Henri and Gascon folded the balloon, gathered up the scrambled remnants of their baggage, and placed everything in a pile. Henri found the rifles, which had gotten jammed into the sand underneath a broken piece of the basket. Cautiously, moving so that everything he did could be seen and not misinterpreted, he wrapped the rifles in a blanket and placed them inside a basket that was to be loaded on one of the pack camels. One of the Tuareg, a man called Buzu who wore all-white robes, waved them away brusquely when it was time to load the camels. He handled the task himself, hissing and cursing and goading the animals to do his bidding without excessive complaint. Buzu was the only one working, while the other Tuareg sat in silence in the shade. If they were not overtly hostile, they seemed withdrawn and unfriendly.

When at last they were ready to depart, Henri found himself provided with a riding camel of nasty disposition. The camel is an animal of contrasts, able to adopt a demeanor that is either terribly awkward or immensely dignified, depending upon its mood. It further possesses the ability to look altogether natural in either guise. As Henri's mount rose from its knees to a standing position, a process in which the rider is first thrown violently backward, then forward, then backward again, it jerked viciously, nearly toppling Henri in the process and causing him to slide sideways around the neck, until he was hanging on in a most precarious fashion. It was at that very moment that Serena, already mounted, rode up.

"Well, monsieur, I believe you looked better in the balloon," she said brightly, and it took all of her effort to keep a straight face.

Henri looked at her sheepishly and felt himself flushing. He struggled back to an upright position and settled himself in the leather webbing of the saddle. As he did so he noticed that his pouch had fallen on the ground. For a long moment he just stared at it, wondering how to get it back without the complete loss of his dignity. Gascon was already up, as was everyone else. Then Serena saw it too and quickly appreciated his dilemma. "I'll get it," she said. She slid off her mount in an instant, snatched it up, handed it back to him, and remounted her camel without its kneeling again. Her movements were lithe and graceful, and Henri watched her appreciatively.

"*Merci,*" he said, nodding in gratitude. "How many days' ride to Arak?"

"Eight."

"After eight days I will be the picture of grace at this."

She laughed. "Or the camel will be riding you."

They rode hard, setting off in single file through the narrow wadi that wound its way off the plateau. Mile after mile passed by and they did not stop or slow or talk. The camels were superb animals in top condition. They kept a rapid pace, maintaining a steady rhythm as their hooves plodded through the soft sand of the wadi. Henri watched the Tuareg ride, crossing his legs over the camel's neck as he saw them do, but his animal would not respond to the movements of his feet. His mount occasionally tried to break away to graze on brush or the sparse foliage they passed, but he reined it in tightly. As he pulled on the nose ring the camel glared at him balefully, and once tried to bite him. He could only hope that during the journey he would be able to settle into a strained coexistence with the beast.

Henri pulled a small notebook from his pocket and tried to make sketches and notes as they rode, but the rocking motion of the camel made it impossible. He put the book away and contented himself just watching, enjoying the view from the great height of his camel's back. After a time the wadi broadened, and soon he found himself next to Serena.

"I am pleased, Monsieur deVries. You have stayed on the camel all this way!"

"He is waiting until tonight to unload me as he wishes," Henri admitted ruefully. "I think he would rather I'd stayed in the balloon. I shall have to remember not to turn my back on him."

She showed him the Tuareg manner of sitting in the saddle and holding the rein, and how to make the camel respond to his feet, a task for which he had to remove his shoes. But the camel wouldn't cooperate. It complained loudly and spit in disgust, much to her delight. "It must be your French toes," she said.

"How is it you speak French so well?" Henri asked her.

"In the spring of my tenth year a small group of us traveled to El Gassi," she said. "I became separated from the group and fell from some rocks. I broke my leg so badly the bone came through the skin. No one with us knew what to do. The marabout who would normally care for such an injury was not with us, and I could not travel. There was a White Father living in the town, a French missionary from Algiers. He knew what to do and set the leg. And when I developed fever and nearly died, he tended to me. I was there a long time, and could not rise from my mat. It was then he taught me to speak the language."

"He did it very well."

"He was a kind man. He grew vegetables and gave them away though he had not enough to eat himself. He tried to convert me to his religion, as he tried with others. But for all his effort he made not a single convert. And then one day someone cut the father's throat. My lessons were finished." He was startled by the matter-of-fact way she said it, as though it was the most natural thing in the world.

"Who?"

"I don't know. The Shamba, I think." She used the word as a curse. The Shamba were Arabs of the north central oases, while the Tuareg were Berbers. For centuries there had been a blood feud between them, with caravan raiding and looting of camps embittering one generation after another. "They are devout of Islam and have no patience for the White Fathers. It was only a matter of time until someone did it."

"How is it the Shamba left you alone?"

"They are *ben haloof*," she said, "but even sons of pigs will not harm a girl. The father had hidden me anyway, to be sure. He was worried about my safety. In the end he worried about the wrong throat. They would have taken me hostage, I suppose, had they known I was there, and traded me back to my people. The Shamba despise us worse than . . . well, than *you*, and would do anything to bring us harm. They have never been able to master us or bring us to their ways. When we meet in battle they always get worse than they give. It is intolerable for them. They call us the abandoned of God, but God has not abandoned us, as you see. He is all around us." With a sweep of her hand she indicated the remarkable country through which they traveled. To their west lay a long, low range of dunes, their slopes rippled with hard sand that shimmered like copper in the sun. To the east a flat was strewn with pebbles in colors ranging from salmon to deep purple. A plateau rose before them, its face fractured with jagged gorges to whose sides clung stubborn thorn trees on which bright flowers blossomed. There was no monotony to it, nothing bleak or empty. For Henri it was a world of variety and surprise.

The wind had blown her hair into her face. She brushed it back, and as she did Henri found himself staring at her. He was struck by the complexity of this woman of the desert, who spoke so frankly and whose spirit was so free, who could laugh so easily and completely enjoy herself with simple things, and yet in the next moment deal just as readily with death. The Sahara was a harsh environment that bred tough people. He had no doubt that if need be she could kill a man just as easily as—just as easily as kiss him. She was fresh and a little insolent. He liked that, the insolence, for it was so apart from what he always experienced. He was accustomed to women who fawned over him for his money or position. This woman would be unimpressed by both. She seemed to have everything she needed atop her camel.

With a start he realized that he hadn't been listening to what she was saying. She caught his gaze and held it for a moment, then dropped her eyes as she continued talking.

". . . the northern oases, and there I had a chance to practice the language with the French settlers. Then two years ago I accompanied my uncle to Algiers. He is a great marabout, and has taught me much." She explained that marabouts were holy men who taught religion and served as physicians and instructed the Tuareg in astronomy, geography, botany, reading and writing. "I waited there while he made the pilgrimage to Mecca. It was there I saw a balloon. One that flew, that is."

It was springtime in the desert, warm but not hot. They rode comfortably as midday became afternoon, and the long afternoon hours stretched into early evening. They talked without stopping, riding alongside each other and all but oblivious to the others, who had stretched out into a long languid procession. The countryside gradually flattened, the ground changing from the coarse sand of the wadis to a blend of finer sand mixed with colorful stones. Henri and Serena talked easily and endlessly about scores of things, about birds they saw and plants that could be eaten and plants that would kill you, about the sultan in Istanbul (was it true, she wanted to know, that he bathed in a golden tub?), about ships that plied the Mediterranean, about horned lizards and snakes, about the desert and its weather, its nights and its floods, its quirks and its beauty. She seemed to know everything about it, and saw it all through eyes that were observant and sensitive and engaged. Once she spotted something in the distance and without a word rode off to get it. When she returned she held a delicate sand rose, a desert blossom sculpted by eons of wind. She held the gift out to him as they rode. He had to lean to take it and nearly lost his balance, but she caught him and steadied him with her free hand, and pressed the rose to him with her other, and their palms touched lightly. The touch was a fleeting one, but there was a moment of magic in it for them both. Gently he murmured his thanks and looked at the rose. Its crystals blazed brilliantly in the sun. He placed it carefully into the inside pocket of his cloak.

They traded tales of the places they had seen. She held her breath at his description of the Seine, flowing in a slow lazy arc past his home, of the snow that covered the peaks of France, and of the icefields he had crossed in Scandinavia. She told him of the great caravan routes and of caves where ancient rock paintings showed that what was now her desert home had once been a fertile jungle full of animals. She delighted him with tales of ostrich hunts that lasted two or even three days, and pointed out places where there would be water, places he would never have thought to look, and she told him of the thunder noise that the dunes made when the sun was coming up. There was too much to say, so much to share, and it all came in a rush between them that consumed the whole day.

Twice Tamrit rode back to her and told her to stop her foolish talk with the Frenchman and to conduct herself with more dignity. Twice she responded with fire in her voice and sent him away, sulking and miserable. He despaired at the chasm that separated him from what he desired and what he could have. Serena had spurned many suitors over the years. Tamrit knew that he had come closer than any of the others to winning her, but this afternoon he had suddenly seen with startling clarity the contrast between the way that she responded to him and the way she behaved with the Frenchman. He loved to hear her laugh, it was true, but it tore at him to hear the difference in the tone of her laughter with this accursed *ikufar*. She never sounded like that with him, never acted that way or laughed so easily. She was always so distant, so unattainable. And her talk! Tamrit had trouble getting twenty words out of her, yet she hadn't stopped chattering all day to this devil-of-the-sky. At first there was more ache than anger in him, but each passing hour he was forced to endure it shifted the balance until he was seething inside. He spurred his camel viciously and rode ahead for a while, but gave that up when he realized it made him look foolish and feel even more isolated from her. It would be better to stay closer in order to keep an eye on things. He selected a position to ride from which he could not help looking at them, even though he hated doing so. The afternoon wore long on his patience. Gradually his focus shifted away from her indifference and toward the interloper, his anger simmering against the Frenchman.

Gascon rode near the rear. He was puzzled by the behavior of the count, who was overly preoccupied, he thought, with the Tuareg woman. Gascon was still wary of their escort but took some comfort from the fact that while the rifles were out of reach on the back of a pack camel, he had at least succeeded in keeping the count's valise with him, which contained a pistol.

When at last they stopped for the night, Henri found that he was quite sore from the ride. It was with a great sense of relief that he was able to get off his camel without making a spectacle of it. He realized that it mattered to him that this graceful desert woman not witness another bout of clumsiness on his part. When he acknowledged the thought he blushed privately and shook his head at the crazy notion. *Why should it matter?* he wondered.

Camp was quickly established by Buzu, who once again did all the work while the others did nothing.

Henri and Gascon tried to help but he brushed them aside. "He is Irawellan," Serena explained. "A slave. It is his task to mind the needs of the camp." She explained their caste system to him. Except for Buzu all the men of her party were noblemen, warrior-overlords who acted as guides and guardians to caravans, and patrolled their districts against attack. In other Tuareg camps there were marabouts. The *imrad* were vassals who worked the land and tended the herds and paid levies for protection, and sometimes accompanied the nobles as their squires. At the end of the chain were the slaves who cultivated gardens and tended to the livestock and saw to the needs of travel. The social order she described, like the appearance of their men, struck Henri as medieval.

Buzu unloaded and hobbled each of the camels by folding a foreleg up and tying it with rope, then leaving it to wander as it sought its meager pasture. Henri watched the slave start a fire, a process that required no steel or flint. He rubbed a small green stick sharpened like a pencil down the length of a dry stick, creating a small channel into which dry bits of wood fiber were rubbed off and collected at one end. The small pile grew and began to smoke, finally igniting. He put a battered tin pot on the fire for tea. Then he heated a thick millet porridge, which started as a paste to which he added a small quantity of nearly black water from his goatskin.

The group squatted around the fire, Henri and Gascon with them. They passed the bowl of porridge around a circle, each person taking a bite with a wooden spoon before passing it to the next. The Tuareg revealed nothing of themselves as they ate, for they did not lower their veils to eat, but rather lifted them and turned away as they brought the spoon up under the cloth covering their mouths. The porridge was filling, but brackish and dry and full of sand. Henri didn't notice. He was watching her. For dessert they ate dates that were kept fresh in leather pouches, and drank tea. As Serena translated Henri answered a thousand questions from the Tuareg men, who, except for Tamrit,

seemed to have gotten over their initial hostility and had
accepted their presence. Soon they were all laughing.

Tamrit kept to himself, hunched over by the fire. He
sat quietly, ignoring the chatter. He was no longer angry at the intruders. His anger had been replaced with a
plan. He knew what to do. Their journey to Arak had
brought them very near Shamba country. He had a
Shamba knife taken from a corpse during a raid. It
would be a simple enough matter to steal up on the
French devils in the middle of the night and silently cut
their throats. He would leave the knife where anyone
could see that the perfidious Shamba had been at it
again. Only Serena would have doubts or even care, and
he would deal with her.

Gascon looked about for the best place to sleep. He
didn't want to camp close to the Tuareg. He would not
trust what he could not see, and their faces were hidden.
He had shared his concerns with the count, who had
only shrugged. It was not like the count to let his guard
down, Gascon reflected, but he seemed truly uncon-
cerned. Well, then, he would watch for both of them.
He selected a spot on the opposite side of the fire from
where the balloon and their other supplies sat in a pile.
While he knew he couldn't easily get to the rifles, he
didn't want anyone else getting to them either. He satisfied himself that it was the best position available. He
would sleep with the valise as his pillow and keep one
hand on the gun.

When darkness fell and the moon had not yet risen,
Henri took his sextant and with Serena at his side
walked over the gravelly plain toward a dune. The pebbles blended with sand and the sand became deeper,
making for hard work. The dune was much higher and
farther away than it had looked from camp. When they
arrived at the top he sat cross-legged and began his
sightings. He explained to her the workings of the sextant, making diagrams in the sand to illustrate how
knowing the time and the position of the stars could tell
him where he was. She grasped the concept quickly and
eagerly, nodding her head in excitement, then sighting
the stars herself. He pointed at the different stars he

sometimes used. "That is Vega," he said, "and Cepheus, and there—"

"Is Rigel," she interrupted, "in Orion," and she went on and on, pointing at other stars and constellations, here Pegasus, there Cassiopeia and Delphinus, names that to his astonishment were the same or similar to those he knew. Though she couldn't tell him where the names came from, she knew them all, it seemed, knew more than he did, and she had stories for some, taught her by the marabout.

By the low light of a candle Henri marked their position on his map. He sketched the rough features of the terrain they had passed that day, and showed her where he had marked Bou Saada and the Grand Erg. She took his pencil and with a hand that was swift and sure drew more for him on the paper, much more, adding Timimoun and Arak and beyond it the great Tassili Hoggar, the high volcanic massif in the deep desert that was her home. She sketched in riverbeds and mountains and prominent features of the land, hesitating only slightly as she gauged where to place them. She worked quickly and confidently, and even without a sextant, Henri had no doubt that her markings would be reasonably close. She knew her subject well.

He was surprised at the extent of the mountains she drew. "I had thought there would be more . . . emptiness," he said. "More sand."

"There is plenty enough of that," she laughed, "but there is much more to this land than the dunes. It is a wondrous place, as rich with life as it is with death. If you have a bigger paper," she promised, "I will make a better map."

The moon rose huge over the plain before them. They looked at it through field glasses and gazed at the majesty of the view. The campfire flickered in the distance. The cold made them shiver and Henri pulled a blanket over their shoulders, and produced a flask of wine. She coughed when she drank but it warmed her, and they sat there for hours, chattering and laughing. When it was very late they reluctantly came down off the dune and said good night.

Tamrit burned inside as he watched them return. His eyes had never left them. He pretended to be asleep as she passed his mat.

Later Serena lay awake on her mat and stared at the moon, dazzling white overhead. Her mind was on fire with the Frenchman. She felt the sweet stirrings of something beginning and reveled in it, for beginnings were such exquisite times. She struggled with her feelings, unsure and a little uncomfortable, knowing that everything was wrong with a relationship between cultures, yet not caring, not really caring at all. She only knew that she loved his company, that she had never felt so warm and happy beside another man. *These are the foolish thoughts of a stupid girl,* she told herself. *How can I think these things? I have known him for less than a day. But such a wonderful day.* She would let it develop as it would, in its own way.

Suddenly the soft strains of a flute broke the night silence of the camp, and for the thousandth time since the balloon had fallen a smile came to her face. She hadn't seen him with an instrument, but she knew at once it was he who played, and not Gascon. There was something in the melody that was the Frenchman, something gentle and sweet and warm. It was the custom of the Tuareg for a man to compose poems for the woman he loved in the ceremony of *ahal,* to demonstrate his feelings for her with a gift of verse. She knew that Henri would not know this, but she chose to make his music her private *ahal.* She let herself imagine that he was playing just for her, that they were alone under the moon and the stars, and she closed her eyes and lost herself in its magic. It was enchanting to her, that this man from Europe could know so well how to capture this place with music. It was a desert song he played, a song that brought to mind the lovely chant of the muezzin calling the faithful to prayer from his minaret, a song of mystery that sang of the flowing of the sands and the passage of time and the beautiful slow steady rhythm of life.

And then the music stopped, and she slept.

Much later, just before dawn, Tamrit set his cover

aside and rolled silently off his mat. He listened for a moment to be certain no one stirred in the camp. A wind had picked up. It would help cover the sounds of his movement. Carrying the Shamba knife in one hand, he began his stealthy crawl toward the sleeping Frenchmen. The killers would leave no trail, for the ground was hard and rocky. There would be no way for anyone to determine from whence they had come, or where they had fled. There was nothing he could do about the moon, but he would be operating away from the rest of the sleeping Tuareg, and knew that if the Frenchmen saw anything it would not matter, for it would be the last thing they saw. He would kill deVries first, then the other one, and leave the knife and crawl back to his mat. After dawn someone else would find the bodies and raise the alarm. It would be someone else who would accuse the Shamba. Tamrit would be outraged along with the rest of them, and it would be done.

He moved quickly through the silent forms and baggage of the camp. No one moved and the camels were quiet. He stayed in a crouch as he approached the Frenchmen, his feet sure and steady. He had done this a score of times before, in caravans and camps, to the Shamba and his other enemies. It was pathetically easy at this time of night, when men slept most soundly. The blade was sharp and would slice cleanly through the flesh.

He arrived at the sleeping form of Henri, which was covered by a cloak. Tamrit steeled himself. He reached forward to draw back the edge of the cloak.

The voice hissed low and deadly and stunned him like a blow.

"If your word is so easily abandoned, Tamrit, do not abandon mine." The dark form of Serena stood behind him. She held one of the lances and was poised to use it. "By all that is holy to you, touch him and I will run you through." The hard steel tip of the lance prodded the folds of cloth at the nape of his neck. At the same instant she spoke, Gascon's blanket moved. His pistol was cocked and pointed squarely at Tamrit's forehead. He had watched them both coming. He had no idea what the woman had said and briefly wondered if he would have to shoot her too, but when he saw the position of her lance he understood.

Then Henri stirred and startled them all. He was not under the cloak on the mat, but had been sitting with his back to the basket of the balloon. More than an hour earlier, unable to sleep and unheard by anyone, he had moved to the packs to sit and watch the sky. He was awake and held a knife.

The magnitude of his defeat shook Tamrit to the quick of his being. He had been completely humiliated by two *ikufar* and the woman he loved. He made no pretense of innocence. Dishonored and alone, he left the camp before dawn. He took one camel and his simple possessions and headed off across the plain. He rode without a destination, his mind in turmoil. When the sun came up he dismounted from his camel. He prepared himself in the ritual manner, placing his prayer mat toward Mecca and using sand rather than water for his ablutions. His voice rang strong through the emptiness as he recited his litany of prayers. When he had finished he added a silent vow of holy vengeance upon the infidel Henri deVries, upon his life and his descendants and his possessions. He swore it in the name of Allah, and swore it for his sons unborn. Afterward he scooped out some sand to make a hollow and with dried vegetation made a small fire. He brewed a pot of tea and ate a handful of dates. Once again he mounted his camel and began to ride. It would be more than twenty years before anyone in the deVries family would see him again.

T HE NEXT NIGHT SERENA TOOK HENRI BY THE hand and led him out of camp. No words passed between them, for words were not needed. They climbed to the top of another dune, this time where no one could watch. Henri threw down his cloak and made a soft bed in the sand and they made love under the stars, oblivious to the cold, touching, exploring, clinging to each other, laughing and crying quiet tears of joy.

They stayed awake all through a night of whispers and promises and shared hopes and watched the sun come up over the gravelly plain.

They moved through the rest of the journey to Arak as if through a dream, where all the edges were soft and everything felt both real and unreal and fragile and desperately wonderful. They lost all sense of time, except to notice that it seemed to pass too quickly. One day stretched into the next. They slept little, instead sharing every moment, fighting sleep for fear of missing even one second of it, then holding each other tightly when at last sleep came to take them. Neither of them had ever known anything like it, ever felt so consumed by the fire and ecstasy of love first discovered. They shut out the Tuareg and Gascon and moved through the days in a private place that only the two of them shared, eating alone and riding together as they embarked on a slow passionate journey of discovery of each other's minds and bodies. They played games in the sand, tumbling down the sides of dunes. He taught her how the French danced, and she taught him how the Tuareg danced, and they mixed it together and collapsed in hilarity at the end of it all, and made love again.

Their approach to Arak was announced by a sudden riot of color and wild geological turbulence. Serena pointed out highlights of a landscape that looked to Henri as though Dante must have made it. It was the gateway to the Hoggar, a massive basalt plateau of the high desert that was the fortress of the Tuareg during those times of the year when the rains and forage were good. There were sudden steep walls and massive boulders strewn upon the sands, and Henri was struck dumb by the beauty, by the oddity of it all. Spectacular cathedrals of rock stood before him, towering great monuments of violet and mauve with spires and parapets, and he moved before them in a silence approaching reverence, as he might have moved through a church. For two days more they passed through valleys and across plateaus, until they stood in the camp of the Hoggar Tuareg.

THE AMENOKAL OF THE HOGGAR TUAREG, SULTAN El Hadj Akhmed, lord of the Tuareg tribes, master of the central Sahara, sat back on his haunches in his red-roofed tent and thundered at his sister. He was a man accustomed to having his way. His commands affected the lives of entire villages and tribes. His whims altered trade and commerce in vast regions of the desert. Yet now he sat nearly impotent before his sister, who would not listen. He had been making preparations to break camp, to travel with a salt caravan over the southern route to Bilma, when Serena had suddenly announced her intention of marrying a foreigner who had fallen from the sky in a balloon. She would leave everything— her family, her people, her way of life, and return with him to France.

Just like that.

And in all of this she had not asked. She had decreed.

At his side sat the marabout Moulay Hassan, a revered and wise man who was also his uncle. Across from them sat Serena, and next to her sat the source of the amenokal's present troubles, Count Henri deVries.

The count sat quietly; there was nothing Henri could say. He knew only that the discussion was heated, and he could guess the content easily enough without knowing the words or seeing any face but hers. She was tough, he thought, and she was standing up to them, taking a terrible verbal beating, but giving no quarter, setting her jaw and leaning forward, sometimes clenching her fists, shrugging, waving, shaking her head. He watched her with admiration. *She is a wondrous woman.*

They had been arguing for the better part of the afternoon, and for the amenokal it was not going well. He had tried everything: persuasion, bribery, orders, threats. Nothing had worked. He had begun at the logical place, by simply forbidding it.

"You cannot!" she retorted.

"I can and will! I will have him killed and take you prisoner!"

"Raise a hand against him and I will cut it off! If you

lock me up it will have to be until the day I die, for I will have no other man but this one." She looked at Henri and spoke with fierce conviction. "Accept my word, Brother, for I have given it."

The amenokal sighed. Had Serena been able to see behind the blue cloth, she would have seen a face that was weary and discouraged. He was often certain that the Arabs knew better when it came to the treatment of women, w'allahi! When a man decided his daughter or sister was to be married, or not married, that was that. The discussion was limited, simple, the transaction finished. Life lived in such a manner was manageable, predictable, serene. A Tuareg woman could be more contrary than a camel, and Serena could be more stubborn than any ten of them together.

The amenokal regarded Henri. *He looks strong enough. His face shows character. But he is ikufar. He is wrong for Serena. He is trouble. And if they marry I shall be rich, but I shall never have an heir.* It was true that the Frenchman had pledged a dowry unheard-of in his memory. Six hundred camels, he had promised. Six hundred! A vast fortune! Henri had started with four hundred, and at that stupendous amount the amenokal had gasped. Assuming the gasp meant his initial offer was too low, Henri immediately raised it. Then he had presented the amenokal with a pouch of gold and silver coins and a rifle with ammunition. The delighted amenokal had fired it with stunning inaccuracy, missing a huge boulder at a hundred paces, while everyone smiled and pretended he'd shot well.

But more than dowry, more than any wealth the Frenchman might bestow, the amenokal wanted an heir, someone to command the *tobol* of the Tuareg after he died, to preserve their standing as princes of the desert, to retain their traditions. It was on this matter that he could tolerate no union between them.

"You could marry so well! Men of a hundred families would give all to have you!"

"Hah! They care nothing for me. They would marry me to father the next amenokal. Nothing more."

"You are both wrong and too harsh, Sister. You are a

woman to treasure. Yet that is not the point. This man
is of a different world. He looks solid enough. But it is
neither he who concerns me, nor your contentment. It is
your unborn son."

"There is no son!"

"There will be."

"When there is we will discuss it."

"Then it will be too late, when what is done is done.
Now is the time to consider his life. There *will* be a son,
Serena. And he will not be of us, and he will not be of
the French."

"He will be of *me*. He will be of his father."

"It is not enough. A man needs a tribe. A man needs
to belong. Bring a son into the world who does not
belong, and you condemn him to a life in between. That
is a life no mother should choose for her son. That is a
life no child should be forced to live. It is a cruel thing
to do, Serena. A selfish thing."

She lowered her head when he said that, so that he
could not see her eyes. He had found that place inside
her that was the most vulnerable, through an appeal to
her sense of duty to children yet unborn. Was she being
selfish? Which mattered more, that she follow the longings of her heart, or that she provide the amenokal with
a perfect heir? There was no guarantee that her own son
would even *be* the heir. While succession to leadership
of the Tuareg was matrilineal, there were others who
might succeed El Hadj Akhmed first, including her own
cousin Ahitagel, the son of Serena's mother's sister. But
fate might someday make her son that leader. To become amenokal was a desperately difficult path for any
boy or man to follow, all the more so if his veins carried
the mixed blood of her union with Henri. She knew all
that, yet there was no argument within her strong
enough to overcome her feelings for the man sitting beside her. She knew what she must do.

"If it is the child's destiny to be amenokal, if he is the
right one, then his blood will not matter. And if he is
not the right one, pure blood will not help."

"Speak sense to her," the amenokal said to the marabout, raising his hands in supplication. Moulay Hassan

had been Serena's teacher, her guide as she grew from infant to girl to woman. He had been her surrogate father since her own had died. He was as close to her, as influential with her as anyone among the Tuareg. She had been one of his prized students, a quick study whose questions soon outpaced his answers, whose mastery of Tuareg lore and the sciences outstripped his own. It was because he knew her well that he knew it was useless. He had seen her set her mind, as he had seen her do so many times before. She would not be deterred. But to please the amenokal he tried mightily, and failed miserably. Serena was master of her will.

"I will miss you, child," said the marabout when he finally gave in. His eyes misted. "But promise to bring the boy back to know his own one day. Bring him back to know his great-uncle."

CHAPTER 3

THE HOLY MAN OF THE SAHARA TOOK THE UNION of Henri and Serena with far more equanimity than a holy man of France, Monseigneur Murat, the bishop of Boulogne-Billancourt.

At the time of his father's death, Marius Murat was too young to understand the events that led up to it. His father was a merchant of modest means. The family had a little money and a littler house. One day a visitor came, an arrogant man with a top hat and silk cloak and shiny black boots. He arrived in a closed calèche that had a driver and was drawn by two matched chestnut horses. Carriages like that did not come often to their *quartier*. Murat stared at the beautiful horses and the rich carriage in wonder. Then he heard his mother crying hysterically.

The stranger brought terrible news. Murat had vivid memories of huddling in the corner of a room with his mother and his sister while the man and Murat's father argued. The details were hazy: investments and property and bad luck. His father had gambled on a land deal. Not only was the original investment lost but the house and all the family's possessions as well. Men would be coming to take everything—the meager furnishings, the wardrobes and dressers and the oak table in the kitchen and the carved maple washstand that had belonged to Murat's grandmother. Murat flushed with shame as his father dropped to his knees to plead, and the stranger laughed with scorn. His father clenched his fists and shouted things about frauds and swindlers. There was violent pushing and the man threw Murat's sobbing father to the floor. Murat saw a look on the stranger's face that he never forgot. It was not a look of pity or anger. It was a look of smug superiority.

That night Murat's father went out and was gone a long time. When he came back he was raging drunk and carried a pistol in his belt. His eyes were blood-red and wild. Murat felt his spittle as he talked and swore and whimpered his rage. His anger built, until Murat and his mother and sister had to cower again in the corner. They listened in terror while his father waved the pistol and said frightful things—that he ought to kill the man, kill himself, kill them all. Sobbing, he took another drink of rum. He wiped his defeated eyes and wandered into the kitchen. A terrible loud bang shook the house and left a smell of powder and blood. Long minutes passed when the only sound was a haunted noise coming from Murat's mother. The boy was the first to brave the kitchen, to see what his father had done.

The stranger returned even before the funeral, accompanied by the prefect of police. There were other officials, sullen-looking men with rifles and mustaches and papers with wax seals. The family was allowed to gather its clothing, nothing more, and leave.

At the time, Murat understood nothing of what had happened. As he grew from child to boy, from boy to youth, he began to distill the lessons he had learned. He drew them from memories of his father. He drew them from his passage through the slums of Paris, where the rats lived better than the cats and the cats lived better than the children, and where he had to stand aside while nobles passed in their carriages and splashed him with the filth of the streets. He drew them from his job carrying heavy bales of cloth and sweeping the floors of the little hat factory where he worked twenty hours a day for thirty sous. He drew them from cynical adolescence.

It is better to be the man evicting than the man vanquished.

It is better to wear the black boot of power than to die beneath it.

Only fools have no money and live like dogs.

Murat did not grieve for his father, for he was a boy who did not feel things as others did. There had always been an empty place inside him. He puzzled at other children who cried when possessions were broken or lost, or who disintegrated in tears when classmates called them names. Murat could call the names, or be called them, and it didn't matter. Pets died; Murat was indifferent. He did not make friends easily. His appearance was forbidding. His eyes were penetrating, wolf gray and cold. His manner was aloof. When he did make friends they soon tired of his brooding and sullen nature, of his authoritarianism, and they left him. Murat didn't care. He didn't need friends, not their approval or their confidence. Intimacy was trivial, unimportant. He found his own company entirely satisfying and kept to himself.

Time strengthened his resolve that no man would ever come and take away his possessions. He would not live as his father had lived, in a futile pursuit of meager means, all acquired under rules made by someone else. *I will not be my father,* he told himself. *I will have influence and wealth.* He swore it to himself at every meal, when his stomach growled in hunger before his near-empty plate. He swore it to himself at night when he went to sleep. He swore it to himself every morning when he woke up. He swore it to himself when his mother made him sit next to her while she cried; and he despised her for her sniveling and her weakness. He hated having to sit that way, hated having to pretend to comfort her. He stared off into some distant place while she cried herself to sleep.

I will not be my father. I will be my father's master.

Murat had a coldly practical personality, given to detailed planning of everything he did. He looked for ways to make his resolution a reality. There were precious few means open to him. In most areas of French life, merit was of far less importance than birth. As he was not noble born, whatever he might achieve would have to come from his own effort. Commerce was not practical. He was quite clever enough for it but lacked capital, and disdained a life fighting for scraps somewhere in a pathetic netherworld between poverty and success as his father had done. The military might bring him power but no wealth, and even the power would be limited without a birthright with which to secure the highest ranks. Besides, he had no desire to risk his life in the pursuit of his goals. The trades? Only bare sustenance. The professions were just a shade better, and quite costly to study. He had no talent for the arts, in which no money or power was to be found anyway. He racked his brains and bided his time in the wretched apartment and pushed his broom in the factory.

And then one day when he was seventeen it came to him.

It was an epiphany.

It was the Church.

His uncle had come to visit. He was a religious man, and Murat's mother had insisted the family accompany him to a Christmas mass. Murat had not been to church since he was baptized. They went to Notre Dame on a cold, crisp morning. The streets of Paris were busy, but nowhere so much as near the church, where there was an excitement, an energy in the air. The sanctuary was crowded to overflowing. Murat and his family were jostled about rudely and had to content themselves with standing behind a pillar to the rear of the railing of the nave. Murat could see nothing. He held on to the pillar and climbed onto the railing, and there he saw things that made his spirit soar as high as the magnificent vaulted ceiling.

The archbishop of Paris himself was conducting the service. He stood in the chancel before the high altar. The church was so big he looked to Murat as though he were a mile away, and all heads were turned reverently toward him. Even from a distance, Murat could see the flowing robes and brilliant sashes, and perceive the majesty. The archbishop was flanked by priests and servers, and his voice rang out above the crowd of worshipers, who sang their hymns and bowed their heads and looked up to that man standing above them all, a man whose open arms promised glory for those who would accept his truths. Murat couldn't understand the words.

They were Latin, unintelligible to his unpracticed ear, but they had the certain ring of omnipotence, settling over the hushed congregation, the word of God Himself. The prelate's voice boomed off ornate columns and echoed in the alcoves. The sun shone through glorious windows of stained glass and fell upon the gold miter on his head and upon his white and purple robes.

Murat saw the plush red carpets behind the altar and the precious stones gleaming in the chalice that a priest held to the archbishop's lips. He saw the parishioners, even the poor ones who had only rags to cover the holes in their rags, slipping their alms into the collection plates, and he saw that the plates were made of silver. He watched the throngs of faithful who stood as the bishop beckoned, and sang as he sang, and prayed as he prayed. Everything was perfect, everything divine: the geometry, the light and the space, all the energy and life and worship focused on the archbishop and the altar behind him—the stone arches soaring overhead, massive and powerful; the mighty chandelier, hanging, it seemed, all the way from heaven. The choir sang and golden bells pealed the glory of God and, for Murat at least, the even greater glory of His church and His ministers.

That Christmas morning Murat came closer than ever before in his life to feeling something deeply. It was a glorious sensation that filled him up and brought a smile to his face. Had his mother seen him at that moment it would have frightened her, for it was the same smile another man had worn in her kitchen years before—a smile of smug superiority, a smile of chilling certainty. Murat had found his way, a path to power that even a poor child could follow, and the door to it was wide open. The Church had suffered from a severe shortage of priests since the Revolution, when those not deported were executed. Their ranks had never again been completely filled. Vacancy meant opportunity. Less competition meant more room to advance. Murat knew at last where he was going, and where he was going had nothing to do with God.

He entered the Seminary of St. Michel in his eighteenth year. He had no difficulty with seminary life, adapting quickly to its requirements and dedicating himself to its conventions. He developed a perfect understanding of what it took to become a priest, coolly calculating the expectations of the Church hierarchy and the parishioners themselves, and took great pains that every word and deed might make him appear to be that priest. Religious thought rarely entered his mind. When it did, it was as rote, not as belief. He hadn't the slightest belief in God. When he prayed it was to nothing, empty words to fill a void. God was never expected to answer his prayers. God never did. He never looked for God in his surroundings, never wondered whether He was there. It wasn't important. The priesthood was a commerce of sorts, a commerce that trafficked in men's souls rather than goods, and no more required a belief in the underlying premise of God than a broker required a belief in the underlying premise of the Bourse. All that mattered was whether it worked. If others believed, he granted them their faith. If he himself did not, who was to judge him harshly so long as the conventions were kept? He was a clever chameleon who did not suffer the inconvenience of a moral base.

It was in the confessional that his talent for adaptation reached its greatest height. There he feigned agony and invited the most severe acts of contrition. There he admitted those things that he knew his confessor on the other side of the screen needed to hear. He conceded at least some of the sins of his life; and where he thought they might be lacking, he burnished them for effect. He sought a realistic balance. He admitted greed, but left out ambition. He admitted the empty place inside, but left out his failure of faith. He admitted anger at the man who had brought death to his father, but left out his envy of that man. He said all the things a penitent his age would be expected to say. And he knew where to stop. A certain amount of candor in the service of his aims was one thing; candor in the service of plain truth was another, and further than he cared to go. So he did not acknowledge the women he still had on his occasional trips outside the seminary. Nor did he confess the man. Each Monday after final prayers had been said and the seminary had fallen silent for the night, a priest slipped quietly into Murat's small room and stayed until just before dawn. Such revelations would have been too much for the priest behind the screen, so Murat kept them to himself.

Murat was convincing in his demeanor. He struck a pose of pure humility as he knelt. His prayer voice resonated with conviction. He took the conventions of his apprenticeship seriously, applying himself diligently to the study of the Scriptures, Church history and doctrine, and the decorum of the Church. Latin came easily to him, as did the ritual ceremonies. Whether Murat stood before a parishioner or a peer, a bishop or a king, he struck exactly the right note; and over time, his brilliant act of deception took on the reality of repetition. Hours of practice brought the Holy Spirit to his voice and the wrath of God to his gestures and made righteousness run fast in his veins. He delivered the charade so convincingly that he himself began to believe it; and his message grew real to his audiences, which in turn reinforced him. At last one could not tell, standing in front of Murat and a man whose soul was pure and whose existence was truly devoted to religious thoughts and good works, which was the believer, and which the pretender.

Murat went from the seminary to the diocese of Boulogne-Billancourt which had two other priests, with whom he worked out a comfortable if unspoken arrangement. They worked on the souls of the parishioners, while Murat worked on their pocketbooks. He was a more effective fund-raiser behind closed doors than in a chapel, dispensing blessings with one hand while accepting thanks with the other. But he was effective in the chapel as well. Where some priests preached hope and salvation, Murat found that a well-developed fear of God and eternal damnation was a more direct route to loosening men's wallets. He pounded the pulpit and his eyes bulged with almighty fervor. His voice was

deep and mellifluous and full of the sound and fury of
the Lord, and that voice fell upon vulnerable con-
sciences like the golden hammer of God. The francs
poured into his coffers.

Yet his great strength lay not in the gospel of fear. He
quickly demonstrated to his elders that he was a gifted
administrator and organizer, talents the Church desperately needed. In France, the Church and its bishops
were quite independent and received no help from
Rome, and little enough from the state. Murat found
ways to make the diocese money, and ways to save the
diocese money. He straightened out muddled accounts
and established his own procedures for keeping the ledgers. He began dealing directly with bankers and bro-
kers and vendors, and soon his offices bore a steady
stream of visitors. Gradually, he gained direct access to
the accounts of the Church. At first his access fell under
the close scrutiny of the bishop. But as time passed his
freedom increased. It was then that he began to demonstrate what was perhaps his greatest gift, the one most
highly prized by his elders. He was a genius at finance.
He speculated on the Bourse, somehow knowing when
to buy and when to sell. It was all very small at first, for
the bishop was a man whose nerves were easily frayed
and whose appetite for a gamble was well under control. But each success brought Murat more liberty, until
at last he stopped asking altogether. Murat showed similar genius at acquiring and selling property. As with
stocks, he always seemed to know just what to do with
property, and when to do it. He could bring more
money into the Church with a single land transaction
than he could in twenty years behind a pulpit.

If Father Murat was shrewd, even ruthless in his
dealings, no specific complaints ever reached the ear of
the bishop. There were rumors, it was true, rumors
of dark dealings and transactions on the slippery edge
of the appropriate, but the bishop showed little interest
in the ledgers so long as things ran well. If Murat was
disliked by the other priests, well, it was of little consequence. If the bishop himself did not like Father Murat,
if he found his stares cold and empty and devoid of

Christ inside, if he felt a certain chill when the priest talked, he dismissed the notion and turned his attention to more pressing matters of the diocese, for the bishop was a man who understood performance and could judge ambition. Above all, he was a man who could count. His diocese had always possessed a surplus of debt, never a surplus of cash; yet within two years of Father Murat's arrival, the first renovations to the cathedral in two hundred years were made, and improvements and repairs followed, even to the bishop's own castle. There had even been enough money for contributions to the workingman's fund and to the orphanage. The bishop was well pleased.

There was also money for accounts that even the bishop didn't know about. These accounts were private, established by and known only to Murat. In the beginning, they contained modest amounts, but each success made him bolder and the amounts grew. Murat needed the money to make things work in ways that sometimes troubled the squeamish. Difficult bargains had to be sealed, and bureaucrats purchased: matters that his less practical superiors might not approve. It was all perfectly justified, he reasoned. Without him the Church would not have the money anyway, and as he used it to further his ends in the name of the Church it was all quite appropriate. Over time, the line between the interests of the Church and the interests of Murat began to blur. He began using the money for his own personal needs, needs that grew steadily in number and were quite insatiable.

For years Father Murat worked that way, developing contacts among government functionaries, civic officials, lords and ladies of the realm. He gave tips and received them. He granted favors and asked them, storing up obligations for later use. He learned secrets and remembered them. He learned others and divulged them. Along the way, he thundered at the moral infirmities of his flock, exhorting them to saintliness and damning the sins of flesh that crept through the night streets of Paris. He did it even as he slept with whores, even as he slept with men. He threatened hell and sold maps to paradise, and found his parish brimming with souls eager to buy the maps. France was a nation of realists and doubters and skeptics, but Murat was not deterred, for he knew something of men's nature—that in crops of doubters could be found a rich harvest of souls.

He dealt and he damned. And he ate. Upon entry to the seminary he had been scrawny, the product of long years of near starvation. At the seminary the food was plentiful if not fancy, and he gained a little weight. At the parish he took charge of the matter personally, and soon the food was as fancy as the wine, and both were abundant. He filled out and ordered new robes, and filled out some more. Within a few years, he grew corpulent and sprouted an extra chin. The bulk added timbre to his voice and his voice added funds to the coffers.

Father Murat had come far from the kitchen where his father's life had ended. People paid him homage and asked for his blessings and showed him deference and respect. His life was bountiful and he lived well. But he was neither content nor finished. He had only begun. The first step on the road he had chosen had been taken with his eyes fixed firmly upon the robes of the archbishop. He would not stop until he wore them, and after that the red robes of a cardinal.

Murat advanced along his path by ingratiating himself with ministers and bureaucrats of the government—men who needed the money he could give them, men who in turn gave him the information he required to make the money. The president was Louis Napoléon, nephew of Bonaparte. Murat had supported Louis Napoléon from the first. Each time the man sought more power, Murat was there to help. Finally, a coup led to Louis Napoléon's installation as emperor. The development suited Murat well, for it was the emperor, not the pope in Rome, who named bishops in France. Murat already knew most of the emperor's staff and had made several of them rich. Beyond that, Murat had tailored his own political views of matters concerning Church and State to suit the emperor's needs. That the emperor required the loyalty of bishops above any they might feel to Rome was perfectly logical to Murat. Rome did nothing for him.

It was simply a matter of time until he could exchange black robes for purple. He would have to be patient, however, as there were no vacancies among the ranks of the bishops except in the provinces. Murat disdained such posts, which were hopelessly poor and consumed with spiritual drudgery. He preferred the opportunities and connections of Paris and bided his time. Then a new bishop was transferred to the see. He was a kindly man who avoided politics and whose courtliness and simple devotion to the teachings of Christ had won him deep love and respect among the parishioners of his diocese. The bishop was healthy, a relatively young man of fifty-four, and Murat knew he was likely to be bishop for many years to come. Murat chafed under the gentle hand of the new bishop, who would not let him use his talents the way he had done before. He was diverted from finance to the priestly tasks of visiting the sick and tending to the salvation of the parish.

"Yes, my son," the bishop agreed when Murat protested, "it is true our temporal needs are pressing. But the good Lord will provide for those. It is your task to do His work among men's souls." No amount of argument made a difference; and at least on the surface Murat was forced to comply, but he was growing impatient.

His opportunity, when at last it came, was quite unexpected, as near to an act of God as he had ever seen.

Terrible springtime floods had swollen the Marne and Seine Rivers to overflowing, and parish houses had been destroyed across the river. The bishop asked Father Murat to accompany him as he looked after the needs of his flock, and to lend assistance where possible. Murat was not given to fanciful acts of goodwill on his own. He detested the thought of spending hours in a downpour in a futile quest to save men's dwellings or comfort their souls. It was his preference to send money and other priests, better-suited than he to provide this kind of help. But the bishop asked, and Murat assented.

The storm raged furiously around them as they boarded the little ferry for the short trip across the river. The wind whipped their robes about them and they had to hold on to their hats. The surface of the water was angry with whitecaps. It was dusk, the coming of night hastened by the thick dark clouds overhead. The ferry was not much more than a raft, a low wooden craft that had been built before the Revolution and rendered faithful service in the decades since. Now it strained against the flood waters as its operator pulled on the ropes that were suspended across the water to guide them to the opposite shore. They were nearly halfway across when a large tree floating downstream caught the ferry on its corner and turned it partway around. The tree broke free and continued floating, but the raft did not immediately straighten itself in the roiling water. A wave caught a corner of the port side, which dipped slightly under the water. That was enough to brew disaster. The load of crates on the ferry shifted. A mule lost its footing and slipped toward the side, which sank the endangered corner even more. Pandemonium erupted. Amid the shouts of the ferry operator and the braying of the mule and the noise of the storm, the edge of the craft dipped completely under, tilting the boat and hurling its occupants into the water. The ferry was held tight by the overhead rope and dragged against the current at an impossible angle. One of the passengers disappeared downstream, holding on to the back of the frantically braying mule.

Murat went under, swallowing great gulps of icy black water as he flailed about looking for the edge of the ferry. He caught a rail beneath the surface and was able to pull himself partway up to where he could hold on. Gasping, he used his free arm to work the raging current and keep himself upright. Water had gotten in his nose and mouth and he coughed violently. The lower half of his body was still submerged. At that moment he saw the bishop's arm break the surface of the water, and then his head. The brave father struggled furiously, but his robes were heavy and prevented him from moving freely.

"I cannot swim!" he half-cried, half-spluttered as he saw Murat. "Help me!" A brilliant burst of lightning illuminated the scene, freezing it in a brief eerie glow. The bishop had lost his hat. His head was gashed and bleeding.

At that instant Murat realized a decision was at hand. He could reach out, and the bishop would be rescued. Or he could just watch, and trust in the Lord to save His faithful servant.

"Help me!" cried the bishop again, and the heavy clouds poured and the lightning flashed once more over the terrified face and its river of blood. To Murat he looked grotesque, a pathetic old fool who could not swim. He was choking, and when he opened his mouth he took in more water. Murat looked around. There was no sign of the ferryman or the other passenger. There was no one at all. Murat's heart raced as fast as his thoughts. Then his brain took control, and he calmed himself.

He knew what to do.

"*Hail, holy queen, mother of mercy, our life, our sweetness, our hope. To you do we cry, poor banished children of Eve . . .*"

The bishop went under, his outstretched hand inches from Murat, who could have reached out to him easily. He came up once more, a desperate, beseeching look on his face. Murat caught hold of a piece of wood floating on the surface. It was sodden and heavy. He raised it up over his head. A terrible flicker of recognition dawned in the bishop's eyes as he realized what was happening. With all his strength Murat brought the club down. He felt a dull *thunk*. He raised the club again, and again he struck. The bishop went limp and sank.

"*. . . to you do we send up our sighs, mourning and weeping in this valley of tears . . .*"

Murat felt something bump against his legs underwater. It frightened him. He kicked viciously, to push it down and away toward the bottom. It was soft and yielded to his blows. For a long moment of dread he waited for it to bump him again. But it didn't. It was gone, swallowed by the current.

The storm raged and rain ran down his face and Father Murat clung to the side of the ferry. On the shore he could see men waving lanterns and shouting for other boats, and he knew help was on the way. As he waited the automatic litany took over. He repeated the words, and the words became the truth: *It was the hand of God that tipped the ferry. It was the will of God that he struck his head when he fell.*

God's will be done. God rest his soul.

THE BODY OF THE OLD BISHOP WAS NEVER FOUND. Within a fortnight word came directly from the Tuileries Palace: by the grace of the Emperor Napoléon III, the see of Boulogne-Billancourt had a new bishop. Marius Murat, the son of a poor merchant, humble servant of God, loyal friend of the empire, had arrived at last at the threshold of his dream. The first time someone kissed his ring a delicious shock ran down his spine, and he savored it, like a sexual sensation. Later, in the privacy of his palace—*his palace!*—he was giddy, it was grand!—the smile he permitted himself was a real one. He was overlord of thirty parishes, forty-one curacies, and two hundred eighty-five subcuracies. The trappings of office were exquisite. He had private apartments and reception rooms with crystal chandeliers, and a vast courtyard with a garden that had a fountain in the center. A greenhouse made of cast iron was stocked with exotic plants from all over the world. There were velvet cushions and quilted cloaks and violet robes and coachmen to transport him in eight different carriages. Cooks prepared pheasant shot by his own huntsmen. His wine cellar was superb. Legions of curés and sous-curés surrounded him and busied themselves doing his bidding. He no longer had to hide the transactions he made on behalf of the diocese, for after all, the bishop *was* the diocese, and the diocese was the bishop. For Marius Murat, the arrangement was splendid.

He had been bishop nearly a year when word came to his palace that Count Henri deVries had returned from Africa with a heathen woman at his side. The bishop had solidified his hold over many aspects of his diocese, taking a direct interest in its more notable people and their affairs. He sought influence and control at every level. Count deVries was a prominent resident of the diocese, if an independent and not particularly religious one. His landholdings were vast, his estate among the largest in France. Both his father and grandfather had been deeply religious men and quite generous to the Church. They had given land and money for the construction of schools and chapels. Henri might be expected to do the same, and now he had chosen a wife. It was, therefore, natural that the bishop came to call, and perhaps inevitable that a woman of Serena's strong will and independence would arouse the bishop's ire.

The first time she did so it was over a matter of conscience and form, something of less import to the bishop than his daily menu, but something to which he must attend. It was her position concerning baptism and conversion to Catholicism, requirements for a Church-sanctioned wedding. Henri himself was not particularly helpful.

"She must convert, Count. Of course you will insist."

"It is not for me to insist, Monseigneur. It is not a thing I will force. She is a free woman of another culture."

"It is not I who wish it, Count. It is the command of the Lord God that the sacrament of marriage be kept holy. She is a pagan. Without baptism there is no conversion. Without conversion she is lost, and your marriage will lack the sanction of the Church. In the eyes of God, you will be unwedded sinners. It is not for you to question. She must do this thing."

"Whatever she chooses, she will be my wife. And she will make this decision herself."

"And then what of children? You would forfeit their souls for the sake of a woman's choice? You would let her condemn souls yet unborn?"

"Nothing is forfeit, Bishop. But she will help make that decision when there are children."

"I find your attitude careless, Count deVries. It is not fitting for a man of your station."

"My station has nothing to do with it. It is my belief."

"The Church will not countenance this!"

Henri sighed and shrugged. "You have my permission to speak with Serena. There will be no coercion. If it is her desire not to convert, Monseigneur, then so be it. In that event we will have a civil ceremony." His tone was final and clear.

The bishop had no desire to alienate the count and accepted his requirements. It was a time of great spiritual independence in France, and of hypocrisy. Many were antireligious, but followed the forms: They had their children baptized, and married in the Church, and were desperate to receive the last rites from a priest. It was spiritual insurance they sought—the comfort of tradition without restraints on their behavior. It was the sort of transaction the bishop understood perfectly and exploited for his treasury. If the count wanted to keep a pagan woman but remain in the Church and give it money, then the bishop would certainly not deny him his wish. But he must try for the woman's conversion. It was the proper form.

The first meeting did not go well. Serena disliked the bishop immediately. "God has sent me for your soul," he announced imperiously. He extended his hand for her to kiss the ring, but she did not. It was plain to her that his mouth said one thing, his eyes another. He spoke polite words, yet regarded her with a look of scorn that fairly shouted "heathen." He uttered pieties while staring openly at her breasts, at her body.

She found him repulsive, but she put up with it. She had come to live in Henri's society. He had told her that they could isolate themselves in the château for a year or two until she felt more comfortable, and thus keep her contact with outsiders to a minimum. But that was not her way. "If I live here it must be with your people, not apart from them," she said. She was determined to deal with the traditions and customs of France, and that included its marabouts. She was nervous and uncertain, but kept the feelings to herself, determined to be strong; yet she was overwhelmed by the new sights and sounds of Paris, everything coming so fast, the world moving so swiftly after the gentle rhythms of her desert. Paris was so light and bright, the only real city she'd ever seen. Algiers was a mere shadow next to this city with its gaslights and cancan and the carriages and the noise. She wanted desperately to do well for Henri, to fit in, and her first real test was with this fat pompous man who reeked of wine and told her she must obey or face the wrath of his God.

She was not intimidated by the bishop or his God, and determined not to let her dislike of him interfere with a hearing of his position. So she tolerated him, and listened. Like many Tuareg, she was not Muslim and had an uncomplicated belief in God. Had it been anyone other than the bishop who tried to convert her, he might have succeeded, for she wanted to make things as easy as possible on the difficult path she had chosen. But she would not be bullied. There had never been about Serena any soft compliant edges, and she was not about to start with Marius Murat.

The bishop's sessions with Serena went off and on for days. He talked for hours of the religion, but in his words she heard only darkness and fear. He offered visions that were terrible, visions that frightened, visions that left her with a sense of dread rather than comfort. Nothing he said felt right.

In her darkest moments of doubt she wondered if she was making a mistake. Maybe her uncle had been right, and the gulf between European and African was too great. Maybe they shouldn't have children at all. But at the end of each meeting, when the bishop had finished, her head was still high and there was Henri, gentle and solicitous, and he kissed the back of her hand. She loved him to distraction and knew it would be all right.

The bishop tried to wear her down, to let fatigue or resignation forge the victory he could not win with threats. But she was stubborn. He had never reckoned with such a strong woman. She was insolent and impertinent, and he told her that her soul suffered from the mortal illness of sin and that the only cure lay in conversion.

"You must do it for the sake of your soul."

"My soul is not chattel for your Church."

"Then you must do it to preserve the holy sacrament of marriage."

"My marriage does not require your sacrament."

"The count's marriage does. You must do it for him."

"The count expects nothing of me in this matter. It is for me to decide."

"Then you must do it for your children."

"Why must I? They will do it for themselves, when they are ready."

"You must do it because otherwise you will burn in hell, and they will follow you there."

"But I have done nothing to earn entry to your hell and the children are unborn." Serena shook her head. "I knew a White Father in the desert. He spoke without threats. He spoke of beauty. You speak of terror, yet you both profess the same religion. How can this be?"

"God has many faces."

"As does his priest, I think."

"Insulting me will not change the point. You must do it because it is the law of God."

"*You* say it is. I say it is your own law, and I will not follow you. The God I know is within me. I do not require your blessing to keep Him there."

"He is a false God!"

"He is mine."

He led her in circles for days, through every conceivable argument. She gave him no satisfaction, and their dislike for one another deepened. Their final session was acrimonious.

"The difference between you and a scorpion, Priest, is that a scorpion has no artifice. You see the tail, and you have seen the scorpion. I see the cross around your neck, yet I have not seen you. Your tail is well hidden."

Had anyone else been in the room to hear the insult,

the bishop would have reacted differently. Now, he simply gave up. He needed the count. "I wash my hands of you, woman," he said darkly. "You have turned from Christ in your descent toward hell. May God have mercy on your soul."

Henri and Serena were married in a civil ceremony.

The bishop told himself she was but a mosquito to his thick skin: irritating, perhaps, and she drew a little blood, but she was more an annoyance than anything else. Underneath, however, he was seething. The bitch had mocked and insulted him. By refusing to keep the forms she had committed a sin against his authority. If she was a mosquito, one day he would swat her.

It was Serena's second sin against the bishop that aroused his permanent ire, for it was no mere spiritual matter. It was a matter of property.

The city of Paris had undergone a metamorphosis under Louis Napoléon. The emperor had commissioned Baron Eugène Haussmann to transform the city, and transform it he did. Like a great couturier, Haussmann ripped off the city's medieval cloak of dust and neglect, and exchanged it for a magnificent gown of brilliance and glamour and gloss. Massive public works projects turned the city upside down.

Haussmann began with the slums. From the Middle Ages they had festered all over Paris, insidious cancers that grew everywhere without proper regard for her dignity, from the doors of the Hôtel de Ville to the shadow of Montmartre, slums that troubled the emperor and blemished the empire. So Haussmann tore them down and swept them away, until the old ones were memories and the new ones were concealed. In their place rose a grand geometry of circles and squares and triangles, drawn with new boulevards and bridges and parks and public places, and dotted with public buildings and private mansions protected by wrought-iron gates. Glorious places, fitting jewels to outshine Vienna and Berlin and Prague, adornments to which the emperor could point with pride.

If it was all simply a facade, it was a damned fine one, for the unpleasantness was now out of sight.

The four-fifths of the city living in misery now had to be miserable somewhere other than the city's center. Paris could not look truly great while children competed with dogs for the garbage on the main thoroughfares.

Nothing stood in the way of progress. If the poor suffered in the process, if their meager possessions were ripped from them without compensation, if their mud-colored hovels were knocked down around them, it was a price the city would tolerate. This was Paris, and Baron Haussmann's broom was progress.

Paris needed everything, and in an affirmation of self-regard, Paris got everything. For the living, new churches. For the dead, new cemeteries. For the hungry, new markets. For the bored, new theaters and an opera and a racetrack at Longchamps. For the traveler, new railway stations and roads to link Paris with the rest of France, and France with the world. It was change on a monumental scale. Aqueducts brought fresh water from the provinces; sewers carried the effluent back. Notre Dame was renovated, and after seven centuries, the Louvre was finally completed. Thousands of trees were planted, hundreds of fountains added. Five streets converging on the Arc de Triomphe were not enough, so more houses were torn down and the five became the twelve streets of the Place de l'Étoile. Thousands of new gas lamps lit dozens of new parks and thoroughfares until at night the city glowed like a field of diamonds.

The bishop was everywhere in the transformation. Information about neighborhoods to be demolished and new buildings to come was traded secretly and carefully. It was information that made men wealthy. The bishop and the baron knew each other well. Where there was the baron, there was the bishop. Where there was the bishop, there was the baron. Never in public, of course, and never in ways that might later prove troublesome. But throughout it all the bishop was engaged in an orgy of buying and selling and trading.

Through his normal channels on the baron's staff he learned one day of an immense opportunity, the creation of an outer boulevard in the southeastern quarter that would join others encircling the city. It would be a massive undertaking, underwritten with a separate bond issue, so large that he confirmed the location and timing with the baron himself. Yes, the baron agreed, this was what the emperor had conceived, and this is what the emperor would have. The new boulevard would be imposing and wide, with parks and shops and housing. The bishop immediately set his curés to the business of acquiring land: a parcel here, a section there, a row of houses, a farm, a factory. The scope of the project was overwhelming, the largest scheme the diocese had ever attempted. It required the investment of huge resources, resources that first emptied the accounts of the see and then tapped the bishop's private reserves. Still it was not enough. He borrowed money from friends at the Crédit Foncier, where funds were supposed to be restricted to departments and communes, but where his influence ran deep. He persuaded investors to join him as minority partners. He drained money from the parishes of the diocese and demanded more. He was obsessed with the project. He would make a fortune the instant the new route was announced.

Then the unexpected happened. He received an urgent summons from Monsieur Portier, his liaison on the baron's staff: he must come at once. Monsieur Portier was a mousy little man with a pince-nez. He was highly agitated when the bishop entered his bureau.

"The project has changed, Eminence! The boulevard has been moved!"

"Moved!" roared the bishop. "How can it be? The baron himself assured me!"

"*Oui,* and so he intended, Your Grace! And so it was to be until three days ago. It was the emperor *himself* who changed the route! He took a ride in his carriage and decided he did not like the lines of the boulevard! They were not straight enough! When the baron heard of it he was granted an audience with the emperor. He even argued the point. *Argued!* But it was no use. The emperor's mind was made up."

Portier was frantic. He had put his own pension into the project. He saw everything crumbling because of an emperor's whim. *Voilà:* a sweep of the hand, a turn of the great mustache; and suddenly instead of here, the new rue would be there, and fortunes would be lost. Sudden, unbelievable. The *lines*, indeed!

"You fool!" said the bishop.

"Alas, I cannot read the mind of the emperor, Your Grace!"

"*Merde*," the bishop said, forgetting himself.

"Your Grace?" Even in his panic the clerk was startled to hear such an utterance from the bishop. Portier hadn't known whether to cry or to throw himself off a bridge before he summoned him. He was afraid of the man, of his bulk, his temper, his power and vengeance. He was ruined, he was sure. But the bishop said nothing more. He was pacing, lost in thought.

Portier turned to a large wooden bunk of drawers in which detailed maps of each arrondissement of Paris were kept. He drew out a map and spread it on a table. As the bishop was preoccupied, Portier studied. He raised his eyebrows when he saw it. It was just the slimmest possibility, but he called out.

"Eminence, look! Perhaps all is not lost. This is where the route will now be placed." He traced a line on the map with his finger. "If Your Grace can somehow acquire the land here"—he pointed to a large tract—"and here, and here, then your earlier acquisitions will retain their value." The bishop looked carefully at the map. It was true, he saw. The land Portier indicated would join his holdings to the new route.

"Who owns the land?"

Lit with new enthusiasm, Portier hurried to the land records section of the bureau. He climbed a ladder and pulled a massive book off the shelf. He pored through it page by page, squinting where the writing was old and faded, nodding and mumbling to himself, until he arrived at the proper section.

"*Voilà!*" he fairly shouted, pointing eagerly. "*C'est ça!*"

There was but one owner for all the land: the count Henri deVries. *DeVries!* The bishop cursed himself for the weakness of his position.

"We must have the land condemned," he said.

Portier shook his head. "Alas, it is not possible, Your Grace."

"And why not? Land is condemned regularly by the baron for public works!"

"*Bien sûr,* Eminence, what you say is true—*except* for land belonging to the nobility. The emperor has no wish to alienate them. His orders have been explicit from the beginning: If it cannot be purchased, it will not be condemned. Besides, a condemnation would never work. The count's land is not essential to the new route. It is only essential to preserve your . . . should I say . . . *our* investment."

The bishop resigned himself to approaching the count. There was at least one thing in his favor, he thought, congratulating himself that he had kept his temper when dealing with the count's woman. Henri deVries surely valued his immortal soul, like any other man. A donation of the land to the Church—or even its sale—would ease the pain he must have felt at entering into marriage without the blessing of the Church.

So it was that he came to call on Henri. "The project is important for the vitality of the new city," the bishop told him. "Your family has been more than generous to the Church and served France with distinction for generations. It is fitting that this tradition should continue now, when so much progress has been made. The diocese considers this project good for the city, and good for the diocese. As you see, there will be a park here." He pointed to the map. "And here, a school. The emperor intends that a wide boulevard be—"

"Who owns this land?" Henri interrupted. He pointed to a part of the bishop's new holdings. The bishop hesitated. He thought about lying, but saw no harm in the truth. "It is owned by the Church."

"By your diocese, perhaps?"

"*Oui,* Count."

"And when did the diocese acquire it?"

"I do not see where that should concern you."

"So that I may know your intentions, Monseigneur. I wish to understand why you are here."

"Very well. The diocese has owned the land but a short time."

A tight smile crossed Henri's face. "Then I understand, Monseigneur. This is an investment for you. Without my land yours is worthless."

"This is not a question of worth, Count deVries. The diocese is engaged in the Lord's work. It is a matter of the highest use for the land. The emperor has transformed the city. The Church supports him in his efforts when it can. If it is not advantageous for you to donate the land to the city, the Church will of course consider a purchase, and the Church itself will donate it to the city."

"Then will you be donating this other property as well, or holding it for sale?"

The bishop thought quickly. *Damn the man!* So quick to the point, so direct. Well, if he had to, he would disclose the Church's business intentions. It was certainly not unheard of for the Church to engage in commercial transactions. He decided it would be good form to admit to certain commercial aspects of the transaction and to donate a portion of the land to the city at the same time. But before the bishop had a chance to answer, Serena walked in. Her eyes fell upon the visitor. A look of distaste crossed her face but quickly passed. The bishop rose but made no attempt to proffer his ring. She greeted Henri brightly and saw the map they were studying.

"We were just discussing a gift of our land in Montparnasse for the new outer boulevard," he explained. She looked at the map.

"Is that near Vaugirard?"

"*Oui,*" he replied, smiling. She was still new to the huge city of Paris, yet already knew her way around. She had always been clever with maps.

"I have just been to Ramiza's shop." Ramiza Hamad was an Algerian woman who had opened a dry goods shop in Montparnasse. Serena had met her soon after arriving in Paris and bought material for clothing there. Ramiza knew the oasis of El Gassi, where Serena had

broken her leg as a girl. She and her family were regular
guests at the Château deVries.

"It is horrible what is happening there! She is losing
everything. Her family paid rent for three years in advance and lost it all. She said they lost it to the Church!
I was going to ask you if there was anything to be done,
Henri." She looked innocently at Murat. "But now perhaps the priest can help them."

"Is this true, Monseigneur?" Henri asked.

This time, Murat knew he had to lie. "No. The
Church has had nothing to do with any such difficulty,
and would not be party to it."

"Do you say my friends are mistaken? It is they who
live there! It is they who know!"

"I say only that they have made an error, that is all. I
am certain they are well intentioned," the bishop replied
with ice in his voice. "If you will permit me to say so,
perhaps the countess should mind matters of her household and leave matters of property to the count."

"Perhaps the priest should mind matters of religion
rather than matters of property," she shot back.

Henri stood up. Serena's enmity for the bishop had
been clear since the prelate's unsuccessful efforts at conversion. He saw no hope for an amicable reconciliation.
The best he could try for was a strained peace between
them. "Thank you for coming, Your Grace. I will consider the matter of a gift directly to the city."

"It is all I could ask," the bishop replied.

"Are you going to give him the land?" Serena asked
after he left.

"Probably. The boulevard is a good project. But first
I will see about Ramiza."

The next day Henri went to Vaugirard. He talked
with the Hamad family, and then with others who had
shops in the same area. The picture they drew was disturbing. They had paid heavy advance rents, only to
find their homes and shops later condemned for use in
the construction of a new street or park. They had not
been able to get their money back. They never dealt
with the landlord, only with agents. They weren't even
certain who the landlord was. Some said the Church,

some said not. The agents told them nothing and said they should raise the matter with the city. The city refused to help and would not permit them to examine the property records, which were confidential. They had lost their money and their property and weren't even sure to whom.

If powerless tenants could not obtain access to the records of the city, Count Henri deVries had no such difficulty. He was soon poring over the records and discovered that the landowner, once having collected money from the tenants, had then been paid by the city for the property. The landlord had in fact been paid twice: first by the tenants, then by the city. It was a clever scheme inflicted upon the helpless, repeated hundreds of times.

There were other papers to see at a different bureau. Henri examined them himself, to be certain there was no mistake. One landlord was dominant, not the owner of every property, but of scores of them. Leafing through the heavy book, Henri saw the name on document after document.

Msgr. M. Murat, évêque de Boulogne-Billancourt.

There could be no mistake.

Henri was furious. He rode to the bishop's palace and went directly to his private apartments over the strident objections of the housekeeper. The bishop was occupied with a tradesman who was installing new Cordovan leather walls in his private dining room. The emperor had installed imitation leather walls at Fontainebleau. Not to be outdone, the bishop had ordered real ones. He looked up in surprise as Henri entered.

"Count! An unexpected pleasure."

Henri's countenance was grim, his voice a whip. "No pleasure, Bishop. You lied to me."

The bishop motioned to the workman. "Leave us," he said. The man dropped his tools and hurried from the room. The bishop turned to Henri. He spoke in a low voice. "Do not forget yourself, Count! I will not be addressed in this manner!"

"What Serena said was true. Your diocese has stolen money from families. From shopkeepers. It is fraud!"

"You are talking to God's servant in this diocese, Count. I do not lie."

"I have been to the city offices. I have seen the papers for the rents. I have seen the papers for the purchases. They bear your signature."

The bishop nodded his head and gave him his most understanding smile. "My signature is on many things. A hundred papers are presented to me every day." He picked up a folder from his writing desk. The folder was tied with a ribbon and bulged with documents. "The diocese owns a great many properties. Much is left to the discretion of the curés who attend to these matters for the Church. I trust them when they present me with something. I confess that I do not read them all. If what you say is true it is possible one of the curés may be responsible. If so I will find out. I assure you I will get to the bottom of it."

Henri looked at him scornfully. "Are you telling me you don't know what is happening in your diocese? Once or twice I might understand. But a hundred times and more? Over two years? And then you would place the blame on a *curé*?" Henri shook his head, and looked the bishop straight in the eye. "I said it before. I don't believe you. You are a liar."

The bishop reacted in the only way he knew how. He took the offensive. A thousand times before he had done it with those who challenged him; a thousand times before they had backed down. He raised himself to his full height. His face was flushed with anger, his gray eyes savage. His hand trembled with rage as he shook his fist in Henri's face. "You speak this way in peril of your immortal soul, Henri deVries! Until now I have treated you with some leniency in deference to your station. I have been reasonable about your marriage—"

"You dare to threaten me over my marriage?" Henri was incredulous. "This has nothing to do with my marriage!"

"I only remind you of the pain of excommunication! I remind you of your precarious position! I remind you that I have shown more tolerance in this matter than the holy Church requires I show! What has been done can be undone! Your title and your money and all your self-righteousness will not protect you from the wrath of almighty God!"

Henri stared at the bishop and felt ashamed. What a fool he had been! He had never seen the man behind the robes. He had never felt the need to look. He had only humored Serena when she criticized Murat. Now what he saw filled him with revulsion. He spoke quietly, the anger gone from him. "I will have no part of your project. For that and for my marriage, do as you will, priest. Do as you will." He turned and strode from the room, his boots echoing down the hall. The bishop listened until the noise was gone.

That night the bishop sat in his darkened bedchamber, hunched over in a chair. The palace was hushed, his passion spent. Two bottles of wine lay empty at his feet. His eyes were red and his tongue was thick. His head was pounding; the wine would not make it stop. The storms of his fury had thundered throughout the afternoon. Word of his mood passed rapidly among the secular and clerical staffs at the palace. Curés quickly found business in other parishes. The servants moved silently through the back halls, trying to remain invisible. All dreaded a chance meeting or a summons. His vengeance could be swift and horrible.

Some had not moved quickly enough. He saw to it that Monsieur Portier was fired that afternoon, filling a note to Baron Haussmann with enough threats to guarantee it. He summoned the clerk of the diocese, a meek but capable priest who had dutifully carried out every instruction of the bishop's without fail. The man was summarily transferred to Vanves, the poorest parish in the diocese. He fired the housekeeper who had let Henri into his apartments. Yet the anger continued to build inside him, a great bilious anger that consumed him with hatred and spite, and in its fires he found the only other person he could hold accountable for the disaster.

"Serena said . . ." Over and over he heard the count's accusation. "Serena said . . ."

The she-devil. Serena deVries. The pagan whore.

It was her fault.

When he knew it was true he lay exhausted in his stuporous fog and the voice came to him as it always did, soothing and sure.

God will punish her for thwarting His works. And I will be His instrument.

He rose to his feet and staggered. A boy of eleven peered out at the great bulk of the bishop from beneath the silk comforter on the bed. The boy was terrified. The bishop could hurt him so when he was like this. He had lain there for more than an hour, afraid to say anything, afraid even to move. He wondered whether the bishop had forgotten him as he drank and drank. He saw the old man's head nodding and heard him talking to himself. He wondered whether to run. But then the bishop saw him. The bishop had forgotten it was Friday. There was a boy every Friday. Such a sweet young body, this one had. His favorite. But now he could not focus on the child through his rage. He wanted only to be left alone.

"Get out!" the bishop swore. "Get out of my sight!" The bottle he threw broke just behind the bare feet of the boy as he fled through the door.

CHAPTER 4

Berlin, 1870

"I T IS FINISHED."

Count Otto von Bismarck, minister-president of Prussia, took a drink of schnapps and sat back heavily in his chair. He was in a dimly lit room on the second floor of the Schloss Charlottenburg in Berlin, eating a late dinner of blood sausage and bread with his ill-humored but brilliant chief of staff General Helmuth von Moltke and the minister of war, Count Albrecht von Roon.

It would have been difficult to find three more crafty, powerful, or intelligent men in a room anywhere on the Continent that evening. Over a six-year period they had reshaped the balance of power in Europe, redrawing maps, playing royalty like puppets on strings, throwing hundreds of thousands of men into battles that would fashion the future of two continents.

Yet the mood in the room was somber, for there was very real danger of peace with France. Peace would upset Bismarck's plans. Peace could end the grand scheme he had carefully tended for years. He was possessed by the dream of a united Germany, a reich dominated by Prussia. A reich of which he would become chancellor. To accomplish this he had to unite swarms of independent principalities and dukedoms, many of which had tiny armies and lone generals. The process had begun with a war against Denmark, which the German confederation—of which Prussia and Austria were the strongest members—had won handily.

His plan flowered at Sadowa, a massive and bloody

battle on the Bohemian plain that pitted the Prussians
against their former ally Austria in a struggle to become
the preeminent power among German-speaking people.
Sadowa had been a huge gamble. Under the Hapsburgs,
Austria was regarded, after France, as the most powerful nation on the Continent. There was no assurance
whatever that Prussia would win, or that Bismarck
would not end up on the gallows. But Bismarck was not
one for the safe path. He had gambled, and in a few
short weeks he had won. From the victory he had
forged the North German Confederation. The balance
of power had shifted again. Europe trembled.

What remained of his task was to bring the southern
German principalities into the union. This he intended
to accomplish by drawing their common enemy, France,
into a war. The opportunity presented itself when a
junta of Spanish generals overthrew Queen Isabella of
Spain. Bismarck had connived with the generals to offer
the Spanish throne to Prince Leopold, the nephew of
Prussia's King Wilhelm. France already faced Prussians
in the northeast. If Leopold accepted, she would have to
face them in the southwest as well, and German influence would spread on the Continent.

And that, Bismarck knew, would lead to one of two
outcomes. The first was the humiliation of Louis
Napoléon, whose position, already weakening among
the powers of Europe, would deteriorate further. The
second was that France would refuse to suffer such
provocation and would instead declare war. Bismarck
was banking on the latter.

"The French ego," he had assured the generals, "will
never tolerate bratwurst on two borders. They will puff
their chests and draw their swords and test your armies
again."

"The French army is larger than ours," von Moltke
reminded him. "They will not fall so easily as the
Austrians." The president laughed derisively. He had
once shared the popular opinion that Napoléon was a
man to be feared and respected. But no more. He had
seen him vacillate in international affairs and stumble
badly. His court was corrupt. Reports of his illnesses

and dissipation were widespread. He was a man who preferred to follow the flow of events, rather than to shape them as had his uncle Bonaparte. A feeble man at the head of an unraveling empire.

"I have looked into the emperor's eyes," said Bismarck. "They are empty. He is a sphinx without a riddle. His country is no better. From a distance France is stunning, but when you get up close there is nothing there at all. And when they realize we have insulted their precious dignity, they will do as they always do. They will fight. Only now they will show up for battle wearing nothing but honor for armor and pride for a sword. And we shall raise the whole of Germany against them."

Bismarck's generals needed little persuasion of their own superiority. They were confident of their troops. For four years, since Sadowa, they had been rearming, preparing, planning. As generals always did, they wanted more time. But when time ran out, they would be ready.

Now events—and their own sovereign—were threatening their grand plans. The French had indeed puffed their chests and rattled their swords. They had been outraged. They had been insulted. Their foreign minister had threatened war.

King Wilhelm did not share Bismarck's enthusiasm for war with the French, at least not over this issue. Prince Leopold himself had been lukewarm about taking the Spanish throne, for the situation there was unsettled.

So Wilhelm had blinked.

"It is finished," Bismarck repeated, the resignation heavy in his voice. "The king has backed down. Leopold has renounced any claim to the throne."

"I thought you had secured the cooperation of his father," said von Roon.

"As did I. I persuaded his father by appealing to his sense of duty as a Prussian. And his father persuaded him. It was done. Leopold had asked King Wilhelm to allow him to accept, and Wilhelm agreed. But then Wilhelm changed his mind."

Bismarck shook his head in anger. "*Gott in Himmel,* Wilhelm lacks spine. He has buckled under his fear of the French. He has no stomach for the unknown. If the king grants further concessions to the French, I shall have no choice but to resign."

At that moment an aide appeared through a heavy paneled oak door. He approached the table and saluted.

"Herr Minister, an urgent telegram." He held out a tray to Bismarck, who took the envelope from it and opened it.

"It is from the king, through the foreign office." The king was taking the waters at Ems. Bismarck silently read a few sentences. "It appears the French ambassador approached him today." He read further, shaking his head in wonder. "*Mein Gott,* but they are insolent. Evidently the king's assurance that he is withdrawing his support of Leopold is not enough for them. They asked Wilhelm to guarantee that Leopold will never seek it again. And they have asked Wilhelm to apologize."

"Apologize?" said an incredulous von Roon. "For what should he apologize? The king has done nothing in this matter but what the French themselves have asked!"

Bismarck was not paying attention. He was still reading. "His Majesty has rejected their demands," he continued. "He has decided not to receive the French ambassador again. He wants to know if I think we should communicate the latest demand and the king's rejection to the press." He passed the telegram to the others and fell silent, thinking.

"Even for the French, unbelievable arrogance," spat von Moltke. "Of course, Excellency, this should be reported to the press at once. The public will see their demands as outrageous."

"It will accomplish nothing," said von Roon. "It is mere posturing now. The cause is lost."

But a smile was taking shape on Bismarck's face. There was new light in his eyes.

"Gentlemen, this telegram should not be released to the press."

"I think you are wrong, Exc—" started von Moltke. Bismarck raised a hand to silence him.

"I said *this* telegram should not be released." He rose and walked to a desk at the side of the room, from which he retrieved a fountain pen. He returned to the dinner table and pushed the dishes aside. He laid the telegram down and carefully began to edit it. For a few moments his pen made the only sound in the room as he scratched through a few words and added others. When he was done he straightened up in his chair. The look on his face was impassive as he held the revised telegram out for the others.

"Gentlemen, *this* is what the world shall read."

Von Roon and von Moltke studied Bismarck's work. The realization of what he had done dawned slowly upon them. Their eyes took on a look of admiration as they understood. He was an artist. He had taken the king's simple refusal to see the ambassador and turned it into an outright insult to the French. It would be more than the French could bear. They looked in awe at Bismarck. No one but he would have dared.

No one else had the balls.

"It is brilliant," was all that von Moltke could say.

"A red rag for the Gallic bull," acknowledged Bismarck with a modest smile. He poured them each more schnapps, and raised his glass in a toast.

"To a united Germany," he said. "Gentlemen, we shall have our war after all."

GENERAL BERNARD DELACROIX ENTERED HIS CARriage in the courtyard of the Tuileries, the palace of Napoléon. The general was a member of the emperor's elite Imperial Guard. He was heavyset with a round face and florid features from too many days of leisure and too many nights of excess.

"Le Château deVries," he ordered his driver, and settled back to enjoy the drive. It was a beautiful summer evening. The sky was cloudless and deep blue. The shadows of the setting sun lengthened across the courtyard.

The general was bone tired. For weeks he had barely ventured from the Tuileries. Tonight he would take a welcome break from the relentless pace and attend a party. Count Henri deVries was returning from Russia and had passed through Berlin along the way. The general wanted to get his sense of the preparedness of the Prussians. But there was another reason, a far more compelling reason he was attending: it was Elisabeth, luscious Elisabeth, the wife of Colonel Jules deVries, the count's brother. Elisabeth, lovely Elisabeth, blond and willing. Elisabeth, wild and ambitious and brazen. The general stirred in his seat and felt himself growing excited at the thought of her. He smiled at her persistence, wishing his own officers had her spirit. With the Prussian situation the general was accepting no social invitations, but Elisabeth had taken great pains to ensure his presence, first sending a note and then stopping by the Tuileries personally. Brandishing her parasol like a sword and her resolve like a club, she'd bullied his aide into accepting her invitation on the general's behalf. The general didn't mind, not at all. He was ready for Elisabeth. He would have her. Tonight, in the count's home, with her own husband nearby. The thought brought a smile to his lips and a shiver to his groin.

His carriage turned to the east outside the palace gate. The route to the deVrieses' would take him past the best of the city. There was the Palais Royal, and the Garden of the Tuileries, where the band from his own Imperial Guard entertained men and women enjoying the fresh air and strolling along the paths among the flowers and trees and fountains.

He passed beneath the long branches of the chestnut trees that lined the rue de Rivoli and into the Place de la Concorde. His carriage joined a never-ending stream of vehicles rolling along the streets in a dizzying parade of élan and excitement. Coachmen's whips lashed magnificent purebred English horses drawing the elite of society to and from their affairs: an endless procession of top hats, gowns, capes, and jewels feeding an unlimited supply of parties, masked balls, dinners, operas, musicals, and plays. All the formidable resources of finance, intellect, and culture were brought to bear to prevent that most horrible of French maladies, boredom. The refrain of *Paris at Play*, a popular musical revue, was heard everywhere: *"Without finery and pleasure, we must agree, life is just a stupidity."*

The pursuit of pleasure was insatiable, permeating every aspect of French life, consuming every waking moment: for the rich, an evening at the opera; for the middle class, the cancan at the Bal Mabille; for the poor, a drinking den and twelve-year-old prostitutes, or, more likely, nothing at all.

The general passed through streets that were a carnival of jugglers and magicians and potion peddlers and harlots. Sidewalk cafés were everywhere. At the Café Guerbois one might see Renoir or Zola, while at the Nouvelle-Athenes, the general thought grimly, the traitors Clemenceau or Gambetta might be heard roasting Napoléon. They were becoming bold to the point of disloyalty. They ought to be banished, like the writer Hugo. General Delacroix thought the emperor was too soft on dissidents. He had stopped cleaning France's house too soon. He should have done to the intellectuals what Haussmann had done to the poor, only instead of the suburbs he should have shown them the guillotine. Even banishment was too easy, an unsure fix that could come undone. Blades and bullets: these solved problems more permanently. Delacroix would have been only too happy to deal with the writers and the painters for the good of the empire, painters like that dandy Manet who slopped the excrement of thinly disguised insults to the emperor onto his canvases, and composers like Offenbach, the half-Prussian who wrote operettas satirizing empires and armies and—yes—generals. It was humiliating. Liberty had gone too far when one couldn't attend the theater without fearing another assault upon one's integrity or sovereign or profession.

But it would not come to pass, the general knew, for the emperor was sick and weak, a slave to his Spanish empress, Eugénie, and her intrigues. His hold over the empire was slipping, his prestige among the other rulers of Europe at a low, a low that meant danger for France, for where there was no respect for a sovereign's fitness or judgment or resolve, there was danger of war. Even in the best of times, Napoléon had never been imposing. Now his miseries were clear to anyone who looked. He could barely walk for his kidney stones. The eyes had lost their luster. The whispers at the palace were louder now. The man was disengaged, drifting in pain, losing his grip. There had been violent strikes and street riots in the spring as a struggle developed between authority and liberty, the poor and the rich. Attacks on the emperor were growing commonplace. The newspapers were full of it, full of the fury of discontent, full of the lies and license of the malcontents. The general shook his head at the outrage.

He passed through the shadow of the Arc de Triomphe in the Place de l'Étoile. In all the world this was his favorite place, a memorial to the great wars of the empire, an affirmation of the might of France, its frieze depicting a procession of conquerors bringing the spoils of war home to the motherland, full of glory past, full of glory present, full of glory to come. As always, the Place was vital and alive and surging with humanity. Here one could find reassurance in troubling times. Here one could see and hear and touch that which the general felt would forever preserve France: men-at-arms, men of power and pomp, men with plumed helmets and golden breastplates and swords and guns; the sky blue tunics and jackboots of the Cent Gardes; Lancers on white horses; officers of the Guides, aristocrats in green and gold with their sabers gleaming in the sun; hussars; the Chasseurs d'Afrique and the Zouaves on their Arabian horses; the Spahis from the Sahara. Everywhere, the mighty trappings of a nation that could deploy a half-million men under arms, fighting men who were the envy of the world. From North Africa to Tahiti, China to Somalia, Madagascar to the West Indies, the armies of France rivaled the English as they sought to fulfill their destiny of acquiring and civilizing the world. Yes, reflected the general, kings and emperors would come and go, but France could always look to her military to serve her interests and protect her God-given role as civilizer of the world. France would muddle through, as she always did.

And muddle through she now must, for there was something new in the air of Paris this evening, a special energy and excitement and sense of danger. One could always find something in the air of Paris—love or lust, revolution or intrigue. Now it was the prospect of war with the Prussians, whose king had insulted France. The affront filled the sidewalks with cocky, swaggering crowds, full of the giddy self-assurance that comes so easily to those who don't have to fight. Parliament was hot, the press on fire. On street corners and in parks, crowds gathered to listen to impassioned speeches. Notices papered every wall. Rumors fed gossip, and gossip became news, and the news made all France indignant.

It was wonderful to be a military man just then, to enjoy the respect and awe of the masses, who saluted anything wearing a uniform. True to form, the general's passage brought tipped hats and excited waves amid feverish cries of *"Vive la France!"* and *"À Berlin!"* and *"Vive la guerre!"* After four wars and progressively increasing rank, Delacroix had gotten farther from the battlefield but closer to the glory.

E LISABETH WAS IN ECSTASY. THIS WAS HER PARTY, the party she had worked and hoped for. It was not the party of the year, or even of the month, for this was Paris, after all, but the party of the week perhaps; and for the wife of a colonel, the guest list glittered with promise for advancement for herself and Jules. She had tirelessly leveraged the guest list, first convincing one notable to come, then using that name to persuade someone else, then using both to obtain yet another of even higher stature, until the collective assurance grew that the party would indeed be worth attending.

Henri had been out of the country in Russia, on one or another of his explorations. She didn't know where or what, but what she did know was that his absence allowed her to dominate the household and take control of its budget and to begin to move things along in her own way. Move them she had. For tonight there was an abundance of help: butlers and cooks, servers and maids, all frantically keeping up with her commands and setting table just so, taking care that all was dusted and arranged and that the candles were lit and the gaslights polished and rugs beaten and floors mopped and shined. There was *so* much to undo.

She detested the way Henri had, as she put it, "savaged the château." He was uncomfortable with the affectations of Paris. Upon the death of the old count, he had done away with everything he considered ostentatious or silly, which was to say most of the contents of the house. Stone and wood took the place of frills and satin. Fine carpets were replaced with African rugs. Out went the overstuffed chairs and gilded picture frames and baroque consoles and enameled tables.

She could only watch in dismay as, despite her protests, her brother-in-law stripped the house of its soul. She rescued what pieces she could, and furnished her private rooms in the château as richly as leftovers and a military salary would permit. Not one sou remained after her budget was spent on clothing and furnishings. As a colonel, Jules was well paid, but only as emperor would he have been rich enough for Elisabeth. Had the count not fed them they would have starved, for there was no room in Jules's salary for Elisabeth's fashion *and* food.

Now, with Henri away and a party at hand, the house was hers to remake. She had been clever and determined. Carefully she searched the storerooms and four different attics and found what she needed in dusty trunks that had belonged to the old count; the old man had had a greater appreciation for show than Henri. In the attics she uncovered riches she hadn't known existed: enameled glass goblets, deep blue in color, with hand-painted miniature portraits from the court of Louis XIV; matching hard-paste porcelain dishes with exotic patterns of cherubs and carriages and forest scenes; a table of painted pine inlaid with Belgian marble and ebonized fruitwood; overstuffed couches and chairs with carved legs; a tapestry of woven wool and silk. Everything she chose was dusted and cleaned and polished and arranged until the whole house more closely suited her tastes and sense of propriety.

Through all these preparations Serena had stayed out of her way, caring little for the party or the budget. There could not have been a greater contrast between the two women. Serena had been born and raised a nomad. Comfort to her was found by looking inward, while comfort to Elisabeth was strictly an external proposition. Serena was content sleeping on the floor; Elisabeth required a Louis XIV canopied bed in which to recline. Serena was an excellent horsewoman; Elisabeth complained of the beasts' smell. Where Serena dressed plainly and wore no makeup, Elisabeth changed her clothes six times a day. Each season demanded a fresh set of clothes. Once a month she visited the specialty salons in Paris: first, to be seen doing so; second, to purchase the latest rage—cashmere shawls, cosmetics, or scarlet shoes. She had seven parasols and twenty-three garters and thirty-one pairs of shoes. Innumerable hats filled countless boxes stacked in deep rows in her closet.

Elisabeth found Serena an embarrassment, so painfully . . . *foreign.* Elisabeth had trouble introducing her to her friends, for Serena seemed to have no gift for the small talk so central to parlor life. As for her clothes—well, the woman had no sense at all how to dress. At least she had dropped her desert rags and adopted the French style, but she wore her gowns unadorned. Yes, Elisabeth granted, she was ravishing; and it troubled Elisabeth not a little that even without hairdressers and hours of preparation, Serena still managed to look so fresh and beautiful. Elisabeth noticed the way men stole looks at Serena. It was impossible not to notice. However the military men and their wives might criticize Serena behind her back for being so different, a heathen and all, the men all looked at her *that* way. All of them did, the pigs. Elisabeth was particularly incensed when, on one occasion, she was certain she'd caught her own Jules looking at his sister-in-law. She'd refused to sleep with him for a month, as though somehow that might dim the flames of passion she was convinced he harbored for Serena. If logic was not Elisabeth's strong point, sex was a weapon she used wisely and well. Owing to his military service, Jules was away for long periods, so that when he came home he was naturally eager to renew the bonds of marriage. If she had anything at all to resolve with him, any scheme or program or plan in which she needed his intervention or cooperation or connivance, that was the time to do it. For in the heat of passion Jules was an animal, and prone to promise anything.

Years earlier, Elisabeth had given up on transforming Serena into a lady, or instilling in her the social graces, dressing her and teaching her the proper demeanor of a countess. An early instinct to help her sister-in-law had been replaced by the realization that the Château deVries needed a lady, a proper lady. *She* was that lady, and whatever polish Serena lacked added luster to her own. Yet Elisabeth felt somehow cheated by Serena or, more accurately, felt that she and Jules had been cheated by Henri and Serena. For it was Jules who had the bearing of a count, not Henri, and Elisabeth who looked the countess, not Serena. It was only by fault of birth order that Jules was untitled and penniless, whereas Henri held the name and family fortune. The title was entirely wasted on the man. Why, if Jules were count—how she longed for it!—the Château deVries would be returned to grandeur and life would be fine.

Instead, she fumed, she was relegated to the second tier. Instead of a noble wife she was a military wife, forced to spend her time in circles that glittered less than those to which she aspired. Therein lay yet another injustice, a bitter fact of her perpetual orbit at the second level: as the wife of a colonel she could dominate the other wives, the lesser wives, and mold their opinions for them and tend to their attitudes and actions. But as the wife of a colonel she would be forever subservient to the wife of any general, however second-rate or unde-serving. That thought was simply too dreadful to bear. So one of her primary missions in life was to promote Jules, to help him think, and to do what she could to keep others out of his way as she pushed and goaded him into becoming all that she needed him to be. He had become a lieutenant colonel at the age of thirty-one, a colonel a few short years later. She required more, much more. She required it faster. Marshal of France by forty would suit her perfectly.

Now her guests filled the great house and affirmed her standing. The party was a huge success, the drive lined with gorgeous carriages and horses, the rooms full of gorgeous people, officers in elegant uniforms, ladies with deep décolletages and elaborate coiffures and jew-els, and gentlemen in their knee breeches and silk stock-ings and evening jackets. The whole house was alive with color and gaiety. If there was fear of the war it did not show here. Here there was only optimism and the sublime glow of self-confidence.

Elisabeth had panicked earlier in the evening, for Henri had not yet arrived, and it was the promise of his presence that had lured some of the guests to her party. She had cut it very close, knowing how far Henri had to travel, and in fact she wasn't at all sure he would arrive tonight. She stood greeting guests with Jules beside her, and kept looking nervously at the door and making ex-cuses to those who inquired after him. But at last there he was, amid great commotion in the entryway as Moussa flew into his arms. There was a quieter, whis-pered greeting from Serena that produced a wonderful smile on his face, and then he worked through a succes-sion of guests with Serena at his side. Count and Countess deVries passed easily through the crowd. Henri was a lean, handsome man with strong hands and thick black hair and deep blue eyes alive with intelli-gence and curiosity and wit. His boots were dusty, and he carried his cape on his arm, but even in traveling clothes he had a presence, a force of personality that dominated the room. At last he stood before Elisabeth, a wry smile on his face. He made a gesture that took in everything: the party and the people, the resurrected furnishings and her defiance of his customs in his absence.

"Well, Elisabeth, I see you've managed to stay occupied while I've been away."

"*Henri!*" She smiled grandly and kissed him on the cheek. "I'm *so* glad you've arrived! I do hope you're not *too* exhausted from your trip. There are so many people who can't *wait* to see you!" She knew from his look that he was not really angry, that he would tolerate her tonight, and tomorrow promptly restore the house to the wretched medieval state he preferred. But no matter. This night was hers.

"I marvel at the way you make me feel like such a welcome guest in my own home," Henri said with a laugh.

"But you *are* a welcome guest, dear Brother! Come now," she said, taking him by the hand. "You shall have something to eat and drink, and then there are some people with whom you simply *must* speak."

"A moment, Elisabeth." He turned toward his brother. "Hello, Jules."

"Henri." Jules shook hands stiffly. His voice boomed and his handshake was like iron. He was a heavyset, muscular man. He had a square jaw and bushy mustache and heavy eyebrows over eyes that were dark and forbidding. He never relaxed, not for a moment. He stood erect as though supported by a steel rod, and walked as though in a parade. There was tension and formality and a certain pomposity in his manner, leaving his junior officers joking among themselves that "the colonel even craps standing up."

The military meant everything to him. He lived it, breathed it, dreamed it. He was always in deadly earnest, his every action directed toward the fulfillment of his command responsibilities. He was narrow-minded and believed absolutely in the superiority of all things French. He had been born with no sense of humor and smiled only rarely. This often put him at odds with his brother, whose admiration of things French had been tempered by his travels and whose sense of humor was intact.

"How was Berlin?" Jules asked.

"Indeed, Count, we are all curious!" It was General Delacroix, who emerged through the crowd with General Raspail. They were the senior officers present but dissimilar in every other way: Delacroix a big extrovert, Raspail short, slight, and frosty. Delacroix was relaxed and jovial, Raspail tightly coiled and intense. Delacroix's hair was bushy and thick, Raspail's parted in the middle and slicked back. Delacroix had a walrus mustache; Raspail's was pencil-thin, highly waxed, and pointed at the tips. Jules saluted his commanding officer first and then Raspail. The eyes of Delacroix were upon the women. He returned the salute with a perfunctory wave and handed Jules his coat. Raspail quickly followed suit, adding his hat to the top of the pile. A barely perceptible frown crossed the colonel's face. It was a brief moment of humiliation, being treated like an aide, but there was nothing to be done. He found a passing lieutenant and handed the stack to him. At the same time he diverted a butler with a tray of champagne toward the group.

The generals made their greetings. Delacroix bowed deeply to Serena and kissed her hand. "*Madame la comtesse,* as always I am honored in the presence of the Saharan jewel."

"General."

Delacroix turned to Elisabeth, who blushed as their eyes met. She hoped no one noticed, and extended her hand. "I'm *so* glad you could come, *mon général.*"

"It could hardly be otherwise, madame," said the general with a smile. "My aide informed me of your summons. It was quite unnecessary. I would not have missed it."

Raspail shook hands with Henri and gave him a vacant smile. Raspail didn't like the count. He considered Henri a frivolous vagabond without a proper sense of the obligations of nobility, a man who as a count should represent authority and order, yet seemed to disregard both. Raspail had served in the Crimea with Henri's father, and found little similarity between the two.

Now Raspail's mind was on Bismarck. "You were going to tell us of Prussia."

Henri's face went grim. He'd spent six weeks traveling from Moscow and on the way had passed through Prussia and finally France itself. It was clear both countries were preparing for war, and the contrasts he had seen disturbed him deeply. "Of course, General, but understand my observations were limited. I spent only two nights in Berlin. I have old friends there, but Prussian enthusiasm for French visitors is limited. I looked around as best I could. What I saw was a country urgently preparing itself for war. There were troops and munitions everywhere."

"There are troops and munitions everywhere in France," said Jules.

"Of course. I have seen them myself. But there's a difference."

"And that is?"

"The Prussians seem quite prepared. They are serious, deadly serious, while Paris seems to be having one of her parties." Henri took in the room of revelers. "Like this one."

Raspail dismissed the comment with a frown and a wave of contempt. "Perhaps we can afford our parties more readily than the Hun. We are always ready for war. Just this morning the minister himself assured the emperor that we are prepared to the last gaiter button."

"Perhaps the minister should have another look. We are not armed like the Prussians. We are not ready like the Prussians. In Berlin, I saw the troops drilling. Their artillery was polished. Their barracks were painted. Ours are run-down, and our men are drunk."

"Their *barracks?*" The general's voice was laced with sarcasm. "You judge them by their *barracks?* Their *barracks* will not bear arms against France! Their *barracks* will not fire a shot, or protect them from our infantry. Their *barracks* will not plan strategy or save them from the finest army on earth."

"Pride will not win a war, General," Henri said, "not against the Prussians. Or have you forgotten Sadowa?"

It was an unpleasant reminder for anyone in the military. Half a million men, more than a thousand artillery pieces. Only eighteen days. Eighteen days for the illusion of Austrian military power to be shattered by the steel spike atop Bismarck's helmet. France, the only power strong enough to do anything about it, had done nothing. And now Prussia was knocking at France's door.

One simply didn't acknowledge such unpleasantries. A proper Frenchman mustered little but disdain for the notion that the Prussians were anything to be feared.

"You make a grave error comparing the Austrians to the French," said Raspail.

"There is no error about the German armies and their armaments," said Henri. "In Essen the factories of Krupp are working around the clock. They are not making strudel, General. They are making breech-loading cannons, thousands of them. The railroads are full to overflowing with them."

"I have seen their cannons," said Raspail with a dismissive wave. "They had the arrogance to bring them to the Paris Exposition and show them off."

"Well, then you know they are heavier than anything we use and are quite as deadly as anything on the Continent."

"Like their wit?" asked Elisabeth, desperately wishing to lighten the atmosphere.

"No, madame, like their food," replied General Delacroix, and they all laughed.

"Then I fear Bismarck's table is well set," said Henri.

"If so, our army shall eat well, Brother," said Jules. "We are hungry for the glory of the battlefield. We are ready to shed the blood of the regiment for the honor of France."

Henri stiffened. It was an old argument between them. "It is an honor you seek for yourself and for which you would pay with the lives of boys, Jules. There is no honor in this cause. There is not even a cause in this cause. We need no war with Prussia over the Spanish throne. And even if a war served a purpose here, France is not ready."

General Raspail replied with all the derision his voice could summon. "It is extraordinary to hear such military wisdom out of the mouth of a man who has never worn the uniform of his country."

Henri smiled slightly. "I do not need to wear the uniform of France, General, to see that it is made of gold and stuffed with straw."

Raspail turned purple with rage. The tips of his mustache quivered. With visible effort he sought to quell his fury. "You insult me, Count," he hissed. "You insult the honor of France with your treason. If it were not for your father . . ."

General Delacroix put a soothing hand on the little general's shoulder. "I'm sure the count means nothing of the sort by his remarks, General," he said, smiling. "It is clear he has no idea of the true balances here. But let us not fight among ourselves. Let us save it for the Hun."

"You asked for my observations, General," said Henri, unruffled by the general's outburst. "I gave them to you. I regret they do not fit with your own."

"The field of battle will prove you wrong," insisted Jules. "For centuries others have doubted France's will or her readiness. For centuries France has shown them wrong. For centuries France has shown the world she knows the art of war."

"That is your mistake, Jules. You practice the art. The Prussians are making it a science."

"Then we shall humble the Prussian with art," said Elisabeth brightly. "And now that we have slain Bismarck and won the war, let us dispose of this topic and speak of something else."

ABOVE THE PARTY, TWO SMALL VOYEURS WERE having the time of their lives. From one end of the house to the other they crawled, slithering along a dirty wooden floor underneath the rafters, spying on the adults below. Over the years, the hidden passageways that connected the upstairs bedrooms in the Château deVries had yielded new and ever more exciting secrets to the enterprising and endlessly curious boys. Among the surprises was a series of peepholes into some of the downstairs rooms. Even the count, who had spent his own youth crawling through the spaces, had no idea some of the holes existed. They had been cleverly built to blend into the plaster molding that ran around the circumference of every ceiling in the house, and from within any room appeared to be part of the design. The ceilings were quite high throughout the house, so a person standing below them couldn't make them out very well anyway. Painters who saw them assumed they had something to do with ventilation. But they were not part of the design, nor did they have anything to do with ventilation, for one had to lift a piece of wood from the passageway flooring above to expose them. Small finger-pulls were notched into the ends of the boards to allow them to be lifted. The holes were quite deliberate, installed by some forgotten ancestor for some unknown purpose.

They now delighted and amused the boys, who were directly above some of the guests standing by one of the buffet tables in the dining room. They were peering at something that had held their rapt attention for a few long moments: the immense snowy white breasts of Baroness Celestine de Chabrillan, whose décolletage was so low that she seemed brazen to the other women and practically naked to the boys. The tight bodice of her dress squeezed her breasts upward and together, making them appear like two soft melons separated by a deep canyon, into which flowed a river of pearls. The baroness was engaged in conversation with a minor diplomat from the Austrian embassy, who had drunk too much champagne and could not tear his gaze from her chest.

"What do you suppose they're for?" whispered Moussa.

"Jacques says you squeeze them," said Paul. Jacques

was a classmate, ten years old like they were, who seemed to know a lot more about the world than they did.

"Yecch." Moussa made a face in the darkness. "Why would you want to do that?"

"I don't know." He thought for a moment. "They look like they'll pop if you do."

"*Merde*," said Moussa.

"Jacques says you kiss them too."

"Jacques would kiss anything."

"I know. I saw him eat a locust once. He looked it straight in the eye and kissed it before he popped it down."

"*Merde*," said Moussa again, not quite sure which prospect was less appealing, the lady or the locust. He sat up and took a small sip of champagne from the bottle they'd stolen from the kitchen. He grimaced at the taste and wiped his mouth on his sleeve. His head felt light. He passed the bottle to Paul, who remained transfixed at the hole.

"Here," he said. "Take another drink." Without looking, Paul reached for the bottle. He hit it by the neck and it tipped over. He sat up so quickly that he banged his head on one of the rafters, loosing a shower of dirt into his eyes. Frantically both boys grabbed for the bottle. Together they managed to capture it, but not before it had rolled along the floor and spewed forth a great gush of foam and liquid. A small stream of champagne ran straight for the open board over the peephole. Moussa's eyes grew wide as the liquid disappeared over the edge.

"Quick! Stop it!" Paul stomped on the stream, and giggled. His boot splattered the champagne all around.

"Shhhh!!!" Moussa started laughing too, but stripped off his shirt and plopped it onto the escaping stream to make a dam.

"Got it!"

In quiet unison the boys crouched over the hole to see what had become of their champagne. It had filled the low point in the plaster molding and spilled through one hole, and then another, making two tiny and short-lived waterfalls that plunged to the room below. One fell onto the shoe of the diplomat, who didn't notice, the other onto the breast of the baroness, who did. A look of horror crossed her face. With a gasp she stepped back and looked up. The stream died as suddenly as it began.

"Dis*gus*ting," she said, and stormed off, dabbing at herself with a handkerchief and leaving the confused diplomat to his glass of champagne.

GENERAL DELACROIX HAD AT LAST MANEUVERED himself into a corner of the foyer with Elisabeth. It had taken time and patience, for everyone had wanted to question him about the Prussians, and Elisabeth was the charming and gracious hostess. But at last they found themselves together, and alone.

"You look exquisite this evening, Elisabeth," he said.

"Thank you." She smiled, discreetly looking past him as she did to make certain no one was paying attention.

"I need you," he said.

Elisabeth blushed. "Bernard, really, not now."

"Yes, now. I can't wait. Let's go somewhere."

"Please, be reasonable. There's a party! I must attend to the guests!"

"I'm a guest, Elisabeth."

"You know what I mean. My husband is here! We can meet tomorrow."

"I may be gone tomorrow. The emperor will declare war. There is no time, Elisabeth." Delacroix was a head taller than Elisabeth, and as he looked down upon her he felt the irresistible stirrings of lust. She was a beautiful woman. He could smell the perfume in her long blond hair, which was piled high in elaborate curls. Her cheeks were soft and flushed, her eyes alluring and her lips full and red. She wore a tight silk dress. She was overpowering.

"We may all be gone tomorrow, Elisabeth," he

pressed, "including Jules. You know I can help him. I want to keep helping him." Delacroix looked over his shoulder, into the dining room, which was still packed with people. "Besides, he's not paying any attention."

It was true. Jules was engrossed in conversation with another colonel. He clutched a large glass of champagne, of which he'd had too many. He would not notice anything amiss in this crush.

It was so dangerous, so outrageous, so tempting. Elisabeth felt no sexual attraction to Delacroix, at least not in the strictest sense of the word. Yes, there was an attraction, but it was more complete than mere lust: it was the promise of power, of advancement of her cause, of the possibility of attaining all that meant anything to her in the world. Delacroix was powerful, and she was aroused by proximity to power, and *that* excited her sexually; and she looked at the general and her heart beat faster and she began to decide not when, but where.

She was doing it for Jules, of course. It had always been for Jules and his career, for the family, and yes, even for France. They would each do their part, he in the field, she at home, and together they would attain the ultimate mantle she sought, the baton of a marshal of the French army.

She had been sleeping with the general since the Italian campaign, when Jules had received his promotion from lieutenant colonel to colonel. Jules had been assigned to the Italian garrison, and had found himself involved in a skirmish at Mentana. He led a force of nearly brigade strength and had stumbled across a much smaller and poorly equipped company of men who had been separated from their leader, Garibaldi, during a storm. The incident was one of those turnabouts in war that results not from planning or deliberation, but rather from complete happenstance that becomes blind luck. The result said little of Jules's leadership or lack of it, for there was nothing more involved than utter surprise on both sides. Without firing a shot, raising a sword, or giving an order, Jules had simply been swept along at the front of an impressive tide of Frenchmen and horses that swarmed over a grossly inferior Italian force. It was over almost before it had begun.

Yet in a campaign that had been boring, brief, and seriously deficient in action, the skirmish had matured with each retelling. The details took on more luster, with the outcome of the "battle" appearing ever more uncertain, until by the time they arrived at headquarters the word was everywhere that Jules deVries was a cunning hero and his troops valorous indeed. It was a triumph of illusion. Jules, who had remained with the main force, had no idea why such a stir had developed over a trivial incident; but the general who later presented him with his promotion didn't press him for details, and Jules knew better than to protest.

Elisabeth had not known which had been the truly important act: her sleeping with the general, which she had resolved to do before Jules had even left for Italy, or Jules's own good fortune in the field. It didn't matter, really, for the result was what counted. General Delacroix had been quick to claim credit for the promotion—and in fact had endorsed it enthusiastically—and had since made it clear to her that he had taken to looking after the colonel, to keeping him out of trouble and making certain that opportunity met him square on. The promotion had brought with it assignment to more sedentary duty at Imperial Guard headquarters in Paris, which meant Jules would travel less than before. Elisabeth liked that. It meant he could spend more time with her and Paul.

Not for an instant did Elisabeth consider her trysts with Delacroix an act of infidelity. She was not unfaithful, just practical. When they slept together the first time, in the Hôtel de Ville, in a suite the general had arranged with silk curtains and thick Persian rugs and a stunning Louis XIV four-poster bed, she had begun with some trepidation, for while she knew what she was doing, this was an unknown road full of danger. Her butterflies had flown quickly before his advances. And as she took him inside her that first time, and closed her eyes and realized with whom she was sleeping—that this powerful man sat at the emperor's side and commanded the legions of France—she grew hot and frenzied and made love like a madwoman. Her long fingernails left deep gashes down the back of the astonished general, who had never known such turbulence and lust in bed.

She had not stopped loving Jules; nor did she love him any less. In fact she felt the opposite had occurred. She felt closer to him than ever, knowing that she had played a pivotal role in their mutual quest to advance his career. She knew Jules quite well, suspecting that his military skills were uninspired and that his past promotions had had more to do with his ability to follow orders without hesitation than with his qualities as a strategist or leader of men. There was nothing wrong with that, for the military depended upon obedience. It was simply that his career could use every possible advantage in its progression. It did not matter to her that in the councils of power, from the Tuileries to the parliament, from the emperor on down, flesh was the currency of the moment, that other women, many of them, were doing the same thing she was to curry favor here or there. She drew no comfort from having so much company, nor did she need it to ratify her own actions. What others did was of no consequence to her.

Elisabeth stood there in the foyer with the general and savored the danger and the thrill and the arousal she felt in a room full of generals and diplomats and nobles. She glanced again over the general's shoulder. Her pulse quickened. She made her decision.

"Follow me," she whispered, touching his hand lightly. Briskly she turned and walked to the far side of the entry hall, around the corner toward the kitchen. There was a door to a little-used pantry. As she approached it she hoped she appeared composed. She dreaded the thought of seeing Madame LeHavre, the cook she despised, but the object of her fear was loudly occupied at the far end of the kitchen directing the efforts of the help. Elisabeth opened the pantry door and slipped quickly inside. The general appeared a moment later, closing the door softly behind. There was no latch on the door, but there was a small wooden ladder used to reach the highest shelves. He slid it in front of the door, wedging its cross-brace beneath the handle so the door couldn't open.

Elisabeth threw her arms around him. The sounds of the house dimmed. Dishes and glasses clinked in the kitchen. There were muffled voices and an occasional shriek of laughter. They kissed long and passionately. Elisabeth fumbled at the general's clothing while he worked at the catches of her dress. He pulled it off her shoulders and partway down.

They froze as someone jiggled the doorknob to the room. The person gave up, and they heard footsteps disappearing down the hall.

"*Ce n'est rien,*" she whispered. "Someone's got the wrong room. But we must hurry!" The general surveyed the room. Two walls were covered from floor to ceiling with brown wooden shelves which held hundreds of cans, bottles, and jars. A canning table stood along the wall at one end of the room. With powerful arms he lifted her off her feet and carried her to it, pulling some aprons from a stack on a shelf as he went and throwing them on the table for a cushion. Frantically he unbuckled his trousers and dropped them, struggling to get them past his erection. He was panting. He lifted her skirts and petticoats and she lay back on the table, arms outstretched.

"Come to me quickly, Bernard," she said in a low voice, and an instant later he was in her, his hand on one breast, his mouth on the other as he half-stood, half-lay upon her and their bodies began to move together in the steady unison of passion.

MOUSSA AND PAUL SAT IN THE SEMIDARKNESS OF the secret passageway, comparing notes on the evening's espionage and sharing the last of the champagne. They were not drunk, for the spilled bottle had left them little, but they felt content, fuzzy and warm.

"*Une soirée magnifique!*" announced Paul. He had

never seen a party at the château, or anywhere else, but his pronouncement was delivered with the authority of a true connoisseur.

"*Merveilleux*," agreed Moussa. "Especially the goose."

They'd had a wonderful party. They'd spent most of the time in their second-story haunts enjoying their private view, looking down upon bald heads and feathered hats and baroness parts. But they'd also hidden underneath the buffet table, staring out at shoes and pants and petticoats. Paul had started to tie a banker's shoelaces together, but the man had moved away before he was done. They'd poured vinegar into several open bottles of champagne, and put horseradish in the cake. They'd stuffed their pockets with hors d'oeuvres and gone out behind the house where they sat in the woods, their backs to a tree, and watched the comings and goings of the guests. The shoelaces inspired Moussa to try something similar with the horses. They'd sneaked behind a group of liveried footmen standing near the carriages. Crouching low, they'd tied the tails of some of the horses to the carriages behind them, and then tied harnesses to other harnesses, and managed to create a massive tangle without getting caught.

And then there had been the goose. The boys had been downstairs in the kitchen when it happened. A mongrel dog had slipped through a forest of guests' legs, underneath the buffet table and through a door to the kitchen, where it had boldly seized an entire cooked goose ready to be carved by Madame LeHavre. She was a stout woman who always wore a plain black dress and a starched white apron, and she could get deadly serious when the mood took her. Her eyes caught fire at the sight of the thief. She grabbed a butcher knife and gave chase to the scrawny dog, which weighed barely as much as the goose flopping around in its mouth. They disappeared through the back door, which had been propped open to keep the kitchen cool, and across the lawn. Madame LeHavre was not a young woman. She moved more quickly than the boys thought possible, but not as quickly as the dog. She took the theft personally and would have carved up the beast if she could have caught it, but the dog was lucky and got away clean. For the boys, if not for Madame LeHavre, it was the high point of the evening. They howled at the memory.

"Thinking of the goose makes me hungry again," Paul said. "I'm going to the kitchen. I'll bring something back."

"Your face is a mess. You'd better let me go, or wash up first." Even in dim light Paul's face was covered with dirt and streaked with champagne. It was the kind of attic grime that wouldn't wipe off, but smeared instead. It wouldn't do to appear downstairs looking as if he'd been dragged through the dirt, and washing wasn't something that appealed to Paul just then.

Moussa wasn't much better. His upper body was covered with dirt, which highlighted a long scar that ran underneath his rib cage where the boar had gored him four years earlier. His shirt, the one he'd used to mop up the champagne, lay in a heap somewhere down the passageway. But his face was still relatively clean. "*D'accord,*" Paul nodded. "You go. Here. You can wear my shirt. While you're gone I'll go back and get yours." He slipped it off and gave it to Moussa, who pulled it over his head and crawled through the trap-door into their bedroom.

Paul started back down the passageway. He crawled next to a wall that ran around the back stairwell and continued down the passageway. Along the way he stopped to look through each of the spy holes. He peered into the count's study. The room was dark. He watched the help in the kitchen, and saw Moussa talking to Madame LeHavre. He noticed a notch in a board that he didn't remember ever lifting to look through. He lifted the board and knelt down and put his eye to the hole. He saw part of a table and two hands, a man's and a woman's. He guessed he was looking into the pantry. He shifted his position to get a better view. Then he saw it clearly, at first not comprehending what he was seeing. But then his brain caught up with what his eyes were seeing and his eyes went wide.

He saw his mother lying on her back on a table, and

a man in a uniform—it was a general's uniform, Paul could see the sash of the Imperial Guard—a general bending over her, his pants down around his ankles. They both were moving back and forth and making grunting noises. And then everything came to him in a blur. He saw her breasts, breasts he'd never seen before, at least not that he could remember, breasts like those on the baroness, but these were his mother's breasts, breasts uncovered, and her dress was pulled down off her shoulders and the man was holding her and rubbing them and kissing them—*he was kissing them*—and his mother's eyes were closed; Paul knew the man wasn't hurting her, but he couldn't tell what he was doing, couldn't tell what that expression on her face meant, and he didn't know what was happening, except that his mother was with another man in a strange way. And then she kissed him. Paul knew what that was; he'd seen his father kissing his mother one time when they didn't know he was looking, but this was a different kind of kiss, a lot different than when she kissed Paul. Then he saw his mother's eyes fly open wide. She groaned and bucked and said, "*Oui! Mon Dieu! Oui!*" and looked straight up at the ceiling, right to where he was looking back. He panicked and thought she must be looking at him, but then he remembered she couldn't see him, not through those little holes, of course not, but he jerked back anyway and sat up.

He was breathing hard and his face felt hot and his heart was pounding, pounding so much he could feel it in his ears. It was like the time he'd fallen out of the tree house and had the wind knocked out of him. That time his breath had finally come back to him in great gasps. Now he felt the same way, but there wasn't a tree house, or a fall. Just his mother and that man. He was terrified too, all tingly and scared. He had no idea what he had seen, only that it seemed to be something private, something his mother shouldn't be doing with a strange man.

He closed his eyes, which stung with grime, and rubbed them as he tried to make sense of things. He felt ashamed for spying like that, and knew that somehow he'd done something wrong, something terribly wrong, that he shouldn't have done it, shouldn't have been looking, but now it was too late, he couldn't take it back, and he wished he and Moussa had never come here at all, wished he didn't know about the stupid peepholes and the passageways, wished he were back in the tree house, right now.

Down through the darkness he heard Moussa calling for him in a low voice. "Paul!" There was a pause, and silence. "Paul, where are you? I brought the food! And I got another bottle! *Paul!*"

Paul didn't answer. He sat in silence, staring straight ahead. He drew his knees up to his chest and buried his dirty face in his hands, and tried his hardest not to cry.

FOUR DAYS LATER NAPOLÉON DECLARED WAR. Jules prepared to leave for the front. His days were a blur of activity. He left for the Tuileries early in the morning and didn't return home until late at night, barely taking time to eat. Even at home, when everyone was asleep except Jules and the boys, officers and soldiers came to see him. The boys watched from their window overlooking the front drive. Everyone was in a hurry. Couriers rode up fast on their horses, right to the front door, and carried messages inside. Their boots clomped in the front hall. There was silence in the house as they waited, and then boots clomped again as they carried messages back out.

Sometimes at night the boys heard Henri and Jules arguing. They didn't understand what was being said, except that it was something to do with the war. Moussa wanted to go into the passageways to listen, but Paul wasn't interested. He was finished crawling around in there, he said.

Paul stood in awe of his father, and with the coming of the war supposed he was probably the most important man in Paris just then, excepting maybe the emperor. Jules was the biggest, bravest, most powerful man the boy had ever seen. Paul swelled with pride when he saw other soldiers salute him, or stiffen in his presence, or run to carry out an order. He loved to watch him put on his uniform. His father was meticulous about it, every movement precise and well ordered, every centimeter of cloth pressed, every button shiny, everything just so. When the colonel was out Paul would touch his dress uniform, the sword and pistols and crimson sash, and wonder what it must be like to be a soldier. He dreamed of the uniform he would wear one day.

When Paul had turned eight two years earlier, Jules had begun letting him polish the sword. Paul handled it with reverence. It was over a meter in length and had an ivory handle with an eagle's head carved in it. It had belonged to his great-great-grandfather, who had used it in the Revolution. He ran his finger down the long blade, lightly so that the razor-sharp steel wouldn't cut. He used polish and a soft cloth to make it shine until he could see his reflection. After he was finished and was sure he had it perfect, his father would inspect it with a critical eye. The colonel always found a blemish, and lectured him like a recruit.

"Your sword is your companion, your friend. It is an extension of your honor. Show your pride, son. Make it look so."

Sometimes, no matter how hard he tried, Paul couldn't see the defect, but he would start over just the same, often having to repolish it three times before the colonel would accept it.

Now, as Jules stood in his bedroom and packed his bags with uniforms and toiletries and papers, Paul polished the sword again. Moussa was with him. The boys shared everything, but not sword duty. Paul let Moussa assist by getting the cloth or holding the polish, but he wouldn't let him touch the sword.

"Where are they going to have the war?" Moussa asked as Paul worked.

Paul shrugged. "I don't know. Somewhere they can find Prussians to kill. Prussia, I guess."

"I bet your father kills a lot of them."

"About a thousand, probably."

Moussa whistled. It sounded like a lot, even for Uncle Jules. "How can he get so many?"

"I don't know. He'll stab them first. Like this." Paul lifted the sword with two hands and ran a Prussian through. "I suppose he'll shoot them, too. Just to be sure."

"What if they shoot back?"

Paul frowned. "Everybody knows Prussians can't aim. Prussians are sissies."

"Didn't they beat the Austrians?"

"Austrians are sissies too."

Moussa knew that was true. Everybody said so.

At last Paul finished the sword. He was certain it had never looked so fine. He had Moussa check it first, and even though Moussa didn't touch it, Paul buffed it again. With great trepidation he took it to Jules, who held it up for inspection. Paul held his breath, expecting the inevitable order to do it over. Jules turned the sword to see both sides. He held it up to the light of the window. The blade gleamed. Paul had done well. It was perfect. But he was not a warm or demonstrative man. He could not permit himself a smile of acknowledgment. He addressed Paul as he would a private.

"Well done." He nodded brusquely. "It is acceptable." He set the sword on a table and returned to his packing.

Paul was in ecstasy.

The next morning Jules left before the sun came up. Elisabeth and the boys rode with him to the Gare du Nord. Paul sat in the front of the carriage with his father. Moussa rode in the back with Elisabeth. Since the party, Paul had been distant with Elisabeth. He didn't know how to look at her or what to say. Being near her made him feel awkward, so he did his best to avoid her. She was preoccupied and didn't seem to notice.

Even at dawn the teeming streets burned with the fever of war. Their carriage could barely make the passage for the traffic. Hawkers peddled papers filled with Gallic passion. Dogs barked and roosters crowed the cocksure confidence of a defiant Paris. Throngs of

soldiers went this way and that, each in a different
direction, each on some private mission. Wagons full of
ammunition and supplies clogged the roadways and created massive traffic jams.

All the activity of the streets funneled into the railway station. Ordinary traffic had ceased as train after
train, regiment after regiment, boxcar after boxcar of
supplies was loaded and departed. A ceaseless stream of
armed men entered the station. There was no order,
only confusion. Men didn't know where they were going, or where the rest of their units were, only that they
were supposed to report to the station. Some were early,
some were late, some were at the wrong station. Many
were drunk. Some had passed out on the platforms and
were pushed aside roughly by the crowds. Women clung
to men, and cried their farewells.

Jules made his way angrily down the platform, disgusted by the chaos. Elisabeth and the boys hurried
along behind him, waiting as he stopped to chastise a
drunk or order men to move wagons or boxes to make
way for the traffic. It was hopeless, but Jules was Jules,
and he would try: "You there! Move those crates!
Corporal! Have that man picked up and brought into
the station! See he's placed on report. . . . Where is
your commanding officer? . . . Where is your
rifle? . . . Who's in charge here?"

None of it did much good. Some of the men sneered
and made rude gestures as the colonel passed. Paul saw
it, and wondered and worried. Moussa gawked at everything. Elisabeth wore a pained expression. She
stepped gingerly around the drunks and the garbage and
the boxes and did her best not to let any of it touch her,
and wished she'd had the sense to bid Jules farewell at
home. But at last they arrived at his platform. The train
was just backing in, so they had to wait. Paul stood next
to his father and watched as the locomotive belched
smoke at the ceiling. Its shrill whistle echoed through
the great hall. Clouds of steam billowed out from between the cars, enveloping the platform in a white misty
shroud.

Without thinking Paul started to take his hand, but the colonel pulled away. "You are too old for that," he said, without looking down. Paul dropped his hand and felt his face flush. The excitement of the day was being replaced by the reality of his father's departure. It was just beginning to sink in: he was going away. Paul wouldn't see him for a while, maybe a long while. Paul didn't know how long wars took. He'd asked Moussa, who hadn't known either but suggested they ask Gascon, who usually knew everything. But Gascon had only shrugged and said, "As long as it takes." Paul felt a lump in his throat. He wished he could go.

Elisabeth stood next to Jules. Her face was bright and showed no strain. She had long since stopped worrying about his dying in battle. She was so certain that he would become a marshal of France that death must, of course, take a back seat to destiny. This war was a blessing. It was what she needed, what *they* needed. War sped promotions as peace never could. She was saying *au revoir* to a colonel, and would greet a general upon his return. She smiled at her husband as he was about to leave.

"I am certain you will bring us honor, Jules."

Jules kissed her stiffly on both cheeks. Public displays of affection made him uncomfortable. "I shall write as affairs permit," he said.

"Kill lots of Prussians, Uncle Jules!" said Moussa.

Jules waved. As he was about to step up into the train, Paul rushed up to him.

"Wait, Father, I forgot! I made you a present!"

With a broad smile he held it up to the big man. He had carved it himself from a piece of oak. It was crudely done, but recognizable. It was a toy soldier. An arm had broken off, so Paul had taken a straight piece of a twig and fashioned it into a rifle with a bayonet, and pasted it where the arm would have been. He painted a face on it, and the buttons of a uniform down the front. He used a walnut shell for a hat. The soldier had a small smile on its face.

Jules turned it over in his hands. It touched him

deeply, and he knew how long Paul must have labored over it. But his expression remained impassive. He regarded it with the same eye he used when Paul polished his sword.

"It is chipped," he said. "And our troops don't wear hats like that. You should pay more attention." He slipped the soldier into his pocket. "Very well," he said. "Make the next one with more care." He turned and disappeared into the train.

CHAPTER 5

W E WILL CROSS THE RHINE IN A WEEK AND BE IN Berlin in a fortnight," Jules had predicted confidently in Paris. For the better part of two centuries, that is exactly what the French army would have done. But not this time, not with Prussia. The war news was desperate. Disaster had followed debacle with stunning rapidity. The expected invasion of Prussia never occurred. Delay and indecision had paralyzed the French army, while Prussian troops and artillery poured into the Alsace and Lorraine regions of France. A small French victory at Saarbrücken had been followed in rapid succession by humiliating defeats at Fohrbach, Wörth, and Weissembourg. Suffering from ill health, Napoléon had given up supreme command to Marshal Bazaine, whose own army had become trapped in the fortress town of Metz near the Prussian border. More than fifty thousand Frenchmen had been killed, wounded, or captured there. The Prussians had surrounded the town in an iron vise, cut the telegraph wires, and were building a makeshift railway to facilitate troop movements during what everyone expected to be a lengthy siege.

Line after line of defense had been abandoned: first the Saar River, then the Moselle, then the Meuse. The town of Nancy was relinquished by French troops without a fight, to be occupied by four Prussian soldiers. The passes of the Vosges had fallen. Strasbourg was being shelled; Toul was under siege. At Givonne, French troops panicked at the sight of the approaching enemy and fled into the woods. At Gravelotte, braver French troops blew their trumpets, and stood their ground, and died. The skies had opened up over France and all the thunder and lightning was Prussian, and all the rain French blood.

Everywhere it had been the same as collapse followed calamity, until the Third Army of the crown prince of Prussia had chased General MacMahon halfway across France, and threatened to strike at Paris itself. Exhausted, hungry, and stunned, MacMahon's army had retreated to Châlons.

It was not Jules's custom to dwell upon reports of setbacks and defeats. He had always drawn strength from adversity, determination from defeat. Around him stirred the four corps of a new army, more than one hundred and forty thousand strong, moving to join forces with General Bazaine, who had wired his intention to break out of Metz.

France would show the Prussians yet, by God.

She would show the world.

But although there was reason for optimism, Jules's mood remained black. Great armies had clashed and thousands of men had given their lives, yet his own sword was dry, his pistol polished, his rifle silent in its scabbard. He had not seen a Prussian, not even a prisoner. Instead, his regiment had been relegated to the rear of the new army, where it arrested looters and set fire to French stores to keep them from the enemy—numbing duties that only worsened the soldiers' morale.

Where that army had passed, nothing remained, not a twig or a bush or the stalk of a plant or the low limb of a tree. Anything that had been growing was ground into the earth. Anything that had not moved was crushed by wheels and hooves and boots into unrecognizable mulch. It was as though a massive swarm of locusts had passed, devouring everything in its path. Through this eerie desolation Jules led his regiment, looking for stragglers and keeping a careful eye out for the Prussians, of whom there was no sign. The plan to meet Bazaine depended upon speed, but the elements and the terrain conspired to slow the procession. A storm found the army and camped directly overhead, drenching it with torrential rain. Wagons broke down in the muck and had to be tipped over and pushed out of the way. Artillery was abandoned. Without dry wood to start fires, the men ate cold rations and drank bitter wine and huddled in miserable wet tents.

Each hour, Jules had more to deal with in the rear than before. There were deserters in growing numbers, who when caught were arrested and returned to Châlons. Stragglers were falling behind everywhere, first scores, then hundreds of them. Many were drunk and fell senseless into ditches. The army had passed through Reims without collecting enough rations. As a result, the men pillaged the countryside through which they moved. French farmers lost everything to their own army, from livestock to the stores of grain in their barns to the contents of their larders. They were left with nothing but their rage, which fell hardest upon Jules and his men.

It was no duty for a proud colonel of the Imperial Guard, to clean up behind a demoralized army. Where was the enemy he came to face?

Jules knew there was only one way to shake his mood.

He needed to find some Prussians to kill.

BONJOUR, COLONEL."
Major Dupree saluted as his squadron rode up to meet Jules. "Everything quiet, sir. The night patrols have reported back. They made it ten kilometers to the rear, there and there." He pointed to the southeast, to a low ridge, and to the south, past a stand of trees barely visible in the distance. "If they're coming, they'll be coming from there."

"They're coming all right, and they won't be long." Jules nodded at the line of cattle disappearing into some woods behind the army. "We're not exactly streaking across France," he said. He looked over his shoulder. "At least the rains have kept the dust down. We can see what we're about." He drew a spyglass from his pack and scanned the horizon to the southeast in a slow, steady motion. The Prussians were out there, of that he was certain. For a day now they had heard the roar of distant artillery, and occasional bursts of rifle fire. But he saw nothing. It was unsettling.

From the northeast a messenger rode up, out of breath and in a hurry. "Colonel, sir. General MacMahon is turning the army north, to reprovision at Rethel. You are to concentrate your patrols on the southeast. He expects close Prussian contact there."

"*Rethel?*" Jules repeated it, to make sure he had heard correctly.

"Yes sir, for the supply train. The Seventh Army still has no cartridges, and there is not enough food. We can't provision ourselves from the countryside. The general wants four days' worth. The entire army is to detour. Sir." He saluted, and was gone.

"My God, it is madness to turn north, Colonel," said Major Dupree. "We're already going too slow. Now we're changing direction, and going the wrong way. The Prussians will put us in a box. We'll never get to the general in time."

Jules couldn't believe it himself. "I suspect you're right, Major. But Rethel it is. Let's get on with it."

THE SMALL FARMHOUSE SAT IN THE ARGONNE hills, surrounded by rocky potato fields and broken patches of birch and ash trees. A barn sat behind the farmhouse. The buildings were old and shambling and run-down, with leaky roofs and cracked windows and doors that didn't close. The place was parched and poor, and had never provided more than a meager living from a grudging land. A small streambed ran behind the house, which in the spring and early summer carried runoff from the hills to the Meuse River. Now it was dry. The main body of the army had missed the place, passing some distance to the west, so the fenced yard still contained horses, an ox, a pig, and some chickens.

The barn was on fire. The animals were frantic, moving in circles around the yard, shrieking and squawking, and charging at the fence. There were six saddled horses tied near the front door of the house, but outside there was no sign of people.

From a vantage point several kilometers away, Major Dupree saw the thick column of smoke rising from the fire.

"Prussians?" he asked, pointing to the smoke.

Jules looked through his glass. "Maybe. Let's have a look."

Quickly they made their way to the farm, keeping a careful eye on the woods as they went. The woods were still and seemed empty, even the birds not moving. They approached the house cautiously, and saw the horses tied at the front door.

"Those aren't Prussian mounts," the major said. "Or French army." He thought for a moment. "Irregulars?"

"If they are they shouldn't—" Jules began, but he was interrupted by the sound of men laughing, followed by a horrible low moan that grew in intensity. From out of the back door of the house burst a young woman clutching a small child to her breast. Her hair had half-fallen down and nearly covered her dirt-streaked face. Even so Jules could see that she was very pretty. Her dress was torn at the neck and hung from her shoulder. As she ran she kicked up dust, half-dragging one leg. Jules saw she had a clubfoot. The woman began running toward the front of the house when she suddenly caught sight of Jules and his men. Terrified, she drew up sharply. Her moan became a shriek. She looked desperately around and then ran the other way, toward the burning barn.

Jules dismounted quickly and started toward her. Major Dupree dispatched two details to check the perimeter of the farm. At that moment a man appeared through the back door of the house. He wore the uniform of a captain in the *Francs-tireurs*. He was laughing loudly and clapping, as if to the rhythm of a dance.

"*Ma chérie!*" he called after her. "You leave so soon! We have just begun!" Her wail never stopped. She disappeared around the side of the burning barn, dragging her foot as she made for the gate. He started quickly after her. Other men, dressed in gray uniforms, came out of the house behind him, clapping and laughing and drinking brandy from a bottle they passed around.

"Captain!" Jules's voice was like a thunderclap. Startled, the captain turned. He froze as he saw the colonel, the broad smile on his face disappearing. Jules didn't take his eyes from the man. With a terrible feeling in his stomach he felt he knew what was going on without looking further. He had heard much of the *Francstireurs*. They were irregular troops, guerillas who had been mobilized after the first French defeats to harass the Prussians, to ambush them, to cut their lines of communication, to create confusion and engage groups of the Prussian Uhlans who had been sent forward in small, detached parties to sow terror among the populace. The *Francs-tireurs* were men who had rejected the discipline of the ordinary military in favor of roaming the countryside, engaging in unconventional tactics. They were vicious fighters, and had been accused of great excesses, not only against the enemy but against the civilian population as well. It was said that they cut the throats of Prussians they caught with uncommon zeal, that they took body parts for trophies, and that the tortures they devised were grisly and drawn out. Jules didn't know what was fact and what was myth about them. He had run across them in Châlons, and found them to be unruly and rude. Half of them ought to be court-martialed, he thought, and the other half sent packing. The group before him now were still laughing, although more quietly, and they continued to pass the bottle. They looked upon Jules and his troop with obvious contempt.

"Major Dupree, get some men to do something about that fire. Take care of these animals. Get them out of here. And see if the woman is all right." Jules turned his attention to the captain of the *Francs-tireurs*. The man was disheveled and stank of alcohol. He was a large, strong man with a full, jet black beard that contrasted with his shock of gray hair. Thick brows cast a shadow over eyes that were red-rimmed from brandy but still arrogant and forbidding. He had the sullen look of a man who'd been robbed of his purpose.

"You! What the devil is going on here?"

"We were passing by and saw some—"

Jules roared at him. "I'll be addressed as Colonel, Captain! You've forgotten how to salute? What's your name? What unit is this?" The man scowled and flung him a contemptuous half-salute. "Captain Victor Delescluze, Colonel, Third Vouziers Irregulars." He said it slowly, his voice laced with sarcasm, drawing the last word out: "Irrrr . . e . . g . . g . . g . . ulars." Some of the men behind him chuckled.

"As I was saying, Colonel, we saw some Prussians."

"Here? You saw Prussians here?"

"I said it, didn't I?"

"Colonel!" It was Major Dupree, his voice filled with urgency. Jules left the captain and strode around the side of the barn. The woman was there, with her child. She had sagged down onto the ground with her back to the fence. Next to the fence lay the body of a man, no doubt her husband. He wore the clothes of a poor farmer. He lay flat on his back, his arms and legs splayed out as he had fallen. He stared through sightless brown eyes at the sky. He had been shot once through the forehead.

As Jules approached, the farmer's wife drew her knees up tightly and began rocking in the dirt. Her moans had become a steady deep lowing, sounds like an animal might make. She clung to her daughter so tightly that the knuckles of her hands were white from the pressure. The child was about three years old, a little girl with doe eyes and long lashes, her eyes puffy from crying. At the sight of Jules and Major Dupree, she buried her face in her mother's chest, and they rocked softly together, back and forth, back and forth.

A shadow fell over them, and the woman looked up. Her eyes focused on something behind Jules. She stiffened and rocked faster. Jules turned. Delescluze stood behind him.

"Wait over there, Captain," Jules said.

"What for?" Delescluze asked.

Jules's eyes blazed at that. "Major Dupree! Escort this—" Delescluze scowled and drew back before the command was issued. Jules knelt again.

"Madame," he said, touching her arm gently. She pulled away from him. He drew his hand back. She looked at him through haunted eyes.

"Madame, I must know. The captain"—he indicated Delescluze—"the captain says that the Prussians were here. I must know, madame. Is it true? Did they do this to you? Did Prussians kill your husband?"

The woman quivered. Her whole body shook like a leaf. She said nothing. Her eyes had lost none of the terror he had seen in them earlier.

"Madame, *s'il vous plaît*. You are safe now. Tell me what has happened here. If there are Prussians we must find them quickly."

Silence.

Jules tried a few more times, but to no avail.

"See what you can get from her, Major," Jules said to Dupree, and then he returned to Delescluze.

"Did she tell you lies, Colonel?" Delescluze asked.

."Why would she do that?" Jules's voice was sharp.

"She's hysterical. She could say anything."

"What could she say that would be of concern to you, Captain?" Jules gave him a cold, appraising look.

"She's a cripple, Colonel. Just a crippled peasant woman. It doesn't matter what she says."

"You disgust me, Captain. She's a Frenchwoman. You should busy yourself with the Prussians."

"We were."

"There's no sign of them. No sign they were here."

"They were here, Colonel, I tell you they were. Four of them. Uhlans. I saw them. My men saw them. We chased them away. And what about the dead man, Colonel? You think he shot himself?"

"I wonder, Captain. Why weren't you chasing them?"

"We were about to chase them when you got here."

"It looked to me like you were beginning to chase *her* when I got here."

"Hell, Colonel, I was just having some fun."

At that moment one of the lieutenants Major Dupree had dispatched to reconnoiter the area around the farmhouse rode up and stopped before them.

"Any sign of Uhlans?" asked Jules.

"No sir, no sign at all. We've made two circles. *Rien du tout, Colonel.*"

Jules looked long into the eyes of the captain. He was certain Delescluze was lying. He was certain he was looking at a murderer and a thief, but there was nothing he could do, not as long as the woman would not talk, and Major Dupree appeared to be having no luck. Besides, he couldn't afford to get tied up here. He needed to be moving.

"It appears your Prussians have disappeared into thin air, Captain," he said.

"They're clever bastards all right, Colonel," Delescluze said with a smirk.

Jules got his face up close next to the other man's. "I think you're a liar, Captain. I think you're a killer and a coward."

Delescluze stiffened, his face reddening. His hand dropped to the hilt of his sword, but he stopped himself.

"Get your swine out of here, Delescluze. Get the whole stinking lot out now. If I see you again I'll have you arrested if I have to make up a reason. I would love nothing better than to see your smile beneath the blade of a guillotine."

Captain Delescluze saluted with another of his waves of amused insolence. "Yes sir. *Je t'emmerde.* Fuck you, Colonel, sir."

The lieutenant, still on his horse, heard the insult and started to raise his rifle. Jules felt his blood run hot. In a lifetime of military service he had never been so abused. In Paris he would have seen personally to the man's arrest and court-martial. Even in Châlons, in field camp, he would have done the same. And had this man been a member of the regular French forces, Jules would have done so now.

But in that moment Jules was to make the greatest mistake of his life.

He held the man beneath contempt and did not

consider him part of the military establishment. He was a thug in charge of bandits and bullies, and wasn't worth hot spit. Jules could not afford the men required to place him under arrest and return him to Châlons or Paris for trial. Jules had no doubt that the mangy group of assassins would kill its share of Prussians, and that, in this mistaken moment, outweighed his own need for justice.

So it was that Jules did not act, that he waved off his own officer and let the group go. "*Laissez*, Lieutenant. It is not important. These . . . these *men* are leaving."

Delescluze smiled broadly. "That we are, Colonel, that we are." He turned to his men. "*On y'va, messieurs*," he said, bowing slightly to the colonel and waving his men along. They laughed and joked among themselves as they left the yard. In a moment they had mounted their horses and were gone.

"Ugly lot," said the lieutenant.

"Bastards," said the colonel.

A detail buried the farmer in a shallow grave. The woman watched them with no expression on her face, never moving from where she sat. Her daughter peered out from under one of her arms. As they were about to leave, Major Dupree helped her up and into the house.

The fire burned itself out quickly. There was nothing left of the barn or anything that had been in it. A few wisps of smoke rose lazily from the rubble. Jules went briefly into the house after he satisfied himself about the other arrangements. The woman sat in the semidarkness of the sparsely furnished room. Jules stood before them. He felt terrible for what had happened, but could think of nothing to say.

Gently he reached out and touched the little girl's hair. It was soft, and reminded him of Paul's hair when he was a baby. After a moment he turned and left.

HALF AN HOUR LATER JULES WAS ATOP A BLUFF with Major Dupree where they had a commanding view of the surrounding terrain. To the north they could see the great crawling black and gray mass of the army, still moving slowly along toward Rethel. The Prussians would be off to the east somewhere, although he could detect no trace of them. He had dispatched two squadrons to the northeast and another to the southeast with instructions that they rendezvous later that afternoon at a small village called Marchault.

He finished scanning the horizon and turned his glass to the area beneath where they sat. He could see the farmhouse. He was still haunted by the look in the woman's eyes, by her child. He felt the bile rising in his throat as he thought of the *Francs-tireurs*. It was not enough to have the Prussians with which to contend. They had to cope with these animals as well.

How I wish I were at the front of this army, and not the rear.

Suddenly the major touched his sleeve. "Colonel!"

Jules looked where the major pointed. The sun was behind them, and from their vantage point they could see for kilometers. A smile grew on Jules's face as he looked. The sun, behind his shoulder, illuminated it all: the lance carried by the lead rider, the gold emblems on the helmets, the white sashes across the chests, the crimson bands around their necks and waists, the red-rimmed blue blankets on the horses. As distant as they were, there was no mistaking it: six Uhlans, threading their way carefully through a section of trees below them. The Uhlans would not be visible from the road, but from where Jules sat the view could not have been better.

"Any more behind them?"

"*Non, Colonel, c'est une partie seulement,*" the major said. The Prussian patrol was alone, in keeping with their practice of employing small scouting parties. Jules felt his spirits soar and his blood race. Prussians, by God, there were Prussians at last! His horse felt his excitement, and stirred his feet impatiently.

"Let's have a go at them, Major!" He continued scanning, and stopped abruptly as his scope fell once again upon the farmhouse.

He swore. "*Merde!*"

"Colonel?"

"*Les Francs-tireurs.* They're back."

Delescluze and his five men had waited in the bush, and once believing the way to be clear had returned to the farmhouse. Through his glass Jules watched them dismount. Delescluze led his men inside. Jules knew what they wanted. He knew what they would do. His blood ran hot as he thought about what was going to happen.

He thought quickly. As much as he wanted the Prussians, they were a small group. Dupree could take them easily.

He would deal with Captain Delescluze.

"Major. I'll keep six men. I'm going back to the farmhouse. You take the rest and have after the Uhlans. You'll take them neatly if you wait for them there, in that stand of trees where the road bends to Attigny. After you have them, wait for us there." Jules indicated a broad arc in the road.

Dupree nodded, a smile on his face. It was all the same to him. Prussians or Delescluze—after weeks of nothing, they had something to do at last.

The two parties split and disappeared down opposite sides of the bluff. Jules thought of the woman and knew there was no time to lose. He urged his horse on. Sure-footed and eager, the horse negotiated the rocky terrain easily as they descended. They made their way quickly down a ravine, through a light wood, and straight through the rocky fields. As they entered the potato fields belonging to the farmhouse the men following Jules moved abreast of him, so that they rode in a line, shin to shin. The hooves of their horses made a muffled rumble as they raced across the field.

Inside the farmhouse, Delescluze had picked himself up off the body of the woman and buttoned his fly. He was furious. The bitch had kept him from his pleasure. She wouldn't let go of the little girl, so he had ripped the screaming thing from her arms and shoved her at one of his men like a sack of provisions. From that moment, the woman had fought like the devil, fought like no man he'd ever seen, fought him well and viciously. She had clopped him on the side of his head with her fist, making his ears ring. As he grabbed one arm, she tried to scratch his eyes out with the other, raking a fingernail across his eyeball. He roared in pain and hit her hard across the mouth. He hit her again and again, hearing something in her cheek breaking, but she wouldn't stop fighting, wouldn't give in. So he had reached for his pistol, to hit her with that, when she kicked him hard in the groin with that damned clubfoot. That was when his erection—so strong until then, so driven by her fury and the vigor of her blows—that was when his erection had gone from him. And once she had done that, once she had stolen his moment and changed it for pain and made him double over in agony, once he heard his men laughing behind him, laughing at his impotence in the face of this crippled woman's battle, he had snapped, his mind cold with fury, his eyes bugged out in rage. He threw her down and pinned her beneath him and dug his fingers into the base of her throat and pressed down, pressed past her gasping and choking, pressed deep down until he could feel her spine with his thumbs, and she looked at him through awful eyes of hatred, eyes that were bulging but would not submit, and her lips turned purple, and finally, after what seemed an eternity, her arms went limp little by little and her legs weakened, until at last she stopped struggling and the life went from her and she died.

"Fucking whore!" he roared at her as he struggled up. "Bitch!"

One of his men laughed. Delescluze turned and hit him, knocking the man to the ground, and that is when the captain looked through the broken front window and saw Jules and his men storming across the field. Delescluze knew he and his men could not run. There was no choice.

He knew what they had to do.

No one in Jules's squad was expecting a battle. They expected a bit of a dustup with some drunk and poorly disciplined irregulars, and multiple arrests. They looked forward to it, confident, even arrogant as they rode side by side—proud men of the Imperial Guard in their white uniforms and red breeches and black jackboots and epaulets, the fearsome Guard, the plumes on their golden helmets streaming behind them in the breeze. They would romp through it quickly, and rejoin the major where the real action was.

They were drawing close to the farmhouse when the roar of the first fusillade erupted from within, killing four of them outright. The colonel's horse took a bullet in the chest and went down. Jules was thrown to the ground and knocked unconscious. Stunned, the remaining two men pulled up desperately, their horses rearing in fright. The men reached for their weapons but there was no time. Rifles roared again from within the house. Both men went down, one wounded horribly in the face, the other dead. It had all taken less than thirty seconds from the first shot to the last. The man with the face wound writhed in agony, his screams the only sound remaining.

The door to the house opened. One of the irregulars peered cautiously out. Satisfied that there was no one else, he made his way to the screeching form on the ground. He raised his rifle and fired.

In the potato field before the farmhouse, all was quiet once more.

JULES REGAINED CONSCIOUSNESS WITH HIS FACE down on the dirt floor of the farmhouse. It was the smell he recognized, something familiar about that smell, pungent and irritating. Still stunned from his fall, he saw the irregulars moving about the room, as if in a dream. They had dragged the bodies of his dead Guardsmen in from outside. Jules could count them, all hazy and fuzzy counting, one-two-three-four-five-six dead, all dead, heaped in a bloody pile of white and red, thrown on top of one another like dolls, arms and legs all jumbled together in a big mess, rivers of blood running onto the floor. He could hear laughing, talking, and then two of them came over to where he was slumped against the wall. One of them kicked him in the mouth. Jules tasted leather and grit and blood, and then they grabbed him beneath the arms and hauled him to his feet. Through his daze Jules saw the body of the woman, her dress ripped from her shoulders and hitched up around her waist. Across her chest lay her daughter, the little girl facedown, the black handle of a carving knife protruding from her back.

Then he realized what was making the smell. One of the irregulars had sprinkled kerosene over everything in the room, over the furniture and the walls and the bodies, God, all the bodies, drenched in the stuff. And then the man knelt and lit a match, and Jules roared through his fog and lashed out, his hand finding something soft, but then someone hit him from behind, and as the flames began their work he was out again.

When he awoke it was after dark. He couldn't move. He was stiff all over. Everything hurt. His hands were tied tightly behind him. He couldn't feel his fingers, couldn't tell if they moved when he told them to. He tried to roll over but couldn't. He groaned.

Delescluze sat across from him in the darkness. He sat on one of the red blankets taken from a dead Guardsman. He was sipping from a bottle of brandy.

"Well, well, our guest is awake. Sit him up," he snapped. A soldier grabbed Jules by the shoulders of his uniform. As he did one of the epaulets ripped off. The soldier stared at the little silk cords dangling in his hand. With a laugh he reached for the other and ripped it off too. There followed Jules's medal from the Italian campaign, a ribbon from Algeria, an insignia from St. Cyr; all the dressings of the colonel's rank and history, and the soldier pinned them on his own plain shirt or stuffed them in his pockets.

"There," he said, "I'm a right proper officer of the Imperial Guard now," and he pranced around, puffing his chest and holding the epaulets on his shoulders.

Jules tried to get his bearings. He had no idea where he was. There was no fire in the camp, but a full moon in a clear sky provided light enough to see. They were in the country somewhere, but it was impossible to tell how far they might have come while he was unconscious. He shook his head to try to rid it of the haze. His mouth was swollen, his lips split and bloody. His head pounded, the blood surging in his temples. As the moments passed his head began to clear, and it started coming back to him, and he felt his fury rise once again.

"Would you care for a refreshment, *mon colonel?*" Delescluze extended the bottle to Jules, who kicked it away savagely. His action brought a shake of the head from the captain, who rose calmly and retrieved the overturned bottle. "A shame to waste such fine brandy," he said. "It is from Charente. You should be more discerning."

"I demand you release me at once," Jules said. For all he had been through, his voice rang strong, with absolute authority. "You must surrender to me."

At first Delescluze was silent, as though he hadn't heard. And then a broad smile crossed his face and he and his men roared with laughter.

"It is hugely funny, your joke," he acknowledged, nodding his head in clear admiration. "But I am afraid, *mon colonel*, that you have become confused. It is you who have surrendered to me."

"The devil I have. I will see you roast in hell for this outrage."

"Perhaps you will see me in hell, Colonel, but not for this." He shook his head. "No, Colonel, for this I will suffer nothing. For what has passed today, I shall take a bow on some great Paris stage, at the Comédie Française, perhaps, before crowds of those who will applaud and throw me flowers and kisses."

Jules could not comprehend what was being said. His tormentor's head was bowed. Every so often he would look up, and in the bluish light of the moon Jules could make out his face. Behind the brandied glaze of his eyes there was force and purpose and terrible anger. *Delescluze is not a drunk*, he thought. *He is a lunatic.*

"You are mad, Delescluze."

The captain laughed delightedly.

"Mad indeed, Colonel, mad indeed. Through and through. Astute of you to notice." He sat back against a great log that lay across the clearing in which they sat and lit a cheroot. The smoke rose languidly in the air.

"Yes, *mad* is the right word, the precise meaning. Mad, but not crazy. Mad I am, mad I am . . ." His voice grew fainter as his mind drifted in some faraway place. He said nothing for a few moments, and then he looked at Jules.

"I despise you, Colonel. You are disgusting. You and all your Imperial Guardsmen are swine, for you guard the Imperium. The great, the grand, the mighty Napoléon and his court of thieves, and you stand at his side and lick his boots and do his evil work. The empire is corrupt and you—you . . . bastard . . . you protect it! You preserve it!" His anger flared and his boot lashed out, catching Jules on the shin. A sharp pain shot up Jules's leg, but his face remained impassive.

"You talk drivel, Delescluze. You mean to say you killed my troops because you dislike the emperor?"

Delescluze looked at Jules with contempt. "Don't be an ass, Colonel. I killed your troops because we were having a party and they tried to interfere. But if I'd thought about it for a minute, I guess I would have killed them because I dislike the emperor, yes. Yes, Colonel. I would kill anything that would prolong this wretched empire. Your emperor killed my father. First he stole his land. His Baron Haussmann, the great master builder, decided he needed a street. To get that street he took away my father's life. Everything. His house, his shop, his livelihood. He tore it down and built a street in its place and put a sewer under it to carry all the royal shit out of Paris. A fucking street for my father's life! He got nothing in return. No money, no note, no position to make up for his loss. Nothing. When my father protested they laughed in his face. No court would hear him. And when he took to the streets because there was nothing left, they shot him dead like a dog, and left his stinking corpse in that street for my mother to cart away. A street and some shit for my father's life."

Delescluze took a long swig from the bottle. If he had not been drunk before, it looked as though he was intending to get there now. He sat silent for a minute, looking up at the moon and lost in thought. In the distance they heard artillery fire, the low rumble of a war that for the moment had passed them both by.

"You hear that, Colonel? That is the sound of the Prussians kicking our backside. They are going to win this war, Colonel. They have won it already. Bismarck and his fucking plans—he's doing for us what we haven't been able to do for ourselves. He'll stick that spike on top of his helmet right up Napoléon's ass, and save the rest of us the trouble."

Delescluze took another drink. "I would kill you all if I could," he said, "but I cannot, of course. I will go off to the woods and kill Prussians, because right now that is what I have to do. I hate them even more than I hate the grand ass imperial. Even more than I hate you. But I cannot kill enough of them to matter, and you and your scum are too weak to do it. They will win in the end."

"What do you intend to do with me?" asked Jules.

The question appeared to take Delescluze away from the camp. His eyes glazed. For a long time he did not respond, and Jules thought perhaps he had not heard. But then Delescluze focused again, and looked at him with eyes that seemed fevered in the moonlight.

"Since we took you prisoner I have devoted considerable thought to that question, Colonel. Of course, I considered immediate execution. I could have just left you inside that house, provided you with a little kerosene refreshment, and offered you one of my cheroots. I almost did that. Almost did. But I got to thinking that that was too honorable an end for such a pompous bastard. Somebody might think that the fine and noble and brave colonel had died in battle. I couldn't have that. I couldn't leave your children with the thought that their father was a hero who died fighting Prussians. I would hate for them to think that, Colonel, for there are no heroes in your empire. Plenty of idols, but no heroes."

He put a hand to his forehead. "And then it came to me, and it was like thunder in my head. I am a simple man, yet even I have to admire its beauty. You are the perfect instrument for my revenge. You ask what I

intend to do with you? I am going to give you back to
your own." He smiled. "I am going to send you back to
Châlons! I am going to send you back and let you be
eaten by your own dogs. I will send you with a little
amusement that should make your life interesting, at
least for a while."

Jules stared at him blankly, not understanding.

"You see, Colonel," Delescluze said, "it is not you I
wish to destroy. It is your honor."

Delescluze barked at one of his men. "A lantern! And
see its light is kept low!" Delescluze searched his ruck-
sack and drew out some paper and a pencil. When the
light was set next to him on the ground, he leaned forward to write.

"What is the date?" he asked.

Jules said nothing.

"No matter," Delescluze shrugged. "I believe it is the
twenty-fourth." He bent over the paper:

> To the commanding officer, Châlons camp,
> I, Captain Victor Delescluze, commanding of-
> ficer of the Third Vouziers Irregulars, hereby
> transmit into your custody one prisoner. On the
> 24th of August, in this year, in view of our unit,
> this officer sent his troops into battle against a
> strong Prussian regimental patrol in the vicinity of
> Marchault. My own troop was too far from the
> action to join the battle, and could only watch the
> progress of the engagement from a height. As his
> troops were committed, they at first seemed to do
> well against the Prussian foe. They stood bravely
> against furious fire, and I myself will recommend
> that they receive a unit citation for bravery.
> However, as we watched the tide of battle turn-
> ing against them, we could see that the colo-
> nel, one . . .

He looked up. "What is your name, Colonel?" he
asked.

"DeVries. Jules deVries."

"Ah, a noble name as I expected, Colonel. A fine name indeed." He returned to his writing.

> . . . one Jules deVries of the Imperial Guard, who had been watching from a hillock as his men were being slain, turned his horse away from the action and departed at a gallop.
>
> It was our assumption that the colonel was going to rally other troops of his command who might as yet not be visible to us from where we stood. But as we made our way down to help in the cause of France, we discovered him still fleeing, and that there were no other troops for him to join. When we surprised him in his flight, the awful reality of what he was doing sank in. He had stripped off the jacket and blouse of his uniform, with the intention, we can only surmise, of exchanging it for one belonging to some civilian. When caught in the act he refused to answer our repeated questions, and engaged in a lengthy deception. But as to the character of his crime, as to the certainty that he abandoned his men and had fled the battle like a coward, there can be no doubt.
>
> It is only because of this officer's high rank that I have elected to return him to your jurisdiction instead of trying him in the field. I lack adequate rank to do what begs to be done, what must be done to preserve the honor of France and her sons who this day have shown such courage and willingness to die in her cause.
>
> I, and all of the men in my command who witnessed this act, will cooperate fully with an official court-martial when one can be convened. But owing to the presence of Prussian troops in the immediate vicinity, I cannot in good conscience remove myself or my men from the service of our nation, even for a moment, solely in order to dispose of a repugnant matter such as this. Consequently, I shall contact you by wire or post at the earliest possible opportunity so that we can bring this matter to its just conclusion.

*I trust that my actions meet with your under-
standing and approval.*
   Vive la France!

                    Victor Delescluze, Captain
                    Third Vouziers Irregulars

When he had finished he sat back against the log and
took a drink of brandy. In the dim light and with a
steady voice he read the letter back to Jules, a look of
satisfaction on his face.

"On the whole I believe it is rather well done, don't
you agree, Colonel?"

Jules's attitude as he listened had shifted from disbelief to near-amusement.

"You are a fool, Delescluze. This will never work.
They all know me. They know what I am."

Delescluze smiled and shook his head. "Your world
is finished, Jules deVries. When this war is over, nothing
will be the same, nothing ever again. You live among
jackals, and there will be no emperor to protect you. No
empire. Your own kind will forget you. They will turn
on you, and eat you alive."

"You are mistaken, Captain. But no matter. What
you do here"—he nodded at the letter—"is the feeble
act of an idiot. If this is the best you can do, I overesti-
mated you. You'd do better to shoot me. Because as
long as it takes, I will find you and repay your treachery
and murder."

Delescluze returned an amiable smile.

"I think not, Colonel. We shall see. Your confidence
in your world is greater than mine. If nothing else, this
will provide you with some interesting times, of that I
am certain. And I do not worry that you will find me.
We will never see each other again, Colonel, not on this
earth. Of that, too, I am certain."

THE GUARD DISPATCHED BY CAPTAIN DELESCLUZE
to accompany Jules to Châlons treated his prisoner
roughly and with contempt. He bound Jules's hands in
front of him with a rope, so tightly that he drew blood,

and on two horses they made their way down the road. There was heavy traffic, mostly caravans of wretched refugees fleeing from the desolation of the war taking place to the east. Jules had to wait as long trains of carts driven by oxen and filled with piles of bedding and worn furniture and pots and pans and clothing all vied for position on the dusty road. Women and children huddled together and rode on carts when they could, and walked when they could not. They had no idea whether the war was being won or lost, and trudged along in dusty silence.

A few looked at the prisoner with curiosity. They could tell from his bearing, if not his uniform, that here was a man of position, of importance. At first he ignored them, lost in his own thoughts, but then, embarrassed, he tried to catch their gazes and hold them when he could, as if to reassure them that this was all a mistake, that he was undeserving of what they saw him endure. But none of them read it in his look. None of them understood. They always averted their eyes, and left him to ride in silence. After a while he gave up trying and stared straight ahead.

The August afternoon blazed hot. Jules wore no helmet. The sun baked his head and dried him out. He was desperately thirsty, but would not permit himself to ask his captor for anything: neither food nor water nor assistance of any kind. He would sooner speak to the devil. The guard, hungover from his long night at the brandy with his companions, paid no attention as he half-rode and half-slept while they traveled. Occasionally his head would slump as he nodded off. He would catch himself and suddenly snap awake again. They passed hours that way, never stopping.

At length they came to an obscure trail that was little more than a path but which provided a shortcut to Châlons. The guard took it, to be rid of the mass of traffic on the main road. The noise of the road faded as they left it behind. The new road was lined with trees that provided welcome shade and cooled the air. Near five o'clock they came upon a stream. The guard led them down an embankment alongside the narrow bridge to rest and water the horses. He dismounted and then pulled Jules roughly down, dumping him on his rear.

"Right on your asshole where you belong," he laughed.

The man turned his back. Jules struggled to his feet and looked around. There was no one near that he could see. He hadn't been thinking about escape, for he was certain that rational minds would prevail in Châlons, and that he would quickly turn the tables on his captor. But as the guard turned, Jules saw his opportunity and acted almost without thinking. This was his chance! Swiftly he ran forward, raising his bound hands and bringing them down around the guard's neck. Energized by his own sudden movement, enraged by his captivity, by the brutal murders of his men, by the despicable slayings of the farmer, his wife and child, Jules felt all the emotion of the past twenty-four hours come to the surface as he lifted the man off his feet from behind, his wrists under his chin. The guard struggled fiercely, choking, unable to cry out, grasping at his neck in an attempt to loosen the vise grip Jules closed around him. His arms and feet flailed helplessly as Jules held him up. Jules intended to choke him into unconsciousness, work the knife from the man's belt, and cut himself free. The guard gurgled and sputtered, but was powerless against the strength and fury of Jules's attack, and he began to sag as his strength left him.

Jules felt the heady excitement of triumph and knew that he would soon be free. Just then a powerful blow stunned him from behind. He lost his balance and crashed to the ground, the guard still within his grip.

"Hold!" came a sharp voice. Jules could not see who was there, but held on as tightly as ever, until a vicious kick to the back of his head brought a gasp to his throat. His arms went limp and he let go. The guard rolled away from him, choking, coughing, and spitting. Facedown, he panted in the dirt.

Jules recovered his own senses and looked around. A wave of relief swept over him. It was a sergeant of the Dragoons who had hit him.

"Sergeant, thank heavens you've come," he gasped as he struggled to his feet. "You have—"

"Shut up, you! Who the devil are you anyway? I saw you assault this man!" The sergeant looked at Jules's wrists, which were still bound, and at the prostrate form of the guard, still gasping on the ground. The sergeant helped the guard to his feet. He still couldn't speak for the damage to his throat. As the man gathered his strength Jules tried again, knowing that he must take command of the situation quickly or not at all.

"Sergeant!" he roared. "I am Colonel Jules deVries of the Two Hundred Twentieth Regiment of the Imperial Guard! This man has imprisoned me falsely. He's a killer, part of a group of irregular troops operating near Vouziers. They took my squad by surprise. They murdered them all. They murdered civilians—"

"Shut up, I said!" the sergeant snapped. He regarded Jules with uncertainty and suspicion. He couldn't quite make out what he had before him, except that the man bore no resemblance to a colonel of the Imperial Guard. He had the bearing, it was true, and the manner of an officer. But his physical appearance—the ravaged face, battered and puffed and black and blue above the tattered remnant of a uniform, torn where epaulets and medals might have been—said otherwise.

"A colonel, eh?" he said. "I can't rightly say what you are by the looks of you, but if you step out of line once more I'll clomp you again! I'll have order here, by God I will!"

The guard found his voice at last. "This man is a prisoner, Sergeant," he croaked. "You saw him! He tried to kill me! He's done it before, I tell you. He's full of treachery. I have orders to transmit him to the commanding officer of the Châlons camp. Here, here, you'll see . . . I have this." He pulled the letter Delescluze had written from his pocket and handed it to the sergeant.

Jules raised his hands in frustration. "Sergeant, those are lies!" he said, but as his hands came up the Dragoon, now thoroughly suspicious, pushed him away and stepped back. He opened the letter and read it slowly through. Several times he stopped and looked at Jules, and then took up his study of the letter again. When he was finished he shook his head.

"A bad business," he muttered to himself. "Terrible."

"Sergeant—" Jules began, but the man cut him short.

"Silence! You have already admitted you are this man's prisoner. Do you now deny it?"

"No, Sergeant, but if you'll—"

"Shut up! Do you deny you were trying to escape?"

"No, but—"

"Enough!" He turned to his horse, opened his pack and drew a pen from it. "It is simple. If you are innocent of these charges, you shall be acquitted. In the meantime, I must allow this man to carry out his orders, and I must report what I have seen with my own eyes. Justice demands it. I can do nothing else . . . Colonel." The sergeant wrote quickly on the back of Delescluze's letter. When he was finished he handed it back to the guard, whose countenance bore a smug grin of satisfaction at the turn of events.

"There you are, man. I've told them what I've seen today. You're lucky I came along. You're a sloppy one, all right. I doubt your rabble could have surprised the Imperial Guard. You wouldn't make it ten minutes with the Dragoons. Watch he doesn't get behind you again. Now be off, both of you."

Jules watched his guard pocket the sergeant's new condemnation. For the first time since his nightmare began, he felt the forebodings of disaster.

CHAPTER 6

MOUSSA AND PAUL LAY ON THEIR BACKS IN THEIR tree house and smelled the smoke and stared at the flocks of birds streaming by. Below them, away across the open field, Henri and Gascon had spent the morning cutting trees. The two men had been at it for days, using a great saw whose teeth were huge and hungry. When they had one firebreak cleared, they set fire to a whole section of the old forest. Serena had come to join them, to bring them lunch and help. She stood next to Henri with her arm around his waist as he ate. They watched the magnificent shade trees of old and solid oak, some more than a thousand years old, go up in flames, and there were tears in her eyes.

All around Paris it was the same. At Fontainebleau, at Vincennes, at the foot of Mont Valérien, forests burned and the skies filled with smoke. During the past few days the destruction had reached the Bois de Boulogne, the splendid park the emperor had created next to the Château deVries. The Bois had been desolated, all its trees cut, its wonderful heavy gates removed. Workers were preparing huge stone ramparts with loops for rifles and embankments for artillery to stand in their stead.

The defense committee had convened in Paris and had decreed that the fires must be set to deprive the advancing Prussian armies of their protection. In the east, near the Prussian border, enemy troops had found refuge in the forests and, from their cover, had wreaked terrible havoc on the French forces. Marshal MacMahon had asked Napoléon for permission to torch the forests, but the emperor had refused, saying he didn't want to see the beautiful woods destroyed. Thousands of French casualties had resulted. Paris would not make the same mistake. She would offer the Prussians no shelter.

Yet few in Paris really believed the Prussians would make it to the city's walls. Conflicting reports flowed in by the score from distant fields of battle. Elisabeth argued with Henri when he announced the decision of the defense committee and told her he would begin torching the vast forests of the château itself. She was struggling to maintain her optimism in the face of mounting evidence that the French cause was in serious trouble.

"Really, Henri," she said, "I expected you to show a *little* more spine than to buckle under to Trochu and his *sissies!*" Trochu was the military governor of Paris. "Why, just last evening I dined with the Baroness de Chabrillan. She told me that Count Palikao told her that he had it on impeccable authority that the crown prince of Prussia had been brought before the emperor and shot himself."

"I heard that as well," Henri remarked dryly, "just before the announcement that Beaumont had fallen." At Beaumont the Prussians had surprised the French at lunch and routed them before dinner. Early press reports had gloated over a great French victory.

"That was a lie, Henri! Must you swallow Prussian propaganda whole?"

"You're deluding yourself, Elisabeth. Have you seen the refugees streaming into Paris? Where do you suppose they're coming from? Have you noticed the defenses they've started to mount around the walls of the city? What do you think is going on out there if we are doing so well?"

Elisabeth struggled to maintain her composure. She hated to argue with Henri. He was so calm, so . . . so *logical.* It was infuriating. "You're just panicking like all the rest. Really, I expected more from you."

For weeks she had carried on tirelessly, searching out reports of French victories and repeating them to anyone who would listen: reports that Bismarck himself had nearly been caught by French Zouaves as a whore serviced him in Montigny and that he had been forced to jump out a second-story window; reports that Marshal Bazaine had sent an entire Prussian army corps crashing to a grisly death among the rocks of a quarry at Jaumont in a rout so total that only bloody pieces of the Prussians and their horses remained. Through August she clung to each hopeful story, and embellished it, and above all else wished fervently that it be true. She had one letter from Jules, received soon after he left, in which he told her a little of the gathering army and the upcoming campaign. On the whole he sounded optimistic, if vague. She re-read it a thousand times. She talked to his portrait in her bedroom and clipped articles in the papers that looked promising and ignored the others, and fought the war herself in drawing rooms and at the social gatherings that were still common but that had begun to lose some of their gaiety.

If a feeling of gloom was descending over certain quarters of Paris, it settled nowhere more heavily than on Paul and Moussa. But for them it wasn't the war, or the Prussians. It was the end of summer, and the beginning of school. Determined to preserve as normal a life as possible for its children in the face of war, most of the cathedral schools of Paris opened, as did some of the government schools.

Moussa was desolate. He hated school, and couldn't believe there was even talk of it. They had missed four days of school the previous winter when a snowstorm had blanketed the city and shut it down. They had missed school when the Seine had run over its banks and flooded the basement of St. Paul's, the cathedral where their classes were held. They had missed school when Sister Angélique had been killed by a runaway horse.

So why was it, he wondered, that the Prussian army couldn't put a stop to it? He worked on Henri incessantly, taking every opportunity to chip away at his father's determination that he attend as usual.

"Father, in light of the international situation"—he had heard the words from his aunt Elisabeth, and loved their sound—"I should help you and Gascon with the forest, don't you think? We'll need to be ready."

"What I think is that you need to go to school," said the count.

"But Father . . ."

"We'll stumble along while you're in class. You'll do more about the 'international situation' if you can read about it."

Moussa was indignant. "I can read, Father! You know that!"

"So I do. You need to read better."

It was terrible, made the more so by the fact that they had had such a wonderful summer. He and Paul had done everything. They were old enough to explore Paris, at least during the daytime, and had spent glorious days wandering her streets and learning their way around. They swam in the lakes and spent lazy afternoons fishing from the banks of the Seine, which ran through château property. With the help of Henri and Gascon they made a wooden raft that they put into the water near St.-Cloud and floated all the way to Malmaison. On the way men and women on the shore hailed them and saluted the tricolor atop their mast. Gascon met them with a wagon to transport the raft back home. It was heady stuff for two ten-year-olds.

The count placed great importance upon the boys' training with weapons. He and Gascon spent an hour before breakfast every morning teaching them to shoot a Chassepot, the new military rifle with which both Paul and Moussa were excellent marksmen, and to fight with wooden swords, at which both boys were dreadful. Swords clunked harmlessly on arms and heads as the boys clumsily sought to control them. Gascon grimaced as he watched. "It's a good thing we started with wood, sire," he remarked to the count, "or we'd be picking up little body parts all morning." Each boy suffered countless lethal blows from the other before practice improved their agility and they began to show some signs of skill, however slight. With great patience, their tutors taught them to duck, to feint, to anticipate; when to thrust, when to parry, when to advance, how to retreat, the four of them working up a sweat and sometimes ending up in a great heap on the ground, everyone laughing, all tangled and dead. At length the wood was replaced with steel, which Gascon blunted on a grindstone so that mistakes would raise a lump but not cost an arm or a hand. As the boys hefted the heavy blades their muscles grew stronger, their footwork became more deft, and they began to develop a keener awareness of the subtleties and finesse of combat.

"He's sharp with a blade, that one," Gascon noted one late summer morning, as he watched Paul thrust at Moussa. "He's got an instinct for it." Paul was the matador, Moussa the bull; Moussa was stronger, confident, more methodical as a fighter, wearing his opponent down through sheer determination, where Paul would taunt and torment his adversary into making a mistake.

"That he does," Henri nodded. "They will both make formidable fighters." He watched with pride, well pleased with their progress with swords and the other weapons. They learned to throw knives and even to shoot rocks from a slingshot, a skill at which Moussa excelled. And in the afternoons, if the weather was right, the count would take them out to hunt with his hawks.

A glorious time, if only school didn't have to ruin everything.

I AM SISTER GODRICK. THE LORD GOD HAS blessed me with this cathedral and burdened me with this class. If you do precisely as I say, if you work hard, if you mind your manners and keep the devil at bay, He will bless you too. If not"—she pulled a flat oak paddle from the folds of her habit and raised it high, smacking it so hard on the tabletop at the front of the class that even though the boys saw it coming they all flinched in their seats—"if not, *this* shall be His instrument of correction, administered through my humble hand."

All they could see of her was an imperious black shroud wrapped around a thin, sharp face and harsh dark eyes. She was a smallish woman with no figure beneath her habit, just a mystery in black except for that cold face and bony hands that gripped the oak instrument of the boys' obedience.

"You shall bow your heads as we pray," she announced, and immediately the roomful of heads complied, save one. Sister Godrick began to prowl the aisles between the desks of the boys as she prayed in a firm but slightly shrill voice.

"Merciful Father, through Your perfect grace we have come here to share in the teachings of Your blessed son Christ the Good Shepherd, to learn of the wondrous world You have created in Your image . . ."

Whack!

Without warning the wood crashed down on Moussa's hand. He gasped in pain and yanked it away. The blow left an angry red welt. He looked up at her in shock. Her eyes were closed as she continued to pray. He had watched her approach, yet her action took him completely by surprise.

"May you, almighty God, nourish these small souls with Your grace, and may Christ our divine teacher grant us His light and everlasting love."

Whack!

Again the wood screamed down. Again it caught Moussa on his hand, this time the knuckles of the other one, which he hadn't drawn away quickly enough. A tear came to his eye and he put his knuckles to his mouth, his eyes full of fear at the specter before him.

"Amen," said Sister Godrick.

"Amen," repeated the class.

She towered over Moussa like a mountain of black terror, the lightning in her hand poised to strike again.

"And now, young man, perhaps you will share with the rest of us the reason why you cannot bow your head in prayer."

Moussa didn't know what to say. He never closed his eyes when others prayed. He didn't pray himself. He had when he was younger. He had prayed with all his heart for God to make the other children leave him alone. He had prayed for them to stop making fun of him. It had never worked. He had prayed for other things too, for boy things, for toys or for luck or for some trouble to go away. He didn't mind that it never worked, for he had stopped expecting it to, and he didn't blame God or anything like that. He had simply concluded in his ten-year-old way that God wasn't there, or that at least He didn't listen to children. So prayer was useless. It didn't produce anything, so it didn't mean anything. Sometimes, to be polite, he would move his mouth and mumble along when other people prayed, but he'd be mumbling about fishing or something, not God. Sometimes he would actually say the words he'd been taught, to see if they worked any better. But usually he would just observe what was going on around him rather than close his eyes for a prayer that wasn't there.

In class he had simply been doing what he always did.

"I . . . I'm sorry."

"Sorry!"

"Yes, Sister. I didn't mean to offend you."

"It is not I you need to concern yourself with, young man, it is the Lord God."

Moussa doubted it, for she was the one with the oak paddle. He looked over at Paul, who occupied the seat next to him and was trying his best not to attract Sister Godrick's attention. He had his head down and was intently studying the wood grain on his desk. Moussa could make out the faintest trace of a smile at the corner of Paul's mouth. He would get even later.

"What is your name?"

"Moussa."

"Again?"

"Moussa."

"What is 'Moussa'?" she asked.

"It is my name, Sister."

"Yes, but what is it?"

Moussa didn't know what to say. He shrugged.

"I'll tell you what it is," Sister Godrick said. She was addressing the rest of the class now. Her voice was mocking. "I'll tell you. It is a heathen name. It is a godless name. It is the unholy appellation of an infidel!"

"It is my name, Sister," he repeated.

"Moussa, Moussa, Moussa!" Her voice sang it out, scornful and hard. "It is a savage name, and this is a Christian class. Do you have any Christian names, *Moussa?*"

Miserably, he shrugged his shoulders.

"I didn't hear you, *Moussa!*"

"I don't know," he said meekly.

"Don't know! Don't know a Christian name, or don't know if you have one?"

"I don't know," was all he could think of to say. He looked down at his desk. He wished he were dead.

"Well then, what is your full name? Or do you know it?"

"Yes, Sister. It is Moussa Michel Kella deVries."

"DeVries! So you are the deVries boy!" She said it as though it meant something to her. "Well, deVries, the name 'Moussa' shall be stricken from this house of God. We shall call you Michel. Michel, the guardian archangel of the Jews, who are themselves only a half-step up from heathen, but a step *up* nevertheless. I suppose it's the best we can do." It was settled, then, and she turned her attention to the rest of the boys.

"Now class, you have just met Michel, who shall certainly not forget himself again. The rest of you—stand and introduce yourselves. One at a time. Let us begin!"

SISTER GODRICK COULD REMEMBER WHEN SHE was called Celeste. Nearly all the memories were horrible, and could still wrench her awake at night and constrict her chest with terror and send her to her bare knees on the cold stone floor, where she prayed that God would forgive her, and that she might forget.

She remembered her mother—a sad, pretty woman who braided her hair in the tiny fifth-floor attic where their only furniture was one wooden chair and a pile of blankets for a bed. There were no windows; the room was always dark. The roof leaked, and it was cold in the winter and broiling in the summer. There was never enough food all the year round. One winter when Celeste was six a fever came. Her mother caught it and coughed up blood and hugged her daughter and died.

She could not remember her father but she knew who he was. Her aunt Philomena had driven the evil name into her again and again, to make certain she would never forget: Gerard Flaurens, *Father* Flaurens, the sanctimonious priest lured from the righteous path by lust, and who, having committed the great sin of fathering Celeste, had embraced God anew and abandoned them both—but not before rising to the pulpit to publicly condemn and humiliate the mother, that pretty whoring parishioner, for leading him astray. Celeste had never seen him, nor he her.

"He's a righteous one, that," said Philomena repeatedly. "Forgot God, fucked your mother, found God, and forgot you."

Philomena was a woman embittered by life. Her resentment over having to raise a six-year-old with no resources to do it forever poisoned her against the child.

When Celeste was twelve, her aunt braided her soft golden hair and rubbed rouge on her cheeks and sold her to a cloth merchant for thirty sous. The man kept Celeste locked in his apartment for six days, never letting her outside, tormenting and raping her whenever the mood struck him. Philomena beat her without mercy when she complained. After the cloth merchant there was a blacksmith with huge dirty hands and foul breath, then a drunken lawyer who weighed nearly three hundred pounds, and a series of soldiers from the local garrison, mostly officers who passed her around for days without end. After that there had been three years of it, one gross encounter after another, each, to her, more horrible than the last. Her aunt counted the money and beat her with a cane and searched for the next customer.

One of the men gave her some rum and she discovered that the act wasn't so ugly if she drank enough of it. One drink beforehand soon turned to three or four. That was followed by some drinks afterward, and that by drinks at night, and that by drinks in the morning when she awoke, and then it all ran together into blackness. Six months or a year passed that way, the girl forever in a stupor, until finally one winter day she awakened to find herself holding an iron poker matted with blood and hair. Next to her on filthy sheets lay the cold dead form of a man whose skull was bashed in. She supposed she had bludgeoned him to death. She didn't remember.

She stumbled out of the room and down some stairs and out into the snow. For days she ran in circles through nameless streets, lost and cold and soaked. She had nowhere to go. At night she slept under piles of trash, or in the sewers where it was warmer but where the rats ran over her legs. She was desperate for a drink and begged for food. Near death from fever and exhaustion, she slipped into unconsciousness in the alcove of a great stone building.

She awakened in the care of the nuns who found her. There were days of delirium as she battled fever and drifted in and out of nightmares. She would awaken shrieking, fighting furiously against the gentle hands that restrained her. After the fever broke she said nothing, unwilling to talk to anyone. She withdrew into a silent world where she cried herself to sleep every night. One of the nuns had always been there, holding her. They brought soup and fresh clothes and nursed her back to health. They asked her nothing of who she was, or what she had been through, or what she had done, or how she had come to be on their step.

Murderer? Whore? They seemed not to care.

For months she lived among them. They let her help in the vegetable garden, where she found she had a talent for making things grow. She helped them put whitewash on the walls of their little cubicles. She worked in the kitchen, cooking and cleaning up after the meals. At first she ate alone in her room, but later she began to share meals with one and then another of them. There were chickens in the yard. She mended the coop wire and changed the straw and gathered the eggs. She washed the floors, and her own bedding and clothes in a stream. She would do anything except run errands that took her outside the four walls of her sanctuary.

She found she loved living that way, among people who asked for nothing and didn't care who she was. She loved living simply. Most of all she loved living away from men. She began to speak again.

After nearly a year Celeste died and Godrick was born. The floodgates of heaven had burst open for her, and she was awash in the perfection of her new life. Like so many converts to a new cause, she became intoxicated by it, and blinded to all else. She immersed herself totally, without moderation, equivocation, or doubt, in her complete devotion to God.

She became a driven woman, determined to purge herself of her past life and to rid herself of all that was unholy, to strip her heart of material things, to live in detachment and poverty, and to reject her own will, her inclinations, her whims and fancies. When the rules of the convent proved insufficiently strict, she discovered that she could debase herself even more, that she could deny herself even more, that she could rid herself of all worldly pleasure and comfort.

"*Mortify the exterior senses,*" said Mother Superior, and Godrick discovered that it felt good, and moreover that she had true talent for it. At first, when eating her simple meal, she would think of something unpleasant so that the taste would not be too agreeable. When she found she could still enjoy the flavor of a tomato or a carrot she would sprinkle it with alum, to render it bitter and dry. If she tasted something sweet, she would spit it out. If she caught herself admiring a picture, or a piece of furniture, or even the cover of a Bible, she would quickly shift her gaze to the dreariest part of the room, and seek penance in something drab.

"*Offer up your suffering for Our Lord in the World,*" said Mother Superior, and Godrick excelled at finding ways of subjecting her body to discomfort, and exposing herself to repugnant things. She permitted only poor sandals on her bare feet, even in winter, when she would pray in the snow until she lost the feeling in her toes. She would stand on one foot while she meditated until her muscles screamed, and she would collapse on the floor, only to rise and repeat the exercise on the other. She slept without enough cover in the winter, so that she would be too cold to sleep well, and with too much cover in the summer, so that she would bake in sweat. She sewed her habit from used cloth, and then threw it away because the material wasn't coarse enough and didn't chafe. She bathed only in cold water, using abrasive soap that left her skin raw.

"*Avoid frivolity of mind,*" said Mother Superior, and Godrick learned to concentrate primarily on spiritual and academic books, rather than books that could excite her imagination. Too much curiosity was bad for devotion to God; this was the lesson of Eve.

"*Avoid vanity,*" said Mother Superior, and Godrick cut her hair to ragged wisps that she hid away. She shaved off her eyebrows and shortened the eyelashes that so many men had remarked upon back in the black days before Godrick was born. There were no mirrors in which to gaze, no reminders of the earthly visage she had so loathed.

"*Be obedient,*" said Mother Superior, and Godrick did what she was asked without question. It felt good, for obedience deprived her of the need to think for herself.

In her zealous pursuit of perfection as a nun, there arose a problem for her. As she practiced self-mortification, as she shunned vanity, as she found new ways to suffer, she realized that the more she abused herself, the better she liked it. The more something hurt, the better it felt. The better it felt the more guilt she carried, for feeling good was a pleasurable act of vanity, and ran contrary to her teaching. So she devised new ways to punish herself for feeling good. She fasted for days on end. She kept herself from sleep at night by sitting on the cold floor of her cubicle. She refused to make friends among the other nuns, for friendship made her feel warm inside, and feeling warm inside was wrong because it was self-gratification. One must be a friend only to God and to His son Jesus Christ. That was more than enough.

After five years of convent life, never-changing and serene, Mother Superior ordered Sister Godrick to begin teaching in the cathedral schools. At first she hated it. She felt awkward being out in the world again. Social contact terrified her, even though she was teaching young boys. That world, the world of men, had been lost to her for a very long time. But at length she was rescued by her quandary: when she realized how much she disliked it, she realized that it felt good, and knew that she could do it.

When the call came from the bishop of Boulogne-Billancourt for a fourth-form teacher, Mother Superior chose Godrick. So it was that she came to teach Moussa and Paul and their classmates that year in the cathedral of St. Paul.

A S YOU HAVE BEEN TOO HAUGHTY TO BOW YOUR head in prayer with us, Michel deVries, you have perhaps been occupied contemplating the nature of our studies this year. Can you tell us what they will be?"

Moussa shook his head.

"I thought not. Does the word *trivium* have meaning for you?"

"No, Sister."

"Ah, a well-*educated* haughty boy." There were anonymous snickers from the back of the room. She raised her hand for silence. "And quadrivium? What of that?"

Nothing.

"I thought not. I see your education has not kept pace with your self-esteem. Well then, perhaps you can clear your head long enough to pay attention. For the next year your lives shall travel the crossroads: the trivium of grammar, rhetoric, and logic. And you shall have an introduction to the quadrivium: geometry, astronomy, arithmetic, and music. Nothing too demanding for your empty heads, but we will work on it together. You shall do it for the glory of God, and I shall lead the way."

It went that way the whole morning. In three more encounters Moussa was the subject of her attention. Three times it did not go well. What was worse, Moussa reflected glumly, was what he knew would come next, as soon as class let out for the morning. Every year the same thing happened on the first day of school. They would taunt him, and tease him, and maybe there would be a fight. Some years were worse than others, but it always happened. Moussa figured that getting so much attention from Sister Godrick was bound to aggravate things. He was right, for recess was less than five minutes old when it began. Another student, Pierre Valons, stood in a corner of the yard with a group of friends. He pointed and laughed when Moussa emerged from the doorway with Paul.

"Half-breed dumbbell! Infidel's going to hell!"

"Why 'Michel'? Why not 'Imbecile'? That's a good Christian name!"

Some of the others caught the spirit and heaped vicious names on silly ones. Soon a rock flew through the air and struck him on the shoulder.

The days when he had taken insults passively had passed, as had the days when he would melt in tears. He had never understood what made the others do it, only that he was somehow apart from them, somehow different, and that he would never fit in. From the time Serena had first held him after it happened, when he was only five, his mother had counseled patience.

"Ignore them," she said. "Deny them the satisfaction of seeing you rise in anger." She too had suffered this way. "Pay no attention to them. They are only jealous of your noble birth." She had tried to soften their insults. "When they call you half-breed you must remember what it really means, that you are the best of two worlds, the best of the French and the best of the Tuareg."

Her advice felt warm and wise while he was on her lap, but evaporated quickly in the schoolyard. His patience only drove his tormentors to greater creativity in their taunts, and then they accused him of cowardice, of being a sissy. If he cried it drove them to new heights of viciousness.

And then one day when Moussa was eight Henri had seen his bruised cheek and asked about it, and Moussa had poured out his sorrow and his dilemma.

"Your mother is right in her way," Henri agreed after listening, "but just now I think they need a good thrashing. You need to teach them a lesson. I wish it weren't so, but they respect only strength."

After that Moussa tried hard not to forget his mother's advice, but he found that fists often worked better. At first he lost most of the fights, but a bloody nose from fighting back felt better to him than a bloody nose from doing nothing. And with practice, along with the instruction he received from his father and Gascon, he got better. Before long the students learned to taunt him at their own peril, for even if they might finally beat him, they would pay a heavy price.

So it was that this morning he was all over Pierre, fists flying. Pierre was down on the ground on his back, Moussa pummeling him without mercy. Pierre's lip was bloody and he flailed back. Three of Pierre's friends joined in, which prompted Paul to enter the fray. It was the two of them against the four, Paul and Moussa raining blows on the other boys, the other boys outnumbering them, starting to hold and kick them, when Sister Godrick and her paddle appeared from nowhere. She waded into the pile of fists and feet and began whacking mightily, yelps of pain mingling with the sound of wood on bare skin and heads and elbows. Finally she brought them to bay, and stood them up in a chastened row before her. The boys were all breathing heavily.

"It was his fault, Sister," Pierre said as soon as he could talk, pointing at Moussa. "He started it." The boys with Pierre nodded their agreement.

"DeVries started it!" one said.

"Yes, that's right! DeVries threw a rock!"

Sister Godrick regarded Moussa with eyes of fire.

"Is it so?"

Moussa refused to answer. No nun, no teacher was going to settle this thing, and he would not seek the refuge of her protection. He would resolve it later, himself. Paul started to say something, but Moussa angrily ribbed him.

"Your silence is eloquent, Michel deVries." She appraised him coldly. He had no idea what *eloquent* meant, but knew enough to worry about what was coming next. He tried not to show it in his eyes. He held her gaze, not defiantly but not chastened, either, until finally, intimidated, he looked away.

"You seem stricken with an excess of pride, Michel. You sneer at the world through it. It will be your destruction. You refuse to bow your head to the Lord in class, you resort to violence in this yard. . . . Very well, then, come with me. We shall see what we can do about it. We shall help you discover whether you are the center of the world." She marched Moussa back into the building. She rummaged through a closet and found a large pail, some brushes and old rags, and a container of lye. Then she took him out behind the school, to the building where the latrine was housed. Without knocking to see if anyone was inside, she marched him in. They stood before the long masonry trench and the holes where the boys relieved themselves. The day was hot, the stench overpowering. Moussa hated to go in there, even for a moment. It was vile. His face scrunched up in displeasure. The sister set the pail down and indicated the room with a sweep of her hand.

"Let us see how your pride fares while you labor on your knees. I will return in an hour. Cleanse your soul while you cleanse this room."

The work was slow and smelly. The brushes splattered in his face, and he even got some on his tongue. He gagged and spit until his mouth was dry. As he cleaned he kept an eye out for spiders. He hated all spiders, but was particularly afraid of the ones who lived in the latrines, for they were ugly and black and poisonous. Sometimes they hid under the edges and bit the unwary in the worst of places.

He took stock of his situation as he scrubbed. It

didn't look good. He could tell he was going to have his hands full with this nun. She had no sense of humor, and seemed to have something against him. He wasn't sure what he'd done wrong, but it seemed to him that everything he said or did—*merde,* even his *name* seemed to set her off. It wasn't fair. She hadn't paid half as much attention to anyone else in the room as she had to him. And then she had blamed him for the fight. No, he guessed that wasn't right, she hadn't taken sides, but he was the only one punished. Still, she was a difficult one.

Halfway through his labors the other boys came in. He guessed Sister Godrick had deliberately excused them to the bathroom early, to subject him to still more humiliation. Moussa bent over his work. His face flushed as he heard the giggles and jokes.

"Is that *Count* deVries's boy, cleaning shit?"

"I don't know. All I can see is his ass!"

"That couldn't be *Mouuussssaaaa.* Africans don't clean up pee, they *drink* it!"

"He's half French. Maybe Michel cleans up half, and Moussa drinks the rest!"

"Do Africans eat shit?"

Moussa's temperature rose, but he kept his head down. Their insults and the hurt echoed off the stone walls and rang in his ears. He felt a lump in his throat and his lip quivered. His eyes started to mist and he knew that tears weren't far behind.

I'm too old to cry! I will not cry, I will not! He drew big white circles of suds on the gray filth, his arm moving in a clockwise direction.

"*Ignore them,*" his mother said. "*Don't let them see you rise in anger.*" He changed directions and scrubbed counterclockwise, pressing harder and harder.

"*Thrash them soundly,*" his father said. "*Make them pay for their fun.*" He dipped his brush in the water and sloshed it onto the floor and made more circles. The bristles made a scratching sound. Laughter reverberated through the room as insult fed outrage. Their voices faded and grew indistinct as he stopped listening and drew into himself. He was learning to do that, to shut the world out, to go someplace in his head where no one else could go.

He told himself it didn't matter. He told himself he didn't care. But he knew it was a lie. He *did* care. He cared what they thought, cared what they did. He hated them for this, hated being the butt of their jokes. He desperately wished they liked him. He longed to be ordinary, to be like the others. He didn't understand why having Henri and Serena for parents did this to him. He loved his mother and father, but sometimes he found himself wishing that they were . . . well, he didn't know, exactly, but that they were *normal,* that they were like everyone else's parents. Mostly he wished the other children would just leave him alone.

After much reflection he decided what to do. During school he would obey his mother, and suffer his penance in peace. After school he would obey his father, and beat their brains in.

As the boys chattered and joked Pierre moved away from them, casually inching closer to where Moussa worked. Moussa didn't see him coming, but soon he was wrenched from his reverie as Pierre let loose right next to him and he felt the warm splash of piss in his face. Pierre howled in laughter.

"Drink that, deVries! *Le meilleur de France!* Take a cup home for your mother!"

The laugh died on his lips as Moussa was upon him. He had no time to react or defend himself before Moussa hit him squarely in the nose, and then dunked his head straight down into the bucket of dirtwater. None of the other boys went to his defense. They read the rage on Moussa's face. Stunned by the fury of his reaction, they dared not interfere. The water in the bucket turned from its sickly brown to brownish red as the nosebleed fed it. Pierre struggled and gurgled, but Moussa held him fast. His face was red; he was breathing hard. He had never felt such wrath. He intended not to let go.

"Stop it, Moussa! Stop! Let him go!" Paul shook him roughly. "Stop it, I say! You'll kill him!" Moussa ignored him. He had Pierre by the base of his neck and pushed down. Pierre's arms were waving wildly, helplessly. With a huge effort Paul grasped the back of Moussa's collar and pulled him back onto his rear end. Moussa let go. Pierre's head popped out of the bucket like a cork. He lay on the floor and sputtered and bled and coughed and cried, his eyes shut from the lye and piss in the water.

Sister Godrick was at her desk when she heard a cry from the bathroom. She stopped writing and listened. A miserable wail, as she expected. She nodded her head, certain her solution had worked out satisfactorily. There would be no further trouble from the deVries boy. By the time she returned to the latrine to inspect Moussa's work Pierre was gone. He was absent from class that afternoon. When she asked about him no one seemed to have any idea where he'd gone. She shook her head in disapproval and wrote a note to herself in her logbook. She would deal with the truant in the morning.

That afternoon the class studied Latin. Moussa decided he liked it about the same as cleaning the latrine. Godrick gave them each an exercise book with stiff covers, and told them to write their names inside. He paid no attention as the class droned conjugations. They chanted in unison. *"Rego, regis, regit, regimus, regitis . . ."* His lips moved, but it was the make-believe kind of movement he used at prayer. He doodled with his pencil inside the cover of his exercise book. He didn't feel good about what had happened that day with Pierre, but he didn't feel bad, either. He guessed his troubles would ease up a bit, and for that he was glad. Maybe this year wouldn't be so bad after all. A few of the other boys had already tried to make up to him, the ones without any spine. They at least would stop bothering him for a while. It was something.

"Superatus sum, superatus es, superatus est, superati sumus . . ."

He stared at the name written on the front page of the exercise book. "DeVries," it said. "Michel." It had felt funny writing it. It sounded like somebody else. He never wrote that name, never used it. No one ever called him Michel. It was an extra name he'd never needed until now. He doodled around it, the loops of his pencil getting closer and closer to the clear block letters. "Michel." He said it to himself, turning the word over and over in his mind. He didn't like it. It was his name, but it wasn't. Sister Godrick had no right.

"They respect only strength," his father had said.

Finally he scratched over it and through it, scratched until he made a hole in the paper and the name was gone. He tore the page out and made a new one. He wrote in bold, clear letters across the middle of the paper, taking care to stay within the lines and doing each letter twice, so it would stand out better:

DE VRIES, MOUSSA.

He felt better. It looked right again.

At the end of the day the students turned their books in to Sister Godrick. She sat at her desk as they stood in single file to hand them in. She opened them one at a time to be certain their names were in the proper place, that the assignments were complete. Moussa's heart beat faster as he got closer to the front of the line. At last he stood before her. She opened the book. She looked down at it for a while without saying anything. He couldn't see her face, only the black crown of her habit and the white rim above her forehead. She looked up at him and for the second time that day, their eyes met. He shifted from one foot to the other, but held her gaze. Looking into her eyes was like looking into the eyes of one of his father's hawks. They were narrow and cold and had no eyebrows. He couldn't read them. They focused somewhere inside him, somewhere even he'd never looked.

The class was still. Sensing that something was going on, the other boys watched quietly. Without a word Godrick began ripping the pages from his book. One at a time, she tore them up and dropped them into the wastebasket next to her desk. When all the pages were gone she held the book over the basket and dropped it in as well.

When at last she spoke her voice cut through him like a sliver of ice.

"If you don't begin turning in your assignments, *Michel*, you will fail this class," she said. "And then, God and the bishop willing, you shall have me again next year."

I WONDER IF I CAN JOIN THE ARMY," MOUSSA SAID to Paul on their way home. They had stopped and were skipping rocks on the Seine. The sun was still high in the sky in what Moussa was sure had been the longest day of his life. The war couldn't be any worse than school, and the Prussians could probably learn something from Sister Godrick.

"I don't think so. I think you have to be sixteen." Paul whipped a rock across the water. It danced five times before it sank. "That's five!" he whooped.

Moussa threw next. He thought he had it just right. But in keeping with his day, the stone sank immediately.

"At the rate things are going," he said miserably, "I don't think I'm going to *make* it to sixteen."

CHAPTER 7

THE LITTLE WOODEN CART SEEMED TO FIND EV-
ery hole in the road. Two of its spokes had broken
and had been repaired with baling wire. Then the
repair had broken and had itself been mended with
leather straps. Each new break brought the cart closer
to total destruction as it jarred and rattled along. It was
pulled by a mule that looked in worse shape than the
cart itself. Behind came some supply wagons and behind
them, a line of men in a double file, seventy-three of
them, each attached by an iron ring to a chain that ran
from the back of one of the wagons and dragged in the
dirt and kicked up dust with a constant clanking and
rattling sound. At the front of the column rode a sergeant of the Garde Mobile, while on the sides and at the
rear rode several mounted guards.

Jules sat alone in the cart, riding while the others
walked. It was a cruel concession to his rank, for it set
him apart and drew attention to him, lending him a
freakish air as the procession made its way on the road
from Meaux to Paris. His legs were shackled in iron
rings. He was thankful that his shackles could not be
seen from the road, but an onlooker could be left with
little doubt that he was a prisoner along with the rest.

Châlons was a blur in his mind. He had arrived with
his guard to find the encampment very nearly deserted.
Most of the regular garrison and its officers were gone,
the town a shadow of what it had been just a few days
earlier. The streets were empty and peaceful, the residents able to move about with a freedom they hadn't
enjoyed for a long while. Jules had expected a quick

resolution to his situation, once he could simply talk to anyone with a level head. He expected that to be General Ducret, the commandant of the encampment and a fair man who had been an instructor of his at St. Cyr, but the general had been called away. Colonel Merrier, the next in command and also a man known to Jules, had gone to Orléans. No officer remained above the rank of Major Cabasse, who didn't know Jules and was unmoved by his protestations of innocence. The major had read the letter from Delescluze describing Jules's desertion, then turned it over and read the note from the sergeant who had thwarted his escape. The major had no desire to become involved in what was clearly going to be an ugly situation.

"There is a train leaving for Paris with other prisoners," he said. "You will be on it." Jules protested vehemently. The farther he got from his men, from the scene of the crimes at the farmhouse, from this part of the country, the more difficult it would be to demonstrate his innocence. His objections fell on deaf ears. And then the humiliation of it all struck him full force. There he was, addressing an inferior officer, a major, a man who ought to feel some fraternity, and in the middle of Jules's impassioned argument, the major simply turned his back on him and without a word strode out.

This cannot be happening to me, he thought as they led him away. *This is not possible.*

The sergeant in charge of the band of prisoners was not a rude or unkindly man, and he alone showed respect for Jules. He had apologized as he put Jules into the cart and secured his leg irons. "I have to do it, sir. Orders." As he finished he passed him a fistful of cigars. "Something for your journey, Colonel," he said.

"Thank you, Sergeant," Jules replied, glad to have something to smoke, and gladder still for the momentary show of humanity. They set out for Paris, the sergeant on the horse, the colonel in the cart, the supply wagons behind, and the rest of the prisoners—murderers, mutineers, and deserters—trudging in the rear on foot. They followed a small road that ran alongside the river Marne. An hour out of Meaux they stopped for the night. The walking prisoners collapsed in dusty fatigue on the ground, while Jules tried to make himself comfortable in the cart. There was water, but still nothing to eat. Jules didn't care. He was past hunger.

It was that time of late summer when the days were still hot but the nights could get cold. Jules spent long sleepless hours shivering under a beautiful harvest moon. Several times he sat up and lit a cigar, and stared out into the ghostly black moonshadows. His mind was in turmoil, fixed on the dark mad eyes of Delescluze. He saw the bodies of his men, doused in kerosene. He saw a little girl, dead on her mother's belly.

He chewed furiously on the end of his cigar. He had no doubt, none whatever, that justice would be done. He had friends, powerful friends. This sham would be exposed. The real criminal would be caught and prosecuted. Jules himself would affix the blindfold and stand the man against the wall. He himself would give the order to the firing squad. He himself would administer the *coup de grâce*. A hundred times that long cold night he watched Delescluze die.

The next morning as the sun was warming them, a farmer pulled up. He was carrying grain to Paris. The rear wheel of his wagon had gotten caught in a bridge support and was hopelessly broken. Each time it turned the whole load bounced and threatened to come off. A wounded soldier lay on top of the load. There was a bandage wrapped around his eyes. It was dirty and bloody, but the blood was dry. His right leg was missing below the knee.

"Can you transport this soldier to Paris?" the farmer asked the sergeant. "I'll not be going any farther with this rig, not for a while, and he's got a ways to go." The sergeant shrugged. He didn't have to ask Jules, of course, but he was a polite man.

"Colonel? You got any objections? He'll have to ride with you."

"No. It's fine. Here, bring him in."

Jules backed up as the sergeant and the farmer

shifted the boy from the top of the wagon into the cart. The boy grimaced as they moved him. He was weak and clearly in pain from his injuries, but he helped as best he could. They laid him on his back on the bottom of the cart. He was a pale youth with sandy hair and white, even teeth. He was big and strong. Even through his pain he managed to occasionally find his smile, and it was that contagious sort of grin that belonged to someone people instinctively liked. After they had settled him in the sergeant threw in his bag. "There, Colonel, maybe that'll work as a pillow."

"Colonel?" Jules saw the boy stiffen. "Are you a . . . a *colonel*, sir?" He said it with a mixture of respect and awe. He seemed not to know what to do. He struggled upward, to sit at attention, trying to decide through his bandages which way to look. Then, flustered, he remembered himself and started to salute. Jules put his hand on the boy's shoulder to put him at ease.

"Don't bother, Private. Rest easy. Colonel deVries, Imperial Guard."

The boy gave a low whistle. "I'm sorry to put you out, sir. I hope I haven't taken up room you were using." The boy was clearly in earnest, more solicitous of the colonel's comfort than his own. "Gosh, Colonel, sir, I've never been this close to a real officer before. I mean, nobody higher than a captain, sir, Captain Frossard that is, and we only used to see his backside on a horse. Never saw none like you except from a distance, sir. Somebody as low as me, you don't see important people except from a distance."

"Well, I guess I'm pretty much like anybody else. What's your name?"

"Millarde, sir, Private Etienne Millarde, Colonel." Even beneath his bandages his face was expressive. His skin was still a boy's, smooth and fresh. He hadn't started shaving. There was down on his chin. Jules guessed him to be sixteen or seventeen. The boy was still working out the magnitude of his company.

"Imperial Guard, Colonel? Does that mean you've seen the emperor himself? I mean, up close?"

"Many times. I'm based . . . I was based in the Tuileries."

"The *palace?*"

"*Oui,* the palace."

Etienne digested that for a few minutes. He struggled against his blindness to imagine the man who must now be in front of him, a man who'd seen the emperor before, and not just at a parade, when the great man was so far away that he was just a little toy figure.

"I sure appreciate the ride, Colonel. I've hitched all the way from Fohrbach. I've done pretty well. I want to get home. They let me go when they saw how my injuries were and all; they said I couldn't do them no good and that if I felt like it I could make my own way. Don't know how long I'd have had to wait otherwise. I was just stuck in a tent. Outside a tent actually, after they got my leg, since there wasn't enough room inside." He said it matter-of-factly, without any trace of lingering emotion.

"You're going straight to Paris, sir? I mean, it's all right with me if we're not, I don't mean to . . . I just . . ."

"Yes. Straight to Paris. You'll be there tomorrow."

"*Merveilleux.*" He was clearly pleased. He was almost home.

"This transport must have important business for them to send a whole colonel."

Jules smiled in spite of himself at the youth's naïveté. And then, thinking about the question in the statement, a strange new feeling swept over him, an extraordinary one he had never before encountered. It was awkwardness. He was a colonel and this was a boy, blind and crippled. And the man didn't know what to say to the boy.

"It's a prisoner transport," was the only way Jules could find to explain it.

It was enough. Etienne was satisfied.

"If you ask me, Colonel, you should just shoot them instead of taking them prisoner. They're animals, and would do the same to you or me." Clearly, the boy thought he meant they were transporting Prussian prisoners. Again, Jules felt the terrible turmoil of the lie, of a situation too bizarre to explain. He had done nothing wrong, and this boy was only a private. It shouldn't matter. But somehow it did, and once more he had no idea what to say.

"You smoke?"

"When I can get it, yes sir, I do."

Jules handed him a cigar. The boy took it in his hand and felt it. It was fat and fine. He passed it under his nose. A satisfied grin blossomed on his face. "Thank you, Colonel, it's a fancy one, that." Jules lit it for him and the boy leaned back, contented. He took a puff and burst into a fit of coughing. The coughing sent him into spasms of pain. Jules could read agony all over his face, but there was nothing he could do. Etienne took a minute to recover, breathing deeply until he regained his composure.

"Sorry, sir. I guess it's been a while since I've had something as good as this."

"That's all right. The next one will smoke easier."

The cart bounced over the road. Each hole sent a jolt through the cart that telegraphed itself through Jules's body. It was a rough enough ride for him, and after a few hours of it his back and arms and legs were aching. He knew it must be hell for the boy, but Etienne didn't complain. The hours passed slowly, like the country-side. The caravan settled into a sleepy rhythmic march. The Marne was full of driftwood that floated lazily past them. He watched it as they talked. Jules welcomed the boy's company. It was nice to have someone to help pass the time. Jules answered eager questions about Algeria and Italy, and talked about military history. Not given to small talk, Jules was uncomfortable at first, but the boy's nature was so easygoing that soon Jules re-laxed a bit and felt almost at ease. The boy listened raptly, engrossed in the stories of foreign campaigns, of generals long dead and battles long won. He talked a great deal himself, with great enthusiasm on every topic. He was the only child of a carpenter and a cleaning woman, a poor family who lived in Montmartre. He had been unemployed before joining the army. He had been in the army only three weeks before they put him on a train for the front.

"I'm a substitute," he said proudly. It was a grand word for him, and he waved his cigar in the air as he said it. "There was a broker's son got a bad number in the draft. He had insurance, and it was my turn. I got to go." He took a puff off the cigar and didn't cough. "I got fifteen hundred francs for my mother. It was more money than she'd seen in a long time, that's sure. She had to lie some about my age to get me—" He caught himself and his face flushed red as he realized his gaffe. "Oh, Colonel, sir, I know it was wrong, but my mother needed the money so bad—"

"Don't worry," Jules said. "Your secret is safe with me. Anyway, it was a brave thing to do." It was a common enough practice. If a man's number came up in the military draft, another man could be paid to fulfill the service. Fifteen hundred francs was the going rate, and there were even insurance companies that sold cheap policies to those who could afford it. A substitute would be found, glad to have the money, and the question of military obligation was satisfied.

"Where were you wounded?"

"At Spicheren, sir. At least I think it was. Nobody had maps. Somebody said it was Giferts. That's a forest, I know, so it might have been. But I guess it might have been somewhere else, too. We were lost most of the time. We did a lot of wandering around."

"I know the forest of Giferts. I've been there." Jules had passed through it some weeks earlier, before the battle. The woods had been empty and still, no different than all the other places he'd been in those early weeks.

"Giferts or anywhere, I guess we saw the Prussians, by God," Etienne said. "We whomped them for a while, too, Colonel. Gave as good as we got. There was lots of rain, and it was hard to make out what was going on, but we could see enough, I guess. The battle messengers told us where to go, and then they changed up and told us somewhere else to go, but it didn't matter. We could see the Prussians coming up the hill. We had our Chassepots, and we popped a bunch of them without their even knowing where the fire was coming from."

Etienne paused for a minute, as if wondering how much to exaggerate to his audience.

"I don't think I actually got any of them with my rifle," he admitted, guilt in his voice. "I shot a lot and my gun got hot, but I never actually saw anybody I was aiming at fall down or anything."

"It's hard to see that in a battle. You don't know. Nobody knows. You just fire. I imagine they knew you were there."

Etienne smiled at the thought. "Yes, sir, I guess they did at that. They knew I was there. We had a *mitrailleuse* too, but nobody knew how to use it right." Jules had seen demonstrations of the gun before the war. It was a terrible weapon, accurate and deadly, modeled after the American Gatling gun. It was far in advance of anything the Prussians had, but had been developed in such complete secrecy and released for use so soon before the outbreak of war that few units knew how to use it to advantage.

"We killed some with it, I know, but then it was getting dark, and after that nothing we did mattered much. They said we had thirty German companies out there in front of us. The First and Second Armies, right there in the woods, on the other side of a ravine. By God, we thumped them for a while too, before their artillery came. After that"—he shook his head—"they were all over us, running through us and around us, and there was smoke where some of the artillery shells had set some trees on fire, and that's when . . ." He hesitated, swallowing, and took a puff off his cigar.

"That's when I met my Prussian, Colonel. The one I *know* I got, I mean. He was right there on top of me. Thought he'd surprised me, but I saw him coming. I didn't have time to fire, so I stuck him with my bayonet. Stuck him like a pig, just as he was there on me, and *he* knew sure enough he was dead. I held him up on the end of my rifle and I could feel . . . I could feel him squirm." Etienne was breathing heavily as he relived the moment, not in terror but in pride. He had done what he was supposed to do for his fifteen hundred francs. He had found himself a Prussian with the end of his bayonet.

"I could see his eyes. They were real scared like, and his mouth was open, and I could see his tongue, all swollen and moving like he was trying to say something. Only he just kind of choked and threw up on me. That was the last thing I saw, was when he threw up. I had him up there when the shell came. I heard it coming, and I guess if I hadn't had him where he was I'd be killed now. He took most of the shell bits. Knocked him clear off me. But you know, Colonel, I'm sure I was the one killed him, not the shell. I'm sure of it." It was vitally important to him, that distinction, something he'd worked over in his mind. No shell, especially not a Prussian shell, would steal that kill from Etienne.

"I'm sure you did," Jules reassured him. "A bayonet wound like that isn't something a man walks away from."

Etienne nodded eagerly, cheered by the colonel's affirmation.

"No, sir, he didn't walk away from it. The shell blew a dead man off me, but I caught some of it anyway. They said it chewed up my eyes pretty good. One was all minced up and I felt the other one was hanging out. I shoved it back in quick as I knew what it was, but I guess it wasn't enough. Don't guess I'll be seeing much anymore."

A kind of shadow passed over his expression. It was the closest Jules had seen him to reacting—to crying, to yelling, he didn't know what—but Etienne tensed for a moment, as if he were ready to let go. And then it passed, and he relaxed.

"I was out there all night in the woods. Never passed out." Again, pride. "Tied my shirt around my leg. I couldn't see it, but I could tell it was pretty chewed up too. Stayed there all night and listened. It was all I could do. There were bugles everywhere, up that hill and all around. The bugles got some dogs to barking, and they'd bark like they were talking to each other, talking about the fighting, talking back and forth through the woods. It went on and on all night. Then I heard someone talking German, and I did my best to look dead, because I knew they'd kill me if they found me like that. I guess I looked pretty dead because they never stopped. They just kept running by. After the fighting was over I heard lots of crying, Colonel, lots of hollering and carrying on. I think that was worse than all the rest put together, the carrying on. I didn't. I mean I didn't say a word or let out a yell or anything. Not even when they took my leg, sir," he said, shaking his head emphatically. "Not even when they took my leg."

As the boy talked Jules fought off a sense of acute discomfort. This man-child of sixteen, this surrogate soldier with no education and three weeks of training, had found the war Jules had missed. He had sought it out and faced it bravely and paid a heavy price. Yet he looked up to Jules, venerated him and felt awed in his presence, and that made Jules miserable with deceit.He felt humbled before this child. He felt like a fraud.

"I'm proud of you, Private. You have served with honor and done your duty. It is all a man can do. You're a good soldier."

Etienne swelled with pride. "They said I'll be getting a medal, Colonel. A ribbon or something. They didn't have enough while I was there, but the captain said I'd get one in Paris."

"That's right. You'll get a ribbon."

"I'll bet you have lots of them, Colonel," he said. "Do you suppose I could touch one, just to . . . just to feel?"

Jules looked down at the tatters of his uniform blouse. His medals, his ribbons, all the symbols of his life, all the marks of his achievements and his honor, even his gun and sword, had been stripped from him by Delescluze and his men. Now he had only shreds. So for the third time that day he found himself telling Etienne a part-truth—no, it was a lie, he knew, telling the youth something that was more convenient than true.

"I'm not wearing any just now."

Etienne nodded in understanding. "It's all right, Colonel. I don't guess they'll give a private the same kind, anyway."

He finished his cigar and threw it over the side of the cart. Jules pulled the rest of his cigars out of his pocket and pressed them into the boy's hands.

"Here. These will help you pass the time."

Toward noon they left the path they had been following along the banks of the Marne and joined the main road to Paris. The road was crowded and noisy, a dusty stream of wagons carrying supplies and refugees. It was a bright, beautiful day of late summer, the sky clear and blue, a pleasant breeze rustling through the trees, nature belying the worried stream of humanity passing by. Horsemen raced by, and at last they began to bring news. Wave after wave of revelation washed over them, one report after another. Soon they were drowning in it, for there was too much, and it was all the same, all bad.

Capitulation at Sedan . . . deadly trap. . . . Surrender, complete defeat . . .

Through the dust and the heat of the day the riders kept appearing, their grim faces broadcasting the story even before they said anything. With each new report Jules closed his eyes as though he'd been hit in the stomach with a mighty blow.

Thirty thousand casualties . . . hand-to-hand combat, every road and garden a battlefield. . . . Bazeilles burned, women and children shot down like dogs . . .

"They got to be wrong, Colonel," said Etienne, frowning after one of the riders had left. "It couldn't be. Couldn't be what they say." His face had grown pale with concern. He was looking for reassurance from the colonel, from the highest authority he could imagine, that it was not true, that it was a damnable lie. But there was no such certainty within Jules. In the incessant recital of disaster Jules heard the ring of truth.

The emperor's been taken captive . . . MacMahon wounded . . . it rained artillery shells . . . nowhere to hide. . . . The entire Army of Châlons taken prisoner and sent to Belgium . . .

Jules asked each rider for news of the 220th, of Major Dupree and his men. But the men didn't know or, seeing him in chains, simply ignored him.

Margueritte's cavalry . . . massed in a heroic charge. . . . The general dead . . . all thrown to the slaughter at Flöing. . . . Two-thirds of the men dead, the rest wounded or captured . . . no one left, nothing . . .

Margueritte! The 220th might well have fought under his command in a major battle. He kept trying.

"Have you news of the Two Hundred Twentieth?" he asked one last rider, and the man pulled up next to the cart and walked his horse alongside. He was a surly hussar wearing a blue tunic whose white trim was stained with blood. The blood was apparently not his own. From the look of him and his horse Jules guessed he'd seen much and ridden hard for days. The hussar looked disdainfully at Jules's uniform, and then at his leg irons.

"And what are you, pray tell, asking me of a fighting unit?"

One of the guards of the procession drew up next to him. "Fucking coward, that's what he is," the guard scowled. "Why should you care for news of the Two Hundred Twentieth?"

Etienne stiffened. "What?" he said, straightening himself up. "What? How dare you address the colonel that way!"

"Colonel?" The guard gave a derisive laugh. "You mean coward! I address all deserters that way! He's a prisoner!"

The color drained from Etienne's face as he struggled to digest what he was hearing.

"What do you mean? How can you say that?"

"You're blind, sonny, you can't see! I suppose he's been entertaining you with war stories, eh? Well, your colonel here is a prisoner! His legs are in chains! He's under arrest for desertion. And if that wasn't enough for him, he tried to escape, and nearly killed a guard. More like a Prussian colonel, by God!"

Etienne recoiled in horror. Jules groped for words,

wanting to explain, wanting to unload his terrible story, but the words were not there, would not come, and he said nothing. Each moment of silence made it all seem more horrible in Etienne's mind. "Colonel?" he asked, pleading. "Colonel?"

"It . . . it is true that I am under arrest, Private," Jules said at last, his voice cracking, "but I did not do what they—"

"You go to hell! You bastard!" Etienne spat it out, shrieked it at the top of his voice. "You lied to me! All this time, you're nothing but a coward, a quitter! Have you been laughing at me? You swine! How could you lead me on so?"

"Private, listen to me! It's a lie!" But Etienne was shaking his head, trembling all over, moaning and talking to himself and rocking his head left and right. If they had arrested a full colonel, he knew it must all be true.

"You're the lie! They don't arrest colonels by mistake! You bastard! You cheated me!" With tremendous effort the boy drew himself up to a sitting position, and from there, using his one leg, pushed himself up the side of the cart. He did it quickly, with great strength, placing a hand on the side of the cart to steady himself as they bounced along. He reached into his pocket to grab the cigars Jules had given him. He wanted nothing to do with Jules, nothing to do with his cigars, nothing to do with sharing the cart they were in. Tears of rage and anguish spread beneath his bandage, staining the cloth and running down his cheek. The tears were pink, tinged with blood. Etienne cried as he struggled with the cigars. He spat out the words.

"*I . . . will . . . not . . . ride . . . with . . . a . . . coward!*"

Jules's head was pounding. Each word ripped him to the quick of his soul. He sought the words to help the boy understand, to get his attention, to calm him so they could talk. And then it happened, so suddenly that it was over before Jules could react. As he leaned forward to help steady the boy, the cart hit another pothole and gave a great lurch upward. Without a sound Etienne toppled over backward out of the cart, waving

his arms wildly, too late to catch himself. There was
nothing Jules could do. Etienne rolled out of sight on
the opposite side from Jules, who because of his leg
chain couldn't get over to see what had happened.

"*Arrêtez!*" he roared to the sergeant. "Stop now!
Quickly!"

The sergeant looked around, not sure what was happening. He pulled on the reins of his horse, but for a
moment the mule behind him kept on. It was all too late
anyway. There was a terrible bump as the cart jolted up
and down.

"*Arrêtez!*" Jules raged again. He pulled furiously on
the chain holding his leg. The metal clanked on the
wood slats of the cart. The sharp iron edge cut into his
ankle, but it would not budge. He strained toward the
edge but couldn't get a clear view. He saw just one leg,
twisted and still. Around it were scattered a half-dozen
cigars.

Horrified, the sergeant rushed to the boy's still form.
He knelt down and Jules could see him grimace and
shake his head. The wheel of the cart had run over
Etienne's shoulder and neck, nearly cutting him in two.

"No!" Jules cried softly. "It isn't true! None of it!
No, no!" And he collapsed on his knees in the bottom
of the cart, taking a big splinter in one of them, but he
didn't feel it. He could only cry out again and again,
crushed, broken, horrified. He had seen a thousand men
die. It had never hurt so much before.

For the first time in his memory, Colonel Jules
deVries of the Imperial Guard of the Empire of France
felt like crying.

"It isn't true," he whispered. "Don't believe them,
Private! It isn't true, isn't true. . . ."

VIVE LA RÉPUBLIQUE! DOWN WITH THE EMPIRE!
Death to the emperor!"

The roar grew in intensity in the Place de la
Concorde. It was Sunday noon. Paul and Moussa
watched wide-eyed from their perch atop a stone wall

as the throng surged through the square. The boys had
been coming into town every Sunday, but never to a
scene like this. This day everything was upside down
and chaotic. Men were everywhere on ladders, perching
them precariously against statues and symbols of the
empire. Saws cut through marble necks and decapitated
the hated heads that toppled down and were tossed
along on the hands of the jubilant crowd like balls until
at last they reached the Pont Neuf over the Seine, where
to great roars of approval they were hurled into the
water.

Steel bayonets of the National Guard glittered everywhere. Golden eagles were torn from fences and columns or were covered with paper if they couldn't be
removed. Statues were overturned. Stone lions of the
empire smashed to the pavement. Top hats flew in
the air and men waved the tricolor in exuberance. At
the Hôtel de Ville portraits of the emperor were ripped
from their frames and thrown out the windows into the
streets, where they were stomped and danced upon by
people drunk on the glorious spirits of the republic.

"Did we win the war last night?" Moussa asked,
watching the party.

"We must have," said Paul, "except that your father
said we lost."

"I know. So what is everyone so happy about?"

"I don't know. A republic, I guess."

"What's a republic?"

Paul shrugged. Moussa was asking too many questions. They could see over the gates into the Garden of
the Tuileries, where Zouaves were nervously patrolling.
The imperial flag still flew above the palace, which
meant that somewhere behind the ancient walls was the
Empress Eugénie, regent of France in the absence of the
emperor. Only she wasn't regent anymore, or empress,
or anything but in trouble from the crowds around the
palace, crowds who would have their republic.

"To the guillotine with the witch!" cried a reveler.

"Shoot them all!" shouted another, waving a musket
high overhead.

A part of Moussa and Paul wanted to stay, but they saw the weapons and felt the menace beneath the outward gaiety of the crowd. Despite the jubilation, they were afraid. Neither wanted to admit it first, but when a rifle shot went off just below them Paul spoke up. "I think we're supposed to be home."

"I think so too," Moussa said, and together the boys slipped off the wall and disappeared into the milling crowd.

ACROSS PARIS AT THAT MOMENT A GRIM PROCESsion was entering the city along the Cours de Vincennes. The little caravan drew attention to itself by the scraping of the leg chains of the men who trudged along behind the little wooden cart. The chains bit deeply into their legs, leaving a trail of blood. The prisoners were hot and sullen, their mood further blackened by the reception they had been accorded since arriving on the outskirts of the city. The air crackled with passion, all Paris in agony over the destruction of her distant armies, yet in ecstasy over the new republic. No matter the mood of the surrounding masses, however, the prisoners were reviled. Crowds of hooting onlookers tormented them as they passed. The mounted guards made no attempt to protect their charges. They would permit no murder, but made no move to stop the humiliation. The ripe contents of a chamber pot flew from a second-story window, barely missing Jules and splattering to the ground beside his cart. Children threw rocks that drew blood. Someone hastily scribbled signs that were hung around the necks of some of the prisoners. Jules was one of them. He struggled against them as they climbed into the cart, but one of the sentries cuffed him savagely with the butt of his rifle. Gasping, Jules sat back as they draped the sign around his neck.

"I RAN FROM THE ENEMY," proclaimed the sign for all the world to see.

"Deserter!" shouted an old woman who saw it. "Shame!" Her husband stepped forward and spit at

Jules. "Swine!" he shouted. "My grandson is at the front fighting for the likes of you!" Someone found an egg. "Something to eat, coward!" Jules saw it coming and turned his head, but the egg caught him on the forehead. It ran down his face and stung his eyes and dripped from his chin.

Jules endured the ignominy with his gaze fixed straight ahead, his eyes unseeing. The noise of the crowd, the jeers and scorn and spit and contempt that were heaped onto him became like a dream, a slow surreal dance of loathing in the background. He looked down at his bound hands. Since the death of the boy Etienne, Jules had been holding the toy soldier Paul made him. It seemed so long ago that he had stood on the platform in the train station, saying good-bye to his wife and son and nephew, people who expected him to go whip the Prussians all by himself; and now he was returning to them like this. . . . He shook his head, disgusted with himself, determined to pull himself from his grotesque reverie.

You are Jules deVries. You are a colonel in the Imperial army. You will conduct yourself in that manner. You have done nothing wrong! You have served your country in two wars. You will stop this pathetic self-pity and act like an officer!

He held the toy soldier that had a crooked grin on its face and a twig where its arm should have been and said the words again.

You have done nothing wrong!

The procession made its way across the Pont d'Austerlitz, down the Boulevard St.-Marcel, and along the Boulevard Montparnasse as it clanked and scraped its way toward the Ecole Militaire, which had been pressed into service as a stockade, both for Prussian prisoners of war and for French military prisoners. Everywhere was a city giddy with the notion of republic, but everywhere the procession passed, the revelry stopped for stares and jeers and the curiosity of revulsion.

It was at the Avenue de Breteuil where it happened.

Moussa and Paul were making their way home when Moussa saw the commotion. He almost didn't bother looking, for it had been a day of such excitement as few men had ever seen, and another demonstration hardly seemed worth the effort to look. But he felt bolder and safer now that he was away from the Place de la Concorde, so he climbed up onto the base of an iron lamppost where he could see over the heads of the throngs of people and into the street beyond. There were horsemen and a cart, and a long line of men trudging behind.

"What is it?" asked Paul.

"I don't know. Soldiers. Prisoners, I think."

"Prussians?" Paul's voice was excited. He wanted to see Prussian prisoners. He wondered if they were human, or had two heads and ate children. He had heard stories of both. He ran to the pole and looked for a place to pull himself up.

"No, not Prussians. It looks like French prisoners!"

"French? Why would there be French prisoners?"

And then Moussa saw the man in the cart. At first he didn't recognize him for the filth, and he certainly never expected to see him in such a setting. He thought he was away at the front. But no, he looked carefully again, and his heart froze. It was Uncle Jules.

"Paul, look!" It was almost a whisper, full of dread. Paul finally hoisted himself up and wriggled into position where he could see. He looked where Moussa was pointing, to the cart.

For a moment there was silence. And then the sound that came from the boy was one that no one who heard it ever forgot.

CHAPTER 8

"AH, THE COUNT COMES TO GLOAT."

General Raspail looked up from the desk in his study at Count Henri deVries. It had been less than two months since the party at the château, where the two men had argued about the readiness of France to fight a war with Prussia. On that day Raspail's uniform had been woven from the pure silk of arrogance. He had boasted and bragged and strutted France's might. He had scorned Henri's warnings and nearly fought with him. Now the little general looked frail, weary, his eyes bloodshot, his posture and mustache slumped, his shoulders sagging under the combined weight of defeat and disbelief. Henri saw the agony in his eyes. Raspail's voice was bitter as he confronted the memory of his unsupported vanity.

"You can save your breath, deVries. You were right. I admit it."

"I would not come to gloat, General," Henri said. "The war is a tragedy for all France. I deeply wish it was I who had been wrong, and not you. But that is not what brings me. I have come about Jules."

Raspail motioned him to a chair. "Of course. Sit down."

Henri sank into the chair. It had taken all his influence and the better part of a day to make it as far as he had through the confusion to find his brother, and then to sit before this exhausted man. No one had known anything about where the prisoners might have been taken. The attention of Paris was on other things. The boys hadn't followed Jules, but had run straight to the château, Paul in bitter tears, Moussa breathless and afraid, where they told the story of what they had seen.

"He was a prisoner, Father," Moussa told Henri. "He was in chains. I could read the sign he wore. It said he ran away."

Paul was miserable. "We couldn't get near him. They pushed us away."

Henri set out immediately. He went first to the Tuileries, to the headquarters of the Imperial Guard, arguing his way through the chaos to the inner offices that had been his brother's post in Paris. The place was deserted except for a soldier who wandered through the rubble that had been picked through by servants of the palace and by the crowds outside. Papers had been carted away, furniture stolen, wallpaper ripped from the walls. Henri told the soldier what he wanted. The man looked at him as if he were mad. "Imperial Guard? But there *is* no Imperial Guard anymore, monsieur. There is no emperor!"

He made his way through the crowded streets to the Hôtel de Ville, the unofficial headquarters of the new republic. Henri found rumors of a general amnesty for prisoners, but no prisoners. He was referred to the Chamber of Deputies, a teeming mass of confusion where no one knew anything. Finally a helpful officer of the National Guard suggested the Ecole Militaire. Henri bribed his way inside and found his brother in a make-shift cell in a common yard, separated from the other prisoners only by wire.

Their meeting had been brief and painful. To the hooting of the other prisoners, the brothers clasped arms, Jules's hands restrained by chains, and for several moments no words passed between them. Jules struggled to maintain his dignity as he stood unwashed in tattered clothing before his older brother and sought the words to explain. His story poured out but his voice cracked twice, betraying him.

Henri listened with a sense of unreality, his outrage tinged by the great sadness he felt, that such a proud man should be so humbled before the world. He knew how difficult it was for Jules even to speak. "You must not despair," Henri said, his own voice thick and his words somehow hollow. "This cannot last for long. They will find the truth and set you free." Jules nodded without conviction.

Before leaving the École, a furious Count deVries had sought out the commanding officer, ready to horsewhip the man for the extraordinarily harsh conditions of his brother's confinement. But to his astonishment he found no one in command. "There was a major here," one of the guards told him, "but he left." Ordinarily, private quarters for an officer would have been automatic. Even captured Prussian officers were granted such amenities. But the soldiers guarding Jules were a rough and angry lot from Paris, radical patriots to the core who took delight in delivering small humiliations to any representative of the old order. Jules earned their special attention on three counts: as an officer, an imperialist, and a nobleman. They roasted him mercilessly. "Three roads to hell you've trod," they taunted him. "The only thing you've gotten right was your desertion. And for that you'll be shot," they gloated. They shorted his food and made him dump his own slop.

So Henri had emptied his pockets to buy his brother better treatment from the mob. His thick wad of francs swiftly overcame their political and social concerns and their need for petty amusements, and they promised the count that the colonel would see better care.

Intending to return later with more money and fresh clothing for the colonel, Henri had gone at once to see Raspail at the general's home.

"It is absurd," Henri told him. "They have arrested him for desertion. He is being held like an animal."

"Absurd? Today everything is absurd, Count. I heard of his arrest from a colleague in Châlons. A bad business. Madness heaped upon madness."

"Then you must help him!"

"Help him! Help him!" His voice was mocking. "Count deVries, let me explain a few things. The reports I have say that our front-line forces who are not dead or wounded are being sent to Belgium. The emperor is prisoner of the Prussians. They say the empress has fled to England. There is a mob at the Chamber of Deputies, everyone scrapping for control. For the moment everyone's in charge and no one's in charge. Ten pretty speeches for every empty thought. Bismarck's armies are marching toward Paris. They'll be here in a matter of weeks if not days. Who will defend Paris and the new republic? Marshal Bazaine is holed up in Metz, trapped like a rat."

Raspail paced back and forth across the little room, pausing to look out the window upon the courtyard. His voice was laced with scorn.

"The streets out there are running wild with rabble calling themselves the National Guard. Most of them are drunk. They cannot shoot straight or march in a line. They cannot wipe themselves! And then after all that I have an officer under arrest for desertion. Under the circumstances, Count, you'll forgive me if the colonel's troubles have not received my utmost attention!"

"I understand the magnitude of the trouble at our gates, General. But Jules is an officer of the Guard, unjustly charged. He could never be guilty of this!"

"Guilty! You misunderstand me, Count. I have known the colonel for a long time. I was in Italy when he was decorated. He is a solid officer. He lacks the brilliance of your father, to be sure, but he is no coward. But it doesn't matter just now whether he is guilty or not."

"How can you say that?"

Raspail looked at Henri as though he were a particularly stupid schoolboy.

"You don't seem to grasp what is happening here! This morning I was in my carriage and a woman—*a woman!*—stopped me on the street and accused me of cowardice. Me! Of treason, for remaining at my post in Paris while our armies were slaughtered in the field!" Raspail's voice rose shrilly. He slammed the table with his fist, and a carafe of water crashed to the floor. "For thirty years I have served France. I wear the uniform of its emperor's guard! And now that he is disgraced, so are we all in the eyes of France. A Frenchman has no pity for failure. There will be retribution. There will be punishment for the defeat. People will have to be found to be responsible. Many people. Jules is in a bad position, Count. He is a good place for the mobs to begin."

"But the mobs won't be trying him."

"Won't they? I wouldn't be so certain. I don't know anymore. I have lost my command. There is nothing to command anymore. It is why you found me here, in my home. I have no office, no post. I will offer my services to the National Guard. I don't know whether they'll have me. Whether they do or not, I have no authority to deal with Jules. I don't know who does. I suspect no one else knows either. It will take some time to sort out."

"Then we must fill that time finding the people who could help him. Jules told me there was a man named Dupree serving under him. A major who saw what happened. He could clear this up."

Raspail snorted. "If Dupree is even alive after the massacre at Sedan, he is probably in a prisoner of war camp in Belgium. Or, very well, let us suppose he escaped. If so he'll hardly be headed for Paris, knowing we'll be the next target of the Prussians. He'll look to join other units still operating in the provinces. I remind you that we are not yet defeated by the Hun. Until we are—God forbid—there will be other armies. He would try to join them." Raspail shook his head. "Long odds for finding him, I'd say."

As the general spoke Henri knew what he said was true. Raspail was hammering away at his hope, relentlessly shattering his illusions that this outrage might be resolved easily. Henri had another thought.

"There is his accuser. Delescluze."

"*Oui, le Franc-tireur.* A drop of dirtwater in a big sea, I'm afraid. A guerilla, waging war by stealth, using treachery against the Hun. Unlikely his unit was involved at Sedan. Even if he weren't the coward the colonel makes him out to be, his unit would be in hiding. If the Prussians caught him he'd be shot, not taken prisoner. The Hun will have no more patience for his ilk than would I. You'll never find him. And it is certain he won't show up for the trial."

Henri shrugged. "Then we should be able to have the

charges dismissed! Surely a letter isn't enough to support formal charges. And without testimony there could never be a trial."

"Have you read the letter?"

"No."

"It is specific. Signed by a French officer. And it is accompanied by a second charge, from a sergeant the colonel encountered while he was under arrest and being escorted back to Paris. The sergeant's charge of attempted escape makes Delescluze's look stronger. It is not enough, I agree, to make a perfect case against the colonel, or maybe even a good one. But it is too much to ignore. There will be a court-martial. It may come down to nothing more than the word of Colonel deVries against two letters. If that is so, then his fate will depend entirely upon who sits in judgment upon him. If these were normal times, then I would call his chances good. The military takes care of its officers. But these are not normal times. The revenge seekers may carry the day."

For a while both men were silent.

"You are not a man to give up easily, General. Surely you will not leave him to the wolves."

Exasperated, Raspail threw his hands up.

"Do you not hear me, Count? The wolves pay me no heed! *I have no influence!* What I have not told you is that yesterday I tried to see the colonel. I was denied entry to the stockade. By a corporal. He looked at my uniform and told me I had no right! A *corporal! Me! No right!*" The indignity thundered from him. Abruptly he stood and went to the window, his back to Henri. For days his moods had swung wildly. One moment he was the fighter, ready to take up a rifle himself and find the bastard Bismarck. The next he was ready to retire, discouraged and outraged by those who questioned his fitness. He had never known such a time. It was one thing to suffer at the hands of one's enemies. It was another to do so at the hands of one's countrymen.

He paced and fumed and finally assented. "I will try to help, deVries," he said. "I doubt whether I will be of much use. But I will try."

COUNT OTTO VON BISMARCK RODE IN THE CAR-
riage along the dirt path. He loved this part of
France, with its charming valleys and picturesque
towns. The woods were fragrant and still. A kingfisher
hunted above a quiet rivulet. Beyond, in the lovely river,
a lone heron diverted its attention from the muddy waters to watch the chancellor pass. Bismarck was on his
way to meet General von Moltke, whose armies had
been so superb and whose successes had so astonished
the world, bringing Bismarck so deliciously near to realizing the grand schemes that raced in his brain.

Behind him lay the smoking ruin of an iron tempest.
He had mounted the hilltop overlooking the little fortress town of Sedan in the valley where the French army
and its emperor were trapped. There he had stood
throughout the long day, next to King Wilhelm and the
American general Sheridan, who had come to observe.
From their camp above the river they watched the
methodical slaughter unfold. The French armies were
surrounded and outmaneuvered, defeated before the
battle began, yet unwilling to yield. The carnage had
been horrible, even for the victor to behold, beginning
in the morning mists that rose from the Meuse. Deadly
fire rained onto the French cavalry from the hills of
Flöing to the north. Down into the valley and across the
river, the German artillery screamed death through the
day, butchering everything in its path, scorching the forests of the Ardennes with powder and iron. King
Wilhelm had been much moved by it, and had shaken
his head in pity for the enemy. "Gallant lads," he said,
watching as they threw themselves in waves on the long
knives of Prussia until their blood ran to the Meuse and
flowed red to the sea.

After the battle, in which twenty thousand had died,
Bismarck had greeted Louis Napoléon, the pathetic
husk of an emperor, ravaged by the pain of his kidney
stones, nearly unable to move. He had tried hard and
unsuccessfully to die among his troops. But the fates
had been unkind and the bullets had flown around him,
and he had lived to shoulder the awful burden of the

white flag of surrender. They had met at a little weaver's cottage at Donchery, the emperor in his general's dress, polite and solicitous. He had not desired war, he wanted the chancellor to know, but had been forced into it by public opinion. He apologized that he could not surrender for his nation, since Eugénie was regent and the legal government was in Paris. But he placed himself and his army at the unconditional disposal of the king. Afterward he had met briefly with Wilhelm. And then in the heavy rains of dawn he had climbed painfully into a brougham and ridden under escort into captivity.

Now that business was done. Before Bismarck lay all of France, and beyond her a continent cowering at the might of the German war machine. The rout was almost complete, but Bismarck knew it was not over. The French were beaten but would not yet admit it. Their pride would raise another army and their honor would defend Paris to the death. That was all right, he thought. The new army would be unworthy, and he had already decided not to invade Paris. It would be a shame to destroy such a beautiful city, and he respected the ability of the Parisians to fight in the streets. There was no need to shed so much German blood. Instead, his armies would surround the city and place her under siege. She would strangle, cut off from the world. Her residents would quarrel among themselves in a slow rot. He would plunge the City of Light into darkness as the rest of France watched helplessly. He would settle himself and the king into—into where? Versailles! Yes, perfect! What luxurious irony, to sit in the palace of French kings and wait for the pearl of France to die!

He ordered his driver to pull over. Across the river he could see wagons and artillery of the army of the crown prince of Saxony. They were rumbling toward Paris, to make his vision of a Second Reich come true.

Maman? Maman, listen to me. Maman, are you there?"

Paul shook his mother. Elisabeth sat in the darkened

room, the shades drawn. Paul wanted her to turn and look at him, to acknowledge him in some direct way, but she only sat there, listening to other voices inside, voices that were louder than his, voices that for days had kept her sitting alone, unable to comfort her son, unable to leave the room. She nodded dumbly, so he knew she could hear him, and once she squeezed his hand, but she said nothing and wouldn't look at him. She had not eaten or slept since the boys brought the news. All the color had left her face and there was no life in her eyes. The room was black with her despair. For two months she had been talking to the portrait of Jules on the wall. Now her chair faced away from it, and she was silent.

When Henri came to tell her that he had seen Jules, and that Jules had asked about her, she could not respond. She could not respond when Paul came. She didn't know whether she could ever respond again. She wanted to say something to Paul, to comfort him, but she couldn't look him in the eye, couldn't face the humiliation she felt, not even with her ten-year-old son. There was nothing to say.

It is so unfair! How could they do this to me?

She had never known defeat or failure, or anything but the gay certainty of a woman whose husband was a man of destiny. Now the dream was shattered; only a nightmare remained. She sat in the gloom and rocked in her chair, wrapped in rage and covered with helplessness, her soul as cold and dark as a crypt. She could not imagine the emptiness of life without position. She was obsessed by thoughts of the social snubs she would receive, of the drying up of invitations to important social events. Never once in those first few days did her thoughts turn to what Jules might be going through, or to imagining the hardships of his confinement. Never once did she wonder about the charges against him. The charges didn't matter; she blacked them out. What mattered was that the war had turned personal, that it had turned personal against *her*.

Now Paul was desperately worried for her, even more so than for his father. Somehow he knew that his

father was made of iron and would be all right. But he
had never seen his mother this way, just sitting and
rocking in silence. She was always so cheerful, so full of
energy, so alive; but now his father was locked away
and his mother seemed all used up. Paul was afraid. He
wondered if it was all his fault. Nothing had been the
same since he'd seen his mother with the general at
the party when they were—what, he didn't know for
sure, except that he shouldn't have seen it, shouldn't
have been spying, and now he felt so distant from her.
He moped around the château, shaking his head when
Moussa asked if he wanted to go to the river, paying no
attention to his lessons with Gascon. Serena tried to
comfort him.

"Your father is a strong man, Paul. I do not know the
French way in these things, but they will see it is a mistake. They will let him go, I am certain of it. He is a good
soldier. You must be a brave boy. Your uncle Henri is
doing everything possible. He will get him out."

Paul nodded. There was a painful lump in his throat.
Tears welled in his eyes and he tried to hide them, but
she brushed his cheek with the back of her hand and it
was too much for him. He collapsed in sobs and buried
his face in her chest. She rocked him and stroked his
hair.

Later she went into Elisabeth's room. Elisabeth sat in
her chair and ignored her. A bowl of soup, now cold,
sat on a nightstand. Serena was a practical woman of
the desert who had no patience for self-inflicted frailty.
She ripped open the curtains and the dying sun of the
September afternoon streamed into the room. Elisabeth
blinked and turned away, but Serena took her by the
chin and made her respond. Elisabeth pulled away, but
Serena pulled back harder.

"Elisabeth, stop this! Your son needs a mother," she
said angrily.

"He needs a father," Elisabeth sniffed.

"Quit sniveling! Wake up! You must come out of this
room!"

"Stay out of it. It is not your affair. Leave me alone.
Go read your books."

"Elisabeth, I'm sorry for what has happened to Jules, I truly am. I have no wish to intrude, but Paul needs you."

"What *I* need is for you to leave me. You have suffered nothing. I have suffered it all."

"*Mon Dieu,* your son is in tears and your husband in prison, and all I see in you is wretched self-pity. Stop it!"

"You don't understand," Elisabeth said in a faint bitter voice, shaking her head. "You don't *need* to understand. You were a countess before this war. When it is over you will still be a countess. I will be nothing. Nothing at all." Once again she pulled away. "You simply don't understand what I have lost."

Serena gave up. "I don't know what to do for her," she told Henri that night. "She is there, but she does not hear me."

"There isn't anything you can do," Henri told her, "except to help Paul. I know Elisabeth. She's a child, and quite vain. She'll need to have her hair done soon, and then she'll come out of it."

GENERAL TROCHU, THE MILITARY GOVERNOR OF Paris, gravely announced that no armies remained to stand between the Prussians and the city, and so the city quickly made ready. Paris had been fortified since 1840 with a massive defense system, including a high wall with more than ninety bastions and a moat. Fifteen forts stood outside the walls, guarding the approaches. The forts and bastions had fallen into disrepair. In a blur of activity men brought stones and earth for reinforcement and carpenters repaired heavy wooden doors. Three thousand heavy guns were brought in on wagons and mounted or left in reserve, while workshops in the city became factories for the manufacture of armaments. A tobacco factory made rifle cartridges. At the Louvre the *Venus de Milo* was moved underground. Sandbags were stacked before the windows, while in the great exhibit halls craftsmen made shells for the big guns. Coats of plaster were applied to paintings and sacks of earth were heaped around the art treasures of France to protect them from artillery. Books and manuscripts were boxed and stored. The Grand Opéra became an observatory and a military store. The Gare de Lyon was pressed into service as a cannon foundry. Barricades were raised at the ends of the grand boulevards, and deep trenches cut. Palaces and public buildings were readied to care for the wounded. A factory for the manufacture of clothes was established in the Gaîté.

Troops from the countryside poured into the city. Thousands of marines and sailors and regular troops from General Vinoy's Thirteenth Corps stood alongside two new corps of untrained conscripts—merchants and workmen and farmers who knew nothing of war but accepted their rifles and drank their wine and waited for orders. There were Gardes Mobiles, mostly made up of undisciplined conscripts, and the National Guard, a loose militia. Artillery units bivouacked in the Jardin des Plantes, and the Garden of the Tuileries became a campground for the soldiers.

The massive preparations were directed by the defense committee, a group of civic leaders who met daily at the War Office. General Trochu was chairman; Dorian, the minister of public works, was the vice-chairman. Among other notables who served was Monseigneur Marius Murat, the bishop of Boulogne-Billancourt. The bishop displayed his usual genius at matters of commerce and supply, which were of critical importance to the city. The range of his acquaintances was vast, the extent of his influence seemingly without bounds. He was able to find goods and materials that others around the table held to be in short supply or impossible to obtain. He located seven tons of saltpeter for the manufacture of armaments. He found blankets, and straw, and wax for candles. His emissaries combed the countryside, collecting vast stores of food and materiel.

The bishop thrived, for war was a magnificent trading ground. Fathers seeking to buy military exemptions for their sons had found that the bishop could invariably come up with the necessary document or certificate. Owners of factories seized for defense purposes had found that the bishop could help them obtain compensation. If the fees he collected for his benefactions were extravagant, if the favors he exacted in return were steep—well, it was wartime, and costs were high.

No transaction was too small for his attention, no prospect of profit overlooked. He sent his managers of the landholdings of the diocese out to visit each of the tenant farmers. There were hundreds of them, some who worked sizable plots of land. The managers produced written orders from the committee confiscating their sheep and cattle and grain for the defense of the republic. Little if any compensation was paid them. The bishop, through his agents, then sold the livestock and grain to the city at exorbitant prices. The Bois de Boulogne became an ocean of wool; droves of cattle spilled beyond the Bois and filled the long slope of the Champs-Élysées; a flour mill was established in the Gare du Nord. Parisians were hoarding preserves and salt and vegetables. Whatever the concerns about the adequacy of the food supply, there was a virtual sea of wine stored in casks and bottles and kegs beneath the city, wine in every cellar and cabinet and bin.

As quickly as supplies and soldiers and refugees were streaming into the city, some of the wealthier families were streaming out, either going to their summer villas in the Midi, or leaving the country altogether. Henri and Serena talked about it at length. They agreed it was out of the question.

"I cannot leave Jules in a prison cell," Henri said. They were walking near the edge of the château grounds along the banks of the Seine, across from the palace of St.-Cloud. It was deserted where they walked, and peaceful. For a blessed moment they were alone, detached from the siege preparations. They sat down by the water's edge, their backs against a massive chestnut tree. "It might take a long time to get him released. I have already seen three different generals and two ministers. None of them has been able to help, at least not yet. With the Prussians coming no one is paying attention to this. One suggested that I was better to leave things alone for the time being, that the sooner a trial is held the more danger there is in it for Jules. He may be right. I have requested a meeting with General Trochu."

"We will stay, of course." Serena had never doubted it. In the desert, approaching enemies did not announce themselves as the Prussians were doing. Stealth and surprise were the common deceptions of Saharan battle. European war was frontal and direct. If one could see the enemy coming, one could prepare. "Do you think the Prussians will invade the city?"

"No." Henri found a stick and used it to make a map in the wet riverbank. He began with the junction of the Marne and Seine Rivers and drew the arc of the Seine as it swept through the city. The river then looped back through the château property and around the Bois de Boulogne as it flowed toward the northeast and the Genevilliers peninsula.

"The château is here," he said, making a mark, "and the walls of the city here. You see we are protected by the bend of the river. It provides a natural barrier against invasion. The bridge to St.-Cloud will be destroyed. *En plus*, we have the guns of the forts of Mont Valérien, here, and Issy, here, to watch over us." Mont Valérien rose from the Seine. At its summit stood a citadel whose guns commanded a huge area on the western reaches of the city. Henri pointed across the river to St.-Cloud. "The Prussians will stop there," he said. "They have no need to attack the city. They have already shown their inclinations at Metz. Marshal Bazaine and his army are still trapped there. The same will happen with Paris. They will draw an iron noose around the city and pull it tight. Then they will camp and wait us out."

"The city will starve," she said.

"Maybe. I think it will end before that."

Serena felt completely comfortable and safe sitting next to Henri, as though he were an extension of her, and she of him. *It has always been so with us*, she thought, and with the thought came a sudden rush of fear, inexplicable fear that washed over her and constricted her chest. She turned to Henri and took his face gently in her hands and held him close. "When I lived in the desert there was a part of me that did not know a husband or son. War never frightened me, or death. But now"—her eyes glistened, and she threw her arms around him, and her voice broke—"now I cannot bear the thought of losing you or Moussa. You are my life, Henri deVries. If anything happened to you it would kill me."

He held her tightly and stroked her hair and blessed his luck at having found such a woman. He had spent long hours analyzing their situation. Nothing was ever certain, but he was as confident as anyone could be. He had considered sending her away with Elisabeth and the boys but he knew she would never consent to it. So they would stay. They would have food. The stores in his cellars were amply stocked, and there would be small game to hunt. If it became necessary they would find protection from shelling below the thick stone walls of the château, the château that for thirty generations had helped the deVries family withstand wars and sieges and the Revolution. But he had meant what he said—he did not believe shelling would occur. It was a sad thought, but he felt Paris would go with a whimper, not a shout.

"Nothing will happen to us," Henri said, and she heard the conviction in his voice. He kissed her on her ears and neck. "We will try to make life as normal as possible for the boys. And there is another reason we must stay. A delegation from the committee for defense came to see me. They have asked for my help."

Serena straightened up. "To do what?"

"To make balloons."

"Balloons!"

"*Oui.* The city will be cut off from the world. They want to maintain contact with the rest of France. Balloons can carry mail and people."

She looked at him with mischief in her eyes, recalling a time long ago in the desert.

"You did not tell them then," she said.

"Tell them what?"

"That you have no idea which way the wind blows and that your balloons crash."

"That was no crash." Henri laughed. "I told you, it was only a hard landing. Besides, I'm not supposed to fly them. I'm only going to build them."

Moussa was miserable, stuck in his private hell with Sister Godrick. It was only September, and already it was the longest year he'd ever lived. He guessed the world would have to explode for school to end, since the Prussians didn't seem to be able to get the job done. But his father was adamant. "If we let the Prussians force us to close our schools, then they've won." Moussa pointed out that other schools had closed, most of the public schools, anyway. The count wasn't having it. "As long as we can keep the school open, we will," he said.

At recess Moussa and Paul wandered to the edge of the schoolyard and climbed to the top of the fence. In vain they looked across the river for signs of the Prussians.

"They'll never get here," Moussa said grumpily.

Paul didn't say anything. He'd been quiet for days, but Moussa didn't bother him about it. They knew each other's moods well.

They came in from recess with all the other boys to face the last hot boring part of the afternoon, which would be devoted to math, and to the inevitable prayers about math, in which Sister Godrick would implore the Lord to ignore their big defects and sharpen their little minds. He opened the top of his desk to get his exercise book out. He frowned. His books were there, but his book bag was gone. It was a leather bag with a shoulder strap. It was a gift from Gascon, and was the only one like it in school. He remembered leaving it there that morning, and hadn't taken it out since then. He looked around the classroom but didn't see it anywhere, not up on the hooks at the back of the room or on anyone's desk. Someone had taken it. Before he could investigate, the imperious shroud of Sister Godrick entered the room. Her habit rustled as she walked to her desk. The chatter of the boys died instantly as she faced the class and began.

"Merciful Father, through Your perfect grace we have come here to share in the teachings of Your blessed son . . ."

Moussa moved his lips, but did not close his eyes or bow his head. He knew that Sister Godrick would see. He knew it would cost him something. Every day it was the same, like a ritual between them. But this time Sister Godrick did not notice. She finished the prayer and crossed herself. "Sit."

As one the class sat and waited as she opened her desk drawer to withdraw the lesson book. She did it automatically, without looking, putting her hand into the drawer, feeling for the bound edges of the book. But what she felt was not the book. She gasped in horror and gave out a little shriek. Like lightning she drew her hand back. She jumped up so quickly that she knocked over her chair, which crashed to the floor. Sister Godrick rubbed her hand back and forth on her habit and stared at the abomination. There, in the middle of the drawer, was a snake. It was a little one. It had been coiled comfortably in the dark until she startled it, and now regarded her with alarm. It was a harmless garter snake, but she didn't know that. She knew only that it was a serpent.

For a moment Sister Godrick was speechless. The fright had sent shock waves coursing through her all the way to her feet. The fear tightened her throat. But outwardly her demeanor before the class was as icy as ever. She closed her eyes and clutched her rosary. With steely resolve she composed herself, determined that the students not enjoy her discomfort. She crossed herself quickly.

"Look, a snake!" Pierre said, as he and the other boys crowded around. "I'll get it out!" The nun nodded dumbly. He reached in the drawer and grasped it behind its head. He lifted it out of the drawer, its body writhing under his hand. Sister Godrick took a step back, and Pierre carried it quickly from the room. In the silence the other boys traded glances, eyes regarding eyes to see who knew.

"Take your seats." The shock had passed. Sister Godrick recovered her composure as the boys obeyed. She picked up her chair and set it upright, brushed off her habit, and took her seat. Carefully she opened each of the remaining drawers of her desk. She examined each of them, all the way into the back. She used a ruler to lift her papers and poke around. Satisfied at last that no other surprises lurked inside, she probed the drawer where she'd found the snake. She put the end of the ruler through something and lifted it out. Gingerly, as though it were a load of dynamite, she placed it on top of her desk, square in the middle where everyone could see it.

Moussa felt his face flush when he saw what it was. She looked straight at him, and from the distance he could feel her eyes burning. He knew that she could see him flushing. He wished he could teach himself not to do that, to stop the tingling sensation that washed over him when he was nervous or embarrassed and turned his skin red. More than once, when he was guilty, it had gotten him in trouble. Now, when he was not, it could do the same.

"Michel," she said. "Come here."

Heart pounding, mouth dry, he stood up from his desk and approached her. As he always tried to do, he accepted her gaze, and held it. The room was deathly quiet.

"You forgot your book bag during your little prank, Michel," she said, indicating the missing leather bag. "Or were you afraid to take the serpent out of it?"

He was nervous and not thinking, and the first thing out of his mouth was a defense of his own bravery. "It was a garter snake, Sister. I am not afraid of garter snakes." It was the worst thing he could have said. He realized his error immediately and started to correct himself, but she spoke first.

"Apparently not, as that is what you put in the bag. So you *did* know about it."

"No, Sister, what I meant was—I was only trying to

say that garter snakes don't bite. There's nothing to be afraid of. I didn't mean—"

"The Lord is your witness, Michel deVries. Do not compound your situation by lying before Him."

"But I did not do it, Sister. Someone took the bag from my desk."

"And you said nothing about it."

"I only just noticed, Sister." He wished that a Prussian bomb would land on them right that second.

" 'Someone' took your bag, you say."

"Yes, Sister."

"And do you know who that might have been?"

Moussa debated with himself. He knew well enough, but preferred to deal with it after class. And yet he was tired of getting in trouble for things he had not done. He decided to try something different.

"I think it was Pierre, Sister."

"Pierre! Come forward!"

Pierre rose from his chair and hurried to the front of the room. His face was impassive as he stood before her.

"Did you steal this bag from Michel's desk?"

"No, Sister."

"Did you have anything to do with the serpent?"

"No, Sister."

She turned her hardest stare upon the boy. Her eyes were narrowed and severe. Sometimes it unnerved a child, and served to get at the truth. Sometimes it just scared them, or made them cry. "God is your witness, Pierre. Do not jeopardize your soul by lying before Him! *Did you know of this?*" Pierre looked at her, then down at the floor. He was one of the boys who got scared. His voice quivered when he answered.

"No, Sister. I swear it before the Lord God."

Moussa closed his eyes. He should have known better.

"Very well. Take your seat."

With a silent sigh of relief, Pierre returned to his desk with a wry glance at his friends.

Moussa tried again. "Sister, I too swear—"

"Do not!" she lashed back, before he could say

more. "A boy who does not bow his head in prayer before the Lord God will not now swear an oath in His name! Do not dare it before Him!" Sister Godrick stood up. "For your lie, Michel, you shall suffer God's punishment in the hereafter. For the serpent, you shall suffer mine now. Drop your trousers."

"Here?"

"Here."

Moussa was determined not to show his fear, and he heard his father's voice. *They respect only strength.* With great effort he summoned the courage to look stronger than he felt. There was no defeat in his eyes. He would submit, but he wasn't beaten—not by Sister Godrick, not by a whipping, not by the treachery of another student. She made him lean over a desk and take hold of the side bars. Then she had the other boys line up in a row so that they could watch and see clearly what was happening. Moussa would be humiliated before them, as they in turn would be warned and humbled by his punishment. In that manner everyone would profit. She made him turn his head toward his classmates, so that he could watch them watching. Only his shirt covered his buttocks. Moussa could see the boys smirking at his exposure. The oak paddle screamed down. She wielded it with terrific force, so that some of the boys jumped when it hit. It was to be no ordinary whipping, then. They saw it in the way she held herself. She was small in stature, but she put her whole upper body into it, and took care with her aim. After five blows she stopped, panting.

"Confession will earn you the Lord's mercy, Michel," she said.

"I didn't do it, Sister." She set her teeth and the oak screamed down again. Seven, eight, nine times. The room was filled with the terrible sound of the paddle. *Whoosh! Whack! Whoosh! Whack!* Again and again the sharp edge of the oak found its mark, biting into his flesh. No one said anything, or dared move. The room was hot, and Moussa fought to keep from crying out. The burning was terrible. He wanted to reach back, to touch his flesh and hold it together.

After twelve she stopped again.

"Confession will earn you the Lord's mercy, Michel," she repeated. Moussa's knuckles were white where he held on to the chair. Tears welled at the corners of his eyes and he clenched his teeth. *Be strong, be strong, be strong.* He made no sound.

"Very well. Your pride is your undoing, Michel. Pride is the devil inside you." The oak lightning struck again. Paul looked away, ready to cry. He knew Moussa was strong, but he didn't know how he could take such punishment. Three strokes was the usual, five the most anyone had endured, and those were never delivered with this kind of force—not even by the curé himself.

Whoosh! Whack!

A stain of red blossomed on Moussa's shirttail. A trickle of blood ran down the back of his left leg. He tried to swallow but his mouth was too dry. The fire burned white hot. He closed his eyes tight against the world. *Be strong, be strong.*

Whoosh! Whack!

The trickle ran into the crook of his knee and made a tiny pool. When the count reached fifteen Moussa knew he could not take another blow. He was about to cry out and confess when suddenly it stopped. His entire body trembled, waiting for the next blow. He expected her to say something, to offer him some more mercy, but she was silent. Sister Godrick dropped the paddle to her side. Her blood was up, her excitement high, the Lord's vengeance running hot in her veins. But she saw the blood and caught herself. She didn't want to maim the boy, and the paddle had not drawn a confession. God's punishment was not yet complete, but for the moment hers was. Moussa's strength was as extraordinary as his pride. She said a silent prayer, that the Lord might give her the wisdom to deal with this boy.

"We shall see whether you have learned your lesson, Michel," she said when she got her breath back. She straightened herself up and brushed her habit. She looked at the boys standing in line, watching. They were deathly silent and afraid. The exercise had been fruitful. It was time to restore the normal order of things.

"Return to your places. Open your exercise books to page seven," she said, and the boys moved as if they'd been threatened by the snake.

THE PRUSSIANS OBLIGED MOUSSA THE NEXT WEEK, if only temporarily. Moussa and Paul heard a huge explosion just after dawn, and with Gascon raced to the river's edge. They climbed a tree and saw smoke rising from the bridge to St.-Cloud, which the defenders of Paris had blown up. Across the river, up past the trees and out of their sight, huge clouds of dust rose from the advancing columns of troops under the command of the crown prince of Saxony, who had approached from the east to encircle the southern part of the city. At the same moment in the north, the crown prince of Prussia marched his own troops. Between them, the princes commanded more than a quarter of a million men, who drew their investing lines in a circle around Paris. Great booming noises shook the air as different forts around the city tested the range of their guns and fired at the Prussian positions. There was no returning fire. The Prussians were careful to stay out of range. Distant explosions signaled the end of other bridges. Train and boat traffic stopped completely, and the gates of Paris were drawn shut. The Prussians cut the telegraph wires leading out of the city. At last the two armies joined together in the west, and the circle was complete.

The siege of Paris was under way.

Henri's days were hectic. General Raspail helped him locate a soldier, a hard wiry man named Blanqui who had served with distinction with the Chasseurs in Algeria. Blanqui was tough, lean, and observant, and had spent several years in the town of Sedan, an area he knew well. He laughed at Henri's idea of finding Jules's witness, Major Dupree, but for a fee of fifty thousand francs down and an additional fifty upon his success, agreed to take two men and set out on a search. He would trace the steps of Dupree and his regiment all the way from the farmhouse to the battlefields of Sedan, checking the hospitals and interviewing soldiers.

"Even if I find Dupree, it may not benefit the colonel," Blanqui said. "Your brother is in the hands of lunatics. I know men who could easily bring him out of the École tonight, and it would cost you a lot less money."

Henri had thought of that, but only as a last resort. He knew his brother. Jules would never permit it. His honor was at stake. To flee under the shadow of false accusations, to dishonor his family, to live in exile, would not be something he could bring himself to do.

"Perhaps another time," he said.

"Another time may be too late, Count," Blanqui shrugged. "But I shall do as you wish."

Blanqui was also to look for news of Delescluze, but he was certain the search would be futile. All of his work would have to be done without arousing the suspicions of the Prussians who controlled the countryside in which he would be operating. The veteran soldier had gray hair and a short bristly beard, and walked with a limp from an Arab scimitar. "The Prussians will think I'm just another impotent old Frenchman," he said. "I'll get by them."

Even if Blanqui were successful, he would have to smuggle Dupree all the way back through occupied France and then sneak him into the city through Prussian lines. Blanqui shrugged when they spoke of it. "If I find him, Count, I will think of something. That will be the least of my problems." Blanqui and his men left five days before the Prussians sealed off Paris.

That done, Henri turned his attention to the matter of the balloons. It was an audacious plan of the committee's, to set a balloon aloft every second or third day, carrying mail and dispatches and the spirit of Paris between the capital and countryside. The French had invented balloons a hundred years earlier, and knew more about them and flew them better than anyone in the world. Now they would fly them in the face of the

Prussians, out of their reach. "When they look up at us we will spit in their eye," said the committee about the Prussians. At least that was the plan.

Henri and the other experienced balloonists recruited by the committee had little to work with. Only a few balloons remained in Paris, most of them left over from the Great Exhibition of 1867. Their envelopes were in shreds and their baskets in tatters. They would have to be repaired, and new ones manufactured. Henri was to work in the Gare d'Orléans, the giant station whose trains lay dormant under the siege. He walked through the eerily silent great hall with its soaring arches and iron beams. He was satisfied. It would be big enough to accommodate such an undertaking. He would need more than seventy volunteers for the task, among them some to fly the balloons.

There were few qualified aeronauts in the city. Volunteers would have to be found and trained, but of those there would be no shortage. Departing the besieged city in a magnificent balloon would be heroic, a feat that would beckon mightily after the short inglorious war. It was a dangerous undertaking, yet there would be ten men clamoring for every spot. Henri figured to lose as many men from inexperience as from Prussian guns or capture.

There was little time for sleep as he set about the tasks at hand. Supplies of coal gas had to be secured, along with the piping required to deliver it to inflate the balloons. There was no silk available in the city. Cotton cloth had to be used instead. The cloth was cut into strips and sewn together by seamstresses working at long tables. Each seam was inspected and tested. Henri tried different mixtures of varnish to be applied to the cloth. The first attempts left the cloth too stiff, so that it cracked. "No, no," he said as he saw what his assistants had produced, "they'll never fly that way," and they tried again. Other mixtures left the cloth too soft and permeable, allowing the gas to leak through too quickly. Finally he stumbled on a combination of linseed oil and lead oxide that seemed to do the job. A laborious process began of treating each section, letting it dry and then rotating the cloth so the next section could be done. When the envelopes were ready they were pulled over to one side of the cavernous hall where they were partially inflated to be tested again. Rope webbing was pulled around them to secure the balloons to the baskets. The baskets were constructed of wood and wicker, and were then suspended from the girders. Henri rigged up a full training set complete with rigging and ballast, and began training his Balloon Corps. Most of the volunteers were sailors. Those not busy learning the techniques of flight were put to work braiding halyards and filling sacks for ballast.

The spirits of the men and women in the hall were high, their chatter excited, all of them glad to be doing something instead of simply waiting in gloom. It was one of the few places in Paris where people were not preoccupied with thoughts of enemy superiority and battlefield defeat.

Henri watched proudly as the first of his balloons was inflated. "They aren't pretty," he said to a member of the defense committee who had come to watch with him. "But they'll fly."

CHAPTER 9

L ET'S BREAK HIM OUT."

"What?"

"I said let's break him out!" Moussa and Paul were sitting in their tree house. Moussa was trying to hit a pigeon with his slingshot. The bird stood well out of range and danger. Moussa aimed a few rocks at other things, watching the bird out of the corner of his eye and hoping to lull it into a moment of incaution. Paul was carving a piece of ash. There were shavings scattered all over the floor of the tree house, and a passable sailboat was taking shape in his hands.

It was a lazy Saturday afternoon, warm and humid and oppressively boring. They were bitterly disappointed with the Prussians, who had turned out to be a dull lot. Since the morning Paris had been surrounded, the boys had ventured to the water's edge a hundred times, expecting a pitched battle to unfold before them on the banks of the Seine. Each time they had come away disappointed. There was nothing to see, nothing at all. There had been a terrible battle to the south of the city, at Châtillon, but they knew it was a battle only because Henri told them so, and because the floor of the château shook from the heavy artillery. But hearing wasn't the same as seeing, and seeing was all but impossible: the count had sternly forbidden them to leave the château grounds except to go to school or, with permission, into Paris. That meant they couldn't inspect the situation themselves. The whole world was blowing up, and they were stuck in a stupid tree house.

A siege just wasn't very exciting.

"Break who out?"

Moussa grimaced as he let a rock fly. "Who do you know who needs breaking out? Your father, idiot!"

Paul didn't say anything for a few minutes. Moussa was crazy. Paul wanted desperately to see his father, it was true, to talk to him and make sure he was all right. But they wouldn't let him visit.

"You can't get in," Henri told him. "It's a military stockade. No civilians are allowed inside."

"They let you in!"

"I'm a count. It's almost the same thing as being in the military."

"I'm a count's nephew!"

"It won't work, Paul. I'm sorry." In fact, Henri was lying. He could easily have gotten Paul inside the stockade, for the guards there were indolent and corrupt. He had thought it a good idea to take the boy to see his father, but he had first raised the idea with Jules, who was vehemently opposed.

"No! I will not have my son see me this way," Jules said. "He will never see his father in a cage." Henri had managed to get a new uniform and toiletries to his brother. Jules looked and felt like a different man, but he was still a colonel confined to the stockade, surrounded by an unsavory bunch of guards and prisoners. There was too much a boy Paul's age could not understand. Jules was firm: he could face anyone in his situation, from the court-martial to the mob. But he could not face his own son. Not yet. "You must lie to him, Henri."

"He believes in you, Jules. Seeing you locked up won't alter that. He knows what has happened. He has already seen you in the cart. Certainly the stockade is no worse than that. He's a strong boy. I think it would be good for him."

"Well, you're wrong. I will not permit it. I will see him again when I am free. Not a moment before. I will not discuss it further."

And so Henri had honored his brother's wish and told the lie, and Paul was locked out of his father's confinement, left to imagine things. He thought about him all the time. He wrote a note and gave it to Henri to deliver.

> *Dear Father,*
> *I hope you are well. I will see you soon, when they let you go. I hope you killed a lot of Prussians. They're camped out across the river, but we haven't seen any. I caught a frog with Moussa, but it died. It was a big one. It is waiting for you in a box at home.*
> *Your son, Paul*

He missed his father terribly. He was angry at everyone, and understood nothing. He hated the Prussians for winning so much. He hated the Frenchmen responsible for his father's captivity, hated the people in the street he'd seen torturing his father. He just wanted things to be like they used to be. He just wanted him back. Now his lunatic cousin was talking about setting him free.

"Don't be crazy," he said to Moussa. "We could never break him out."

"*Oui!* I heard my father talking with a man who said it would be easy. You have seen the Ecole! It's just a big yard, with a wall around it and some fences for the prisoners! They're all outside. We can crawl along the wall and drop a rope to him. He can climb out, and we'll all leave!" It was simple for Moussa, who in matters of intrigue possessed a limitless supply of self-assurance. If an adult could do it, he reasoned, so could they, only a little better. They were ten, and invincible.

Paul considered it. At first the idea was insane, just one of Moussa's big plans, but the more he thought about it, the more it intrigued him. He didn't think they'd actually be able to get him out—that part sounded impossible. But maybe at least he'd be able to see his father, to know that he was all right. Maybe he could even talk to him.

"What do you think they'd do to us if we got caught?"

"Well, they wouldn't shoot us, I don't think."

"They'll probably lock us up for a hundred years with Sister Godrick."

Moussa frowned. "Then I'd rather get shot, I guess," he said. "But look, we won't get caught. I know how to do it." He flung more rocks at the pigeon, which seemed to know just how far away from the boy was far enough, and spelled out his plans in detail. After he finished talking, Paul mulled it over. He suggested a few refinements, which were to Moussa's liking.

"*D'accord*," Paul said at last. He felt the butterflies that he always got when he was about to do something wrong and knew it. "Let's break him out."

They spent the afternoon getting ready. "We have to make a map," Moussa said, and even though they knew every inch of the route he drew one, which Paul laboriously colored with pencils. They went to the river to pick up their raft, and hid it in the woods. That night they hurried through dinner, and surprised Serena by going to bed early. "Big day tomorrow," Moussa told her vaguely. Henri was away in the city at the train station, finishing his preparations for a balloon launching the next day, and would not be home that night.

At ten o'clock the lights of the château had all been turned out. The house was quiet. They opened their bedroom window and crawled out onto the roof. They slid down the roof tiles to an inside ledge where they could catch hold of a branch and then climb down the tree to the ground. They'd left the house that way a hundred times.

At the base of the tree they stopped to make their final preparations. They dug up four knives they'd buried, two for each. "Hide the extra one in your boot in case we get captured," Moussa ordered. "They never look in your boots." Paul picked up a coil of rope they'd hidden behind a bush and draped it over his shoulder.

They were dressed in dark clothing that Moussa thought would make them harder to see. They knelt and rubbed their hands in a batch of mud they'd made and smeared it on their faces. Suddenly Moussa realized how much light Paul's hair reflected. "Spread some up there," he whispered, afraid his cousin's nearly white hair would give them away.

"I won't!" Paul protested. "It's too cold! Put some on your own hair!"

Moussa sighed and thought for a moment. "Wait here." Quickly he shinnied back up the tree and disappeared into the house. A little later he reappeared with two stocking hats that belonged to Gascon. "Put this on," he said.

There was still a light on in the carriage house, but no one about. The night was cool and cloudy. To the northeast they could see the new electric lights at Montmartre reflecting off the clouds. Somewhere dogs barked. A light breeze rustled the leaves in the trees and carried with it the smell of distant cook fires. Paul leaned against the tree and looked at Moussa. Standing still was giving him a chance to think. He was beginning to have second thoughts. Before he could say anything, Moussa signaled the all-clear. "*Tout est bien!*" he whispered. "Let's go!" Paul watched him running silently into the trees toward the Bois, and shook his head. He took a deep breath and plunged after his cousin into the darkness.

They passed along the edge of the Bois de Boulogne, where they gingerly made their way through masses of sleeping sheep. The stench was overpowering. Occasionally a startled sheep would bleat a complaint. They knew their way well, using tree stumps and hedges and ditches to mask their passage. There were occasional patrols of militia, but instead of patrolling, the men were gathered around small fires behind the newly constructed redoubts. Their heads were down in conversation, their hands clasping bottles of wine. It was a quiet night and the men were bored. The boys could hear their grumbling murmurs.

The first challenge of the night was to enter the city proper, which meant they had to get past the great wall that surrounded it. The means of their passage had generated most of the argument that day. Paul thought they should simply walk through one of the gates, for which they carried safe-passage cards, but Moussa rolled his eyes at the very thought of it. "We can't go through the *gate,*" he said. "*Merde,* this is a secret mission. What do we tell the guards? That we've come to help a prisoner escape? Besides, we have to have some way to get back *out* again, when we have your father."

Actually, no one would have questioned them at all at the gates, even at that hour. No curfew had yet been established and a great deal of foot traffic still passed back and forth at all hours of the day and night. Being questioned, however, was hardly the point. Moussa wanted their mission to have a certain flair; and one couldn't have the same kind of adventure strolling through a gate as one could have sneaking into the city under the very noses of its guards. It wasn't creative, or brave, or even very French to be so straightforward when subterfuge would serve so much better.

"I see what you mean," Paul finally agreed, although he grew more nervous and less enthusiastic about the plan with each step. Yet he wasn't a coward and couldn't stand the thought of Moussa's taunts if he refused to go through with it.

At the edge of the Bois they stopped at a culvert to pick up the secret transport they'd hidden earlier that day, their small wooden raft with two paddles. They had floated it many times on the river near the château. Their plan was to carry the boat to the Seine. There was a break in the city wall where the river passed through. They would put the raft in, paddle across in the shadow of the wall, and come ashore inside Paris on the left bank.

"It will be easy," Moussa promised.

"What about the water gates?" Paul asked. There were large gates that swung across the river to halt traffic.

"There's room at the edge. The raft is small enough. We can get around them."

The boys carried the raft and neared the base of the thick stone wall. It was awkward going. The wood bit into their hands while the bushes scratched their faces. They had to stop often to rest. They were careful to stay in the shadows, but had to cross two roads before reaching the river. They entered the first road too quickly and were nearly spotted by a patrol of Zouaves. They reversed their course hurriedly and disappeared back into the brush until the patrol passed. At the next one they were careful to wait, watching and listening until they were certain there was no one about. After they were clear of the road they hurried down the gentle slope toward the river. The wall towered high and dark above them. On its ramparts were more guards, ready for the Prussians with cannons, *mitrailleuses*, and rifles. At one of the bastions they could make out the face of a guard as he came to the end of the walkway and paused. They could see a small red glow from the cigarette he was smoking. He threw it into the water, and they watched its long lazy descent. After a while the guard turned and disappeared. Across the river in the opposing bastion they could see other guards.

"They're paying more attention than the guards in the Bois," Paul whispered.

"I know." Moussa nodded excitedly. He was highly pleased with their mission so far. The city was an armed camp, and they were about to foil its defenses. "Be quiet. Let's go!"

Together they slipped the boat into the slow-moving water and crawled on board. They made barely a splash, but to Paul it sounded like thunder and trumpets. He was certain that every noise they made would be their last, and that the next noise he heard would be a rifle fired at them. He wondered what a bullet felt like. Then a terrible thought occurred to him. His whisper to Moussa was louder than he intended it to be.

"Do you think we might look like Prussians in the dark?"

"Paddle!" Moussa hissed, and Paul hastily picked up his paddle and started working on the water, careful not to stir it any more than necessary. They had to go upstream, but the current was gentle. They were at home on the water, and Paul's nervousness faded as he concentrated on the task at hand. They were midway across the river and passing the plane of the wall itself when he looked up. He saw the bright flare of a match that illuminated the face of the guard high above them. Unconsciously he tried to become part of the bottom of the boat. It seemed impossible that he could see the guard so clearly, and that the guard couldn't see him. Paul had no idea why he'd agreed to this crazy stunt, especially since it must be done in the dark. He *hated* the dark, always had, hated its terrors and its mysteries, hated it when Moussa used it to scare him, hated it when he heard things in it, hated the things he imagined. Now it was their shelter, but it was awful shelter, and it was too late to go back. He promised himself he'd kiss a girl before he'd listen to one of Moussa's half-witted ideas again. He closed his eyes and said a silent prayer for invisibility and paddled softly along.

Suddenly, Moussa accidentally slapped the water with his paddle. Paul caught his breath. "Shhhhhh!"

"I know, I know," Moussa whispered. They had both stopped paddling for a moment, and their raft began to turn and float downstream again. "We're drifting! Keep paddling!" They dug their paddles into the water again, but Paul had shifted his attention, up to where he had seen the guard. Absently he started paddling the wrong direction, making the raft turn in a circle. "Not that way," Moussa hissed. "Go the other way!" Hurriedly Paul corrected himself, and once again the boat turned in the right direction. His palms were wet with perspiration. He wondered how they could be so wet when his mouth was so dry. He hated the feeling, and wished he were home.

The boys worked softly, steadily. The little raft moved upstream.

Up on his post, a National Guardsman waited. Marcel Julienne was a forty-four-year-old blacksmith. He had been a soldier for six days, and on the ramparts for five. He blessed his luck at drawing guard duty on the wall. He could stay warm, and the solid earthwork and stone of the wall offered a lot of protection in the event the Hun actually tried to do something. Officers rarely showed up to check on them after dark, for after all, officers had better things to do than worry about an invasion everyone knew wasn't coming. Yet Marcel was never overly casual. Even if no one else expected the Prussians to come pouring over the walls, he didn't want to be surprised by a bayonet in the belly. Every so often he actually drew himself to his feet and shouldered his rifle and wandered off to the edge of the rampart to have a look.

Paris was eerily dark for a Saturday night, her windows all blacked out for the siege. Away from the city he could make out the outline of the fort at Issy, a glow of new electric lights on its far side. All the forts around Paris had them. Beyond Issy there were Prussian watch fires, too distant to make out anything other than the fiery glow. Below him the river was dark and quiet and full of shadows. He was tired. He rubbed his eyes and shifted his musket to his other shoulder. He lit a cigarette, waiting just an instant too long to close his eyes before the match flared. For a few moments he was blind to the night. It didn't matter. There was nothing to see anyway. As he was throwing the match away he stopped abruptly. He thought he heard something, and listened. The city was quiet behind him, the clouds acting like a great muffler. It sounded like something splashing in the water below him.

Marcel unshouldered his weapon and leaned over the edge of the wall. He couldn't see clearly. There were still bright spots in his eyes from the fire of the match. He took his cigarette out of his mouth and set it on the wall next to him, to keep the smoke from bothering him. He strained forward once again, cocking his head a little sideways, and listened. His finger found the trigger. He stood perfectly still. He was certain there was something.

Another guard walked up behind him. "*Qu'est-ce qu'il y a?* Do you see something?"

Marcel raised his hand in caution. The guard fell silent and listened. He peered downstream, to where the river separated and made an island. He could make out the faint outline of its shore, and a stand of trees. His eyes ranged along the dark clumps of bushes near the shoreline closer to the wall, and along the roadways visible from their post. The river was inky black beneath them. The night was alive with a thousand shadows, and some of them made noise. But none of the shadows, he felt certain, were Prussian troops.

"Come on," the guard said irritably. "It's nothing. You're holding up the game."

Reluctantly Marcel nodded. He had been so sure. He shouldered his musket once again. He opened his jacket for the flask of brandy and took a deep drink. They walked back to the card game. It would be a long night.

Below him on the water the boys were just beginning to make out the murky outline of the water gates. The raft moved steadily forward. As they drew nearer Moussa began to discern something that didn't look right. He slowed his paddling, and Paul followed suit. "What's that?" Moussa whispered. Ahead, just in front of the gates, there were dark bulky objects floating in the water. They were indistinct, big, nothing more than shadowy phantoms. Smokestacks loomed above them, bobbing slightly on the river, and then they could see what looked like cannon in one end. As they drew closer they began to see the scattered forms of men. Moussa's heart froze as the dark shapes took form in the darkness and he realized what they were.

"*Gunboats!*" There was a small flotilla of them, all tied together to form a boom on the water in front of the gates. They had not been there before, but had been brought in to defend against an enemy approach on the water. The boys were almost upon them by the time they realized what they were.

"Quick! Turn around!" Paul said. In his panic he forgot to whisper, and his voice carried across the water.

"*Qu'est-ce que c'est?*" From one of the boats a deep voice rang out, its stern authority plunging cold fear into the boys. A sailor jumped up and looked out across the water. Instinctively Paul and Moussa hunched down and started to paddle as quickly but quietly as they could, turning their raft back the other way. The sailor heard the noise they made quite clearly, but saw nothing.

"Who is there? Identify yourselves!" he demanded. Others stood to look. The voices floated over the little craft as it moved away from them in its quickening flight downstream. "Craft in the water!" came a shout. "Fire the engines!" came another. "Man the guns!" The gunboats came alive with sailors who had been asleep in them. The boys paddled madly, listening in dread to the commotion growing behind them, abandoning caution and paddling harder, ever more furiously as the noise of the alarm drowned out the sounds of their passage. There were metallic noises and the clank of tools from the boats as sailors scrambled to start the engines. Firing the boilers to full steam was a slow process, and the crews wasted no time. No one knew exactly what was out there, whether it might be a sneak attack by the Prussians or Bismarck himself on a night cruise up the Seine.

A bosun roused from a deep sleep quickly realized that the steam engines would take too long to fire up, and determined to make chase immediately. He led five men in an awkward dance over the tops of the gunboats. They made their way to one of the iron-plated shallops, a small open boat with long oars and a single gun. They would row after the intruder. The shallop was moored between two of the gunboats, poorly positioned for a quick departure. The bosun shouted orders as the sailors worked furiously to free it. "Cast off that line," he roared in frustration as one of the sailors fumbled with a rope. They were wasting precious time.

"*Faites vite!* Quickly! Quickly!"

With barely controlled panic fueling their arms, Paul and Moussa were paddling as fast as they could move, terrified by the explosion of activity behind them. "Are they chasing us?" Moussa asked. Paul looked around. He couldn't see anything on the water, and wasn't about to wait and look. "I can't tell," he puffed. Paul's face was dripping, splashed each time Moussa lifted his paddle from the water. Their arms were aching from the effort. They were just passing the wall of the city, the raft moving rapidly as it passed into the open water.

Marcel Julienne was sitting at the card game with a good hand when he heard the shouting. So there *was* something after all! Without a word he picked up his musket and ran back to his post at the edge of the rampart, where he could get a view of the water and the gunboats. The other guards threw down their cards and ran to their own posts. "Is it a general attack?" one asked nervously. A night assault was something they all feared.

Marcel saw sailors moving around on the gunboats, their forms backlit by the fires awakening the boilers. He couldn't make out what was happening, except that there was a commotion. Something was out there. His eyes began searching the water, methodically passing back and forth from the near bank to the far one, his search starting at the gunboats and moving back downriver. Without diverting his eyes he unslung the musket from his shoulder and nestled it under his left arm.

I'm going to bag a Hun! he told himself, too excited to be afraid. He felt his pulse quickening, the effects of the brandy washing away in the excitement. His eyes moved systematically, quickly. Damn! Nothing but darkness! He stared again at the gunboats. A few lanterns had been lit on their decks as the crews worked furiously. He could make out a shallop as it moved away from the group, its long oars like fine wings waving from its sides as the crew maneuvered into position. There was a shrill whistle, and more shouting.

Cold black water from the river splashed over the front of the raft as Moussa dipped and leaned and leaned and dipped, pulling with all his might. He could feel Paul in the back doing the same, the raft bobbing slightly against their movements. They were making great time, he knew. The noise behind them was terrifying in its effect. All hell was breaking loose as the whole of Paris seemed to be awakening and coming after them. Moussa didn't want to imagine the trouble they were going to be in, the look on his father's face when the militia dragged them home to the château. *We have to get away!* He pushed the thoughts out of his mind. There was no time for thinking, no time for anything, just flight down the river, exhilarating and horrifying at the same time, his body flushed with adrenaline, his mind fixed on the rhythm of his motion, no time to look left or right or anywhere but straight ahead, downstream. He kept to the middle, not wanting to chance heading for either shore too close to the wall. There would be men on foot or maybe even horseback out there, looking for them. There was an island in the middle of the stream not far ahead. He would steer them there. Dip, lean, dip, lean; the boys paddled with all their might.

Marcel searched the river a section at a time, letting his eyes adjust each time he moved them, his every sense alert. He desperately wanted a cigarette, but dared not take his eyes from the water. *Where are the bastards?* He fidgeted with his musket, wondering if it would fire properly when he needed it. Sometimes they didn't, and blew up in the faces of the men firing them. He wished he had one of the new Chassepots, instead of the old *tabatière*. And then he saw a movement in the water and held perfectly still. What was it? A wave? A log? His eyes ached as he sought a focus. He rubbed them, but it was too dark. The water was full of tricks from his angle. Everywhere he looked there was something; everywhere he looked there was nothing. But there it was again! It moved!

"*Oui!*" he shouted, to no one in particular. He raised his weapon and shouldered it, supporting himself on his elbows as he leaned out on the parapet wall. He took aim at the spot, blinking to clear his eyes of the liquor and the smoke. He felt the hair tingling on the back of his neck, and squeezed the trigger.

The bullet zinged into the water next to the raft. Both boys heard it, but neither realized what it was until an instant later when the rifle shot registered.

"Moussa, they're *shooting* at us!" Paul croaked, his throat so constricted from fear that he almost couldn't speak. The realization was stunning, the fright crushing his chest so that it was hard to breathe.

"Go faster!" Moussa said. "We've got to get out of range!"

"No, let's tell them—!"

Before he could finish Marcel had reloaded and fired again. The bullet was closer than the first one. Its sound shook Paul with the terrible understanding that their harmless adventure had gotten all twisted and turned deadly, that behind and above them were soldiers determined to find and obliterate the occupants of the little boat. *They don't know we're just boys,* Paul thought. *They don't know we're not Prussians.* His heart was going wild. He closed his eyes and felt himself peeing in his pants. *No one knows we're just kidding.*

"Shut up and paddle!" Moussa hissed, and the little boat fairly flew down the water as they pulled for their lives. In the distance they could make out the dim silhouette of the island looming out of the river. Far behind them, on the other side of the city wall, they heard the *chunk-chunk* of one of the gunboat engines as it steamed at last into life.

For a mile up and down the wall, the alert was confused but gathering momentum. Lanterns went out and guards raced to their posts. Soldiers in the bastions hailed others down the line. Men shouted orders into the night as the drowsy and half-drunk garrison sprang into action. There had been no drills, so few of the men knew what to do but to run half-panicked to the edge of the wall and peer into the night at the unseen enemy. "What's the trouble?" they asked each other uncertainly. No one knew anything except that *something* was going on. Gun barrels poked uncertainly at the blackness as hundreds of eyes strained to see.

On the ramparts near Marcel two other guards came racing up after the first shot to see what was happening. "Down there!" Marcel shouted as they drew near.

"Where?" one asked. "I don't see a thing!" Marcel himself was still firing more at a suspicion than at a clear target, but he knew the position of his suspicion, and pointed. "*Voilà!* There, you see? In the middle!" His tone of certainty removed all doubt in the others, who aimed their weapons in the general direction where he pointed, and fired. A moment later they fired again. Then they stopped and listened, to see whether their fire would be returned. "Do you see anything?" one asked. Marcel shook his head. He cursed the blasted muskets they used. They probably couldn't hit the river with them, much less something on it. Below their position the nose of the shallop pulled past the wall, its crew straining at the oars, its dim form heading swiftly downstream in pursuit of the intruders.

"Hold fire!" shouted the bosun from the shallop. Just as he spoke more gunfire erupted and drowned him out. He waited until the shots died away and then tried again. "Hold fire!" he shouted up at the wall. "Shallop in the water, making chase! Hold, I say!" He listened for a response. He heard nothing and shook his head in disgust at the trigger-happy green troops on the wall. "Ship your oars," he ordered, "else we'll be taking shot from our own troops!" His men needed no persuasion and quickly pulled their oars from the water.

The first fusillade from Marcel and his two companions was the last as far as Moussa and Paul were concerned. The bullets splashed wildly around them in the water. If they stayed where they were they would be hit. They both had the thought at the same time.

Jump!

They flung their paddles aside and dove overboard just as the second round was fired from the ramparts. A bullet smacked into the raft, sending splinters of wood flying. One splinter caught Paul in the cheek as he went over the side. Moussa felt a violent tug on his shirt. The next instant he was swallowed by the cold wet blackness. The splash of their entry into the water was lost in the pandemonium of the city's defenses. Gunboat engines turned over and men shouted on the wall. Volleys of gunfire all ran together, shattering the quiet of the night.

After the firing stopped, the crew of the shallop set out again. The muscular sailors pulled at the oars as the boat glided downstream. The bosun crouched in front, staying as close to the bottom as possible so that the light armor on the side of the boat might protect him from enemy fire. He held a pistol, and his eyes were alert for surprises. No one had actually seen anything, so no one knew exactly what they were looking for. At the rear sat the gunner, his weapon at the ready. Behind them the first gunboat was passing the wall. Two others were almost at steam, ready to join in the chase. The shallop was still well out front, slicing through the blackness. For long moments it hunted alone in the dark water. On the shore toward Billancourt horsemen raced along the soft turf near the river's edge, alerted by the disturbance at the wall. A huge electric light flared on in the distance at the fort at Issy, much too far away to do any good.

For the next two hours the defensive forces of the republic were on full alert on the southwest edge of Paris. Seven hundred men on the walls commanded fourteen cannons and a *mitrailleuse* and scores of Chassepots as they waited and looked and listened, every man itching to fire on the cursed Prussians.

The shallop passed once around the islands near Billancourt, then worked back upstream on the other side, patiently searching. At one point, it passed within a few meters of the little raft, empty except for a coil of rope. No one saw the raft as it floated along with the current.

Two hours after the first shots were fired the major in charge of the guards on the wall appeared at last. "It was at least three boats, Major," Marcel reported, "full of Prussians. I seen them clearly, their faces all black. They must have had explosives. Must have been trying to blow the gate for a larger attack!" The other guards chimed in. "That's right, Major! Bastards cut and ran when we fired at them."

Five hundred meters downstream, the bastards in question had dragged themselves up onto the island in the middle of the stream. They were exhausted and deathly afraid, and lay in the low, thick bushes along the shore. They watched as the shallop went by, and then the gunboats. Once some of the crew from one of the boats tramped around on their end of the island, searching mostly up in the trees. The boys held completely still, their chins mashed into the mud as they tried to keep from being seen. For more than an hour they heard the crews of the different boats calling back and forth, or hailing the horsemen ashore. It was, Moussa guessed, the most commotion he'd ever seen about anything, and it didn't die down much for a couple of hours. Terrified, they lay there without moving the whole time. They were both soaked and shivering, cold deep to the bone.

"You hurt?" Moussa whispered when they'd caught their breath.

"Just a scratch on my cheek," Paul replied. He was as low and miserable as he'd ever been, and still not over the fear. "I peed my pants, though. What about you?"

"I'm all right." Moussa was silent for a moment, thinking. He decided it was okay to admit it, but only to Paul. "I peed mine too."

"Good," Paul said. "That was a stupid plan."

Moussa nodded. Things hadn't gone exactly as he'd hoped. "I guess so."

They watched the river and their teeth chattered. A gunboat passed by, leaving a small wake that came at an angle and lapped at their arms. They waited until an hour before dawn. No night ever took so long to finish. When the activity died down a little they cut some branches with their knives and covered themselves against the cold. It didn't help much, but it felt good to move around a little. The defenses relaxed slowly. The boats disappeared toward their berths on the other side of the wall. The shore patrols stopped, and the area slipped back into silence. When they thought it was safe they slid back into the water and swam across. They made their way through the dying night back to the château. With relief they saw the house was still all dark. They climbed up the tree and back through the window into their bedroom. After the long night that seemed it would never end, the room felt warm and comfortable and safe. They had never been so glad to be home. They were both a mess. Their faces were scratched from the bushes, especially Paul's cheek where the splinter of wood had gouged it. They were too tired to think up a story just then, and would have to work on some serious fiction when they woke up.

"Look at that!" Moussa said as they were getting undressed. He held out his shirt for Paul to see. There was a neat hole under the right arm, and another near the left chest. One of the bullets had passed straight through the shirt, right to left, while he was diving into the water. The boys stared at the holes, wide-eyed. Moussa inspected himself again to be sure there weren't any surprise holes or anything. As he did he saw that the bullet had caught one corner of his amulet, nicking the leather.

Wearily they collapsed into bed. Paul was asleep the instant his head touched the pillow. Beneath the warmth of his covers Moussa held the amulet. He ran his finger over the edge and felt the nick. *It was lucky again,* he thought. His mother had told him it was blessed. Mostly he had believed her, but never as much as he did now. He closed his eyes and clutched it tightly, and saw himself going over the side of the raft in a hail of bullets. He had a last thought before exhaustion tugged him under.

It saved my life.

Outside their window roosters crowed and the sun came up and Paris was safe once again.

CHAPTER 10

As Henri predicted, Elisabeth eventually emerged from her room. She was ravenously hungry and weary of her mood, even if she could not shake it. Her tears were finished. She could be a very practical woman. She realized that she needed to find some alternatives, and the dark places of her melancholy held none. She had to face the realities. Jules was in prison, and did her more harm there than out of prison. If he could not be a marshal, at least he need not be a felon. She would busy herself with seeing him freed, and then rebuild her life. *Our lives,* she corrected herself, without much conviction.

But it was not the same Elisabeth who came out of the room. The bright canvas of their future that had once been so glorious had been painted over with the bleak colors of scandal and shame. Whatever might become of Jules, she knew deep down that her fairy tale had died. Its death took the sparkle from her eye and put a heaviness in her step. She was bitterly disappointed with the lack of sympathy and understanding shown her by Henri and Serena. She expected commiseration and shared tears; she expected *something*. Instead they were unfeeling and harsh. She was betrayed and alone.

A hairdresser and manicurist were summoned to the château to tend to her cosmetic needs, enabling her to venture once again into the salons of her peers. At one she encountered a friend who, blessedly, had not heard of Jules's arrest, or at least did not suggest an awareness of it. The woman chattered mindlessly about the current amusements to be enjoyed courtesy of the war. From a safe distance, she told Elisabeth, she had witnessed a battle at the village of Bagneux, applauding enthusiastically as the French troops advanced to test the Prussian lines, then moaning and declaiming in disgust at the subsequent if smartly executed French retreat. "Really, dear Elisabeth, it was grand opera at the city gates. How ever could you have missed it?"

Elisabeth was only half-listening. The time had come when she must see Jules. She dreaded it, but there was no choice. If she were to influence his release, she would have to apprise herself of his situation, and find out what she could about other officers of the Guard. Henri arranged everything for her visit.

Her mood sank as she approached the cold facade of the Ecole, then plummeted as she walked through the penal compound inside the courtyard. It took all her effort to keep her gaze forward and hold her head up as she passed between the rows of fenced-in prisoners. It was a smelly, vile gauntlet she walked. She felt their eyes undressing her, and heard their lewd invitations and disgusting suggestions. What distressed her most was not their crude lechery, for she expected that, but the mortifying thought that anyone might associate *her* with one of the prisoners. She kept her eyes forward and walked quickly and told herself that Henri would *have* to find a different entrance if she were to return.

There was one small blessing, she reflected: at least she wouldn't have to see Jules in public, in the common pens. Henri had seen to that, thank heavens. Jules had originally been confined outside, in the common pens with the others, but had since been moved inside the Ecole. His room was small, barren except for a cot and chamber pot. Henri had brought books that stood in a small pile next to the cot. It was not much, yet it was a vast improvement, and left Jules a measure of dignity he had not felt in a long while.

Jules was surprised to see her. The private who had escorted her smirked at the colonel and left the room, shutting the door and leaving them in privacy. Henri had seen to that too. Jules sprang to his feet and moved forward to greet her, for an instant almost losing his military restraint, his stiffness. The delight in his eyes was real, but she noticed that something was missing from them. The hell he had been through had stolen their stern fire. *He's a ghost of himself,* she thought. Her own smile was cold and tight, her manner restrained. She offered him her cheek, and pulled away as he tried to embrace her. Confused, he backed away.

"Elisabeth! Aren't you glad to see me? I thought you would be glad."

For a moment the actress in her was missing. She did not feel strong enough to sustain a deception. "How could anyone be glad of this?" She waved her hand and looked around. "I'm sorry, Jules, but how could *anyone* be normal here? It's so *appalling.*"

"I did not choose the room, Elisabeth," Jules said with a trace of sadness. "It is wonderful to see you, to know you are safe. I thought you weren't coming."

Elisabeth sat down on the cot. The little lies still came easily. "I have been so busy, Jules," she said. "The theaters are being converted into hospitals, and they need *so* much. I've been helping them."

He nodded. "It was the right thing for you to do, of course. You have always been so giving of yourself." They talked of Paul and traded small talk, avoiding the war, the siege, and the arrest. When she didn't ask he finally volunteered the story of what had happened. He recounted it in detail, leaving out nothing except the humiliations he had suffered in captivity. She listened in silence, stunned by the unfairness of it all. His tale brought back all the disgrace, the grief, and her mood descended into blackness once again.

She stood when he finished, and paced the little room. "Oh Jules," she said, "I am so *fearfully* unhappy. How could you let this happen?"

"How could *I?*"

"I love you. I have always loved you. But I must tell you that this is so . . . so low. I am so disappointed, so *terribly* disappointed. Wasn't there a time you could have done the honorable thing out there? Wasn't there a time you could have . . ." Her voice trailed off.

Stunned, he stepped back. "You would rather I died?"

"Wouldn't *you?*" Her wail was from the heart. "Wouldn't you, Jules? Do you prefer this to death? Do you, really?"

"My God, Elisabeth, what I *prefer* is to clear my name."

"Don't you see? That's just it. Our name will never be clear again. Even if they let you out—"

"*If?*"

"All right, you know what I mean. *When* they let you out, your name will be destroyed. People will believe the worst!"

"To the devil with what they believe! What matters is that the truth be told. I did not do this thing!"

"Jules, you're such a simple man. You see things so clearly that aren't clear at all. The truth doesn't matter! It doesn't matter whether you did what they say or not. Everyone *thinks* you did it! Don't you see that? Don't you see that this has ruined us?"

"I—" Jules looked at his wife, and saw a complete stranger. "My God," he said sadly. "I don't . . . I cannot believe . . ." He couldn't stand any longer, and sat down heavily on the cot. He had never felt so weary. There seemed to be no end to this tunnel of his. No light, only more darkness and surprise. Everything felt so heavy and confused. He put his head in his hands and closed his eyes.

Elisabeth looked at him with sad condescension. She actually felt sorry for him. He really didn't understand. She moaned, hating the ugliness and the shame. "Oh Jules," she wept, "I'm sorry, I didn't mean it, I'm so confused, it's all so unfair, I don't know what I mean anymore, or what I want. I—I just don't *know*." Her voice dropped, and she sagged against the wall. "I only wonder whether death would not have been better than dishonor."

Jules could not answer. If he hadn't known exactly what to expect from Elisabeth, he hadn't expected this. He realized that he didn't know his wife, didn't know her at all, and it shocked him into silence. He had never paid as much attention to her as he ought to. He knew it, and regretted it. The Guard had always come first. He had always been so busy. Their lives together were perfunctory. He gave her position and security. She gave him her body, and was the mother of his son. Was that all? Was it really that empty? He wondered whether love was a part of it, whether it had ever been, or whether it was simply show between them, a slow empty dance.

Now he did not know what to say to his own wife.

Better death than dishonor.

He had said it himself before. He had said it to his troops. And now the word *honor* had gotten all fuzzy in his mind and he didn't know what it meant anymore.

Everything I touched is dead. The woman, her child, my troops. The private, young Etienne.

And now us.

Now we are dead too.

I t was kind of you to see me, Your Grace."
Elisabeth knelt before him and kissed his ring, and took the chair he indicated. The chair was velvet and soft, like the palace, a quiet island of peace in a mad place. She found herself in his palace because she had nowhere else to go, and because in the end it was the best place to be. Bernard Delacroix, the general with whom she had slept to seal a bargain of favor for Jules, was dead, slaughtered at Flöing with his cavalry division. She greeted the news of his death with indifference, except for a sense of waste. He had never seemed the sort of general who would die with his troops. *Such a pity*, she reflected. *All that effort lost with an old man on a battlefield.* There were others she knew, men of prestige, but they too were gone, dead or missing or in Belgium. No one was left to help, and there was no time

to build new alliances. The war was so maddeningly disruptive. As she had asked questions and sought her way, the subtle signs kept pointing to the bishop of Boulogne-Billancourt. He was everywhere, on committees for defense and committees for provisions, and it was said that he bought and sold men like cattle. The tentacles of his influence ran deep with the generals and politicians. His power ran far beyond the realm of the Church.

So Elisabeth came to him in desperation, to strike a bargain for Jules's freedom. She did it with no idea what she might use to buy what she wanted. She had no illusions about the bishop's charitable nature, and little money with which to improve it. There were rumors about his sexual appetites, rumors that, as she looked across the room at him, she hoped were not true.

"What can an old bishop do for you, my child?" he said. His smile was fixed, the expression in his icy gray eyes impenetrable. *I know those eyes,* she thought. She was afraid of him, and knew instinctively that the stories of the bishop's abilities were true. *I have come to the right man.*

"I need your help to free my husband from prison, Your Grace. He is a colonel, Jules deVries. He has been accused of desertion. Falsely, of course."

"Of course," Murat said. "I have heard of the case. Most unfortunate. But I am afraid you presume a great deal, madam. I am a bishop, not a general. I will remember him in my prayers. But beyond that, what can I do?"

"You are too modest, Eminence. I have spoken with officers who regret in these times that they are generals and not bishops," she said, smiling. She leaned forward. "They believe you can do a great deal in my husband's case, Eminence. A great deal."

"They have had more than their share of troubles with the Prussians, it is true," the bishop acknowledged, "but I fear they underestimate the Church's own difficulties. The war has caused so much upheaval. Nothing works as it once did. Men have turned away from God's

peace to pursue the devils of war. Nevertheless, it is true
that with the help of the Almighty I have tried in my
own small way to be useful to those in need. Madame
deVries"—he looked at her with a knowing eye. He
knew of her liaisons with the late General Delacroix,
whose discretion had never been complete—"I know
that you are a woman of intelligence. You have not
come here without something quite specific in mind.
What is it exactly you wish of me?"

Elisabeth did not hedge. "General Trochu will be ap-
pointing a panel for a court-martial. I have learned that
he will do this within a fortnight. There are three men
who I believe would look favorably—fairly, that is—
upon my husband's situation." She named them. The
bishop nodded. He knew them all. Elisabeth continued.
"It would be . . . useful to have them selected as the
panel for the court-martial, Your Grace. And once appointed it would be—how should I say it—most fortunate if they . . ."

"—knew which was the just and proper path," he
finished for her. "Of course. I understand." A simple
business.

Murat rang a bell and a male servant appeared. "I
will have brandy," he said curtly. "Would you care for a
refreshment?" he asked Elisabeth.

"Thank you, Eminence, perhaps I will join you." The
servant disappeared and quickly returned with a crystal
decanter. Murat dismissed him with a wave, and poured
a glass for Elisabeth. She took a small sip. She drank
rarely and the brandy burned her throat. The bishop
downed his in one swallow, and quickly poured more.
He turned to her and smiled, and Elisabeth braced herself. The delicate moment had arrived.

"It is not outside the realm of possibilities that I
might be of some use in your cause. Let us say for the
moment that I am willing to try. I do not believe you are
naïve in these matters. So let me simply say it is customary for those who come to pray in the cathedral to make
an offering to the Lord, in order that His servants might
carry on His good works. I must ask, madam, what it is
that this house of God might expect for your prayers?"

They said he was direct. Elisabeth flushed, and took a large swallow of brandy. It burned all the way to her chest. "Your Grace, I am afraid I have little to offer. I am not a woman of means. My husband was—is—a career officer who has been paid modestly for a life of service to his emperor and his country. What little I have, of course, is available." She saw him look away as if bored. "But perhaps Your Grace might suggest something—?" She wailed inwardly at her lack of resources. All these years, and she had nothing to give but *that*. The bishop rose and walked to the window. He was silent for a moment, and then he spoke.

"There is a thing, madam."

So now it comes, she thought, certain she knew what was coming next. *Men are men, whatever their uniform—only lust underneath.*

"Yes, Eminence?"

He turned to face her, and their eyes met. *Dear Lord, he is grotesque,* she thought. There were angry veins on his face and he was hugely fat. She thought of what it must be like underneath him, the sweat and the breath and the gropings of pushy jeweled hands. Bernard had at least kept himself fit.

"You still live with your brother-in-law, the count," the bishop said.

The unexpected direction took her by surprise. "Why yes, Your Grace."

"He has something of value to me."

Elisabeth shook her head. "I am afraid the count does not consult me in the matter of my own husband, Eminence. But if he has something you wish then I could certainly approach him—"

"It is not something he would give willingly," Murat interrupted sharply. His eyes were intense and held hers directly. "It is something that must be taken."

"*Je ne comprends pas.*" Elisabeth looked at him uncertainly. She had no idea where he was leading her.

Marius Murat had never forgotten the land that Henri had withdrawn, or the deep hatred he felt for the countess. The land didn't matter anymore, not financially. The emperor's outer boulevards had all been

built, and already had outlasted the emperor. The diocese had recovered from its monetary setback, which
had been serious but temporary. Murat wanted the land
because it would finish something unfinished. It was a
matter of his pride. Victory was an impulse, a habit that
required feeding as he himself did.

"You know where he keeps his papers. The important ones, I mean, for his holdings."

Elisabeth blinked. She had never paid much attention
to such matters. "I suppose so, Your Grace, but the
count has not—"

"Never mind the count. I want you to find certain of
those papers. I will tell you exactly which ones, what
they will say and look like. You will bring them to me."

"Your Grace, I—I don't quite know what to say,"
Elisabeth stammered. Taking papers from Henri—well,
it was wholly unexpected.

"Madam, let me be blunt. You wish your husband
freed, whatever the inconveniences of the facts in the
matter. I am perhaps more familiar with his circumstances than you might realize. I must say that his pros-
pects are not appealing. The military is in the hands of
rabble who cannot distinguish between a fine officer
and a corrupt one. The distinction is not one that will
assume much importance in their deliberations. It will
be the empire on trial, fueled by the despair of an inferior lot who have lost in the field to the Prussians. Justice has little bearing on these matters. You have asked
me to do a thing that can be done, God willing. But to
complete the task I must go to great lengths. General
Trochu himself cannot be approached directly. There
are back doors and side entrances to such a thing. It will
have to be done with great delicacy. These papers are
the only thing that interest me sufficiently to extend myself so. You must obtain them for me. I will see to certain changes in them, and then I will require you to
witness those changes, as the count's sister-in-law, so
that there can be no question later as to their authentic-
ity. There is a notary with whom I work most closely on
these matters, Monsieur Pascal. He will prepare every-

thing. That is how your husband will be saved, Madame deVries. That way and no other."

Her heart raced. To deceive Henri! To steal his papers, and after a forgery to witness them! Her signature, on paper! He would know everything. He would cast her out. It was too much. She could not do it.

"Your Eminence, it is impossible! The papers, *oui*, perhaps I could get them, but to sign something, to witness it as you suggest, would be evidence he would see! He would know! He would ruin me! I cannot do that, I cannot risk it!"

The bishop shrugged. "It is of little consequence to me, madam, if you cannot bring yourself to the task. It is a choice you must make. All of your choices are difficult. Do as I ask, and yes, you may forever incur the wrath of your brother-in-law. There are worse things, I suppose, that could befall you. Do nothing, and—well, your husband may pay with his life. I do not envy you your dilemma." He poured himself a fourth glass of brandy, and took it again at a swallow. He did not bother to offer her any.

"But I would have nothing left." She said it with a voice as empty as the prospect.

"You would have a husband."

Elisabeth's brain reeled. She didn't like it. The one certainty remaining in her life was her home. She would always have shelter and food for herself and Paul so long as the count considered her family. But to betray him, to do as the bishop asked? Sadly she shook her head.

"Eminence, I cannot. I must think of my son, of his support and future. The count—"

"There is something else." He knew what was in her mind. He could see it clearly, as he saw all things that people wanted, things that they would give and not give, things that they would do and not do, things that they must have in return. It was his gift to see them.

"Perhaps it will help you make up your mind. There is, of course, some considerable value in this transaction. Enough that I could assure you and your son an annual allowance from the proceeds. Assuming, of course, that you could deliver the papers I require, and that you sign everything as agreed. There would be no going back." As he anticipated, his words sparked a light in her eyes. He watched her carefully.

No going back, she thought. No chance to change her mind later. It would have to be substantial.

"Forgive me for asking, Eminence, but how much of an allowance would you be suggesting?"

"Four hundred thousand francs."

Elisabeth gasped inwardly. It was more than she and Jules had in ten years.

"You will guarantee this in writing?"

"Of course. With suitably vague reasons for the payment, naturally, but I will give it to you with the seal of the diocese so that my successors are bound by my act."

"The allowance will run forever?"

"For as long as you or your husband live," Murat replied, the brandy warming him and making him feel generous, "and half that amount for your son as long as he outlives you both." It was a pittance compared to the worth of the land, but it wasn't the money that drove him. It was the having.

Elisabeth weighed the offer. Never in her life had she done such a thing, but never in her life had she faced such a threat to everything she knew. Never had the stakes been so great for Jules. Once uncorked, her bottle of reasons for going through with it flowed like champagne. She told herself that it was for Jules, that it was best for Paul, that Henri could easily withstand such a setback, as his holdings were vast and this would make no difference, none whatever. She told herself that she deserved it, they all did, that she could do no less for her family. A last problem nagged. Jules would eventually find out. He would never countenance her action. But after the thunder and lightning of his discovery passed, after the storms of his fury had abated, what would be left? She had always been able to lead him where she wished. If she could not do it again, he would leave her and Paul. But she would still have the money, and the money would be her freedom. She and Jules would never be the same again anyway. *Would that be so bad, really? Can't the death of one dream give birth to another?*

And finally she knew her mind. She felt a great weight lifting, a burden that had not eased since the humiliations of Sedan. She leaned forward to the bishop, her eyes more alive than they had been in weeks.

"I believe I'll have another brandy, Your Grace."

Léon Gambetta is a horse's ass, Henri thought for the hundredth time. He'd known the man for years, and for years had found him pompous and full of himself. He was a lawyer-politician with a glass eye and golden tongue, flamboyant to the bone, and at the moment was minister of the interior, preparing to climb aboard a balloon. For all his dislike Henri wished him success. It was a moment of great drama for the country and the city, as Gambetta departed to raise an army to come to the relief of Paris. It was a long shot, Henri thought, but if anyone could do it, it would be the horse's ass Gambetta.

Henri had worked nonstop as one balloon after another took flight with the hearts and hopes of Parisians, who cheered the balloons and their aeronauts from every vantage point in the city. Count von Bismarck also watched them from Versailles and was infuriated. He ordered Krupp to make a special cannon to shoot them down, but the cannon was a failure and still the balloons flew, one every forty-eight hours or so, balloons that carried men and mail and carrier pigeons in little cages, to be released later from the provinces to fly messages back into Paris. It was the only way possible, for the Prussians had a virtual stranglehold on the city. For safety, the balloons started to fly at night, but they flew defiantly, a triumph of the French spirit.

The balloons suffered every fate, but most of the fates were kind. They were shot at by Uhlan troops who

chased them from the ground, but the bullets fell short.
They were lost at sea. They suffered sudden descents
and bad landings in trees. Some were dragged along the
ground, injuring the pilots. One carried photographic
equipment aloft that was used to record enemy positions on the ground, another dogs trained to return to
Paris with dispatches tied around their necks. The
occupants of nearly every balloon delightedly pissed on
upturned Prussian faces. One carried two boxes of dynamite for disposal on the Prussian lines, another opti-
cal equipment for studying a solar eclipse. From their
launching pads in Paris the balloons floated out to every
corner of Europe, once even crossing the North Sea to
Norway. A few balloons were captured, but most arrived safely, carrying hope and military secrets and the
messages of the besieged residents to their loved ones on
the outside.

Gambetta was a stout man. He wore a heavy coat
and fur-lined boots. He had some difficulty getting into
the wicker basket, but the gift of making it look easy to
those watching. The mood in the Place St.-Pierre in
Montmartre was festive. Large crowds had gathered to
see the minister off. The flight had been delayed for two
days because the winds weren't right. Now two small
trial balloons had gone up, and conditions were perfect.
Henri was talking with the pilot Trichet, giving him
last-minute instructions. "Don't worry," Henri said,
motioning toward Gambetta, "if you run short of lift
the minister's got gas enough to get you all the way to
Tours." Gambetta roared with laughter, and the pilot
joined in uncertainly. The minister could poke fun at
himself as easily as the next man, and for that at least he
had Henri's respect. "Well said, Count," he beamed,
"but don't tell him what to do if he needs to lose ballast."

Henri smiled. "I wouldn't dream of it, Minister, but
he's a good pilot. He may think of it himself. Godspeed
to you. Bring us back an army."

"That I will, deVries, that I will."

The ropes were cast off and the great yellow balloon
soared up above the crowd. Ever the showman,

Gambetta waved his sealskin cap to the throngs below, and unfurled the tricolor.

"*Vive la France,*" he roared, his voice triumphant.

"*Vive la république!*" they roared back, and Gambetta was gone.

THAT NIGHT AFTER DINNER, AN EXHAUSTED HENRI sat outside the château on the large porch swing with Serena. Elisabeth was away in the city. Paul and Moussa had been conducting frog races on the lawn. Paul's frog had won seven times straight and he had emptied Moussa's pockets of every marble and sou. Eventually, the boys tired and climbed onto the porch. They sat with their backs against the railing and drew up their knees and watched the sky, and traded stories about great frogs they had known.

The October evening was unseasonably warm and humid. A massive bank of white clouds had gathered during the afternoon, large thunderheads that puffed and billowed like cotton and towered as high as the eye could see, so luminous that not even the approach of darkness could swallow them. The setting sun had suffused them with deep crimson that faded to soft pink and finally to purple. As night fell the clouds suddenly came to life once again, streaked through with bright flashes of yellow and red. At first no one could make out what it was, but then it dawned on Henri. "It's the light of cannon fire," he said.

It was beautiful and looked eerily like a dry lightning storm of summer, only there was color and no sound and they knew they were witnessing the awful distant flicker of death. Every so often one of the windows would rattle in the carriage house. The horses whinnied nervously in the stables.

"Do the Tuareg have sieges like us, or just plain battles?" Moussa asked his mother after one spectacular flash.

"Most often battles. But there was a siege, once, a very famous one."

"Tell us!"

"Surely you've had enough of sieges and war. There is so much trouble in the world. Wouldn't you rather hear the story about Tahat, the mountain that—"

"Yecchh." Moussa grimaced. "Not another love story, Maman. We've heard that one already. We want to hear about the siege." Paul nodded his agreement.

Serena looked at Henri. His head had slipped onto her shoulder and his eyes were closed. She did her best to cover him with her shawl without disturbing him. "Very well," she said with a sigh, "I'll tell you the tale of Tashmani, a boy who saved his people. He lived long ago in the Hoggar, the desert mountains where I grew up. Tashmani was a Targui of the Kel Rela, the noble house of the Tuareg to which Moussa and I were both born. Even when he was very young he proved himself to be a skilled hunter who knew how to trap hares and even gazelles. Like all young boys he was impatient to grow up. He longed to go out with the men, to guide and protect the great caravans of gold and salt and slaves that passed through his land, and one day to make his sword famous in battle. But every Tuareg boy, no matter how nobly born, must first learn to care for the goats and camels that belong to his tribe. So Tashmani would spend all day in the mountains where his goats could graze. Often he would stay out all night too, for to live with only the stars for a roof is to be Tuareg, and to be Tuareg is to be free, and that is what Tashmani valued most of all."

Moussa was intrigued. "Is that all a Targui has to do, is go out and watch some animals? Doesn't he have to go to school?"

"The Sahara is a land of many lessons. A boy studies the world around him."

"But there aren't any teachers?"

"The women all teach, and so does the marabout, sometimes."

"Isn't he like a man nun?"

"Something like that."

"Not much of an improvement," Moussa grumped. "But I like the idea of watching goats better than sitting in a classroom all day."

"You would learn it is not easy, Moussa," Serena said, "just as Tashmani did. One day he fell asleep and a lion attacked his goats, and ate them."

"There are lions in the desert?" Paul asked.

"Not anymore, but there were then," Serena said. "You can still see pictures of them, drawn in the caves. Tashmani should have been more careful, but when he woke up and saw the lion, he ran away without trying to protect his goats. When he went back to camp to tell his elders, no one believed him. Lions were very rare and they all thought he had lost the goats to his own carelessness, which of course was partly true.

"Tashmani was very discouraged. His father told him that he would have only one more chance, and that if he lost any more goats he might never overcome the shame. Tashmani, as you can imagine, was worried that he would never wear the *tagelmust*."

"When does he get to wear the veil?" Moussa asked.

"Usually when he is sixteen, when he is thought to be a man."

"What does he wear before that?"

"Until he is a little younger than you he goes naked," Serena said, and the boys were appalled at the notion.

"After that," she continued, "nothing could keep Tashmani from his duty. He tended his goats very carefully. He practiced with his lance for hours, in case he might encounter another wild animal. He never slept until his goats were safe. For a long time he made no mistakes. But no one ever forgot the goats that he lost. A whole year passed, and Tashmani's head remained bare.

"Then one day he wandered far from camp, looking for pasture. He came to a high plateau where he'd never been. He was near a cave when he heard a horrible noise. When he went to look he saw the most frightening sight of his life. It was a beast, bigger than this house." The boys' eyes widened as she indicated the château.

"Tashmani crept silently as a breeze into a corner of the cave. He knew it was a tharben. He'd heard of them, of course, but no one among the Kel Rela had ever actually seen one. It was a reptile, like a giant lizard. Its eyes smoldered like the embers of a fire, and it had long tufts of soft hair growing on the back of its head. Its sides were layered with scales that glittered like jewels. On each of its feet there were six claws, curved like scimitars, only sharper. Its mouth held three rows of teeth, each as long as a dagger, and its tail was spiked like a cactus.

"The tharben didn't see Tashmani, who held deathly still as the creature crawled past him to the entrance of the cave. He saw it leap into the air like a bird. It sprouted wings from behind its front legs, and soared up and away into the sky, making a gust of wind as strong as a *simoom*. Tashmani was afraid to move.

"Before long the tharben returned, carrying four wild camels in its claws. To Tashmani's dismay he saw that the creature also clutched two of Tashmani's own goats, which in his fright he had left untended outside the cave. But by then it was too late. The tharben breathed fire, cooking the camels, which he ate whole, one by one. Tashmani's goats were dessert.

"Tashmani cowered in the shadows, afraid he might be next. When the tharben went to sleep he slipped away and raced home to tell his elders. But no one believed him. First a lion, and then a tharben—were there no bounds to his wild imagination? His father told him not to return until he found the goats he'd so foolishly let wander away.

"Tashmani returned to the cave, thinking the tharben might catch more goats and that somehow he might snatch them up and run before the tharben got to dessert. As he approached the cave he heard an awful shrieking, and then he saw that the tharben's wing had gotten caught between some rocks. Tashmani almost ran away, but he couldn't ignore the terrible cries. Bravely he took up his lance and stepped forward, to pry the wing free. The tharben roared and tried to catch him in its jaws, but then it saw he was only trying to help. Tashmani freed the wing, which was broken. The tharben could no longer fly, and without help it would starve. Knowing all the ways of the Tuareg to mend sick animals, Tashmani fashioned a splint from the branches of a tamarisk tree, and carefully bound the wing. While the tharben was mending Tashmani hunted for food, for lizards and hares and gazelles. In return the grateful creature promised not to eat him.

"When the tharben recovered the very first thing it did was to let Tashmani fly on its back while it tested its wing. Tashmani was thrilled to find himself flying above even the desert hawks. Later they went hunting together. Seeing that Tashmani was a shepherd with his own goats, and preferring the taste of wild goats anyway, the tharben agreed not only not to eat any more of Tashmani's goats, but to let them graze on its back, where a rich grass grew. And the tharben even gave Tashmani half of the wild goats it caught, so that Tashmani's herd might become stronger.

"All of this kept Tashmani from his home for many weeks. While he was away, the Shamba from the northern oases invaded the land of the Hoggar with a great army. Their numbers were too many for the people of the veil, who fought valiantly but found themselves overwhelmed. Finally the Tuareg were trapped on the slopes of a great mountain called Tararat. The Shamba soon realized they could never prevail with arms, so they surrounded the mountain, cutting off every route of escape.

"Of all the Tuareg only Tashmani had not been caught in the siege of Tararat, for, of course, he was still away. With the tharben fully healed and his herd of goats stronger than ever, Tashmani proudly returned to camp to tell his father the wonderful news. When he found the camp deserted and realized the terrible dilemma of the Kel Rela, what do you think Tashmani did?"

Moussa snorted. "I would have gone to the city to buy a *mitrailleuse.*"

Serena smiled. "There was no such thing in those days. And the people of the veil never fight with guns."

"I'd make a balloon out of camel skins and use it like Uncle Henri," Paul said. "I'd fly them out."

"That is almost exactly what Tashmani did," Serena

said, "only he didn't need a balloon at all. He raced back to the cave and told the tharben of his trouble. The tharben knelt down at once so that the boy could climb up. Holding his lance, Tashmani pointed the way. The tharben swept through the sky to Tararat, where the Tuareg and the Shamba were still fighting. Everyone feared the tharben, but when the people of the veil saw Tashmani on top they raised a great cheer. The tharben landed in their midst and one by one they climbed up. The Shamba could only watch, for the tharben kept them away with its tail.

"By then the tharben was quite hungry from its labors, so before soaring away it scooped up a score of Shamba for a snack. While flying the tharben breathed fire to cook them. It tried one but had never tasted anything so vile as a Shamba. So instead of swallowing the rest, the tharben spit them all out. They fell to the earth, where they landed in a petrified forest near In Salah. I have seen them myself. Their shocked faces still peer out at the sky, trapped forever within the stone.

"The disgraced Shamba retreated to their homes from Tararat, passing their fallen warriors on the way. Neither they nor any other tribe ever dared return to invade the enchanted land of the Hoggar, fearful of the spirits they might find there doing the bidding of the people of the veil.

"All over the Hoggar, the Tuareg wrote poems and sang songs about the brave boy who had saved his people. Tashmani acquired many camels and became a great warrior. He married Alisha, the descendant of Queen Tin Hinan, the first and most noble of all Tuareg women, and together they had many children. I am a descendant of Tashmani and Alisha, as are you, Moussa."

But Moussa was lost in thought, idly wondering how long it might take a tharben to cook a nun, and whether his family connections might be sufficient to get the job done.

Later that night, after the boys had gone to sleep, Henri looked wryly at his wife. "Are all Tuareg women so adaptable with their legends, or is it just you?" he asked.

"What do you mean?"

"You've told me the story of the tharben, only there wasn't any siege, and it didn't eat any Shamba. As I recall it had something to do with a whole caravan that disappeared over a woman's jealousy."

"I thought you were sleeping," she protested.

"I could never sleep through a tharben. I could use one just now, and a pilot like Tashmani."

"That was a different tharben," Serena said, her eyes twinkling. "Just for you. Besides, the boys didn't want to hear a love story."

CHAPTER 11

I T WAS THE DAY.

Paul awoke in the twilight before dawn and lay in his bed, staring at the ceiling. The room was quiet except for Moussa breathing heavily in the next bed, still dead to the world.

Paul felt good under the covers. All the world was at peace on this side of the bedroom window. But the butterflies were back, the ones that flew in to announce trouble or danger. Only this time they weren't for himself. They were for this day, for his father. It was the day he both prayed for and dreaded, the day his uncle told him to be patient for, the day that never seemed to arrive.

It was the day his father would stand before a court-martial. The day Paul was determined to see him at last. It was a Monday, and he was supposed to stay away from the trial and go to school. "The trial is not something for children," Henri had told him. "I will be there myself. I will tell you everything that happens exactly as it occurs. I promise." Paul had agreed, but his insides got all knotted up as he thought about it.

He had heard his aunt and uncle talking, late one night when they thought nobody was listening. But he was awake and heard them through the vent, and what they said filled him with dread. If things didn't go well for his father they might take him out and stand him by a wall and shoot him. Uncle Henri had said so. He'd said it twice. If Paul didn't quite understand how that could happen, he certainly understood what it meant.

And he wasn't about to let that happen while he was sitting in some lousy class staring at a nun. He never—well, almost never—directly disobeyed his uncle. There was just too much trouble when he did. But this was different. If it meant punishment, he would take it. He and Moussa had talked about it the night before. Usually it was Moussa who came up with the big ideas. This time it was Paul who forged ahead, daring to do the forbidden.

"I'm not going to school tomorrow," he announced. "You can if you want. I have to see what they're doing to my father."

Moussa thought it was a grand idea, one that required them both to be there. "But they probably won't let us in," he pointed out.

"We'll sneak in."

"They'll probably throw us out."

"So we'll sneak back in. I'll watch through a window, or listen from behind a door. I'm not missing this." Moussa's grin of adventure gave Paul another thought. "We're going into the city through the *gate* this time," he said in a tone of voice that meant no arguments. Moussa pretended to be disappointed.

Paul watched the dawn light slowly fill the room with another autumn day. When it was time he awoke Moussa. Acting as if everything were normal, they left at the regular time for school. The count was late himself, busy with paperwork. Paul was pretty sure he felt the count's eyes on his back from behind the window of the study as they disappeared down the lane toward St. Paul's. Moussa didn't seem to notice. They got to a junction in the road where they should have turned right, and turned left instead.

A month and a half of siege had dulled the sharp gay edge of Paris. People walked more slowly and talked more softly, and there was less laughter than before. Even the boys noticed something was different.

Long lines of people waited in front of the grocers they passed; food was getting scarce and expensive. The boys walked through the Champ de Mars, a huge

encampment filled with guardsmen who looked haggard
and hungover. The Ecole loomed huge across the com-
mons. Paul's heartbeat quickened when he saw it. They
were making their way quickly along the side of the
street, staying out of the path of carriage traffic when a
familiar voice froze them in their tracks.

"Have you forgotten the way to school, or do you
test my patience?" Paul's hair stood up on the back of
his neck. He flushed and looked sideways at Moussa,
who was studying the ground. The count never had to
raise his voice to sound angry, Paul thought. He knew
how to make you miserable without yelling, how to get
right inside of you with his voice of velvet thunder.
They turned to face him, and had to look up to see him.
The sun was behind him and it blinded them. He looked
as though he had a ring of fire around his head.

"It was my idea, Uncle Henri," Paul said quickly. "I
made Moussa come—"

"You have no mind of your own, Moussa? Your
cousin thinks for you now?"

"Yes . . . I mean, no sir," Moussa stammered. "I
couldn't let him come alone."

"He wasn't to come at all, and you knew it. You
heard us talking." Moussa nodded, red and ashamed. "I
thought we had an understanding," the count said to
Paul. "I take you at your word, as you must take me at
mine."

"I had to come, Uncle Henri," Paul said, and he
thought about it and remembered that he was right,
that he was sure, and he stood straighter and felt less
guilty. "I know I said something different yesterday. But
it wasn't enough to just hear. I have to see what
they do."

Henri looked down on the two anxious boys. They
fell mute, awaiting his judgment. He had known where
they were going from the moment he'd seen them leave
the house, just as he knew what he would do now. But
if he was to prevent anarchy in his household he had to
let them stew a bit in their broth of nerves and guilt.
Paul was fidgety, moving up and down on anxious feet.
Moussa's hands fiddled with twigs, but his expression

was a masterpiece of innocence. *He gets that face from his mother,* Henri thought fondly. *The guile is his own handiwork.*

"Climb in," he said at last. The boys scrambled into the carriage, which started forward at once. They still didn't know whether he'd keep going straight or turn around for St. Paul's. With the count it might go either way. Henri regarded them sternly. "I will get you inside. Keep absolutely quiet and stay out of the way. Understood?" Paul's eyes brightened, and a smile of triumph and relief crossed his face. He adored his uncle. The boys both nodded eagerly.

The carriage threaded its way through a throng of people and turned into the courtyard of the Ecole. A guard recognized the count and waved them along. As they made their way inside the building, Paul watched his uncle moving easily through the crowd. Whether people wore uniforms or not, the count was greeting them, shaking hands and chatting. He seemed to cause a stir everywhere he went. Some in the crowd stood apart from him and scowled, looks of hatred on their faces. They loathed his influence, his nobility, his money. But no one was indifferent to his passage. Paul felt a surge of pride that he was with a man so commanding, so sure, so significant. It made him feel big and important himself. It had to mean good things for his father. He saw the count hand one of the guards some folded-up money, and they were waved inside.

The court-martial was to be held in a makeshift courtroom with a high ceiling and windows that ran along the top of one side. There was a bare spot on the wall where a portrait of the emperor had been. A tricolor had been hung in its place, but was smaller and didn't cover the spot. The room had been chosen because of the large number of spectators expected, both military and civilian. It was the only room large enough. There was a long table at the front with three chairs, one in the center with a high back much larger than the others. Two smaller tables were set in front of the big one, with more seats. A podium stood to one side. Along the back of the room were scores of chairs and benches jammed close to one another for the audience. The civilian spectators were chosen by a lottery held in the courtyard. There were ten applicants for every seat. The boys watched as they streamed into the room, some noisy and rude, others quiet, others laughing, ready to enjoy themselves at the trial deVries, one of the few entertainments left in the city. "I wonder how come they're letting so many in," Paul whispered. He didn't like it, didn't like the press of people filling the room, didn't like the whiskers and jokes and rough manners and the smell of stale wine. He didn't like what he saw in their eyes. It was like they were coming to watch the elephants at the zoo, Castor and Pollux. Moussa felt it too. "It's like a carnival," he whispered.

Henri indicated two chairs at the back of the room. His look left no doubt that he expected to find them there next time he looked. This time they would obey. They sat down as the count moved forward to one of the tables at the front of the room. He started talking to two men wearing uniforms that Paul didn't recognize. Others came into the room, big men in other uniforms, uniforms that they didn't recognize, and those men took their places at the table opposite Henri. The one in the middle carried a stack of papers. He had a large Adam's apple and dark brooding eyes and a shock of unruly gray hair. Instinctively Paul didn't like him. *That one is the enemy.*

A door on one side of the room opened, and Paul's heart leapt with joy as his father came through. He looked pale and tired and not like himself, but he was still big and powerful and stood like a mountain in the boy's eyes. Jules's gaze swept the spectators and the officials, but he did not see his son. Ramrod-stiff, head high, he strode to his seat. At first his entry made the room fall silent, and then Paul heard the crowd beginning to stir to ugly life around him. *"Voilà le poltron! Traître!"* They reminded Paul of his classmates, when they dared to test authority: just loud enough for the words to be heard by all, but soft enough for their source not to be identified. Jules ignored them, and sat conversing with the count and the others at his table. The room was alive with a hundred conversations.

After a few moments another door opened and three men walked in, important-looking men, officers, and everyone stood. Paul and Moussa were unable to see over the crowd. They climbed up on the bench, but all they could see were bald heads and an occasional mustache up front. The day was a blur for Paul, who paid attention but couldn't understand a lot of what was going on. It started with the prosecutor, the man with the gray hair, who stood and read from a paper detailing the charges against his father. He said once again all the terrible things, using words like *treason* and *shame* and *cowardice*, and talked about the conduct of an officer and unfitness for duty and dereliction and desertion.

When Paul lost the meaning of the words he focused on the man and his mannerisms. He reminded Paul of a street performer he'd seen at the Place de la Concorde, a man who had a monkey and a flute and strutted back and forth and told stories and hooted and made fun of people in the audience. The prosecutor swaggered and glared, and pointed and stared. He stood next to Jules as he spoke and leaned down and put his face up close to the colonel's, and carried on in his voice of accusation, Paul fascinated and repelled by the man's bobbing Adam's apple as it punctuated his sentences. *"This sneak, this deserter . . ."* His voice droned on as a long finger indicted the colonel and waved in his face. Paul was astounded that anyone would have the guts to do that to his father. Didn't he *know* how that infuriated him, how that could get him knocked on his backside? Didn't he *know* he was addressing Colonel deVries?

The hateful words kept coming. " . . . *this wanton disregard for his men, leaving them to the Prussian sword . . ."* As Paul watched he prayed fervently that the prosecutor would have a stroke and drop dead right there on the floor, but instead the man produced a letter from an officer named Delescluze. It was evidently very important, because he read it twice out loud as he walked back and forth in front of the judges. The prosecutor's voice was slow and soft, but full of menace as he quoted from the letter.

" '. . . as to the character of his crime, as to the certainty that he abandoned his men and had fled the battle like a coward, there can be no doubt,' " the prosecutor said, halting after each word to give it emphasis.

"He reminds me of Sister Godrick," Moussa whispered glumly.

Paul jabbed him. *"Shhhh."*

The prosecutor's delivery was devastating, at least as far as Paul could tell. People strained to hear. They shook their heads and muttered among themselves, and had to be quieted four times by the judges. He saw eyes filled with hatred and vengeance, all fixed upon his father. Most of the time he watched his father's reactions as people spoke. Paul could tell if someone was lying just by watching his father's face, because that face had been turned toward *him* when he lied. The colonel had a nose for it and his punishments could be terrible. But for some reason in court he just sat there and listened.

Paul could tell when his father was upset, though, or when he was ready to explode in anger. He saw his eyes narrow and his skin color change, and his shoulders shift. *Why don't you say something,* Paul wanted to shout. *Tell them this is crazy, that it's all wrong!* But he didn't. He kept quiet like Uncle Henri said and sat on his hands and wished it would end soon.

He could tell it was trouble when the prosecutor produced a thick blue enrollment ledger from Vouziers. "It is clear from these documents," he said, "that Victor Delescluze is indeed a captain in the Irregulars, and that"—he held the letter up at eye level, and shook it with each word, as if they would hear him better or believe him more—*"this . . . is . . . his . . . signature.* No forgery. No mistake. Proof that his letter is genuine. . . ." There were more murmurs from the audience, more warnings from the judge for quiet.

The lawyers bickered about something. They did it all the time, with bad manners and big words. They couldn't agree about anything. One said yes, another said no. One said today, another said tomorrow. Paul didn't like any of them, not even the ones who were supposed to be working for his father. They just sat there and took it, the insults and the lies and all, and when they were done taking it they stood up and dished out some of their own. Paul wanted them to *do* something instead—to draw some swords and have at it, clear the air with a good fight that would leave some guts on the table and a head or two rolling around on the floor, but the bunch of them didn't seem up to it. Even Uncle Henri just sat there and listened to the ugly business.

The room was hot and smelly with perspiration and old tobacco. By late morning it was nearly unbearable, but the proceedings wore on. Another storm broke when the prosecutor called a witness he said he had not expected to locate, "owing to the unfortunate progress of the war."

"That's one way to put it," Moussa whispered, "when the Prussians are whipping our ass."

Paul recognized the uniform of a sergeant of the Dragoons on a towering man, full of power and presence, a cavalry officer who looked the absolute picture of French glory. His uniform was crisp and dazzling. He wore a red tunic with a white sash. There were scarlet epaulets on his shoulders and gold buttons at his sides, and shiny leather boots that rose almost to his knees. He removed his gold helmet and placed it under his arm, and stood at attention until the judge bade him come forward. All eyes were upon him as he walked to the front of the room. The prosecutor had him introduce himself. Paul could tell from his father's look that he was unhappy to see the sergeant.

The witness began to tell his story, and it was a story of damnation delivered with calm assurance. *Oui,* he told the prosecutor and the judges and the court full of people, it was he who had written the note on the back of the letter from Delescluze. *Oui,* he said, it was he who had observed the colonel trying to escape from his guard. *Oui,* he assured the court, this was the man—he pointed at Jules deVries, pointed with authority, without the slightest shred of doubt or hesitation—this was indeed the man, and he said it in a voice that was firm and rang with conviction and truth. *Oui,* the court heard, he had pulled this man off a hapless guard who was merely attempting to follow orders and do his duty and escort the prisoner to Châlons. *Oui,* he said, he had witnessed the assault from its beginning, had seen the colonel sneak up behind the guard and assault him viciously. *Oui,* he said, the colonel had admitted to him right there that he was trying to escape!

Oui, Paul heard, *oui* over and over, *yes* guilty, *yes* he did, *yes sir, yes yes* until he wanted to cover his ears and cry, wanted to jump up and smash the man in his stupid face, smash him until his filthy lying brains were spilled all over the floor. After a while Paul didn't listen to him anymore. He closed his eyes and shut him out. Moussa watched his cousin and saw a lone tear trickle down his cheek. There was nothing to say. He put his hand on Paul's shoulder.

The sergeant had just been excused when a major burst into the courtroom and rushed to the front. The newcomer whispered excitedly into the judge's ear. The judge went pale and raised his hand for order, to silence the room. Gravely he stood to address the court.

"An announcement has been made by the Government of National Defense," he said. He cleared his throat and the room fell silent, all eyes upon him. "Marshal Bazaine has surrendered his forces and the town of Metz to the Prussians," he said. "The marshal did so unconditionally, without a fight. The Prussians have entered the city. Our valiant troops are captive. This court is recessed for two hours. *Vive la république!*"

An uproar shook the room as all three judges left hurriedly. Angry spectators shouted passion and fire, hurling their outrage at everyone and no one. "The last perfidy of the empire! The coward!" one shouted. "Bring him to us! We'll show him how to surrender!" One man, an ancient figure sitting bent and alone on a bench, wept bitter tears. Guards began herding the spectators toward the door, and the courtroom emptied quickly. Paul had heard of Bazaine and had been to Metz once, but beyond that it didn't mean much to him except that he wondered miserably whether this was somehow more bad news for his father.

Jules conferred with Henri and then rose to be escorted out by a guard. As he stood he saw Paul for the first time and froze. Paul got to his feet. Father and son regarded each other across the room. Uncertainly at first, Paul walked toward him, and then in a flood of emotion fairly flew the last few feet, and banged into the colonel and hugged him hard round the waist. Jules was embarrassed. He looked to see if anyone was watching. No one but Moussa was paying attention. Jules permitted himself a pat on Paul's back.

"Father, Father!" Paul cried, and tears were pouring down his face, and he hugged him tightly, not wanting to let go, not even as Jules tried to pull him away, gently at first, then with greater firmness. "Paul, that's enough," he said. "Control yourself. This is a public courtroom." Paul looked up at him, half-crying, half-smiling. "I missed you, Father," he said. "I want so badly to help. I want to do something but I don't know what. I want to make them stop telling their lies. I want to make them let you go. I want to kill all the Prussians, and the guards and judges and the lawyers too. I want you to come home."

Jules was afraid to say anything for fear his voice would crack. He had never felt such a need for anyone as he did that moment for his son, but he didn't know what to do just then that wouldn't look . . . weak. So he did nothing, said nothing. Feeling hopelessly awkward, he could only nod. He motioned to Henri to come get Paul, to take him away. Henri put his hand on Paul's shoulder. "Come, Paul," he said gently.

"I'm not leaving," Paul said. "Don't make me leave, Father, please don't make me. I won't do it, I won't."

Jules sighed. He wished desperately that Paul hadn't come, that he didn't have to see any of this, that Elisabeth had had the grace and good sense to keep him away. But, of course, it was too late. "Very well," Jules nodded. "You may stay if you wish."

After Jules was gone the boys wandered around outside. Paul was suffused with happiness that he'd spoken to his father at last. Just touching him had made him feel better, made him feel that things would be all right. After a difficult morning his spirits soared. He and Moussa wandered through streets teeming with agitated people fired up about the news of the war, of which Metz had only been the most recent debacle. The government looked soft and inept, and Paris was smoldering, ready to catch fire from its own anger. Irate orators stood on boxes and raised hell before eager crowds. "We'll have a new government!" a man shouted from his pulpit to the cheers of the crowd. "The Commune forever!" Hats flew in the air and bayonets glistened, and people hugged each other and cried tears of joy. *Vive la Commune!*

Someone threw a rock at the speaker, but it missed and landed at Moussa's feet. He jumped back and looked at Paul. "It's like the day the empire fell," he said, and they scurried back to the École.

That afternoon the courtroom was sweltering. Paul's attention was riveted on the proceedings. He noticed every word, every sound and motion. It was his father's turn, he guessed, because the prosecutor had fallen silent for a change, and the witnesses were ones called by the lawyers sitting with Uncle Henri. And the witnesses were saying nice things.

"A fine officer, deVries," said a little man with a mustache whose name was Raspail. *He seems awfully small to be an officer,* Paul thought. *I'm as tall as he is. Well, almost.* Yet not only was the man an officer but a general. The prosecutor jumped up and complained about his uniform. "Out of order!" he cried. "There is no Imperial Guard anymore. This witness has no standing!" One of the judges told him to shut up and sit down, and Paul thought nothing finer had happened in the courtroom all day. After Raspail there were other officers, another colonel and then a major who said wonderful things, things about Italy and Africa and the service of France. It was heady stuff and Paul savored every word.

Near the end of the day Jules deVries himself rose and spoke to the court. Paul nudged Moussa to make certain he was listening as hard as he ought to be. *This will shut them up,* he knew. *There's no way they can doubt him now.* His father's voice was not loud but strong and firm, its tone captivating the room as no other voice had. It was a voice Paul had heard a thousand times, a voice that had told him to stop doing this, or to start doing that, a voice that invariably scolded or taught some lesson.

Paul listened raptly as the voice described what had happened since he left Paris on his way to the Prussian front. He told the story carefully, in great detail, missing nothing, from the look of the smoke over Châlons to the Uhlan patrol in the forest near Attigny to the position of the bodies in the farmhouse. He looked straight at the judges as he spoke, head erect, shoulders up, and to Paul he looked a million times better than the officer of the Dragoons. The stories he told were confusing, though. Instead of cavalry charges his father spoke of drunken soldiers. Instead of secret patrols there were French supplies put to the torch. Instead of great battles there were French soldiers, murdering women and children. It was all wrong, all mixed up. Paul didn't know what to make of it.

Paul saw that the judges listened carefully as his father spoke, all three of them leaning a little toward him and tilting their heads as if they might hear better. But the spectators paid no such attention. He could hear the jokes and the doubts and the mean things they said, undermining every word, every statement, laughing and shaking their heads and keeping up a steady murmur of distraction and disbelief. He glared at them. *This is my father speaking.*

"Delescluze took me prisoner when he realized I'd caught him in the act of murder," he heard his father say. "He was a twisted man. He wrote the letter for revenge against the empire. He did it drunk as we sat by a campfire. He wanted nothing more than to destroy my honor, and wrote the letter in the specific belief that the empire would fall at the hands of the Prussians, that this very trial would be the result. . . ."

He spoke for nearly an hour, and when he was done his voice was hoarse. "I am not guilty of these charges," Paul heard him say. "I am not a coward. I have told you the full truth about what I have done, and what has been done to me. I stand ready to fight for my country. I stand ready to die for her."

It was the best speech Paul had ever heard. He wanted to jump up and shout, but the words didn't seem to have the same effect on the others in the court-room, who hung far more intently on the closing words of the prosecutor.

"The whole history of France is covered with military glory," the prosecutor said. "For two centuries she has held Europe in her hands. It is impossible to consider that she should have fallen in the field so thoroughly without the duplicity, the treachery, and the desertion of key officers. We have seen it in Sedan, with the despicable acts of a man who pretended to be emperor, yet who then raised the white flag to the Hun. We have seen it in Metz this very day, behind the spineless actions of a *poltron* whom we cannot in good conscience call *Maréchal de France*. And then"—he stood once again before Jules and leaned down, his face within inches of the colonel's—"we have seen it in Jules deVries. In *this* man, we have seen the mighty spine of France crumble. For him there can be but one end. From you, honorable panel, the honor, the glory of France demands nothing less than a bullet to the brain of this most low and cunning coward."

The crowd erupted at that, exploded like nothing Paul had heard all day. The awful feeling of dread settled over him again, the one that brought the panic and the fear. He reminded himself it didn't matter what the audience thought. His uncle said it was the judges who made the decision. But he looked at the audience cheering, and he looked at the judges who allowed it, and his uncle's assurances didn't help. Didn't help at all.

When quiet returned there were others who spoke,

but it was too hot and too much and it all ran together in Paul's mind. In the end the judge in the middle spoke and said all the evidence had been heard and to come back in the morning for a decision.

Why do they need until morning? he wondered, but he stood when everyone else did, and then at last it was over for the day.

Regret to inform you Major Dupree killed at Flöing. Unable to locate balance of unit. No sign Delescluze. Still looking.

Blanqui

Henri received the note after court that afternoon. It had arrived in Paris three days earlier by pigeon post, and was contained with thousands of other microscopic messages on photographic paper. The authorities had taken several days to transcribe them all for delivery. Miraculously, it had finally made its way to the château. Henri's heart sank as he read it. He debated whether to give the message to his brother, or spare him the awful news. His chances were withering, or gone. Henri cursed himself.

The great Count deVries has tried everything, and it has all come to nothing.

He should have listened to Blanqui in the first place, when he suggested breaking Jules out. Now it might be too late.

He decided to give the note to Jules anyway. He couldn't lie to him. As he rode across Paris to deliver it he heard a chilling sound. It was the rhythmic drumming of the *rappel*, calling the National Guard to arms. A sound of tumult, of terror, a sound that had last been heard in the city during the Great Revolution, a sound that preceded death. In the afternoon and evening hours, the city had come to the precipice of a new insurrection. The blows of Metz and Le Bourget had been quickly followed by talk of an armistice with the Prussians. The government was considering the payment of a massive fine to end the war, and the cession of

the provinces of Alsace and Lorraine. A mob at the Hôtel de Ville had had enough of the government, and had
taken General Trochu and his ministers hostage. The
troops in the working-class district of Belleville were in
full mutiny. The Committee for Public Safety had declared the government finished, and proclaimed the establishment of the Commune. Loyalist troops waited in
the Place Vendôme for the order to quell the uprising.
The siege was less than two months old and Paris, as
Bismarck had prophesied, was already ripping at her
own throat.

In this atmosphere my brother awaits a verdict,
Henri thought grimly.

Jules read the note his brother handed him. He crumpled it and dropped it to the floor, nodding his head as
though he expected it. In the weeks of his confinement he
had listened as other soldiers were marched away from
the compound. He had heard the volleys of the firing
squads, and the prisoners did not return. The last one
had gone two days before. His thoughts were morbid.

"I heard drums before," Jules said at length.

"I'm afraid it's bad." Henri explained the situation
as best he knew it. "There may be civil war before it's
over. I don't know who will be running things in the
morning, or whether it will affect your trial. If it does, it
can only make things worse."

"I don't know how they could get worse. My God,
the Prussians outside the gates and now *le spectre rouge*
inside. I never would have believed that so much could
go wrong so quickly."

A rainstorm settled over the city and lasted through
the night. Jules listened to the steady downpour and
didn't sleep at all.

At the château Paul prayed alone in his bed, silent
prayers mingled with oaths and promises and declara-
tions. It was the first night he had ever spent in fear.

"You asleep?" he whispered to Moussa.

"No."

"You think they'll let him go?"

Silence. The rain pounded on the window. "*Oui.*
Do you?"

More silence.

"*Oui.*"

By the light of a candle Henri and Serena held each other and listened to the storm. Henri told her of his doubts.

"No one could have done more," she protested.

"I could have broken him out."

"And I would have helped you, and then we'd all be in the cell with him, or outcasts. Then who would be left to help us?" She squeezed his hand. "It is not the way. You have done what you can, *mon amour*. You have done what you must. And I believe it will work. Tomorrow he will be free."

Alone among the deVrieses, Elisabeth slept soundly that night. She had not attended the trial. It was simply too embarrassing, and there had been no need. She had sealed her bargain with the bishop. Her part was done, and the rest was just show. She had found the papers, her heart nearly stopping when Serena entered Henri's study while she had the papers out on the desk, but she had managed to cover them up, and had gotten them out successfully. The notary had done his work, the bishop his. The judges were the right judges, and they had received their instructions. The bishop was efficient.

She wished she could share her knowledge with the others, with Paul at least; but of course, it was impossible. She told him not to worry, but he dismissed her with that awful look she'd seen in his eyes of late. He seemed so distant just now, and wouldn't talk to her. He spent all his time with Moussa and when he talked to adults it was to Henri or Serena or Gascon, never to her. She supposed it was a phase, that he would get through it. She would fix it later. Everything would be better later, when this business was done.

COURT WAS SCHEDULED TO CONVENE AT NINE o'clock the next morning. By seven the crowds were assembling in the courtyard, larger than the day before, fueled by newspaper accounts of the trial. Some had spent the night outside the Hôtel de Ville, where an

uneasy compromise had been reached in the hours before dawn. Elections were to be held, and there were to
be no reprisals against the leaders of the uprising.

For the moment, civil war had been averted.

Half an hour early, at eight-thirty, the prisoner was
shown into the courtroom. His lawyers and the prosecutor had been hurriedly summoned from their homes
by special messengers, and were hustled into the court
through a side door. The court was empty except for
Jules and the lawyers. Suddenly the judges filed in and
took their seats. Jules was puzzled. Obviously not even
Henri had been informed. It was clear the judges had
decided not to wait for the crowds. The prosecutor
started to object, but the judge silenced him and told
Jules to stand. The judge spoke only two more words.

Non coupable. Not guilty.

Jules heard it with numb relief. It was done that
quickly, without speeches or explanation, a swift climax
to his long nightmare. He closed his eyes. Again the
outraged prosecutor leapt to his feet, but the judges
were already departing. Outside, the crowd sensed that
something was developing, and a few spectators entered
the courtroom. Like a brush fire the news spread
through the assemblage, producing disbelief and shock.
They had come for blood and had been denied. The
morning's ennui was to have been punctuated with a
firing squad. All the smart money knew it. Only pay offs
and corruption could have managed such an outcome.

Henri and the boys were approaching the court just
as Jules was leaving. He was under an escort of guards
who pushed their way through a crowd pulsing with
malice. From atop the carriage Paul saw his father in the
middle of the throng. The boy must have absorbed
more than he thought the previous day, because he read
the mood of the crowd and knew instantly what it
meant.

"They're letting him go!" he cried in jubilation. He
leapt from the carriage and plunged into the multitude,
ignoring the count's shouts to stop. He made his way
through a forest of legs and arms to Jules. "We're going
home!" Paul said in a half-question, half-statement.

"*Oui*," the colonel nodded. "We're going home." He said it dully. His eyes were listless, his spirit low. His happiness at seeing Paul could not overcome the awful sadness that engulfed him. During the long dark hours of his captivity he had often wondered how it would feel to be set free. It wasn't to be like this, not at all. The glorious delight of liberation he had expected was missing, choked away by the loathing of the crowd. He felt cheated and empty.

Paul followed him closely as he made his way to the carriage. The shouts got uglier as they went. "*Déserteur! Traître! Allez au diable!*" The crowd was becoming a mob. People jostled and pushed and ripped at Jules's uniform. One tore an epaulet from his shoulder. The motion startled Jules from his reverie. Without thinking he hit the man, whose jaw shattered with a crack. He collapsed on his back, the crowd around him incensed at the colonel's brutality. With growing concern for Paul's safety, Jules took him by the hand and began shoving his way along, pulling Paul in his wake.

"Quickly!" Henri called desperately, seeing that the situation was getting out of hand. Jules heaved his son onto the carriage and leapt aboard himself. Henri lashed the horses, and the carriage lurched against the crowd that was surrounding it. The guards had melted away altogether, abandoning the square to its own passions.

"It was all fixed!" a man shouted. "Justice bought and paid for by the Count deVries!" "*A bas la noblesse! A bas le gouvernement! Vive la Commune!*" The crowd roared and the horses drawing the carriage whinnied in fright. Pebbles began to fly. The colonel took one on his forehead that drew blood. Terrified, Paul and Moussa huddled on the floor of the carriage. Determined hands grasped the sides of the carriage and tipped it back and forth, hoping to overturn it. Henri pushed relentlessly on, turning his whip on two men who tried to grab the harness. They fell away and the carriage moved out of the square.

As the angry gauntlet faded behind them Jules looked to be sure the boys were all right, then down at his hands. With surprise he saw they were trembling. They hadn't ever done that before, not in Africa or Italy or in the face of Delescluze. His temples were throbbing. The carriage passed quickly through the city. He stared out into the cold November day. It was a different Paris than the one he had left on his way to war. He didn't know her anymore, nor she him.

CHAPTER 12

THE PANGS OF HUNGER BEGAN TO GNAW AT THE belly of Paris. November passed and milk ran out. The massive herds of sheep and cattle that once filled the Bois de Boulogne and the Champs-Élysées were depleted. Private livestock was confiscated. Donkeys and mules disappeared. The dog population began to shrink, while cat carcasses were decorated with colored paper and hung in butcher shop windows above signs that proclaimed the delicate pleasures of the "gutter rabbits" for sale inside. Butter and cheese were only fond memories. For one franc a day men ventured into the neutral zone between French and Prussian lines, ducking bullets as they pulled roots and vegetables and stuffed them into sacks before scurrying back to safety. Goldfish in the ponds of the Luxembourg Gardens were caught and eaten. Women waited all night in food lines that stretched for blocks. Only wine was plentiful and still cheap, so that except for the well-to-do most of the city went to bed drunk and hungry.

On one of their Sunday morning explorations Paul and Moussa saw a crowd gathered around a vendor's stall in the Place de l'Hôtel de Ville. The vendor had a patch over one eye and wore a seedy jacket. Before him were piled stacks of wooden cages full of red-eyed rats whirling madly around inside, desperate to escape, nipping at each other and working on the wood of the cages with long sharp teeth. The rats were fat and brown with pink ears and feet and tails. A bulldog lay on the sidewalk next to the cages, occasionally opening an eye to inspect the rats or the gawkers, but otherwise rock-still.

"What do you do with the rats?" Moussa asked.

"Eat them," grumped the vendor.

"Why would you do that?" Paul asked in wonder.

"Because you are hungry, *naturellement*." The man shrugged.

Moussa couldn't imagine it. "How could you ever get that hungry?"

The vendor looked at the boys with their fine clothing and full faces. He was tempted to shoo them away, but they were just stupid children and meant no harm. He spat in the gutter. "By being born in this hellhole of a world," he said. As he spoke a woman approached the stand. She was frail and gray. Two small children clung to her skirts. For a few moments she regarded the occupants of the cages. The rats quarreled and stared and turned in circles. She shivered and drew her shawl more tightly around her shoulders, unable to make up her mind. For a moment her resolve deserted her and she began to leave. She had gone only a few steps when she hesitated and then returned, a look of despair on her tortured face. At length she raised a bony hand and pointed. The man used a stick to goad her purchase through a little gate into a smaller cage. The bulldog stirred itself from its languor and sat up attentively, waiting to do its duty. The vendor opened one end of the little cage and tilted it at an angle toward the waiting dog. The rat turned and tried to run, but it was a poor uphill climber. The vendor shook the little cage, the rat slipping and clawing and scratching, and finally it fell out the end to the waiting animal, who caught it in powerful jaws before it hit the ground. With a quick motion the dog tossed it in the air and caught it by the head. The dog shook it once. The rat went suddenly limp, neck broken, body dangling from the dog's mouth. Dutifully the dog dropped it at the feet of the vendor, and promptly plopped down again, bored. The boys watched in awe. They'd never seen a smarter dog. The vendor bent over and deftly picked the rat up by the tail, wrapped it in a piece of newspaper, and passed it to the woman. She paid him two francs and left. Paul was shocked.

"You mean people *pay* to eat them?"

The vendor smirked at his ignorance. "*Oui*, little master, as I will pay you. If you've the courage and the stomach for it, go hunt some and bring them to me. I'll give you fifty centimes apiece."

"Fifty centimes? That would be easy money," Paul scoffed. "Gascon catches them all the time in the stables." Gascon set out traps filled with glucose to attract the rats, which became trapped in pots. He drowned them and threw their bodies behind the woodshed, where the neighborhood cats finished them off. Sometimes Moussa assisted with his slingshot. He didn't like the rats much, but he wasn't afraid of them, either.

Moussa's mind raced as he pondered the possibilities of becoming a rat magnate. "I know a place we could get more," he said to Paul. "A lot more."

"Where?"

"A place Sister Godrick showed me, without meaning to."

The cellar of St. Paul's was a dark and ancient place of stone that Moussa knew well. There was a basement beneath the crypt where they buried old dead bishops, and another basement below that, all of it built centuries earlier with huge stone blocks quarried from beneath the city. After the latrines it was Godrick's favorite purgatory for him, down there in the dark where some penance or another with a broom and dustcloth awaited him. When she wasn't checking up on him or he was tired of the work, he spent the time exploring. There were boxes of old leather-bound books, their pages brown and crumbling with age, filled with illustrations that showed men with horns and animals with human heads. One book showed graphic pictures of men and women—saints, he guessed—who had haloes and were shown meeting various horrible deaths. They were gored and speared, drawn and quartered, beheaded and hung upside down. Riveted, he turned the pages, concluding it was a tough business being a saint.

There were stacks of old paintings leaning against

the walls, covered with dust and tied together in bundles. Some were taller than he was. He cut them apart and found more gruesome pictures, oils that were cracked with age and depicted gargoyles and giant winged monsters being flown by men in armored suits. On the whole he liked them better than the portraits of cardinals and bishops that hung upstairs in the cathedral.

One day Moussa found a staircase made of stone that descended from the lower basement. The opening was almost completely obscured by a faded woolen tapestry that hung on the wall. Moussa discovered it by accident with his broom. He took a lantern from its wall stand and started cautiously down. His insides tingled and stirred. He kept the lantern up and his head down, fearing only that he might run into a colony of spiders who, when not working in the school latrines, hid there waiting for people to come downstairs. To his vast relief there were none at all, not even any old cobwebs. Too dark and damp, he guessed. He descended one flight, and then another, and another. At the bottom stood an old rough-hewn oak door, heavy and worn. He tried to push it open but it didn't budge. He set the lantern down and heaved with all his might. At last it moved, its old iron hinges complaining with rust and neglect. When he had gotten it open a little he stopped and listened. He could hear a faint rustling noise. He picked the lantern up and put it through, past the door, and looked inside. A wide corridor stretched away in the distance to where the light was swallowed up by the blackness. The walls were made of rough stone. Along the floor were piles of dirt and rubble.

And amid the dirt and the rubble he had seen the light of the lantern reflected in a thousand tiny eyes, eyes that were now bringing fifty centimes a pair on the street. A perfect hunting ground. He hadn't finished describing it to Paul before their decision to go hunting was made.

"I don't want it to be dark," Paul said nervously as they gathered up what they needed. "I want to be able to see what I'm doing. We'll catch more that way." He wondered whether Moussa could read the fear in his voice, whether he knew Paul was afraid of the dark. Probably not, because when Moussa suspected such things he said so, just before gleefully rubbing it in. Paul had no idea of the terror lurking in Moussa's soul about spiders, for of course Moussa never revealed it. Paul thought Moussa was absolutely fearless.

"It won't *be* dark," Moussa said. "We'll have a lantern." Paul wasn't as sure as Moussa sounded, but then he rarely was. Still, it seemed easy enough, if the rats were as plentiful as Moussa promised. They'd have quite a treasury by dark. They had glucose and tins and burlap sacks for their catch. Moussa brought his slingshot and a bag of pebbles, "in case the hunting gets too good for the traps." They slipped into the cathedral through one of the side doors. No one paid any attention to them. They hurried through the hallways and toward the basement. It was all territory that Moussa knew well. Down the stairs they went, then down some more, until they were in the room with the tapestry. Paul's heart beat a little faster, and he wondered if it was time to get a stomachache or something. But so far Moussa was right—there was plenty of light, and Paul figured at least the tunnel wouldn't have Prussians in it or, worse, trigger-happy French guards. He decided to keep going.

They slipped behind the tapestry and descended the stairs, one flight after another, Moussa leading the way and Paul right behind. It got colder and damper as they went down, the stone walls seeming to weep with the ages. The stones were smooth and felt slimy to the touch. Their shoes made little noise on the solid steps. At last they reached the old door.

"Push it back," Moussa whispered. His voice sounded loud in the confined space. Paul set his lantern and sack down and pushed. The door gave way with a creak. They stepped through the opening into the blackness, the air musty and still and cold on their necks. Paul closed the door again behind them, taking care not to let it go all the way. He was afraid the latch would catch and trap them there forever, in a lonely dungeon filled with devils and dread.

"This is it," Moussa said. He lifted his lantern, which cast a dim glow over the shadowy realm of mystery and the rats. "And they're still here." Paul saw them everywhere, little red eyes shining among the piles of dirt, eyes cautiously surveying the intruders. They stayed back out of the way, hiding at the farthest edges of the light.

Waiting.

The boys ventured farther into the room and busied themselves setting out the traps. It helped to be moving around, as if the noise they made might banish the demons of the darkness. They set the lantern on a ledge while they worked. Paul scooped out hollows between stones on the floor where they could set the tin traps, into which Moussa then poured glucose. When they were done they surveyed their work with satisfaction.

"Two hours and I guess they'll be filled up. We ought to get about a hundred," Moussa said. He looked around. The area they were in was a room that narrowed into a corridor. "I wonder what's down that way."

Paul didn't share his curiosity. "I don't know. But I'll be all right just waiting here."

"You can't wait here. The rats won't just jump in the traps while you're staring at them. You've got to give them some room."

"Then we can go upstairs."

Moussa replied using his long-perfected tone of voice that made Paul feel small and gutless. "You go upstairs if you want. I'm going exploring."

Paul groaned inwardly. It always went this way. Moussa would have an idea, Paul an objection. Moussa would argue, Paul would give in. After they had done it and it was all over Moussa would agree what a stupid idea it was in the first place. The ideas never got any better, yet the pattern never changed. Paul's dread of dark places was not as great as his concern over Moussa's disapproval, even though Moussa never openly belittled him. He didn't need to, since Paul always caved in before it got that far. Sure enough, Paul felt his resolve dying along with his objections. He cursed himself for going along, and then did.

"Oh, *d'accord*, I'm coming with you."

Moussa held the lantern high. They made their way down the blackness of the corridor, tentatively at first. The ceiling was arched and quite high enough for their passage, but the darkness made them want to duck as they walked, as if something might suddenly appear from out of the gloom and hit them on the head. A cloak of cold and silence settled over them as they crept along, their senses fully alert. They tried not to make any noise, even though the tunnels were deserted and there seemed no need for silence.

They walked for a long time. They passed through mid-sized rooms, then great galleries where vast quantities of stone had been mined. In some places the walls were smooth and perfectly straight as if cut with a razor, while others were scalloped, as if scooped with a spoon. They found old rusty tools, chisels and parts of saws, and wood handles that were worn smooth with use by long-dead craftsmen. Cart wheel tracks were ground into some parts of the stone. Planks from the carts were scattered among iron casings for wheel spokes. It had been a city beneath a city, the tools and wheels silent testament to the activity that had taken place there.

Sometimes corridors branched off, or rough stairways disappeared up into nothingness. Some were blocked off with piles of stone. They passed through a junction where six corridors departed like points of a star from the one in which they were walking. They decided to keep going straight through. "If we don't turn," Moussa said, "we won't get lost." Once when they stopped they heard water rushing in the distance, but they couldn't find it. There were other sounds, nondescript noises of the dark that their imaginations magnified a thousand times. Their eyes played tricks on them too as they walked. They'd look at the lantern, and then little floating lights of different shapes would dance around them as their eyes darted through the blackness, shapes of heads and bodies, Moussa's spiders and Paul's demons, things that wouldn't go away when they shut their eyes. But they stayed close to each other and touched a lot and got used to it after a while, although their step was a little quicker than usual.

At length they arrived at a set of rough stairs. They weren't evenly carved like the ones that descended from the cathedral. They might not even be stairs for all the boys could tell, but they looked like they went somewhere. They climbed up easily at first, but then had to take turns holding the lantern while they pulled themselves up over ledges that grew steeper and farther apart. They had gotten quite high when their way was blocked abruptly by a stone wall.

Paul had had enough. "Let's go back," he suggested after they'd climbed back down. "The traps are probably full by now."

"Just a little farther," Moussa urged, and they continued down the corridor. They passed through an area where the floor was rough and uneven, their footing uncertain. Paul tripped over something and fell to the ground. Whatever it was rolled a little way, like a light stone.

"What was that?"

Moussa raised his lantern and looked down at the floor. At first they couldn't tell what it was. But then Moussa gave a little squeak of fright. It was a human skull, smirking at them from the place where it had come to rest in its soft bed of dust. In a flash of panic they looked around, wondering if there were other parts, or killers with long silent blades and blood in their eyes. But there was nothing. No one else, no stray arms or legs or ribs. Just a skull in the dirt, disembodied and alone. Moussa moved closer.

"Don't touch it!" Paul hissed.

"Why not? It's just some old bones." Carefully, delicately, Moussa nudged it with the toe of his boot. It toppled over and the boys jumped back. The skull regarded them sideways.

Satisfied that it wasn't going to move on its own,

Moussa knelt next to it and held the lantern near. The light cast deep shadows. They could see through one eye into the empty interior, and the little zigzag lines on top where the bone was fused together. The nose was a gaping hole, the teeth intact. The skull had a quizzical, friendly expression. Moussa decided it was harmless. He set the lantern on the ground and gingerly picked up the skull. It was dry and lighter than he expected. He briefly wondered if he was committing a sin somehow, just by touching it. Fooling around with what used to be someone's head was probably near the line. But he turned it over and over in his hands, and decided it wasn't any different than a piece of old cow bone. Whoever had lived in it was long gone and probably wasn't even Catholic.

"I'm taking him with us," he announced. "We can get him a hat and keep him in the tree house. We can call him Napoléon the Next."

Paul came closer, his initial queasiness melting before his curiosity. He was not amused by Moussa's choice of names. Napoléon had caused enough trouble. "How about Fritz? We can say he was a Prussian we killed." Moussa giggled. It was perfect. "*Très bien.*" He held him up at eye level. "*Fritz, je m'appelle Moussa, et voilà Paul.*" He bowed politely, from the waist, and took Fritz in his hands. He tossed him lightly in the air. Fritz grinned. Paul decided Moussa's idea to explore hadn't been so bad after all.

Their attention shifted back to the passageway. It was getting late and they needed to keep moving. A little farther along there was another widening, and then a huge cavern that must have been a major collection point for the quarry. They could tell the room was large only by the way sound echoed in it, because the light from their lantern was lost in the gloom long before it lit the ceiling or the other side. Near where they stood another set of ledges resembled a steep set of stairs. Old fragments of rope were wound together in huge braids that cascaded down the ledges like cotton waterfalls, and were still attached to slings of dried leather from old stone harnesses. From the size of the room and the ropes it was obvious they had come to a station where stone had been hoisted to the surface. Moussa set the lantern down and peered up, waiting for his eyes to adjust.

"Look!" he said. "Light!" At first Paul couldn't see it, but he waited and saw it too, a diffuse glow that barely lit the walls above them. They set Fritz down next to the lantern and began climbing up, eager to discover where their secret passage had brought them. The ropes made it easy to climb, and they ascended more quickly than before. They had gone up a considerable distance when they heard a piece of metal striking another. They stopped and listened, hardly daring to breathe. They heard it again, and then other noises, lower and indistinct—a voice, a man's voice, although they couldn't make out anything he was saying. He laughed. They looked at each other. Careful not to make any noise of their own, they crawled up. The climbing was growing easier, the steps closer together than before, and the ledges were covered with dust that muffled their passage. The voice became more distinct, and then they made out others, four or five altogether. Moussa could tell from the light that they were just below the top. He put his hand on Paul's shoulder and they stopped. He could hear more clearly now, and what he heard brought a flicker of recognition. At once it came to him, and he knew what he was hearing as certainly as he knew his own name. He saw from the look on Paul's face that he knew it too.

The voices were speaking German.

Cautiously they worked their way up, sliding up on top of each step, then moving again, being careful not to dislodge any rocks or stir up the dust. Their hearts were pounding. The stairs grew less distinct until they became a ramp, and they were at the top. Moussa raised his head to look. They had arrived at the edge of an alcove that was the size of a large parlor. The room was empty. Two sides were natural stone. The third, from which the light was coming, was a wall made of stone blocks, carved and stacked nearly twenty feet high to the ceiling. The stones at the bottom of the wall were quite large, with smaller ones higher up. Daylight filtered through gaps in the wall. Someone had intentionally blocked off the entrance to the quarry a long time earlier. The boys were in the back half of the entrance to the quarry. The voices were coming from the front half, on the other side of the wall.

When Moussa realized they couldn't be seen, he motioned to Paul to follow him, and they crawled into the alcove. They waited to be sure no one heard. There was no break in the conversation. They could smell the smoke from a fire and the aroma of cooking food. Hair standing on end, they crawled on hands and knees to the wall of stone and peered through one of the cracks. On the other side, not ten feet away from them, six Prussian soldiers were gathered around a small fire. They were sitting under an overhang of what resembled a cave, which was the outer opening of the old quarry. They had removed their boots and were laughing and smoking. They drank liquor straight out of a bottle they passed among themselves. Two of them played a card game. One of the soldiers tended to the food cooking in a tin pot that balanced on the stones at the fire. It was a comfortable, peaceful scene, the men sheltered from the chill fall wind, the siege momentarily forgotten.

It took a few moments of silent observation for the enormity of their circumstances to sink in. They were in a cave with Prussian troops! *Prussians!* After the shock passed and the realization set in, Paul stared intently at the faces of the ones he could see. He had never seen Prussian soldiers, not up close. He was surprised by their common features and simple bearing. He didn't expect them to look so normal. One was an old man with snow white hair and kindly eyes, who smoked a pipe and reminded Paul of a portrait of his great-grandfather. Another, a baby-faced youth with bright pink cheeks, the one tending the fire, might have been his grandson. But Paul was not fooled by their simple look. He knew theirs was a clever disguise.

These were the men who were at least partly responsible for what had happened to his father, men who had brought war to his country and nearly destroyed it.

These were the men who were now choking his city, who would first starve it, and then plunder it to rubble. These were the very men who people said ate babies and raped women. He had no idea what *rape* was, but it sounded awful and thoroughly Prussian. *No,* he told himself, as ordinary as they might pretend to be, theirs were the faces of evil.

As Paul's hatred simmered, Moussa peered out past the opening, trying to determine where they were. His range of vision was limited by the mouth of the cave and there were no visible landmarks. From the position of the sun he could tell only that he was looking to the south. He could see down the slope of a long gentle hill. Beyond that the roofs of small farmhouses were scattered among the trees, with smoke blowing sideways from their chimneys in the strong winds. There was a road in the distance. It wasn't enough. They could be anywhere. The only thing he knew for certain was that the tunnels ran all over the place. There were miles and miles of them, and they ran underground all the way from St. Paul's to the enemy positions encircling the city.

He looked at Paul and saw his intent expression. He tugged on his sleeve and motioned that they ought to leave. Moussa had no desire to toy with a bunch of Prussian soldiers. The longer they stayed the greater the chance they would be detected. The memory of their close call at the hands of French troops still made his insides flutter. It was time to go. He thought Paul would be eager to leave, but Paul shook his head stubbornly and gestured at Moussa's back pocket. Puzzled, Moussa looked around. The band of his slingshot was hanging from one pocket, a sack of pebbles bulging in another. The color drained from his face. Could Paul actually be thinking that? A slingshot? Against a half-dozen Prussian soldiers?

Angrily he shook his head and turned to crawl away. Paul grabbed him by the sleeve, and drew his face up close. "If you won't do it then give it to me!"

"Do what? *Merde,* it's a slingshot, not a gun!"

"We have to at least hit one with it!"

"You're crazy!"

"Well, you're a coward." The word struck Moussa like a blow. He didn't know what had gotten into his cousin. Paul's face was red, his look deadly earnest. Paul had never, ever called him that before. Moussa was bigger and bolder, always the one in front. He was not the one who usually needed persuading, even though just now he thought it wise to gather up Fritz and be gone, while Paul had some notion about taking on Bismarck's infantry. Although he wasn't about to admit it, Moussa had realized something as he peered through the stones. Up close, the Prussian soldiers scared him to death. But there was no way he'd let Paul think him afraid.

"I am not a coward," he hissed, "and you know it!"

"Then do it!"

"What do you want me to do?"

"Just hit one in the eye with it," Paul whispered.

"*Just* hit one in the eye?"

Paul nodded eagerly. "*Oui*. That will be enough. Then he'll have to go home."

Frustrated, Moussa looked around. He couldn't let Paul do it. They both knew he was a lousy shot. He'd bungle the job and get them both caught. He looked at the wall again. It would protect them for a long time, even if the Prussians decided to give chase. They'd have to tear the wall partly down, and the boys would be gone long before that. Still, the whole idea was insane, even for Moussa. Yet his choices were limited. His cousin was determined, and now his own honor was at stake. At last Moussa gave in. "*D'accord*," he said, "but just one try. If I miss we get out of here anyway."

"All right," Paul agreed. "But don't miss."

Together they crawled back to the wall, their knees stirring the heavy dust on the floor of the quarry. Moussa fished for his slingshot and drew a few pebbles from his pouch. He chose a rose quartz with a jagged edge. *A sure killer,* he thought. Carefully he loaded it into the leather sling, feeling the edges and moving the rock around until it nestled just right between his fingers, the fat part in back for a good grip. He'd done it a thousand times without looking, but this time he looked anyway, to be absolutely certain. Satisfied, he stood up and rested his elbows against the stone. He could see the heads of a couple of the soldiers. He stepped to the left a little, to find an opening big enough. He was thankful for the blustery fall wind that blew outside the mouth of the quarry. He could hear it whipping the branches of the trees. It would mask any noise he might make.

He chose his target, the soldier with the baby face. As he did he flushed hot. He was actually going to do it. Slowly he drew the sling back until it was stretched taut next to his ear, all the way to the breaking point, farther than he had ever pulled it. He squinted and framed the face of the soldier between the posts of the slingshot, judging the range carefully, measuring, moving his hand a little up, then a little down until he was sure he had it right, and his eye had the other, dead-on. The soldier was perched on a stone with his back to one wall, his profile exposed to Moussa. He held a big spoon in one hand and gazed blankly into the cook pot, his expression lost in reverie. At last Moussa was ready.

He swallowed hard and held his breath, and let go.

The stone streaked through the opening in the wall and found its mark, striking the soldier in the cheekbone just below his right eye. Startled, he brought one hand to his face and jumped to his feet. His spoon flew from his hand and clattered on the rocks.

"*Gott in Himmel!*" he bellowed in rage, blood gushing from the wound. "I've been shot!" He spun around and staggered toward the opening of the cave as the others sprang to their feet in a panic, scrambling for their weapons and helmets. Moussa and Paul kept looking just long enough to see the blood, and then dropped to the floor and fled, terrified, on hands and knees. They slithered over the edge and down the stairs into the dark protection of the deep quarry, and were gone.

In the front of the cave the wounded soldier danced and hollered in pain, the skin of his cheek laid clean away from the bone. The others looked around uncertainly. There had been no gunfire, no sounds of assault. No one had seen the stone or heard it drop to the ground, where it fell among a score of others. They peered out the opening of the cave, in the opposite direction from which the stone had come, none of them with the slightest idea what they were looking for. The hillside below the cave was deserted. They looked up, wondering whether something might have dropped from the ceiling of the cave. Nothing. Shrugs met puzzled looks. One of the soldiers walked around the perimeter of the cave, stopping at the wall where the stones were piled up. He climbed up on one and peered through an opening. Looking in that direction, with the light behind him, he could barely make out the void behind the wall. Empty.

Nichts, he decided. Nothing there. He climbed back down.

The old man examined the boy's injury. "It's not a bullet wound," he said. "Quit whining. Your eye is all right. You probably stabbed yourself with the spoon." The boy groaned. The others laughed and sat back down, the excitement forgotten.

Moussa and Paul heard nothing. They moved as if the entire Prussian army were at their heels. They fairly flew down the ledges, slipping and sliding, bumping and scraping, desperate to reach the corridor that would lead them to the safety of St. Paul's. They clung to the ropes, flaying elbows and skinning knees in their mad descent. They listened for footsteps or shouts, gunshots or cannons, and heard nothing but the clatter of their own escape echoing around them. When they hit bottom Paul tripped and fell to his stomach, letting out a cry as he hit the ground. The lantern glass rattled loudly, filling them with dread that now they'd been heard for sure. Paul struggled to his feet and snatched up the light, which luckily hadn't broken. Moussa picked up Fritz and carried him under his arm like a kick ball, and they ran as fast as their limited light permitted. On and on they plunged through the corridors, straight through past the widenings and the yawning black holes of other corridors that departed for places unknown. For twenty minutes they kept up their headlong pace, never slacking. They abandoned their efforts at running in silence, and as each moment passed with no sign of a pursuit their fright turned to ecstasy as they decided they'd gotten away with it.

"Did you see him? Did you see?" Moussa gasped when they stopped to catch their breath. They were laughing as quietly as they could, their chests heaving from their flight, their slight bodies trembling all over in ecstasy mingled with fear. They'd both forgotten the accusation of cowardice, the tension in the cave. Everything had melted away except the vision of the little rose quartz flying through the air and striking its mark. There was no mistaking their success. They had blooded the enemy.

"You got him! Right in the eye!" Paul whooped. He was filled with pride, happier than he'd ever been. He realized he'd done something brave, or rather that he'd made Moussa do it; but it amounted to the same thing, he thought. That's what officers did, they got busy thinking things up and then appointed someone else to actually do the work, afterward keeping most of the credit. He didn't mind sharing the credit, because he knew that some was legitimately his too. For as long as he could remember he'd been afraid, often of the most trivial things, desperately wanting to do the brave things that seemed to come so easily to Moussa, but then always backing out at the last moment, or cringing the whole way through. But this had been different, and he knew it. It was like the day of the boar, a day in which there had been no time for fear. He felt strong and savage and utterly invincible.

When they'd listened for a while and knew for sure that no one was chasing them, they relaxed and sauntered down the corridor again, Moussa and Paul taking turns explaining the battle to Fritz. Paul announced he was fairly certain he'd seen the soldier's eye popping out and rolling around on the floor like a marble. Moussa said the man would probably die soon from his wounds, if he hadn't already. Fritz listened attentively and smiled appreciatively and didn't argue their claims.

They talked about whether they should tell anyone. They knew in the instinctive way that boys do that none of the adults were likely to share in their enthusiasm for what they'd done. Gascon would understand, and might even secretly approve, but they figured that after he was done congratulating them he'd probably get out the cane. In the end they decided it was wiser to add the afternoon to their long list of secrets.

When they arrived back at their hunting grounds beneath St. Paul's, they were delighted to discover that the rat business had been brisk. They heard their catch before they saw it, mad claws scratching against tin pots. By the dim light they saw the traps all full and swarming. Scores of trapped eyes regarded them with malevolence and fear. Carefully they lifted them by their tails to avoid the long slender teeth that nipped and flashed, and dropped them into the burlap bags. When they had two sacks full, and the sacks were as heavy as they could carry, they lugged them back up the basement stairs.

On the way Moussa stopped and pulled some cloth out of a box in one of the storerooms. He made a wrapper for Fritz, and they emerged into the daylight. It was late and the afternoon had grown bitter cold. They had no jackets and shivered as they walked. The rats in the sacks made a terrible commotion, squealing and flopping around inside. All the movement and the teeth and claws that occasionally poked through the sides made progress slow and difficult. People they passed on the streets regarded the two urchins with looks of puzzlement and disdain. As they arrived at the Place de l'Hôtel, dusk was forcing the rat vendor to begin packing up. At first he didn't recognize the boys, all bloody and torn.

"We brought your rats," Paul told him proudly, and suddenly the vendor remembered. "Ah, the noble hunters." He looked at their wounds and assumed they'd gotten them catching the rats. He shook his head in pity for the hapless children of the bourgeoisie, who could manage to make a hundred francs of trouble out of a fifty-sou problem. And from what he could see, they hadn't even gotten it right.

"But look here," he said, "why have you kept them

together like that, in those sacks? Don't you see what they've done?" He pointed at the burlap, which was covered with dark stains. The boys hadn't noticed. They loosened the drawstrings and looked inside to find a terrible mess of fur and blood. Jumbled together and panicked to escape, the rats had attacked one another. Nearly all of them were wounded, or dead.

"I can't sell them that way," he told them, aware of what they must have gone through to fill the sacks, but certain that no one would buy a damaged animal. "Next time don't put so many in the same bag. No more than six, do you hear?"

When they had finished separating out the rats that were still healthy, the vendor counted out their pay. Moussa and Paul looked at the little pile of centimes and their hearts sank. The rat business was tougher than they'd thought. Yet they'd found Fritz and whipped the Prussians.

It hadn't been such a bad day after all.

U H OH," MOUSSA SAID AS THEY APPROACHED THE château. "It's your father." He could see him there in the drive, near the kitchen door. If it wasn't late enough at night to use their rooftop approach, it was the way they slipped into the house when their appearance might land them in trouble, as at the moment. Madame LeHavre, the cook, would cast them a disapproving glance, but she never told on them, and let them creep up the back stairs to clean up. But this time it wouldn't work. Jules was sitting outdoors in a chair, trying to light a pipe.

They approached the colonel as inconspicuously as they knew how, hoping he would ignore them. There was a time when he would have, but no longer. Paul looked on the ground next to where the colonel sat, hoping he wouldn't see it, not this time. His heart sank when he saw the bottle, and he knew it was trouble. His father was drunk.

"Where've you been?" The colonel's voice was cross.

The boys hung their heads and shuffled near. Jules was slumped in his chair, draped in it almost. It was cold but he sat without a coat, seeming not to notice. His eyes were glazed and bloodshot. The alcohol thickened his tongue and mangled his speech.

"Just out, Father. No place special."

"Just out? Looking like that? You look like pigs, filthy pigs! How dare you come home that way? You're bloody and crude! Don't you have any pride? Speak up, Paul, and look at me when I talk to you. I asked you a question."

Paul avoided his eyes, and stared at the ground. He hated it when his father got this way. Lately he had to hate it all the time, because Jules had been drunk for a month, and it was getting worse. His temper was foul, and sometimes he drank so much he passed out in his plate of food, right at the table in front of Uncle Henri and Aunt Serena.

Once he had disappeared for three whole days. Henri and Gascon took a carriage and went looking for him in the city. It was late when they brought him home. Paul woke up and watched from the top of the stairs as they tried to get the colonel to his room. The smell of vomit filled the house.

Jules snapped at everyone in the château, and even had Madame LeHavre in tears, which was nearly impossible to do, because the cook was tough as a mule and accepted trouble from no one. But Colonel deVries could deliver a devastating tongue-whipping, and his cruelty flashed bright and often. It was a side of him no one had ever seen, and it frightened Paul to death.

Lately he had taken to slapping Paul if the boy didn't move quickly enough. It took only the slightest offense to provoke him, like forgetting to comb his hair. Jules would lash out with the back of his hand and slur something, and then he would turn red and get quiet and walk away. But he never said he was sorry. The first time it happened the shock of it was so great Paul burst out crying, even though he wasn't hurt. "I'm sorry, Father, I didn't mean to do anything wrong," he said, although he hadn't done anything at all. Once when Jules slapped him, Henri saw it. The count's face darkened and he moved to intervene, but then he checked himself. Later Paul heard them arguing. Their voices were loud and some glass broke, but all the details were muffled behind closed doors.

After the first few times Paul learned that avoiding him altogether was best. Paul didn't know what to make of it all. The transformation had been so fast, so complete. His father had taken to drink just as quickly as he'd set off for war, with the same vigor and drive for vengeance. He watched his father grow cold and hard, and from the way Jules snapped at him he was certain he'd done something to cause it.

"It will pass," the adults told him, trying to cheer him up, but they really didn't know what to say to the boy. "He's a tough man, the colonel," Gascon told him. "He'll get over it." Serena seethed, and once tried to talk to Jules about Paul. Her timing was terrible; he was drunk. "Go back to where you belong," Jules thundered at her. "Go meddle in some camel shit. Something you understand." She slapped him so hard that it hurt her hand, but he laughed and staggered away. No one else saw it. Serena wept alone. She dared not tell the count. The next day Jules didn't remember. "He doesn't mean it," she told Paul. "He isn't mad at you. He's ill."

Elisabeth was almost never home, getting in late at night if at all. Paul didn't know for sure, but he thought his parents weren't sleeping in the same room anymore. Elisabeth watched Jules deteriorate and felt she had to say something to Paul, struggling to find an explanation. "It's those articles," she told him.

The Paris press had treated Jules viciously, and had not let him alone for a moment since the trial, when they trumpeted their charges of influence and bribery and corruption in the infamous case of the colonel who ran. They excoriated him on the front pages. They got hold of the Delescluze letter, which they printed in its entirety with no rebuttals. The prosecutor fed them details that were richly embellished before they ran.

Jules's likeness appeared in nearly every edition until

his face was as well-known as that of Gambetta or Trochu. He was recognized readily in the street and run off like a mad dog. Interest in his story was heightened by another, about a simple sergeant named Ignatius Hoff, who sneaked out of the city at night to the enemy lines, where he cut the throats of German sentries and returned with their helmets as trophies. His kills were counted carefully, nearly thirty in the month of November alone. His exploits were legend, the contrast irresistible.

Within ten days of his release Jules began attacking the bottle. He'd returned to the château after trying for the fifth or sixth time to volunteer his services to the forces defending Paris. The brigades were ill-trained and poorly organized and needed officers like Jules. "They didn't want me," was all he said when he came home. "Didn't want me, and wouldn't have me," and he would clean off whatever mess had been thrown onto his uniform, eggs or worse, by the proud men of the defense forces. And he retreated into his rum.

Paul did his best to shut it all out, to pretend that it wasn't happening, and his mind clung to the hope it would be over soon. He'd seen his mother come out of her own shell when Jules had been in prison, and expected the same thing would happen with his father. In the mornings when he woke up he started fresh, anxious to see his father, to see whether his storm had passed, and if he could polish Jules's sword again or do him some favor. But the first look of the morning from Jules would kill the hope quickly, as Paul could see from the angry eyes that nothing would be different that day than the day before, and the day before that.

But now it was the early evening, the dreaded time when the colonel's furies were strongest, and Jules was building a rage against him for being late, for coming home bedraggled and torn.

"I'm sorry Father," Paul said. "We were playing in some—"

"Shut up! I don't want to hear about your amusements! The city surrounded by Prussians, people beginning to starve, and you're playing! Playing! Where is your sense of respect? Where is your honor?" For long hot moments Paul withstood his withering scorn. Moussa stood helplessly by, wishing he could either leave or do something to help. Now he knew how Paul felt, having to sit there while Sister Godrick worked on Moussa. Nuns and colonels learned how to address people from the same books, he thought.

Paul forgot himself then, and tried to ease his father's harsh impression of their activities. He broke his promise to Moussa about the secrets of the afternoon. "Wait, Father," he said, "you don't understand. We were in the tunnels below the city. We saw some Prussians, in a cave. We hit one of them in the eye and hurt him. Hurt him bad. He'll have to go home, Father! He'll have to go back to Germany! We were helping, really we were!"

The colonel absorbed some of it and rose from his chair on shaky legs. His face was reddening as he listened to the tale, his eyes narrowing, his teeth clenching. His hands were shaking and he dropped his pipe to the ground.

"You too?" he said. "You would humiliate me? My own son wishes to show me how a *man* fights Prussians? And with a wild tale like that? A ten-year-old who does what the colonel did not? How—dare—you—" He was out of words, his mouth working in silent rage. "You little bastard!" he finally said. He lashed out with his hand and caught Paul on his cheek and knocked him to the ground. Paul raised his hands as if to ward off another blow. His cheek was bright red where Jules had struck him. "No Father, please, that's not it. I didn't mean anything by it. It's not a lie! Ask Moussa. We did it, we really did! I thought you'd be proud!"

Jules wasn't listening. His eyes were on the cloth wrapping Paul dropped when he fell. The cloth had fallen away, exposing some of the skull inside. Jules bent over unsteadily and picked it up. "And I suppose this is the one you killed?" he said, lifting it out of its wrapping. "My God, Paul, what have you boys been doing? When did you begin stealing from graves?" And with that he flung the skull away. Moussa and Paul watched, helpless and sad, as Fritz hit the stones on the side of the house. He was old and dry and shattered into a thousand pieces. Only the jaw was left intact, and it came to rest in the dirt.

Fritz was still smiling.

AFTER THREE MONTHS OF SISTER GODRICK AND the fourth form, Moussa was learning to live with his hell in class. His existence was about the same, he guessed, as being a soldier on the fortifications, dodging bullets and eating grapeshot. He thought he had an understanding of the nun, with whom he had settled into an uneasy coexistence. Their relationship was still full of fireworks and friction and tests of will, but he thought he gave as good as he got, and sometimes, in little ways, he even thought he won. He knew he would flunk the class in the end, because she still refused to mark the papers on which he wrote "Moussa," which was all of them; but he decided that he would talk his father into letting him quit school altogether. They were rich, he knew, very rich, and there didn't seem much point in his continuing at St. Paul's. He could buy a school, and hire the teachers he wanted. There were some details to work out with the words and the logic he'd use on the count, but he was sure they would come. Time was growing short. In another month class reports would be issued, and his day of reckoning with the count would arrive.

Except for Pierre, the other boys in class had left him alone after his beating for the snake. They hated and shunned him, but gave him grudging respect for the way he had handled his punishment, and the way he stood up to Sister Godrick. They knew they couldn't have done as well; and more important, perhaps, they knew he could still whip them.

Aside from the certainty of his flunking, therefore, he saw the year working out pretty much like any other year in school. He knew he'd make it through, and as the weeks passed he even grew somewhat complacent.

But then Sister Godrick saw the amulet.

She was leading the class in daily prayer, beseeching the Almighty first to watch out for the young souls of St. Paul's, and second to slay the Prussians besieging the city gates. It was a good prayer, Moussa thought, although he felt that if her connections were as good as she made out, the enemy ought to have keeled over by now. As she prayed his head was bowed but his eyes were open as always. It was one of his little victories, and one of hers. If he did not close his eyes but did bow his head, she felt as if adequate respect had been shown the Lord, and he felt as if adequate liberty had been granted. They hadn't discussed it, but instead had settled into the compromise.

Moussa had gotten dressed hurriedly that morning, and the amulet was hanging outside his shirt. During the prayer he was absently playing with it.

Whack!

He jumped, his reverie shattered. Her paddle still carried the shock of thunder when she used it.

"And what is that you toy with during prayer, Michel?" Sister Godrick asked him. She nudged the amulet with the end of her paddle.

Moussa pulled away. She had no right to touch it. "It's nothing, Sister," he said, and he quickly started to slip it back under his shirt, but she caught the cord near the back of his neck, and pulled on it so he couldn't.

"It is not 'nothing,' Michel. I am not a fool, and by the grace of God have not gone blind. I can see it clearly enough. I asked you what it is, and you shall tell me."

"It is my amulet, Sister."

"Ah, une amulette! A trinket for unbelievers. And what evil is deterred with this amulet, Michel?"

"I—I don't know, Sister. It's lucky, that's all."

"Lucky!" Her voice was full of scorn. "Give it to me."

Moussa's face flushed and his heart raced. Why hadn't he put it where it belonged? Why did she care, anyway? "It's mine, Sister. It belongs to me. I need it. I don't take it off, ever. It saved my life."

"Did it, indeed! So this remarkable amulet has God-like powers!"

"It saved my life, Sister."

"Give it to me."

"I won't!" He couldn't believe this was happening. Anything but the amulet. He jumped up from his desk and broke for the door, but she caught him by the shoulder and pushed him down roughly. She set her paddle down and with her free hand lifted the amulet from around his neck. Moussa was squirming, his face red with anguish. He clutched it tightly as she pulled, but then let go for fear she would break it.

Sister Godrick held it up for the class to see. It dangled from her hand, a dark leather cord with a pouch at the end that was sewn around the edges, its contents hidden. It was to her a tool of devil worship, a heathen offering to false gods, an adornment of evil that belonged with voodoo rituals and savage sacrifices. Worst of all, it was a direct denial of the power of the Almighty.

"This is an abomination under God," she said, her voice rising. "It is a violation of His commandments. It is a sacrilege. There is only one Church and one true God, and this"—she shook it in her fist—"*this* is not His sacrament. Michel has jeopardized his eternal soul by wearing it, and by ascribing to it false powers, and by bringing it among us." Moussa's eyes were riveted on her fist, desperately afraid of what she might do.

Unlike Moussa, Sister Godrick was not resigned to letting things continue along as they had been. If there had been lengthening moments of peace between them, she knew the boy was far from broken. He was still the lamb of God with a disease that could infect her entire flock. He was poisoned by an independent streak that remained as noxious to her as the breath of the devil himself. She had been ready to destroy the amulet right there, to take scissors to it and shear it to pieces in front of the class. But she read the expression on Moussa's face and instantly understood that she held in her hand the instrument of his submission to her will. His eyes were vulnerable as they had never been under punishment or threat. She could see the amulet meant everything to him. She let him go, and walked to her desk. She found paper and hastily drew a picture. She turned and walked to the lesson board, where there were nails for displays. She spiked the picture on the nail. It was a crude likeness of Satan, and the nail poked through his forehead. Then she hung the amulet over it, and it appeared to hang around the devil's neck. Satisfied with her handiwork, she turned to the class.

"The coin that does not bear the image of the Prince of Heaven has no place in His Kingdom," she said gravely. "The works of man that do not have the love of God stamped upon them, have no value in Heaven. This is a work of blasphemy, of magic and sorcery, and has no place in this life. It is a sign of weakness, of submission to evil. You will see it hang there on the proper neck, and you will remember that they belong together. Over the weeks as it hangs there you will observe Michel, and see that he does not need it for luck as he believes. One has no need of luck when one has the Lord."

She opened her desk drawer. Looking carefully before she reached in, as she now did every time she opened it, she withdrew a small rosary. She took it to Moussa and held it out to him. "Idle hands that have need of occupation can do no better than this, Michel. You will learn that lesson and one day bless the Lord for His light." He made no move to take it from her. She set it on his desk and turned her back on him. It was time for the day's other lessons.

Sister Godrick could not have stricken more directly at Moussa with a spear to his heart. For the rest of the day he sat dumbly in his seat, devastated and in shock. She had taken from him his protection, his shield against a hostile world. It had saved him from the boar and from French bullets, from fevers and accidents and he didn't know what else. It held the spirit and goodwill of his uncle, a man he had never seen. His mother had told him about the amenokal, and Moussa saw him as a great and powerful man, just and wise. Such a man would never have given him the amulet without being certain of its effectiveness. Moussa believed in its power as surely as he knew the sun rose in the morning.

At recess he sat at his desk, refusing to go outside until she made him leave, and then he stayed just outside the room. He didn't want to go where the other boys were. He felt naked. He looked to be sure it was still hanging there. He was desperately afraid she'd throw it away while he wasn't looking, and that it would be gone and he wouldn't know where. He paid no attention during lessons. She spoke and he heard nothing. She gave instructions and Paul had to nudge him to comply. The amulet hung on its devil, and Moussa tried to think of what to do.

After school he waited until the other students had left, and in one of the hardest moments he could remember approached Sister Godrick, who was writing at her desk.

"Yes, Michel?" she asked without looking up. "What is it?"

"Sister, I'm sorry I brought the amulet to school."

"As am I." The words were delivered sharply.

"Sister, if you will just let me take it home, I promise I won't wear it, and that I won't bring it back—" There was pleading in his voice, a desperate tone she had never heard. She was pleased. Her assessment had been correct. His weakness was within her grasp.

"Get to your knees, Michel," she directed. "Bow your head. And close your eyes."

He had guessed she would do something like this. He told himself she would soften if he complied. He hesitated for a moment, to make it look to her as if he was deciding, but his decision had already been made. He sank to his knees and closed his eyes. He rested his elbows on her desk and clasped his hands.

"Let us pray." She led him through the Lord's Prayer, and after that an act of contrition. He repeated the words after her, with the promise to sin no more. Then she told him to say a prayer out loud, a prayer of his own making. He felt awkward and struggled to find the words. He hadn't made up a prayer since he stopped praying, and he'd never made one up for someone else to hear.

"Father, forgive me for my sins," he began. Those

were easy words, that started many prayers. "I know it was wrong to bring the amulet to class. To St. Paul's, I mean. I know it is Your house and I meant no harm by it. I've learned my lesson, God, I promise, and I won't do it again. . . ." He didn't say, "if You'll just make her give it back." After all, she wasn't stupid. She was just a nun.

When he finished he almost forgot. "In Jesus' name, Amen," he said.

"Amen," Sister Godrick repeated. He opened his eyes. They were filled with hope that all had been rectified.

"May I take it now, Sister?"

"You have a great distance to travel, Michel, on the road to God's salvation. I find your words self-serving and your motives transparent. You value your pride more than your soul, which stands in mortal peril." She rose and dismissed him with an icy wave. "The amulet will stay where it is."

"Sister, please," he beseeched her, his voice trembling. "I'll do anything you ask."

"It is not what I ask of you, Michel, it is what the Lord asks. When you understand that, when you truly believe it, then I will know. And I will give the amulet back to you, and you will destroy it yourself. Go now. I am busy."

He shook his head and tried to absorb it all. He felt betrayed and full of hatred. He got to his feet, shaking with anger. "You tricked me! You're worse than the devil! I hate you! I hate you!" She didn't flinch. Her eyes were penetrating and cold and steady, and she knew she had him. He would not be long now, coming to the ways of the Lord.

Moussa ran from the room, blind with tears and rage, alternating with promises to himself that he'd kill her, that he'd steal the amulet back, that he'd burn the cathedral to the ground if he had to. He didn't know what to do. He wanted to die.

CHAPTER 13

"YOU LIVE AMONG JACKALS. THEY WILL FORGET you, and turn on you, and eat you alive."

Every night Delescluze came to him, mocking, taunting. Every night he said it again: "Your world is finished." The colonel laughed at the absurd notion, secure in his empire, unafraid, unbelieving, and spit in his face. A gust of wind blew up and turned the spit around in midair and it landed back on Jules's cheek. Delescluze shrieked with laughter when he saw. "You wear it so well, Colonel."

He awoke in his recurring fog of pain. His head screamed and his temples pounded. His tongue was thick. His throat and mouth were dry and tasted hideous. He squeezed his eyes shut in dread of the new day. He had no desire to face it. His days were running sores that ran together, one after another, the next just like the last, tomorrow more of yesterday, today just the same, stuck in between. He hated waking up. The room was dark. He was alone now, the other side of the bed empty. Had Elisabeth been there? He didn't remember. He doubted it. She didn't sleep in their bed anymore. He wasn't sure if she slept in the château, either. It didn't matter.

He dragged himself from his bed to a sitting position, and with a supreme effort stood up. Too soon, too dizzy. He sat down again and held his head in his hands. How could it hurt so much? He had no idea how much he'd had to drink the night before. Where had he been? In? Out? Had someone been there with him? Dim memory, of Paul and dinner. No, that was the night before. Someone was yelling, someone's face was in his face, and he'd gotten angry and—had he hurt anyone? He didn't think so. But he didn't know. That was the worst part, not knowing whether the savage had struck or not. He couldn't imagine striking someone in his family. As angry as he'd gotten over the years, he'd always kept his temper under control, neatly buttoned up and stored inside, and when it was too much there were always his troops to take it out on. But even they had never felt the back side of his hand. They got extra drills or short rations or stood all night in the rain. He shuddered, feeling it deep down to his soul. He'd hit Paul. He knew it. He didn't remember doing it, couldn't see it in detail, but he knew he had. What in the name of all reason would make him hit Paul? There was nothing, nothing at all, but he got so angry and he fed the anger liquor and the liquor took over and he couldn't stop himself, didn't know what was happening. There was a stranger inside him, a stranger who lived in the bottle and came out with the liquor, a stranger with a face of wrath and powerful hands and terrible venom, and the stranger's fury built up until it was blind and then nothing on earth could stop it.

When he was conscious he felt old and tired and lost. It was an effort to do even the simple things, like dressing or eating or brushing his hair. His appetite, always so robust, had left him. He wandered around the house, entering rooms without knowing why he went in. He leafed through Henri's journals but the pages were blurred, the subjects lost. He stared at the labels on the cans and jars in the pantry. He sat in a chair and listened to the squirrels running on the roof.

When he could he avoided his son, whose company he desperately wanted, but he didn't know how to talk to the boy. He had no idea what to say. He had had no idea for years, really, and the words had always come in a trickle. Only now the words had dried up altogether, and when their eyes met it was the father, the stranger, who dropped his gaze first. It was the most horrible of feelings, to be mute and ashamed before one's son.

He sat on his bed and was sick. It came quickly, the

bile rising in his throat. He stood too quickly and staggered a few steps to the chamber pot. He sank to his knees and put his arms around it, his face just above it, and threw up again and again, retching a horrid yellow vomit that wouldn't stop, wouldn't let him alone and racked his guts and made him cough and heave. He rested his cheek on the cool brass until the misery passed. He got to his feet and poured water into a washstand to rinse himself. The water felt soothing, but nothing would truly diminish his agony but time. He didn't know anymore if time would do it, either.

He saw the blinds were not drawn. It was still night out. The château was quiet. Exhausted, he returned to his bed, and then he saw the papers crumpled on the dresser. In a wave of horror it all flooded back; he remembered the night before, at least some of it, and he felt the despair welling inside him once again.

Elisabeth would not be there. Not tonight, not ever again. He had discovered what she had done. He had been looking in a closet for one of his bottles when he overturned a box with papers in it. The seal of the diocese was imprinted in bright red wax, and when he saw his own name on it he had read it. He had already been drinking, and it took a few moments before he was certain he understood. He read it and then re-read it, until there could be no mistake. An extraordinary amount of money to be paid by the Church so long as either Jules and Elisabeth deVries lived, half that much to Paul should they die.

When Elisabeth came in he showed her the paper. The color drained from her face and she snatched it away.

"It is nothing for you to be concerned about, dear," she said lightly. "You have enough on your mind. I am taking care of it," and she turned to go.

"Do not tell me it is nothing to be concerned about," Jules thundered. "I have read it. Tell me what it means. I have a right to know."

"You're so difficult when you're drunk," she said, once again turning to leave, but he grabbed her by the shoulder and spun her around.

"You will not do this to me! I am not so drunk I can't understand there is something wrong in that paper. Tell me what it is!"

Elisabeth sighed. So he had found out. She knew he would, sooner or later. So it was to be sooner, then. "Very well," she said, "you are right. You have a right to know what has been done for you." She sat on the bed and calmly told him of her business with the bishop. She was light and matter-of-fact and told him everything. Jules was so stunned he forgot his bottle and collapsed heavily in a chair. For a long time he couldn't speak as he tried to absorb it.

"How could you do this to Henri?" he asked at last. "How could you? He is our family. He has provided us a home."

"He has done nothing for us. This was your father's home. How *gracious* that your brother should deign to share it with you and your family. *He* keeps the family fortune, which he has not earned. What a great and good and noble man he is, your brother." Her voice was bitter and laced with sarcasm.

"He is the count. It is all his by right. You know that."

"What I know is that you made a terrible mess of things, Jules, and that you were in prison, on trial for desertion. I did what I did to get you out of that. I did it for our family. *Our* family."

"Henri is our family," Jules said dumbly.

"Your family, perhaps. But he has done nothing for me, or for Paul. And besides, he can afford what has been done. It makes barely an *iota* of difference to him, and all the difference to us."

"Why didn't you simply ask him? He would have done anything. He would have helped, of course. He did everything in his power for me."

Elisabeth laughed scornfully. "He is weak, Jules. He does nothing that is not *proper*. He reeks of order. He never would have interfered to save you from a firing squad in the way that I did, the way it had to be done. *Mon Dieu*, Jules, he was counting on *justice* to set you free. He was blind to what was happening. Would you rather have faced the firing squad? I did what had to be done. Your brother hired the lawyers but it was *I* who saved you. And in the process I provided for our future. I did it for us, Jules. Don't you see that? Don't you know it? I want us to be whole again. I want us to be free. I want our family to have what it deserves." She stood and crossed the room. She knelt before him and tried to throw her arms around him, to persuade him into acceptance of what she had done.

Savagely he pushed her away. He was reeling at her revelations, not the least of which was that she had bought his freedom. She had shattered his belief that he had been acquitted because it was right, and because the charges were ludicrous, and because he was not guilty. But the ugly allegations of the newspapers and the crowds had been right all along: the verdict had been purchased. Jules had always lived his life by the book, and if he had been stuffy or stilted, there had been no fuzzy edges. Now he trembled at his own naïveté. He knew nothing of his world, or anyone in it.

"You think I could countenance this? Did you think for a moment that I would turn my back on my own brother?"

"I thought only that you would care for your wife and son, Jules."

"My God, Elisabeth." He looked at her through heavy eyes. His shoulders sagged and he slumped in his chair. "I had no idea. You have always worked your little intrigues with the world, always tried to have your way. I let you do it myself, more times than I can remember. But this—this is evil, what you have done. Truly evil. I honestly don't know whether I am more upset discovering you are capable of this, or finding out what a stupid man I am." He shook his head sadly. "I shall tell Henri, of course. What you have done will be undone."

The sense of finality in his voice was clear, his tone unmistakable. His mind was made up, and he would not waver. Elisabeth knew she had lost, that further argument was futile.

"You will only do harm to your son and wife."

"You are not my wife, Elisabeth. My wife died a long time ago, and I never knew it. I will provide for my son as I have always done. He will never be wealthy, but he will be fine, in spite of this, in spite of what you have done to him. To our name."

Elisabeth stood, her eyes flashing in anger. She clutched the precious paper in her hands. "Tell him if you wish. It will do you no good. It is done already, and will not be undone by you or the count. You are an idiot, Jules, a little man. I despise you. Go bury yourself in a bottle." The rest was blurry in his memory. He knew he had exploded in rage, and that he had struck at her, struck with all the pent-up fury and helplessness he felt. There was a broken table. Her violet drapes were crumpled on the floor, and a plate lay shattered at the foot of the bed. He couldn't remember how that had all happened. He remembered the shouting. And he remembered that she had not shed a tear, and when she left the look she gave him was one of hatred and satisfaction. He had had a lot to drink then. He knew because of the way he felt now. The bile came again, sudden and furious. He curled up on the floor around the chamber pot, gagging and heaving until his insides hurt.

When it had passed he felt better. He lay there for nearly an hour without moving, his eyes open but unfocused. He got up and cleaned himself again. He wandered around his room for a few moments, unsure of what he wanted to do. *Aimless, always aimless.* It was still early, just after midnight. Sleep would not come again, not without the bottle. He looked at it on the dresser and reached for it but then stopped. The thought of more made him nauseous. *Extraordinary. Even I have had enough.*

He stopped in front of the mantel, where his sword had always hung, the sword with the ivory handle and eagle's head. The weapon had belonged to his father, and his grandfather, and his great-grandfather before that. Its long blade had shed the blood of the enemies of France at Waterloo, and in the Crimea. It had shed the blood of the sons of France, during the Great

Revolution. He himself had carried it on three continents. For all the flesh and bone the sword had carved, its blade had always gleamed razor-sharp, ready to bring honor to the man who wore it.

Now there was an empty spot where it had hung. He had lost the sword, like so much else, to Delescluze.

He had another sword, one that had been presented to him after the Italian campaign. He took it from its wooden box in the closet, and sat in the chair by the window. He had a view out through the great stand of chestnut trees that ran down the long drive toward the river. A crescent moon gave just enough light that he could see the naked branches stirring in the breeze. The leaves had all fallen and the trees were barren, ready for their white mantle of winter. He pulled open the window. The wind was cold and filled the room with the late autumn night. The papers on the dresser blew off in a flurry. It was quiet outside, peaceful. He sat there for hours without moving, his head aching horribly but clearing with time.

He found himself holding the toy soldier Paul had made him a lifetime ago. From the day Paul gave it to him in the train station he had kept it with him. While it had been in his pocket an empire had fallen and Delescluze had worked his demented scheme. It had been his companion in a cell, and had seen his career die, and his marriage. He turned it over and over, the little soldier with a twig where its arm should have been and a walnut shell for a helmet and buttons painted down the front. The soldier gave him its silly grin. Jules had gotten fond of looking at it, that grin, and over time the face had taken on character, and had its own stories to tell. The piece of wood he had received from his son had become something more with time. Paul had done a wonderful job with it.

The hours passed slowly for the colonel in the chair. He wondered how it had all gone so horribly wrong, what he had done to have made things so desperately bad for so many people. He despaired at ever making it right again. His men dead, all dead. The private Etienne too. His marriage over. His own brother cheated by his wife. His son a stranger to him. The Imperial Guard, to which he had devoted his life, disbanded and discredited. His very identity, his sword, unwanted even as Prussians stood at the gates of the city. His name cleared by a court that had been paid for its verdict. His name reviled by the public, a public that was fickle and cruel and made his life hell. Delescluze had done everything he had set out to do. Somehow the crazed words of the curse had come true.

It is not you I wish to destroy, Colonel. It is your honor.

The hours crawled with his nightmares, and his devils swirled around him and fueled their fires until the flames licked hot at his soul. His eyes and his hands kept coming to rest on the sword. It had been a long and monstrous road, and now, with the steel blade in his hands, he began to allow himself finally to see its end. The thought had come to him more than once during the last few months. He'd always pushed it away, at first with outrage and revulsion and absolute conviction. But over time the thoughts had come more often, and his protests had grown weaker. He grew less frightened of it, and then, he didn't know exactly when, he stopped protesting altogether. As he sat before the window the thought persisted and wouldn't leave him. When at last he allowed it in, when it washed around him and through him, he felt its blessed relief, and his sadness almost passed from him. He was so tired of it all, so tired of fighting, so tired of his living death. So easy to end it, so easy except for Paul, and Paul alone. And yet he knew that Henri had always been as much a father to the boy as he had. A better one, in many respects, and Serena spent more time with him than his own mother did. Paul would suffer, yes, but in the end he would be better off.

He rose from his chair and with a sense of purpose he had not felt for months made his preparations. He sat at his desk and drew out writing paper and a pen. He wrote a letter to his brother in which he explained what had happened with his property, in as much detail as he could remember from what Elisabeth had told him. He apologized for the burdens he had placed upon them all, and was placing upon them yet again. He asked that Henri continue, as always, to watch out for Paul. When he was finished he wrote another letter, to Paul, and sealed them in separate envelopes.

He went to his wardrobe and carefully laid out his dress uniform. It was pressed and clean, the jacket bright white next to the crimson pants, the gleaming belt and red sash, the ribbons and decorations colorful markers of his life. He dressed with precise movements and careful attention to each detail, making certain that everything was exactly as it was supposed to be.

When he had finished he looked critically at himself in the mirror. Everything was perfect. He took his pistols from their cases and strapped on his sword. He shut the window to his room, so that the rest of the château would not be chilled. He closed his door quietly and went down the hall. He set the letters on a stand in the entry where he knew they would be seen, and then he went upstairs.

He walked softly down the long dark hall. He needed no light for he knew it well, this hall that passed by rooms so full of memories. He and Henri had played there as boys. They had grown up and sons had been born and mothers and fathers had died. He found the doorknob and turned it silently and went inside.

Moussa was asleep, snoring lightly. Paul was in the other bed. The curtains were open, and the moon cast its pale light into the room. Jules went to stand beside Paul's bed. He stared at his son, at the tousled hair so bright against the pillow, at the face that could be so expressive, that had so much innocence. He felt himself losing control, his throat constricting with anguish. He wanted to wake Paul, to talk to him, but he knew the words would not come, that it was better this way. He leaned down and gently brushed back the hair from Paul's forehead. He started to kiss him, but drew back. For long moments he stood there, fighting with himself. And then he turned and walked silently to the door. With his hand on the knob he hesitated for just an instant, as if he was going to turn around. But then his shoulders straightened, and he walked out and pulled the door closed behind him.

In the stable he saddled one of the horses. It was an old stallion that had once been full of temper and pride, but whose fires had dimmed with time. *Like my own,* he thought. He went through the motions automatically, without thinking. Blanket, saddle, cinches—everything checked and double-checked, everything just so, the way that he had taught a thousand men to do. When he was ready he took the reins and led the horse outside and closed the doors. Effortlessly he mounted, adjusting the sword at his side. Horse and rider moved slowly past the château. Jules knew the trees, the roof, every inch of the grounds. He had always loved it. It didn't matter that it had not been his on paper. It had always been his anyway.

The eastern sky was streaked with the first glow of dawn as Jules passed through the Bois de Boulogne. He rode quickly, wanting to reach his destination while night was still on his side. He passed camps of soldiers whose sentries were barely awake, and who watched him pass in silence. At a trot he passed Neuilly, and Villiers, and St.-Ouen, and around the base of the great Fort de l'Est near St.-Denis. When he arrived at the outer limits of the French lines, a lone sentry stood at an outpost to block his way, uncertain why this man would be about at this hour of the morning, and, more particularly, why he would be going in *that* direction.

"You cannot pass here, sir," the boy said nervously. "This road is closed to all traffic. Orders of the commandant, sir."

"Get out of my way, Private," the colonel responded, and the boy, hearing the unmistakable voice of authority, did as he was told. Jules rode by without breaking stride. He left the road and passed earthworks and old artillery encampments and through empty fields. It was all deserted, eerily quiet. No one ventured between the lines, not here, not anymore.

The sun was almost up when Jules stopped and pulled out his spy-glass. Slowly he scanned the horizon until he found what he sought. There was a peasant's cottage, with low fortifications to each side. He could see a sentry wearing the distinctive helmet, sitting with his back propped against a wall of the cottage. For long moments the sentry didn't move. He was sound asleep. *The pride of the Prussians,* Jules thought. He placed the spyglass back in its sheath. He gauged the angle of the sun, calculating exactly where it would rise, wishing to use it to best advantage. He drew his sword and leaned over to pat his horse on the neck. It was something he always did before a battle, to calm the animal's nerves, to let him know it would be all right. "We're a small regiment, you and I," Jules said. "We'll have to do this alone, and well." He sat silently, erect and motionless. He closed his eyes and smelled the morning air. He smiled. The first rays of the rising sun struck wispy light clouds along the horizon and shot them through with pink. He felt the welcome warmth on his back. The sun would be behind him, square in the eyes of the enemy. He watched as its light found the roof of the cottage, then crept downward until it gleamed off the sentry's helmet.

With a furious kick Jules spurred his horse. The old animal stumbled but then found its footing. First a trot, then a full gallop as they raced across the plain, gathering speed. *Arms at order,* Jules told himself in the litany of a cavalryman's preparation as he flew into battle. The horse's hooves were muffled in the soft soil. *Ranks tight, all together.* Jules became oddly detached from himself, as though he were an observer, not a participant. He felt a floating sensation, the lightness of a bird in flight. *Knees close, find the next boot.* The wall was before them. *Set your mark.* His sword came up, and they took to the air.

The Prussian sentry never knew what hit him as Jules and his horse soared over the fortifications. His head had been severed before he could raise the alarm. His helmet clanked to the ground, the sound lost in the roar of thundering hooves. Some of the men inside the cottage stumbled out, astonished looks on their faces as they were cut down, one after another, by the mad colonel of the Imperial Guard whose sword swung repeatedly through the air. He fired at them with a pistol and hacked at them with his blade, no sound coming from his lips, his eyes set in savage determination beneath his helmet as he waded through their surprise and confusion, a fearful dervish raining terror and death in the dawn. Four had fallen by the time one got off a shot. It struck Jules in his arm and he dropped his sword. With his other arm he raised his pistol and fired back, and a fifth infantryman died. Then there were other shots from the cottage and the Prussian rifles began to find their marks as horse and rider whirled through the camp. Jules took a bullet in the chest, and another in his thigh. His heart pounded and he fired and fired. He was hit again and felt numb. The world swirled around him and his horse staggered to its knees, and they both crashed to the ground, Jules hearing nothing as he floated downward through the dust, a strange silence settling over him, a heaviness overtaking his arms and legs as men shouted and he came to rest on his back. He tried to move and couldn't. Nothing worked anymore. He stopped firing, stopped hacking. His fingers twitched and his eyes settled on something in the sky. There was peace now. He was warm and calm. A Prussian stood over him, pointing a pistol at his face. Jules tried to move his lips, to say something, but then the gun roared.

Later, going through the pockets of the madman, one of the Prussians found a toy soldier. He looked at it and thought what common craftsmen the French were. No wonder they'd lost the war. *A toy.* It was pathetic, not worth keeping. He tossed it away. It fell into the trench, the trench being dug to bury the men killed by the lunatic who had shattered the breaking dawn with such fury.

CHAPTER 14

WINTER CAME EARLY TO PARIS, RAW AND GRAY and depressing. Streetlights winked out as coal gas was rationed for balloons, and the night streets became so dark and boring that people complained they looked as bad as London. Plans for a counteroffensive had been in the making for weeks. The Second Army of Paris under General Ducrot was to break through the Prussian lines and rendezvous with Gambetta's Army of the Loire, which had been raised in the provinces and was battling to the aid of the capital. Enormous hope was pinned on the success of the sortie. Ducrot issued a stirring proclamation to his troops as they readied for battle.

"As for myself," the general said, "I have made up my mind, and I swear before you and the entire nation: I shall only re-enter Paris dead or victorious. You may see me fall, but you will not see me yield ground!" The campaign did not go as well as the proclamation. Inexperience was led by incompetence. The element of surprise was lost completely as the eager troops massed inside the city, their movements as visible to the Prussians as to the Parisians themselves, who gathered on the ramparts to watch. The city's gates were shut and ambulances ordered to stand by, further clear signs for the Prussians to read. A massive bombardment began from the forts that shook Paris to her core. Not a Prussian on the perimeter was unaware that an offensive was coming. A balloon was launched with information for Gambetta, to let him know the army's strategy. Unkind winds kept it aloft for nine hours. It landed in

Norway, and Gambetta remained ignorant of the city's plans. Then, just as the sortie was to begin, nature intervened a second time as the level of the Marne rose, preventing the laying of pontoons, which were necessary to allow the troops and their supporting guns and supplies to cross the river. The pontoons were too short. There was no choice but to wait for the water level to fall. The resulting delay allowed von Moltke to position his Saxon troops exactly where they needed to be, while French forces mounting feints to the south were not informed of the delay, and fought and died for nothing.

When at last the French crossed the river, they attacked Brie and Champigny in an effort to capture the heights of Villiers. The fire of the guns in the French forts was murderous as it softened the way for the advance, but the shells were indiscriminate and killed as many French as Prussian troops. Ducrot's forces were successful at capturing their objectives, but then an attack by the Prussians along the length of the front caught the French, who were having breakfast, by surprise. During the long and bloody day that followed, the ebb and flow of battle turned in favor of the Prussians, then the French, then the Prussians once again. During the night men froze to death, and flesh stuck to iron. Finally it was the bitter cold as much as Prussian guns that drove the French back toward the city, for the Second Army had brought no blankets. The only thing that slowed their retreat was the search for food. When horses were shot dead on the field of battle, soldiers stopped to carve the meat from their bones. They stuffed it in their sacks or chewed it raw, and retreated in the heavy fog. Behind them, twelve thousand officers and men lay dead.

The wounded were loaded onto boats and unloaded at the Pont d'Austerlitz, where they were carted off to surgeries or, nearly as often, straight to the Père la Chaise cemetery. Morose crowds lined the boulevards and watched the immense tide of carnage flood back into the city, the broken and shredded bodies like bloody flotsam on the river of ambulances and wagons and carriages. The stench of death mingled with the smell of smoke from the cannons that had fallen silent in the forts.

The magnitude of the defeat was felt in every quarter. Neither victorious nor dead, General Ducrot reentered Paris at the head of his dispirited army. Paris looked for scapegoats and hoped for a miracle from Gambetta. But at that moment the Army of the Loire was being defeated at Orléans. Word came later, by pigeon. Gambetta was not coming. Orléans was lost, Rouen about to be. General Bourbaki and his Army of the North were retreating, and the government had been forced to move from Tours to Bordeaux. On every front, disaster.

The food situation grew worse. Stocks of grain were dwindling. Prostitution spread to pay for hunger. Hooves and horns and bones were ground into *osseine* for soup. Animals from the zoo were sold for slaughter. The chefs of Paris cooked buffaloes and zebras, yaks and reindeer, wapitis and Bengal stags, wolves and kangaroos, and—when there was nothing left—Castor and Pollux, the elephants.

The arctic cold led to the burning of doors and furniture. Women and children scavenged bushes and tree limbs and roots and bark. Smallpox and typhus began to kill, along with respiratory ailments that filled small coffins with the children of the poor. Clothing was scarce and peasants made shirts of newspaper.

Yet all was not lost. France had a seemingly limitless ability to find new men for new armies to raise against the Prussians. So Paris waited. It was a source of great pride that no one in the world had expected the city to hold out so long, and the spirit within the gates remained high. Her citizens were determined to hold out against the hard winter, and to fight the harder Hun.

At the Château deVries no one knew what had become of Jules. The night he left the two letters in the entry hall, Elisabeth had returned home to collect some clothing. Wishing to avoid a confrontation, she came just before dawn, expecting to find Jules passed out and the rest of the house asleep. She saw the letters on the stand and recognized Jules's handwriting. She opened the one addressed to Henri and sat in a chair to read it. For a long time she sat there without moving, without tears. She told herself it was for the best, that Jules had finally chosen death over dishonor. It was a pity that he had done so without anyone noticing. She put both letters in her reticule, collected the papers from the diocese, and left the house.

The sentry who had seen Jules said nothing, for there was nothing to say, really. An officer had ridden by in the dawn on his way to the Prussian lines and had not returned. He might have gone anywhere. Might have gotten drunk and fallen from his horse, might have gone off to Versailles to shoot Herr Bismarck. What officers did was not his concern. Madame LeHavre was sure Jules was out slopping drunk in an alley somewhere as he had been before, at no loss to the household. At first Henri thought Madame LeHavre might be right, but then Gascon told him one of the horses was missing. Henri went into Jules's room. He saw that the sword and uniform and sidearms were gone, and suspected the truth. He rummaged through the papers and found no notes, nothing that would tell him for sure. It was unlike Jules to leave no word. Henri was heartsick at the tragedies that had befallen his brother, and agonized about what he might have done differently. Gascon asked him whether he wanted to mount another search in the city as they had done before. Henri shook his head. "This time we'll not find him," he said.

"We mustn't tell Paul," Serena said. "Not now, not yet. You may be wrong. Anything might have happened." Henri agreed.

Paul himself decided that either his father had gone off to get drunk somewhere, or he'd finally become so angry with him that he didn't want to live at the château anymore. Mostly he tried not thinking about it at all. A week passed, and another, and he couldn't help noticing that life was easier when his father was gone. He loved his father and hated himself for the thought, but it wouldn't go away. If only he could have his old father back, and things could be the way they used to be.

Elisabeth was living somewhere in the city. She came and went without explanation. If she had to visit Paul she did it when she knew Henri was unlikely to be there. She had not seen the count. She had no idea whether he had found out about the property and no wish to be there when he did. She thought not, because she had intercepted the pathetic letter from Jules. But the count's contacts were legion, the discovery just a matter of time. In fact the count's property manager had volunteered for the National Guard, and had gotten himself shot by a subordinate. The count's affairs were in complete disarray. Henri was too busy to tend to them himself, and not particularly concerned.

Elisabeth hadn't moved out, but she was never there. She told Paul she had business to attend to in the city, and that she would be back; things were just temporary. One day when it was snowing Paul saw her riding in a carriage next to a man with an elegant top hat and a fur collar and a trim goatee. She snuggled next to him as he draped his arm around her. Paul called out and chased her carriage, but she was laughing and didn't see him, and disappeared down the boulevard.

Henri worked feverishly on his balloons. It was something to do, something that kept his mind off his brother and the deteriorating situation in the city. The *Volta* was launched, carrying equipment and instruments to be used in making observations in Algeria of the approaching total eclipse of the sun. No one knew whether the balloon got there, but to launch it at all was a little victory over the Prussians, a triumph that proved French science and will thrived even in the face of war.

One night in mid-December when the boys were asleep he snuggled with Serena, exhausted. "I want to take you to the opera," he said. "There is a performance on Christmas Eve. A benefit." Henri was not much fond of socializing, especially not during the siege, but he loved the opera and it would be a welcome break from routine. A benefit performance was being held to raise money for the hospitals. Many performers and musicians remained in the city, and a noted director had been persuaded to mount the production. The city was desperate for ways to sustain morale during the siege, to remind itself that it was still the glorious center of civilization.

"The opera? Which one?"

"This one is perfect for you." He showed her the invitation. "It is called *L'Africaine*. I saw it once before. It is about an African woman named Selika."

"Selika? Very like mine."

"She pretends to be a slave, but is really a queen of her people."

"Why would a queen pretend to be a slave?"

"For the story, and so she can fall in love with the hero. He is a great explorer. She can read maps, and shows him the way to India."

"Who cannot read maps? And this man, if he is such a great explorer, why does he need help to find India?"

Henri smiled. "Did I know the way to the heart of the desert? He is not the first man who needs a clever queen to guide him. Anyway, the opera has everything. It is a great spectacle. Ships and storms at sea. A poison tree and a grand inquisitor."

"A grand—?"

"Inquisitor," he said. "A heckler, who works for the Church and has people tortured and put to death."

She arched her eyebrows. In her experience Henri's Church seemed to have a lot of unsavory characters in it. "How amusing. Does he sing too?"

"Everybody sings. It's a very pretty opera. There are flutes and oboes and violins. It's very moving. And graceful, like you."

"The more you describe it the more it sounds silly."

"Of course it's silly. But it's beautiful. You'll love it, I know you will. Except in the end the queen lets the explorer sail off in his ship with another woman." Henri squeezed her gently. "Of course, you know I would throw the other woman overboard, and come back for you."

"There would be no need," Serena said. "I would see that her bed was crawling with scorpions. She wouldn't live past the first night."

"You see? You understand the opera perfectly. And then she would sing even as she died from the venom."

Serena giggled. "That's a lot of singing."

"They say writing it killed the composer. I met him once. A man named Meyerbeer. He died the day he finished."

"A difficult business, this *Africaine*."

"Yes, all around. I want you to dress up so all Paris can see what a true African queen looks like."

It was a sore subject with her. "Your countrymen have no desire to see me dressed up or otherwise, Henri. You know that. They think me a Prussian spy." Her treatment at the hands of Paris had never been warm. She had never felt at home, never accepted. But since the beginning of the war it had been much worse, by turns humiliating and infuriating.

Just before the siege the civil authorities had rounded up and expelled from Paris a large number of citizens whose character or demeanor was judged less than exemplary. As a consequence, people in the poorer quarters of the city were arbitrarily forced into carts and driven to a distribution point near the Point Du Jour. They made up a long and pathetic procession as they filed out of the city's gate.

Serena had been returning from a visit to her Algerian friends in Montparnasse when a gendarme stepped in front of her carriage and blocked her way. With no attempt at courtesy he forced her to descend to the street. He regarded her with suspicion. She wore a plain dress and a light cloak. Her hair was pulled back in a thick braid. If she was elegant and noble in her bearing, she wore none of the trappings of wealth, no jewelry or furs. A woman of means would never have driven herself, as Serena invariably did. Her looks were vaguely European, but just as vaguely Mediterranean. She spoke with an accent and had no papers. Henri had warned her to carry them, but she was uncomfortable with the notion of a free woman needing papers to travel. The officer noted her expensive carriage and concluded she must be a servant, a whore, or a thief.

"Where have you stolen this carriage, woman?" he demanded contemptuously.

"I don't know what you are looking for, sir, but I am the Countess deVries," she responded icily. "The carriage belongs to me. Now you will get out of my way."

He roared with laughter. "*La comtesse!* But, of course, why did I not recognize you immediately? How foolish of me. Please forgive me, *Comtesse*," he said, bowing with deep irony. "And now you will kindly proceed to that gate, where the royal procession is even now leaving the city." He shoved her roughly into the forlorn line of human refuse being ejected through the gate, and ordered her carriage confiscated. Serena stumbled and found herself caught and supported by a woman who was painted in loud and lascivious colors, and they held on to each other as they passed through the leering crowd toward the gate. "It will be all right, dear," the woman said to her. Serena was not frightened, but she was shocked by her treatment. The procession was filled with diseased people, blind women and crippled children, street urchins and whores, misfits and thieves—people the authorities preferred to see outside the city gates.

The procession passed in the shadow of a large building. Standing on one of the low balconies, watching the targets of their decree pass as they might watch effluent drift by in the Seine, stood a few members of the committee of defense. Serena saw them watching. Among them, in the center, she saw purple robes on a corpulent figure. He saw her at the same instant, and looked straight at her. Their eyes met, and in that silent moment between them they understood each other well. Without an outward glimmer of recognition or a move to help her, the bishop turned away from the rabble.

Most of the city's rejects accepted their fate at being consigned to the line, but Serena saw an opportunity and slipped away easily. One of the guards shouted after her, but was unwilling to give chase to the woman who fled so quickly into the trees. Another whore more or less wouldn't matter in a city the size of Paris.

As the siege progressed, paranoia in Paris became rampant. Anyone whose face was not Gallic or who spoke with an accent was presumed guilty of spying for the Prussians, which was to say that half the population of Paris regarded the other half with suspicion. Arrests were common. Serena was quite imperious enough to back down most of her accusers, but not always. On one occasion she was escorted roughly by a mob to the prefecture, where the prefect himself recognized her. The color drained from his face and his abject apologies to her were mixed with a searing tirade against the crowd. He had personally conducted her home, and wrote her a *laissez-passer,* a safe passage with his signature and seal, and he advised her to stay indoors. She thanked him and tore up the paper, and went about her business as usual. Serena never told Henri of her difficulties. She saw no point in upsetting him, and in any event there was nothing he could do. She would not disguise her looks or hide herself away in the château.

As casualties of the siege increased, Serena volunteered to assist in one of the hospitals. She knew nothing of French medicine, but was content to help in other ways. She washed bedding and cleaned floors and provided small comforts to the wounded after the surgeons had finished. She read to one of the men, a private from Belleville who had drifted in and out of consciousness for days. One afternoon he opened his eyes and saw her and heard her voice, and he raised a terrible commotion over the foreign woman. "Get away!" he shrieked. "Get out! You have no right in our country!" He pushed her away and his wound broke open. The surgeon calmed the boy and applied fresh dressings, but then he drew her aside. "We are most grateful for your help, madame," he said, "but perhaps it would be better for all concerned if you were not here to upset the men."

Serena started to protest, but then she checked herself. She would not force herself upon them. She had chosen her path when she married Henri. If it was difficult, it was by choice. Out of that choice France had become her adopted country. If she occasionally found herself hating its hauteur, if she suffered too often at the hands of its bigots, she must learn to deal with it, even as she thought the more satisfying course would be to put some of those bigots to a horsewhip. If her son was to learn tolerance, she had to know it herself. Yet it was not easy. In the deep desert it was said the Tuareg were the world's most arrogant people. But in the deep desert, she thought, they had never met the French.

After that she helped Henri with his balloons. She searched the city for material for the envelopes. She found some through her friends in Montparnasse, and by making the rounds of tailors' and milliners' shops. There was initial suspicion as she made her requests of strangers, but when they heard it was the balloons for which she sought help, their eyes lit up. From them she collected bits of calico and silk, and learned to sew them together. She was content with what she had found to do, and loved being with her husband. Still, when he told her that he would show her off at the opera, it stirred up all the anxieties inside.

"To hell with them," Henri said. "You will be with me. You will be the most beautiful woman there, and the only thing people will think is how jealous they are of me and my Prussian spy."

Serena smiled, and kissed him. She would go to his silly opera.

MOUSSA'S SHOES CRUNCHED ON THE SNOW AS HE walked down the lane toward St. Paul's. The air was still and crisp and his breath swirled in great clouds around him. He drew the collar of his coat around his neck to keep out the winter air. His mouth was set grimly, his teeth clenched against the cold. He felt it stinging all the way down his throat to his lungs, and wondered what it was going to be like to die of pneumonia or consumption or just plain cold. Without the amulet it was certain to happen. Things were beginning to go wrong. He'd already been bitten by a spider in his own bedroom. It left a big welt under his arm, which swelled up and stretched until the skin was shiny. In a desperate search for the spider he'd turned their room upside down, angering Paul when he tore his bedding apart and set all his clothes out in the hall.

"If the spider's in my clothes it'll bite *me*," Paul said irritably. "Leave my stuff alone." But Moussa couldn't chance it, and he emptied drawers and turned out the closets. When he found it hiding under a windowsill he crushed it with his shoe and threw it outside. But after that he couldn't sleep for fear the spider had a relative waiting to get revenge.

Then Moussa had fallen when he and Paul were walking on a wall behind the château, fallen and nearly broken his arm. They'd walked on that wall a thousand times and never so much as teetered the wrong way. Suddenly he'd gotten clumsy, and the world seemed a dangerous place. He was certain it was no coincidence.

Now as he trudged along the path he could already feel some hideous disease burning his lungs. He wondered whether, if he died, Sister Godrick would be sorry when she heard. Not a chance. She'd probably cross herself in thanks, and lead the class in hymn. He considered leaving a note, so that when they chipped his body out of the ice the gendarmes would know who to blame. But the police would never dare arrest Sister Godrick, not even for murder. As far as he could tell people didn't do things to nuns. Nuns did things to people.

The cathedral loomed dark against the gray winter sky. There were lights on and it looked warm inside. He was going there to pray. Nobody knew except Paul, who said it was a waste of time. But Moussa had to try. Christmas was just two days away, and there would be four weeks of holiday after that. He had to get the amulet back before then.

He went inside, the heavy door shutting behind him with a loud *thunk* that echoed through the building. The cathedral was empty, dark except for a few lanterns hung along the walls. It wasn't nearly as warm as it had looked from the outside. He could still see his breath. His footsteps echoed on the stone floor as he walked to the bank of candles. He struck a match and lit one. He put some of his rat money in the wood offering case and said a prayer. Then he went to one of the hard wooden chairs facing the altar. He knelt and bowed his head. He didn't know how to make a proper prayer, exactly, so he started with a few that he knew by heart, and then he just started talking. It still felt awkward, as it had with Sister Godrick, but the words began to come more quickly, and soon he relaxed and was rambling on as if to an old friend. The murmurs of his voice carried up from his small form until they were lost in the darkness of the great nave. His hands and feet were numb from the cold, but he didn't notice.

Without artifice and without evasion the boy poured out his heart. He explained things as they seemed to him, and confessed things that nobody else knew, not even Paul. He admitted how he felt about Sister Godrick, trying as best he could to be fair about it. He figured God already knew about her anyway and would understand his feelings. He apologized for what he'd done to Pierre in the lavatory, although he allowed there might still be trouble between them. He admitted an old crime against a cat in the neighborhood. He tried to tell it all, and along the way to make no bargains he couldn't keep. When he finished he crossed himself and said, "Amen."

That night was full of hope. His earlier doubts about God were erased and he fixed on the certainty growing in his mind that tonight had worked, that soon the amulet would be his again. Before he went to sleep he said another prayer, to be sure. He had never said so many prayers in his life.

The next day he went eagerly to school. It was Christmas Eve, and the day was to be a short one. All classes reported first to the Great Hall for a special program of poetry, prayers, and hymns, which the bishop himself was to attend. Moussa saw him sitting on one side of the room, the curé at his side and most of the nuns arrayed in a circle behind him. The bishop was so mountainous he looked as if he needed two chairs. Moussa read his part flawlessly and suffered through the rest of the program. When it was over the curé gave a benediction and at last they were released from the torture to return to class.

When Moussa entered the classroom he looked on the wall and his heart skipped a beat. The wall was empty by the board. It was gone. The picture, the amulet. Sister Godrick walked in and began talking immediately, so he didn't have a chance to question her. He was overwhelmed with fear that she had thrown it away, or burned it, or that someone else had stolen it. But then it occurred to him that maybe the prayer was working, and that she had taken it down to give it back to him. When the break came at last he eagerly went to see her.

"Sister, my amulet—" he began, his eyes on the wall.

"I removed it, Michel. His Eminence Monseigneur Murat is with us today. You have seen him yourself. One could hardly leave such an abomination on display."

"Where is it, Sister?"

"Do not trouble yourself with it. It is secure."

"I thought you were going to give it back to me. Let me have it, Sister. Please."

"Perhaps when you return next year. It will not happen today. This is not the proper time to discuss this, Michel. Take your seat."

"It *has* to happen today, Sister. I can't wait until later. *Please.*"

"I told you. It will happen in God's time, if at all."

"But I talked to God last night." Moussa flushed. "He said—He said I could have it back."

"The Lord said that to you?"

"Well, not exactly in a way I could hear, but something like that."

"I am pleased you are trying, Michel. Now take your seat."

"Sister, I can't. You must let me have it. Please. *I prayed.*"

She gazed at him levelly. "And it is well you did. The renaissance of your soul must begin with prayer. You have taken the first step on the proper path. And now if you do not immediately take your seat, you shall soon wish you had."

Moussa saw his dream crumbling behind the hateful woman, saw everything falling hopelessly apart, and a great rage welled up inside him. He felt the bitter salt tears pouring down his cheeks, and he was sobbing. How could she still be doing this, after his prayers? Didn't she talk to God? It wasn't right, none of it was right.

His eyes fell on her desk, and he knew it was there, in one of the drawers. She kept everything there. In a flash he jumped for it, but she moved to block his way. She caught him by the shoulders and started to propel him toward his chair. But in a blind rage he pushed back with all his might. His balance was just right while hers was just wrong. She lost her footing and fell backward. She tripped over her chair and went down, striking her head hard against the corner of her desk, then falling to the floor next to the wall. The chair turned over and clattered against the stone. Moussa barely noticed as he made for the desk. He was going to snatch it away. He was going to take it and run away from school and home and everything. Nobody was going to stop him.

At that instant a voice broke the stillness that had fallen over the room. "Stop! How dare you! What have you done?" And Moussa felt a mighty grip on his shoulder, a man's hand, like steel, and the drawer kept its treasure out of his reach. The hand spun him around, and he was looking into the hard face of the curé. Moussa saw someone else. For an instant he took his eyes from the curé to see, and his heart sank. Just behind him stood the imposing form of the bishop of Boulogne-Billancourt.

Sister Godrick struggled to her feet, her legendary composure shaken. "Father, Your Grace, I am so sorry," she said, her face flushed. She straightened her habit, touching her head gingerly where it had struck the desk. An angry bruise was already forming. There was a spot of blood. She dabbed at it as she spoke. "A disagreement that unfortunately grew out of proportion. The boy has forgotten himself."

The curé glared at Moussa. "Leave now," he said. "Wait in my study. I shall summon your father."

"No." The basso voice was firm. The bishop approached and the others stood back. The rest of the boys were frozen, transfixed by the spectacle happening in their very own class. They had witnessed their share of excitement between Moussa and Sister Godrick, but it all paled next to this.

"This is the deVries boy, isn't it?" the bishop said. His wolf gray eyes held Moussa's without wavering. They were the coldest eyes Moussa had ever seen, like looking into a mist. Moussa stared back at him defiantly, but he felt uneasy inside.

"Yes, Your Grace," Sister Godrick said. "Michel."

"Michel?" The bishop looked puzzled. "I thought his name was—I have forgotten." He shook his head. "Some foreign name."

"He uses his Christian name in class, Your Grace."

"Of course." The bishop took Moussa by the chin. He looked long at him, appraising him. Moussa saw something in the eyes. Was it anger? Hatred? He guessed the bishop would be furious about his pushing a nun, but somehow the look was more than that. He couldn't tell.

"Something troubles you, Michel?" the bishop asked. "You would treat a nun so?" Moussa didn't know what to say. He was afraid, and there was too much to say to explain anything. So he said nothing. After a while the bishop spoke again.

"Send the child to me."

Horrified that the prelate himself had seen such a breakdown in her class, of all places, Sister Godrick moved to salvage the situation. "Your Grace, I'm sorry you had to witness this unfortunate incident. It is a small matter of discipline. There is no need for you to trouble yourself on my account. I assure you I will regain complete control of the situation," she said.

"I am certain you shall," the bishop replied evenly,

but he didn't take his gaze from Moussa. Then he said it again, in a tone that defied discussion. "Send the child to me. This afternoon, at my palace."

"As you wish, Eminence," the nun said, bowing her head.

"Go now to my study," the curé said to Moussa.

AFTER SCHOOL PAUL DIDN'T KNOW WHAT TO DO. *Moussa had pushed her over!* Even for Moussa, it was astonishing. Now he was trapped in the curé's office, waiting to go to the bishop's palace. No one Paul knew of had ever been sent there for a disciplinary matter. He wondered what happened there. If Sister Godrick used a paddle and the curé used a whip, he supposed a mighty bishop would use dungeons and racks and dragons. He was terrified for his cousin. He thought about doing nothing, waiting until that night to see Moussa and find out what had happened. But that would be disloyal. Paul had stuck by Moussa through everything, and knew what he was going through. Sister Godrick tortured Moussa, did it all the time. She pushed him past the point anyone could stand. Maybe he shouldn't have knocked her over—although Paul couldn't remember feeling so good seeing anything in his whole life—but somebody needed to know the other side of the story. It was time to tell someone. Moussa needed help. There was only one person who would understand. Only one person he could tell.

Aunt Serena.

IN SHORT, MADAME, THERE IS TOO MUCH MICHEL and too little humility in your son."

Serena stood across the desk from Sister Godrick, who had delivered a long and bitter litany of the sins of her son.

She is not a wicked woman, Serena thought as she listened. *She is a zealot. And zealots are far worse than wicked. I see why Moussa has such trouble.*

"He is out of control," she continued. She touched

the lump at her temple. "There is an evil streak in him. I knew him to be vain, and have suffered his childish pranks, but I had not judged him capable of violence. I was wrong. There is more savagery in him than I had seen. Perhaps it is his lineage."

"I know my son well," Serena replied evenly. "There is no evil in him. His spirit is simply that of a boy. I think he troubles you because he is not docile. He is proud of his lineage, which is noble, and his name, Sister Godrick, which is Moussa."

"In this class it is Michel. You will forgive me for being blunt. His lineage is at least part heathen, and his spirit, as you call it, is self-indulgent and weak. Only his self-regard is strong."

"Paul has told me of your treatment of Moussa. If he struck you it was wrong. He will be punished for it. But if he did so he must have been driven to it. He would only do such a thing because you torment him."

"He torments himself. I am merely God's instrument."

"Perhaps the instrument is too sharp."

"I see where the boy gets his impious fire. You feed his vanity, madame, at the expense of his soul. He is but a heathen, and I see it is you he has to thank."

"You seem determined to offend me."

"If you take offense you should look within, Countess." Sister Godrick was quite unawed by the woman standing before her. Countess, king, or commoner, they were all petty souls before the Lord.

"You are here to teach him, not take charge of his soul."

"You are mistaken, madame. Without his soul there is nothing to teach."

Serena had heard enough. "And without the boy you will have nothing to teach, either. I will take him now. Please show me where he is."

"He is not here. He has gone to the palace."

Serena gave a start. "Paul said he was to go this afternoon. I had no intention that he see—that man."

"The curé had to leave early. He took Michel with him. By now your son is in the hands of the bishop."

THE BISHOP WAS IN A TOWERING RAGE, HIS STAFF in a fright. He had returned to his palace that morning to find the clerk of the diocese awaiting him, a concerned look on his face.

"A moment, Your Grace?"

"What is it?"

"The property you ordered sold, Eminence. I have been to the land bureau in the city, to complete the transaction. It seems there is an error."

The bishop was puzzled. "What kind of error?"

The clerk was afraid, but plunged ahead. "It is most embarrassing, Eminence," he said. "The property we have sold does not appear to belong to the diocese." He laughed nervously at the very absurdity of what he had just said.

"Of course it does. I was personally involved in the purchase."

Relieved, the clerk sighed. "Well then, that settles it. I—I'm sure Your Grace could not have made an error, so perhaps there is a mistake elsewhere. All the same, there is a—a difficulty with the records of the arrondissement. The transaction will be delayed until we can sort it through."

"Have you brought the records?"

"But of course, Eminence."

"Let me see the transaction ledger." Heavily, the bishop took his seat. His housekeeper handed him a brandy, which went quickly. He took another. The clerk placed the ledger on the table and turned it so the bishop could see. A fat finger traced the list of entries for the properties. There were not many for the largest parcel, which had belonged only to the family deVries, and then to the diocese. The entries were all there, quite in order. And then—

"Wait! *What—is—this?*" The bishop's face turned as purple as his robes as he saw the last entry, recorded in the bureau just six days earlier. It was clear. It was done.

"*Vendu par Msgr. M. Murat, évêque de Boulogne-*

Billancourt. Transfer to E. deVries. Tax paid. Witness Prosper Pascal, Notary."

Murat trembled as it sank in.

E. deVries. Elisabeth! The bitch! She had—she had cheated him! And Pascal was in on it! The notary he himself had used a hundred times had turned against him, against the Church, against the very house of God, against God Himself! He was apoplectic with rage. The whore was sleeping with the notary! She had to be! They'd seen the prize, they'd taken it from him!

"Your Grace?" The clerk watched the bishop's color change. He thought the prelate was having a heart attack. He leaned forward to help. "Eminence, are you all right?"

"I am not all right! Get out! Get out!" Hurriedly the man gathered up the books and fled from the room. He closed the door to the sound of breaking glass as the bishop's tempests raged.

The bishop cursed and drank and brooded and drank some more. He had such a full day in front of him, and now this. There were commitments all the rest of the afternoon, then a benefit at the Opera, and after that Mass at St. Paul's. Near midnight he would join the archbishop at Notre Dame. He rang for his housekeeper and canceled the afternoon's appointments. He had to think, to plan. Two amateurs had trifled with the master. What had been done could be undone. He would get the property back, and then he would work his revenge.

There was a timid knock at the door of his apartment. The housekeeper put her head in.

"There is someone to see you, Your Grace. A child."

"I want to see no one. I told you to leave me alone."

"He was brought by the curé from St. Paul's, Eminence. The curé said you wanted to see him. The boy's name is deVries."

The bishop took a long drink. His head was swimming, his blood running hot with brandy and revenge. He closed his eyes.

The boy's name is deVries.

"Of course, so I did. I had forgotten. Show him in. And then I am not to be disturbed under any circumstances." His voice was iron. "Do not disobey me this time."

"Of course, Eminence."

The heir de Vries. Such an innocent child, from such a troublesome family. Aunt and uncle, mother and father. Such trials they'd brought. A pity that the blood of the next count should be diluted by hers. Still, a lovely boy, lovely boy. Such beautiful features. Fine hands, silken hair. So delicate, such blue eyes. And his skin, so smooth, so precious, no taint of her blood . . .

Marius Murat felt his loins stirring, and he set his drink down.

SERENA PUT THE WHIP TO HER HORSE. HER HEART was racing with fear for Moussa, who had passed from the nun to the bishop, from the scorpion to the cobra. She cursed herself for leaving his education so completely to Henri, for not paying closer attention. She had asked about the bishop, and Henri told her the man never came to the school, that he had little to do with diocesan affairs. Moussa would be in the hands of the finest instructors in Paris, he said. He was right about many things, but in this he was wrong. She had had enough of Henri's church and its schools and its marabouts. She wanted to get Moussa out, away from it all. They would find another school. There were civil schools, private tutors. She would find something. They could bring instructors into the château, or she would teach him herself. Anything but this. If Henri wanted to argue, then they would argue, but her mind was clear. The nun was possessed and the bishop was evil.

Her mind recoiled at her vision of the man, and she drove her horse ever harder. She didn't believe he would physically harm her son, but then she wasn't really sure. She didn't know what to believe of Marius Murat. He was a man she judged capable of anything. She had looked into his eyes.

You may torment me, Priest, but not my son!

MOUSSA GLANCED NERVOUSLY AT THE BISHOP from his seat. His chair's stuffing was thick and soft and nearly swallowed him up. He had to lean forward to keep it from devouring him. His mind was running in a thousand directions. He was afraid, but he wasn't sure of what. The bishop just stared at him and said nothing and drank. He drank like Uncle Jules, Moussa thought, only more, and he was huge, about twenty stone. He wondered what would happen if the bishop sat on a horse. *Probably kill the horse.* An unwanted vision of the scene appeared in his brain, the horse squashed on the ground, its legs all splayed out and broken, and Moussa looked away so that the bishop wouldn't see the smile working at the corners of his mouth. The bishop certainly didn't need to see him smirking, and Moussa actually didn't feel like smirking, not at all, but sometimes when a thought like that strayed into his mind it was hard not to. His thoughts turned to Sister Godrick and the amulet and all the day's trouble, and the little smile died by itself. He wondered what was going to happen, what he ought to say. He didn't know what to do around a bishop after the ring got kissed. Should he try and explain, or just wait and take his punishment?

His eyes wandered around the room. The palace was huge and dazzling. There were six doors to the room. He wondered if the bishop ever got mixed up trying to pick one, and what was on the other side of each. He noticed there were even little paintings on the ceiling, but they were of dreary religious subjects. It was curious, how somebody could paint them upside down like that, and so small. He turned his head almost upside down to look. They made him think of the pictures he'd seen in the basement of St. Paul's, the ones of the mutilated saints, and his mind got back to matters of his own punishment. He wondered if bishops were the ones who made saints pay like that. He'd looked for weapons right away. He hadn't seen a paddle, or a whip. He was certain there would be one, probably made of solid gold. There was a poker by the fireplace, but it was black with soot. No bishop would ever touch it. He stole a peek at the bishop and flushed as he felt the bishop's eyes upon him.

"Come here, child," Murat said, his voice soothing. "I have devoted much thought to your troubles. They are not so grave that we cannot mend them together. Come now, and sit with me."

S ERENA ARRIVED AT THE PALACE AND RACED UP the stone steps to the main entrance. She had no idea where to go, where he might be. She pushed through the massive wooden doors. The entry was grand, with marble floors and busts on pedestals and a staircase that wound to the second floor. Wide corridors stretched away from the entry. As she opened the door she saw a priest hurrying by. "Tell me the way to the bishop," she said curtly.

The priest looked at her crossly. "I do not believe the monseigneur is receiving this afternoon, madame," he replied. "You can see his housekeeper."

"Then show me there."

The priest led her upstairs, where they found the housekeeper talking with the bishop's coachman. The woman dismissed the man and listened to Serena's demand. The woman shook her head. She was adamant. "It is not possible, madame. His Grace is not even here this afternoon. Come back next week. Come back *mardi*."

"The priest *is* here, and I will see him now." Serena pushed past her, and began opening doors.

"What are you doing?" the housekeeper demanded. "I told you! He is not here! Stop, this instant!" But Serena pushed her out of the way. She found the right door, and burst into the bishop's apartments.

What she saw across the room on the couch didn't register for a moment. Her son was there, his shirt torn, his pants unbuckled. His face was twisted in anger and fear. His hair was tousled. He was struggling against the huge form of the bishop, who was grasping at the back of his shirt while Moussa was trying to pull away. He saw his mother, and a look of relief swept over him.

"Maman!" he cried. Startled, the bishop let go. Moussa shot out of his grasp. He ran to Serena and buried his head in her dress.

"Go home, Moussa," she said quietly. "Now, quickly. Wait for me there." He nodded and she watched him bolt from the apartment. Then she turned to face the bishop. He was struggling to right himself and was gathering his robes about him. He was half-drunk, she could see it from across the room. An animal, slobbering and grotesque. Her head was pounding.

She moved swiftly across the room. She saw the poker by the fireplace. She picked it up as she went, lifting it above her head to strike him. The bishop raised his arm to ward off the blow. "I will—" she started to say. At that moment the housekeeper rushed in behind her, accompanied by the coachman.

"*Your Grace!*" The housekeeper gasped. "I am so sorry, Your Grace! She pushed me over! What has happened! Are you all right? Has she hurt you? Get back, you! Get away from the monseigneur!" Serena hesitated, the rod high above her head. The coachman stood behind the housekeeper, glaring at Serena. His eyes were on the curved iron hook of the poker. He judged her to be a woman who would plant it in his skull, and didn't relish a test.

"Get her out of here," the bishop said, wheezing. He sat heavily down in one of the chairs. "She's mad. She tried to kill me. Call the rest of the house staff if you must. Just get her out. And then get out yourselves."

Another servant stepped forward hesitantly to carry out the bishop's instructions. It was unnecessary. Serena dropped the poker, which fell with a dull thud on the carpet. Without a word she turned and strode from the room.

SERENA DESPERATELY WISHED HENRI WERE HOME. He was at one of the balloon factories—she didn't know which one—and was not coming to the château first. They were to meet at the opera. She didn't want to go to the damned thing, not tonight. But she had promised, and he would be waiting.

Moussa was all right. He had cried, and wouldn't tell her what had happened, but he was all right. He was safe. She had touched his face, his head, his arms and his legs. She had held him for a long soft moment. Then he pulled away, and ran outside to play with Paul. He wouldn't do that if he weren't all right. She made certain both Gascon and Madame LeHavre would be there to look after him. Gascon read the trouble on her face and reassured her. "If you wish it I shall not leave his side." "I wish it," she said, and he had moved off to watch over the boy. And so there was no reason, really, not to go. She would tell Henri of the situation the next day. It would be Noël, his holiday Noël. They usually went skating then, on the lake in the Bois. She would slip and slide on the ice, her ankles wobbly, and he would try to hold her up, and they would collapse together in laughter. Her memories of it were warm. But this year they would not skate. They would talk. She knew she would have to tell him. She had hidden her own troubles, but this was different.

His rage would be terrible. She needed his rage.

He has tried to harm my son. She trembled at the thought. She tried to concentrate on her dress and her hair. She wore her hair with a ribbon in a thick braid to the side, the way Henri liked it. She wore no jewelry except a ring he had given her. It was turquoise and silver, from Afghanistan. She regarded herself critically in the mirror. She did not paint her face. She thought she was horribly plain, but Henri truly loved the way she looked, she knew he did. The other men seemed to notice as well. But she had learned not to take their attention as a compliment. Frenchmen were not discerning. They leered at anything vaguely female.

She decided she was too plain. She found a hat, a big one with feathers from Elisabeth's room. It was graceful and becoming. She knew it would make him laugh when he saw it. She never wore hats and he would know she was doing it for his silly opera. She smiled. Oh, she loved him so.

He has tried to harm my son. The thought kept intruding, washing over her like a cold wave of horror. *What manner of man would do that to a child?* She would have to stop what she was doing, and catch her breath and think about all of the what-ifs. What if Paul hadn't come to her? What if she hadn't ridden so fast? What if, what if. . . .

He has tried to harm my son. Every time she thought it, her blood boiled and a terrible sick feeling seized her by the chest. She shuddered. Prussians outside the gates, Henri's Church within.

I could have killed him, she said to herself. *I could have buried that iron rod in his brain.* She didn't know why she had stopped. It wasn't the servants. She had simply stopped.

He has tried to harm my son. His flesh was her flesh. His hurt was her hurt. His torment came from her blood, his blood that was her blood, and they were both so foreign here. His honor was hers to protect, his life in her hands until he grew to his destiny. She had made a choice many years ago, to marry the count and have his children. It had been the right decision, but a selfish one. She had known it at the time. The amenokal had known too. He had warned her of the trouble that would follow, the trouble that would befall her child. He had seen it so clearly. It was her own selfishness that had placed her son in peril.

He has tried to harm my son.

And it is my fault.

CHAPTER 15

A HUNDRED GLORIOUS CARRIAGES DREW UP BE-
fore the opera on the rue le Pelletier. The dress of
the women was more subdued than normal owing
to the war, but still there were feathers and lace and
bright faces, gay smiles and quiet laughter. Even with
Bismarck at the door Paris still knew how to have a
good time.

Henri saw her coming. She moved through the
crowd with grace. "As I predicted, you will captivate
them all," he said. He looked appreciatively at her hat
and fooled her by not laughing. "It becomes you."

"It feels as if a bird landed there." She smiled. "I
keep wanting to swat it."

He felt her tension immediately in spite of the smile.
"Is anything the matter?"

She had settled herself for the evening. It could wait.
"Nothing, I'm sorry, it's all right. We can talk about it
later," she said. He took her arm and they walked inside, the count returning a score of greetings, the
countess a score of looks.

The hall glowed with official Paris. Henri pointed
out Governor Trochu and the mayor of Montparnasse,
a scattering of colonels and generals, and the American
ambassador. Even Victor Hugo had come. Serena had
learned to read French with his books, and stared at
him raptly from across the hall. His head with its flowing white hair was just visible over the edge of his box,
and pretty young women were on either side of him.
The audience was alive with excitement and gossip, everyone hoping for an escape, however brief, from the

troubles outdoors. Both sides were celebrating an unofficial Christmas truce. Just after noon the guns in the forts had fallen silent, and the audience would be able to hear.

From the instant it began Serena was enchanted with the production. As Henri had promised, there was grand spectacle and beautiful music. The orchestra was very close. She watched the musicians as they played, their breath visible in the cold hall, yet the temperature not seeming to affect their music. The performers came out onto the stage to huge applause, and there was a riveting solo by a beautiful woman, her voice soaring through the absolutely quiet hall. "She's the one who—" Henri started to explain in a whisper, but she shushed him. She would follow it. At one point the stage swarmed with bishops in their purple robes, the bright red of the Grand Inquisitor in their midst. Serena's heart beat faster at the awful sight of all the high priests, but she reminded herself it was just a performance, and pushed him out of her mind.

At the intermission they went to the lobby, where Henri pointed out the murals, the paintings of famous singers who had performed there. They moved across the crowded room, Henri constantly caught up in greetings and brief conversations. She was looking up at the chandelier when she turned and nearly bumped into the bishop. He was talking with a small group of men. They were fawning, hanging on his every word. He looked to one side and saw her. His eyes were still glazed from the day's drinking, but he was sober enough now. His gaze darkened and his demeanor changed. He turned away from his companions. She realized he was coming to say something to her.

"Why *Comtesse*." He bowed with heavy mockery. "To see you twice in one day. Such a pleasure is more than I deserve."

Serena felt the blood pounding in her temples. Pure malevolence emanated from the man. He was remarkable, that she granted him. That he could carry on so normally after what he had done was all the more damning. She spoke in a low steady voice. "I left too soon today, Priest. I should have used the poker on you. If you come near my son again, I will use it. I will kill you."

The bishop's eyes lit with genuine amusement and he laughed. He leaned forward and put his face near to hers, so that he could speak for her ears only. "Such a temper you display. Actually, I had been planning to have him back one day. I can only wonder how the child could be so fine when he is nothing but the half-breed bastard of a pagan slut. Most curious, isn't it?"

The savagery of his words took a moment to register. She heard the voice and felt the spittle and saw the twisted smile, and all the horror of the afternoon came rushing back at her and her hatred became blinding and passionate.

She didn't think about what happened next. She simply acted. She moved as if through a dream, everything slow, calm, methodical. Behind the bishop stood a major of the Garde Mobile. He wore his full dress uniform, with a red and blue tunic with gold filigree on the sleeves, a képi, and gleaming knee boots. He carried a sword on one side, a pistol on the other. She took two steps through the crowd, its laughter and talk and the tinkle of champagne glasses seeming distant and vague. In a fluid motion she yanked the gun from the major's side. She turned to face her tormentor, everything happening so quickly no one had time to react but the bishop, who alone saw her movements. His face twisted in the horror of slow comprehension. He raised his hands and said something and stepped back. She didn't hear. She couldn't hear anything now. She raised the weapon and drew back the hammer, and she thought of the boar in the Bois that day so long ago, that other malevolent beast that had tried to harm her son, and she fired, and fired, and fired again, fired at the face retreating behind a mask of blood, fired at the huge grotesque creature as it sank to the floor, fired bullet after bullet into the hated brain. After a while she realized that the roar had died. The bullets were all gone, the chamber empty. The gun clicked and clicked as she pulled the trigger. She stopped.

The opera house erupted in pandemonium. Women screamed and men ducked and shouted. At first no one knew what had happened. The people standing close drew back in horror as the bishop fell. Henri had been talking with an American diplomat. At the shots he whirled and saw Serena standing there with the pistol in her hand, a cloud of smoke around it, the bishop of Boulogne-Billancourt lying at her feet. Serena dropped the pistol to the floor, and stared dumbly at the body. Henri was paralyzed with disbelief.

"Get back! Out of the way, quickly!" came a deep voice from the crowd, and the prefect of police pushed his way forward. For a moment he said nothing as his eyes took in the scene. His face turned ashen. He knew the bishop. He knew the count, and the count's wife. It was all there, clear before him, yet nothing was clear at all.

"I am afraid you must come with me, Countess," the prefect said gently. He moved to take her arm. It was enough to shake Henri from his shock. He sprang forward and shoved the prefect out of the way. He caught Serena by the hand and pulled her through the crowd, which was still boiling in confusion. There was no time to think, only to do. He was not going to let them take her. They had to escape. Nothing else mattered. With elbows and shoulders he cleared a way through the throng, Serena following, holding his hand tightly. A man in an infantry officer's uniform stood to block them. Without breaking stride Henri lashed out with a vicious backhand that sent the man reeling. Another few steps and they were at the front doors. All around them there were shouts and confusion, the house shattered in shock. A whistle shrilled.

They raced out the door and down the street, Henri still leading Serena by the hand. It was quite dark. The streets were covered with a thin blanket of snow, their progress slowed by the ice underneath. Henri looked back. A few people had ventured out of the doors behind them into the cold night, and were staring after them. But so far no one was giving chase. They came to his carriage. He lifted her easily and jumped in, and whipped at the horse. "We've got to get Moussa and Paul," he said as the horse responded to the lash of his whip. "We've got to get out."

She nodded dumbly. "I had to do it," she said simply. "I had to."

Henri barely heard. He drove the horse away from the opera, toward the Boulevard Haussmann. The bitter cold air stung his face. He was shaking a little, with the realization of what he had done. His action had been instinctive, but his mind cleared quickly and he knew he was right.

His wife had shot the bishop in cold blood. Of that he was certain. It didn't matter why, not yet. The only thing that mattered was to get her out, out of the city, away from the madness and the masses. He had left Jules in the hands of justice, and had doubted the wisdom of it ever since. There would be no such doubts with Serena. She was his life. He had to protect her, had to get her out of the country, out of Paris at least. He had no illusions about what could happen to her if they stayed. He had powerful friends, but so had the bishop. He was prepared to lose everything for her, if it came to that. He would never let them take her.

Their carriage flew through dark streets. Serena sat next to him, holding tightly. He turned again to look behind. Still no one following, but he knew they would come. Soon. His mind raced with escape, with calculations of coal gas and wind and ballast. It would work, if only there was enough gas, and enough time.

"There's a balloon just ready, at the Gare du Nord. It was to leave tomorrow night. We'll get Moussa and Paul. We'll leave tonight."

THE PREFECT WAS SHAKEN. HE KNELT BY THE bishop, who had collapsed in a pool of blood and purple robes. He was dead. The prefect grimaced at the mess that had been the man's face. He pulled a part of the bishop's robe over his head, to cover it.

The prefect had despised the bishop. There was noth-

ing to like about the man or his methods. On occasion
they had done business together, and the prefect had
made a great deal of money. On other occasions he had
cleaned up after others had finished dealing with him.
There had been suicides, hushed and ugly, and a murder. The bishop was always somewhere at the fringes,
never close enough to be implicated. His death would
leave Paris a better place. Offhand the prefect supposed
the countess had gotten caught up in some nasty business with him, and had finally done what so many others secretly longed to do. The prefect would have
preferred to dump the body into the Seine and lift a
toast to a better city, but, of course, it was out of the
question. He had a job to do. He had to act. A hundred
people had seen it happen. A hundred people had seen
the countess and her gun. She would have to be brought
to account.

The prefect had known the count for years. Never
closely, but from a distance. The count had surprised
him by running, but then he understood that a man
would wish to protect his wife. The count would in turn
understand that the prefect would wish to protect the
city.

The prefect stood and turned to a sergeant of the
police. "You will take two men and go quickly to the
Château deVries. It is near Boulogne, on the road to
St.-Cloud. You will arrest the countess for the murder of
the bishop. If the count resists or interferes in any way,
you will arrest him as well."

"At your order." The sergeant saluted, turned, and
pushed his way through the milling crowd.

SHE STARTED TALKING AT THE NEUILLY GATE.
Henri had leaned down to speak with the sentry. As
the man opened the gate it made her think of the fall
day when the bishop had looked down upon her as she
was being expelled from the city, and the whole story
began to pour out. She told him what had happened
that day, and about her morning at St. Paul's with Sister

Godrick, and about later, at the palace. Henri listened intently but drove like a madman through the Bois de Boulogne. The forest looked eerie in the snow and low light. Everywhere there were tree stumps, the remains of a great forest being cut to fuel the city's fires against the bitter cold. Even the roots were disappearing.

Serena's voice broke as she repeated what the bishop had said at the opera. "I could not help myself, Henri," she said as she finished. "I would shoot him again for what he tried to do to our son." Henri put his arm around her, and the carriage sped through the woods.

At the château Henri talked urgently to Gascon in the front hall. He told him quickly what had happened, holding back nothing. There were no secrets between them. Gascon's eyes widened but he said nothing. "Get me fresh horses," the count told him. "I'm going to take Serena and the boys out of the city."

"Sire." Gascon raced to the stables. He harnessed the two best horses there, and loaded the carriage with supplies that he thought the count would need, including heavy blankets and a lantern. In the château he pulled a rifle and two pistols from the case. He made certain they were loaded and that there was spare ammunition. Then he ran to the kitchen to find food for the trip.

Henri went to the study, where he was startled to see Elisabeth. "You will not take Paul," she said. She had been listening to what the count told Gascon. Henri hadn't seen her for weeks, didn't know where or when she might be coming back.

"I didn't know you were here, Elisabeth. I only meant to protect him. Of course I won't take him. He'll stay with you." He moved through his study, stuffing papers into his bag.

"Where are you going?" Elisabeth asked. Her mind was reeling with the news, but she worked hard to remain calm. *The bishop dead!* It was thrilling. She began to believe, truly believe, that she and Pascal were going to pull it off. Now only the count posed a threat to her plans, and he was leaving.

"I don't know. Somewhere. To the country."

"You're leaving the *city?*" Elisabeth's eyes widened. "I suppose the Prussians have given you their blessing?"

"We're taking a balloon. There's one ready at the Gare du Nord."

"Are you mad?"

"Quite, Elisabeth. Now please let me pack."

Upstairs Serena rousted the boys and was filling a small bag with a few clothes.

"Where are we going?" Moussa asked, rubbing his eyes.

"We're leaving the city. By balloon. I'll explain later. We must hurry!" Moussa looked uncertainly at Paul.

"Leaving? Paul's coming too, isn't he?"

"No. He's staying with his mother. She's downstairs. You'll see him later. Now *quickly!*"

The boys looked uneasily at each other, sensing that something larger than they could understand was happening around them. The adults were racing around, Gascon at the carriage house, the house in a turmoil. Something was wrong, terribly wrong.

"I guess I'll see you later," Moussa said, pulling on his clothes. The prospect of a balloon ride was exciting, but the thought of leaving Paul behind made him miserable.

"I guess so." They both knew the end of the siege was a long way off. They wouldn't see each other for a while. Maybe a long while. Paul took the pocketknife he used to carve wood from his dresser drawer. "Here, you'd better take this. You might need it." Moussa nodded his thanks.

On the way out Moussa had a sudden thought, and panic set in.

"Father, I can't go, not yet."

"Nonsense. Where's your coat?"

"I have to get my amulet."

"*What?*"

"My amulet. Sister Godrick took it. I need it. I can't leave without it."

"Don't be foolish. We're in a hurry, Moussa. You can get another one."

"No I can't, Father. It's the only one. It's special. It's from the amenokal. She took it from me and I need it back."

"I know who it's from, son, but there's no time! We must go! Now! Quickly!"

"It's at St. Paul's. Please, Father." His voice quivered. Henri stopped what he was doing and looked hard at his son. His voice had never had such a plaintive tone.

Serena spoke quietly. "We can stop there, Henri. It isn't far out of the way. Please. It's important."

Henri sighed. If they could escape the château grounds without being caught, he figured it would be a good while before their pursuers thought of the balloons. They ought to have enough time. "All right, but hurry! They'll be coming!"

"I will delay them as long as I can, sire," Gascon said as they hurried to the carriage. "If you need me—"

"Thank you, Gascon." Henri clapped him on the shoulder. His face was grim. "I'll contact you later, when the siege is lifted. Mind things for me."

"Godspeed, sire," said Gascon, and they were gone.

Paul stood in the doorway and with a sick feeling in his heart watched the carriage disappear down the drive. He saw the small form of his cousin in the back and knew Moussa was watching him too. He waved, and choked back a sob. In the distance he thought he saw Moussa waving back.

TWENTY MINUTES AFTER THE COUNT LEFT, THE PO-
lice arrived at the château. The house was in dark-ness, and Elisabeth had retired to her room. The police pounded on the door and shouted. Gascon waited in the dark in the kitchen and let them carry on. At length, when it sounded as if they were going to break the door down, he answered.

"I'm coming, I'm coming!" He opened the door, grumbling and scratching and rubbing his eyes as though he'd just gotten up. "What is it? Who's there?"

"Police," the sergeant snapped. "Where is the countess?"

Gascon shrugged and yawned. "Pardon, monsieur, but I do not know. Perhaps with the count."

"And where is the count?"

Gascon shrugged again. "I have no idea. Perhaps with the countess. I work for him, not he for me. They haven't been here tonight. If they do arrive, perhaps you would care to leave a message for them? I would be happy to deliver it, monsieur."

The sergeant shook his head.

"Then perhaps you would care to come inside and wait? I am certain they will be home later this evening. I can offer you wine, to take away the chill."

The sergeant thought it over. He decided to leave a man at the château and return to the prefecture himself. He wasn't terribly worried about not finding the countess. After all, where could she go? It was one of the few advantages of the siege, he supposed. They would have her soon enough.

"*Oui*," he said to Gascon. "I will leave one man here with you."

The sergeant was near the end of the drive when a figure loomed out of the darkness. The horse almost ran into her, and had to be drawn up suddenly.

"Are you crazy?" the sergeant shouted. "You might have been killed!"

Elisabeth ran to the side of the carriage. Even though it was dark she pulled her shawl up around her face, so that no one could identify her. She had made her decision in the study, and ran out the back door when she heard the police coming down the drive. She would seize the opportunity she saw in Henri's ruin. If Henri were arrested helping Serena escape after the murder of the bishop, his own credibility would be forever destroyed. The bishop's death and Henri's dishonor would seal her claim to the property. She looked up at the officers in their carriage.

"You must be quick!" she said. "The count is escaping with the countess!"

The sergeant laughed. "Not much running to be done through a ring of Prussians," he scoffed. "And who are you?"

"Never mind, you fool! This is the Count deVries you chase!"

"So?"

"Have you not seen the balloons leaving the city? It is he who sends them up! Even now he is on his way to the Gare du Nord, where they are launched! He is leaving tonight!"

Y OU *WHAT*, MAMAN?"

"I shot him. I killed him."

She tried to explain it as they rode together in the back of the carriage. She had thought about not telling him, or lying. But their lives were about to change forever. She had to tell him. He was old enough to know the truth. And when he knew the truth his lip quivered, and he was desperately afraid for her, afraid for them all, and he clung to her and knew it was all his fault, this terrible trouble that was chasing them through the night, and he began willing the horses to run faster.

Serena waited in the carriage while Henri and Moussa hurried into the cathedral through the main door. An acolyte was preparing the church for the late Mass. Puzzled, he watched as Moussa led his father down the aisle and into the sacristy, where they disappeared through another door that led to the back corridors. Henri hadn't been in the passages for years, but Moussa knew his way through the maze blindfolded, and soon they arrived at his classroom. The door was locked. Henri pulled hard at the brass handle, but it wouldn't budge.

"I can go around, and get in from the window in the courtyard," Moussa said.

"No. No time." Henri set his shoulder and rammed the door. It moved and wood splintered, but the heavy oak held fast. Henri hit it again with more force, and the door gave way with a crash. Moussa ran into the darkened room, tripping over a chair as he went, the chair clattering to the floor. Across the courtyard in the rear of the cathedral the count saw the light of a lantern moving their way. "The curé," he said. At the desk Moussa rummaged quickly through the top drawer where he was sure she would have put it.

It wasn't there.

He opened another drawer, and another, his desperation mounting as he ran out of places to look. He was terrified. What if she'd taken it with her? What if she'd destroyed it? He pushed the papers aside, his fingers probing the back of each drawer.

"Hurry, Moussa!" the count said. "They're coming!"

Moussa slammed one drawer shut, and opened another below it. Papers and pencils and books. It wasn't there! He was ready to cry.

And then he had it, his fingers closing around the familiar leather. He pulled it out and looked at it triumphantly. "Got it!" he said, and they ran from the classroom as the curé was fumbling with the door at the other end of the hall.

In the carriage Moussa had an idea. "I know another way out of the city, Father."

"Oh?"

"Through the basement of the cathedral. I've been there, with Paul. There are tunnels that run all the way to the Prussian lines. We could sneak past them."

The voice was a whip. "You were at the Prussian lines?"

"They never saw us, Father."

"We'll talk about that later. But now we need to get past the Prussian lines, Moussa, not just to them. We've got to fly. We'll take the balloon."

Once again the carriage lurched forward into the darkness.

THE SERGEANT WHIPPED SAVAGELY AT THE BIG horse straining at the harness. Steam poured off the animal's neck, its breath labored and deep. The other officer sat at the sergeant's side. He was not much more than a boy, nervous and new to the force, clutching a rifle in one hand and holding on to the edge of the cabriolet and trying to keep from pitching out with the other, all the while trying not to freeze to death. It wasn't easy, police business. Their carriage was light and fast but unstable, slipping and sliding and bouncing through the streets, making a terrible clatter on the cobblestones, the wheels creaking and popping as they went.

The sergeant cursed his horrid luck. He knew he had been lax when he set out to make the arrest. He had barely trotted his horse from the opera to the château, deluded by the notion that a besieged city made a good jail. If he let the countess escape so easily it would end his career.

But he was determined not to fail. Again and again he lashed his horse, spurring it on ever faster. They flew along the narrow passage of the Quai de Grenelle, past the long sloping lawns of the Champ de Mars, where thousands of troops slept in tents or huddled together before small fires, trying to ward off the arctic freeze. Then it was on to the Quai d'Orsay, the horse pounding alongside the river that looked so dark and deep and cold, the great shadowy form of the Louvre looming large across the water. He turned across the Pont Neuf, swerving to avoid a group of startled pedestrians who jumped back out of the way. The Ile de la Cité was a blur, the towers of Notre Dame just visible in the darkness, the crowds beginning to assemble in the great square for midnight Mass. He pressed ahead along the rue St.-Denis, willing his horse to run faster. A sudden blast of wind took his hat and muffler, but he never slowed.

"Just a little farther now," he shouted to his young companion. "We're almost there."

THE ENVELOPE OF THE BALLOON BILLOWED UP against the cold dark sky. The wind flags on top of the *gare* showed just a slight breeze, to the southwest. It wasn't much. The cold had settled over the city like a blanket, and the air wasn't moving. It would have to do,

Henri thought as he looked up briefly. He cursed the cold. His fingers weren't working properly. They were numb, his knuckles bleeding and torn. He pounded at the valve to get it working again, so that it would open all the way for the coal gas. The balloon was nearly full, but he wanted more so that when the temperatures warmed—if they ever did—they'd have plenty of lift for long distance. But something was stuck, some grease frozen or lever caught, he couldn't tell, and there was just a weak hiss as the gas moved instead of the normal whooshing sound. The more he hurried the longer it seemed to take.

Henri had lit two bright gas lamps at either end of the square outside the station, to give them enough light to work. The square was surrounded by a tall iron fence, erected to keep the curious away from the equipment and the gas lines. There was a large gate at one end through which supplies were carried. A sleepy guard tended the gate. He had been surprised to see the count arriving at such a late hour on Christmas Eve, but then the balloons went up at crazy times.

"A launch tonight?" he asked.

"*Oui*," Henri said. He nodded and closed the gate after the carriage entered the compound. A small group of spectators gathered outside the fence to watch. They always came when a balloon was going up. They were used to seeing more lights and more people involved, but they chattered excitedly anyway. A balloon launch was a great event, even to one who'd seen a dozen.

Henri set about filling the balloon, leaving Serena and Moussa to load sacks of ballast into the basket. They hauled them off a big pile and lugged them one at a time across the plaza. They lashed some to the outside of the basket, and simply dumped others inside on the floor. Moussa ran to the carriage and collected the blankets and the sack of food, and carried them back. He slipped on the corner of one of the blankets and tripped, spilling everything onto the cold stone. He recovered quickly and scooped things up, running and dumping them into the basket.

A light snow started to fall. The balloon began to

strain at its tethers as the gas poured in. Henri timed it, his mind calculating the cubic meters and the flow. Three minutes, two minutes. The basket was starting to lift. They needed more weight.

"Serena! Moussa! Get in, now!" he shouted, and they climbed over the wicker railing. The balloon was like a live mass trying to escape its bounds. The halyards creaked above them and the wicker crackled under their weight.

They all heard it at the same time, the clatter of wheels and the relentless rhythm of hooves beating against the distant pavement. Without looking Henri knew who it was. He could take on no more gas. Furiously he started to close the valve, struggling with it as the cold thwarted the movement of the brass and iron.

"The guns!" Moussa's voice choked in panic. "I didn't get the guns!" They were still in the back of the carriage.

"Leave them!" Serena said, but he was up and over the side before she could stop him. She had to stay where she was, to tend the ropes. She looked helplessly on as he ran for the carriage and picked the weapons out of the back. He put the ammunition boxes in his pockets, and scrambled back over the rough stones. Relieved, Serena pulled him up and over the side.

She heard the carriage on the other side of the station. It stopped.

"Henri, come now!" Serena shouted, her voice desperate. "They are here!"

THE SERGEANT PULLED UP ON THE WRONG SIDE OF the building. He had no idea where the balloons were launched, but quickly saw through the station to the lights on the other side. The biggest part of the balloon was hidden from his view by the structure of the *gare* itself, but he could make out the round neck through the windows, and the halyards straining upward. The balloon was ready to go! He lashed at his horse and raced around the side of the building. He cursed. The way was blocked by a wide ribbon of tracks. There was no time to backtrack, to find a crossing to get to the other side.

"*Merde!*" he said. "We've got to go on foot. Be quick now!" They jumped from the cabriolet and scrambled across the tracks. The boy stumbled and fell heavily on the rails. He bloodied his lip on the cold steel, and wiped it with his sleeve as he jumped up and ran. Their boots clomped on the pavement as they ran to the fence. Serena saw them first. Henri was just lifting off the lines that held the balloon to concrete posts at either end of the square. He had two more to go.

The sergeant saw him through the fence. "You there! Count deVries! *Arrêtez!* You are to stop this instant! The countess is under arrest! You must stop now!" He saw the count glance over his shoulder as he raced to the next post. He lifted off the line, turned, and started for the last one. Desperately the sergeant looked for the way in. The gate was all the way on the other side of the area. There was no time.

"Stop or I'll shoot!" he said, and at that the boy at his side raised his rifle.

Henri ignored him and ran full speed to the last of the posts. Off came the line. Now the only rope holding the balloon to earth was under Serena's control. "Cast off the line!" he shouted, and quickly she twisted the line off the post. The balloon lurched upward, then quickly dropped, then started upward again. Serena panicked as she saw how far he had to run, and that the balloon was lifting away from the ground. He was running full out. He would have to jump in.

"Fire a warning shot," the sergeant said to the young gendarme.

The youth was nervous. He was an expert marksman, but had never pointed his rifle at another human being. He had already sighted the count down the long barrel of his rifle, fixing on the retreating back. Perhaps he was *too* nervous, or perhaps he only heard the word "fire." He breathed deeply and squeezed the trigger.

Henri had just reached the basket when the shot rang out. Serena was reaching out to take his arms when the bullet struck. She heard a thud and felt his arms jerk, and his grip slipped away. "Henri!" she screamed. The balloon was lifting away and she was holding him by herself over the side of the basket, his legs dangling free. He couldn't help, and was dead weight in her arms. She knew she couldn't hold on for long. He was beginning to slip, and the balloon was climbing quickly. "Moussa, help me!" she cried. Moussa leaned over the side, and together they struggled desperately to pull him up. Serena could see a red stain blossoming on the back of his jacket.

At last they had him inside. He collapsed in the bottom of the basket, onto the bags of sand. His eyes were closed. Serena slipped down the side of the wicker and took his head in her lap. There was a trickle of blood at the corner of his mouth. He opened his eyes, and saw her there. He squeezed her hand weakly and smiled, then closed his eyes. Her face was next to his, and she saw his color draining. "Oh Henri, no, no, no," she cried. She held him tightly as the balloon began to rise from the yard and soar over the top of the *gare*. "*Je t'aime*," she whispered. More shots rang out from below. "I love you, Henri. *Je t'aime, je t'aime.*"

Below them the two policemen stood helplessly and watched from their position outside the fence as the balloon was swallowed by the night. The guard had rushed toward them on hearing the shots. "Are you crazy?" he shouted. "What are you doing? That's the Count deVries in that balloon! There is coal gas in it! If you hit it it will explode! From here it will kill us all!" The sergeant thought about it, about bringing them down that way, but he'd seen a boy inside the basket.

"To the calèche," he snapped to the one with the rifle. "We'll follow them as long as we can. Maybe the balloon won't make it outside of the city." He didn't believe it, but he had to try. They raced for their carriage.

Moussa was panicked. Things were happening too fast. He didn't know what to do. "Maman!" he shrieked, his eyes moving between his wounded father below and the massive balloon above. The world was falling away quickly and he was terrified of the height and the night and the unknown before him. "Maman, I don't know what to do! I don't know how to fly this! We're in the sky! *What should I do?*"

But Serena wasn't listening. She held her husband's head in her lap and rocked back and forth, gently rocked, stroking his hair, kissing his forehead, squeezing his hand, whispering, her warm tears falling onto his face. She knew there was but a moment left. It was with a balloon that their love had begun. It was in a balloon that it was ending. His breathing became shallow and she felt him slipping away. She cried out desperately but couldn't stop it. There was nothing she could do.

His eyes closed once again and he was gone.

Moussa heard his mother's wail and from the terrible sound knew his father was dead. His heart froze. It was too much to comprehend. He looked out over the edge of the basket and forced himself to deal with their situation. His mother wasn't responding. He had to do it himself. He could see the rooftops below, and lights twinkling in a few of the houses, but he couldn't make anything out clearly. He had no idea where they were, or in what direction they were heading. He tried to calm himself, to think. They had to keep altitude, and he saw that they were already beginning to lose a little, getting a little closer to the ground. He reached over the side and with the pocketknife Paul had given him cut free one of the sandbags hanging around the outside. The bag dropped away, and immediately he felt the difference.

The snow fell more heavily now. He thought it would be wise to get above it, in case the snow might damage the envelope or make it too heavy. He cut loose a few other bags, and the balloon soared upward. The clouds grew thicker, and soon there was no sight of the city or anything else. They were wrapped in a shroud of silence and the clouds.

Moussa pulled in the ropes hanging free and tied them to the side of the basket. After a while the balloon broke through the blanket of snow clouds and rose above them. The sky above was cold and black and full of stars, the brightest stars he had ever seen. The clouds stretched away forever like a carpet at his feet. It looked as if he could climb out of the balloon and just walk across them. It was beautiful. He cut away more ballast. He couldn't feel any wind, but from the clouds he could tell they were moving. He thought it was to the south, but he couldn't be sure. It didn't matter. There was nothing else to be done.

He sat down in the basket, next to his mother and the body of his father. He drew a blanket over them all, and his mother put her arm around him. Moussa gently touched his father's face, and it was only then that he knew for himself, for certain, that it was true. Softly he began to cry.

Far below them, too distant now to hear, the bells in the towers of Notre Dame rang in the joyous day of Christmas, the ninety-seventh day of the siege. The archbishop of Paris lifted the chalice of the blood of Christ to the congregation. Outside the ramparts, French troops froze to death in their trenches. At Versailles, Bismarck stood before a warm fire and lifted a toast to Wilhelm, the next emperor of all Germany, the master of Europe.

The next morning the balloon came to earth in south-central France, in the province of Auvergne. They landed hard in a field, and would have been hurt but for the soft blanket of snow that cushioned their landing. No one saw them come down. Mother and son buried Henri as best they could, under rocks they hauled with frozen hands from across the fields. When they were done they stood holding each other, staring at the mound of stone. Then they set off through the storm to find a road.

Through the long night in the air, the Countess deVries had cradled her husband's head in her lap and thought about what to do without him. She didn't want to go on. There was only blackness without him, only desolation and despair. But there was Moussa to think of.

She settled on the only thing she knew to do. She would take her son away. They would make their way to Marseilles and find a boat to Algiers. From there they would cross Algeria to the Sahara.

In the Sahara they would find the Tuareg.

She was taking him home.

PART 2

THE SAHARA

1 8 7 6

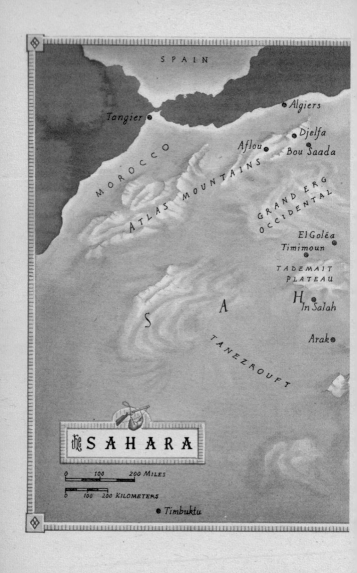

SPAIN

Algiers

Tangier

Djelfa

Aflou Bou Saada

MOROCCO

ATLAS MOUNTAINS

GRAND ERG
OCCIDENTAL

El Goléa
Timimoun

TADEMAIT
PLATEAU

A   H In Salah

S

Arak

TANEZROUFT

THE SAHARA

0   100   200 MILES

0   100   200 KILOMETERS

Timbuktu

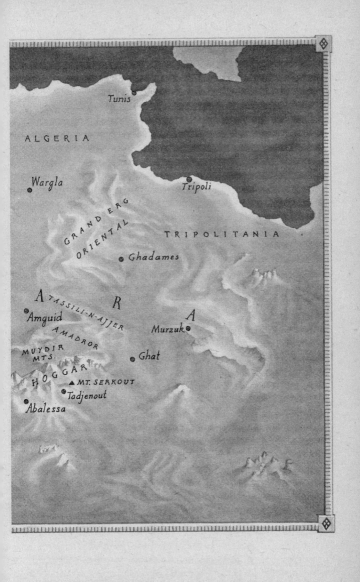

CHAPTER 16

SOMETHING MOVED. SOMETHING WAS THERE.

The great gangly bird stopped grazing and raised its head. Keen brown eyes watched patiently for a sign, a movement. The bird stood quietly in the tall grass of the wadi, a riverbed in the Hoggar, the high desert mountains of the Sahara. The ostrich was a three-year-old male, more than two and a half meters tall. A light wind rippled the grass but there was no scent.

The bird was near exhaustion. For three days it had eluded its hunters, through long awful hours of panic and flight interspersed with calm, as the hunters first found, then lost the track, then picked it up again, and the deadly game wore on. The effort was telling now. Even at rest its heart was pounding, its breath labored, its reserves of strength nearly gone.

The whole flock desperately needed rest. The little ones would falter first, then the adults. At the beginning there had been forty of them. Now only nine or ten others grazed nearby, their long necks appearing through the grass, bobbing up and down as they watched and grazed and wandered along the trickle of water that still ran down the sandy wadi in the wake of the storm. The rest had been caught or gotten separated during the chase, which had led hunter and hunted across the wild volcanic plateau that was torn with violent cliffs and veined with sharp valleys and strewn throughout with boulders. The plateau was a giant maze of natural tunnels and caves and passageways. It held a thousand hiding places to help the birds, but a thousand more traps and dead ends to help the hunters. Survival depended on taking the right turns.

Across the rocks, Moussa raised his head carefully. He wore the blue veil of a nobleman of the Ihaggaren, the master race of Tuareg who ruled the Hoggar. The blue men, the Tuareg were called, for the deep indigo dyes used in their robes and in the sheshes that covered their heads, and that often rubbed off and colored their skin. The soft cloth was wound round his head like a helmet, high and wide on top, then wrapped round and round his head and neck, covering everything except for a narrow slit like a visor, through which only his eyes could be seen. He wore his *takatkat*, the flowing blue summer robes of light cotton that covered everything except his hands and feet, and beneath it *takirbai*, broad trousers. He carried only a lance and club for weapons; a rope; a spyglass that had belonged to his father; and a *guerba*, a goatskin water bag, slung across his shoulder.

He maneuvered carefully downwind from the birds. He chose his steps cautiously, making his way through the boulders that lay upon the valley floor between him and the birds. It was the height of the Saharan summer, and the rocks were blazing hot, blistering the skin of anyone who touched them.

He, too, was near exhaustion. His body ached with fatigue. He had eaten no food since the previous morning, when he had permitted himself a handful of dates. His body had grown lean and hard in the desert. He was accustomed to infrequent meals, but now he wished he'd taken more. His stomach growled with neglect, and his muscles burned with the effects of extended effort. But this was his first hunt, and he pushed the discomfort from his mind.

The hunt was a timeless ritual between old adversaries, the blue men and the big birds. It had been five summers since there had been a chase with so many in the flocks. During two of the summers there had been drought and the birds had not come at all. For three summers after that there had been war in the desert, and no time for the chase. But then one afternoon they looked up from camp and saw the dark storm over distant mountains, and their blood ran fast and the Tuareg sprang to action.

Essamen! Lightning! Like magic, a great siren that beckoned man and bird alike. When the rare summer storms came, the skies grew angry and black and crackled with fire. The birds would see it and some instinct drew them together in pairs and the pairs joined with others until there were flocks and the flocks grew large, and then they would travel vast distances straight toward the fire in the sky, knowing that the lightning meant water to drink, and that water meant flowers and grasses to eat.

From other parts of the desert, the hunters would come as well, teams of them on fast, light camels who would alternate in relays as they wore their quarry down. The meat was a great delicacy, but it was the birds' skins and feathers that were much prized. They would be traded with the caravans that came from the southlands on the way north to the sea, where it was said they were shipped to distant lands to become hats and boots. No one believed the stories, even when Moussa told them of the glorious *chapeaux* seen on the Champs-Elysées. What was not in doubt was that a good hunt meant great wealth for the tribe and honor to the hunters, and often laughter to those who managed to witness part of the chase. It was never certain who looked sillier, the hunters or the hunted.

Moussa found a resting place and stopped. He watched the ostriches and pondered what to do. He had become separated from the others late the previous afternoon. First his camel had died. No, that wasn't right, he'd killed it with his empty-headedness. And then Mahdi had abandoned him, leaving him alone and on foot. Moussa flushed with embarrassment and anger when he thought of it: first his own stupidity, then his cousin's treachery. Moussa had been riding his prized camel, Taba, with a group of ten other men. They were moving in a loosely spaced line to flush the ostriches toward another group of Tuareg who waited near

Temassint. The ostriches would see them and run away, only to be turned again by the other group, the lines of hunters moving closer together as the birds ran themselves to exhaustion and could be caught.

Taba was a fawn-colored Tibesti camel, a present from the amenokal on the day Moussa had become a man and donned his veil. It was a superb animal, agile and cooperative and fast, surefooted on the rocks, and magnificent through the hunt. Together he and Taba had goaded six of the birds into a blind alley. Moussa was riding alone, consumed with excitement and the thrill of closing in on the quarry. He hadn't called for help, hadn't stopped to think. In his eagerness he had ridden up fast behind them, until they ran out of room. They turned around to flee, and found the tall rider and camel blocking the way.

"Be careful," the amenokal had warned him with typical brevity. It was Moussa's first hunt, and his only lesson. "They kick." Moussa knew the amenokal's way with words, and to look for hidden meaning, to think beyond the obvious. But this time he hadn't thought carefully enough.

Moussa had slowed and was gently moving toward the biggest bird, a giant black-and-white male that stood as tall as the camel, when he made the very mistake the amenokal had warned him about. Overeager, he got too close. The birds were tiring, but still had plenty of fire. In a panic the giant one lashed out with its powerful leg. Taba took the full force of the blow on the right foreleg. The bone snapped sharply. The camel bellowed and bucked and crashed to the ground, nearly crushing Moussa, who was just thrown free. Before he'd had a chance to get to his feet the ostriches had rushed past him, a little one in the rear running right over him in its mad flight and knocking him unceremoniously to the ground. Moussa grunted at the impact and fell hard on his back. The fall jarred him all the way through to his teeth. At length he picked himself up again, shaking his head to clear it.

Taba's shrieks and sobs echoed off the big rocks and filled Moussa with anguish. As he brushed himself off he heard laughter. Without looking he knew who it was, and his heart sank. Mahdi had a knack for being there when Moussa did something stupid, and was never shy about rubbing it in. He had appeared just in time to see the disaster. He had come down a steep slope on one side of the rocks, too far out of the way to stop the fleeing birds, who by then were disappearing gracefully back down the wadi, bobbing and weaving, kicking up sand and splashing in the water as they went. They pranced like feather dusters on legs, stretching their stubby wings to help them in their flight. They made barely a sound as they disappeared.

Mahdi watched them go, then paused to savor Moussa's situation before moving on. Mahdi despised his cousin, despised the way his own father, the amenokal, treated Moussa, despised the way he showered him with attention and gifts. The amenokal never treated Mahdi that way. Toward his own son the amenokal was harsh and unforgiving. Mahdi's eyes had burned with jealousy since the day his aunt Serena had brought the soft child from France to live among them. Mahdi could beat him when they fought, for he was two years older and much larger, but he took no real pleasure in such victories. All he really wanted was for Moussa to tire of the hard life of the desert and return to France. Each passing year made that less likely, until all Mahdi could do was make each day as difficult as possible for the intruder.

"Well done, Cousin," he said derisively from his mehari. "Another grand coup for the noble *ikufar*." He used the term for foreign infidel; it was his usual insult. Moussa felt his contempt, and at that moment knew it was deserved.

"I almost had him," he said lamely.

Mahdi whooped at that. "He almost had you, *w'allahi!* Brilliant trade. A mehari for a wisp of dust." He turned to ride after the birds.

"*Ekkel!*" Moussa called. "Wait! I need another mehari! Leave one for me!" Mahdi was leading a dozen spare mounts. He was going to position them on the far side of the hunt, where they would be fresh and ready when needed. He could easily spare one, but had no intention of making it easy on Moussa.

"And let you kill it with more stupidity? Do I look so foolish? If you will have another, walk back to camp and let the women and children see the noble Son of the Desert on foot. It is best to get moving, Cousin. It is hard to catch enough ostriches to make up for a dead camel when one is walking." He snickered and turned to ride off.

Moussa watched him disappear and kicked at the sand. He was angry with Mahdi, but angrier at himself. The amenokal would be disgusted. Oh yes, he would maintain an even gaze and his voice would have no sharp edges. He would not be so impolite as to directly chastise him. But Moussa would know the disappointment in his uncle's heart and feel the failure worse in his own. In the desert, camels were life. Camels were wealth. Camels were everything. The others would talk about it, and laugh and shake their heads, and tell jokes at his expense. Except for Mahdi's, their laughter would be good-natured, but that wouldn't diminish his failure.

Moussa felt wretched and overwhelmed. He had donned the veil only a month before, when he turned sixteen. The veil! So long awaited, the *tagelmust*, so eagerly anticipated, that enchanted moment when the bare face of the boy disappeared forever behind the blue veil of the man. The cloth had come from the south-lands, eight meters of it, a gift from his mother. From seventy leagues around had come the people of the Hoggar: other nobles, and vassals of the Dag Rali, the women and the children, the serfs and slaves and smiths, the marabouts and the chiefs, all there to witness the ceremony, that grand moment when their lives paused and they grew hushed, the moment when he felt at the center of the universe; and from that point on the people watching could only guess at the proud grin blossoming beneath the folds of cotton.

He stood in the sun that day and his great uncle, the holy marabout Moulay Hassan, invoked the blessings of God and with a flourish recorded his name in the register of the Kel Rela, proclaiming him a man before all the world. Before the veil he had received the *takouba,* the heavy killing sword that marked his rank. Swords were handed down through generations, from father to son. The best blades were enchanted, endowed with the strength of the men who owned them, possessed of the best properties of chivalry and honor and bravery that made their owners great. Stories of the battles they'd seen and the virtues they'd defended and the raids they'd repulsed were passed along with them.

As Moussa's closest surviving male relative, the amenokal took the responsibility of finding him the blade. He had dispatched Keradji, the one-eyed *inad* who was the best smith of the Hoggar Mountains, to Murzuk, where a merchant had parted with the blade reluctantly, for it was hard and sharp, made of the finest gleaming steel of Seville. Keradji had fitted the blade to a hilt that was shaped like a cross. He inlaid the handle with jasper, and polished it until it was as bright as the sun itself, and it slid effortlessly into the tooled leather scabbard Moussa slung around his neck. It was a fine work. Moussa pointed out that the handle was too big for his grip, but Keradji squinted at it and then turned Moussa's hand palm up. "You must be patient," he said. "It is like the paw of a puppy. You'll grow into it." Moussa swung it for hours in practice until his muscles screamed, back and forth and over his head until he knew the sound it made as it swished through the air and could behead a *willik* weed at will. After the sword he had received new clothing and stone bands for both arms that would bring him strength and protect him from the swords of others. Afterward had come the finest prize of all, Taba. It was a heady time, the tides of masculine change swirling through his life, and he had reveled in it. For a month he had walked on air, practicing his swagger, strutting and standing tall and mixing with the men and their camels instead of the children and their goats. In a subtle way he thought people treated him differently. Nothing extreme, he thought, simply a new measure of deference and respect.

But that ceremony had been so much easier than this reality. He looked at the camel churning in agony on the sand, and didn't feel like a man. He felt like a stupid boy, just pretending. The desert had shown him its reward for arrogance and inattention. Life in the Sahara was so difficult. One needed to be born to it to fully understand its ways, and even then it took great skill and cunning to survive.

Once he had been allowed to make a march of three nights with some of the men. It was near summer's end, the air still searing during the day. Moussa had been given the responsibility for filling and carrying the water skins. The first day he loaded them on his camel and tended them carefully, making sure not a drop was spilled. That night after the last tea had been prepared, he propped the skins next to his bed on the sand, mindful to keep the tops up. In the morning he awoke and discovered to his horror that they were all empty, their water sucked through the skins into the sand. Because of him six men had gone without water for two days and nights.

The desert was full of such lessons that crushed one's vanities. He despaired of ever achieving a mastery of it. Was he really ready to carry the weapons of nobility? Ready to assume the mantle of a lord of the Kel Rela, responsible for the lives of his vassals and slaves, responsible for their families and property, responsible for leading raids against the Tebu and the Shamba, and against caravans who dared pass through the desert without paying duty, and for trading with the masters of those caravans and for increasing the wealth of the tribe? The list of a noble's burdens went on and on, and he felt only doubt. So much responsibility. Too much, he thought sometimes. More than a man could carry, and he wasn't even a man.

He felt like a fraud.

Reluctantly, Moussa turned to his awful chore, to end his camel's misery. He slipped the blade from its sheath beneath the robes of his forearm. Taba's mouth was foaming, his eyes wild with pain. He struggled to rise, but collapsed and rolled over to one side. He gave a long slow sigh of rage and frustration. Moussa took the knife in both hands and drew a deep breath. He plunged the blade deep and cut quickly. The blood gushed hot and sticky, soaking his forearms and hands and robe. It was too late to get out of the way, so he just knelt there and let it flow and closed his eyes while the life ran out of the beast, into the sand.

It was not possible to love a camel, not in the way one might love a dog or a horse. Camels were quirky and ill-tempered and quick to spit. They could crush a man's head with their bite, or throw up a nauseating green muck that they could aim with stunning accuracy. They cried and complained and carried on. They were awkward contraptions, not properly designed, really, for anything except desert travel. But he had come close to loving this one. Taba had dignity and a gentle nature. He had admired the camel long before it had become his own. He had helped train it, and tended its sores. He saw that it got the best pasture and that its hobbles weren't too tight. He had checked its droppings for disease, and carried water for it when the watering hole was too deep. One day at dawn he had mounted the camel when no one was around. He rode it from one end of a clearing to the other, Taba responding instantly to the pressure of his feet. Moussa had laughed out loud when the animal produced an unexpected burst of speed, but he took care not to push it too hard. Then he'd looked up to see the amenokal watching. He slowed immediately, ashamed at having ridden the animal in such a way without permission.

"I am sorry, Abba," he said. *Abba*, he called the amenokal when they were alone. Father. They were close, the chief and the boy, yet the amenokal could be stern and harsh and cold, and his words could sting like a whip. But that morning he only laughed and waved him on. "Give Taba your wings," he said. "See how he feels in flight," and Moussa's eyes widened in delight. He spurred the animal on, and although the young camel had never been let go like that it ran strong and felt sure beneath him, and the wind blew through his hair and he bounced at first at the awkward gait but quickly recovered and held himself erect and took Taba faster, ever faster until they were at full attack trot, and he imagined himself at the head of a great column of warriors, his new sword lopping off the heads of the enemies of the Ihaggaren.

Yes, Taba, you were a good camel, he thought. A good camel that deserved better than to die at the hands of his incompetence. Eyes still closed, he stroked its head and whispered to it while it died. Hot tears streaked his cheeks. Even if they were hidden beneath his veil, he was glad no one else was there to watch.

When it was over he shook off his self-pity and set about salvaging what he could of the situation. Losing the camel was bad enough. He knew better than to lose the meat as well. Quickly he set about skinning and quartering it. He needed no salt. The desert air would dry the meat quickly enough. It would be tough, but there was nothing to be done about that. He found a natural shelter in the rocks where he could leave the meat and skin. After he had dragged everything to it he piled smaller rocks at the opening to keep the carrion-eaters away. Then he marked the spot with a stone cairn. He would return later with another camel to collect everything. His labors took most of the afternoon. When he had finished he didn't rest. He was determined to redeem himself, and set off on foot.

He climbed to the top of a granite pinnacle that stood like a sentinel above the surrounding landscape. A lone cypress tree stood there. It was a massive, ancient tree that for two thousand years had been an unfailing landmark. Lightning had hit it a dozen times, leaving black scars up and down the knotted trunk. But the tree seemed stronger for it, twisted and scorched but unyielding, overlord of the land below. Its mighty branches had provided shade for a wetter world that once ran fast with chariots and cheetahs and sparkled with pools and streams that were alive with hippos and crocodiles and fish. The Roman legions of Cornelius Barbus had camped beneath it. There were still rare crocodiles and fish and lions, but most were gone now, having given way to the inexorable creeping desert.

But whatever became of the land, that tree would still be there. Moussa sat in its shade and looked out over the vast distances—the heat shimmering off the rocks, the earth before him all gold and black, stretching away to the ragged peaks of the Atakor, the highest part of the desert mountains. The Hoggar was an astonishing world whose beauty he was just beginning to appreciate. The *Bled el Shuf*, the Shamba called it, the Land of Thirst and Fear, but the civilized men of the Hoggar knew them to be ignorant, the Shamba, as empty-headed as they were savage, and quite incapable of comprehending such beauty. There were cones and spires and animated shapes that seemed alive, silhouettes of fantasia that fed daydreams and told stories and spawned legends. They were starkly beautiful, these mountains, each of them male or female, according to Tuareg lore, each with a name, a range of mountains that gave haven to hawks and eagles and mountain sheep, as well as to men. It was a fortress, the Hoggar, cooler and wetter than the surrounding desert, its rocks heaved into a great desert castle, a stone sanctuary in which its Tuareg inhabitants had found safety and food for nearly as long as the cypress tree had grown.

The mood of the mountains changed throughout the day, the colors rich and varied. Dawn was his favorite time, fresh and cool and full of promise. At midday in high summer the sun was master, humbling everything with its relentless fire. After the fire passed the desert seemed softer and the yellows ran to gold and at sunset the sky would flame red and orange before it faded to purple and gave way to a carpet of stars.

That afternoon the rains had washed the dust from the sky, and as the day died, it had no color but a blue so deep it was almost a night sky. The storms had spent themselves, and now there was no trace of them left in the sky, no distant clouds or even any humidity. He wondered if there would be other storms that year, or the next. Whenever it came the rain was savage and poured in torrents from the heavens. The first three years of his life in the desert it hadn't rained at all. Even some of the permanent *gueltas* had dried up. In the fourth year the rain brought floods that wiped out an entire camp of Kel Ulli, leaving swollen corpses to dry in a blazing sun. He had seen their twisted bodies, the children and the goats and the men and women, lying among the flowers that sprang up from the storm. Beauty and life and death, all from a rain.

He peered through his spyglass and listened for sounds of the hunt, for the excited shouts that meant the chase was hot, for the bellows and roars of men and their camels that would reverberate through the rocks, but there was nothing. No Tuareg, no ostriches. Only a light wind, whispering from the east. He waited and watched and listened as the shadows grew longer and the afternoon became night. When it was dark he climbed back down. He made tea and then curled up in a sandy bed in the shelter of a granite overhang, drawing his cloak around him to keep out the chill night air. He was too troubled to sleep, and spent the night looking up at the heavy blanket of stars. He tried to count them but could not, and looked for the constellations his mother had taught him, and watched them turn their slow shimmering arc around him.

He remembered the awe of his first desert night, the dazzling web so clear and bright. He had never seen such a sky when he lived in Paris. The lights of the city were too bright. The lights, such lights . . . it was six long years since he'd last seen them. Or was it seven now, or even eight? The years ran together and time lost its urgency and sometimes he didn't notice its passage at all. But surely it was a lifetime since Paris. He was happy in the desert yet sometimes longed to be back in the city, to see what it was like now. His memories of it were fond, the bad parts seeming not so bad, the good parts seeming better than they were. But the more time passed, the harder it became to remember at all. No matter how he tried to hold on, the treasures of his past no longer burned so brightly in his memory. The details dimmed and the people grew fuzzy, and he couldn't remember what some of them looked like. He closed his eyes and tried to bring them up, Paul and Gascon and Aunt Elisabeth, but sometimes he couldn't do it. It worried him terribly when it happened. It seemed as if he didn't care. He *did* care, he told himself. He didn't want to be unfaithful. He didn't want to lose his other life completely. He asked the marabout for paper and drew pictures of his father with scraps of charcoal. The pictures were crude, but they helped him remember. He promised himself a thousand times that no matter what happened to the other faces and places in his mind, he would never let himself forget his father's face. He folded the papers carefully and put them in a leather pouch that hung from his neck, and at night by the fire took them out to look. After he had folded and unfolded them many times the pictures would smear, and he would draw new ones.

One winter he had spotted a lone viper in the sandy wastes near Amguid, and he pointed at it excitedly to Lufti, his slave, and said, "Look, there's a—" And he realized he couldn't remember the word for it in French, and didn't know the Tamashek word for it, and it terrified him. All the rest of that winter he silently reminded himself of the French word for everything he saw.

His thoughts came in both languages, but more and more they came in Tamashek. He fought the shift but couldn't stop its slow progression. There was no one with whom to speak French except his mother, and as he grew older and spent more time traveling through the desert camps, he saw her rarely. He asked whether anyone wanted to learn the language, but none of his friends had any use for a barbarian tongue. So he contented himself with teaching Lufti, who paid rapt attention to his master's foreign babble but learned nothing at all.

He missed Paul, terribly at first, so much it burned, yet time had dimmed those fires as well. He wondered whether his cousin still thought of him, on those nights when he couldn't sleep. Was he looking at that star this very instant? Had he felt that wind on his face? He'd written him a score of letters, letters he gave to the caravan masters to mail when they arrived at the coast. But no letters ever came back. Maybe Paul had died in the war. Maybe the Prussians had burned the château and everyone in it. He asked for news of France from the same caravan masters. They knew of nothing save the conditions of their routes and the price of slaves in Tangier and word of plague in Hausaland to the south, of new taxes imposed by the bey of Constantine and the revolt in Tripolitania. Some of them could speak six languages, and their knowledge spanned thousands of leagues. But they knew little of France and her wars, and cared less.

And so over time a whole world disappeared.

He talked to his mother about it sometimes, but her eyes misted and her voice broke. He knew that memories were difficult for her, and so the silences about those times grew between them, and they dwelled in the present. Now it was only at night, when he was alone like this, that his mind wandered back to Paris—to brief flashes of the colors and fine carriages, to the white snows and fall leaves of the Bois de Boulogne; and the bitter winter nights when his father sat in his study before a roaring fire, reading a book or writing a letter, or telling a story to the two boys who sat with him; to afternoons spent ice-skating, and to the lazy Seine that carried more water in an hour than his new world saw in a year. It was another life, most of it hard to believe now. Sometimes, as he told new friends about the old world, he wondered which parts he really remembered and which parts he only imagined.

It was an awkward time, when nothing was settled in his life. He was stuck between things: neither French nor Tuareg, man nor boy. He had left France too young to comprehend what had happened there, and he still didn't understand this desert. "You must be patient," the amenokal told him. "You are in such a hurry for your life, for understanding. You are Moussa, and for the moment that is enough."

He slept fitfully at last. The hours passed and the first gray light of dawn streaked the horizon. He shook off the night chill and made a fire for tea, and as he squatted before the flames his mind returned to the hunt. He would continue it alone.

At dawn he was moving again, trotting quickly through the rocky terrain, sometimes following the wadis, other times jumping from rock to rock, all his senses alert. He knew the most likely places to look, places that after the rains had the thickest growth and offered the best shelter for the birds. He alternately ran and walked and ran for hours on end. His feet shuffled softly atop the sand, the rhythm of his motion fluid and smooth as he looked for signs of the flock. At midmorning he drew up sharply. He saw their tracks in some hard-pack sand. He couldn't yet read the signs well enough to know how many there were, or how fast they were moving, or even how fresh the tracks were. Lufti could have told him all that, and probably even what sex and age the individual birds were, but Lufti had stayed in camp, burning with fever.

He had been at it several hours when he spotted the big male, and behind it the others. He tried to contain his excitement, but as he watched the birds he exulted: *This is my flock. It will make up for Taba.* He set his rope and *guerba* on a rock and scouted the area. Carefully he climbed up and around, well out of sight of the birds. As he realized where they were his hopes soared. They were grazing at the narrow end of a glen with steep walls. At the far end the water trickled down from the plateau above, splashing into a small pool. He circled all the way around to be sure. The birds had no way out! Of course, he had to get them to run the right way, and then came the hard part, preventing their escape once they realized their predicament. He had no desire to see what a blow from the big animal would do to his own leg.

He began collecting bits of scrub and brush. There was a surprising amount of growth scattered among the rocks, and before long he had a pile assembled. He used stronger branches to make a framework along the bottom, and filled in the gaps with brush. He used his rope to loosely tie the brush together, until he had a long light pile of it, a little taller than he was and about three meters in length. If he could drag it quickly enough, he could block the entrance to the defile. He hoped the birds were too stupid to realize how easy it would be to get back past it, that to them it would simply look like an impassable wall. Of course he'd be standing there shrieking like ten *djenoums* to discourage their investigations. After that—well, after that he didn't know exactly what he'd do. He'd never hunted ostriches.

When he finished he tugged on the end of the rope to test it. Some of the brush on top bunched up against the rope. Everything leaned to one side, and collapsed to the ground. Patiently he stacked it again, and re-routed his rope. It was a fragile mess, but there was no time to make it stronger.

Stealthily, he moved his little weed fence, crouching in front as he pulled it along toward the opening. He was downwind of the ostriches, who had shown no sign of fright. He could see their heads buried in their work as they pulled at the tender new shoots. When he had drawn as close as he dared, he jumped up suddenly, waving his hands and running straight at the small flock. The heads of the birds sprang up from grazing as the ostriches sensed his presence. As one they turned and shot down the wadi. Moussa whooped and shouted, even though they were deaf. As soon as they had passed the opening that he intended to block, he stopped and raced back to his pile. Furiously he dragged it along, desperate to beat the birds, who would quickly reach the other end of the trap, at which point they would turn once again and race through the glen at full speed in his direction.

The going was tough. Twice a part of the contraption snagged on rocks, but he coaxed and pulled and prodded until he had it to the opening. He dropped his rope and ran to the rear, to pull it around to close the trap, when he heard the birds coming, all nine of them, the heaviest more than a hundred and fifty kilos, the lightest just a baby but still weighing more than Moussa did, and his heart caught in his throat. They ran nearly sixty kilometers an hour, lifting their legs delicately as if striding on air. The big male was in front, two other smaller males just behind, the females and yearlings in the rear. Desperately, Moussa pulled on the weed blockade, and as it closed the gap his heart sank. It was too short to completely block the opening. He could do no more with it, so he turned to face the oncoming horde.

He stood in front of the opening, raising his arms high and wide to make himself as fearsome and large and terrible as he could, then waving his arms as he jumped up and down, choking back his panic as he watched the wings and necks and feathers and feet bearing down madly upon him. He started screaming at them, and at the last second, as he was getting ready to jump for his life, the lead bird turned and headed back the other way.

Moussa's heart was pounding, his throat dry. In the distance he heard a shout. He couldn't tell who it was, but he knew help was near. All of the birds turned with the big male except for one of the other males; it had spotted the opening and was determined to blow right past him. On and on it came, bounding closer with each step. Its mouth opened and it hissed at him. Abruptly it stopped, as if deciding what to do. For just an instant it hesitated, and then started forward again. Impulsively, Moussa jumped and reached out and caught hold of it by the base of the neck. He didn't have any idea what he was doing, and neither did the bird, which madly flapped its wings. Powerful legs swept him off his feet, and he half-rode, half-dragged alongside, trying to keep his balance, trying to pull himself up, to get on top, too startled to do the smart thing and just let go. The ride was punishing, the bird panicky, Moussa's head bouncing up and down with each step. One of the bird's feet caught on his robe, and bird and boy went down. Moussa hung on for dear life, not wanting it to get back up again.

Behind him he heard howls of laughter coming from the other Tuareg, who had drawn up on their meharis behind his brush barrier and were watching his hunting technique with delight and disbelief. With a mighty effort the bird struggled to stand up again. It was too strong for Moussa to hold down, and it dragged him up with it. Moussa was on his knees when the bird broke free, and he fell flat on his face as the ostrich dashed madly away.

Three of the Tuareg on their meharis moved quickly into position in front of the brush, while the others

dashed past Moussa toward the birds at the other end
of the defile. Moussa recognized Taher, and behind him
Zatab, their clubs at the ready. Even with veils, the
Tuareg were easily distinguishable by the way they rode
their meharis, by the way they walked, by the way they
wore their robes and their arms, by their mannerisms,
by the way they wound their veils, by a thousand different things. One didn't need to see a face to know
someone.

"These are my birds, Taher!" Moussa cried. "My
catch!" He didn't want the others to steal his victory.

Taher drew his mount alongside Moussa. His eyes
were alive with merriment. "*Eoualla,* Moussa, of course
the catch is yours. As Ahl-et-Trab is my witness I would
not rob you of your prize. But they haven't exactly been
caught yet. I mean, they don't *look* caught, anyway, not
to me. Do you wish help finishing the job, or do you
intend to ride each of them that way until they drop
dead?"

Zatab laughed. "No, he was trying to scare them to
death with his shouting."

"Shouting? Was that shouting? I thought it was
French poetry," Taher replied. Taher was renowned as a
master poet of the Hoggar Tuareg. "And that perhaps
Moussa was going to lull them to sleep with it. Excellent idea, but more likely they'd die from it."

"You are right, Taher, his words are better than poison. Strong poison. Such a blessing to die quickly and
not have to suffer more French poetry."

"Tell us your poem again, Moussa," Taher pleaded.
"Please. The one where your arms flap like palms and
your mouth runs like loose bowels." He imitated
Moussa's whoops, waving his arms up and down, and
laughed so hard he nearly fell off his camel.

Moussa took their jokes in good spirit, ashamed that
he had doubted them. Had Mahdi been with them the
outcome might have been different, but Mahdi must
have joined up with the other group of hunters after he
left. "*Eoualla,* Taher. I thank you for your help. So
much so that I will keep the rest of my poems to myself
until we get back to camp."

At that the meharis were off, and within three hours there were piles of skins and meat and precious feathers ready to be transported back to camp. It was a rich haul, and Moussa was feeling much better now about his failure with the camel. He had redeemed himself.

There was one escapee, a baby that Moussa cornered and couldn't bring himself to kill. He was ready to club it when he let himself look into its big liquid velvet eyes. It looked so forlorn and innocent that he lowered his club without swinging, and after much posturing and strutting and chasing and cajoling managed to get a rope around the little bird's neck. After that it was a matter of fending off the new jokes as the others teased him. The *amadan*, they called him, the animal keeper; and they all knew it was his great weakness. The Tuareg loved their dogs, but Moussa's love for animals went far beyond that. He was even known to love his goats, when he was young enough to be assigned to tend them. No one knew anyone but Moussa who loved goats, because goats were not lovable. "He must love them in *every* way to love them at all," one of them had joked, but Moussa didn't understand the laughter and didn't care.

And so that day as the caravan left the little glen and began its way back to the Tuareg camp, there were eight weary men; seventeen camels laden with skins and feathers and meat; and in the rear, one prancing baby ostrich led by a rope tied round its neck.

H OT AND TIRED AFTER THE HUNT, MOUSSA BROKE off from the others on the way back to camp to visit his *guelta*. It was his favorite place in the Hoggar, a deep pool nestled in a secret spot among the rocks. Taher promised not to let any harm come to the little ostrich, and took the lead rope from him. Moussa led his borrowed mehari up through the rugged terrain until it could go no farther. He hobbled it and then climbed the rest of the way on foot, following a path that was invisible to anyone who didn't know it was there. Suddenly he was upon it, a deep sheet of blue shimmering in the sun. Winter or summer, the *guelta* never went away, even in a drought. It was fed by an underground spring that sent a constant lazy stream of bubbles to the surface. Clumps of grass clung to the rocks around the pool, out of the reach of the animals. Massive rocks rose above the pool on two sides. One of them formed a natural cave over the water, while on the other side a ledge ran down to the water at a steep angle. The rest of the pool was surrounded by a sandy bank that often bore the footprints of animals that came to drink at dawn or dusk, the wild Barbary sheep or the small herds of goats with their shepherds. A lone oleander tree grew in a pocket of rich volcanic soil, its fiery rose-colored blossoms as sweet smelling as they were poisonous. There were deep shadows around the *guelta* where Moussa could escape the oppressive heat, or rock ledges where he could sit on cold winter mornings and bask in the warmth of the sun. The *guelta* was completely sheltered from the wind by the rocks, and the silence that could be found there was as perfect as the deep blue sky.

No one else ever came to swim with him. They were superstitious about spirits that lived in the water, but Moussa believed they were afraid of drowning. They watched in fear and awe when he swam, certain when he disappeared under the water that he'd never surface again, or that if he did it would be with a *djenoum* riding on his back.

He climbed to the top of the rock overhang and stripped off his clothes, hesitating for a moment when it came to his veil. He hadn't been swimming since the ceremony, and hadn't taken the veil off at all, not even to sleep or eat. A Targui wore it everywhere, at all times. But he couldn't swim with it on, and besides, there was no one to see him. He dropped it in a heap with his robe and pants. He dove into the pool, the icy water shocking his system. The pool was deep and crystal clear. He stayed under until his lungs were near bursting. He took a deep breath and then went under again, exhilarating in the cold, his arms pulling against the water, muscles rippling as he stroked back and forth beneath the surface, sweeping gracefully from one side to the other. Then he took more air and went straight down. He didn't know how deep the pool was. He had never found the bottom. He played a game with himself when he came here, going deeper and deeper each time until his ears screamed and his lungs ached and he had to turn back. Someday he would touch it.

When he tired he floated on his back, closing his eyes and letting the sun warm his front while his backside stayed cold. The water grew calm, and he floated free with his arms outstretched, savoring every moment.

After a time he grew cold and decided to get out. Just then he was shocked by a splash, a deep *kerplunk* at the far end of the pool. Abruptly he opened his eyes and dropped his feet, treading water. Gentle waves rippled the pool. Someone had jumped in and was still below. A long minute passed. Afraid whoever it was had fallen in and might be drowning, Moussa went under to look. At first there was nothing, but then he saw a blur. He came closer until he could make out another swimmer, exploring the rocks. Moussa tugged on the person's clothing. The swimmer turned to face him, and with a shock he realized who it was.

Daia!

She smiled, and said something that came out as a burst of bubbles. She pointed down at something in the rocks, but Moussa was too startled and embarrassed to see what it was. All he could think of was his nakedness. He turned and retreated quickly to the other side of the pool, where he came up gasping. An instant later she broke the surface just next to him. She shook her head, the water spraying off her hair, which she wore in long braids. She smiled, her teeth perfect and white, her eyes gleaming. She seemed totally at ease in the water.

Daia was fifteen or sixteen, he didn't know for sure. She was of the noble Kel Rela clan like Moussa, but lived with a different drum group than he, so he saw her only rarely. She had been orphaned when just a child, her father the victim of a Shamba raid, her mother taken by fever. She was wild and full of life and energy. She could ride a camel better than a man and run faster than a boy. Other than that he knew little about her.

"Moussa!" she said, laughing. "Why did you swim away? There are fish there! I saw them!" She didn't seem to notice his embarrassment. Moussa sank as deeply as he could into the water, and turned his face away from her, showing as little of himself as he could.

"Of course there are fish," he snapped. "The pool is full of them. But you should go away. I am not dressed properly."

"Properly?" she laughed. "You are not dressed at all!" Then she disappeared under the water again. Moussa looked up at the rock overhang, wondering how quickly he could get to his clothes. *Fool! Why couldn't I have gone swimming with at least my pants on?* he thought, but he never had. He couldn't get out, and he couldn't swim with her. He paddled water and tried to stay at one end, turned away from her. A chill ran through him when he realized he'd been floating on his back, exposed to the world. He wondered if she'd been watching him before she jumped in. Of course she had, but for how long?

She swam about for nearly half an hour, by which time Moussa was so cold he could barely move. He swam to stay warm, but it made little difference. He said nothing to give away his discomfort, determined not to show any sign of weakness, convinced that he could stand the cold longer than she could. In the meantime he tried to keep his distance. She was completely carefree and at ease, moving all over the pool, laughing in delight as she explored. Several times she disappeared underwater, and he saw the ripples on the surface as she moved in his direction. Once she brushed against his legs as she passed underwater. He felt an odd thrill from her touch. She was all the way back on the other side before she surfaced. *She must do this often,* he thought. *I'm surprised I haven't seen her here before.* With a start he realized he was staring at her, and that she was staring back. He disappeared beneath the surface.

Finally, when it seemed he could stand the cold no

longer, she got out. He sighed in relief; she'd be going at last. But to his consternation she lay down on a rock by the water where the sun was hot and she could warm herself. As she got out he noticed her body beneath the thin cotton shift she was wearing. She had a very slight build. The wet material clung to her. He saw the line of her small breasts, and the outline of her nipples, and he felt an odd stirring in his loins, a tingling that was confusing but felt warm and wonderful and quivered all the way up to the hair on his neck and into his head, a warm feeling mixed with the cold, and he couldn't take his eyes off her, yet it made him all the more ashamed of his situation. He didn't know what to do. He was shivering, the skin on his hands shriveled. She closed her eyes. Moussa treaded water, waiting.

When he could stand the cold no longer and her eyes had been closed for a long while he quietly slipped out of the water. He started up the rocks toward his clothes. He heard a giggle. Her head was still resting on the rock, but her eyes were wide open and she was watching him, a smile on her face. Anyone else would have looked away, to give him his privacy, but Daia was full of mischief and just stared. Moussa looked down at himself. The cold had made his penis shrivel almost as thoroughly as his pride. It had shrunk as if trying to climb back inside his body. What remained of it looked about the size of a pea pod. The only blessing was that from where she was he guessed it would be just about invisible.

"Turn around!" His voice squeaked from the cold. Another little humiliation. He hoped his voice would change soon. He knew it didn't sound much like thunder.

She said nothing, and made no move to turn her head. The smile stayed. She was enjoying herself, he realized angrily. And besides that she was warm.

He was paralyzed with indecision. He needed to use his hands to get up the ledge. He couldn't do that without completely exposing himself to her, unless he went backward, and he couldn't go backward up the ledge without looking like a complete idiot. He certainly wasn't getting back in the water. He didn't know what to cover, what to do. One hand went automatically to his groin, while the other went to his face. He stood for a moment that way and she giggled again. After another moment of agonized indecision he gave up trying. He dropped his hands and scampered up the rocks. As he disappeared from her view he drew up sharply, horrified. His sword was there, right where he'd left it. His dagger and sandals were there. His *guerba* still hung from the branch of a bush.

But his clothes were gone.

He groaned.

"Daia!" he called over the rocks. "What have you done with my things?"

He heard her laugh. He waited for her to say something, but there was only silence.

"Daia!" he shouted again. His voice echoed sharply over the rocks.

"The *djenoum* must have taken them!" she called back. "You have made them angry, swimming naked in their pool!"

"Stop it! Stop playing games! Where are my clothes?"

Silence.

He stomped around, looking in crevices and between rocks, hoping to spot the pile. He stubbed his toe and cried out in pain. He sat down to rub it. The gravity of his situation began to dawn on him. Would he have to walk all the way back to camp naked, like one of the children? It was too appalling, too horrible to consider. He'd kill himself before he'd do that. No, he would take his sword and wait until a caravan appeared, and then at night—

W'allahi! By God!

"*Daia! This isn't funny!*"

He suffered more silence. He crawled to the edge and peered down and saw her still lying there. She didn't move. He watched her. He could see her breathing. Again he noticed her figure beneath her shift, this time the curve of her legs, the way her hips were beginning to fill out. He wondered if he'd go to hell for looking. The goat girl was becoming a woman. She was very pretty. He felt the stirring again. He forced himself to turn away and sat cross-legged on the rocks, wondering what to do. The sun was warm, blessedly warm, but he was still cold to his core and his teeth were chattering.

A few moments later he sensed rather than heard something behind him. He looked over his shoulder. Daia had crept silently up the rocks and was standing behind him. She was smiling broadly. In her out-stretched hands she held his clothing. "I found them below," she said innocently. "The *djenoum* must have dropped them when they saw me coming."

"Very funny," Moussa snapped. He kept his back to her and drew his knees up to his chest to cover himself better, and looked away. "Just put them there and leave me alone."

"You must come get them," she teased.

"Never!"

"All right," she said lightly, shrugging. "I'll just take them with me back to your camp. I'll tell them I found them—"

"*No!*" In a flash Moussa was up, reaching for them, his modesty forgotten.

She pulled her hand back so that the clothes were behind her, and he had to stop short. She looked him up and down, her eyes wide with fascination. He felt her eyes, looking into his face, and then down—*there!* Mortified, he realized he was getting the feeling again. As much as he willed it not to happen, his little penis was shaking off the cold, and stirring to life. He dropped his hands to cover himself, but not before she'd noticed.

"You should be ashamed," Moussa told her sharply.

"For what? *I* kept my clothes on!" Her eyes lit with a wicked smile. Then without a word she dropped his clothes and turned and ran back down the rocks. He was struggling into his pants as he listened to the sound of her fading footsteps. By the time he had the robe over his head and was working on his veil, she was long gone.

I F MOUSSA WAS MILDLY UPSET ABOUT HIS CLOTHES, his return to camp crushed him. His swim had cost him more than his modesty. In his absence he had missed a *djemaa*.

His slave, Lufti, had been anxiously waiting for him at the bottom of the wadi that led to the camp. Lufti was ill, his eyes rheumy and red rimmed. He wore his veil low, exposing a broad nose that glistened with beads of sweat from his fever. He was chilled and even in the heat he kept an extra robe drawn around his shoulders. His eyes brightened when he saw Moussa. Even though his news was urgent, the slave was first polite, inquiring after his master's afternoon.

"Sire, felicitations on the hunt. It is said you captured many ostriches using only poetry!"

"Master Taher said that?"

"Yaya, sire. It is all over the camp. No one has heard the like of it. And your swim, it was enjoyable?"

"It was memorable."

Lufti took the camel's lead. "But sire! Where is your camel? Why do you ride Master Taher's mehari?"

Moussa shook his head. He didn't want to talk about it.

"Master, you must hurry," Lufti told him, almost as an afterthought. "There was a council. A big one. All the nobles were there. The lord amenokal, he was looking for you! I think you have missed it, sire. The others have been leaving. You should go now, quick-quick!"

"A *djemaa*? Without notice?"

"There was no time."

Lufti led the camel away to be hobbled for the night, while Moussa hurried toward the amenokal's tent. The camp was alive with preparations for the coming night. Young boys were returning from the day's pastures with their goats, while others carried loads of brush for the fires. Naked children played tag before the great rocks against which the camp was nestled. Dogs barked and slaves tended to milking the goats and the cooking. The red roofs of the tents glowed rich in the fading light.

The amenokal's tent was larger than the others, pitched on a high spot from which it overlooked the rest of the camp. Its roof was made from the skins of Barbary sheep. There were no sides to the tent, only grass mats, which could be rolled up to control the winds and the sand. A fire blazed to one side, where the carcasses of two goats had been roasted in the coals and then picked clean. Moussa's heart sank. The feast was over. And so too was the *djemaa*. It would have been the first council he could have attended as a man. As a boy he had been welcome to listen, but could say nothing and had to make tea for the others. Now that he was a man, it would be Moussa's privilege to participate if he chose.

And he had missed it for a swimming hole.

He recognized various drum chiefs of the minor tribes, who were now streaming out of camp. It had been an important gathering, with all the major families and tribes of the Hoggar represented. As he entered the amenokal's tent he saw that only the amenokal and Mahdi remained.

The amenokal was suffering from the same fever that had stricken Lufti. Normally a hardy man, he had been bedridden for days. He was still terribly weak, racked by coughing spells, and was propped against a tent pole for support. "Ah, Moussa, you have returned," he said.

"You enjoyed your afternoon leisure?" Mahdi asked, delighted to embarrass Moussa in front of the amenokal. "There was nothing urgent here for your attention. Simply a matter of war."

"What has happened, Lord?" Moussa asked, ignoring his cousin's barb.

"The Kel Ajjer are up to their old treachery," the amenokal said. "We have learned they are massing for an attack near Ademer. All the tribes are agreed. We will storm the Ajjer before they can raise their hand against us. All the nobles are departing. Every available vassal of the Kel Ulli will be armed as well."

The Kel Ajjer Tuareg lived to the east, near the plateau of the Tassili, along one of the great trade routes between Tripolitania and the southlands. The war had started over the defense of the rights of a small tribe of Tuareg, and had raged for three years in a series of skirmishes and all-out battles.

"Will the Turks help them again with troops?" Moussa asked. The previous year the Turkish bey of Murzuk had provided arms and Arab troops to the Ajjer Tuareg in exchange for the establishment of a garrison in the oasis of Ghat. The Turks, seeking to extend their influence in the region, had nearly tipped the balance against the Hoggar Tuareg in a massive battle.

"I think they want no part of this war," the amenokal replied. "I sent an emissary to the bey. He says he has no wish to invest further in our quarrel. I believe his intention is to weaken the Ajjer now as we ourselves were weakened before. In this way he hopes to keep all the people of the veil too weak to challenge his influence. But his motive does not matter. Our purpose is served."

"So the Ajjer are abandoned by the Turks to our blades," Mahdi said.

"Do not discount more treachery," Moussa said. "I do not trust the Turks. While we tend to the Ajjer in Ademer we should place a reserve force outside Ghat. In case the bey forgets himself."

The amenokal smiled. The boy had learned much. "It is a pity you missed the *djemaa*. Your counsel might have added to our deliberations. That order has already been given."

"Had I known of the *djemaa* I never would have missed it, Lord."

"Had you not been consorting with your fish like a foreigner you would have known," Mahdi said. Moussa flushed crimson, thankful his veil hid it, but the amenokal ignored his son's taunt.

"You have not told Moussa of his duty here, Lord," Mahdi said. Moussa stiffened. He could feel the smirk in his cousin's words.

"The *tobol* of the Ihaggaren will ride with Ahitagel. He has already departed with a force of nobles, and leads in my name." The *tobol* was the war drum, symbol of the amenokal's authority. Ahitagel, the cousin of

Serena and El Hadj Akhmed, was the heir apparent. With the amenokal too ill to lead such a force, he was the logical replacement.

Moussa's heart leapt. "I will leave immediately and join Ahitagel, Lord," he said.

The amenokal shook his head. "You are to remain here, Moussa, with ten Kel Ulli." The Kel Ulli, the people of the goats, were vassals of the Kel Rela. They fought only rarely, carrying weapons with special permission and always under the command of a noble.

Moussa was horrified to be left behind. "But Lord, it is my duty to—" he began.

"It is your *duty* to do as I wish," the amenokal rasped curtly. He doubled over in a spasm of coughing. It was a moment before he could continue. "The Kel Ajjer are not the only predators in the desert. I cannot leave the defense of our camps to the women and children and one sick man," he said, referring to himself. "You will remain here, and mind our backs. You will command the Kel Ulli, of course, after they arrive. *This* is your duty, Moussa, and it has great importance."

"Yes, Lord," Moussa said, bitterly disappointed. Of course, someone had to stay. But it was a humiliation to be the one called. It was not duty as war was duty, to watch over the goats and the children and the vassal camps and slaves. It was second best. He wondered if Abba did it because the amenokal didn't believe he was ready. For three years he had watched as others carried the fight, blooded in battle and returning as heroes. There were many who did not return, but it seemed not to matter. Poems were written about the warriors, both the living and the dead. Songs were composed. Swords were celebrated and legends grew.

But he would be left out of it, his own legend seeming forever stillborn. Already he could feel the blistering ridicule of Mahdi. "So, the noble *ikufar* will mind the babies and the camel shit," he laughed scornfully as they left the tent. Moussa tried to ignore him. That night after the nobles had left for war he checked the camp and then wandered out to brood in the moonlight.

THEY SWAM IN SLOW CIRCLES JUST BENEATH THE surface, passing ever closer to each other with every turn. Her image was blurred, mysterious, and beautiful, the details becoming clearer each time. He could see only that now she wore no clothes, that incredibly, she had come nude into the pool, to join him there. He looked at her, trying to make out the secret places of her body, but the water and the darkness swirled around her, leaving only a graceful mystery that made his blood rush. She beckoned him to follow. He tried to catch up, but each time as he drew near she pulled away from him, swimming faster than he, looking over her shoulder, waving and smiling. She swam so effortlessly, so free. She seemed never to have to draw a breath. He followed her until he could stand it no more. He came to the surface, gasping for air. The moonlight was bright on his face, bright like the daytime, the water shimmering in silver pearls around him. The sand around the pool was deserted, the rocks barren. He knew they were alone.

With a thrill he realized that she knew it too.

He took a deeper breath this time and disappeared again, blinking as he looked about for the soft light of her passage. This time he felt rather than saw her, as she came from below and behind him and reached up to him. Her touch sent a shock through his body. He turned to her and she drew up from below, her fingers delicate and curious and slow. He felt her on his ankles, then his calves. She caressed the hollow behind his knees, and then his thighs, and he closed his eyes and floated with it all, luxuriating in the sensation of her skin like silk against him, her warmth flowing around him in the gentle current. Every hair, every pore of his body felt wild and fired by her presence. She touched him on his hips and ran her fingers lightly up his sides. She drew level with him. Aroused and hard, he pulled her close, feeling her nakedness against him, their bodies quivering. He had never felt anything so soft and smooth as her skin beneath his touch. He ran his hands down her back, using just the tips of his fingers, softly, slowly, both of them lost to the feeling, floating in the water, entranced, the curves of her hips and her breasts pressing against him until without knowing what to do or what he would find he brought himself to her and they clung to each other, and there was a frenzy between them, a frenzy of bubbles and heat and passion as they joined together, and together they rose for breath and burst through the surface and cried in wonder and she shouted his name and he felt himself letting go, felt the fire leaving his loins. . . .

Confused, excited, Moussa awoke in a sweat. He was breathing heavily, still lost in some delicious place that was like a warm and wonderful bath. Soft night sounds flitted into his consciousness. He heard the wind rippling the roof of his tent. Low voices murmured from near the fire. His mind rose slowly from the mists of the dream.

Vaguely he realized he had an erection, stiff and throbbing and warm. He touched it. His robe there was warm and wet and sticky. The touch made him shudder again, the pleasure shooting all the way through him like a bolt of lightning, making him tense and then relax as the feeling washed over him and he came again. He tingled all over.

His head swam in the wonder of it. This had never happened to him before. He still didn't know where he was, or where she was. Was it real? Had she been there? He knew she had not, but let himself deny it for long pleasurable moments. He tried to hold it all in his mind, to recover it all: the feeling, the dream, Daia. But try as he might he could not hold it. He closed his eyes and sought her under the water, but could not see her. He drew the folds of his robe close, to touch her once more, but could not feel her. The world intruded on his private place. She slipped slowly from him, disappearing beneath the surface of his mind, until she was gone, and he slept once more.

CHAPTER 17

18 August 1876
Dear Moussa:

Well, I turned sixteen at last. I guess you know that, though. I thought of you when you turned sixteen in July. You always got your birthdays before me. I sat in the old tower at St. Paul's and looked at the river. It's where I go when things get too stiff around here. They still haven't fixed the cathedral from when it burned during the war. Last month some of us had a party up there, and it was after midnight before we got caught. There was serious hell about it. I couldn't leave the château for a fortnight except to go to school. Then they boarded the cathedral up, but I pried a place open and can still get all the way up to the top.

The party was for Antoine. Did I tell you about him, in another letter? I don't remember. I guess he's my best friend now. We took some girls to the party who knew Antoine's older brother, and we had a bottle of Charente I took from the cellar. My girl was nineteen! I got to feel her poitrine but then I got sick on the brandy before I could get to her good stuff. Antoine said he got all the way with his girl, but I don't believe him. He couldn't even tell me what it was like, except to say really vague things that I think he made up. When the heat dies down a little we're going to find them again and have another party. If I get anywhere I'll let you know. The real stuff, not made-up things. I know you would do the same for me.

I always thought sixteen would be an important birthday for me, but I feel the same as always. I want to be twenty. I think that's a better
age. The best, maybe. Then I can do what I want,
and my mother can only watch. You know her,
though. She'll be on me until I'm a hundred. For
my birthday she took me to the races at Chantilly.
It was the first thing she's ever let me do that
wasn't all stuffy and formal. She was with one of
her "gentlemen friends," as she calls them. She
has a lot of them. She makes me call them
Monsieur This or Monsieur That, but they're all
Monsieur Crap to me. Well, Monsieur Crap gave
me a hundred francs and told me what horse to
bet on, like a real know-it-all. Before the race I
went down and looked at the horses. The one he
told me was wheezing like it had consumption. I
picked a different one and got seven hundred
francs back. Monsieur Crap's horse finished dead
last. He said he lost twenty thousand, and acted
like he didn't care. I think he was just shooting off
for my mother. He's a minister in the government.
Today, anyway. We've had a lot of governments
since you left. They keep them for a week or two
and then throw them out, and Mother throws the
men out just as fast. I haven't liked any of them
yet. I hope someday she'll get to one I can stand,
but I doubt it. Not before I leave here, anyway. I
figure that will be when I'm twenty. Antoine's big
brother went to the military academy at St. Cyr,
and after that he got to go to Indochina or someplace. I want to go to Africa. I think my father
would like that. He was there, and so are you.

One more year at the École. The Jesuits there
make Sister Godrick look pretty soft, but I do my
work and they leave me alone. She's still teaching,
by the way, but at another school since they
closed St. Paul's. Some other poor bastards are
getting the hard side of her board now. I couldn't
believe it when I saw her. She looks just the same,
only I think she's shorter than she used to be. I

wanted to do something in your honor—brain her
with a brick or run her down with my horse, but I
was with one of the priests from school and had
to be polite. As much as I hate the idea, I think
she's the sort of person who's going to die of
old age.

Gascon got sick in March. He got a lump in his
belly that was big enough to see, and he just got
worse and worse. It happened pretty fast. I went
to see him every day at his apartment in Montparnasse. I wished that he was still living with us.
When he was so sick it felt like he belonged at
home, but he and Mother never got along and she
put him out. He didn't have many visitors, just
some old army men and me. As sick as he was, he
told me stories, just like he used to. We talked a
lot about you. One day a priest came and gave
him the last rites, and told me Gascon was going
to have to get buried in a pauper's grave. I guess
Gascon didn't have any money. I couldn't stand
that idea so, of course, I gave the priest enough to
take care of things.

Gascon let me have his old guns then, thinking
he was finished with the world. And then the
strangest thing happened. A day or two later
he said he felt better, and he got up out of bed.
The lump got smaller and pretty soon it was gone,
and Gascon was as good as ever. He didn't want
his guns back, and I never got the money back
from the priest, either, which is all right because
of how it all turned out. Gascon said not to worry
about it, because the way things were if he died
later and didn't get a good grave I could use his
guns to shoot the priest. Now Gascon is my only
grown-up friend. I can tell him things and he
doesn't laugh. As often as I can I steal money
from the butler's house fund and give it to him. I
know it's your father's money, but I'm sure he
wouldn't mind.

I still think of you all the time. I miss you and
Uncle Henri and Aunt Serena. The way everyone

*left me, all at once, well, it was all so quick. First
my father, and then all of you, and it's been pretty
lonely since then. My mother says you're all dead.
I don't know about my father, whether he died
after he walked out on us, but I don't believe it
about you. I wouldn't write letters to a dead
cousin. I wonder why you never write, but I'm
sure it's for a good reason. I'll keep trying from
this end.*

Your cousin, Paul

He folded the letter and put it in an envelope. On it
he marked, as he always did,

Monsieur Moussa Michel Kella deVries
Avec les Touareg
le désert du Sahara
Afrique

He gave it to the butler to mail. Later, as instructed
with such letters, the butler gave it to Paul's mother.

CHAPTER 18

THE SHAMBA RAIDERS CAME IN THE QUIET PART of the night when the moon was low in the sky and life in the Tuareg camp was at its lowest ebb. One after the other they slipped silently over the rocks, stopping to listen and watch, then moving once again. They could see the dim forms of the tents spread over the gentle slope, the rocks looming protectively behind them, with dark shadows between them indicating where narrow passages led toward the wells and meager pastures beyond. The embers of a cook fire still smoldered in front of one of the tents. The Shamba would have preferred a night that was black as death to one that had any sliver of moon, but they had not chosen this time for the raid. The Ajjer, with their war, had chosen for them.

They came from Wargla, a northern Shamba oasis. Their leader, Abdul ben Henna, was the younger brother of a caravan master who led merchants from In Salah to Ghadames. Abdul had acquired his personal hatred for the Tuareg along that route, in the year when his brother had taken ill and put him in charge of a caravan. A caravan was a collection of independent merchants carrying gold or slaves, ostrich feathers or salt. The merchants banded together under one master who knew the route, who could rent them camels when they needed them, who could find the watering holes and the pasturage along the way, who could help them overcome the dangers of the road, and who could negotiate safe passage with the lords of the route, the

Tuareg. Young and full of himself, Abdul had gravely accepted the great responsibility.

As caravan master, Abdul ben Henna was so pleased at the fees he was able to charge on behalf of his brother that he stole a third for himself. He brooded about his theft for nearly a day, and then decided to steal half instead, quickly sending the remainder to his brother before it disappeared altogether. That was the easy part. It was just before departing, while negotiating with a group of the accursed Tuareg, as was the custom, that he made two mistakes.

He paid too much, and he paid the wrong Tuareg.

The caravan was halfway to its destination when he met the true masters of the road, who demanded their just due. At first Abdul refused, incensed by the Tuareg duplicity. Stubbornly, he ordered the caravan to proceed over the objections of the merchants, who knew that one did not deny the Tuareg devils their tribute.

That night Abdul ben Henna's younger brother was slain by hands unseen, and five camels disappeared. In the morning the Tuareg returned, just two of the tall arrogant scoundrels blocking the passage of an entire caravan. They announced that due to rogue bandits known to be in the area, the price for safe passage had doubled. Yet again Abdul turned a deaf ear to the entreaties of the merchants who demanded that payment be made. He ordered the Tuareg out of his way on pain of death. The caravan pressed on.

The next night another man died and four more camels were lost. To the mutinous rumblings of the merchants, Abdul insisted that he could deal with the situation. That night he doubled the guards around the perimeter and kept fires of brush and camel dung burning brightly. He himself patrolled the length and breadth of the caravan, his eyes searching the blackness. Near one o'clock in the morning he nodded off. Near two o'clock one of the merchants died and the throat of Abdul's own camel was cut. No one heard a thing.

With twenty more nights to Ghadames, the merchants had had enough of their brash young caravan master. They told Abdul that the next life given to the Tuareg would be his own. Abdul capitulated, but his humiliation was not complete. Even with the profits stolen from his brother, he had insufficient money. He was reduced to borrowing from his clients to cover the shortfall. It had taken Abdul's brother a year to make up the loss of camels and money, and he had cast Abdul out of the house.

Abdul ben Henna had waited patiently for vengeance. Now his opportunity had come with rumors of the resumption of war between the Ihaggaren and the Kel Ajjer. Seasoned caravan masters shook their heads in dismay at the news. Upheaval among the Tuareg could upset the rhythms and routes of the desert. But Abdul exulted. Any war that pitted Tuareg devil against Tuareg demon was a good war; praise Allah if all the vermin killed each other. Best of all, there was fortune to be found in a war of the blue men: spoils unguarded and camels to steal.

He wasted no time assembling a party of four other men for the *razzia:* his sons Kadder and Baba, and two of his brothers, Bashaga and Hammad. He trusted none of them, but they were tough caravanners who traveled fast and knew the desert as well as he did. Most of all, they shared his hatred of the Tuareg. It was a timeless feud, passed from generation to generation, from father to son, from uncle to nephew. The Tuareg killed the Shamba and the Shamba killed the Tuareg. There was no beginning to it and no end, only widows and orphans and hot angry blood that ran to the sand.

The raiding party stole fast camels and food from a caravan and raced south into the desert. There were forms to be followed before any *razzia,* and they did so meticulously. First was the matter of alms for the needy. Because they were on the road, it was customary to turn their offerings over to their leader, who would pass them on to the intended after the raid. To do this Abdul swore in the name of his father, and his father's father. The others knew he would keep the money, and made certain not to give too much. Next was the solemn pledge of a fifth of their spoils for Allah. In actual practice this might range anywhere from a tenth down to nothing and a promise about the next raid. It was a matter between a man and his God. Finally, they prayed for success, beseeching Allah to be as merciless in their cause as he was merciful to the faithful. Abdul ben Henna led them in prayer, his voice strong as it floated over the barren waste: "Oh Sidi Abd-el-Kader, let us throw fear into the hearts of those who disbelieve, and they will be gathered unto hell, that Allah may separate the wicked from the good." It was a prayer Allah was likely to heed, since the blue men were well known among the faithful as the abandoned of God.

By the time the Shamba party arrived at the approaches to the Hoggar, they were traveling only at night, hiding by day in the rocks, careful always to cover the telltale signs of their passage. They stopped making cook fires, forsaking tea and eating nothing but dates. They made no noise, their eyes ever watchful. Despite their expectation that most of the Tuareg men had gone to war, the Shamba were cautious. Even with Allah riding on one's shoulder, one did not enter lightly into the fortress of the Hoggar, whose rocks and valleys hid a thousand perils. A lowly shepherd girl could give them away, or a dog.

They had found the camp exactly where they expected, near Tadent where the pastures were good and the air was cool. As they had hoped, there were few men. "Only one blue devil," Abdul whispered excitedly, watching Moussa cross the camp. "The rest are slaves, and women and children." His temples pulsed with hatred as he watched the peaceful scene. He longed to kill them all. Yes, even the children, for a dead child could not grow up to wear the veil. He willed himself to keep his discipline, to content himself with the business at hand. The Tuareg man would no doubt die, but Abdul's mission was to find glory with plunder, not with fire. He was there to steal camels. If children also died in the raid, *mektoub*. It was written and a blessing, even if it was not his purpose.

He had ordered his brother Bashaga to slip away and reconnoiter the gorges behind the camp where most of the camels would be kept. Bashaga had returned after dark, out of breath. "*Hamdullilah,*" he gasped, pointing to the upper gorge. "There are more than forty camels near the wells! There are no guards. No shepherds."

Abdul ben Henna blessed his great fortune. Forty camels! How munificent was Allah! Was this not a sign of His blessing? Oh, how the vile Tuareg would feel his vengeance this day. He would take his rightful place at the head of a great caravan once again, and he would do it all on the backs of Tuareg camels!

Abdul issued his orders. "Hammad, Kadder. You will enter the camp and cut the throats of their goats." It was not strictly necessary to do so, but it would make a few enemy bellies cry with hunger. "Mind you, only those far enough away that you will not be heard. You must move more softly than a breeze. Baba, you will collect the camels hobbled near the camp. Bashaga and I will take the camels from the well. We will all meet at the spot where we camped two nights ago. Keep your eyes open! Go now, with Allah!"

The men split into two parties and melted into the night. Hammad stripped and wrapped his clothes in a bundle. He put his pistol inside, leaving the handle out so he could grab it quickly. Then he tied the bundle with a cord and slung it around his back. He saw his nephew Kadder's puzzled look. Stripping was a common practice among the Arabs of the northern oases, of Oran and Morocco, not of the Shamba. "My clothes are too light in color," Hammad said. "It is harder for them to see a naked man. You should do it too."

Kadder snickered. "One of us looking like a fool will be enough," he said.

"Suit yourself," Hammad shrugged. He loved stripping for a *razzia*. It excited him, the wind on his back, the earth under his feet, and the blood everywhere. . . .

T HE HOURS PASSED AND THE CAMP SLEPT. Hammad moved silently among the goats, crouching low, his knife busy, his arms and legs and feet drenched in blood. It was strangely sensual, being naked and slitting throats. He dipped a hand into a fresh wound and rubbed the blood on himself until he was slippery with it. It was wet and warm, and a thrill ran through his body. He worked quickly, slicing deeply. Like willing sacrifices the goats moved to make room for him but made no unusual noise, raised no alarm. There was only a light burbling sound when they died, and no one to hear it but Hammad. Most cooperative, he thought, wiping his hands on his thighs. Hammad noticed that he had moved dangerously close to one of the Tuareg tents. The smell of blood was strong, but there was something stronger.

Incense. Sweet. Feminine. Hammad listened for the sounds of his nephew and heard nothing. He decided he had done enough goats. He crawled closer to the tent, to investigate.

KADDER GRUNTED AS HE SLIPPED AND FELL. ONE of the goats bleated in panic and shot through his grasp. He cursed under his breath and froze, awaiting the sounds of alarm.

Nothing.

He kept on. Ten, fifteen, eighteen. They died quietly and quickly. A shame to waste them, he thought, but a pleasure to deny them to the blue devils. "Work Allah's retribution," his father had said, and Kadder wielded an obliging blade.

Suddenly he stiffened and whirled around in a crouch. Standing behind him was a human shape. It was small but close, and the person had obviously seen him. Kadder had no idea why no alarm had been raised, why there were no shouts, but it didn't matter. Without a sound he leapt forward and up, his blade flashing swift and deadly and deep. As he struck he saw it was just a shepherd boy, aroused from his sleep by some noise. The boy fell to the ground, overwhelmed by his attacker. Kadder felt the familiar things through his blade: the skin, the vessels, the sinews. His heart pounded as he cut. He noticed to his surprise it wasn't much different than killing a goat.

The struggling stopped. The hated thing was dead.

SERENA WAS SHOCKED FROM HER DEEP SLEEP BY A great weight that smothered her. One hand covered her mouth, another moved down her body, then groped roughly between her legs. She felt the hot breath of her assailant, his beard rough against her cheek. A surge of adrenaline swept through her as she realized what was happening. She struggled fiercely, lifting her shoulders, trying to throw him off, but he was too heavy, too strong. He worked to rip away her clothes. He found the end of her shawl and stuffed it in her mouth, muffling her growing cry.

"*Quiet*," he hissed in Arabic. He pressed the tip of his knife against her throat. "Do you understand me, Tuareg whore? Quiet!" Eyes wide, she nodded that she understood. His body was wet with the blood of the goats, his penis hard, throbbing. He took her hand and made her hold it. She could see almost nothing for the dark, but when she felt him the horror of it gripped her and a wave of nausea swept over her, fear and revulsion and disgust all mixed together with hatred, but she felt the cold steel at the same time, and her struggles stopped. Her chest was heaving. She felt him working at her shift. He wrenched at it roughly, trying to rip it away, trying to hurry, stopping only to put her hand back on him when she let go, holding it there, insistent, tugging, showing her what he wanted, then reaching again for her skirt, groping.

Serena closed her eyes and felt the blade at her neck and tried desperately to think. A thousand terrors screamed in her brain. *Have they killed Moussa? The amenokal? Is it the Kel Ajjer? No, no, they would not do this to me, and this man wears no veil. Tebu? Shamba? Yes, they would do this, and either of them would kill me when they finish. They will kill us all!*

With a conscious effort she forced herself to be calm, pushing the hysteria away. She must not panic. She ran

her mind's eye over her tent, looking for weapons. Earlier that evening she had been working on a leather pelt.
Where is my knife?

L UFTI SHIVERED AS HE RETURNED TO HIS SLEEPING mat. The fever had dropped, but he still felt horrible. His head pounded and lights flashed when he closed his eyes. He still woke up often during the night, and had gotten up to urinate. On his way he became nauseated, and his stomach heaved and he vomited, kneeling down and supporting himself with shaking arms as he fought the spasms. The episode didn't pass for twenty minutes. When he felt better he rose to return to his sleeping mat, which he had moved during his illness away across the clearing from the nobles' tents. Head throbbing, he absently made his way. Suddenly he tripped over something. He went down fast and hard, banging his head on the rocks. He groaned, his night going from bad to worse. He sat up and rubbed his forehead, and felt moisture. He smelled it. Blood! He felt around in the dark and his hands found a goat. Then another, and another. All of them dead. His heart began to pound, his fever forgotten, and he was on his knees, his eyes making out the dim shapes of the bodies. They were everywhere! Goats, dead! What on earth—? Then he found Sala. The mute boy, the little Kel Ulli shepherd, his body twisted, his throat cut. Lufti's fingers fumbled at Sala's flesh, his fingers telling his brain something he couldn't comprehend. How could this be? There had been no noise, nothing. Who could do such—

And then in a flash he knew, and he stood.

"*Ouksad!*" Lufti shouted, cupping his hands over his mouth. His voice shattered the quiet night. "*Ouksad! Aradaaaaaaaarrr!*"

H AMMAD KEPT HIS HAND AROUND SERENA'S, forcing her to squeeze him, pushing her hand up and down, up and down, faster, faster, as his hips started to buck. He was everywhere with his other hand, on her breasts, between her legs, pawing, demanding, brutal. He got her shift all the way up and started to enter her. She wailed inside, her mind shrieking in silent helpless fury at the animal she knew she could not stop.

Then Lufti's scream pierced the night. She felt Hammad stiffen for an instant at the sound.

It was enough.

With all her strength she yanked his testicles, closing her hand around them and squeezing as she pulled, ever tighter until her hand shook with the effort. She felt one crush beneath her grip. With a roar Hammad straightened up and she let go. She pushed him back and he fell to the ground. She was up and over him in a blur, ripping the shawl from her mouth as she flew for the leather pouch containing her knife.

Through tears of rage and pain Hammad saw her leaping. He still had the knife in his hand and stabbed at her. He caught her on her leg, his blade finding cloth and soft flesh, but she kept moving, past him and out of reach. One hand on his groin, the other clutching his blade, he struggled to his feet. By God, the witch had nearly castrated him! His balls were on fire, his belly seized with a pain so intense he wanted to throw up. He fought for control. He wanted to kill her, knew he must kill her, knew he must do so quickly. There would be only seconds to get away from camp before the Tuareg were all over him and escape became impossible. She snatched something from the floor and whirled to face him. He couldn't make it out, but knew it would be a weapon. There was no time to get at the pistol in his bundle of clothing. He had to finish her *now*, with his knife. He had killed a score of men and feared nothing from this woman.

His pain forgotten, he lunged.

MOUSSA DIDN'T WANT TO LET HIMSELF WAKE UP. His dreams were rich and soft and new. He was just learning to hold on to them, to feel them, to let his mind weave soft silken threads between reality and fantasy. It was a sweet netherworld, fleeting but for a precious moment he could savor all the rest of the day.

But then he *heard* Lufti, his brain realizing that the shrill scream was not part of the dream, and he was awake instantly. He heard the word clearly at last.

Aradar! Raid!

He threw his cover back and leapt from his mat, grabbing his sword as he ran out of the tent, his senses alert, his eyes sorting out shapes and forms in the darkness. He raced through the camp. There was pandemonium, people running everywhere. There was no sign of the raiders. He didn't see Lufti. He started for the camels. They were after the camels, of course. First, last, and always, the camels.

"Moussa!" He heard his mother's voice, and found her before her tent. She had lit a torch and was wrapping a cloth around her leg, which was bleeding. "Mother! Are you all right? What—?"

"In my tent," she said, motioning over her shoulder. "Shamba, I think, only it's hard to be sure. He's too light to be Tebu. He was carrying this." She held out a knife that had a distinctive curve at the tip. Shamba, most certainly. Serena was trying to control herself, but Moussa saw her hands were shaking, that she was trembling all over. A crimson stain was growing quickly on her bandage. He helped her inside, where she sank to the mat. Automatically, he started to tend to her wound.

"Leave it," she told him. "I am all right. You must see to the others, to the rest of the camp."

Moussa knew she was right. He stood up and saw the body on the floor. A bundle of clothing lay nearby. He knelt and quickly unraveled it. He found a pistol and a small cloth packet with extra ammunition. The pistol was corroded and would certainly misfire and kill a man trying to use it. He cast it aside. A pouch held three silver coins. Beyond that just a ragged shirt, trousers, and sandals. Nothing more of the man. Alms and tatters and rust. The intruder was lying on one side, legs drawn up toward his chest. One hand was between his legs, clutching his groin, the other grasping at the hilt of Serena's knife protruding from his throat. His face was bright red, eyes wide open and bulging grotesquely. He was covered with blood. Moussa shuddered. The man had died hard. The enormity of the attack swept over him in a wave of disbelief. He was shocked to think the Shamba had come so close to killing them all.

That is my mother bleeding, he thought, his anger mounting. *They tried to kill my mother.*

Lufti burst into the tent. "*Hamdullilah!* You are safe, sire, and your mother too! But they have killed Sala. They cut his throat and killed his goats. I have—*aieee!*" He saw the body on the floor and took a step back. "Oh-oh-oh, *Iblis* has been busy tonight!" The devil was everywhere, and Lufti knew he would need more amulets to counter this horrible night, many more, and that he would have to pay the marabout, pay him many times, to remove the spirits. "The camels are gone from their lower grazing area, sire," he continued, his eyes riveted on the naked blood-soaked body. "I . . . I have not yet had time to see the upper."

"They will have them all by now," Serena said. She leaned back on her mat to still the burning in her leg. She grasped their situation before the others did. The camp was nearly defenseless but for Moussa. Slaves were useless with weapons. There were no other nobles nor any vassals to help. All of them had gone days earlier, gone to war with the Kel Ajjer. So cunning, the Shamba, to choose this time. She trembled at the thought that her son had to carry this burden himself. *He is not ready!* Oh yes, he wore the weapons and the veil, but he was a boy, a child. In her mind he would never be ready. She had lost Henri and couldn't bear the thought of losing him too.

Since childhood she had lived with *razzias,* the great awful sport men used to test their virility and that normally had accepted rules. It was not something to think about. It was the way of things. But now she looked at the *razzia* through a mother's eyes, and nothing looked the same. There was only fear.

And if it was not the Shamba it would be the Kel Ajjer or the Tebu, or a scorpion or a storm. She could not hide her son away, could not protect him. There was no choice. There was only Moussa, and—

"The amenokal!" she said suddenly. "Please! See to him quickly!"

"Stay with her," Moussa said to Lufti. "Tend to her leg." Serena squeezed his hand tightly. He left and strode quickly across the compound. He called out at the amenokal's tent.

"Abba?"

There was no response. He pushed back the mats covering the entrance and saw there was no one inside. He continued swiftly up the path, his sword drawn and ready. He found the amenokal just a few steps farther. He was just a dark shroud in the black night, stooped over, holding his sword. Near him, sprawled on his back, was another body.

"Abba?"

The amenokal held up a hand. Moussa heard his rasping breath. He was winded and ill, but not wounded. "He ran straight into me," he said at length. He held out a dagger. "He tried to prick me with this." Moussa heard the note of humor and pride in his voice.

"Come, Abba, let me help you," Moussa said, reaching for his arm. The amenokal waved him off.

"I am unhurt, Moussa. You must go. Quickly. There will be others. They will have the best of our camels by now, from the upper pastures by the well. They'll keep to the rocks as long as possible to make it harder for you to follow. Take Lufti, for his eyes. He knows much of what you do not. They'll have left one of their number to guard their backs. Watch for him as he watches for you."

"Yes, Abba, of course, but—"

The amenokal held up his hand again for silence. "You are always so quick to talk, Moussa. Never quick enough to listen. We are the only two Kel Rela here, and I cannot go. I would only slow you, and speed is your ally. So it is in your hands alone, this thing. When the

Kel Ulli arrive I will send them to join with you, but I have no idea when that will be. There is no time to wait. Speed is everything."

"*Eoualla,* Abba. I understand."

"There will be many of them to your one." It didn't matter, of course. Were there five or twenty Moussa would be expected to bring them to account for their raid, even if his own life was forfeit. He accepted this without thinking.

"Your life will depend on your wits, Moussa, not on your strength. You must remember what the lowly ostrich did to your mighty mehari. That is what you in turn must do to the Shamba." It was the first and only time the amenokal had referred to the incident. It was not a rebuke.

"Do not try to follow them in the rocks. They will be expecting that. Go around, quickly. They will follow the Gassi Touil, through the great dunes. Meet them, do not follow them. Come now. There is something you must have." The amenokal stepped over the body of Baba and returned to his tent, beckoning Moussa to follow. Inside he lit a torch. From its honored place on top of a wooden brace he withdrew a long packet. Carefully he pulled away the outer leather wrapping, and then the layer of cotton inside. The rifle was as shiny as the day Henri, the Count deVries, had presented it to him. Moussa took care of it and saw to its cleaning. He was the only one besides the amenokal who ever fired it. The amenokal treasured it, but after twenty years still couldn't hit a large mountain with it.

"Take this," El Hadj Akhmed told him. "You will need it." He offered it reluctantly, not because Moussa couldn't use it, but because it was not the way the Tuareg fought. There was no honor in killing with guns. Guns were cowardly things, used by weak men who could kill from great distances, not knowing even whether they had killed for certain, or whom. A bullet was anonymous, impersonal. A bullet never flew with the same artistry as a blade. With the same result, perhaps, but never with the same inspiration. It was better that men fight up close, with swords and lances, knives and cunning, so that the victor might know he had fought well and won, and that the one defeated might know his master before he died.

But as the amenokal had feared, their enemies had attacked at their most vulnerable moment. He had planned for there to be no fewer than ten men including Moussa in the camp, but something had delayed the Kel Ulli. Moussa was alone, and the amenokal could do precious little to help. He burned with guilt that he could not go, but at that moment El Hadj Akhmed knew he would be more burden than benefit. His fever was high, his joints on fire.

The odds facing his nephew were long. Small and alone and only half-Tuareg, after all, he faced a task for which he was only partially prepared. Moussa had spent more than half his life among barbarians. His father and his vassal Gascon had taught the boy well, that much the amenokal had always seen. He could throw a knife, and his slingshot was a great novelty, the talk of the desert. His sword work was coming along under the tutelage of Abu Bakar, the master swordsman. Moussa was solid with the blade, a strong fighter. But he lacked finesse, just as he lacked the killer instinct of Mahdi.

Now the amenokal wished it were Mahdi he had kept behind, and not Moussa. Mahdi had been tested in battle many times, Moussa never once. He often found himself comparing the two boys. It was true that Moussa was his favorite. He hated to confess it to himself, never admitted it to others and tried never to show his preference in any way. It hurt him to feel that way about his own son. It felt wrong, yet it was so. Mahdi brought him so much pain.

Mahdi was eight when he first killed. The victim was a Tebu, a straggler from a raid who had fallen from his camel and broken something inside. Mahdi had been looking for a lost camel when he came upon the man, who was semidelirious and bleeding from his mouth, no longer able to keep up with his fleeing comrades. Mahdi did not know of the raid but recognized the stolen camel grazing near the fallen man. He knew the intruder to be a Tebu as certainly as if he had looked directly at the devil. It was enough for the slight boy with the angry eyes.

The Tebu saw Mahdi standing over him. Weakly he asked the child for water. Without warning or mercy Mahdi was all over him, his only weapon the staff he carried. Mahdi beat him until the staff broke, and after it broke began stabbing with the jagged end. He kept on long past the time the Tebu was dead, until one of the Tuareg giving chase came upon the scene. The man called to Mahdi to stop, but the boy was deaf with frenzy and had to be pulled away.

At the age of ten Mahdi fell into an argument with an adult slave from the next *ariwan* over access to a well. All children of the Hoggar, whether noble, vassal, or slave, were expected to take a turn at tending the herds. Mahdi took his turns only grudgingly, and had been caring for a dozen goats. The slave had a larger herd and was watering the animals. Custom permitted him to finish first since he had arrived first, but Mahdi was not to be kept waiting.

"Make way!" Mahdi ordered. "I wish to water my goats!"

"Patience, little master," the slave replied amiably. "All of God's animals must drink. I am nearly finished."

"Make way now, I say, or face the consequences!" Mahdi snapped, eyes flashing at the impertinence. He drew his slight frame erect and placed his hand on the hilt of the knife at his side.

"At your command, little lord," the slave replied, smiling good-naturedly at the imperious child. But he moved slowly and in fact all his animals had finished drinking by the time he'd collected his things and prepared to return to the pastures. Mahdi glared at him as he departed. That night he brooded over the effrontery, which grew in his mind to a full-fledged insult.

Later the slave brought three goats to Mahdi's *ariwan* in payment of his master's land rent. Mahdi saw him and his pent-up anger exploded, and he fell all over the surprised man with a flurry of curses and fists. The slave easily kept the boy at arm's length and did not strike back. The amenokal himself had to pull Mahdi apart from the slave, who fell to the ground as he made abject apologies. "I am sorry, Lord, I appear to have angered your son. I did not mean it." Accustomed to his son's temper, the amenokal nodded and dismissed them both.

A few days later the slave had not returned to his own *ariwan* with his herd. A search was mounted and the body was found, its throat cut. Mahdi denied knowing anything about the death. But the amenokal had looked deeply into the eyes of his son and knew the truth of it.

The years had done nothing to soften the boy. In a fight he was frightening, even to another Tuareg. There was a fire inside him that few men had, a fire that must one day burn out of control and consume everything near it. But fire properly channeled had its use. Mahdi was a killer, ruthless and cunning, born to the desert. No Arab stood a chance against him. He would not rest, the amenokal knew, until the heads of the Shamba were sundered from their bodies.

But it was not to be. Mahdi was gone, and the amenokal could not quickly provide either the finesse or the killer's instinct that Moussa required. Lufti would make up for some of the imbalance. The slave was quick and wise in the little things, the desert things, to which one needed to be born, the things the Shamba would use against them, the things that Moussa might miss. The gun, he hoped, would make up the rest. Moussa was the only one who could use the gun anyway. When they hunted together, Moussa with his hawks and the amenokal with the rifle, it was Moussa's hawks and Moussa's aim that found food.

Moussa looked at the rifle and shook his head. "It is not right, Abba, to fight with a gun. I have heard you say it myself, many times."

"Yes, it is true. You have also heard me say that a jackal without friends does not confront a lion. There are times when one reality must overtake another. This is such a time. Take the gun."

Moussa was secretly relieved. He knew what guns could do. But he promised himself he would not use it if he did not have to.

"Give them no quarter," the amenokal said finally. "They will give you none."

"No, Abba. No quarter."

THEY LEFT QUICKLY IN THE TWILIGHT BEFORE dawn, gathering only the barest of necessities for the chase. Water bags, food pouch, weapons. They hurried through the camp, past the others who had assembled from the tents. He felt their eyes upon him as he walked, the inexorable press of their expectations. He was Ihaggaren; his shoulders carried their burdens. He would recover their camels and avenge the boy Sala. Moussa strode purposefully past them, robes flowing, holding himself tall and straight and noble. He was too proud to be afraid.

The camels were all gone. They had known all along that it would be so, but they looked for strays just the same. It was a good grazing area, for the grasses were thick and the few camels kept there could not wander too far, so it took them only a moment before they knew. Lufti didn't hesitate.

"We must run to the *ariwan* of the Kel Ulli, sire. They will have mounts for us," he said. The camp was two valleys away. One day, by foot.

Moussa hesitated, unsure. He wanted to go back, to talk to the amenokal, to ask. He had never made such decisions by himself. What would Abba do? His head pounded with the pressure of it. The first rays of the sun streamed over the horizon. The new day had begun.

"Sire?" Lufti looked at him expectantly, urgently. "We must hurry, quick-quick. We are losing time."

Moussa knew it was up to him, and him alone. He could not go back to ask. Not now, not ever again.

He was Ihaggaren.

"Yes," he said. "We must hurry," and together they were up over the rocks and gone.

CHAPTER 19

IT WAS LATE AFTERNOON OF THE DAY FOLLOWING the raid. Abdul ben Henna squinted at the sun and weighed the odds and decided to abandon his brother and first-born son to their fate.

Stealing the camels had been almost too easy. He and Bashaga and their forty camels had reached the meeting place with surprising speed, and soon after them Kadder had appeared alone with the rest of the camels taken from near the camp. Abdul's heart soared as he saw the coup had been complete, barely skipping at the news his son brought.

"There were shouts," he told them. "The alarm was raised. Hammad and Baba were still in the camp, among the goats. I did not wait to see what became of them."

Abdul pondered the probabilities. Hammad and Baba might be dead, or prisoner, or on foot. The Angel of Death would come for them, or else the hand of God would deliver them. Abdul ben Henna would not interfere.

Malish, mektoub. Never mind, it is written.

He nervously scanned the rocks, searching for the blue death he knew would soon be coming. Already he could feel them watching, waiting, their eyes hidden in the shadows, their knives sharp. His stomach churned nervously.

"We will not wait," he said, closing his heart. He drew an ancient flintlock, the oldest of the two weapons they carried, from his pack. He gave it to his brother, keeping the better firearm for himself. "Bashaga, you

will stay to the rear, to watch our backs and gather
strays. Do not fall far behind. Tonight we will stop for
only one hour. We must put great distance behind us. If
any of the camels falter, do not wait for them, do not
goad them. Kill them at once." Abdul would quickly
sacrifice those who even began to stumble, lest he lose
them all. And then he would deny the stragglers to his
enemy by cutting their throats.

They moved off quickly to the north, along the trails
and scree of the Hoggar, the camels roaring and grunting and jostling. For three days and nights they barely
stopped to rest. Always the camels looked for pasture,
and always the men looked over their shoulders. Abdul
whipped his mount viciously, kicking, cursing, lashing
the skin of his mehari until it bled, changing mounts
frequently. He sweated and prayed and pushed, the dust
choking, the days blazing, the nights frigid.

From a distance they were a superb sight, stretched
out over the flat, moving in their timeless undulating
rhythm, but up close they were beginning to suffer from
their pace. The Amadror was a blast furnace that
sucked their membranes dry and baked their brains and
scorched the soft feet of the camels. On the fourth day
they lost their first two, young Tibestis who could not
keep up. Kadder cut their throats. Their blood had not
stopped flowing before the rest of the column had
moved on.

Abdul was heading for the wells of Tan-tan; they
would arrive after five days of punishing travel. He
would never have tried such a run were it not for the
wondrous condition of the camels. Abdul marveled at
it. The Tuareg might be dung in the anus of humanity,
the abandoned of God, but as Allah was his witness
they surely knew how to take care of their meharis! In
Wargla he would give them a six-month vacation,
where they could fatten on rich grasses and sweet water
and recover their strength. They would become the
backbone of his new herds; their seed would spawn new
generations that would be the pride of the Shamba.

The glorious visions danced before him in the heat

shimmering off the flat. He saw himself with four wives and a score of sons and clothes made of silk, and he brought down his scourge on the bloody haunches of his mount to drive it on, to make it all come true.

"THE SPIRITS HAVE BEEN FED, SIRE, I HAVE SEEN TO it. You may rest easy now."

Lufti had wandered out into the rocks to find the best place, where he carefully set the bowl of porridge alongside a small gourd of water. No matter how tired he might be, it was his nightly ritual, seen to faithfully and without exception. In the morning the food and the water would be gone. It never failed. "The Kel Had, the People of the Night, get most plenty thirsty, sire."

"I was already resting easy, Lufti," Moussa said through his exhaustion. His body ached with their efforts of the past days. He tolerated Lufti's superstitions rather well, finding them amusing. "I think the spirits will leave us alone tonight."

"Yaya, sire, of course they will. But only because I feed them." His voice was defensive. "Forgive me, sire, but you should not doubt the effectiveness of my measures. Since becoming my master have you had seizures?"

"Never."

"Have you been possessed, or taken ill in the head?"

"No."

"Suffered the bite of a snake?"

"Not yet."

"The fever of the pox?"

"I am free of it."

"Well then, have you died?"

"No, of course not."

Lufti held up his hands in triumph, at the glorious proofs of science. "Yaya, see then? It is because I have taken proper care that such ills have not befallen you."

Moussa grunted noncommittally. "I thought your amulets took care of all that." The slave wore an arsenal of amulets. They were pinned to his robes and turban and hung from his neck. They contained eagle claws and lizard tails, scraps of the Koran, lions' teeth, and wrinkled papers filled with magic squares. What little of worth that Lufti managed to acquire went to his payments to the marabouts for new and ever improved amulets, amulets that would prevent him from falling into wells, amulets that would stave off disease, amulets that would keep him from losing his virility, or his mind.

"The amulets care for *me,* sire, not for you. You will not wear them. Oh-oh-oh, how I implore you to wear them. But until you will, I shall feed the spirits for you."

On a cold morning long ago in a balloon over France Moussa had given up the only amulet he ever wore. So much had happened because of it, so much evil and pain. He knew it was his fault his father was dead. If he hadn't pleaded with him to take the detour to St. Paul's to recover the amulet they'd have been gone long before the police arrived at the Gare. Serena scolded him when he said it, but he knew it was true. The worst things that had happened in his life had happened because of that amulet. Sister Godrick used it for torture, and his father died for it. He didn't need the amulet and he didn't need God. He had thrown it from the balloon, watching as it fell lazily down until it disappeared in a cloud, carrying with it the weight of his father's soul. Now the *taleb,* the holy man, came to camp and brought new amulets, and collected fees for which he dispensed *baraka,* the blessings and guarantees of healthy livestock and successful caravans. The *taleb* with his mystical power reminded Moussa of the bishops and priests, all of them with their hands out and their lips moving with empty promises, thundering the righteousness of their Gods, and accepting the grateful offerings of frightened souls. Now Moussa was the only man of the Kel Rela who wore no amulets. Lufti worried greatly for his master's *baraka* and so saw to the feeding and care of the spirits on his behalf.

"Very well, Lufti. Just see that you don't give them the last of our food."

"Of course not, sire."

MASTER, I HAVE A REQUEST OF YOU."

Lufti had been brewing tea, clearing his throat and fidgeting and shoving the coals around in the little fire on which their teapot bubbled. With growing amusement Moussa had watched him working up to it, and had been tempted to tell him to just come out with it; but it wasn't right to push. Lufti would get to it in his own time.

Moussa nodded. "Of course."

"Forgive me for being so blunt, sire, but there is a woman. . . ." Again he paused. "Well, sire, when we return with the camels I would very much, oh so very much like your consent to . . ." He cleared his throat again. "Sire, if it would be your pleasure to grant me, ah, this—"

"What *is* it, Lufti?"

"Marry." Lufti blurted it out. "Marry her, sire, I would like so very much to become her husband."

"What are you talking about? Marry whom?"

"Oh yes, sorry, it is Chaddy, who is of the *ehen* of Mano Biska."

"Chaddy!" Moussa knew her vaguely. A pretty woman with a bright smile. "Marry her? Why, of course, Lufti. If it is your wish."

"It is not my place to do as I wish, sire. It is my place to do as you wish."

"My wish is your wish, then, in the matter of this woman."

Lufti bubbled at that. "Sire, you are too kind. May Allah's blessings be upon you, as always. The bride-wealth payment, sire, is four goats." He thought a moment, then upped the ante. "Five goats."

It was Moussa's responsibility to pay for the bride of his slave, and then to provide for them and their family. "Five it shall be," Moussa said.

"And a sheep, master. Uhmmm, three sheep."

Moussa smiled. "Anything else?"

"No, sire, nothing more. Five goats and five sheep. That is all, absolutely all. And five lengths of cotton. Nothing else. To pay more would be a crime. Six lengths would be better. She is only a slave like myself, after all, but she will be a most valuable addition to your *ehen*." Again Moussa nodded his assent. Lufti fairly danced with delight, spilling their tea into the coals. The liquid hissed and a cloud of steam rose from the fire. "*Aiyee,* sire, so sorry. It's only that I was busy thinking—"

"Your thoughts seem costly, Lufti. Something else?"

Lufti's sacred duty was the protection of Moussa's property, to see that nothing was wasted or ill-spent. But in the matter of his own bride there was conflict. "It is just that Mastan of the *ehen* of Zatab Mel intends to ask Chaddy to be his own. I do not wish trouble. I only wish to conclude this matter in my favor. A camel, sire, would be—"

"Too much," Moussa said firmly.

"Exactly," Lufti said quickly. "Far too much, just as I was thinking. But a *tirik?* That would be perfect."

Moussa sighed. A saddle was not so much, but his new daughter-in-law was getting very expensive. "Very well. But that shall be the end of it." He felt awkward, as he always did when dealing with Lufti as master to slave. He had never expected to be responsible for another human being, not in this way; and certainly not for a man who was ten years his senior—or was it fifteen, or twenty?—Moussa had never seen his face, and couldn't tell for sure, but he did know Lufti to be a man who knew far more about the Sahara than he could ever hope to know.

When Moussa was just fourteen, he had traveled to Ideles with the amenokal. Lufti belonged to a nobleman who treated him indifferently. The man kept him in clothes and quarters that were less than he could afford, and far less than Lufti deserved. Lufti had been called upon to serve tea to the distinguished guests. All eyes had been riveted on the amenokal except the slave's. He raised the teapot high in the air to delicately pour the ritual glasses, and discreetly observed the young Kel Rela who as yet wore no veil. The boy had an obviously gentle manner and his face was kind. Moussa was a curiosity, discussed among slaves and vassals and nobles alike long before he arrived in camp, the son of the French barbarian balloonman and Serena, sister of the amenokal. Lufti looked to see whether the boy had six toes on each foot, as the rumor about barbarians had it, but was relieved to see that his Tuareg blood had prevailed to give him only five. The boy seemed normal in other ways. Lufti made the impulsive decision to cut off the tip of the ear of the young master's camel, which was hobbled outside the tent. By Tuareg law his action could be compensated in only one way: The slave doing the damage became the property of the injured nobleman.

The injury was discovered, and Moussa had a slave.

"I don't want him," he said simply to the amenokal and to the slave's former owner, when his new property was announced. His objection had nothing to do with Lufti. His life was difficult enough without adding the burden of another human being. From what he had seen slaves were hard work. They were as children, to be cared and provided for. Moussa was too young for children.

"You have no choice in the matter, Moussa," the amenokal said brusquely. "He is yours. It is the law."

"Then it is a bad law, Lord," Moussa said. "I don't need a slave."

"You have no veil and cannot write properly in our language and already you feel fit to judge the law." El Hadj Akhmed sighed. "It is an honor to receive a slave in such a manner. Now he belongs to you. It is finished."

"Very well," Moussa nodded. "If he is mine then I set him free. At once."

"I forbid this foolishness!" the amenokal thundered. "You shall wait until you have at least eighteen years before rewriting the laws of man and the Ihaggaren. Then—but not before—commit whatever madness gives you pleasure. Now hold your tongue. He is your vassal." With that the boy became liege lord of the slave man.

Lufti was carefree and easygoing, proud of his position as a *buzu*, an outdoor slave. He had more status than that of common *iklan*, who tended to menial

matters of the household. Lufti viewed himself not as
slave so much as Kel Ahaggar, a man of the Hoggar. He
wore the veil, and lived in his master's tent, and tra-
versed the desert on his master's errands. There was the
prospect of manumission one day, when he might become *imrad,* a vassal who could own livestock—and
yes, even own slaves. But there was no hurry. Lufti was
content. He had the best master in all the Hoggar, even
if his master himself didn't know it yet. Moussa expected little of him, and even seemed grateful when he
did those things that were his place to do.

Tuareg nobles were not born to do work. They were
born kings of the desert. Born to lead, to command, to
fight. They played games and composed poetry and
raced camels and lived off the labors of their vassals. A
true nobleman would let a fire go out before stirring
himself to its rescue. But to the horror of his peers,
Moussa would toss camel dung on a fire as quickly as
not to keep it burning. He often brewed his own tea,
sometimes even brewing it *for* Lufti. Moussa treated
him like an equal and seemed to find nothing unusual in
it. The other slaves shook their heads privately, embarrassed for the dignity of Master Moussa. Lufti fretted
over it until he could hold his tongue no longer. It was
his duty to help teach his master, after all, for it was not
the boy's fault that his blood was tainted with European
defects.

"The head is the head and the tail is the tail," he had
finally told him in exasperation one day. "You should
accept the end to which you are born, sire, and leave me
to mine."

They had all misunderstood Moussa, however. His
stubbornness had been refined in the schoolyards of
France. The more the nobles jeered and the more the
slaves chattered the more intractable he became. He put
a sharp end to it with Lufti: "I am not so concerned
with heads and tails and such things," he had told him.
"But if it suits you, I give you leave to cut the ear off
another man's mehari." At that Lufti's blood had
chilled. He never said another word about the matter,

and came to accept his eccentric master and to bless his good fortune. He kept a sharp eye out for other slaves who might say by day how unseemly was his master's behavior, but try by night to cut the ear off one of his camels. One could not be too careful, Lufti knew, with unscrupulous slaves.

And every so often, he permitted his master to brew the tea.

They were a good team, the Ihaggaren and the *buzu,* as they hunted the Shamba: Moussa the reluctant leader, pushing, nervous, alert; Lufti, the desert wizard, the reader of signs who could find food almost anywhere among the rocks, knowing which plants were edible and which would kill them, and knowing where to find the water holes, and how to read the evidence of their quarry's passage. The master watched and listened.

Moussa pushed hard, driving until well after dark when the night was pitch and the camels began to stumble, then bowing to Lufti's gentle suggestion that perhaps they had ridden enough and should rest. Once, riding in the predawn hours, Moussa had nodded off, and his mehari had begun to wander off on its own. "Master!" Lufti had called gently, as Moussa jolted awake. "This is the way of the Shamba. And that," he said, pointing at Moussa's path, "surely that is the way to hell." And he clapped and giggled, and Moussa had to thank his good fortune at having such a companion.

When they emerged from the Hoggar onto the plain of the Amadror, Lufti examined dung and pawed at tracks and studied the way the rocks were turned. His eyes noticed everything. "There are three of them, traveling in two groups. Two ride in front. One is behind, a day at least."

"Only three?" Moussa was surprised. He had expected more.

"Yaya, surely three. Is three not enough, sire?"

"It is enough."

A day later Lufti announced they were making up time, moving faster than the Shamba and their herd. It was to be expected for two men against a herd. Besides, no men on earth could travel as the Tuareg traveled, with little food or water or rest. Moussa sat comfortably in his light riding saddle. When the horizon had no limit and the heat rode him like a mighty blanket he permitted himself to slip into periods of trancelike dreams, the only sound the wind and the *shuff-shuff* of his mehari's hooves. He rocked gently to and fro in the saddle and lost himself in thoughts of *her*, of Daia; and he felt himself stirring down there again, and he wondered what it would be like to be with a woman, that way.

And then his pleasant reverie was shattered by images of the cut throats of camels slaughtered by the Shamba. He scolded himself for drifting. *They killed Sala*, he reminded himself sternly. *They tried to kill my mother.*

"They will make for the wells of Tan-tan," Lufti predicted, examining the ground. "They can go no farther than that without killing what they have stolen. The wells are not fruitful. They will be delayed at least a night. We will come upon them there."

Moussa nodded.

"May I ask, sire, your plan of attack? Your plan to slay the Shamba?" Lufti's eyes were eager through the slit of his veil, his faith in his master complete.

Moussa thought about that. "I don't have one yet," he replied honestly.

Lufti did not believe it for a moment, and Moussa felt rather than saw the grin blossoming beneath the slave's veil. Then Lufti laughed and slapped his knee, as though it were the greatest joke in the world. "It is quite right, sire, not to share it with me. I am certain it is a fine plan. When Allah wills it I know you shall tell me, so that I might assist you." He prodded his mehari. "*Bok bok*," he said to it, humming happily to himself as the camel began to move.

Moussa paused awhile before following. His pulse ran faster and his mind was in turmoil. It caught at his throat and constricted his chest.

The wells of Tan-tan were before them, and he had no plan.

THE LANDSCAPE CHANGED AND BECAME MORE UN-even, its windswept face scarred by small wadis carved by ancient rains from the dead flat of the Amadror. Boulders were scattered about, huge chunks of rock oddly out of place, strewn almost casually as if dropped by the gods, and forgotten.

Bashaga watched them coming from his perch atop one of the boulders. He had spotted them almost an hour earlier from atop his own mount, two figures moving quickly along the plain, nearly lost in the shimmering waves of heat, their tall silhouettes wavering ghostlike as they approached.

By God, the devils move quickly! He knew he could not outrun them. He would have to make a stand. Quickly he chose his ground and set about laying his trap, whipping the camels until he had them out of sight. He climbed up on one of the boulders. He primed his flintlock, carefully arranging his spare powder and balls in a pile on a cloth. He would get off one shot, then scoot backward and reload. It was a good defensive position. The Tuareg could never reach him with their blades. He could reload and fire at will until he had them. He wiped the sweat from his forehead and peered down the length of the barrel at the approaching enemy. He was ready, *Insh'allah*, to spill their loathsome blood.

Moussa was riding in front, Lufti well behind when the gun roared. Moussa heard the ball whiz past his ear and ducked instinctively, nearly falling off his camel. Wildly he looked around for the source of the shot, tugging at his own rifle to free it from its sling on his *tirik*. He saw a movement atop one of the rocks and slid from his mehari.

Bashaga cursed his luck when he saw he had missed. He got to his knees and scurried back on the rock to reload. His attention was split and he realized in horror that he was too close to the edge, which sloped and then dropped sharply off. He let go of the rifle, which clattered down the side of the rock, and his fingers scrabbled desperately to get a grip. With a yelp he fell over the side. He landed with a heavy thud and screamed out in pain.

Moussa raced forward, rifle in one hand, heavy sword unsheathed in the other. He heard the moaning. Slowly, expecting a trick, he edged around the rock. Bashaga was sprawled on his back, his left leg twisted under him, clearly broken. A jagged shard of bone protruded through the skin. Bashaga looked up in fear and hatred as he saw the veiled monster approaching. With an effort that made him gasp, he grabbed the dagger from his robe and hurled it. Moussa ducked and the knife thudded harmlessly to the ground. Now Bashaga was unarmed. *Allah, take me quickly,* he prayed to himself. Tears of pain streaked his cheeks. Moussa straightened up as he viewed the broken man before him. He kicked away the flintlock.

Lufti appeared timidly from behind the rock. When the shot was fired he had jumped from his mount and taken its reins and those of Moussa's mehari and had led them to cover. Now he spied the Shamba on the ground, helpless, and his eyes lit up. "*Hamdullilah,* master!" he cried, certain Moussa was responsible for the man's condition. "A fine job!"

Bashaga tried to make out his executioner's face, but could see nothing of Moussa save the hated eyes behind the veil. Nothing more. He cowered and cried.

"You must finish him, master," Lufti said.

Moussa had dreamed of this moment since he was a child. He had listened to the tales of the Tuareg warriors and the stories told by Gascon and had seen himself in a thousand scenes of battle: proud, victorious. He had beaten a hundred foes in the hot terror of close combat, their heads obliging his blade by tumbling from their shoulders.

But there was to have been a fight, not just a clumsy fall. Stupid luck had made him master of this man who whimpered like a child and had no weapon. Yet luck was better than skill, even if it didn't taste as good. Seize every advantage, take any edge. Kill him now with one blow. Blooded at last, his sword would finally begin to build its legend. It was easy.

Prisoners were never taken in the desert. Never.

Moussa handed his rifle to Lufti and took his heavy killing sword in both hands. His brain flooded with endless visions of Shamba cruelty and treachery. *This is the scourge of the desert. The dread enemy. A thief, a killer. A man who helped attack my mother. Maybe it is he who killed Sala.*

A thousand reasons for a man to die.

Give them no quarter, the amenokal had said. *They will give you none.*

He raised his sword, the razor-sharp blade glinting in the sun. His muscles trembled under its weight. He judged the angle, to be sure of a clean blow. Lufti watched expectantly, memorizing every detail to repeat to all the *buzu.* The desert was quiet but for the babbling and crying of the condemned man. Moussa stared at him, at his gray whiskers and chubby cheeks and dirty turban and the bulging eyes of terror. And then he sighed, and lowered his sword.

"We will leave him," Moussa said at last. "Find his water *guerba* and his food. Leave them here, next to him. Take his weapons. Gather all the camels, including his. We will take them all." Bashaga looked at him with fearful eyes, not understanding the gibberish coming from the Tuareg, wondering what terrible fate they might be devising for him. By Allah, was death by the sword not horrible enough to suit the blue devil?

"Forgive me, sire," Lufti said, shaking his head earnestly, determined to keep his master from this folly. "You must kill him. Quick-quick, for the others still flee. This man is *Shamba.*" He spat the word. "He will cut off his own leg and crawl upon his stump in order to hunt you, and when he finds you he will cut your throat in the darkness as he has done to Sala."

"There is nothing left of this man to crawl. He will die here, and it will be his own work, or the work of the desert. We have recovered what he stole. It is enough. Now do as I say."

When they left Bashaga's howl haunted them until it was swallowed by the wind.

As he rode through the afternoon Moussa tormented himself with more of the awful uncertainty that seemed to haunt his life. He was bitterly disappointed in himself. He had recovered four camels, but he failed to finish the job like a man. *Merde,* his own *mother* would have done it.

Riding behind, Lufti had been silent for hours. At first he was certain an error had been made. But as he thought about it his doubts had turned to pride as he convinced himself how thoroughly Moussa had humbled the Shamba. At length he began to nod excitedly to himself and to cackle at Moussa's coup. Only a great warrior could afford to show mercy to such vermin. Such a beneficent man, Master Moussa. So young, and already a wise and great soldier. Tales began to blossom in Lufti's head, where a little flourish here and an embellishment there would transform the day into legend. His thoughts turned to the unfortunate quarry fleeing before them. He hurried to catch up.

"It has been a glorious day, sire," he said as he drew abreast. Moussa said nothing, so Lufti carried on happily. "Oh-oh, how you had him! Such a look of terror in his eyes! Like a child before a snake. Surely he thought he was doomed! And just as surely the others do not know the strength of the storm that follows them! Yaya, they had best flee with their lives!"

Moussa gave him no acknowledgment. He stared straight ahead and listened to him chatter on. He had clearly heard the earlier tone of disapproval in Lufti's voice, and now in his misery and uncertainty wondered if the slave was mocking him, as they would all mock him soon. The thought stirred rage into his shame, and the mix began to boil inside. *I am the master,* he told himself. *It is I who am Ihaggaren. What he feels does not matter.*

"Shut up!" he hissed. "Do you hear me? *Shut up!*"
Stung, confused, the slave hung his head. He slowed

his camel and dropped back once more to ride in silence and shame.

Moussa gritted his teeth. Another mistake. A proper Tuareg did not show anger or speak harshly to another, and certainly not to a slave. There was no dignity in such behavior. Would he never learn?

He felt as desolate as the vast empty Amadror that stretched out before him. His throat was dry and bitter. He ached inside and his head pounded and the hot air baked his eyes.

I am not Ihaggaren. I am a coward, a fool.

Behind his veil he wept.

A BDUL BEN HENNA SCOOPED HEAPS OF SAND WITH his hands from around the wells of Tan-tan, hollowing out a depression from which his camels could drink. Across from him Kadder did the same, father and son working feverishly to provide enough water quickly to the thirsty caravan so that they could get moving once again. As Abdul had feared, it would not be a quick process. Some wells in the desert were deep holes, into which skins attached to ropes were dropped and then lifted out, the precious water then poured into sandy troughs from which the animals could drink. Other wells, like the one at which they labored, relied on seepage. On the surface they appeared dry, but when they were scooped out the water began to appear. They had to wait for water to filter into the depression, and then the camels could drink. The noisy beasts pushed at each other to get at the water and slurped it up greedily. They stomped around in the sand and pissed in it while they drank, until the depression was a fetid wet mess. If Allah was with them they would be done by morning.

Periodically he peered south into the void. "They will not be far behind us," he kept saying.

"Surely Bashaga will stop them with his gun," Kadder said hopefully.

Abdul grunted. "My brother is a fool," he growled. "He will stop nothing but a Tuareg sword."

The sun grew golden in the sky as it began to set. The

colors softened and the shadows of the watering camels lengthened until they stretched out like flat black giants on the plain.

It was from the north, not from the south, that Moussa and Lufti watched them. Once Lufti had been certain that Tan-tan was the destination of the caravan, he had led them on a route that skirted the well, and positioned them in front of it. They had found a shallow wadi that would help conceal their camels, which they double-hobbled and left behind. They had cautiously half-crawled back toward the well and lay on their stomachs as they watched. Lufti carried a short stabbing knife that he had assured Moussa he was ready and willing to use, although Moussa was skeptical.

Moussa's heart pounded as he surveyed the scene. The two Shamba worked with their backs toward them and were mostly obscured by the milling camels. The land surrounding Tan-tan was perfectly flat. They could go no farther without being seen. "There is nothing to give us cover," he said in a low voice to Lufti, who was already clutching his knife. "We'll have to do it after dark."

"Yaya, sire," Lufti said. "After dark, certainly." He paused, thinking. "And what is it, sire, that we will *do* after dark?"

"I'll tell you later."

Lufti nodded. "Of course, sire."

By four o'clock in the morning the Shamba were exhausted and the camels nearly full. Twice during the night Abdul had leapt up, racing to the perimeter of the encampment, certain someone was there. Nervously clutching his rifle, he listened intently, seeing shadows where there were none, imagining the Tuareg flashing before his eyes. He knew the darkness hid death, but could do nothing about things he could not see. They had spent too many precious hours at the well. It was not a good sign that Bashaga had not appeared.

"Kadder," he snapped, kicking his drowsy son. "Get up. It is time to remove the hobbles of the animals. Get your own mehari ready. We must go."

Kadder groaned. His hands were blistered and

bloody from his labors. Every muscle in his body ached for rest. He turned his back to his father's boot.

At that instant the whole world around the well went utterly mad. First Lufti let out a call for the stolen camels, a familiar cry recognized by the biggest of the bulls, which struggled to its feet to respond. An instant later, from the opposite side of the camp, Moussa fired his rifle into the air and unleashed a bloodcurdling scream, and the scene turned to bedlam. Shrieking and panicked, a large Tibesti bolted away from the noise, pulling on the tethers that held it to other camels who joined it in flight. Others rose and followed quickly, all of them moving awkwardly, struggling against their hobbles or their ropes, moaning and bellowing as they stumbled toward Abdul and Kadder. Kadder jumped to his feet, a sword in one hand, a knife in the other, and moved straight toward the onrushing mass of camels, threading his way through their legs and bodies toward the Tuareg he knew were on the other side. In a panic Abdul lunged for his rifle and fired it blindly into the dark. He wounded a camel whose shrieks added to the chaos. He cursed loudly, his fingers fumbling to reload.

Out of the corner of his eye Moussa saw Lufti moving toward the younger of the two Shamba, and then lost him in the jumble of legs and bodies. Moussa concentrated on the one with the rifle, carefully raising his weapon and peering through the darkness, waiting until the mass of camels had passed and he had the man in his sights. The Shamba was helpless and exposed as he struggled with his weapon. Moussa knew he had him. This time there was no hesitation.

His finger squeezed the trigger.

Nothing happened.

He squeezed again. Nothing. The gun was no use and he flung it aside. He drew his heavy sword from its scabbard and raced through the darkness toward the Shamba. Abdul saw the swirling robes and gleaming steel. He raised his rifle like a club to parry the blow of the sword as it hissed through the air toward his neck. The blade took a chunk out of the stock of the gun. Moussa swung again, and once more Abdul parried,

only this time the rifle flew from his hands and fell to
the ground. Abdul's knife was out instantly, its blade
lashing out and catching cloth and flesh. Moussa felt it
nick his side but kept moving, turning and twisting until
he faced Abdul again. They circled each other warily,
Moussa's thoughts on the deadly tip of the Shamba
knife. He held his sword in both hands and heard the
whispers of Gascon and Abu Bakar guiding his steps.
He felt almost light-headed, without fear. Moussa took
a mighty swing and Abdul ducked, the sword just missing his shoulder. Again a swing, again a miss, and before Moussa knew it the other man had lunged into
him, his knife flashing at his throat. The sword slipped
from Moussa's hands and both men fell hard to the
ground. They rolled over. Moussa caught Abdul's wrist
as the blade sought his neck. Twice the blade touched
his skin. Twice he forced it back, not knowing whether
he had been cut. There was no time to think or to feel,
only the strain of muscle against muscle, arms quivering
with the effort. Summoning all his strength, Moussa
kicked Abdul back, and at once his hand found the
stabbing knife he kept beneath his sleeve. Abdul sprang
to his feet and Moussa rose to meet him, knife against
knife.

Abdul lunged and Moussa dodged, but this time not
quickly enough, and the Shamba's blade found its mark.
Moussa gasped as he felt the searing pain shoot through
his right shoulder and down his arm, and it was all he
could do not to lose hold of his knife. He shifted it into
his other hand and kept moving. Abdul gloated at the
strike; he could see the devil trying to keep both arms
raised, but the right one, the strong one, was down,
nearly useless. Then he saw the devil stumble. With all
his remaining strength and speed, Abdul went for the
kill, his blade first in one hand as he began, then in the
other, a feint and a stab, his blade at the devil's throat.
But in a blinding instant he knew he had missed, his
weapon caught in the folds of cloth covering the monster's head and neck. Even before he felt the steel of the
enemy's blade he knew it was over. He had seen nothing

of his opponent's face, save the eyes. It was one of the reasons why he hated them. They killed in mystery.

As Moussa's stabbing knife pushed up through to his brain, Abdul ben Henna's last thoughts were of revenge.

Lufti AWOKE WITH THE DAWN, HIS HEAD POUND-ing. He had been knocked cold by the surge of camels. He struggled to his feet, blinking, and surveyed the scene. Near the smoldering ashes of the fire was the body of Kadder, whose neck had been broken in the same rush.

He saw Moussa sitting near the well, his back propped against a dead camel. Lufti ran to him. Moussa sat dazed. At his feet was the body of the other Shamba. Sometime in the night Moussa had cut a piece of the dead man's shesh into a bandage and wrapped it around his arm. The material was stained with blood. He shivered slightly.

The slave knelt down. "Sire? Are you all right?" The material of his master's shesh had slipped, almost obscuring his eyes. His gaze seemed distant, fixed on something only he could see. "Sire?" Lufti shook his shoulder gently.

Moussa looked at him blankly. Almost imperceptibly, he nodded.

Relieved, Lufti burst into chatter. "That was a wondrous plan, sire. Oh-oh, yaya, wondrous! *Hamdullilah!* They didn't know what hit them! Surely they thought the whole of the Ihaggaren were upon them!" Lufti swelled with pride.

Moussa looked at the dead form before him, his mind taking in what had happened. His knife had done its work. His duty had been fulfilled. He had redeemed himself. He was a man. He stared at his hands, stained with the life of another man.

His hands. Noble hands. The hands of an Ihaggaren.

And then it overwhelmed him and he bent over and the vomit came, wave after wave of it. Lufti was puzzled. He couldn't imagine what was wrong, why there

was no celebration. Only this odd retching illness. Another defect, perhaps, of the master's French side—but
of course, Lufti would cut the throat of anyone who
dared suggest such a thing. The nobleman was a magnificent warrior.

The slave could only turn away, and begin rounding
up the stolen camels for the long journey home. He
would not look again upon the heaving form of his master, and he would wipe the scene from his memory. His
master's dignity would be preserved.

THERE WAS NOT EVEN THE SATISFACTION OF TRI-
umph in their return to the Tuareg camp. Moussa
knew immediately something was wrong, terribly
wrong. The children should have been everywhere, running through the legs of the returning camels, chattering
and screaming and laughing. Instead he saw them
standing mute. There were not the usual fires or activity
in the camp. Small groups of slaves sat talking among
themselves.

He saw Serena, waiting for him near her tent. Beautiful, she stood in the sun, her hair lifted gently by the
wind. He saw the joy and relief in her eyes as she
watched him coming, and her pride at the string of camels he led. But he saw too the sorrow that overshadowed
all else.

"Mother, what has happened?" he said as he drew
near her.

"The amenokal is dead," she said simply.

"*Abba?*" Moussa slipped quickly from his camel. He
put his arm around her shoulder and together they
found shade in her tent. He listened numbly as she told
him.

"Three nights after your departure, the Kel Ajjer
came. There were twenty of them, maybe more. They
attacked the camp of the Dag Rali. There was only the
amenokal to fight them, and three others of the Kel Ulli.
Everyone else is still away. I tried to stop him, to make
him wait until we could get help. He was too ill to go,

but he would have none of it. A shepherd found their bodies this morning."

Moussa held her and gently stroked her cheek. That night, for a second time, mother and son stood in the wind above a pile of rocks and buried a part of their lives.

CHAPTER 20

October 1880

"So you want to go to Africa."

Lieutenant Colonel Flatters sat at the borrowed desk in the commandant's quarters of St. Cyr, the military academy near Versailles outside Paris, and studied the dossier of the twenty-year-old second lieutenant standing at attention. He looked up at the eager face.

"Yes, sir."

"It is said Africa is a good place to advance your career. Is that your interest?"

"That is a well-known theory, sir, but I believe it is also a good place to serve my country. I have no objection if it also helps my career. I believe I could be of use to you on your mission."

"*Oui*, I suppose it is a good place to serve your country. It is also a good place to die."

"I have no intention of dying there, sir."

"I trust not. Yet I wonder how you feel you can be of use to me. Your dossier is painfully brief. Do you speak Arabic?"

"No, sir. Latin."

"*Latin!* I'm certain that will be quite useful in the Sahara, Lieutenant," said the colonel sarcastically. "Berber?"

"No."

"Have you been to Algeria?"

"No, sir." Paul had been to Spain, but felt it wise not to attempt impressing the colonel with the fact.

"Ridden a camel?"

Paul shifted on his feet and stared straight ahead. "No, sir."

"Hmmmm." Flatters settled back into his chair and continued reading. Presently he spoke without looking up.

"I knew your father."

"Yes, sir." People often said that, especially the older officers. It could be good, and it could be bad. Sometimes it wasn't even true, just words spoken about an infamous man to gauge a son's reaction. He had learned not to react, but to wait for the rest of it: the embarrassed cough, the averted eyes, or the commiseration and the spirited defense. The case of Jules deVries still sparked intense reactions, but Paul read no meaning in the colonel's eyes.

"It is as much because of him as your record at St. Cyr, that the commandant has recommended you to me."

"I would prefer that you consider me on my own merits," Paul said stiffly.

"Then my consideration shall be brief at best," replied the colonel, studying the file. "High initiative, which seems your strong point. Acceptable marks. Excellent grasp of history and math, I see, both of which rank somewhere near Latin in usefulness in the desert."

"I believe the colonel himself wrote a book of the history of the desert before the Arabs arrived. It was an excellent work, sir, if I may say so."

"You read it?" Flatters asked skeptically.

"*Oui*, Colonel. You suggested that the Arabs and Islam would never find a foothold in a Berber land."

"And now I propose to see whether the Christian French can do any better. You must wonder at my optimism."

"Not at all, sir. The French *will* do better."

"And why is that?"

"Because it is the destiny of France to rule."

Flatters nodded absently at that. "I hope it is her destiny to rule more than a horrid desert," he muttered so that Paul could barely hear. He was silent for a moment. He shifted in his chair, trying to ease the acute pain of sciatica. He looked at the young man through glazed eyes. "Any other qualifications with which to impress me, Lieutenant?"

"I am excellent at geography, sir, and map reading."

"There are few maps of where we are going. Almost all of them wrong."

"I can help correct them, sir. I am skilled with a sextant and can navigate." Paul was desperate to be accepted by the colonel. "I have not traveled in Algeria, but my aunt was Tuareg," he volunteered. He regretted it the instant he said it.

"Yes, I know of the countess. An escaped killer, I believe," said the colonel dryly. "Hardly in your favor. Do you know where she is now?"

"No, sir."

"Any idea whether she is even alive?"

"I have not heard from her or the count since . . . since the siege, Colonel. Ten years ago now."

"She was presumed dead at the time. I recall an officer swore he killed the count, but they never found a body. She and her son—that would be your cousin?— were presumed lost in a balloon during a storm. Interesting story. Tragic. I suppose she would be of no use to us anyway. Still, she was Hoggar Tuareg, was she not?"

"*Oui,* Colonel."

"It is through the Hoggar that we propose to journey."

"I am aware of that, sir. I have read Minister Freycinet's papers on the subject. All of them."

The expedition proposed by the minister of public works, Charles Freycinet, was the largest ever mounted by France into the Sahara. Lieutenant Colonel Paul Flatters had already led one expedition into the desert and was organizing a second. His mission was to survey a railroad route through the Sahara with the idea of opening trade between France and a hundred million black African customers. The very pride of France rode on the project. The nation had physically recovered from her humiliation at the hands of the Prussians, but the mental wounds were unhealed. There was no better salve for bruised egos than a grandiose scheme such as the one now cooking in the halls of the National

Assembly, where excitement was building over the prospect of such a daring feat. The Americans had completed a railway between two coasts more than a decade earlier, through inhospitable lands. All the world knew that whatever the Americans could do the French could do better and, more important, with greater flair.

Complaints that the American West was no Sahara fell on deaf ears, as did concerns that no railroad could long survive in the shifting sands of the desert, that there was no supply of water, coal, or wood to fuel the trains. "Details to devil small minds," snapped the minister to his critics. The politicians believed that the vast desert must be developed as the critical link between their provinces in the north of Algeria and Senegal and Timbuktu in the south. French interests were quickly altering the map of the interior of Africa, and the Sahara stood between those interests and the homeland. "If France does not move quickly to fill the void," declared the minister to the National Assembly, "the British and the Germans surely shall." Once thrown down, such a gauntlet could not fail to be picked up by the French nation. There were new frontiers to conquer, from Indochina to the shadowy rich forests of Africa. One could not let other nations have it all. If the Sahara itself was not a jewel, it was at least the way to the jewels. "Paris to the tropics in six days!" trumpeted the headlines, and in a frenzy of self-confidence the assembly provided the money.

Several routes were being considered, but the one along which the Flatters expedition would travel seemed the most likely, as it began from Wargla, a desert town to which France had already extended its influence. Flatters had assembled a group of engineers and surveyors, to be accompanied by a military escort made up of French officers, nearly fifty *tirailleurs*—riflemen of the Armée d'Afrique—for firepower, and cameleers from among the Shamba—conscripts who were legendary caravanners and could help ensure the success of the long trip.

There had been mild interest among the graduating cadets at St. Cyr for the one remaining position in the expedition, and now Paul was one of two final candidates. St. Cyr was full of hard-drinking, hard-playing men, most of whom would be content to receive plum assignments in French garrisons around Paris. Paul wanted none of that. A decade earlier he had stood with his hand in Gascon's as they watched Wilhelm and Bismarck lead their Prussians down the Champs-Elysées. That day he had carried the shame of all France on his small shoulders. Then he had cringed with his mother in the cellar of the château as the mad *pétroleuses* poured rivers of fire through Paris and brother fought brother in the civil war they called the Commune. He understood nothing of what had happened, only that he felt like a coward, using his mother's skirts to hide from rabid women and their fire. After that he dreamed only of the army, of the desert. His father had served there. Over his mother's objections he had entered St. Cyr, where he had studied while the others played. From the instant he had heard of the Flatters expedition he could barely contain his excitement. He wanted it. It was a chance to be strong, a chance at history.

The colonel gauged the strength of the young man standing before him. What he had not revealed was another of the trifling troubles with his plans. He had written the amenokal of the Hoggar Tuareg, a man named Ahitagel. Flatters had asked permission for the second expedition to pass through the amenokal's territory. He had received the response only recently and had not shared it with anyone, not even with his own wife.

You are not welcome here, the letter said. *Try another route.*

Flatters had spent years in the Arab bureau, in various northern oases of the desert. The letter was the typical bluster, he decided, of a weak man. One replied to such rudeness with strength. The colonel would first try paying the Tuareg to forget their objections. Everyone knew they lived for the bribe. If that didn't work he would brush them aside, crush them if necessary.

"We may have difficulties with various of the indigenous tribes of the region," the colonel said vaguely to Paul. "Does that trouble you?"

"Of course not, sir. It is what I have trained for."

"I must rely upon my officers to be prepared for anything."

"They will be no match for our forces, Colonel. It is my understanding that you will be using the Shamba with your troops. I have heard that there are no better soldiers among the Arab people."

"Romantic crap, deVries. You had better divorce yourself of such ignorant notions. They are cowards, like all Arabs. But I will grant you they are the best of the cowards. They are barely trainable, like dogs. They will steal one blind. One must watch them constantly."

Paul was disconcerted by the contempt in the colonel's words for the men who would be serving under him, but said nothing. The colonel had spent enough years among them to be entitled to his opinion. Certainly he must know how to handle his men. Yet as he looked at the colonel he couldn't help but wonder about the man, who wasn't at all what Paul had pictured. The colonel hardly appeared the cunning desert warrior. He thought such an officer would have more . . . flair. Flatters carried himself like a man bored by the world, suffering through life instead of savoring it. He was overweight and had a high forehead and short thick neck. He had a neatly waxed mustache, a round face and florid complexion. His temper was legendary, and some said he was given to bouts of depression. Paul had heard rumors of disaster on the first Flatters expedition, of cowardice and poor command decisions. But such complaints were heard about any military venture and Paul shrugged them off. Whether the colonel who sat before him was the ideal French warrior or not, one thing was certain. Paul was determined not to be left behind.

Flatters stared at the anxious junior officer. "You seem to have fire in your belly, Lieutenant," he said. "Well, the desert will put that out soon enough. It will grind you down, the same way it does every man who goes there."

"It will not do that to me, Colonel."

"Hmmmph. So says every man. Still, you seem fit

enough, if somewhat lacking in substance." Flatters made his decision. Without enthusiasm he nodded. "Very well, Lieutenant deVries, I suppose you'll have to do. I will arrange matters with your commandant. We leave in a fortnight. You'd better get moving. You have a lot to do."

YOU ARE DOING THIS TO HURT ME," ELISABETH sniffed. They sat in the study of the château before a roaring fire.

"Nonsense, Mother. I am doing it because I want to. It has nothing to do with you."

"That's just the trouble. Nothing you do these days seems to have anything to do with me. And why some dreary backwater with savages? We have the money, the connections. You can get an assignment here, in Paris. I can arrange—"

"I don't want you to arrange anything, Mother. I don't want connections. I want to do this myself."

"You are so stubborn, Paul. Honestly, I wish you would act with a *little* more dignity, like a count."

"Please don't start, Mother. I'm *not* a count."

"You will be, as soon as the court has ruled your uncle dead."

"You want him dead, don't you?"

"What a horrid thing to say! Of course not. But what I want isn't important. He *is* dead. I only want the court to recognize that, to make it formal. To make *you* the new Count deVries."

It was an old and futile argument between them. "If Uncle Henri is dead then Moussa is the count, not I. It doesn't matter anyway. France is a republic, Mother, in case you've forgotten. The days of counts and kings are gone. There *is* no nobility anymore."

"There are titles and tradition."

"They mean nothing. They're just for show."

"This estate is certainly not for show!" She sighed. "Dear God, Paul, I've told you a thousand times. They died escaping! All of them, including Moussa! No one could have survived. If they'd gotten away they would have written us by now—if not openly, then secretly. You *know* that! Ten years, and there has been not one word! Not one! Nothing but death could have kept them silent for so long! Why do you have such trouble accepting that?"

"Because I am in no hurry to bury them, Mother. I don't want what is theirs. I only want the army. I want Africa."

"*Africa!* The *army!*" She let the words slither from her tongue like repulsive serpents. "What about the army could possibly hold your fascination or respect? Is it not enough what the army did to your father? Is it not enough the army was humiliated by the . . . *Huns?* It is no career for a man of your talents! Besides, you don't *need* a career! Whatever you want, anything at all, is right here in Paris! Madame Deveaux is begging me to convince you to take her daughter Monique to one of the balls!"

"Monique is an idiot, Mother. I wouldn't take her to a cockfight."

"Paul! Mind your tongue!"

"It's true. I'm tired of you trying to find me a wife. I'm tired of you trying to run my life. *You* take Monique to the ball, if it pleases you! I'm going to Africa!"

He slammed the door. Elisabeth sat still for long moments, her heart racing, her hands trembling. *Mon Dieu,* the very thought that he treated her so! She listened as Paul's horse thundered down the drive. She poured herself a brandy and walked to the desk where Henri had spent so many comfortable nights before the same raging fire. She sat in the chair and stared at the drawer.

She hated the drawer, yet was fascinated by it.

From around her neck she drew a slim gold chain, at the end of which was a key. She put the key in the lock and opened the drawer. It was stuffed with letters, wrapped in two bundles. Absently she shuffled through one. They carried dates spanning most of the last decade, the envelopes addressed in a hand that had visibly matured over the years. They were all addressed to Paul. All from a wretched little place in the Sahara called the Hoggar. Elisabeth knew about the Hoggar. The first few years she had read the letters carefully. She had read them just long enough to learn what had become of the count, his wife, and his son. When she realized they weren't coming back to France she stopped reading the letters and simply put the new ones into the bundle. Then two years ago they had stopped coming.

The other packet contained the letters Paul had written to Moussa over the same period. She had read all of those, some of them many times. It was the only way she could keep up with what her son had been doing, what he had been thinking. They were a journal of his life, revealing things he certainly never told *her*. Even though they often hurt her feelings, she read them anyway, finding them useful when she needed to prod him one way or another.

Both bundles sat in the drawer on top of the pathetic little letter Jules had written to his son the night he died. She didn't know why she hadn't destroyed them. She should burn them all, just as she had burned the letter from Jules to Henri. *That* one had been simply too inflammatory.

Now as she closed the drawer and locked it, she worried that somehow Paul would meet his cousin in the desert. Of all things, that he should hook up with this madman Flatters and go to the very place where she thought the past had disappeared forever—it was so unfair! She was terrified that something would happen to upset her plans, the plans she'd worked so carefully. Since the count and his *murderess*—Elisabeth loved the delicious word—disappeared that night, she had been countess in all but name. She had access to the money, to the assets, to everything, and no one to challenge her. The château was hers, her parties grand, Henri's furniture burned and her own installed. But still she coveted the mantle that had always eluded her. Her husband had never been able to obtain it, and now she would have it for her son. She had waited the required nine years before she could begin the process of declaring the missing count dead. There were no other heirs to interfere. If Serena were ever to return she would end up in prison.

Only one danger remained: the wretched half-breed Moussa. She had been delighted to read of him playing like some desert sheikh. She exulted when he wrote of his love for the desert, that he wanted to live there forever. Feeling secure at last, she had filed the court papers. And now she very nearly had it all.

Elisabeth sat alone in the darkening room. One of her half-dozen servants appeared to inquire timidly, "Does the countess care for dinner?" She waved him away and drank her brandy and stared into the fire.

CHAPTER 21

THAT SUCH ECSTASY COULD DWELL NEXT TO SUCH misery inside the same heart was a shock to Daia. For days she had been torn, her mood soaring and then plunging. She didn't know what to do.

Daia lived in the *ariwan* of Mano Biska, one of the minor chiefs of the Ihaggaren. There she had grown from scrawny goat girl to beautiful woman. For several years she had had many suitors, but she turned them all away without interest. Only one man had held her interest, and the interest had not been returned. Besides, she was in no hurry for marriage. Then Mahdi had begun to visit, appearing in her *ariwan* more often than his business in the camp required. He always took the time to call on her. The other women were jealous. Mahdi was of excellent lineage, the son of El Hadj Akhmed, the great amenokal killed in the Ajjer wars. Mahdi was a man in whom all the greatest strengths of the Ihaggaren dwelled, a man who would inevitably make his strong mark in the history of the Hoggar. But the women's jealousy was in vain. Mahdi cared for none but Daia.

If Mahdi might make an exceptional mate, his ways were hard. She knew he could be cruel, that he was quick to temper, and that his tongue was sharper than any blade. He was renowned as a warrior, and his family would never lack for food or wealth. Yet his rages created much trouble even among his family. His own father had publicly chastised him for his eruptions. He was nearly alone among the Ihaggaren in his devotion to Islam, and his eyes burned when he spoke of it.

He was as tightly coiled as an adder, and as quick to strike.

Yet Mahdi seemed a different man when he was near her. He brought her gifts of jewelry and cloth. In her presence all the ferocity melted away, and he seemed gentle as a lamb, yet stiff and nervous too, overwhelmed by her presence.

On a splendid night beneath a winter moon there had been an *ahal*, a romantic gathering at which the women sang to the soulful notes of the one-stringed *imzad* and men read poetry that joined with the quiet rhythm of the night drums. Mahdi's voice became soft as he said surprisingly tender things, things she never expected to hear from a man whose nature smoldered as if it had been forged in the smith's fires. Before the appreciative crowd he recited a poem he'd written for her.

> *My heart is the eagle*
> *Whose wings brush the peak*
> *that is Daia,*
> *but never own her.*
>
> *I stop there to rest, and find beauty*
> *unseen from the air.*
> *Soft edges, silken places*
> *that gladden my heart.*
>
> *Daia, the wondrous peak*
> *becomes now a song.*
> *Sweet gentle rhythms upon my mind.*
> *Who is she, this woman who tames the eagle,*
> *Who holds my heart?*

She knew he had labored with the words, which did not come naturally to him, words that seemed sweeter and more meaningful because of it. She knew that together they would make fine daughters and sons of the desert. In so many respects he was the perfect mate. When she confessed she was troubled vaguely by his hard dark side, which could erupt in such a frightening manner, Anna, the old slave who was like her mother, had scoffed at her doubts. "It is the hard edge that makes the sword great," she said. "You deserve his interest, as he deserves yours. It would be a mistake to turn him away."

Yes, she knew she was lucky. She told herself that her influence could still the fires that raged inside him.

Four days after the *ahal,* Mahdi had sent an emissary to her *ariwan.* As was the custom, Keradji, the one-eyed blacksmith, had come to broach the subject of marriage. Daia had no mother or father or uncle to ask—and one would not discuss such a matter with Anna—so Keradji spoke directly with Daia. She had thought it over carefully. It was not the easy decision she had always expected it to be, but in the end she assented.

That had all been thirty days ago. A lifetime. Before the laughter. Ah, the laughter.

She sat atop her mehari and quietly watched the source of her trouble. Moussa handled the hawk with hands that were long and delicate and almost feminine, his touch as soft as the feathers of the beautiful bird. "Her name is Taka," Moussa told her proudly. "The sword of Orion." She was a small *terakel,* a female, fast and strong and nearly white in color except for a small patch of gray on her chest. He had captured her high in the Atakor, and had spent long patient months training the bird. Daia had learned much about the hawk in the past few days as they traveled together. She had learned much about herself as well.

She had seen Moussa only twice in the four years since the episode in the *guelta,* when she had seen his face and his body and had caused him such acute embarrassment. The image had never left her, and once she had tried to make it clear through intermediaries that she would welcome his company. She didn't know whether it was shyness or anger or whether he simply wasn't interested, but he had never responded. Over time the images of the *guelta* faded, and she had given up on him. Then she hadn't seen him at all for two years, and Mahdi had come into her life.

Moussa had been making a circuit of the vassal

camps of the Dag Rali when word reached him that a *djemaa* had been called. The amenokal Ahitagel had summoned all the Kel Rela to discuss the imminent expedition of the French, who were massing a caravan in Wargla. The meeting was to be held in ten days' time in Abalessa, the amenokal's winter encampment. Along the way Moussa had encountered Daia, who had been making her own way to Abalessa where she was to join Mahdi.

Her initial glimpse of him had provided the first surprise. She had seen him from a considerable distance, and yet knew immediately who it was. She felt herself flushed with the unexpected pleasure of anticipation. He looked regal and proud and magnificent upon his mehari. His robes were light blue, his veil white. A hooded hawk, majestic in her own right, sat upon his shoulder, brooding and alert. As Daia drew near the hawk turned toward her, tilting its head beneath the hood, sensing her presence. At the same time she saw the bright blue eyes of the man smiling behind the veil.

"You have grown well, Daia," he said without prelude when they met. "I am pleased to see you."

There was nothing more than correctness in his voice, but she felt herself blushing anyway. "As I am pleased also. It has been much time."

"You are alone?"

"I was traveling with the *ehen* of Mano Biska," she replied. "I was parted from the others when I stopped to visit my cousin in Ideles. I am going to Abalessa."

"As am I. Do you wish an escort?"

"I need none," she said, a little haughtily. "I am able to care for myself."

"I am aware that you are better with a blade than most men," Moussa said. "Your reputation makes its way to my camp, even if you do not. I meant escort for company, of course, not for protection."

"I believe you meant it for protection."

He sighed. "Very well then. Will you escort *me* to Abalessa?"

"Will you keep your clothes on?" she asked innocently.

Moussa started, caught off-guard by the reference to the incident at the *guelta*. He recovered quickly. "If there are no thieves nearby then yes, I shall."

"There are thieves everywhere in the desert."

"Then, mademoiselle, they had best beware the naked man," Moussa said, mixing languages as he often did, his eyes alight.

Daia leapt at that. "There is but little to beware, as I recall," she said, and they laughed and their journey together began. As their meharis fell into an unhurried rhythm she had her next unsettling surprise. As pleased as she had been to see him, she was even more pleased that they were alone. She chided herself for such thoughts and pushed them from her mind.

They were five days' ride from Abalessa. Moussa traveled slowly, stopping frequently to work with Taka. During the early mornings and late afternoons the bird rode on his shoulder, but the rest of the day when the sun was high it rode in its own shelter. He had constructed a miniature tent on the pommel of his saddle, its front open so that a gentle breeze would pass through and cool the bird as they rode. She was amazed at the trouble Moussa had taken. "I have heard that only the sultan of Morocco rides in such a litter," she said.

"If he weren't so fat and could fly for me like Taka I would gladly construct another for him," Moussa replied.

Several times a day they halted when Moussa spotted game. Sometimes it was a lizard or a snake sunning itself atop a rock, or perhaps a jerboa, a little desert mouse, hopping frantically between hideouts. A scorpion might be scuttling along the sand. Occasionally they would even see a hare. In the rock desert through which they rode such game was plentiful, if only one looked sharply enough. Moussa's eyes seemed as keen as the hawk's.

He had adapted the hunting process quite well to the desert. Usually there was no one to flush the game for which the hawk waited, so he used the tools of his childhood. With a motion that showed infinite practice and patience, Moussa drew his slingshot from his robe and, one-handed, fit a pebble to the sling. Then he would slip the leather hood off the hawk, let loose of its jesses, and launch her into the sky. As she circled on powerful wings he raised his slingshot and quickly let his pebble fly. The sand near the quarry would erupt and the game would be on the move, and the hunt was joined. With grace and speed and power the hawk would wheel and swoop down, straight as a lance, a killer on wings, gauging the path of the fleeing animal as it sought cover in the rocks or beneath the cram-cram bushes scattered across the land. Sometimes the prey would win, disappearing into a hole or beneath a rock without a second to spare, leaving Taka to screech in rage as her wings beat against the desert air. She would rise to Moussa's lure, to sulk and nurse her injured pride as she awaited the next opportunity.

But defeat was rare for Taka. More often her powerful talons would find their mark and she would seize the game and break its neck or, in the case of a snake, rise back into the sky to drop it onto the rocks where it would be stunned or killed. Then Taka would screech again, louder now in victory, *eeeek-eek-eek,* and descend on her kill. Quickly Moussa would offer the lure. Taka would stare at him for a moment, as if deciding, and then reluctantly rise from her kill toward the lure, and end her outing on the leather at his wrist. He would quickly reward her with a liver or brain from the kill and, voice cooing, softly sing her praises. He would slip on her hood and when she was calm again he would return her to her perch atop the saddle. Taka preened herself carefully. First she roused, lifting her feathers until she looked like a duster, then shaking herself violently to settle them into place again. After that she oiled each feather with her beak. When she was finished she stretched each leg, and then her wings and tail.

Moussa regarded her proudly. "She is a fine one," he said. "Mannered and persistent. Her spirit is great. She is the best I have had." Every kill required a slightly different approach, master and hawk working harmoniously together in a seamless blend of Moussa's efforts and Taka's natural skill. Moussa would lay the plan; Taka would carry it out.

"You are a poet with her," Daia said in wonder as she watched. "But why does she always come back? Why doesn't she just leave?"

"Because she knows me. We are comfortable together. She does my bidding as I do hers. I feed her, she feeds me. I suit her needs today, as she suits mine."

"And if she does fly away?"

"Then she is free," he said, shrugging, "a daughter of the desert once more. She *will* fly away one day. I will make her, if she doesn't do it on her own. She was wild once, and will be wild again. I have only borrowed her spirit from the desert. She was not born to live at the end of a jess. She is mine only for a season, and never really mine at all. When she leaves I will catch another, and begin again. That is the way of it. I doubt I'll find another like Taka, though."

There was infinite patience in him as well as passion for the birds and the hunt. She saw it in his eyes and his touch. "My father taught me to hunt," he said. "Nearly every day we went out into the woods near our house for rabbits and quail. One day when I was six we even killed a boar."

"What is a boar?"

"Too much to catch with a hawk," he said, laughing, and he told her of the day near the Bois de Boulogne when Paul saved his life, and of the little fort they had in the grand oak tree that stood near the lake across which he had seen the emperor of France. He chatted on for hours about that other world, a world of top hats and carriages, where the water was plentiful and turned to ice in the winter and where the snows fell everywhere, not just in the highest mountains.

"There are wide boulevards in Paris lined with trees," he told her, spreading his arms expansively. "The buildings are nearly as big as our dunes."

Her eyes widened. "Why on earth would anyone wish to live in such a crowded place?" she asked. "Why would they wish to live in a house built of unmoving stone? Why would they wish a roof over their heads?

How would they know the sky? How would they know freedom?" She shook her head. "It is odd that people choose to live in such a backward fashion. It is no better than the *harratin* who till the soil, forever chained to their plots of land."

He had no answer for that.

But aside from the handicap of the houses that held them down, the French seemed an interesting enough people, and she listened raptly to his descriptions, enchanted by the breadth of his imagination, which, she thought, must surely be the only place where some of the things as he described could exist. He told her of fireworks and cannons and gaslights, of palaces with fountains where water tumbled out of the mouths of stone figures.

"Your stories are beautiful and clever," she said. "I often wonder whether you are but an extraordinary liar," she teased when he told her about the telegraph. He laughed and protested his innocence and assured her it was all true, "except for the parts I make up."

Whether she believed or not, she found herself caught up in the words, in his descriptions, in his zest for the world of his childhood. He was charming and quick-witted and the oddest man she had met. In every inch he was a nobleman, but a nobleman such as she had never seen among the Ihaggaren. He sat erect and moved with easy grace and had the delicate features in his hands and feet that marked his high birth. But the haughtiness and reserve of the race, so highly prized in others, was missing in him. He was instead a blend of irreverence and wit, a mixture that delighted her.

"Your barbarian side is demented," she told him more than once as she laughed at his comments about himself and others.

"Thoroughly," he agreed, not without a note of pride.

His attitude was contagious, and she chattered back with ease. The miles drifted by and Taka hunted and that night they camped and made a fire. He made a great show of cooking for her like a slave, although she wouldn't eat much of what Taka caught. "That lizard

could be your uncle," she reminded him as she warily
regarded the reptile grilling over a bed of coals. It was
well known that ancestors inhabited the bodies of reptiles. No one among the Ihaggaren except Moussa
would ever have eaten such a thing. He scoffed gently at
her superstition and ate it anyway. "It does not taste all
that bad for a relative." He smiled, but made couscous
for her while she made them bread, kneading the dough
and baking it in the sand beneath the coals.

After they had eaten and the camels were tended they
settled before the fire with their backs to the rocks and
drank strong tea. He told her stories until the gray twilight before dawn. They huddled next to each other in
their separate cloaks to ward off the frigid winds. The
sun had just risen when they reluctantly let sleep take
them at last.

Through everything they did ran the strong thread of
laughter. It was easy, comfortable, everywhere. They
laughed at things they hadn't laughed at before, at
things that hadn't been funny until they saw them together at the same moment. They laughed at the antics
of the jerboa as it hopped before the night fire, carrying
bits of bread to its mouse house, and at the grotesque
complaints of their meharis as they were loaded in the
morning, and at Moussa's imitation of an abbess he
called Godrick—a thoroughly sacrilegious display that
Daia only partially understood but which had her
nearly in tears.

For both of them, it was a time that passed much too
quickly.

All the while she knew he was not courting her, that
he realized she was on her way to join her betrothed.
There was no pressure on them and so they were able to
be free, free to enjoy each other without other eyes or
ears nearby to disapprove or to spread gossip, free to be
silly and young, free to say whatever they liked, free to
be alive.

She didn't know when it changed, only that it had. It
was on the third morning when she realized that her
gentle trembling was not from hunger or the night cold,

but that it swept across her like a breeze whenever he came near. In her life there had never been such a feeling. In her life there had never been such a time.

She did her best to hide it from him, and from herself. She found herself staring at him, watching the easy way he rode his mehari, or his hands as they handled the hawk or mixed the flour and water for bread. When he glanced toward her she looked away quickly so he couldn't see she had been watching. After he had fallen asleep at night she lifted herself on one elbow and looked at him until dawn, a tender smile on her face.

On the morning of the fourth day they were standing before the fire, their minds and bodies numb with fatigue, yet somehow completely alive with the adrenaline of happiness. They were chattering and giggling, preparing for the day's journey. For a moment a silence passed between them and their eyes met. On an impulse she began to reach up to him, to touch his veil. The next instant she caught herself. She felt Mahdi's eyes burning into the depths of her soul where things were happening even she didn't understand. A cloud of guilt passed over her. She dropped her hand and turned away and the moment passed.

The rest of that day she strengthened her resolve to stop acting in ways that made the guilt come. She succeeded in pretending indifference toward Moussa, turning away and trying not to laugh when he said something amusing. For the first time there was awkwardness between them.

"Are you troubled?" Moussa asked, his voice gentle with concern.

"No," she said. "I was only thinking of my marriage." It was true, so she didn't understand why she hated herself instantly for saying it. She thought Moussa's head jerked a little at the words. After that he was uncharacteristically quiet and for the first time in nearly four days they rode in a sad unnatural silence that was as suffocating as the desert heat. Suddenly each stride of the camel seemed interminable, and Daia didn't know what to do. One part of her wanted their

journey to end quickly, wanted to arrive in Abalessa
where all the confusion might end. The rest of her, most
of her, wanted their journey to last forever.

Through the long hours it tore at her. Moussa
stopped to hunt. She watched him without getting off
her mehari. When he went to retrieve the game Taka
caught, he found a small patch of flowers growing beneath a bush. He pulled one up and looked at it. Its
petals were bright blue and had bloomed for less than a
day. By that night they would be withered and gone. He
kept the flower, intending to give it to her. But when he
returned to where she waited, he saw her upon her
mehari, and saw the pain on her face, and decided it
would be a mistake. He had no right.

And when he was certain she wasn't looking he let
the flower drop to the ground.

But she did see.

THAT NIGHT MOUSSA SHIVERED IN HIS ROBE BY
the dying fire and watched the brilliant stars. He was
too exhausted to sleep, too numb, his mind too busy.
He listened to the even sound of her breathing as she lay
in her own robe next to him. When he closed his eyes
his world opened up into a kaleidoscope of images of
the last few days. He held on to each one until it faded
away to the next, and then he began again. He felt himself smiling, and once laughed out loud. Later he fought
back a tear. He had never been closer to another human
being; he had never felt so alone. There was so much he
wanted to say to her, and yet there was Mahdi, who
had passed like a shadow, it seemed, between them.
Sometime in the night he finally drifted off into a fitful
sleep.

And then the dream came—a dream he had had before yet a dream so intense he knew it was something
completely different. He felt her there, slipping up beneath his robes, her body soft and warm as she made
her way next to him, and it was a perfect dream, so
much better than the others—a dream in which he felt

every curve, every breath, felt her silken skin against his own, felt her fingers as she explored him and he grew hard, a dream in which he touched her with more gentleness than he knew he possessed, touched her with more feeling than he had ever known, as if she were made of sand and might crumble beneath his caress. And then in a flash of desire they melted together, moaning, whispering each other's name, desperately clinging, and then he was inside her and there were tears of joy and their passion burst in a white-hot instant of sunlight. It lasted all night, the dream, through long, luxurious hours of exploration, of feeling, of enchantment, and in those hours he found everything, found her cheeks with his lips and found the small of her back with his fingertips and found her nipples and all the soft sweet mysterious places he had only imagined before. His heart pounded and he wanted to laugh and to cry at the same time and wanted the dream never to end, never to stop, wanted all his dreams to be this way. . . .

And through it all he knew it was not a dream, and that made him hold on to her even more desperately, and she to him; and they knew that when the night was over it would be finished, that the dream would never be again.

ALL ACROSS THE SAHARA STORMS OF INTRIGUE raged over the French Lieutenant Colonel Flatters and his mission.

In the busy caravan crossroads of Murzuk, the Turkish bey attempted to calm the nerves of the merchants who feared the loss of commerce should the French succeed in building their railway. The bey received instructions from Tripoli and in turn met with his own agents. He dispatched them with detailed instructions and a significant portion of his treasury to In Salah, there to await the amenokal of the Hoggar Tuareg.

In the oasis of Ghat a cabal of Senussi fanatics held council to deal with the infidel threat. Their lives were dedicated to Allah and the *jihad* against the heretic. Their order was small but growing, an army of zealots prepared to sacrifice their lives in the holy cause, which did not stop with exterminating unbelievers. They cared not that the current threat was French. It could have been Italian, or Turkish. All foreigners were devils— even the Turks, who, although they were believers and would surely find eternal comfort at the side of Allah, could not stay the holy wrath of the Senussi. The Sahara was not a free river from which any man could drink. The Sahara was for Saharans, where Allah would one day reign supreme, even among the heathen Tuareg. Until that day, the foreigners must die.

One man among the Senussi had a particular interest in the French. Tamrit ag Amellal had joined the order more than twenty years earlier. Until his self-imposed exile he had been a Tuareg of the Kel Rela. He had attempted to kill the *ikufar* deVries, a nobleman traveling under the protection of the woman Serena. He had loved Serena then more than his life, more than Allah. But he loved her no more. Now the fires of passion that lit his eyes were stoked only by his devotion to God. In the coming of the French he saw the opportunity to redeem himself.

In Morocco, the sultan listened to the entreaties of his subjects as they implored him to intervene, to protect the oases of the Tuat from the French menace. The rebel Bou Amama swore that if the sultan allowed the French to penetrate farther, he would raise his own *jihad*. The rebel Abd-el-Kader traveled to In Salah to await Ahitagel, the amenokal, a man he was determined to bend to his own purposes.

In Wargla, the sheikhs of the Shamba debated their own response to the unwelcome advance of the arrogant and ignorant Europeans who were venturing into the nest of scorpions.

In the Hoggar, the very land through which the French proposed to march, the amenokal and the nobility listened as Mahdi and Attici, the most rabidly anti-French among them, carried the arguments for the death of the intruders, while Moussa and his friend Taher argued moderation.

"As we speak, the barbarian Flatters makes his preparations to leave Wargla," Mahdi reported. "Our spies there tell us he has assembled three hundred camels for his passage. He has announced his intention to pass through In Salah. In Salah belongs to the Ihaggaren! How dare he think he can sully these lands with his band of unbelievers! The Lord Amenokal has told them already the way is not open to them, yet they come even so. Such arrogance must be met with the sword of Heaven, not the palm of friendship."

"You are too quick to strike, Mahdi," said Taher. "We have also heard that his baggage is filled with money and gifts. He has two white horses of the finest Arabian stock. It is only logical that we relieve the colonel of his possessions, then let him pass. His passage can have no effect upon us, while his wealth will be welcome."

"*Welcome!* They will have Shamba cameleers with them. They are hiring them now in the souks, bribing them with ease. *Shamba!*" He spat the word. "Would you permit such men as these, men in league with the devil, to defile the Hoggar in exchange for French wealth? Does the sweet breath of the lion make his mouth any less dangerous?"

"They wish only to pass. Let them pass and take their money, I say!"

"Take their money, yes! But kill them!" Mahdi was livid. "Are they not unbelievers? What infidel has the right to enter this country for any purpose? What *ikufar* deserves other than the sword of Allah?"

Attici raised his hand to caution Mahdi. Pressing the issue on religious grounds was unlikely to carry the day. Among the Tuareg such arguments often fell on deaf ears. Attici wanted to turn the argument on more practical grounds: the Ihaggaren must control the caravan routes and never give way to any outside force.

"Do you believe these will be the last of the barbarians to come?" Attici asked. "That the devil Flatters is

the last of their number who will show an interest in the
Hoggar? Who among you believes the French will not
interfere with the passage of caravans, which until now
have traveled only at *our* pleasure? Who among you
believes the French will not try one day to banish the
trade in slaves? The man who believes this must also
believe that camels may fly!"

"They would not do such a thing," Moussa said,
uncertain he believed the words even as he spoke them.
The fact was that he had no idea what the French might
do. Yet he did not believe them capable of ill will
toward the Tuareg. The French were, after all, his people too, though his memories of them had clouded with
the years. Such memories might not be trusted. But all
afternoon he had defended them against the most outrageous statements: The French would massacre their
men, rape their women, kill their children. The French
boiled their victims. Poisoned wells. Burned date crops
of the northern oases.

"The Hoggar is ours," he argued. "There is nothing
here to interest the French. They would not care to interfere with our commerce. Never! There is no logic in
that, no need! If anything they would wish to increase
commerce, then tax the caravans themselves on the
Algerian end! That is the French manner!"

"Moussa speaks with the French half of his tongue,"
snapped Mahdi, "and without benefit of his brain.
What they touch they steal. What they cannot steal they
corrupt with their heathen ways and barbarian laws. In
Algeria have they not taken the most fertile lands for
themselves? Have they not pushed the *harratin* from
their lands and forced them into their cities, where they
die of filth and rot? Have they not filled their prisons
with the men they have robbed blind? Have they not
destroyed everything they have touched?"

"There is no proof of such things, Mahdi," said
Taher.

"I have proof enough. I have the word of Abu
Hassan, who has been many times to the tell where
these things have occurred. Who among you will cast
doubt upon his word?" His voice challenged them all.

No one would deny the word of the venerated marabout, who had spent much time in the northern provinces of Algeria.

"It is as Mahdi says." Abu Hassan nodded, his voice frail. "When they plundered Sidi Ferouk, their bombs rained for days on women and children. They burned houses and put the torch to olive groves. Women who wore jewelry had their ears and hands and ankles mutilated, their limbs removed by the infidel sword for their silver. Great plantations of the Kabyles were destroyed, their palms cut down. Animals and land were taken without payment. Whole villages were fined, innocents executed. Muslims were banished from their own markets if the French were present. The *harratin* were left with nothing. These facts are well known among those of the tell. There is no reason to believe the French jackal will lose his appetite among our camps."

"It serves the *harratin* right," grumped Taher. "Shame enters the family that tills the soil. Their fate means nothing to us. We are not such farmers. Do you mean the French will seize our land? And then what will they do with it? Will they farm? Nonsense! There is nothing to farm within a thousand leagues of the Hoggar! There is nothing but the way of the nomad, of the Ihaggaren."

"No, they will not farm. But they will seek to control the land, to become masters of the caravan routes we have controlled since the beginning of history! And then they will stop the slaves! Without slaves where will the caravans be? Without caravans where will we be? What is to become of our way of life?"

"I do not believe the French will do these things," Moussa insisted.

"If they have no designs upon our caravans or trade, Moussa," said the amenokal, breaking the silence in which he had been listening to the exchange, "then why do they speak of a railway? Is not a railway for the purpose of transporting goods? Would not such a thing permit them to travel at will through the Hoggar?"

Moussa was puzzled by this himself. "I cannot vouch for their sanity, Lord, in placing a railway here," he replied. He knelt and drew a picture for them in the sand as everyone strained to see. Almost no one among them had ever seen a railway or an engine; in this Moussa's knowledge was respected. "This is the manner of roadbed I remember," he said. "They must lay two rails of steel on blocks of wood. The steel is quite heavy, to support the weight of a train. It would have to be made in France or Spain and shipped all the way across the sea, piece by piece, then transported through Algeria. The same would be true of the blocks of wood, for nothing grows in the north that will support such a line. Then there is the matter of the train itself. Engines employ steam to turn the cranks to push the train along the tracks. They must have water for this, a great quantity of it, and some material to sustain the fires to run the engines. Between Wargla and the southlands there is no water for such needs. Nor is there anything to burn that will keep a train moving. And even if there were, they would have to pass through the great dunes, through the Gassi Touil, where the Ergs move fifty paces in a day. The sand will bury whatever they build. What can stand against it? Certainly not a train." Moussa shook his head in puzzlement. "There is no logic to the French plan, Lord, this I must confess."

Ahitagel considered that for a time. "If we assume that the French are not stupid—and I am not at all certain we can make such an assumption—then these facts suggest they have a different motive for coming."

"Our spies tell us that the French have hired *tirailleurs*, Lord," Mahdi said. "Of what use are Algerian riflemen for the exploration of a railway? The answer is that their purpose is hostile. We must meet hostility with hostility."

"Do we not travel fully armed when passing into another's country?" asked Taher. "Would they not be fools otherwise?"

"Who fears their rifles? What are five Frenchmen to one son of the desert?"

"To have no fear of rifles is to wish a foolish death," Taher warned. "A rifle makes the lowest coward the equal of the greatest warrior. Which Ihaggaren will not feel a bullet?"

"The French are too strong to stop," Moussa agreed. "I myself have seen their weapons as a child. They were fearsome then, and can only have improved. It is best to meet them in peace, to show them there is nothing of interest for them here. We must kiss the hand we cannot cut off. When they want to come, nothing we do will stop them."

"*Nothing we do will stop them?*" Mahdi repeated the words slowly, lacing them with sarcasm and scorn. "Is this the talk of a true son of the desert, or the whimpering of a weak, defeated child? You would expose your flesh for the lion to bite, then take its teeth willingly? Whether the French are strong has no meaning here. They cannot travel in force. There is not sufficient water. They will come in such numbers as will make them vulnerable, as all our enemies have done. The desert will sap their energy, and we will pick the bones of what remains."

"Where is the honor in killing them?" Moussa asked.

"Where is their honor in coming uninvited?" Mahdi replied. He paced angrily back and forth before the group. "Logic and argument are the fetters of a coward. If Moussa lacks the courage to face the French, then at least let him stop hiding behind this pretense. Perhaps French blood runs too thickly in his veins. Perhaps he is in their pay."

Moussa was on his feet before Mahdi could react, the blunt side of his sword clubbing his cousin on the head. With a cry Mahdi tumbled backward, stunned. As quickly as he went down he was back up, sword drawn in rage.

"*Stop!*" the amenokal thundered, and the tent fell silent. Moussa and Mahdi eyed each other angrily, but held their anger in check. Ahitagel's voice lashed at them. "To fight in the *djemaa* is unforgivable."

"It is unforgivable that he calls me traitor," Moussa snapped.

"A lucky blow, Cousin," Mahdi hissed. "We will finish—"

"You will finish *nothing*," Ahitagel said. "There is enough trouble facing us without stirring it among ourselves."

The amenokal was deeply troubled. The debate had done nothing to clear his mind. Every instinct told him to treat the intruders ruthlessly, for if he permitted the expedition other Frenchmen would surely follow. Yet if he stopped it, if he ordered them all killed, would the outcome be different? Were the French not many and vengeful? Could the people of the veil stand alone against them in war? For all of known history the Hoggar had been the inviolate sanctuary of the Tuareg, feared by all who came near, a sanctuary over whose caravans and affairs the noble Ihaggaren had always been the undisputed masters. Always they had been able to defend that sanctuary, to keep it their unquestioned preserve. Always they had known the face of their enemy, and understood it. Now that mastery had been threatened. Grim foreboding flooded over him.

Ahitagel was further troubled by the enigma of young Moussa. Despite his ten years in the Hoggar, despite the blood of his mother, who was Ahitagel's own cousin, Moussa was still part French. Could any man change the fact of his birth? Ahitagel did not believe Moussa could ever raise his hand against the Ihaggaren. Yet what troubled him was that he did not believe Moussa capable of raising his hand against the French. His loyalties would be divided. His mere presence could lead to trouble. Already the strains of division were showing.

"I have heard your arguments," he said to the waiting *djemaa*. "I must now travel to In Salah. The Turks have sent emissaries, and the Italians. Others as well wish to influence our decisions. It seems everyone has taken a sudden interest in Sheikh Flatters. We must consider our course with great care." Mahdi started to object, but the amenokal waved him silent.

"Moussa, there are other matters that urgently require my attention. Regrettably, I shall be otherwise occupied. Therefore I place you in my stead. You will journey to Admer, to meet with the Kel Owi and negotiate the annual salt trades. There is other business as well, which I shall discuss with you tonight."

"But Lord, I should meet the French! I can speak with them as no other can! I can help you to understand their mind in this!"

"We have already communicated with them in Arabic," Ahitagel said. "We shall do so again. And hear me clearly. It is not we who must understand their mind in this. It is they who must understand ours. Now obey me, as I require your presence in Admer."

He rose to leave. The discussion was over.

CHAPTER 22

M Y GOD, IT'S BEAUTIFUL."
     Paul deVries stood atop a dune at the southern edge of the world known to France, exulting in the infinite desert that stretched out before him like a quiet blanket of mystery. Remy Cavour stood next to him. Strong and stocky, the sergeant was a head shorter than Paul. He had bushy black hair, blazing eyes, and a dark complexion. They had met on the boat from France. Paul found the other officers remote and difficult to talk with. Remy was an irreverent NCO from the slums of Paris, opposite in nearly all things from the young second lieutenant and ten years older, but the two men had formed a close bond. Remy had teased him when he found out Paul was from *the* deVries family. "You're the closest I've been to royalty," he said, "except for when I was a boy and stepped in a mess left by the emperor's horse."

     Behind and below them they could see the town of Wargla, an oasis of more than half a million palms, a mighty forest of green planted to keep the great Sahara at bay. It was the oldest of Saharan towns, a pleasant settlement sitting on a plain of brilliant white sand. A rugged plateau rose to the south and west. A *shott*, a normally dry saltwater lake, lay to the north. The evaporating water in the *shott* left heavy salt deposits whose edges when dry were curled, crusty, and bright like frosted white coral, and provided a pleasant contrast to the palms that were planted in a great crescent. To the northeast was the tail end of the range of dunes that formed part of the Grand Erg Oriental, or sea of dunes, of the Algerian Sahara.

The town was surrounded by a moat and two walls to keep out marauders. In the center was a large colonnaded square that served as the central market, lined with small shops whose interiors were dark and cool. Mosques stood on either side of the square. Bright minarets towered above them, from which the hypnotic words of the Koran floated over the oasis as the muezzins called the faithful to prayer. On market days a horde of people descended on the oasis from every direction, there to barter and banter and pass the hot day. There were faces and costumes from all over the desert, sights and sounds and smells Paul had never before imagined, foods he had never tasted, magic he had never seen, music he had never heard.

Remy saw the look in Paul's eyes as he gazed out over the desert. "You're impatient, aren't you?"

"I feel my destiny out there."

Remy snorted. "From what I hear in the garrison you're more likely to find flies."

"Flies are better than waiting. It's a god-awful business getting a caravan organized." Paul was assigned to provision parts of the expedition. In this he was helped immeasurably by his new aide, Hakeem, a skinny Shamba whose clothes hung in tatters and whose teeth had rotted from sugared tea. He was more boy than man but spoke both French and Arabic and seemed to know where to find anything a person could desire in the mysterious labyrinth of streets.

Paul worked from a master list prepared by Lieutenant Colonel Flatters, who checked his progress daily and complained about every expense. "*Trop cher!*" he would invariably grump whether it was or not, and Paul would promise to do better.

Yet as hard as he worked, the pace was slow; there was nothing easy about making large purchases, a process Paul had assumed would be simple. He or Hakeem would ask questions in the souks about a certain kind of merchandise they required. Inquiries would follow, then introductions to the appropriate merchant, who would speak in glowing terms of the excellence of his reputation, and of Paul's good fortune in finding him. Paul soon learned to judge the merchants by these introductions: the more unsavory the man, the more sparkling the terms that bespoke his good name.

But introductions were enough for one day. Only the next day would they visit the merchant in his shop. He would discuss the sterling qualities of his merchandise, assuring them that no finer goods could be found in any part of the desert. He would offer them tea, and tell tales of the oasis. That was enough for the second day.

On the third day, if conditions were right, Paul and Hakeem would get a glimpse of the blankets or the sheep or the stores in question, but the owner would tolerate no discussion beyond the compliments he required. That night the buyers would be left to ponder the proper value of such treasures. Only on the fourth day would price be discussed, in long tea-drenched sessions where laughter mingled with accusations of bad faith or questions of parentage. Hakeem handled most of the negotiations. He was born to haggle, delivering passionate speeches in rapid-fire Arabic. Paul was reasonably certain that with Hakeem's help France was spending only twice what everything was worth instead of four or five times.

Another full day or two might be required to arrive at a price. Then new arguments would crop up about quantities or terms. The merchant would groan and rub his hands and bewail the impending poverty to which the transaction was consigning him and his descendants. After a price had been finally settled, the buyers would return to make final arrangements for delivery, only to discover that the merchant had heard of a better price fetched in some other souk for the same merchandise, and—this was the only thing that happened quickly in the entire business—the original deal was off. The colonel would explode in anger at the wretched pace of the caravan's acquisitions, and Paul would start over. There was a certain maddening predictability to the process, in which endurance counted more than cunning. Impatience was never rewarded with results. The more he sought to hurry, the more he slowed things down.

One afternoon he complained that Hakeem had spent nearly half an hour buying a handful of dates for them to eat while they shopped.

"*Oui,* Patron," Hakeem agreed amiably, "but the dates are better now that they're older, don't you think?" Paul grimaced and Hakeem laughed at his annoyance. "You will please forgive me for saying so, Patron, but you must learn to think more slowly. Does a dune form overnight?"

"Not if an Arab of Wargla builds it," Paul agreed.

One evening after their work was done Paul and Remy were following Hakeem through the market when Hakeem pulled on Paul's sleeve. "*Regardez!*" he said eagerly, pointing. In one corner a performer had drawn a large crowd. They drew near and watched as the man turned his face upward while two scorpions climbed over his forehead and cheeks, heading for the soft cover of his bushy black beard. They moved delicately, a little off-balance. Suddenly the man gave a great yell. In a blur of motion he yanked the scorpions off his face, throwing one down near the crowd, which scattered quickly. At the same instant he tore the tail and claws off the second one and put the squirming body into his mouth, eating it with obvious pleasure. It was at once thrilling and revolting, yet no man could look away. What Paul did not notice was that the first scorpion had scurried to where he stood. Remy saw, and a grin crossed his face. He said nothing and took a few steps back, to leave the scorpion to the lieutenant. Even in panic Paul moved with a certain grace, but he still fell hard in his effort to get away. The arachnid hurried off, its tail high but harmless, its stinger having been removed earlier by the performer. Delighted that a *kafer* had been added to the entertainment, the crowd roared its delight, led by Remy. Paul picked himself up and dusted himself off, laughing and blushing, while the performer scooped up the wayward scorpion and popped it into his mouth.

"Tell me again how they made you an officer," Remy laughed. "Someday I want to be one too, but I think I'll take different courses."

When they could, Paul and Remy explored the huge gardens beneath the palmerie, strolling along the paths built on top of low dikes built for irrigation. Water bubbled softly through the small water channels, which were kept cleared by slaves, men with broad shoulders and bent backs who sang and chanted while they worked. Their music blended with the chirping of the birds and the flutter of the wind against the palm leaves. The oasis was alive with sound, a perfect place to pass the heat of the day while the markets were closed.

They never saw women in the open, only quiet shrouds huddled together in darkened doorways or on private rooftops, figures that shrank away quickly if a man glanced their way.

"I've been from Mexico to Italy in this army," Remy mused. "Never a place where I couldn't get beneath a woman's skirts with twenty minutes and a bottle of rum. But these women seem almost like lepers."

"They are not for the eyes of man." Hakeem shrugged politely. "For you they are best forgotten."

O NE DAY PAUL FOUND FLOOP.
        He'd gone into a shop, ducking his head to clear the low doorway, greeting the storekeeper and bargaining for some of the chickens cooped behind the shop. He began by himself, determined to practice his primitive Arabic without Hakeem.

The merchant seemed agitated and didn't want to sell him anything. Paul understood only a few words and had to turn to Hakeem. The aide asked questions and at times argued with the man, which seemed to drive the merchant into further obstinacy. Finally the man slapped his palm with his fist and rose to his feet, signaling that the discussion was over. Clearly uncomfortable, Hakeem turned to Paul. "I am sorry, Patron," he said, embarrassed. "He doesn't wish to sell his chickens."

"I *know* that already, Hakeem. *Why* doesn't he wish to sell them?"

Hakeem could think of no suitable deception at the moment, as would have been polite. He was stuck with the truth. "He says there is no point in feeding dead men, Patron. Chickens are too scarce in Wargla."

"Tell him I'm not feeding dead men," Paul commanded. "I'm trying to feed the colonel's caravan."

"I did, Patron."

"And?"

"He says it's the same thing."

This was not the first merchant to express such an opinion. All over Wargla one could hear murmurs of doom about the expedition. In the souks bets were made as to how many days' journey to the south the last man would die. While rumors ran rampant, most merchants cared not for the fate of their merchandise, but for how much might be made selling it.

"We need the chickens, Hakeem. Offer him more money."

"I tried that, Patron. But the fool is as stupid as his fowl. He said he'd rather have his birds than your money."

Seeing it was futile to press the issue, Paul shrugged and turned to depart. At that moment there was a great racket behind the store: a hundred chickens in panic. "*Floop!*" The merchant uttered the name like a curse. He jumped up and rushed out the back, Paul and Hakeem fast after him, their curiosity aroused.

Bedlam reigned in the walled yard. Feathers flew everywhere amid clouds of thick dust stirred by panicked wings. The merchant fairly dove into the center of it, pushing the birds out of his way, cursing the whole while. There was a yelp and a moment later up came the merchant holding a scrawny mutt puppy. Its tail wagged wildly, and its mouth was clamped firmly around a chicken twice its size.

The merchant gave the pup a vicious whack across its face. With a yelp of pain the puppy let go. The merchant spied a wicker stick propped in the corner. He picked it up and raised it to strike the thief.

"*Arrêtez!*" Paul stepped forward. The merchant hesitated. The look the man saw in Paul's eyes decided the issue. Holding the puppy by the scruff of its neck, he said something to Hakeem and threw the dog at Paul. The dog was shaking and flea bitten and looked up at Paul with wide eyes.

"What did he say?" Paul asked Hakeem.

"He said, Patron, that since he was going to kill the dog anyway, there was no better way to do it than give it to a dead man. You still may not buy any chickens, but you can keep the dog for nothing."

Paul laughed and held the terrified animal up before him. "Well, Floop," he said, "at least one of the condemned needs a bath."

Floop was an ungainly thing, a pretty gold color but with ears too floppy and paws absurdly big. He was thick with grunge and tolerated the bath with a wounded look. He followed Paul everywhere through the streets, climbing into baskets and food bins and needing rescue more than once. Floop was a favorite with the members of the expedition, who spoiled him with handouts and scratched him behind the ears. But the dog had nearly done him in with Colonel Flatters, who was difficult enough to get along with as it was.

The colonel had invited the agha of Wargla, Abd-el-Kader ben Amar, key members of the agha's retinue, and the captain of the local garrison to dine with him in his tent. His preparations were thorough. There was to be music and exquisite tea. The colonel himself chose the sheep to be slaughtered and gave detailed instructions to the cook. Brame, the colonel's batman, set a beautiful table considering the limited materials with which he had to work.

Toasts were made and the colonel and his guests were seated. The cook entered with a great flourish, the aroma of the steaming roast irresistible. The colonel lifted it to look and permitted himself a rare smile. He dismissed the cook with thanks, adding that he was sure no more tender mutton could be found outside France.

Sometime during the late afternoon Floop had decided the colonel's tent was the finest shelter in camp. He slipped past the sentry and through the flaps, settling on a spot just beneath the colonel's cot. He was used to various comings and goings in Paul's tent, so nothing disturbed his nap. But when the cook produced the mutton, the fragrance was too much to ignore.

Engaged in conversation with his guests, the colonel didn't notice the dog, whose training by Paul did not yet include table manners. Big for a puppy, his front paws could just find purchase on the top of the dinner table, and he was up, nose over the top, tail hard at work in lively anticipation.

Startled, the colonel stood up too rapidly, banging his thighs against the table. The interrupted momentum was enough to make him lose his balance. He staggered backward, half-sitting, half-standing. He fell against the wooden pole that supported the roof of his tent. The pole snapped, bringing the tent, the agha and his retinue, the captain and the batman, and everything else, down with it.

Outside the tent, the terrified cook, thinking that somehow his meal had been to blame, frantically searched to find where the door had been. In the darkness all was confusion. At last he found it, and shouted to the sentry for help. Together they lifted the edge.

Floop shot through the opening and fled into the night, the colonel's mutton clenched firmly between his teeth.

Both Paul and Floop had lain low for the next few days—Paul, because he thought it prudent, and Floop, because he was chained in Paul's tent. Paul wasn't sure that the colonel even knew whom the dog belonged to, but in a small camp such as theirs word of such things had a way of traveling quickly. The colonel, however, seemed no more sour than usual.

It was only days later, after the two had been discussing the progress of provisioning, that the colonel referred to the matter. Flatters had dismissed him, and Paul was leaving the tent.

"By the way, Lieutenant," the colonel said. Paul stopped and turned.

"Sir?"

Flatters was scribbling a note, and left the junior officer waiting until he had finished. He put his pen down, and raised eyes that smoldered like cinders.

"If ever I should see that dog again," Flatters said, "I shall have it shot."

Paul fidgeted, not knowing exactly what to say. Finally he nodded. "Excellent, sir."

Of course, Paul had no intention of getting rid of the animal. It was simply a matter of training. At night he would leave his tent, saddle his camel, and give the dog his bag lessons. Paul would set him hind feet first into the pouch that hung on the side. Floop hated it, squirming out as Paul rode and dropping to the ground with an exaggerated squeal of pain. Paul would patiently pick him up each time and put him back in, and give him pieces of dried meat and then, as they rode, pet him and talk softly, reassuringly, until the cadence of his voice calmed the dog down.

At last Floop decided he liked it in the bag. The camel's side was warm, its motions fluid and perfect for naps. He finally worked out a comfortable position. He sat on his rear, like a human, back legs folded up, front paws just over the top of the bag, making a cradle where he could rest his chin. It worked rather well, Paul thought, for unless he closed the flap, all that could be seen of Floop from the outside was a black nose, resting between two paws.

Hakeem watched Paul's patient training with confusion. Such trouble for a mere dog! The patron threw a stick as far as he could, and then gave the dog a perfectly good piece of meat for bringing it back. The first time he saw it happen, Hakeem couldn't restrain his curiosity. Nonchalantly, he wandered over and stole a closer look, to see what was so special about the stick. It was nothing but a worthless palm frond. He could only shrug, as he did whenever he saw the dog getting meat for lying down and failing to move when Paul walked away. This perplexed Hakeem most of all; if one rewarded the dogs he knew for lying down and failing to move, there would be nothing left for the people of Wargla to eat.

Once Paul asked the Shamba what he thought of the dog. Ever polite, Hakeem thought for a moment, and replied in solemn earnest. "As Allah is my witness," he said, "this will be a wonderful dog, indeed a truly great dog someday." He paused, looking at Floop. "But for now, Patron, he is merely a mouth on big feet."

Late at night, when Paul's business and Floop's bag lessons were finished, the two of them would take long walks. By moonlight they explored the dunes, struggling through the soft cold sand to the top, to rest and look in silence at the beauty of the other dunes around them, quiet and silken under the moon, then run and tumble down the steep lee sides in a mad race to the bottom.

Paul had never known a fuller time, although he learned to avoid the garrison as much as possible. The garrison of Wargla was farther south than any other maintained by France. The strain of isolation showed on the men, who were tough and vulgar, their discipline lax, their uniforms as crude as their manners. There was unease between the men of the expedition and those of the garrison, an eerie tension bordering on hostility. Paul had to visit the quartermaster on business at least once a day, and found the man's attitude discomfiting. He reeked of palm wine and regarded Paul with glazed pity in his eyes, or else averted his gaze altogether whenever Paul came near.

"Is there something wrong, Sergeant?" Paul finally asked. "Have I done something to offend you?"

"Wrong? Nothing at all, Lieutenant. It's just that I get this way every time I see a man napping beneath the blade of a guillotine. Worries me something might go wrong." He slurred his words, laughing at his own humor. "If I were you, I would forget these boxes and blankets and pack more bullets instead."

"You are so certain we'll have trouble?"

"Trouble? *Merde,* your death warrants have already been signed by the Turks and stamped by the Tuareg.

Every piss-ant in the desert seems to know it but your colonel."

"You're drunk," Paul snapped. "I could see you court-martialed for this kind of insolence."

The man whooped in derision. "That'd be a brilliant response, *sir*. Learned that in St. Cyr, I'll wager. Discipline and form, fuck the facts." He laughed to himself. "Anyway, I'm not drunk yet, Lieutenant, not near as drunk as I'll be in another hour. And an hour after that I'll be thoroughly stinking. Hardly walking. After that—well, if I'm unlucky enough to wake up in the morning, I'll start over. I'll admit I fancy death from drink in this godforsaken place. It's better than a Tuareg spear in the belly. One thing is certain, Lieutenant, neither of us will die of old age."

"The Tuareg haven't the strength to touch us."

"Hah! They don't care about your riflemen. You can't shoot what you can't see. They'll wait until your guard is down, until you're looking the other way. You'll think they're in front of you, but they'll be behind you. Or you think they're coming in the night, only they come at noon. The only thing you can count on from the bastards is they'll find a way to gut you, Lieutenant, without getting in the way of your mighty rifles."

"*Le cafard*," Remy said later when Paul repeated the conversation. "The desert madness." He'd never been to Africa, but he'd seen plenty of remote places and what they did to men. "Lots of them get it. They've nothing to do but brood. Time treats them badly. It stretches worse here because the liquor stinks and there aren't any women. The place just uses them up. Even their assholes get raw from the sand."

"I'll never let the desert affect me as it does them," Paul said. "I'll go home first."

Remy couldn't help mocking Paul gently for his naïve enthusiasm. "I think you take it a bit far the other way. Let me see if I understand your point of view. In the market there are clouds of flies competing with swarms of beggars for the pleasure of eating camel shit mixed with rotting vegetables. What they can't stomach the cook picks up. He spices it up nicely with some old spit and smears it on top of a mixture of couscous, pebbles, and sand. Then he dishes it back to you, at six times the price he'd charge anyone else. You know what you're eating—you *watch* him prepare it—but all the same you enjoy it, because it's exotic."

"That's about it." Paul smiled. "*L'haute cuisine d'Afrique.*" Remy roared.

The desert Paul saw from atop the dunes was not the desert of the garrison, but the desert of his aunt Serena's stories, a vast tableau of valiant warriors and grand destiny. Perhaps more than any man helping to assemble the great caravan taking shape on the plain outside the town, Paul felt the fortunes of France resting on his shoulders. He could hear the glories in the cold wind blowing off the winter sands, glories that would be forever lost to the sad men of the garrison they were leaving behind.

TELL ME ABOUT THE TUAREG," PAUL SAID TO Hakeem the night before they left.

Hakeem nodded gravely, pleased to have been consulted. "It is reliably known, Patron, that all Tuareg customs are vile. They copulate with mountain sheep, men, and women alike. Their men hide their faces because they are too ugly even for their own women to behold. Their women are shameless and go unveiled. They are all thieves and brigands, every one. Even the children. There is no honor among them. They will greet you openly into their tents, steal everything you own while you drink of their hospitality, then murder you as you sleep and leave you for the vultures. They are godless, Patron, even more vile than *kafers.*"

Hakeem caught himself and his hand flew to his mouth. "Forgive me, Patron. My tongue runs too fast and forgets my brain. Or is it the other way around? I did not mean—" Paul laughed at the unintended insult and beckoned Hakeem to continue.

"Their land is enchanted, Patron, filled with the most horrible monsters and terrible droughts. The only use one can make of such a place is to pass through it as quickly as possible, and then to forget it. This is why the Shamba have never bothered to take the land away from them. The Tuareg are accomplished warriors, it is true. Yet, except for the amenokal, the best of them are not as deadly as the weakest of the Shamba."

"The amenokal?"

"*Oui*, Patron, their sheikh. He is the firstborn of a union between the devil and a Tuareg whore. He stands as tall as a bull mehari. His arms are as big around as the greatest palm tree in Wargla. He has six fingers on each hand. He talks directly with *djenoums*, as no mortal man can do, and his eyes are the coals of the devil's own fires."

"A remarkable man," Paul said with a faint smile. He was remembering his aunt's stories about her brother, who had seemed not at all as Hakeem described.

"It is also known among the more learned of the Sahara," Hakeem said, lowering his voice, "that he has two penises."

"*Two* penises? He must be a busy man."

"*Oui*, Patron, he is very busy when not murdering people. One is for his women, the other for his sheep."

"Are you afraid of him?"

At that Hakeem drew himself up and took a deep defiant breath. He was no fighter. He had neither the physique nor the inclination for it, but was suffused with Shamba bravado all the same. "I am unafraid of any man, Patron, most especially the Tuareg," he lied. "Besides, for the true son of Islam there is nothing to fear. Allah has already written the date of my death upon my forehead. On that date I will die, be it from the bite of a viper or the sword of my enemy. But until that date, Patron, no harm can befall me. Of what, then, is there to be afraid?" His expression glowed with the simple certainty of his faith, although he omitted mentioning it might not be wise to unduly hurry fate by tempting the Tuareg.

CHAPTER 23

"WE LOST FOUR MORE CAMELS LAST NIGHT, Colonel," Paul reported. Even in the dim light of the tent, he could see the colonel's eyes flash in anger. Visiting the colonel even on minor business was inevitably the least pleasant task of an officer's day. His rages were frightening.

"And what is it you would like me to do about it, Lieutenant? Is there something about dead camels you can't handle?"

"No, sir, of course not. I just thought you'd like to know. They've already been butchered. That makes a total of thirty-two so far."

"You try my patience, deVries. I can count as well as the next man."

"Yes, sir."

"See to it the guides don't sell the meat to a passing caravan. They probably poisoned the camels to make a few sous." The colonel was lying down, trying to still the fires of sciatica that blazed down his backside. He stiffened. "Get Brame," he gasped.

Paul found the colonel's batman, who sighed at the summons. "Another shot," he muttered. It was an open secret now among the officers. The colonel didn't trust his officers, or his guides, or anyone else.

The only companion he trusted was morphine.

Such secrets could be kept in France, or even in Wargla. But on a journey spent in close quarters they withered quickly. When the caravan was moving Flatters rode on his great white camel, alone out in front of the expedition. He sat stiffly, in agony, and rejected company. When they made camp he rarely emerged from his tent. His moods swung like the temperature, from fire to ice. He could be kind or ferocious. Decisions seemed difficult for him. Simple things that should take little thought seemed to tie him in knots. His eyes were often glazed, his look distracted. He wandered alone among the dunes and the rocks, shuffling painfully and muttering. He paid scant attention when Paul or the other officers spoke to him.

It was Remy who had broached the unbroachable with Paul, his superior officer. Only the bond between them kept Paul from reprimanding him, that and the fact that Remy had echoed his own fears.

"The colonel should have stayed in Paris," Remy growled, watching as Brame entered the colonel's tent. "I don't know what made him try this with a bad back. He's obviously got a strong will, but the morphine could get us all killed."

Paul nodded grimly. "He's off his mind half the time, and impossible the rest."

"Yesterday he told me three different times in the space of an hour to have his camel saddled, and then later on he didn't remember," Remy said. "I heard him ask Brame who'd done it. Then he lost his journal, the one he scribbles in all night. He raised hell about it. Turned everything upside down in his tent. He accused Brame of hiding it. It was in his saddle pack all the time."

Reluctantly, Paul was coming to the realization that the colonel was unfit for duty. "The rest of us will just have to make up for him." After the colonel the senior officer was Captain Masson. Lieutenant Dianous, closest to Paul in rank, was cold but efficient. Pobeguin and Dennery were NCOs whose desert experience was vast. And, of course, there was Remy Cavour, who knew nothing of the Sahara but was a battle-hardened soldier with good instincts.

"I've had to do that before," Remy said. "A bad business. It's like expecting the body to carry on after the guillotine's done its work."

By late January the expedition was hundreds of kilometers to the south of Wargla. The engineers carried on their survey work, making endless notes about the terrain. At night they hunched over their tables and by lantern light fixed their position on the detailed maps they were preparing.

They passed the gorge of Amguid, with still no sign or word from the Tuareg, into whose country they were passing without permission. The silence of the Tuareg bred superstition and fear. At night the Shamba were jumpy, the *tirailleurs* wary. Wild shots were fired at ghosts and fears. When they camped near the dunes and the wind blew, a strange humming could be heard in the darkness among the distant sands. "It is the laughter of the *djenoum*," the Shamba said. "The howling of the Angel of Death." The floor of the desert in front of them was filled with tracks, suggesting that a large group of riders preceded them. Speculation ran rampant. "It's the Tuareg," Remy muttered. "Why don't they show themselves? They're toying with us."

Weeks had passed that way. The guides, Iforass Tuareg who had been hired in Wargla, kept to themselves. They lived far to the southwest, between Gao and Timbuktu, and were normally on friendly terms with the Hoggar Tuareg. They were reclusive, almost sullen, and even they feared treachery. At the wells of El Hadjadj the master of a caravan passing in the opposite direction shook his finger at the colonel. "Ahitagel views all foreigners with hatred, and your mission with distrust," he said. "It is the course of wisdom to return the way you came."

"Nonsense," the colonel told his officers that night, "message after message has reassured the amenokal that we mean no harm. He will let us pass. We have come too far for any other outcome. We *will* pass."

"The *tirailleurs'* morale is low, Colonel," said Captain Masson. "Several have been reprimanded for arguing that we turn back—"

"I don't want to hear it!" shrieked the colonel, his face shaking with fury. "To the devil with their morale!

You keep their filthy tongues in check! You will shoot any man who talks this way. Do you hear me?" he shouted at his officers. "*Do you hear me?*"

Two days later the amenokal's answer came on the heels of the eight Iforass Tuareg guides. Normally they rode far in front of the expedition, obscure flecks on the horizon. Captain Masson saw something and drew up his mount. He shaded his eyes, peering forward. The guides were no longer distant, but were riding toward him at a fast trot, all eight of them, quickly growing larger as they approached. They had never done such a thing. The colonel was just catching up. The other officers, Dianous and deVries, pulled alongside.

"It seems," said Masson, peering through field glasses, "that we are about to meet the amenokal. Thirty-two, heavily armed. Spears, shields, swords. Some rifles, I think. I can't tell what else." Behind the guides, much closer now, was a ghostly tall line of blue and gold. From the distance they looked unreal and otherworldly, the superheated air twisting and weaving their figures. The captain handed the glasses to Colonel Flatters.

"Order the *tirailleurs* abreast, Captain. Arms sheathed. Draw in the caravan."

"Dianous, deVries, see to it."

Pulses racing, the two lieutenants moved at once, passing orders to Cavour, Dennery, and Pobeguin, the five of them then riding back through the long column of men and animals, shouting instructions, pulling the caravan into order. Word of the approaching Tuareg flashed like lightning up and down the line. The riflemen formed a line to the rear of the officers, perpendicular to the long caravan behind them, still engaged in the bedlam of trying to close ranks. The camel tenders bullied the pack animals into a tight group behind the *tirailleurs,* their voices cursing and shouting as they sought quick order. It was a noisy formation, but carried out quickly. For months they had talked of little else but the men who now rode toward them. Now that they were to meet face-to-face, they wasted no time.

The line of Tuareg was ten meters from the French

when a man riding near the right side halted. The others followed suit, and the line stopped as if one. The shroud of its dust nearly swallowed the group from view.

Paul watched carefully as the two formations settled to order. Only the camels moved, adjusting their positions, snorting and stretching their necks. The men atop them on both sides sat motionless, studying their opposing numbers. The dust dissipated at last, and the camels settled down. And then there was silence.

The colonel sat erect on his great white mount, ceremonial saber at his side. He carried no other arms but a pistol in its holster. His officers were behind him, near the center. Behind them, the Algerian *tirailleurs* sat at uneasy attention. They had no uniforms but the desert dress to which they were accustomed. Most wore turbans that might have been white at one time, but which were rarely washed and had become varying shades of tan and brown. Others wore fezzes, red and cocked at odd angles on their heads. The variety of their dirty costumes gave them the appearance of a ragtag band of desert ruffians. The image was belied by their faces, hard and desert-worn, and by the deadly black barrels of the Gras rifles glinting dully in the sun. Behind the *tirailleurs* were the blood enemies of the Tuareg, the Shamba cameleers—masters of the northern deserts, called the Haab el Reeh, the Breath of Wind.

Paul was fascinated by the contrast between the two forces. There was nothing remotely scruffy about the Tuareg. In a proud, straight line astride their camels sat the blue men of the Sahara, the Hoggar Tuareg, the noble Ihaggaren, tall and magnificent and swathed in indigo and black. To a man their faces were invisible, covered by the veils drawn up over their mouths and noses. Where most of the Shamba applied their turbans casually, as afterthought, the Tuareg applied their lithams as adornments, as art. The long cotton sheshes were richly dyed in various colors, but all of them were dark. Meters of the soft material were wrapped around their heads, under their chins, the ends draped back over their shoulders or hanging in graceful folds over their chests. Their skin, as much as could be seen of it, was lighter than that of the Algerians who sat across from them. Their eyes were just about all that could be seen of them. Many wore great cloaks of blue, seamed at the shoulder with a hole for the neck and arms but open at the front, the edges delicately embroidered. Others wore finely decorated robes that hung to their calves. Their pants could barely be seen for the robes, but were dark in color and long. Their feet bore leather sandals.

More than half the Tuareg carried rifles, but the weapons could hardly be compared to the Gras. A variety of bores danced in the sun, old muzzle-loaders, flintlocks, or percussion weapons, some nearly a century old. After the rifles, their weapons were more uniform. They hefted shields of tough antelope hide, finely tooled and drawn taut over wood bracing, and brass-tipped spears carried point up, the long wooden shafts intricately carved with linear patterns. All wore swords, big and double-edged, sheathed in leather scabbards. Daggers were hidden beneath every robe, strapped to forearms or hung from neck sheaths. Sabers were slung on the opposite sides from the swords, their blades long and curved, for striking and cutting.

Their number was but a third that of the French expedition, but their sheer presence overwhelmed that of the larger force. Paul saw the men who inhabited the stories of his childhood, and they were everything he had imagined. They were formidable and fierce, proud to the point of arrogance, aristocrats of the Sahara. Where the French simply sat upon their camels, the Tuareg were enthroned upon theirs. Paul could see why they struck such fear into their enemies. Atop their fine racing meharis, armed with fearsome weapons, the Tuareg were larger than life, seemingly invincible. That a man could not see their faces added to the awe and fed the fear.

Paul sat rigidly in his saddle studying the eyes one pair at a time, looking for a hint of familiarity. His gaze traveled the line, one slit after another. He wondered whether he would know Moussa's eyes after so long, or whether Moussa would know him. But if Moussa was among them he gave no sign.

One of the Tuareg moved slowly forward, the same man who had stopped the march. No rank could be distinguished among them, except that a drum was strapped to the back of his saddle. It was the *tobol,* the drum of authority. He nudged his camel with his feet, while the colonel, using his reins, rode forward as well. As he began to move, he said, almost inaudibly, "Madani, forward."

El Madani, a grizzled NCO, left his position among the ranks of the other Algerians, drawing up to the left and slightly to the rear of Flatters. The colonel spoke Arabic but liked to use an interpreter, to make certain he missed no meaning. El Madani was a veteran whose father had been a merchant in Akabli, a caravan cross-roads. As a boy he had learned the Tuareg language, which he could also read, and his French was flawless.

The Targui spoke first. "I am Attici," he said. "I extend the greetings of the Lord Amenokal."

As El Madani repeated the words to Colonel Flatters, Attici reached beneath his robe and withdrew a paper, rolled and tied with a fine leather string. He leaned forward, ignoring Madani's outstretched hand, and passed it directly to Flatters. He waited in silence as the colonel opened it. The message was written with ink of camel urine and charcoal. The colonel glanced at the message, then passed it to El Madani.

As the *tirailleur* studied it, Flatters said, "I am Lieutenant Colonel Paul Flatters, and bring the peaceful greetings and gifts of the government of the Republic of France to the Amenokal Ahitagel and the people of the Hoggar."

El Madani looked up from his reading and translated, adding *lord* before the amenokal's name. When he finished, he read the amenokal's message to the colonel.

"The road to the south is not safe," he read. "There is trouble. The Sudanese killed a whole caravan from Tripoli because they thought there were Christians

among them. Take the most direct road, for we do not
care to see you come into our *ariwans*."

Attici spoke again. "The Lord Amenokal is to the
south, near Abalessa," he said. "He has sent his able
emissary Chikkat to lead you through the Hoggar."
Attici indicated the guide in the line of Tuareg. "He
knows the way as well as Ahitagel himself. He and three
others will guide you. Your own guides are not welcome, and must leave immediately."

There was no stir among the Iforass guides. They had
expected as much.

"We agree," El Madani said for the colonel, "and
thank you for your hospitality."

Paul nudged his mehari forward and stopped next to
the colonel. He spoke so softly that not even El Madani
could hear. "Begging the colonel's pardon, sir, I wonder
if you might inquire after my aunt and cousin. I think it
would be of use—"

"Not now, deVries," Flatters snapped. "Later, when
we are near their camps."

"Of course, sir."

Paul returned to his position as El Madani was inviting the Tuareg to share a meal. "The colonel would be
honored to invite you to stay with us and—"

Without listening to the rest, Attici abruptly moved
forward through the line of *tirailleurs,* stopping in front
of two magnificent yellow Tibesti she-camels being
tended by a Shamba, who regarded him with undis-
guised hatred.

"These are gifts for the Lord Amenokal," Attici said.
It was a statement, not a question.

"The colonel will present camels and horses personally—" El Madani began to say, but Attici already had
the reins, and was leading the camels away. The
Shamba tender moved as if to block his way, but the
colonel waved him off. Without responding to the invitation or acknowledging the gift, Attici rode back
through the line of his men. All but four, the new
guides, turned to follow, and the Tuareg were gone as
quickly as they had appeared.

"Sassy bastards," Remy said.

The Iforass huddled with Pobeguin to collect their pay, and then they too disappeared, to the west.

It all happened so quickly, Paul marveled.

And almost as quickly, the pessimism that had dogged the caravan evaporated as well. Their doubts about the colonel were unfounded. The man knew what he was doing after all. The Tuareg had answered.

The Tuareg had said yes.

THE KILLING GROUND WAS CAREFULLY CHOSEN. Mahdi squatted, squinting into the sun's glare. His practiced eye roamed the amphitheater of rock with its tamarisk trees at the bottom, near the well called Tadjenout tin Tarabine. They would make camp to the west, over the ridge where they would not be seen. From there they could enter the arena at will, with hidden rock defiles obscuring the entrances and providing cover.

His hand rested on the sword sheathed in its ornate scabbard. The leather on the hilt was worn smooth. His hand was comfortable there, more so than on the rifle in his other hand. *Rifles.* Tools of cowards. But Attici had insisted, and Attici was in line to succeed one day as amenokal, and his word had carried the argument.

Mahdi was satisfied. For its sin of arrogant intrusion the advancing French expedition would pay a heavy price. Tadjenout was perfect. Tamrit and Attici would be pleased.

It was the first moment of satisfaction Mahdi had felt in weeks. Ever since the *djemaa* he had been brooding. The night Daia had come to join him, he had greeted her with joy in his heart. He showered her with gifts he had chosen with such care—earrings from Hausaland, a robe from Timbuktu. He had taken great pleasure in giving them to her and had expected . . . well, something more than cool indifference. And then as the night fell and the fire blazed he had seen it for the first time. He was not a clever man around women. He felt awkward with them and did not hope to fathom their mysteries. But he did not need to be clever to see Daia's look of longing, to know it was not for him. Moussa sat apart from them, talking quietly with his friend Taher and drinking tea. He seemed oblivious to Daia. When Mahdi caught the first gaze she was so discreet he nearly missed it. Then, more carefully, he watched until chance was eliminated. She tried to conceal it, but to Mahdi, who worshiped her, who was so acutely aware of her every look and movement, it was something that she could not hide. And then he worried that if he could see it everyone else could as well. Even as he seethed he forced patience upon himself.

Mahdi had no idea that a mere look in a woman's eyes could cause him such pain. He was angered by his weakness. How could any woman affect him so? It was a helpless, dull ache he felt as she unknowingly turned the blade of her indifference inside him. He had no weapons to fight such a look, or such a feeling. He tried to will it not to be, but it would not leave him. He tried to catch her attention, then, to say interesting things, witty and clever things. But he knew he was forcing it, that he was not being interesting and that she was only being polite as she listened.

His hand squeezed the hilt of his sword. Should he kill Moussa? It would be easy enough to take him in the middle of the night, to leave the certain signs of Shamba, so that *she* would not know. No. Unthinkable. He would make a fair fight of it and kill him cleanly, with honor, something he would have to do sooner or later in light of the blow Moussa had struck in the *djemaa*. That he could defeat Moussa in single combat was without doubt. Yet Moussa seemed oblivious to Daia's glances; he seemed not to return them. Did he scheme behind his veil? Did they sneak away at night, mocking him?

"I have seen your gaze," he said to her when finally they were alone, his eyes wounded, his meek voice belying a man so quick to fury.

"I do not understand your meaning," Daia lied, her heart beating quickly at the accusation. Had she been so transparent?

"Tonight in camp," Mahdi said, "during the meal,

even as we talked together, you could not take your eyes from . . . from *him*."

"Your imagination is active," she said, her face reddening. "I have sworn myself to you, Mahdi. Have I not said it?"

"It is so, yet you do not look at me with the same eyes, Daia. Your heart does not live in concert with your words. I will kill him and be done with it."

"*No! You must not!*" She said it too quickly, knowing he was judging her, but she couldn't help it. She feared for Moussa's life. Mahdi had killed men for much less. Somehow it had all gone too far. Her heart had led the way and she had followed, and now everything precious was at risk. Was she such an easy woman? Could she be so easily shaken from her path?

And in that instant she knew she must put the longings of her heart aside, that she must give up her forbidden thoughts and remember her honor. *I must not go farther down this road*, she told herself. *I will not betray Mahdi. Nor will I jeopardize Moussa, who seems anyway indifferent to me. I have cast my lot.*

"He has done nothing to deserve your wrath, Mahdi. Leave him be."

"On your journey with him from Ideles—?"

"It was simply a journey. We traveled together, Mahdi, from one place to another. Moussa conducted himself honorably. That is the truth of the matter. I have pledged myself to you, and so shall it be."

He heard the firmness in her voice, yet did not believe it.

"I forbid you to travel with him again."

At that Daia bristled. "*Forbid!* Is this the lesson your Senussi teach? Is it what makes you disappear with them for weeks at a time, to learn how they treat women? Would you wave the Koran at your wife like a club? I am not some ass, Mahdi, to be prodded before your stick! You may *forbid* nothing! It is not your right to permit or forbid a thing to me! Save your orders for the *imrad*, for those who will obey!"

"Do not slander the Senussi, Daia. They are holy men. Their cause is just."

"Holy men who teach disrespect?"

"I do not wish to argue the matter. I did not mean to order you."

"I would favor it if you learned persuasion, Mahdi. It will serve us better."

Mahdi felt helpless before her. The Senussi would take no such insolence from a mere woman and would mock him for his weakness. But she was no mere woman, and most of the Senussi were Arabs who did not understand the ways of the Tuareg, a people who were too proud, too independent to submit their will to that of another—even fully to Allah. He prayed for guidance but no guidance came. He was her captive, not she his. She would never be pliant. No Ihaggaren woman would ever be, but in her it went further. She was free, too free. Marriage would not shackle her to him, but he prayed it would help.

He sought to make amends. "I am sorry, Daia. I have spoken without thinking. I did not mean to offend you." When she nodded but said nothing, he went on. "We shall be married after the French matter is disposed of," he told her, then hurriedly added, "if that is your wish, of course."

"Yes," she said. Again she told herself she was lucky to have him, but all the same she was glad of the French coming, of the time it would give her. "Of course. I have said as much. After the French." When they parted neither of them was satisfied.

For the next few weeks the conflict consumed him as he crisscrossed the desert, making preparations. It preoccupied him in his discussions with Tamrit, who accused him of inattention. It distracted him even when he prostrated himself in prayer before his God.

His concentration had never failed him. Yet now, despite his efforts, there was only Daia. Yes, he would marry her immediately. But it was not enough.

Moussa. He bristled with hatred for the *ikufar.*

Moussa. Had not Moussa stolen the amenokal from him? His own father? Did it matter whether Moussa had *tried* to do it, or did it only matter that it had happened, that his father had come to banish Mahdi to the ashes of indifference, that he had come to welcome only Moussa in his tent, as if Moussa and not Mahdi were his only son?

Would it matter now, with Daia? Could he now let Moussa take away this woman, as he had taken away his father?

It was not enough to marry. He would have to deal with Moussa.

THE CARAVAN PRESSED ON, HAVING NEARLY COM-pleted its passage through the Amadror, the vast sizzling flat of gravelly desolation. The mountains of the Hoggar loomed at last in the south. The instant Attici's guides had arrived the procession had changed course twenty degrees more to the east. The officers noted the change and were uneasy, since the Iforass had been so steady in bearing, but fell silent when the colonel asked which of them might show the way instead.

The Amadror began to lose its anesthetizing sameness. Occasional patches of sand and even some acacia trees were visible. Every so often they would see a bird, or several flying together, and a great shout would arise, men pointing and laughing and talking.

The flat became more rolling, and the rolling became hills, and the hills became the Hoggar, its odd volcanic peaks and spires struggling through the almost iridescent violet haze that seemed to emanate from them. They had never seen such a place, and rode enraptured. The camels stepped tenderly through the rocks, which had changed from smooth gravel to rough cobbles to razor-sharp stones, at first spaced well apart but then closer and hard to avoid. It slowed their progress, and at times the caravan stretched out over two kilometers, a great undulating jumble of humps and baskets and bags and men, winding through the craggy passages and long wadis. The camels groaned as if mortally wounded when they cut their feet, their cries returning in haunted echoes from the rock walls. They shifted themselves in exaggerated motions to favor their feet, sometimes losing their loads altogether or having them slip out of place until their tenders had to stop and adjust them. In the worst places the men walked, leading their mounts by hand.

Late one morning they arrived at a large open shelf in the mountains. They were close to a huge peak, called Serkout by the guides, who answered questions rarely, and then grudgingly. One of them stopped to talk with Flatters. He pointed to the edge of the shelf, where a water-stained basin had been cut into the granite.

"We had hoped to find water in this *guelta*," he said to the colonel while El Madani translated. "The rains have been light and it is dry. We cannot continue without water. We have been four days since finding it, and on our path there is no more for seven days." He pointed to a valley that disappeared into the mountains. "There is a well there called Tadjenout. An hour and a half by camel. We must fill the bags."

"Very well then," the colonel replied, gazing up the valley. "We shall make the detour."

"No." The Targui shook his head firmly. "The route is too difficult for meharis carrying packs. You must send them with only water bags and leave the other supplies here until our return."

As El Madani translated he felt compelled to offer the colonel a bit of unsolicited advice. He was normally silent, but on matters that affected his men he had no fear of speaking. "Begging the colonel's pardon, sir," he said.

"Madani?"

"If the colonel pleases, perhaps it would be better to go to the well in force. I do not trust these men. This is a well-known ploy of the Tuareg. They seek to split our force, to weaken it. There are no scouts on our flanks to—"

The colonel bristled. "That will be quite enough, Madani. You are out of place." It wasn't the first time they had made a similar arrangement for obtaining water. It seemed reasonable in difficult terrain. "When I require your instruction on deployment I shall ask for it." His voice was cutting, piercing the front ranks of the men listening behind. Some of the *tirailleur*'s men heard the rebuke, but accepted it with no change of expression, no thought of argument. He had raised the point; the colonel had rejected it. There was no disgrace in that. The colonel turned to Captain Masson, who agreed with El Madani about not splitting the force but had long since stopped arguing with the colonel.

"Captain! Unload the baggage here. All camels to carry water skins. Cavour and Dennery with fifteen men to provide cover and load water. DeVries and five more to stand watch on the *piste* to the well. Dianous to stand command of the base camp with the rest of the men and supplies. You and I shall take the horses. The doctor and engineers may accompany us as they please."

With that the colonel started up the hill, toward the well of Tadjenout.

IT WAS THE FOURTH WEEK OF MOUSSA'S JOURNEY. Since his departure from Abalessa he had handled the negotiations for a trade of salt and camels with the Kel Owi in Admer. He had then escorted a small caravan from that village to Timissao. After that had been the resolution of a dispute over arable land between vassal families of the Dag Rali and the Iklan Tawsit. All of it the normal business of the Ihaggaren, yet all of it meaningless. He was livid at having been ordered on such errands to the south at the very instant the French were approaching from the north. He knew what it meant to his reputation and felt the stain upon his honor. *The amenokal doesn't trust me.* He had done nothing to deserve the mistrust except to be born half one thing and half another. It was the same disease of the blood that had plagued him all his life.

There had been one bright spot in his journey. A trader in Admer had showed him a rare manuscript, carefully crafted and beautifully bound, a collection of fables the trader said had been transcribed by a marabout in Egypt. Moussa didn't know the truth of it, for he could not read Arabic, but as he turned the tooled-leather volume over in his hands he instinctively knew its richness. He thought of Daia when he saw it, of the hours she spent teaching the children of her *ariwan*. He could imagine her reading to them from this book, and the vision brought him pleasure. He wrapped it in oil-cloth and intended to present it to her as a wedding gift.

His weeks of travel had not dimmed the sadness and longing he felt when he thought of her. Mahdi had come to him late at night after the *djemaa*. Moussa expected a fight after the blow he had delivered in the amenokal's tent, but Mahdi was strangely subdued. He began to ask Moussa about his intentions, but it was clearly difficult for him and his question died of awkwardness before it was asked. Moussa understood what he wanted.

"She has made it plain to me that you are to be married. Is it not so? I will not interfere, Cousin." The wedding had been announced the next morning by the amenokal himself. Events had been set into motion. Difficult as it was, he would give her what she wanted.

But then, as he was leaving the camp for his trip to the south, he had stopped to bid his mother farewell. They had talked about trivial things. Serena had known the look in his eye. "You seem preoccupied," she said.

He shrugged. "It is nothing."

"Oh," she said, working at her leather. "I thought it might be Daia."

"Well, it is not," he said too quickly. Moussa tried to escape his mother's gaze, but he had never been able to do that successfully. Now he saw no need to pretend. "She is Mahdi's woman. They are to be married. She has said it, and Mahdi has said it." Serena put down her knife.

"And what have *you* said?"

"That I will not interfere."

"I am not asking of your head, Moussa. I am asking of your heart."

"It is the same thing."

She smiled at that. "I don't know how you can be so quick to show a camel your feeling for it, Moussa, and so slow to show a woman." She stood and began preparing tea, stirring at the ashes of the fire until they glowed. "When I met your father the amenokal told me I was being selfish, that I was thinking only of myself when I said I wanted to marry him. He said what I wanted to do was wrong. The other nobles and the marabouts all agreed with him. My own head knew he was right. My heart alone did not. But I knew from the moment I met Henri that I would listen to my heart. Do I have to tell you which was right?"

He had thought about it every day since then, about what might have been, about what might be. *Malish, mektoub*, the imam would say. Never mind, it is written. He shrugged to himself. Is anything ever written? Is anything ever done? He dumped his cold tea into the ash of his fire and rose to hunt with Taka. He sensed rather than saw the mehari approaching across the desolate stretch of plain through which he had been traveling. He pulled his brass spyglass from the bag slung at his camel's side and steadied his arm on the saddle as he trained it upon the rider's blurry image. It was Lufti, riding like a man whose mount was on fire. Eventually the slave saw him and waved.

"*Hamdullilah*, I found you, sire, praise Allah!" The mehari was wild-eyed with exertion, its breath labored and hard.

"You push your mount severely in this heat," Moussa said, concerned. "Is all well in the *ariwan?*"

"Yaya, sire, all is well, but the Mistress Serena threatened me plenty if I did not find you quickly. I missed you by only a night in Timissao. Then, as Allah is my witness, I lost your track!" There was a mixture of pride and incredulity in his voice. For Moussa to have obscured his passage sufficiently to lose his teacher in such things was a matter of some note. "You have learned well, sire, if your servant may say it! No Tebu devil will find you, that is sure, yaya! There was a time . . . but never mind, never mind!" He slid quickly from his mount and drew a leather pouch from beneath his robe. He opened it and carefully withdrew a letter.

"The mistress sends you a message, sire, and asks that it be read in haste." Moussa saw the clear hand of his mother on the paper:

Moussa, I hope this letter finds you well. I write in French in order that no one else may know this news. I have been shown a letter by the wife of the amenokal. It was received from the French expedition, addressed to Ahitagel. He had already departed for In Salah, so I was asked to open and interpret it. The letter was in response to an earlier message from Ahitagel. It dealt with a point of rendezvous, with a route proposed by the French. There was also a request for a meeting. At the end there were names of some of the officers of the expedition. One of those names—I had to read it over and over to be certain—was Lieutenant Paul deVries. I could not believe it! His age would be right, of course, for him to have become an officer in the army. How well I can see him in uniform, even after what happened to his father. It has been the way of your father's family for generations. And it would be like him to have found his way here. Oh, Moussa. After these many years of silence, can it be anyone other than our Paul?

There is yet another development. I have received word that Tamrit ag Amellal is among those joining the amenokal at In Salah. I have never spoken of him to you before. It was not important, because I thought he had disappeared forever. He is a man who tried to do harm to your father. It is said that he has joined with the Senussi, and that they mean to prevent the expedition of Colonel Flatters. I do not know the truth of it, but Tamrit is a man whose spirit is hard and filled with hate. He knows only treachery. Nothing good can come from his involvement in this.

I sense that much is happening around the French expedition that cannot be seen or heard. I have never known such secrecy among the Ihaggaren. If you can learn of their route, I believe you will learn much of our intentions. If the French are turned to the west, it will be a good sign. They will pass near Abalessa and then freely to the south. But if they are turned to the east, toward Serkout, it means they are doomed.

How I wish the amenokal were alive! Your Abba would know how to counsel you in this. I must confess I do not. If there is trouble, the fact that it is the French themselves who bring it does not make it less painful. That our Paul might be among them makes me afraid for him. It may already be too late to do anything.

I think of you always. May you travel in safety.

Moussa sat down and reread the letter.

Paul!

His heart leapt with joy at the thought of his cousin. A flood of memories and excitement washed over him. So long he had wondered what had become of Paul, so often he had thought of him. For him to be here, in the desert! It was extraordinary. He looked at the date on the letter. Three weeks had passed since it was written. Damn the amenokal for keeping him from the French! He knew immediately what he must do.

"Rest your mehari, Lufti. Then return to the *ariwan*," he said, lashing his belongings into place on the saddle. "Tell no one you have seen me."

"Not even the demon Kel Asouf could pry it from me," Lufti promised. "But sire, where are you going?"

"I don't know exactly. To find the French." Moussa had a sudden thought and withdrew the oilcloth packet from his pouch. He sat down with a paper and pen and wrote quickly.

Daia—

May it please you to read to the children from this book, and bring them its light. Perhaps one day you might teach this child as well, the life in its words. I wish you much happiness in your marriage.

Moussa

There was much more he wanted to say, but he didn't know how to say it. It was all too delicate. The note would have to do. Then he shook his head and tore it up. On a second piece of paper he wrote the same message, except that this time he left out the words *in your marriage*. Perhaps his mother was right. Perhaps his heart was not yet ready to yield.

"Give this to the Mistress Daia," he said, folding the paper and slipping it under the string of the oilcloth.

"Yaya, sire."

Moussa urged his mount quickly to the northeast. Lufti watched until his master was but a speck, and then the speck was gone.

CHAPTER 24

THE SUNLIGHT DANCED ON THE WATER AS IT sloshed down the rock trough, its reflection diffusing into vague yellow shimmies on the golden necks of the animals who stood side by side above it. They drew in liter after liter, sucking noisily, greedily, the muscles in their long throats rippling in tandem with the sunlight in a journey up their sloping necks. Two noisy red Bengali birds were playing games in the branches of the tamarisk trees, swooping among the leaves, undisturbed by the activity below them.

The Frenchmen sat in the shade of the trees facing the well of Tadjenout. They watched the Shamba sweat through their labors, filling the trough and the goatskin bags. The well was deep. A Shamba dropped a bucket tied to a rope into the blackness, waiting until it slapped the bottom, then shaking the rope to tip the bucket until its edge dipped below the water, feeling the heavy pull as it filled and sank, then raising it up fist over fist, muscles bulging under his dirty robes until he had it, and draining it off into the goatskin bags held open by a helper. As he did so, another Shamba took his turn, dumping his wet cargo into the trough for the animals. They worked quickly together, but it would be another hour before they finished. Thirsty camels were still filing down the steep hill to take their turn. The horses were watered right away. They were impressive thoroughbreds, but unable to survive the heat like camels and therefore always watered first. Attici's guides had led them off when they finished, to graze on the rare tufts of grass scattered about the floor of the rock valley.

Captain Masson set down his tin cup. He had been
absently watching the entrancing flicker of sunlight on
the camels' necks and nursing his water, lost in thoughts
of soft Paris nights. Something disturbed his reverie.
Something didn't feel right. The nape of his neck felt
warm and tingly, as if someone were lightly touching
his hair. He was certain of the feeling, having had it
before, but uncertain of the source. He looked around
quickly.

The colonel was engaged in conversation with
Doctor Guiard and the engineers Beringer and Roche.
He was sipping some tea he'd ordered prepared as they
waited for the Shamba to finish. The *tirailleurs* were
relaxed, chattering quietly in scattered groups, leaning
on their rifles. Remy Cavour and the others were up
over the ridge, seeing to the procession of camels, which
seemed to be coming to an end at last. He could see
Remy's figure at the top; the man gave no sign of any
problem. The camels were calm and the Bengali birds
played on.

The captain shrugged inwardly, and lost himself in
the clang of the buckets and the sloshing of the water.

Rᴇᴍʏ Cᴀᴠᴏᴜʀ ꜰᴏʟʟᴏᴡᴇᴅ ᴛʜᴇ ʟᴀsᴛ ᴏꜰ ᴛʜᴇ ᴄᴀᴍ-
els up the hill. The sergeant was on foot, leading his
mount behind. As he topped the east ridge, he looked
down onto the camels milling below, some drinking,
some just standing, some kneeling on all fours as only
camels could. The colonel and the others were sitting
near the well. He saw Captain Masson turn to look at
him, then turn back. It was hot but peaceful. He saw
two of the guides leading the horses away from the well.
The horses were trying to graze, but the guides kept
yanking at their reins, not letting them stop to eat. It
was odd, he thought.

He started down the steep winding path that zig-
zagged down the slope to the floor below. In rocky
country like this he wished for a horse. The wretched
camels carried themselves with an ungainly grace on flat

sand, but in rocks their grace vanished, leaving them just ungainly. As his mount was stepping over a large stone, Remy's eyes were drawn to a movement below and to his left. He looked up and saw one of the guides riding his mehari hard, toward where the two guides were now disappearing with the horses into some boulders that obscured the west side of the bowl. *Is there a passage?* he wondered. *Are they stealing the horses and abandoning the group here?* He dropped the reins, cupped his hands over his mouth, and shouted. The guide looked over his shoulder at him and whipped his camel for more speed. Should he shoot? Uncertainly, confused, he unshouldered his carbine. He glanced at the officers below. They'd noticed nothing, their vision blocked by the camels milling about the well. The *tirailleurs,* damned fools, had their backs turned. No one heard him yell.

He raised his rifle.

DOCTOR GUIARD SMILED AT SOMETHING ONE OF the engineers had said. He hoped it was funny. He hadn't really been listening. His mind was preoccupied in a battle with his intestines, which had been cramping for days. It was the water, of course; and he, the wise doctor, had not been boiling it. He deserved the torment his bowels were bringing him. The tea hadn't soothed him at all. He grimaced. He'd have to go behind one of the rocks.

He was holding his cup in front of his knees, which were drawn up to his chest to help the cramps. He leaned forward on the balls of his feet and started to set the cup down. As he was looking at it, the cup seemed to explode in his hands. It jerked away and flew backward, toward his chest. His forward motion stopped, and he reversed. He'd heard nothing, nothing at all. He thought someone had slammed his sternum with a board. He couldn't imagine why they'd do that. He had no idea what on earth had happened to the cup.

―――――――――

PAUL WAS JUST ABOVE THE MIDPOINT BETWEEN the base camp and the well. He'd ridden the route twice, top to bottom. The going was tough, as the Targui had said it would be, but Paul's mount seemed steadier than most, and was sure, if slow.

Floop was everywhere, running free, exploring the natural caves and following scents and racing over the terrain, dashing underneath Paul's mehari whenever he thought he might get away with it. He'd been kicked once by the camel for the offense, but had learned nothing from the lesson except to increase his speed.

Paul stopped to talk to El Madani, who, with the other four *tirailleurs,* had found a perch just above the midway point on the trail from which they had a commanding view. Paul liked the crafty old *tirailleur.* The man was nearly fifty, but was as wily and tough as any man in the caravan. He'd been two decades in French service and was full of desert stories and tales of the old days in Akabli. And he was the only Algerian who seemed to like Floop's personality, or notice it. He had kind brown eyes, and normally was quick with a smile. But he had not smiled for days.

"*À votre santé, Lieutenant.*"

"*Santé,* Madani. Anything?"

"No, but I don't believe it," he growled, his eyes searching the countryside. "Things don't feel right. The day is too quiet."

Paul laughed. "I would think you'd be glad for the quiet."

"I'll be glad when these mountains are but a memory," Madani said. "These Tuareg are vile sons of whores. You can trust the ones who live in graves. In Akabli they used to trade what they'd stolen from the men they'd butchered. Whole caravans. Then other caravans would pass through and buy what the Tuareg had traded. Later the same merchandise would appear back in Akabli—again in the hands of the Tuareg." He shook his head. "And those caravans stayed together, too. Not like this one." He spat and kept watching.

"Well, things look all right so far."

"No, they don't. Look there." El Madani pointed to the south of camp, where a mehariste was riding at full speed, the expedition's Saluki dogs running behind. It was the guide who was to have remained at the base camp.

"What's *he* doing here?" Paul wondered.

"They don't ride like that in this heat for exercise," Madani said. "He's running."

"I think you're right. We'd better alert the colonel."

As they turned to leave Floop trotted out from behind some rocks, a lizard's tail dangling from between his teeth, like a tongue.

"The bag, Floop!" The dog hesitated and whined, pleading.

"The bag!" Paul's voice cut sharply; his camel was moving. The dog dropped the lizard and scrambled forward, leaping upward when he got to the right position. They'd gotten good at it. Paul caught his front feet in one hand and used Floop's momentum to swing him up, turn him around, and drop him into the bag. Floop wriggled into position, and stared sullenly from between his paws at the retreating lizard.

As the camels started moving and found their stride, Paul heard shots, and a sound like the low rolling thunder of a distant storm.

MAHDI SMILED. HIS RIFLE WAS THE NEWEST, AND he'd been practicing, but he knew the truth of it: it was a lucky shot.

Attici had given him the honor of beginning it. The *tirailleurs* were the closest, simple targets leaning on their guns, but they were believers as well. He preferred one of the infidels drinking tea.

He chose the tin cup as the target. The infidel was holding it just right, its rounded edge catching the sunlight, like a beacon pointing the way. He smiled under his shesh, and pulled the trigger.

Doctor Guiard crashed backward, the bullet deflecting off his sternum and spending itself in his heart. There was little blood from the wound, for there was no heart left to pump it. His arms were flung out behind him, his legs splayed awkwardly. He stared at the sky through lifeless eyes, a puzzled expression on his face.

At Mahdi's shot the tranquil valley suddenly roared with the noise of a score more shots and the shrill screaming of a hundred Tuareg throats as they poured out from their position on the west end. Their camels' hooves rumbled, their frenzy fired by the deep, rhythmic beat of the *tobol*, the drum of war, echoing down from its station hidden atop the ridge. Each of the sounds, intimidating by itself, built with the others into a wall of sonorous terror, amplified by the rock walls of the valley.

Colonel Flatters and Captain Masson reacted instantly when the doctor was hurled back, their long training and instincts taking over from the more natural inclination to freeze at the terrible sound of the attacking Tuareg. They rolled away from the body, grabbing at their rifles and ending in a kneeling position, already firing into the howling blue mass riding toward them. They looked for their horses, to fight mounted and mobile, but saw no trace of them. It would be like this, then, their backs to the well, on foot. Their hands were sure, their motions smooth, their aim deadly, but the number of Tuareg was overwhelming, pressing forward through the raging fire. As fast as the officers could shoot, the Tuareg came faster, camels and men falling at their feet. Those fallen in front brought down others behind, their riders leaping off and over the massive jam, hurling themselves at the Frenchmen, who fired, and fired, and fired again.

The colonel paused slightly, reaching for more ammunition in its pouch on his belt, wrenching furiously at the metal snap. It was too long. From over the top of the mass of bodies in which he stood, a Targui flew at him, shoving his lance before him, driving it hard until it found the gray shoulder, piercing it through. Flatters felt no pain, just a heavy thud that wrenched the carbine from his grasp. He staggered, tripping over the bodies at his feet. He recovered his balance, reaching for his sword with his good arm, and then he had it out, slashing, stabbing, parrying at the Targui before him. As the man fell another was in his place, and another, and the colonel was overwhelmed. A great sword flashed and found his neck. Less than three minutes had passed since the doctor had fallen.

Captain Masson had also run out of ammunition, but had reached his pistol and was firing point-blank into the press of Tuareg. The jumble of bodies was almost a hill, but he knew it was hopeless. He'd seen Sergeant Dennery fall, and the *tirailleurs* near him were being overrun. The Shamba at the well behind him had been dead almost as quickly as the doctor, caught in the fire of the fierce Tuareg volley. Still, he fired. There was no time to aim for the slits in their sheshes anymore, but there was no need, either; he could hear their panting and the rustle of their robes, and their horrid shrilling sound as they were upon him. A sword smashed into his collarbone, ripping a great gaping hole across and down his chest. Stunned, he felt another blow behind him. It had done something to his back. There was no pain to tell him what, just a heavy tug and then some awful internal sound of cutting. He kept squeezing at the trigger and smelled the blood and the powder and fell over something soft, his head hitting the ground. His eyes looked past the blue and found the tamarisk trees. The Bengali birds had gone.

REMY FIRED ALMOST SIMULTANEOUSLY WITH Mahdi, bringing down the fleeing guide. He prayed he'd done the right thing. But then he heard the rumble and saw the blue stream cascading out from behind the same boulders where the horses had disappeared, and he knew.

He found a small flat area and tried to get his camel to kneel, but the pandemonium below had the animal's nostrils flared in terror. The beast wouldn't budge and started pulling at the reins to get up the hill. The animal nearly lifted Remy off the ground. As he clung to the leather, he heard a sharp ring on a rock somewhere behind him. He needed cover.

He pulled his pistol from its holster and shot the

camel dead, jumping out of the way as it collapsed. Its massive body hit the ground hard and slid downhill, coming to rest against a small shelf of rock. Remy was crouching behind it the instant it stopped.

He tugged at his belt buckle, unfastened it, and pulled his ammunition pouch off, throwing it on the ground. He worked the bolt of his rifle, turned to the slaughter below him, and opened fire. At first it was easy. Most of the Tuareg were mounted, riding much higher than the camels around them, and effortless shots to his practiced aim. He fired steadily, accurately, grunting with satisfaction at the falling targets, counting them off to himself, *six, sept, huit,* stopping only to grab more cartridges. Some of the Tuareg below saw him and charged up the hill but he took them easily, almost casually. He was alone, but on good high ground. He thought he could stay like that for hours, until all the godless blue bastards were dead.

I N THE FIRST TEN SECONDS, THE EXPEDITION'S CAM-els massed in the valley went mad with fright. They howled and bucked and ran in every direction, retreating at the echoes or running from some new advancing mayhem, finding no way out of the terror. They ran into each other, some falling, bellowing when others trampled over them, snapping their legs. One fell partway into the well, its front legs dangling in the blackness, throat just over the edge, chin resting precariously on the rock ledge opposite. Frantically it tried to free itself, front legs kicking for a hold, but another camel ran over the top, stepping just behind the fallen camel's head, snapping its neck and forcing it down into the well. Its hindquarters dragged on the rocks until they were gone, and the dead mehari splashed heavily into the water below. The second camel plunged down after the first, howling as it went.

Some tried to run up impossible inclines, legs pumping furiously at the rocks until they lost their footing and fell backward, running into others climbing behind them and toppling them too, legs entwining with other legs, bodies colliding and sliding and falling, until they were a great golden avalanche of terrified fury. Two of the *tirailleurs*, kneeling and firing at the Tuareg, were caught in one of the mass rushes, their weapons flying, their bodies crushed to the ground.

PAUL REACHED THE TOP OF THE RIDGE FIRST AND saw the sea of death churning in the valley below. The reek of blood and powder and sweat made him flinch.

It took him a few seconds to absorb the teeming color, the dead *tirailleurs* and officers and engineers, the crush of blue, the camels rushing madly about. He could imagine what the valley must have looked like before he'd arrived. What he could not comprehend was the one before him now. It wasn't the disorder, or the stench, or the defeat. It was what the Tuareg had begun once they'd won.

Their blood lust seemed to have increased as they gathered around the bodies of the expeditionary force. That the men were already dead was clear; their bodies were twisted and bloody and still. But the Tuareg seemed to be just beginning. They stripped rifles, swords, rings, and whatever else of value they could find. Then they ripped the clothes off of the corpses, heaved the nude bodies into a pile, and began hacking and stabbing and sawing and mutilating, severing limbs and heads and fingers and turning the pile into a viscous bloody muck. Plumes of smoke billowed lazily from the clothing, which they'd torched but burned poorly for all the blood.

Suddenly the resonant voice of Tamrit ag Amellal rose from some obscure spot hidden from Paul's view. Paul didn't understand the words of Tamashek that floated over the amphitheater, words that echoed off the walls and stopped men for a moment in what they were doing. But he didn't need to understand the words to interpret their ghastly tone. When Tamrit finished he repeated the words in Arabic, his message for Shamba and Tuareg alike.

"And those who disbelieve will be gathered unto Hell, that Allah may separate the wicked from the good. The wicked he will place piece upon piece, and heap them all together, and consign them unto Hell. Such verily are the losers. And Allah said I will throw fear into the hearts of those who disbelieve. Then smite the necks and smite of them each finger. . . ."

Paul vomited, unable to stop, unable even to lean one way or another to get it clear of his camel. It came too quickly and too violently, and covered his mehari's neck. He leaned forward, clutching his stomach, shutting his eyes, gagging, choking, coughing.

El Madani arrived at the ridge, his four men close behind him, and saw the retching officer and the scene below. El Madani felt the familiar bite of bile, but he had learned to keep it away until the danger passed. The firing had all but stopped. Only Remy remained, crouching behind his camel. His situation was hopeless. El Madani was unslinging his rifle by the time his camel had stopped moving, but there was nothing he could do now except give away their position. He held his fire and motioned for his men to do the same.

Alone, Remy was confronting the mounted Tuareg from behind his dead camel. He'd run out of ammunition, but not before leaving a score of dead on the rocks before him. He grabbed the barrel of his rifle to use it like a club. He stepped up onto the belly of his camel to get sufficient height, and the first rider was upon him. He dodged the Targui's lance and brought the rider down with a terrific upward swing, catching the man full in the chest and flipping him off his mount. He kept hold of his rifle and swung it again, but then was engulfed in a crush of swirling blue.

Paul heard the Tuareg shrilling and looked up. He saw Remy swinging the rifle, and a great sword rushing down. Remy's left arm came off, the hand still clutching the rifle as it spun slowly upward, Remy's force behind it, the arm and rifle twirling together in a long slow arc to the ground. In the same instant he was speared through the chest, the momentum knocking him off his feet, the force of the spear pushing its point all the way through him and into the ground, where he died pinned like an insect. The swarm of blue warriors was on him in an instant, the bloody ritual of stripping and butchery beginning once more.

Paul heaved again, nearly falling from his saddle. El Madani reached over to steady him. There was nothing he could say to the boy. Paul was ashamed, but the paroxysms of nausea left him unable to move. He heard El Madani almost whisper to himself: "*Les chameaux.*" At first it didn't register. His mind was consumed with what his eyes had seen, and his body was trying to purge it. But then he understood, in a flash: *the camels!* The killing was over below, but there were still men back at the base camp, on foot. Without camels they would die too, and the Tuareg might not have to fire a shot to accomplish it. They had to get the camels back. It was the only thing left, the only thing to do. The thought wrestled with his nausea for control. Paul breathed deeply, concentrating, and then straightened up, his face ghostly pale, bits of vomit clinging to his chin. He looked once more into the valley. The camels were milling everywhere, spread out from east to west in bunches. Yes, it was possible, it could be done if they could get down behind where Remy had fought. There was hope. He looked at Madani, who was studying the valley.

"You stay here," Paul gasped to the old *tirailleur*. "We're going down." He expected an argument, but Madani nodded. What had to be done was for younger legs. He could be more help from here.

"You must hurry," El Madani said. "They have begun." He pointed at the boulders near the west entrance. Some of the Tuareg were starting to lead the camels out. Paul jumped down from his camel, grabbing his rifle and issuing quick orders to the *tirailleurs*. They dismounted quickly, understanding the urgency. Without another word, the five of them started down the hill. Paul had taken no more than a few steps when he stopped, cursed, and turned, racing back up the hill to his camel. He put his hand on the bag.

"Floop, *stay.*" The command was unnecessary. The

noise and the smells had convinced Floop that the bag was a fine place to be just then.

El Madani dismounted, pulled ammunition from the supply bag, and looked for a rock with a view.

The five of them half-ran, half-fell down the hill, moving as quickly as they could on the rocky slope. They were well past the Tuareg clustered around Remy's body before they were spotted, and heard frenzied yells as they disappeared into the teeming mass of camels. They shepherded, cursed, screamed, pulled, and cajoled, trying to gather up clusters of the animals and get them moving uphill. At first they had no luck. All was confusion and the camels didn't know which way to go. But the massive noise in the valley was tapering off considerably, and the camels, regaining some of their composure, started responding to their voices. As the men gathered reins and got one or two of them moving, some of the others followed along.

Paul was the farthest to the east, working alone. He had gone down the hill in an arc rather than straight as the others had. The camels provided plenty of protection as he worked. He was careful to keep them between himself and the Tuareg.

Gathering as many precious reins as he could hold in one hand, he used his rifle as a prod, too roughly at first, so that one of the animals bolted, then more gently, beginning to walk and tap flanks, first right, then left, until he got two going the right way, then four, and before long others were carried along in the sweep, the animals finding a calming influence in the pack.

Paul soon found himself in the midst of fifteen camels, stunned to find them actually going in the direction he wanted. He kept talking, swatting, prodding, persuading, every so often half running in a crouch, bending to peer through the forest of legs to get his bearings. The first time he did it all he saw was camel legs and rock. The second time he nearly shouted in glee. He could see the *tirailleurs,* covered by El Madani, beginning to make their way up the hill with at least fifty camels among them. Best of all, he didn't see any Tuareg.

As he was straightening up, one of the camels he was leading bolted, and he lost his grip on the reins he held. The camels stopped, stared arrogantly at him, then turned and trotted in the other direction. Paul cursed and ran back after them, trying to keep his voice calm as he did so as not to frighten them. Eventually he had three of them, but gave up on the last when he turned and saw that a group of Tuareg forty yards away had spotted him and were running in his direction.

Adrenaline racing, Paul tugged the camels along as fast as he could until he found his way back into the larger pack of animals, who had simply come to a standstill where he'd left them. Once again he had to get them moving in the right direction, a task complicated by their lost momentum and the fact that he had to keep looking for blue robes. Over and over again he heard the reassuring crack of Madani's Gras rifle, but had no idea where the man was shooting. He looked under the legs again, to his right, concerned because he didn't see any blue. They should have been on him by now. He kept low, always prodding, glad for the cover of the animals but frustrated by the blindness they brought.

And then he heard voices and knew. He had been too long getting the strays. The Tuareg had had time to cut him off from Madani's position, and had simply run in front of the pack he was driving. They were turning the animals aside and standing there, waiting for him, their swords drawn.

A GRIN CREASED EL MADANI'S LINED, DUSTY FACE as he squinted and fired. They'd nearly done it, *w'allahi!* The Tuareg couldn't stop them now. He could just see his men's legs in the moving herd as they drove their charges uphill.

The Tuareg had stopped firing. El Madani's weapon made the only noise now. He understood the silence at once, and reveled in it: the Tuareg had run out of ammunition for their ancient weapons, and then for the Gras rifles they'd taken from the victims of the massacre.

El Madani fired carefully, steadily, until the camels and men began pouring over the ridge to his right. Once the four *tirailleurs* were out of danger he turned his attention to Paul. Between passing heads and humps he could see Paul's herd, and El Madani caught his breath—there were nearly a dozen Tuareg just in front of the lieutenant's camels. The Frenchman was isolated, about to die.

El Madani swung his rifle toward Paul's position and tried to take aim. He cursed. The stream of camels was blocking a clear shot. He'd have to get to the other side before he could help. He jumped to his feet and dashed forward, ducking his head, shoving with his rifle, trying to move quickly, but it was impossible. The camels were crowded closely together, four and five abreast, heads to hindquarters, hurriedly obliging the shouts of the *tirailleurs* trying to keep them moving. El Madani had just gotten into the stream when he tripped over a leg and fell painfully to his knees. He struggled to get to his feet but fell again, bumped and shoved and half carried along by the swiftly moving flow of camels, his frustration mounting by the second. There was no time! Enraged, he hit out at the beasts, cursing them, trying to make himself a little space so he could get up and keep moving. He shouted desperately, hoping his *tirailleurs* would hear.

"The lieutenant!" he screamed. "Help the lieutenant!"

THE INSTANT PAUL REALIZED THE SITUATION HE was in, he felt the warm flush of fear. "Jesus," he whispered, eyes wide, mind racing. There were at best six or seven camels between him and the waiting Tuareg, only seconds until his cover was gone. He had run out of time.

Still in a crouch, he let go of the reins of the camels following behind him, and drew his pistol from its holster. He peered between the legs before him, for the timing. Four camels, three . . . now!

Clutching his rifle tightly, he stood erect. Thrusting with all his might, he jammed his rifle barrel hard at the anus of the camel just in front of him. With a shriek of pain, the animal shot forward into the Tuareg, knocking four of them down, then tripping itself on one's robes, and falling heavily onto two more. Paul fired his pistol into the air and screamed as loudly as he could. The other camels bolted at the eruption, straight for the Tuareg.

The surprise all his but his cover now gone, Paul ran for his life. He went straight to his left, his eyes scanning the rocks for shelter. If he could get into the big pillars at the east end, maybe he could work his way back up toward El Madani. It was his only chance. Looking back over his shoulder, he saw a confusion of animals and blue—and four Tuareg, hard after him, less than fifteen meters away. He had more than a hundred to go before he reached the pillars. He swore. Where was El Madani? His rifle had fallen silent. There was no time to turn and fire. He might hit one or two, but then the others would be on him.

His boots gave him an advantage over the Tuareg. They were at home in these mountains, but he wore no robes or sandals to slow him down. He concentrated on the course before him. If he tripped, he would die. If he slowed, he would die. If El Madani didn't help soon, he would die. So many ways to die, but his flight brought him an odd sense of exhilaration, and he knew he wasn't going to die, he was going to reach cover, he was going to live, he knew it, watching the rocks and forcing more speed, and his feet fairly flew on the wings of his will.

NEAR DESPAIR, EL MADANI PUSHED HIS WAY through the last of the camels and was out the other side. Moving faster than he had known he could, he ran forward and threw himself on his stomach to a prone position just behind the edge of the ridge. Propping himself on his elbows, his rifle swinging toward where he'd last seen Paul, El Madani took in the scene below. Somehow the lieutenant had broken away and was running for the east end of the canyon, a group of Tuareg close behind him.

The old warrior steadied himself, took aim, and began firing.

The other *tirailleurs* who had brought the camels up the hill heard El Madani resume firing, and turned to look downhill—toward their own pursuers. Out of breath, nearly exhausted, they knew they had to deal with the Tuareg below, who had advanced up the hill to within thirty meters of their position. Automatically, the *tirailleurs* spread out in a line and began firing.

Once atop the ridge, the camels were packed together, with little room to move. The slopes were precipitous in every direction. The trail on which they had arrived from base camp was treacherous, winding, and steep. To the animals it was no trail at all—just an abrupt drop, like the rest. There were almost sixty of them, a great milling mass that had lost the trail. When the roar of rifle fire erupted and rekindled some of their earlier panic, the fear spread through them.

Intent on the Tuareg below, the *tirailleurs* weren't paying attention. At the outer edge, away from the well, two camels precariously close to the slope lost their footing and fell down a steep incline, bellowing as they went. The camels closest to them reared back in fright, trying to find flatter ground, pushing those behind them in wild-eyed fear. The motion spread through the entire skittish group like a wave, intensified by the deafening noise of the rifles.

It was enough. An animal closest to the well was crowded from behind, and took off back down the hill, toward the well. Instantly others followed, and then more, and then in a flood they were all gone. Too late, the *tirailleurs* jumped up. They watched helplessly as all they had worked for, all they had risked, fled back down the hill. Short of running right into the midst of the Tuareg below, there was nothing they could do.

El Madani heard the noise but didn't look. He was firing at Paul's hunters. He hit one, but the shot was lucky—they were distant, running away from him and after their quarry, their retreating figures bobbing erratically as they dashed between the rocks. Again and again El Madani fired, again and again in vain. He saw Paul nearing the rock columns at the east end. The boy seemed fleet as a gazelle and had widened the distance between himself and the Tuareg, but to El Madani what he was running into looked like a dead-end trap of rock.

But Paul kept straight on and disappeared into the pillars. Cocking, firing, cocking, firing, El Madani pursued his three targets relentlessly, but with each second his hope dwindled, and then it died. They too were gone, swallowed by the rocks.

El Madani laid down his rifle and wiped the sweat from his brow. Dejected, he sat up and looked over his shoulder toward the ridge. The noise he'd half-heard became a clamor in his head. He couldn't believe his eyes and felt a blinding rage within. Down the hill, the Tuareg were administering the *coup de grâce* to his chances of survival. They had the camels again!

El Madani grabbed his rifle and raised it once again, to shoot as many of the departing animals as he could, to at least deprive the Tuareg of them. But he stopped himself. It would be a meaningless gesture, the second slaughter of the day. They were gone. His shoulders sagged. He set down his rifle.

Then another thought occurred to him. He gazed at the retreating camels, scanning them quickly. And then he saw it, and for the first time that day allowed himself to feel total defeat. It was just a little thing, he knew, an almost pathetic concern on this day of so much death.

Near the rear of the retreating camels, caught up with the rest, was Paul's mehari. El Madani knew it by its saddle and by the bag on its side. The bag with Floop inside.

P AUL COULD NEITHER SEE NOR HEAR THE TUAREG behind him, but he felt their deadly presence like a lance at his back, pushing, goading, terrorizing him to greater speeds than he'd ever run before.

He would not die that way!

The thought consumed him, drove him, fueled the fire of his passion to get away. He dared not look back. The rocks at his feet thumped and clattered, grated and gave as he fled up the valley. In every stone there was a hazard, in every hazard he saw the arm, that horrible, lonely arm, twisting and twirling through the air, clutching an empty rifle.

He would not die like Remy!

He didn't slow his pace when he reached the cover of rocks. He weaved and raced through the columns, each moment expecting to lose his running room and be trapped, but each time seeing yet another passage between more pillars. His eyes moved quickly as he ran. He had entered what appeared to be a continuing canyon, filled with great volcanic pillars and spires that had obscured the entrance and even now made a view of the whole canyon impossible. It was an eerie place, swallowed in silence, the sunlight catching the shiny tops of the monoliths, reflecting down onto the sandy floor into soft pools of light through which he fled. The pillars were like some massive petrified forest of trees whose dark gray bark was sculpted in spirals of swirling layers winding dizzily to their tops. Between them grew sporadic acacia trees and scattered bunches of grasses. Butterflies flitted softly in the stillness, their large colorful wings glowing iridescently in the mirrored light of the sun.

As he raced along, the sides of the canyon grew perceptibly steeper, until they were almost vertical walls, punctuated by occasional steep narrow gorges cut deeply into the rock that disappeared out of view.

The rocky floor was growing progressively sandier—a light sprinkle at first, then a thin layer that crunched under his feet, finally a thick bed of it that sucked at his boots, slowing his progress and making him work harder for it. The muscles in his thighs began to feel the drag, aching with each stride, his lungs hurting, his breath strained and ragged, spots of light dancing in his eyes. He'd been sprinting flat-out for fifteen minutes. He was in good shape, but the Hoggar was high above sea level, its air thin. Finally, unable to maintain the pace, he had to stop to catch his breath. Chest heaving, he rested his arm with the rifle against one of the pillars and looked back over his shoulder. Nothing but the pillars met his eyes. His ears were ringing with his effort, and he heard nothing. For an exhilarating instant he thought his pursuers had given up. Surely they could not have kept up his pace. The thought lasted only an instant. Around the last pillar, sword in one hand, Gras rifle in the other, came a Targui, hot after him. The man had removed his sandals and was bloodying his feet for speed.

They saw each other simultaneously, both half-expecting it, but both surprised nonetheless. The Targui drew up sharply, dropping his sword and raising the rifle. Paul was gone before the deafening shot came, protected by the rock he'd rested on. The Targui gave a high-pitched cry, picked up his sword, and ran on. Within seconds another was there, and then the last.

They all shrilled. They knew what the Frenchman was running into. They had him.

Paul ran on, astonished at the speed and determination of the Tuareg. Consumed with his own efforts, he'd given no thought to theirs and had believed himself much farther in front. He would have to go faster. He ran just a few minutes more when he stopped short. There were no more pillars before him. He'd run through the last passage. The canyon was no canyon at all. It was a box, and he'd found its end. His eyes raced along the wall, exploring shadows, niches, looking for something, anything to let him continue. There was only sheer, jagged rock before him, with steep gorges, ledges, and outcroppings. He was no mountain climber. He thought about trying to cut back through the canyon, to lose himself in the pillars and slip by his hunters, but the canyon was too narrow for that. Undoubtedly they knew what he now faced and would be spreading out, ready. He had no idea how many there were, or whether they all had rifles or just the one. Regardless, this was no place to defend himself. He had to go on.

In desperation he saw his only chance—one of the steep gorges, cut by the raging waters of the millennia, barely big enough for a man at its opening, and very, very steep. Its course was lost to view less than ten meters up. Maybe it wouldn't be too steep to climb. Maybe it would lead him up to the ridge of the canyon, nearly a hundred and fifty meters over his head. At least it would give him the high ground and better cover. He had to try.

As he raced for it, another shot came. It was nowhere close to him. At least one of them, he thought, was a poor shot. He turned and fired his pistol three times while he ran, wildly, quickly, not aiming, simply meaning to force them to cover. Amplified by the rocks, his shots nearly deafened him, sounding more like a cannon than a pistol. He reached the gorge and leapt up the first few steps. They were easy and short, like large stairs, but as he bounded up they were taller and closer together. He quickly found his weapons a hindrance. He needed at least one hand free. He slung his rifle over his shoulder and around his neck, so that it hung against his back. Still holding the pistol, he started to pull himself up a long series of the steplike rocks. Except for the faults, the stone was worn smooth. He hoisted himself up, ran across the top to the next ledge, and repeated the motion, climbing steadily up.

He reached the halfway point when another shot came. The bullet smashed into the step above him, showering him with chips of rock. He let himself drop to the slab below, raised his pistol, and turned. There was nothing, only the steep steps twisting down. He waited, crouching as low as he could without losing his balance, holding the pistol extended, ready to fire. There was only one place they could be. The range was too great for accuracy with a pistol, but unslinging his rifle could be a deadly delay.

Then he saw the dull black barrel, and the soft edge of a black shesh, low, at the bend. He aimed and waited a second longer, until the cloth became a head and a shoulder. He fired. He missed the head, where he'd aimed, but the rock next to the shesh exploded, peppering the Targui with rock shards. He heard a terrible scream and saw the shesh disappear backward, the rifle falling. Paul fired once more at the same spot, then turned and hoisted himself up two more of the slabs. The gorge was still curving as it led him upward. He'd soon be out of their rifle sight again, and perhaps find a place where he could use his own rifle. The Targui's awful shrieks tore at his concentration as the sound of agony engulfed the gorge. Paul swallowed hard, grimacing at the noise. The rocks must have shredded the man's eyes. He kept moving, pushing the thought from his mind.

The incline and height of the rocks increased sharply, making his climb more difficult. He needed his other hand totally free, as he knew his pursuers would as well. He holstered his pistol. He'd gotten more than three-quarters of the way to the top when even two free hands were barely enough to continue upward. The steps began sloping on top, so that there was less and less to stand on. His legs pushed, toes searching for holds, arms pulling, fingers clutching, each new ascent more difficult than the last as the steps began to disappear altogether, until he found himself clinging to a nearly vertical slab of granite. Still he pushed upward, his chest and stomach in constant contact with the rock beneath, his hold growing more tenuous each moment. He looked up. Rock walls soared above him on both sides. He prayed there was somewhere to keep going, because he couldn't see it now. Up and up he climbed, every so often finding a small outcropping to grasp, but having to stretch more for each one, his legs almost dangling free as his boots sought purchase in the rock niches. Several times small rocks he tested for support broke free and clattered down the mountain. They fell, hit, split apart, and hit again, until they made a distant thud at the bottom. He shut his eyes, thinking he might sound like that, only softer. If it got any steeper, he knew, he couldn't hold on any longer.

He stopped and looked down through the hole between his armpit and the rock, past his boots, and saw two blue-clad figures twenty meters below, scaling up

behind him. He closed his eyes. The view downward
was dizzying, spreading a rush of fear from his belly to
his limbs. He had never climbed before, never known
the terror height could bring. It was insane, he thought.
They could see each other clearly but were powerless to
do anything except cling like flies to a wall. Perhaps the
hunters would have abandoned their quarry, perhaps
the quarry would have stood and fought had they
known where his flight was leading, but with each successive rock, each new handhold, their course had become fixed, irrevocable, and they were forced to go
on. He choked down the fear, opened his eyes, looked
upward, and kept climbing.

He reached a ledge at last. His fingers found it first, a
body's width away. He gently felt with his right boot
for a hold, tested one, rejected it, then found one that
worked. Jamming his boot in, supporting his full weight
on his toes, he pushed himself up, stretching precariously across the distance, and held on to the ledge as he
shifted across. He pushed up until his right leg was
straight, then worked his left knee up between his body
and the rock and onto the ledge. He shifted most of his
weight onto it and carefully brought the other knee up,
all the time trying not to lean even a millimeter backward in the certainty that it would be too much and
he'd be gone. His entire body trembled from the exertion and the electric clamor of his nerves. He stood up a
bit at a time, spread-eagled, his face brushing the rock—
the only way his body could stay close enough to the
wall. Just turning his head threw his balance out. He
scraped his nose on the rock, comfortable only when his
cheek rested flat against it.

The ledge coursed gently upward toward the wall
that formed one side of the gorge. He could see another
ledge above him, probably at or near the top. He could
see the branches of a tree! Heartened, he began sidestepping up the ledge, left foot groping out, body shifting
along sideways, right foot following, left foot moving
up once again, his hands trying to find small holds, his
cheek pressed to the rock.

When he had nearly reached the wall he stopped and

stared. There was no way across. There was a chasm more than three meters wide that dropped down out of sight. He tried to still his terror. If the ledge didn't continue around the corner, he knew he'd never be able to turn around and get down again—not with the Tuareg, not without wings. Slowly he made his way to the end of the ledge, carefully looking around the corner. His eyes shut tight in despair. The rock was smooth. The ledge disappeared.

Shaking, he turned to look the other way. One of the Tuareg, rifle slung over his shoulder, had already reached the ledge. The other followed close behind. Desperately, Paul's hands explored the surface above him, searching for a hold, for anything to help him go up. He felt a hole. He couldn't tell how deep it was, but it gave him an idea. Pressing hard against the wall, he raised one hand back over his neck until he felt the strap of his rifle. He brought the strap up and over his head, each movement slow, drawn out, and terrifying, and then let the strap slip down his arm until it reached his elbow, and he could reach the gun with his hand. Gripping the rifle near the stock, he brought his arm up along the rock, the barrel scraping as it went, until he had the weapon over his head. He held the rifle to the wall and pressed on it while he worked his way up the barrel, until his hand was halfway between the stock and the end. He slipped his fingers behind the steel, gripped it firmly, and braced himself. He swung the stock end of the rifle away from the wall, its weight making him gasp as it pressed hard against the fleshy web between his thumb and forefinger, his knuckles white and wrist straining as he fought to keep the stock high. As it swung outward, he slipped the barrel into the hole he'd found, and worked the tip in. He nearly lost his balance as the end disappeared, the weight of the stock still pulling his arm back, then he had it. He worked the rifle deeper and deeper until the barrel was jammed in the hole as far as it would go. It would have to do. The Targui was sidestepping toward him.

Paul grabbed the protruding stock with both hands. His feet lost their hold on the ledge, and with a horrible lurch his full weight dropped onto the rifle, his feet swinging clear. Barely five meters away, the Targui watched him silently. He saw Paul swing, looked up and saw the ledge above, and looked back at the Frenchman, dangling from his rifle. Waiting for the swinging to stop, Paul saw the Targui's brown eyes through the slit. They were coldly intent. The Targui reached a decision. Using the same slow, careful motions that Paul had just finished, the man began to unsling his rifle.

Paul knew he had only seconds to get up. He pulled hard, muscles shaking, until his chin was over the top of the rifle. Red-faced, straining, he pushed more, until he had first one elbow, then the other on top, then pushing farther still until his chest was up, then his stomach. Their eyes were fixed on each other in the deadly race, their motions slow, cautious, deliberate, each man clinging to his own precarious balance. The Targui's gun was now down to the crook of his elbow. His hand was working to clasp the stock.

Holding his arms rigid, his eyes steady on the Targui, Paul drew himself up until his knees were over the top. With his left arm he reached up for support on the wall. With his right he reached slowly for his holster. His knees pressed painfully into the steel and wood, but his mind was focused on the man before him, and his rifle, beginning its upward swing, his hand on the trigger. Paul's fingers, shaky from the strain, fumbled desperately at the snap and opened it at last.

They heard the noise at the same instant. Without looking they knew what it was. Each of them stopped dead still, not daring to move, pressing close to the wall to stay out of the way. Small pebbles came first, with sand, then bigger rocks, smashing down, their noise preceding them. Paul clenched his teeth, sucked in his breath, and closed his eyes. He felt small pebbles hit him on the head, and expected to die.

He heard a cry and opened his eyes. One of the rocks hit the Targui's shoulder, knocking the rifle from his hand. The shock knocked his arm sharply downward, destroying his balance. In horrified fascination, Paul watched as the arm waved frantically to recover, but there was no hope, and he was gone—his head dropping first, then his feet, his robes rippling in the rush of air. He hit the rock below with a horrible crunching and snapping noise, arms and legs flopping, and kept falling. The first blow loosened the end of his shesh, and as he continued downward the material streamed out behind him, waving like a long flag in the wind. He hit again, the sound more muffled, and kept falling, his body turning over and over as it slammed into rocks and fell through the air. After what seemed an eternity he came to rest on one of the small steps, his shesh trailed up to the one above. From the beginning, the man had uttered not a sound.

Paul swallowed, his mind numb. More loose pebbles fell. He looked at the remaining Targui, still frozen in position and staring at the heap of blue far below, transfixed.

Shakily Paul stood up on his rifle, his stomach churning, the rifle wiggling a little under his feet as he straightened up, but then holding steady. He reached for his pistol, unholstered it, and raised it. He couldn't miss. The Targui's gaze left the rocks below and went slowly up to the Frenchman standing on his rifle. Without flinching, he waited.

Paul felt the trigger beneath his finger, his eyes fixed on the target's head. He hesitated. The Targui had no rifle, no firearms at all. Just his great sword, still sheathed, useless against him here. For a full minute Paul held him in his sight, his aim unwavering. He dropped his eyes to the rifle on which he was standing. Slowly he lowered his pistol. Still the Targui did not move. Using hand signals, Paul showed him what he wanted. At first the Targui made no move, but when Paul started to raise his weapon again, he carefully drew the sword from its sheath. He held it for a moment, then tossed it over the edge. The steel flashed. The blade clanged against the rock and was gone. His eyes never left Paul.

When the silence returned, Paul put his pistol back in its holster. He boosted himself up onto the upper ledge, his body nearly collapsing in relief as he felt solid ground at last. The shelf was wide, the top an easy few steps up. He rested a moment, then turned around. He leaned down over the edge, stretching as far as he could. His toes fought for a hold in the rocks behind him as he worked the rifle free. He nearly lost it as it came out, but he had the barrel, and pulled it up onto the ledge, scooting back until he was on flat ground again. He peered over the edge. The Targui hadn't moved. Paul was satisfied. The man couldn't follow him, and couldn't turn around to get down without a rope. He would learn to fly or grow old on the side of the rock.

Paul stood. The barrel of his rifle had bent. The gun was useless. With all the force he could summon, he flung it out over the edge, as if the effort might shake off the terror. He turned and climbed the rest of the way up.

He thought he'd never seen a view as beautiful as the one he faced when he reached the top. He stood on a plateau, a massive bed of rock surrounded by low mountains. Serkout rose behind them to the northeast, dwarfing everything before it. Large boulders and rock formations were scattered over the plateau, looking oddly out of place on the flat surface, as if gathered by the gods from their rightful places and set down. The mountains were rugged as always, but here their coarse line was broken by spectacular mantles of sand spilling out from between them, some dropping like waterfalls, collecting in pools on the mountainsides as water would, others like magnificent glaciers, pushed by the ageless hand of time through the passes, creeping down the valleys, inexorably smothering everything in the way. The rock was dark gray, the sand a rich light mixture of gray and gold. The sun was low in the sky, its light mellowing the colors. Paul thought he could be looking at snow and ice on Alpen passes at home. The sky glowed eerily through the light haze in the atmosphere, pink and purple bands of color seeming to radiate from the rocks.

It was getting late. He was weak from hunger and fatigue. As much as he wanted to stop and rest a few moments, there was no time. He had to make his way to the southeast, back to the base camp.

He began walking, but hesitated. His pistol was nearly empty. He stopped to reload it, sitting cross-legged on the ground. As he was slipping the shells in, an uncontrollable trembling seized him. His arms, hands, legs, shoulders—everything refused to work, to do anything but submit to violent shuddering. It was frightening. His hand went numb and he dropped the pistol, unable to maintain his grip. He slipped to his back and stretched out and stared at the sky, trying to regain control, but the shaking grew worse. A torrent of fear and wonder washed over him, a sense of unreality coursing through his awareness. He began to think of the immensity of what had happened. He couldn't measure the change that had taken place in his life, or even quite define it. He could only barely comprehend its scope, and feel helpless in its magnitude. That morning he had been one man among many, a minor officer safe in obscurity and the illusion of the Hoggar's serenity. His life had been so easy, so absurdly easy. Until today. Until Tadjenout. He shut his eyes to close out the sky, and for a moment felt vague tentacles of dread settling over his mind, reaching down into the places where all was blackness and he could not see.

The wave washed over him as quickly as it had come, and all was calm again. He opened his eyes. The trembling had gone. Drained, he lay quietly, and shut his eyes again. His head felt cool, his world at peace. He floated easily, breathing deeply.

He awoke with a start. The sun was setting over the mountains. It was near dusk. He sat up, angry with himself for drifting off. He finished loading his pistol, stood up, and started for the southeast, jogging slowly. It made him feel better, and he picked up the pace a little—not fast, but steady, the running without the pressure of pursuit a release for him. He passed a succession of massive rocks, their shapes merging with their shadows in the twilight, the sand in the passes beginning to lose their subtle shadows and wind-formed shapes.

He stopped suddenly and listened, cocking his head to one side. He thought he had heard a camel, but there was only silence. Then he heard it again, he was sure of it. Dropping to his knees, he looked through the rocks. Nothing. He crept forward, pulling out his pistol. The animal had sounded distant, but the rocks could play tricks with sound. He had to be sure.

He hid in the shadow of a rock slab, scanning the area. In the dim light he saw them, a hundred meters away. It was a group of Tuareg atop their meharis, moving directly toward him at walking pace. He couldn't tell how many there were, for their forms were vague and they rode close together. He was sure they hadn't seen him. They were talking among themselves, laughing. He would have to get clear of their path and work around them. Still crouching, he raced for the next boulder, knowing he was completely exposed as he ran through the open space between. If they looked, they'd certainly see him. At the boulder he stopped again. They were still laughing. He slipped to the next boulder, and the next, darting quickly, each time expecting a cry of alarm, but never hearing it. When he was certain he was out of their sight, he straightened up and started to run. Glancing frequently over his shoulder, he ran easily in the failing light, twenty minutes, then thirty, until finally he knew he was safe. He passed into a large formation of rocks, thinking he would spend the night in their protection.

As he came around a corner, the shock before him brought his heart to his throat.

In the twilight a lone Targui was cutting the throat of his mehari, which had broken its foreleg. He heard Paul coming, picked up his rifle and rose to meet him. Paul's surprise was complete, but he acted swiftly, automatically, raising his pistol to fire. It had all taken only a split second. With blurring speed the Targui swung the stock of his rifle up and out, clubbing Paul on the side of his head. Paul felt the blow all the way through to his feet and pitched forward, the sound of his pistol roaring in his ears.

As he fell his mind raged against the blackness overtaking it. He realized he was going to die without a fight. He crumpled to his knees and crashed to his stomach, pushing back the blur that was taking him, pushing it away and watching the images of the day playing before him—the hacking, the chopping, the fires and the blood, the smell of the acrid smoke, and Remy, brave Remy, mighty arms swinging until one suddenly separated, going its own way, its blood spilling out as it whirled through the air, splattering blue robes and gray rock and the cold dead belly of the camel at his feet, and Paul was racing down the mountain through the fire and the smoke to pick up the arm and give it back to his friend—it must be hurting him so, and he'd be needing it—and then Paul had it, picking it up by the hand, the hand letting the rifle go and coming along willingly, but Remy wouldn't take it, dammit, he wouldn't get up, his eyes stared blankly, stupidly up past the shank of the spear in his chest at Paul, *Oh God, Remy, I'm sorry, it must hurt so, here, take it, please take it back,* and the Tuareg, all drawn back to watch, saw that Remy didn't want it anymore and pressed in around him, a ring of crimson steel and blue and slits of fiery eyes, coming to take yet another. . . .

CHAPTER 25

FOR WHAT MIGHT HAVE BEEN TEN MINUTES OR ten hours, Paul felt himself hovering in a gray netherworld between consciousness and the dark. Everything was so vague, so *almost* something. He couldn't breathe. There was a great heaviness on his chest, or maybe it was nothing. Noises . . . shouting, men shouting!—no, just the wind playing games, there's only silence here. Wait, those were camels he heard . . . no camels now, but blood, the sweet smell of blood. His? No, it was the smell of desert air, and it was good, always so good. He wished the pounding in his head would stop, a thousand drummers on a thousand drums, pounding slowly, in unison, hurting him so—no, those were waves pounding! There he was with Moussa by the sea, little boys playing relentless surf tag, the water retreating before their advance, then advancing before their retreat, and he loved the sea so, but it wasn't *time* now, he only wanted to sleep, but the hawk wouldn't let him, it was screeching in triumph after his kill, wings flapping, beak ripping at the flesh of the little lizard.

Then buzzing, insistent, blurry buzzing in his ears, and, trying to shut it out, a fleeting instant when he saw it all again so clearly, the swords flashing, hacking, mad blue butchers at work in a human slaughterhouse, the smoke of gunpowder burning his eyes. The arm, oh God the arm, cut off and alone, spinning through the air, then the crippling nausea sweeping over him, doubling him over, and everyone dead, or dying.

And then the blackness took him again, snuffing out the terror.

Much later, the crushing weight on his chest woke him again. He shook his head and opened his eyes. There was light but no detail. He groped for awareness. He flexed his hands. They still moved. With much more effort than he would have believed necessary, he managed to bring one toward his face, and he felt another hand. A cold one, dead.

The realization jolted him awake. He grunted, pushing at the body lying on top of him, and as he did so things focused at last: he was looking into the eyes of a man he had shot. The eyes were open. A pretty blue, he thought, but lifeless, unseeing. He stared at them dully, barely comprehending. He knew he had done it, but for now that was all.

Head racked with pain, stomach heaving and queasy, he made a superhuman effort this time and pushed the body off onto the rocks. Winded, he sat up and looked around. At his feet lay a camel, its leg horribly broken. Next to it was a huge double-edged sword and a blood-stained knife with a leather-wrapped hilt in the shape of a cross.

He shivered. It was either dusk or dawn. He couldn't tell yet, for the cold and light could belong to either one. The chill had settled deep into his marrow. He wiped his face with his sleeve. His mouth tasted vile. Swallowing didn't help. His tongue was swollen, mouth dry, and no saliva would come. He looked down at the front of his flannel shirt. It had turned from gray to dark reddish black, dyed in blood. Another man's blood.

Weakly he stood. He stretched, then wrapped his arms around himself and squeezed for warmth. He had no idea where he was. He could see only sky and dark rocks that towered in the distance. He wondered how long he'd been unconscious. He bent over the body to take the Targui's cloak. The man's clothing was caked with dried blood. He tried not to look at the ragged, burnt hole in the cloth as he worked. The body was rigid, like a heavy wooden marionette, and removing the cloak was difficult. Paul's pistol fell out from among the folds and clattered to the ground, startling him. He sat down again, dizzy from the exertion.

Another noise made him look up. From atop a high rock a lone raven, big and sleek, gave him a baleful black stare. Paul was delaying its meal. He picked up a pebble and threw it. The bird took off, cawing angrily.

He closed his eyes and tried to gather himself, to think. It was all still jumbled, but pieces of it were coming back to him. *Tadjenout!* The massacre, the chase. He shivered again.

The hammering in his head began to subside. He needed water. Picking his way carefully over the corpse and the camel, he made his way to the Targui's gear. He found a goatskin water bag. Eagerly he pulled the leather stop and took a long drink, too quickly, so that the water spilled down his chin and onto the ground. The water was brackish, but to his drought tasted cold and perfect. He rinsed his mouth and spat.

There was a soft leather bag, drawn tight at the neck. He opened it and found dates, flour, salt, sugar, tea, and a small brass bowl. Ravenous, he stuffed a handful of dates into his mouth, chewing greedily, spitting out the pits, then had another, and another, washing them down with more water.

He knew he must get moving. He slung the two bags over his shoulder and recovered his pistol. He took the Targui's sword and dagger as well. He wiped the knife on his pant leg and shoved it in his belt. He started to leave but then stopped suddenly, arrested by a flush of shame. He turned around.

In his life he had never hurt another human being, yet had just finished stealing food, water, and cloak from a man he had shot dead. He didn't know how he was supposed to feel, but imagined it should be different than this: no sorrow, no tears. He had killed and was leaving, finished. It might have been his body lying there now. The Targui would have stripped and mutilated it and left, indifferent. He knew he was no Targui, yet standing there so cold, so unmoved, was wrong. The death at his feet ruined the easy justifications.

Face flushed, he dropped to his knees and leaned forward to draw the man's veil over the open eyes. He bowed his head and shut his eyes.

Our Father, who art in heaven. . . .

No! He couldn't do it. The prayer died on his lips as his rage boiled inside.

Not after Tadjenout.

Oh sweet Jesus, what the Tuareg have done!

Remy! The colonel and Masson! Dennery! Dead, all dead! I will not pray for this animal.

He flicked back the veil to expose the face. *Let the crows know the face of evil before they dine.*

He took the cloak from his shoulders and dropped it. He would not wear the enemy's clothing.

I am at war.

He collected the food and water, and started out. It was dawn after all. The sun was up into a perfect, clear blue sky, rising over a distant peak, a great jagged monolith visible up and past one of the valleys. Like the other mountains it was a fantasy sculpted from a dream—all the Hoggar peaks were weird and playful, storybook shapes, distant castles and spires and heads in profile, mountains like none other, unearthly and mysterious. A home for dragons and fairies.

A home for death.

He remembered now. The big mountain would be Serkout. They had passed in its shadow that last day, and Floop—his mind seized on the thought desperately. He looked around in a panic. He'd completely forgotten the dog. He'd left him in the bag.

"Floop!" Nothing, nothing but his voice coming back to him from the mountains, alone. "Floop!"

He sat down and the tears came at last, washing over him in great waves of grief. His insides knotted in agony and he cried until it hurt. After a time he shook himself out of his wretched reverie, the streaks on his cheeks where the tears had dried like tight scars, pulling at his face as he squinted into the day.

He embarrassed himself with his tears. He knew he had to get moving, or die like a grieving fool. The sun had climbed higher. The chill he'd felt earlier had disappeared. It would be a hot day. Not blistering, for it was only February—or was it March now? He couldn't remember.

I will kill them all.

He looked around, starting at the giant Serkout, letting his gaze drift slowly along the horizon, stopping at each peak, each escarpment, each formation, hoping that one of the wild, weird shapes might look familiar. There was nothing, nothing at all. His eyes came to rest again on Serkout.

Is Dianous looking at that mountain? Or is he dead too?

No. He survived. He's in charge now, with the colonel and the captain dead.

What would he do?

Paul kicked a rock absently.

You know what he'd do. Chase the bastards.

Insanity! Outnumbered two to one.

So what? Got to pay them back.

Don't worry about revenge yet. Survive now. Revenge later.

Fight now! What else for a soldier?

Run, that's what. Run north. Run like hell.

Dianous wouldn't run. Would you?

Hell no. Hell yes. I don't know. The Tuareg probably attacked in two places. They're probably all dead now anyway.

Dianous? Not dead! On the way to Wargla. Get moving. Catch up.

Which way is Wargla?

Don't know. North.

Don't know much. Never paid attention. None of these mountains looks familiar. Why didn't you pay attention?

Because there was always a guide to do that for you. No need to pay attention.

How could they make you an officer when you don't pay attention? Things don't come to you like they're supposed to come to officers. Remy knew you were a fraud.

Ah, Remy.

Doesn't matter anyway. No compass or rifle or camel. You can't catch them on foot. Officers die just as dead as enlisted men.

He shuddered. The sun was getting warm on his back. There was only infinite emptiness, and silence.

I'm afraid.

Face the fear. It will pass.

I'm going to die.

Stop it! Whining bastard! North! Amguid, then Wargla! North to water. North to life.

What if they're still nearby, chasing the Tuareg? Go north and you'll miss them. Die lost somewhere, alone.

Going to die anyway. Always lost.

Better getting lost going north than south. Better getting out of here.

And almost before he had finished playing it out in his mind, almost without realizing it, he was walking, his pace growing readily longer, stronger, propelled by intense purpose and terrible fear.

I am lost. Afraid. I don't want to die.

He quickened his pace still more, legs pumping fast, ever faster, pursued by the demons in his mind. He shut it all out. No time for theories, no time to mourn Remy, no time for dogs, no time for fear. There was only the north, and Wargla.

I am at war.

The grim realities of his situation left him blind to the beauty of the country he passed through; the mountains and rocks had become only obstacles to pass. When he did look, they refused to yield even a flicker of recognition. So his course was all his own now. He dedicated his thoughts to speed, to progress, eyes wandering over the myriad routes before him, selecting the ones that would slow him the least. It became a game, his mind judging distances, calculating angles, feet sure, steady, carrying him swiftly over the terrain. Hour after hour he went on, his pace unrelenting, his concentration complete, his body melding with his mind, mind melding with the rocks, rocks melding with his shadow, and his shadow moving north, ever north.

Only as the sun dipped toward the horizon did he feel the fatigue and stop to rest. He set down the food and water and fairly sagged to a sitting position. He munched on a handful of dates as he pondered an

unfamiliar problem: what he was going to do with the
flour. He'd never cooked a meal in his life. It was whole
flour, flecked with what appeared to be insect parts, but
grainy and rich. All he knew was that one made bread
and cakes from it. For that, he'd need heat, and for that,
he'd need wood. There'd been lone trees scattered along
his route that day, but where he'd stopped there was no
vegetation at all. He was sitting on a bed of sand next to
a large black rock that still felt warm from the sun. He
wondered whether it might be hot enough to make
something happen with the flour.

He shook some of the flour into the bowl, sprinkling
in water from the goatskin. He added a handful of salt,
and then, thinking that was too much, two of sugar. He
started mixing with the fingers of one hand. It didn't go
well. One part was sticky, another lumpy, another dry,
all of it hard to work, the whole of it refusing to accept
its parts. Globs stuck to his fingers, which, no matter
how he manipulated them, couldn't get the flour involved that was still dry and powdered. Finally he gave
up on a one-handed effort and plunged in with the
other, clasping them together, squeezing, kneading,
rubbing.

He realized that he'd used too much water. The paste
was getting everywhere. It seemed to creep up his arms
as he worked. He tried to get it into the bowl, but much
of it stuck to his hands. He forced it down off his palms
and the back of his hands, then squeezed it down off
each finger, one at a time, shaking them at the end to
dislodge the blob at the bottom. When he had gotten all
of it off that he could, he stared at his hands. They were
still coated. Not daring to waste anything, he started
licking, which was difficult because a lot of the flour
had already dried hard as a rock, and clung to the hairs
on the back of his hands. In disgust he resorted to his
pants.

He set the blob on the warm rock, removed his shirt
and covered it carefully, and waited for something to
happen. After a time he poked at it. It wasn't doing
anything. His finger left a hole. *Not much of a cake,* he
thought. He gave it half an hour, and poked again. He

figured it was as ready as it was going to get. He picked it up, noting with satisfaction that at least it didn't stick to anything. The outside was hard, the inside gooey. He hadn't gotten it all mixed properly and encountered clumps of sugar, or of salt. Somehow the whole thing had gotten full of sand, which crunched in his teeth. Gamely he devoured it all, noting with satisfaction that it was the best meal he'd ever cooked.

He looked at Serkout through the dusk. It had receded during the day's march, but not nearly enough. Venus was already bright above the horizon. Above it, a few degrees to the east, there was a crescent moon that would give him enough light to walk a few more hours.

He loaded his food and water and set out. He was glad to be moving again, to shake off the chill that began at the instant of sunset. His progress was much slower in the twilight. Mindful of the fate of the Targui's camel, he picked his way carefully over the terrain, stepping cautiously, not always certain whether the shapes in front of him were something solid or just deep shadows. He kept Venus behind him, to his left, using it until the night grew darker, when he could more accurately use the stars. As he glanced at the dazzling planet, his eye took in the shapes of the rocks on the horizon, their forms beginning to melt into the deep purple sky.

Stopping at the site where Paul had made bread, a Targui dismounted and examined the ground, seeing traces everywhere of the Frenchman's passage. Satisfied that he was on the right track, he mounted again and prompted his mehari to its feet. The Targui felt no chill, his shesh and robe and the camel beneath him keeping him warm. He was quite comfortable, his feet resting on the camel's neck. He could go all night if necessary. *"Bok bok."* The sound carried little farther than the camel's ears. The animal turned obediently to the nudge of the rider's foot, to take them north.

PAUL WALKED ON FOR TWO HOURS. THE WIND BE-gan an hour after dark, a strong, unwelcome visitor from the east, noisy and cold. The moon was not yet big enough in its cycle to light the desert. He reckoned he had made five or six kilometers—not bad for a night march in difficult terrain, he thought, but negligible in the vastness he needed to cover. As the moon dipped toward the horizon, he decided to find a place to spend the night, before the moon disappeared altogether and left him in blackness.

He found a large boulder, hollowed out on one side, nestled in a bed of sand and pebbles. He set down his load of food and water and collapsed onto the ground, using the bag for a pillow, his eyes closing in fatigue. Within ten minutes he knew that no sleep would come. The wind was too cold, blowing around the edges of the boulder. He had only the clothes on his back for warmth and no brush for a fire. He would have to make a shelter.

In the waning moonlight he gathered flat rocks, stacking them on top of each other in a semicircle stretching out from the hollow. He knew better than to pick up rocks casually, better than to stick his hands underneath to lift them, without moving them first with his boot. El Madani had warned him to check, always to check. Fatigue and the dark and his hurry for warmth made him careless. He was nearly done, his wind wall knee high. He was putting up the last row, the rocks making a sharp hollow sound as he piled them in their arc, trying to fit them together as tightly as their shapes permitted, so that no wind would get through.

The big scorpion was sluggish, but not immobile in the night air. It reacted instinctively to the intrusion, its tail full of lightning, and striking just as quickly—around, forward, and up, until it found the warm flesh of danger and planted its poison. It withdrew and scurried backward, more slowly than it would have during the day, but still quick, and retreated into the protection of another rock.

Paul felt the fire and knew instantly what it was, the

burning searing its way up his hand and wrist and into his arm, the realization of his stupidity flashing to his brain. He jumped back with a loud cry, clutching his hand to his stomach and bending over it, praying that it hadn't really happened. But it had, the fire paralyzing his hand. He made his way into his shelter and dropped heavily onto the bed of sand, not feeling his head strike the rock; not feeling, for the moment, the cold on its wings of wind, flying through his wall as though it didn't exist. He felt nothing but the fire.

The poison worked quickly. He huddled on his side in the sand, drawing his knees up to his chest in a fetal position, cradling his hand. The wind howled like another living presence in the little space, intrusive and abrasive and rude, and seemed to intensify his agony. He shivered and moaned. His armpit began to swell. He longed for the dead Doctor Guiard, for his medical supplies and help. He cursed himself for abandoning the Targui's cloak, an act of foolish anger. He tried to concentrate through his torment, to force his mind into the refuge of warmer, gentler surroundings: anything, anywhere, to get away. But his mind refused. Wild fire and bitter cold slammed the door of his escape.

Lying on his side became unbearable. He tried sitting up and rocking, his legs folded underneath. He concentrated on the motion, finding comfort in its sway, slowly at first until that stopped working, then faster, the break in rhythm a respite, until faster didn't work either, then slowing once again, lengthening the motions, exaggerating them, until his face touched the rock wall before him. When that stopped working he tried his side once more, writhing slowly in the sand, as if to dig himself a grave and be gone.

He talked to himself, finding comfort in the sound of his voice.

"*Damn it's cold, oh God, God help me. DeVries, you are a fool, a stupid insane fool, try flexing the arm it will help, Oh Jesus, holy Mother Mary that's worse please make it go away, don't let me freeze to death Father just stop it and make this night be over, please God, let it be day, make it stop hurting, please make me warm, Hail Mary, full of grace, the Lord is with thee. . . ."*

His teeth clenched until he thought they'd break. He rambled through them, his voice a whimper in the shrieking wind.

Fever came with sweat that evaporated in the wind and deepened the chill. It raged inside him, bringing convulsive shivers. He opened his eyes and saw the north sky, watching the Dipper creep in its slow arc to empty itself over the horizon. It had never moved more slowly. He despaired for the night's end, for the handle seemed to have stopped moving altogether, its contents frozen.

He screamed, a rough and ragged scream that built from the belly and rose through his chest. Everything was swollen, useless, his hand puffed up until the skin stretched red and shiny and he thought it would burst. Just breathing was torture, but the worst of it was the shivering, which seemed to exaggerate itself down his arm into his hand.

I'm going to die. I want to die. Please God let me die.

The screams came and went, tapering off into sobs, angry bitter choked sobs, his throat thick. His back ached from his twisted posture. His legs cramped. He reveled in the sensation because it was a different pain and kept his mind off the other, and he almost laughed with relief. But then the cycle of pain and fever and cold began again, violent eruptions shaking his entire body, beginning deep inside, working outward, traveling down his arm once again, to be amplified in his hand.

Outraged, desperate, sweat dripping from his brow, salt stinging his eyes, he smashed his swollen hand against the rocks, knocking them down, and scourged it in the sand until the sharp pebbles drew blood, and screamed and cried again at the new agony, while the stars still crept too slowly through God's forsaken night.

At last the cycles lost their sharp edges, and he drifted in and out; the fatigue fought and clawed at his brain to take over. His eyes grew heavy. His screams died to soft whimpers, and the stars faded from his sight, his body rocking, rocking into the night, and at last relief washed over him, great waves of blessed relief, and he slept.

T HE WORLD CAME SLOWLY INTO FOCUS. THERE WAS darkness, but he was no longer outside. He started to sit up but fell back again, dizzy. He groaned. His head ached horribly. He opened his eyes and saw a rock ceiling above his head, reflecting the flickering light of a fire. He was warm at last; the cold had gone.

Slowly, it dawned on him. A fire, a cave. He blinked, and shook his head to clear it. Above him he began to make out a figure. *I am not alone.* The shape wavered, as if he were seeing it through a pool of water. Gradually his vision cleared. White cotton, blue robes. A shock raced through his body.

Tuareg!

His hand flew for his pistol. The Targui caught it and held it easily. Paul struggled fiercely to get up.

"Paul, stop it! It is I, Moussa!"

"The hell you say! Get away!" Paul struggled weakly, half-delirious, his body racked with pain.

"I know you, Paul deVries! I thought it was you, from your hair, and I know it now for sure, from your eyes! And you know me!"

"Take away your mask, Devil!" Paul gasped, still trying for his gun.

"It is not a mask! It is I!"

"No!"

"Yes! We found a skull, beneath St. Paul's! We named him Fritz. I hit a Prussian with my slingshot. Here, look, I still have it—and even the knife you gave me, the night I—" Moussa fumbled in his robes, but by then Paul knew it was true.

"Moussa! By God, it *is* you!" Paul was so relieved he wanted to cry. He pulled himself to a sitting position and tried to hug his cousin but gasped in pain when he lifted his arm. Moussa helped him back down. "Careful. You aren't strong enough to be moving yet."

Paul didn't recognize his own hand. It was bruised

and purple, swollen to twice its normal size, the fingers all puffed and shiny like some grotesque balloon. It wouldn't move properly when he willed it. The skin was ragged, scabbed and oozing. Near the wrist there was a cloth bandage stained dark with blood.

"You did more damage to your hand than the scorpion did," Moussa said. "You must have smashed it on the rocks."

"I don't remember."

"The scorpion was quite poisonous. It might have killed you. I had to open up the wound. I put something on it. You'll feel miserable for a few days. You need water and rest. You look horrible." Paul's hair hung in limp strands over his wet forehead, still flushed with fever. Dark circles set his eyes deeply in his haggard, ashen face. Moussa shook his head. "But you look wonderful just the same. It is good to see you. Good to hear French again. *Merde,* how often I've thought of this moment."

"And I."

"I thought you'd have sense enough to outwit a scorpion. They're more stupid than a chicken, you know. You should be embarrassed."

Paul laughed weakly. "I wish it had been a chicken. I'd rather have had a meal than what I got."

"I'm fixing something for you." Moussa moved to the fire and squatted. Paul could see a teapot steaming, and a lizard on a spit, its skin blackened. It smelled delicious. Paul looked at his cousin in wonder.

"I didn't know if you were alive! You never wrote!"

"Of course I did. A dozen times I wrote, a dozen times a dozen. I sent the letters off every time a caravan passed by. I never heard back."

"I never got any of them. I wrote, too." Paul gathered his strength and pulled himself up to a sitting position. He looked around. They were in a large natural sandstone cavern with a domed ceiling. There were paintings on the walls, ancient drawings of antelope and elephants and crocodiles, eerily illuminated by firelight. Stains from the smoke of old fires had obliterated some of them. There was an arch near the fire, a doorway, and beyond it the blackness of night. Gradually Paul saw more detail. Other paintings, brightly colored ones. Trees, a forest. Birds. People had once lived in the cave. There were shelves carved into the walls, and flat stones that had served as benches.

"What is this place? It is remarkable. It must be ancient."

"There are others like it all over the plateau. This used to be—never mind just now. Rest easy. There is tea. We can talk."

Their voices echoed softly off the walls, the words pouring out in torrents to fill the voids. The count's death, the flight of the balloon, the voyage across the sea and the desert, the victory of the Prussians, the Commune, St. Cyr. There was so much to say, such hurry to say it. A sea of words awash in old memories as questions were answered and mysteries solved, and they hurriedly filled the deep places of wonder they had both had over the years. They laughed and remembered and finished each other's sentences and felt all the warm rush of friendship they'd missed for so long. They drank their tea, cup after cup, the hot liquid restoring in Paul a measure of strength, and they ate slices of lizard meat, and the night passed outside the cave as the hours and years flew by.

"Your mother is well?"

"She hasn't changed a bit since you last saw her, except that she thinks of herself as *la comtesse* deVries now. There's no one to tell her otherwise. She spends the deVries money like water and still tries to tell me how to dress in the morning. Busy all the time doing absolutely nothing. She was sure you had all died. Oh, I cannot wait to tell her!"

"I guess she is the countess now, at that. My mother will never go back."

"But what about you? It is yours, you know, the château and the land, and all the money in the world. Still there, waiting for the Count deVries. What my mother hasn't spent, anyway, and God knows she spends quickly. Lord, she wanted *me* to be count, thinking you dead. Can you imagine?"

"Better you than I. I have everything I desire right here. I want for nothing." Moussa shrugged. "Besides, can you see their faces at the Hôtel de Ville if I were to appear like this?" His hand swept over his robes and he laughed. "Do I look like a count? Surely they would call the *gendarmes* on such an apparition."

And with that gesture, it was as if a spell broke. Paul fell silent and looked down into his tea, as the world outside the cave overtook the giddy heights of reunion. He was ashamed, laughing so easily after so much blood had been spilled. He had forgotten himself, becoming Paul instead of Lieutenant deVries.

He looked up at his cousin, his smile now uneasy, uncertain.

"I wonder how you have changed, Moussa, and it is impossible to see. I ask you once again to take off that hideous veil. Why do you hide yourself from me?"

Moussa's hand went absently to the material. "It is almost a part of me now. I wear it always. I don't think about it anymore."

"Well, I do. Please don't wear it in front of me. It makes you—it makes you one of—them."

"I am not comfortable without it."

"I am not comfortable *with* it." Paul studied his cousin, and wondered to whom he was really talking. "*Merde,* Moussa. This is wrong, all wrong! We sit here talking as if nothing had happened out there. Gossip and old times, and all of them dead! Slaughtered. It was horrible, like some *abattoir*. My God, I never saw anything like it. They cut off—" His voice cracked.

"I know, I saw. I got there after it was over. I could do nothing to stop it."

Paul's head began to pound. "I need to know something, Moussa. And I need to know it now."

"Of course. What is it?"

"Are you French or are you Tuareg?"

"I am both. You know that."

"No, not in this. In this you cannot be both."

"I cannot help what I am. I am just Moussa."

"It is not enough! You cannot keep your hands clean

of this by hiding between! Either you are a part of it or you aren't! You must choose."

Moussa sighed. "It isn't that simple."

"And why not? What is complicated in the choice between slaughter and peace? Between honor and dishonor? Or have you become a butcher yourself? Have you come so far from our world? Has this life so destroyed the person I knew?"

"I am not the person you knew, that is true. I have changed. But I am still the son of Henri and Serena. And I am not a butcher. I had nothing to do with Tadjenout. I argued against it."

"So you knew it was coming."

"*No!* They talked about it, but it was one of many choices. I thought—"

"Spare me this! You dodge so well, and serve yourself so smoothly. If you knew it was even a remote possibility and did nothing to stop it then it is the same as if you yourself held a sword!"

"It is so easy for you to say that. You don't understand."

"Then make me understand! Why didn't you stop them?"

"The amenokal sent me away, on other business. I was not here. He ordered me to go. And now I tell you this honestly, because it haunts me: I knew he was sending me away because he feared I might create trouble."

"You knew he was doing that, yet you left? You allowed yourself to be sent away?"

"I didn't believe they would do this. Never! Ahitagel himself told me as I was leaving that this would not happen!"

"Are you so stupid? Don't the Tuareg do this to everyone? I have heard what the Arabs and the Shamba say. What caravan ever passed this way without meeting death or disaster? And I thought they were exaggerating!"

"It is not as simple as that. The Shamba have fought with us for centuries. The caravans are quite safe if they pay to pass through our land—"

"There, you see? You say 'fought with *us*.' You say *'our* land.' You make your choice clear with every word!"

"I am explaining the position of the Tuareg in the desert, Paul. I am not trying to play word games with you. The Hoggar belongs to the Tuareg, as France belongs to the French."

"Do the French massacre those who wish to travel through their land?"

"My last memories of Paris—before they shot my father, anyway—were of French soldiers shooting at Prussian invaders. Or have you forgotten all that? Where is the difference?"

"We are not Prussians, and we did not come to make war!"

"Why *did* you come then, if not to put a railroad through land you do not own? By what right did Flatters ignore the amenokal's letter that told him he was not welcome, to go another way?"

"I don't believe you. No such letter exists."

"Of course it does. I was there when it was written, more than a year ago."

"Then why did the amenokal send us four guides with an offer to lead us through the Hoggar? A man called Attici brought the letter. I heard it read. It was signed by Ahitagel and said we could pass. They led us all right, straight to Tadjenout! Do you expect me to believe the letter was a forgery? Or that this was all a mistake?"

Moussa was caught short at that. He hadn't known.

Paul sneered at his silence. "I thought so. Treachery is how you deal, all of your kind."

"I didn't know, Paul. You have to believe me."

"I have to believe nothing other than what I see before me. I see a man dressed like a savage, hiding from the truth behind a veil. I see a man who has made his decision."

"I have decided nothing. I have not been given the chance."

"I give you that chance now, to make a choice you must make. I want your help. To find the survivors and help them. And then to help me track down those responsible for the butchery, so that they can be repaid in kind."

Moussa groaned inside. "I cannot help you kill them, Paul. I will help you find your men. I will find you camels. I will lead you out of here, back to Wargla. I will do all that, and you will need my help or you will die. No man can make that journey without camels, and yours have all been taken."

"It isn't enough."

Moussa was heartsick. When he spoke his voice was low. "What was done to the expedition was wrong. But I did not help the Tuareg raise arms against you. I will not help you raise arms against them."

"Then you have chosen against me, Moussa," Paul said. "God in heaven. *Moussa. Moussa.* Did I never hear that name until now? Do you remember what Sister Godrick said about it? A godless name, I think she said. A heathen name. And you always insisted on keeping it! Always chose Moussa over Michel. By God, maybe Sister Godrick *did* know what she was saying. She knew what was in your veins, only we never—*I* never—believed her until now."

Moussa shook his head sadly. "Don't say this to me, Paul. I have done nothing to earn your hatred."

Paul closed his eyes and the bloody demons of Tadjenout roared up before him. "You son of a bitch! What do you think you've earned?" In a rage he struggled to his feet, drawing the pistol from his belt. He took short unsteady steps toward Moussa, holding the pistol so close to his face that Moussa could smell the oil on the barrel. He flinched, feeling instinctively for the dagger hidden in his sleeve, but stopped short. He would never use it against Paul. He wondered if that was how death would come, at the hand of his cousin.

Paul wavered, his body fevered and weak, his chest heaving as he tried to still the confusion and the pain racing in his brain. Finally he slumped to a sitting position. His hand trembled, the gunbarrel still pointing at his cousin's head. He didn't know what to do. He only knew that he could not stay where he was. He lowered his gun.

"I am sorry you have forgotten who you are, that you have somehow lost your soul. You think you have not made a choice. But not to choose is to choose. If you will not help France, then you have joined with those who have declared war on her. If you are with . . . *them* . . . when the time comes for justice, I will not be responsible for what happens, Moussa."

Paul felt old and heartsick. He pulled himself slowly to his feet. He found his bag and half-walked, half-stumbled to the opening of the cave.

"You shouldn't go yet," Moussa said. "You're still too weak. The sun will act with the poison. You won't last the day."

Paul turned. "Go to hell."

"Take my camel, then. And at least let me give you this," Moussa said, reaching for a bag. "You'll need it for—"

"I want nothing from you but what I've asked. If you cannot give that, then stay out of it. If you haven't the spine to choose, then I don't want to see you again. Don't test my goodwill, Moussa. Don't test *my* blood. It is French, every drop. I am an officer in my country's army. I have a duty. I will fulfill it, if it means I have to kill you to do it."

For a long sad moment they held each other's eyes.

Without another word, Paul turned and disappeared into the dawn.

THE SUN WAS HIGH AND HOT AND BURNED IN HIS skull. He lay still in the heat, without shade, waiting for his mind to clear. It wouldn't. It seemed lost in fog, as if he were drunk. He sat up and looked at his knees. Bloody. Must have fallen again.

He didn't feel like eating but drank insatiably from the goatskin, not caring if he ran out. He couldn't stop. He got to his feet for the tenth time, or perhaps it was the twentieth. He couldn't be sure. Each motion was long and awkward and drawn out. The light was blinding and made his head hurt worse. He scanned the horizon. He'd never seen anything so vast or desolate. The sky was empty, even of clouds. The rocks were barren, even of wind. No trees, no grasses, no life of any kind. He felt as vulnerable before the emptiness as a leaf before a hurricane. The prickle of fear returned, the same one that touched him on the mountain, but it was dulled by the fever.

He tried to remember where he'd been. He tried to remember where he was going. He tried to remember what course of action he'd decided upon yesterday. Was it yesterday? Go east, to pick up the trail of the caravan? West? It was so hard to think. . . . North? He'd come from the north, he knew that much. But everything looked familiar, and then nothing did. He was tired, so tired. He just wanted to sleep.

He saw a speck in the sky and shaded his eyes with his hand. It was a bird of some kind, a hawk perhaps, soaring high and easily to the north. He couldn't tell what it was, but it made him remember. North. That was it, north.

He labored to pick up the food and water. He couldn't carry any weight on his right side, so he put the bags over his left shoulder. Each step hurt, jarring his arm and hand. The glands were swollen in his armpits, neck, and groin. It hurt to swallow, it hurt to walk, and the leather straps cut into his shoulder. He forced himself forward, one foot after the other, yesterday's speed impossible, the rock games forgotten. He dragged through patches of sand in the wadis and twisted his ankles on the stones. Each time he tripped he gasped in pain. Each time he got up more slowly than the last.

The sun rose higher into a windless, hot day. Sometimes its warmth felt good, helping against the chills of fever, warming his back and neck. But then the chills left him and he became unbearably hot, his feet baking on the bed of black rock. Whenever his shirt touched his back or chest it came away soaking, only to be sucked dry by the desert air. He stopped frequently to rest, gulping at the water that would soon be gone.

In the afternoon he left the mountains of the Hoggar

behind him and entered the hilly part of the Amadror. His fever raged through the long hot hours, further dulling his senses. At first he had been able to focus on rocks, on his feet, on the gravel, on rare blades of grass. But there came a time when he couldn't do that anymore, when he couldn't think at all; the great shimmering plain through which he walked was as dead as his mind. He kept walking, walking north, one foot before the other, time and again. He went up the long sides of the hills, his cloudy eyes seeing nothing but the next one, and at the top of that, yet another.

Once he thought he saw tracks, lots of them, but his eyes weren't working right, and they were hard to make out. He got down on his knees and looked, his nose close to the ground, and reached out with his left hand to touch one. The track was black and shiny and burned his fingers. The track was a pebble. He picked it up and threw it, barely feeling the pain. Disgusted, he got up and walked on.

His sense of time grew hazy edges and disappeared. He wasn't sure when he ought to stop and drink, so he did it whenever he felt like it, sitting down and wrestling with the stopper and feeling the hot water empty into his scorched body, where it steamed off as quickly as it went in. During one of the stops he lost the water bag. He set it down beside him while he rested, and when he got up to go he simply left it there. He was trying to take the stopper out of the food bag before he realized what it was. The food bag didn't have a stopper. His hand felt the dates inside and no trace of water. He couldn't imagine what he'd done with it. He felt his pockets, looked under his feet, and over the top of the hill, and wandered in circles. He tried to whistle for it, as though it might come, tail wagging, only his mouth was so dry the whistle wouldn't come. Oh well, he shrugged, north, north, he had to move north. Maybe the bag would follow later.

He started walking again but then stopped. Wandering in circles had gotten things all confused. He couldn't remember which way his shadow was supposed to go. Left to right? Or was it right to left? He struggled with the problem. He stared at the sun, then turned to look at his shadow, trying to make out what time it might be.

And then he knew what to do. He'd go ask Remy. Remy would know. He was the smartest man he'd ever met. Remy knew everything. Wobbly but pleased with himself, Paul started walking toward the sun.

CHAPTER 26

BELKASEM BEN ZEBLA WAS A BUTCHER BY TRADE. He was an ugly ball of a man, corpulent and hairy with a round fleshy face that jiggled when he walked. His arms were huge, with biceps as big as most men's legs. His beard and mustache were as ragged as his manner. His foul temper had been distilled with rum, his face scarred in a thousand brawls.

The sun was nearly down but it was still hellishly hot. Belkasem's mood was dark. Sheer lunacy, the lieutenant posting him out on the flank when there were plenty of good *tirailleurs* in the column. It was their business to do this, not his. He'd signed up to help with the cooking and the camels because the pay was nearly double what he could make in the souks of Wargla. Now there was nothing to cook, no camels to tend, and riflemen with nothing to do. Worse, they made him carry the colonel's ceremonial sword. It wasn't half the tool his cleaver was. It was too heavy and lacked a proper edge. He'd not even be able to trim camel meat with it, much less use it to take off the head of one of those blue devils. He carried it in his belt, keeping watch for a sharpening stone.

He had his eyes to the ground when he hesitated. Something caught his eye, a dark shape at the base of a hill. Something out of place. His eyesight was poor, it was true, but in this part of the desert dark shapes meant trouble. He wasn't going to let it get much closer. He took the carbine off his neck where he'd been resting his hands on it like a yoke. He raised it and narrowed his eyes. He waited nervously, wondering if he should shout to the column. Instead he kept his rifle high and walked cautiously forward, squinting harder to see better.

THE MEN SQUATTED AROUND SIX SMALL campfires, warming tiny portions of dried meat and rice over the wood they'd collected and carried during the day. Conversation was subdued around the fires, the mood grim. El Madani sat before one of them, absently scratching Floop behind the ears. The dog was lying listlessly on his stomach, head between his paws, barely opening his eyes at movements around the fire. The men chewed the tough meat slowly, trying to draw out the flavor as long as possible. El Madani slipped a piece to Floop. The dog hadn't been hunting and was surely starving. Floop nosed at it indifferently.

A group of men from another fire, finished with their portions, came over to join those around Madani's fire. From the darkness one of them spoke.

"Leftovers? Anyone got leftovers?" It was Belkasem the butcher.

"Back at Tadjenout," someone said. "Take your lard ass back there and bring us all some." Belkasem glared at him. The group around the fire opened up to let them in. They would talk awhile and then try to sleep for three hours, and march again before dawn.

Suddenly Floop's head jerked up. El Madani felt it and looked at the dog. Floop whined as if unsure, his head cocked, tail moving slowly. He got up and trotted over to the newcomers, sniffing. Then he barked excitedly, his nose at Belkasem's feet, poking around under the butcher's robes. Belkasem kicked savagely at him, but Floop bounded back undeterred, tail cranking wildly, his barking more excited. The butcher kicked again. The mutt was all over him, and the others were laughing. Face flushed, Belkasem reached for a rock.

"*Where did you get those boots?*" Belkasem dropped his rock and looked up. El Madani towered above him, his wizened old face drawn tight in anger. The chatter around the fire died.

"Answer me."

Sweating, Belkasem looked at the men around him for support. All eyes were on his boots. Like them, he had never worn anything but sandals. A deadly quiet settled over them. Jowls quaking, Belkasem looked up at El Madani and saw the fire in his eyes.

"They . . . they're mine," he stammered weakly. "I . . . I've had them—"

"Liar!" El Madani roared, his pistol in Belkasem's face, the cold barrel stabbing at the fleshy cheek.

"I found them!" said the butcher quickly, shrinking back in terror. "As Allah is my witness, I found them today! Someone left them on the trail! It is true, I swear it!"

"What's the meaning of this?" Lieutenant Dianous stepped quickly through the ring of men and saw the pistol. "Madani, what's going on?"

"Belkasem's boots, Lieutenant. He has a new pair. I think they belong to Lieutenant deVries." Floop was sure of it, sniffing and pawing at them.

Dianous looked at the boots, then at the dog, and finally at Belkasem's face, now quivering with fear. His voice was deathly quiet. "You have precisely thirty seconds to explain yourself, Belkasem. If what you say isn't satisfactory, I shall direct El Madani to interview you privately. Away from camp."

RACING THROUGH THE MOONLIGHT, NOSE TO THE ground and barking loudly, Floop found him first. The others followed more slowly. El Madani led the way. Behind him, a barefoot Belkasem stepped painfully through the sharp rocks, carrying the boots. Hakeem's face was lit with excitement as he walked alongside Sergeant Pobeguin, a tough veteran from Brittany. Two *tirailleurs* brought up the rear. They heard the dog's pitch change. Hakeem, the youngest, broke away from the group, running up and over a hill.

"He's here!" he cried. "Here, here! The patron is alive!"

El Madani glared at Belkasem with a look of rage

and relief. The butcher saw only the rage. He held up his hands, imploring, holding the boots like a shield. "I swear I thought he was dead. I swear it! Praise be to Allah, the lieutenant lives!" Belkasem was near tears, his voice shaking. El Madani hurried ahead.

Paul was lying on his back, head cradled in Hakeem's lap. The boy was giving him water, mumbling, "*Ça va, Patron, ça va, ça va*," and trying to swat Floop away. The dog was beside himself, all tongue, paws, and tail. Next to Paul's feet lay Belkasem's sandals. The food bag had spilled, leaving dates and flour everywhere.

El Madani knelt by Paul's side. Paul coughed weakly. "*Hamdullilah*," Madani whispered. The *tirailleur* touched Paul's face. "He's burning with fever." He stripped off his turban and soaked the cotton with water, then draped it over Paul's head. He saw Floop licking Paul's hand. He lifted it and carefully unwound the bandage. "*Agrab*," he muttered.

Belkasem arrived, puffing. "*Hamdullilah*," he said when he saw Paul. "It is true, he is back from the dead! A miracle!" The others stared at him. He avoided their eyes.

They picked Paul up and set him onto a blanket. Hakeem spread another one over him, and the six of them picked up the makeshift litter by the edges and hurried into the night, Floop barking at their heels.

The men at camp had expected to see a burial detail. When they saw the group returning with Paul in the blanket they raised a jubilant cheer. It was the first good omen they'd had in the four days since the massacre. One of their number had been snatched from Tuareg death, and they all felt the triumph. A lean-to was hastily constructed with blankets and rifles. With the doctor's supplies and Hakeem's help El Madani set about attending to Paul. In the next few hours Lieutenant Dianous stopped by frequently, his eyebrows raised in question. After a time El Madani, looking stark naked without his turban, his silver and black hair shining in the moonlight, was able to look at him and smile. "*Ça va, Lieutenant*," he said. "*Il va vivre.*"

Paul slept through the night, sometimes dead to the world, other times drifting, wonderfully warm and comfortable, feeling Floop's body next to him or dimly seeing El Madani, giving him a cup of something. He swallowed its contents gratefully and slept again.

They carried him on the next day's march, the men taking turns at the blanket, ignoring the heat and shading his head from the sun. Paul slept the entire time, awakening only to eat the broth Hakeem brought, and to drink. Outcast and scowling, Belkasem walked at the end of the column, his old sandals showing under his robes as he walked. He still carried the colonel's sword, but Lieutenant Dianous had taken his rifle. Had he stolen from a fellow Muslim and not been in the service of the French, his hand would have been forfeit as well. "You will be dealt with in Wargla," Dianous told him.

They marched after dark until they lost the moon and had to stop. Fires were started with the last of the wood, and the meals began cooking. Paul got up and joined the officers and El Madani at their fire, a blanket wrapped around his shoulders to keep out the cold. He looked worse than he felt.

"The dead man walks," said Dianous. Paul sat down and took a cup of tea and a small plate of food. The night was cold and clear. A steady breeze blew from the plain, fanning the fire.

"What happened back there, at base camp?" Paul asked. He nodded toward the mountains. "I never thought I'd see you again."

"They won," El Madani shrugged. "Our effort was for nothing. The camels bolted about the same time you did. They got them all. And then"—there was an edge to his voice, as if he wanted to say something but didn't—"and then we just . . . waited at base camp all the rest of that day. Didn't even try to get them back until that night. By then it was too late."

Dianous stiffened, but his eyes didn't leave the fire. "I expected another attack. It never came."

"When we finally tried we lost twelve more men. It was another slaughter. Of ninety-eight men we have fifty-three left. Fifty-four—you came back from the dead." El Madani thought of something lighter. "Floop was the only one to escape. He must have found himself in their camp and decided to leave. I imagine he got out with some of their food." He smiled. "More than that, *w'allahi*. He coughed up blue thread for a day."

"We have four or five wounded," Dianous said. "They can all still walk. We have water, enough until we arrive at Temassint the day after tomorrow." It was the last well the caravan had stopped at on the way south. "We have food for two or three days, and then it's done."

Paul thought of the small helping of rice and dried meat he'd just eaten, and of the mountain of provisions he'd assembled in Wargla. He felt guilty for eating at all. Floop was crunching contentedly on the bones of some small animal he'd found and didn't notice the shortage.

"We're nearly a thousand kilometers from Wargla," Dianous said. "If we don't get lost, that is. If we can average twenty-five kilometers a day that's forty days. Forty days on foot, without food. I don't know about the water. If we can even find it, we'll have to carry what we need."

"How much water can a man carry?" Paul wondered.

"I don't know, with weapons and the heat. Twenty or thirty liters. Not enough. It doesn't matter anyway. We lost most of our water bags at Tadjenout."

A silence fell over the officers. One could walk the whole of France the longest way, and not travel a thousand kilometers.

"Thank God it isn't summer," Pobeguin said.

El Madani snorted. "You'll think it's summer."

"The only thing we have plenty of is ammunition," Dianous said. "Everyone has a rifle, some more than one. Most have pistols. We haven't seen the Tuareg since Tadjenout. Maybe they're content with their camels and the horses, and will leave us alone."

El Madani grunted. "Don't be such a fool," he said. "They will be content with our blood."

Paul flinched at the obvious disrespect. Yet Dianous

let it pass. El Madani's views of the Tuareg, always expressed openly on the way south, had taken on considerable weight since Tadjenout. Dianous thought too much of the man's experience and cunning to treat him like an enlisted man in any event. The old man was an intimidating presence. If in some perversion of standard military practice competence somehow aligned with rank, it would be General Madani giving the orders, and they all knew it.

"If Madani's right and the Tuareg are nearby we should find them and fight," Paul said. "Take our camels back."

Dianous shook his head. "We'll never find them."

"We missed our chance," El Madani said. "Now they'll find us."

"That's enough, Madani," Dianous snapped.

Pobeguin asked Paul about his own experiences. As best he could remember, he told them everything that had happened since he'd fled from behind the camels. Almost everything. He didn't know how or what to explain about Moussa, so he said nothing, leaving out the cave. He ended his story with the loss of his water. He couldn't remember anything after that.

"*Mais, mon lieutenant,*" Pobeguin said, puzzled. He was a cheerful, hearty man with a full thick beard and lively eyes. "You didn't lose your water. I found your Targui's water bag just next to you. It's the only one like it we have. It was nearly full. The ground was wet around your head. You'd poured the water all over yourself before you passed out." Paul gave him a blank look. El Madani was deep in thought and said nothing of the camel tracks he had seen.

Dianous was puzzled. "The first night you were unconscious under the Targui. The second, you were bitten. The third, we found you. *N'est-ce pas?*" Paul nodded at the summary. "But we didn't find you until the fourth day after Tadjenout," Dianous said. "You lost a night somewhere."

Paul hadn't thought to account for the extra night. He shrugged. "I guess I might have forgotten the harem." He grinned. "They kept me longer than I thought. The women here are crazy for love."

El Madani joined in the laughter, but his mind was on the tracks.

That night as Paul drifted off to sleep, he thought of the water. He had warned Moussa to stay away, and obviously he had not. It changed nothing.

In the morning he not only felt but looked better as well. El Madani was pleased. Paul's hand had returned to nearly its normal size, but the *tirailleur* told him to watch it closely. "It can rot," he said, "like your brains must have already done when you went poking around those rocks in the first place."

Paul laughed sheepishly. Madani studied his face. "May I ask, Lieutenant, where you learned to treat the wound of the *agrab* in such a manner?"

"I don't know. I don't remember what I did, exactly. I must have put something on it."

"That is most interesting," El Madani said. "The only people I know who do it that way are the Tuareg."

"Lucky coincidence, I suppose."

"Amazing, is more like it. From your reaction that was a highly venomous scorpion. Should have killed you. I found a paste in the wound where you had cut it, from a plant called the *effellem*. It is extraordinary you would know to use it, Lieutenant. Even more so that you would have it with you."

Paul shifted uncomfortably. "I told you—there's a lot I don't remember."

Madani nodded. "*Oui, Lieutenant,*" he agreed. "A lot."

THE COLUMN STIRRED TO LIFE IN THE BLACKNESS before the dawn. Sergeant Pobeguin was the first up, checking that the sentries remained alert, making flank assignments and seeing to it that all the food and water was collected. Excess clothes and blankets were abandoned. The men had begun their retreat carrying as much as they could hold, but they had been fresher then, and their eyes for what was important had been bigger then than their resolve after five days of walking. They jettisoned everything they could and still struggled with their loads.

Paul watched them, disturbed. "Only five days. Already they look worn out, and they still have water and food," he said to Dianous. "They don't look in shape to make it another week."

Dianous said nothing. His silence made Paul think wistfully of Remy, whose company he missed terribly.

Paul carried a new rifle, food and water, a blanket, and a robe. He tied everything together and slung it over his good shoulder. He'd lost his broad-brimmed hat that had been specially made in Paris. It had provided excellent protection from the sun, but only Pobeguin and Dianous still had theirs. Paul knelt at one of the abandoned piles of clothing and ripped a shirt into lengths, tying the ends together and wrapping it around his head.

He noticed Sandeau, one of the engineers, struggling to keep up at the rear of the column. He was a frail, slender man, his bony frame lost in the too-big clothes he wore. He had a bookish, kindly face and was well into middle age. His shoulders sagged and his spindly legs wobbled as he fought to control the bags on his back. His face was drawn and pale. A cloud of flies hovered around him, invading his eyes, nose, and mouth. The engineer's hands were occupied with his load, so he was trying to blow them off, blinking and squinting and working his face to get them away with little success. Paul strode up to him and brushed them away.

"Here, let me carry those for you," he said.

Sandeau looked sideways up at the younger, taller man and shook his head. "*Non, merci,*" he said, "you've had a harder time of it than I, Lieutenant. I'll be all right. Just slow, that's all."

Without arguing Paul lifted the water and food bags off Sandeau's shoulders. The man started to protest, but the relief in his eyes was evident as he felt the load lift.

"Bless you, Lieutenant." He sighed. "Just when one thinks he can go no farther, the Lord sees his burden and lightens it." He looked out at the plain and at the long line of men stretching out before them toward the horizon. He brushed at the flies that had returned to plague him. "I'm going to die here." He said it lightly, matter-of-factly, as he might have said, "It's cold this morning."

Paul scoffed. "Nonsense, Sandeau, we're all going to make it back." He thought his own voice sounded hollow as he said it. He hoped Sandeau hadn't noticed.

The engineer only smiled. "Don't worry about it on my account, Lieutenant. I don't mind. Really I don't. I've drawn my bridges and planned my roads. My wife died last year."

He waved his hand as Paul started to say something. "It's why I came along. I've nothing left at home, nothing to keep me. And I'm tired of drawing, actually. I think I liked bridges best. Roads are so boring. You don't ever really think much about a road, except where it might be taking you. But a bridge—ah, now there's a work of art. Something to admire, something solid spanning the impassable." His eyes were animated.

"I did the bridge over the Seine at Rouen. Do you know it?" Paul shook his head. "No matter; it's lovely. The river's wide there. They used ferries before. Pay and wait, wait and pay. Sink and drown, sometimes. But no more. It was my best work, I think. I have a photograph of it at home. Steel and concrete, a perfect design. It's beautiful, free, fast, and won't sink." He limped along, trying to hurry as he talked, but they were dropping farther back from the column.

"My wife thought this railroad idea was just the thing. She read about it in the papers. She was quite sick for a long time, confined to bed, and read a lot. Talked more than ever, which I'd have thought impossible. Talked my ears off at night. She said I ought to show them how a railroad was done. She knew she was going to die. I think she wanted to be sure I had something to do afterward." He was quiet for a moment, remembering. His eyes misted. He waved at the desert. "I didn't understand this place before. Just what she read me. Even without the Tuareg, I've seen what fools they are in Paris. They'll never put a railroad here, Lieutenant, not in two hundred years. Oh, you could build one, all right, but it wouldn't last. The dunes would smother it, and the rains would wash it away. The only things that survive here are things that can adapt. A railroad can't adapt. It's why I'm going to die; I'm afraid I can't, either." He stumbled on a rock. Paul helped steady him.

"Thank you, Lieutenant. Would you care to pray with me?" Paul shook his head. Sandeau shut his eyes and held Paul's arm for guidance as he walked. "Hail, holy queen, mother of mercy, our life, our sweetness, and our hope. To you do we cry, poor banished children of Eve, to you do we send up our sighs, mourning and weeping in this valley of tears. . . ."

The engineer's voice had a pleasing, soothing rhythm. Paul remembered the words. He'd said them many times at St. Paul's. But now he felt as empty as the plain, and no words could fill him up. Sandeau crossed himself and opened his eyes. They were brighter.

"Thank you for your help, Lieutenant. I'll be fine."

"Call out if you need anything." Paul squeezed him on the shoulder and walked ahead. The sun was barely up over the horizon, but already promised a blistering day. Paul knew most of the men he passed, greeting them by name. Most were subdued, their expressions grim. When he passed Belkasem, puffing hard from the strain of walking, their eyes met. The butcher looked away. El Madani had told Paul what the man had done. Paul felt no bitterness, but no particular forgiveness, either. He was glad the man hadn't killed him instead of just stealing the boots.

Within an hour Paul was sagging under the extra weight of Sandeau's bags. He had tried to do too much too quickly. Hakeem saw it and reproached him. "Even camels have enough sense to complain when overloaded. Surely the patron is shrewder than a camel?" Paul laughed and gave up one of the bags. The boy shouldered it effortlessly.

Of all the men in the column, only Hakeem and Pobeguin seemed to treat the situation as if it were an adventure. Their spirits were chronically high. Pobeguin sang as they walked, loud and off key, stopping only when a pebble struck him on the back. He turned and glared at the silent line of Algerians trudging behind him, but then he laughed, and sang even louder. He was a practical man and quickly took over the rationing of food and water. He announced when it was all right to drink, permitting it much less frequently than they would have liked, but occasionally going without himself, to offer an example. The man's energy was boundless. Even when broiling he seemed to bounce when he walked. By noon, his vitality was annoying.

The two French troopers, Brame and Marjolet, stayed close together. Brame was a lanky, good-looking Parisian with a shock of black hair and a slender face. He had been Flatters's much-abused batman. For him, the quiet retreat was a blessed contrast to serving the volatile colonel, and he seemed almost content. His chin showed the first sproutings of a beard. The colonel had insisted he shave, as had Brame's father before him, so the first personal items he abandoned for the return march were his shaving things. Marjolet was a tall, strapping dark-skinned youth from southern France who'd enlisted when his family's vineyards died of disease. He cooked for the French members of the expedition, selected by Flatters for the task in that sacred military tradition of choosing only men who couldn't cook to be cooks. Paul supposed that only he himself would have been a better choice.

Pobeguin's singing eventually died. Those who had listened didn't know whether to feel grateful or not, because in the silence the sun seemed to press in more than ever, the plain shimmering with relentless fire. Weary feet shuffled on endless gravel, making the only noise except for an occasional dry cough or murmured conversation. With no reference points on the horizon, there was no way to mark their progress. It appeared as if they weren't moving, that they were trudging along some massive and cruel treadmill, going nowhere at all.

In the afternoon Dianous called a short rest halt. The men gratefully collapsed on the ground, and Pobeguin let them drink. Men propped blankets over rifles or swords to make shelter. Some tried to sleep but found it impossible. Others sat motionless, staring into the void.

Suddenly one of the sentries approached at a run, raising a distant shout. His figure looked oddly compressed by the distortion of the heat, the light playing tricks with his body. At first he seemed to be running with no legs, and then he was running on air. The effect might have been comical except he was clearly alarmed, waving his arms and yelling. Paul and Dianous ran to meet him. Out of breath and sweating hard, he pointed east.

"*Les Tuareg, Lieutenant,*" he panted.

"El Madani! Pobeguin! Quickly!" The four of them followed the sentry. After a few minutes they came to a fault line where the plain dropped sharply away and then stretched out into the distance. The sentry motioned them down and they crawled to the edge.

Below them, a few hundred meters away, rode a long column of meharistes. Paul drew in his breath. There were nearly two hundred Tuareg, all mounted, riding on a course parallel to their own. He could faintly hear their conversation and laughter.

Dianous studied them through his field glasses. "*Merde,*" he said quietly. He handed the glasses to Paul, who rested on his elbows to stare through them. The long column was well provisioned, equipped with extra pack camels, all fully loaded. A few of the Tuareg carried the Gras rifles they'd captured. As his glasses swept along the column he was overtaken with rage.

The Tuareg had taken six prisoners at Tadjenout. The men were walking in a gap between the ranks of their captors. It was the manner in which they were forced to walk that was so horrible. Paul nearly cried out for them. None of them wore shirts. Even from the distance, their skin showed blistered and raw. Leather hoods had been forced over their heads. Paul could only imagine the agony they caused as they squeezed tightly, blinding them and magnifying the terrible heat.

The first man in the line of prisoners had had a metal ring forced down under his shoulder blade. His back was covered with blood and he was clearly the weakest of them all. Two ropes were attached to the ring. One led to the tail of the camel in front of him, the other back to the second prisoner in line, where it had been tied tightly like a noose, and the rope passed from him to the next, on to the end. Each movement of the camel had a ripple effect down the wretched line. If the lead prisoner couldn't time his motions to coincide with those of the faster camel, the rope pulled at the ring, and he screamed under his hood, lurching forward. The motion would jerk at the nooses around the necks of those who followed, choking them. If one of them stumbled the others fell, and only when the whole group was down would the Targui on the lead camel stop to let them get up.

"God have mercy on them," Paul whispered. He let the field glasses down, thought for a moment, then turned to Dianous. "We've got to take them. We've got to attack."

"Don't be a fool," Dianous said. "They outnumber us four to one. They've got camels. We're on foot. There's nothing we can do except guarantee the prisoners will die."

"They can't have much ammunition. We've got plenty."

"You don't know what they have. We cannot mount a direct attack."

"Then we could do it tonight. Raid their camp, steal some camels, and set the prisoners free."

"And kill some Tuareg," El Madani muttered. Pobeguin grunted in assent.

Dianous shook his head. "They know exactly where we are. They know we're well armed. Do you think they won't have guards posted? Do we just walk into camp, excuse ourselves and simply walk off with everything?" There was scorn, but something more in his voice. Paul couldn't quite make out what it was.

"We could mount an attack from the far side of their camp," Paul insisted. "Divert them, then send in some other men from this side."

Dianous was having none of it. "They'd be expecting

something like that. The prisoners would be dead before you could even find them."

Paul pointed at the tormented line of prisoners staggering below them. "Look at them, for God's sake. They'll die anyway, if we don't try."

Madani agreed. "I think we could do it, sir," he said. "Two hours before dawn. It's worth a try."

Dianous straightened himself up to a sitting position. His eyes narrowed, his temper flaring. "I'm telling you it's stupid," he snapped. "I won't permit it."

Paul sat up beside him, his teeth clenched. "All right, forget the prisoners," he hissed. "That column is going to follow us until we have no more strength. Do you want to fight them in twenty days, where *they* choose, or fight them now, while we still can? It's a hundred degrees. We're on foot and just about out of food. How many days do you think we can do it? How many days do you think Sandeau can make it? We can *ride* back to Wargla on those camels, Dianous. At least we'll have a chance!"

"That will be enough, Lieutenant," Dianous said coldly. He waved at the flat below them. "This isn't the time or the place to attack. It's too flat, too exposed. We will continue marching north until we find a more appropriate location. That's an order, Lieutenant. I have permitted too much discussion already. Now I'm through talking about it. Get back to camp."

" 'A more appropriate location'?" Paul repeated the words incredulously. "What are you talking about? Don't you remember the ride south? It's *all* like this, until Amguid. It won't get any better. For God's sake, man, we've got to do *something!*" Paul had pulled himself up close to Dianous, their faces nearly touching, the anger about to explode.

"Shut up, damn you!" Dianous was seething, his voice icy. "Perhaps you didn't hear my order, Lieutenant. The matter is closed. We will march north. *North!* If you persist in challenging me, I'll have you arrested. Is that clear?"

"Come on, Dianous, surely—" But Dianous waved him silent and raised his voice.

"I said, *is that clear*, Lieutenant?"

For a moment Paul only looked at him, trying to comprehend. Embarrassed, Pobeguin looked away. At last Paul nodded. Dianous stood up and took the field glasses out of his hands.

"Now get back to the column, all of you." He turned and strode off. The others watched him go in silence. Stunned, Paul shook his head.

"It's the heat," Pobeguin said lamely.

"Camel shit," snapped Madani. "It's Tadjenout all over again. The man is a—"

"A what?" Paul asked.

"Nothing. Forget it."

They turned back to look at the Tuareg column. For a long time no one spoke. They watched the prisoners struggle in their torment.

"Maybe we should shoot them now," Paul said. "We could each take two. It would stop the agony for them, anyway."

El Madani laid his hand on Paul's shoulder and shook his head. "It is not for us to take their lives," he said quietly. "If they die at the hands of the Tuareg, *mektoub*. It is written."

Paul bit his lip and stared below. Madani gave him a gentle shake. "Leave it for now. It is for him to command. If we forget that, it is anarchy. We will all die then."

He and Pobeguin rose to go. "Are you coming, Lieutenant?"

"I'll be along after a while." He watched until the Tuareg column became blurred by the distance and heat. The pathetic figures of the prisoners were lost behind the camels. He lay on his stomach, resting his head on his arms. He stared out at the empty plain, trying to make sense of it.

Suddenly Floop ran up and pounced on him, licking wildly through Paul's protests, nuzzling his nose into Paul's armpits until he couldn't ignore him anymore. They wrestled, rolling over and over each other on the gravel. When they were tired they lay back down and rested. The sun was low in the sky when they returned to the column.

There were no fires in camp that night. They'd run out of wood, and had found no camel dung during the day. They ate their portions of rice raw, crunching noisily on the grain. Most of the men turned in early, exhausted, while others sat around talking. The news of the Tuareg and their prisoners had traveled quickly through the ranks, as had word of Dianous's refusal to attack. El Madani tried to quiet the talk, but with only partial success. Paul was standing at the edge of the camp, looking out onto the plain, when one of the *tirailleurs,* Mustafa ben Jardi, approached him. The *tirailleur* was clearly nervous, and spent more than twice the usual time inquiring about the state of things in Paul's life. Normally on the expedition their greetings were short and to the point, but Mustafa took advantage of their solitude to be more circumspect, more Algerian, in his approach.

"*Bonsoir, Lieutenant,*" Mustafa said. "*Comment allez-vous?*"

"*Bien, merci, Mustafa.*"

"Very well? Praise God, after your most terrible trials alone."

"*Oui,* very well. And you?"

"I am very fine tonight, Allah be praised, for it is very beautiful under His sky. Your wonderful dog, Floop, he is in good form?"

"Yes, he is."

"And your father, his health is good?"

"My father has been dead many years."

Mustafa looked truly wounded. "A great tragedy. Yet it is Allah who is enriched with his presence now. But your mother, all is well with her?"

"She is well."

"*Hamdullilah,*" Mustafa said. "May she live long and well, in Allah's beneficence. And your brothers, they too are well?"

"I haven't any."

"Ah, a pity, truly. All men should be blessed with

brothers. Surely your sisters are plentiful, and are well with their children and husbands?"

"I haven't any sisters, either," Paul said, hoping the response would bring the interminable politeness to an end. Once Hakeem, seeing his impatience with the custom, had advised him to simply say, "My family and relatives all died of the plague ten years ago," thus shortening the formalities.

"Your wife is fine, I pray?"

"I have no wife, and no children, either."

"That is indeed too bad, Lieutenant, that the world does not yet know the produce of your excellent line." Mustafa shook his head sadly. "A man such as yourself, to be unmarried, not to leave the world his offspring. . . ." He reflected a moment on the tragedy. "I have heard the president of France is a brave and wise man," he said. "I hope he is well."

Paul murmured a vague assent.

"And his wife—"

Paul could take no more. "There is something on your mind, Mustafa?"

The man lowered his eyes to the ground. "*Oui, mon lieutenant.* If you will permit me to speak frankly." He looked around, as though someone might be listening.

"Of course."

"We have heard about the prisoners with the Tuareg."

"Yes."

"We think that the *mokkadem* is among them. He was at the well. No one saw his body afterward. Without him we have no one to lead us in prayer."

Paul nodded. "He may have been with them," he said. "I couldn't tell. They all wore . . . hoods."

"*Oui,* Lieutenant, that is my point. If he is dead, *mektoub,* but if he is among them and being treated in this manner by the godless sons of camel turds the Tuareg, it is infamy that must be avenged. We cannot leave him in their hands."

"And what do you want?"

"Well," he said, lowering his voice, "we have heard that Lieutenant Dianous has refused to attack the

Tuareg." He cleared his throat. "And that you, well, that you felt differently." Paul fought to control his anger. The sentry had talked. "We want you to know that we are willing to go with you, to fight like men. We wish to take the prisoners back."

Paul looked at him. "Who is 'we,' Mustafa?"

"There are twenty-five or thirty others who feel as I do. Lieutenant Dianous would not attack after the massacre. He will not attack now. He will not attack tomorrow. He is—how should I say it?—too apprehensive. We are ready to obey your commands. We can leave tonight."

Paul didn't want to alienate the man, but he was growing uncomfortable with the way the conversation was heading. "I understand," he said at last, "but for the moment there is nothing I can do. Lieutenant Dianous is right. No attack is practical just now."

Mustafa eyed him for a moment, a skeptical look on his face. "But we heard that you—"

"I don't care what you heard, Mustafa. It was untrue. I agree with the lieutenant. We shall have the prisoners back. We shall avenge the *mokkadem*. But we must wait. There is no other way."

Mustafa clearly didn't believe him, but he was not leading a mutiny, simply making an inquiry. He knew of nothing more to say. "Very well, Lieutenant," he said, leaving, "but if you change your mind, you must please to let me know."

After the others had gone to bed Paul tried to raise the subject once again with Dianous, who abruptly got up and stalked off.

Paul's sleep was troubled, his mind in turmoil. First El Madani, then Mustafa had subtly or openly accused Dianous of failure to act at Tadjenout. Of—cowardice. But Paul hadn't been there and couldn't make a judgment. Yet he *had* been there a few hours ago.

He found no answers that night.

BY WHAT RIGHT HAVE YOU TAKEN THIS COURSE with the French?"

Moussa thundered out the words. He had ridden hard into the camp of the Ihaggaren, riding his mehari straight through the swarms of Tuareg until he stood over the central fire of the camp. He looked down upon Attici, who was sitting at the fire. Next to him sat Mahdi and a man Moussa did not know. Attici looked up at the intrusion.

"I will forgive your rudeness, Moussa, as you are clearly agitated. It does not become a nobleman of the Kel Rela to forget himself so. This courtesy, even the smallest child of the Hoggar has learned." Mahdi filled his cup with tea, and then the others'. "Come down from your mighty mehari. Join us for tea." He spoke as if to a child.

"I ask again," Moussa said, not moving. "By what right have you become a butcher?"

"Regard the back of my mehari," Attici said pleasantly, "where the *tobol* now rides. Have you not seen it?"

"Then it is the amenokal who told you to do this to the French? This was his decision?"

"If it is your business, Moussa, the amenokal was not specific, and left the matter in my hands. He told me only to 'discourage' Sheikh Flatters. I believe he is thoroughly discouraged now." There was laughter around the fire.

"Did he tell you to hack them to pieces? Is this your notion of honorable battle, to surprise and butcher an enemy? Even *mouflon* we do not mangle so."

"What *ikufar* is worthy of being butchered so kindly as a *mouflon?*" Tamrit asked. There was more laughter. "Is it that the Frenchmen are dead that troubles you, rude one, or that they are in pieces?"

"Who is this man, Attici, who sits at your right hand?"

"Tamrit ag Amellal," Tamrit replied. "And you would be the tender son of the barbarian deVries?"

Moussa slid from his mount, his hand on his sword. "Hold your tongue, Tamrit, unless you are ready to lose it."

Tamrit stirred angrily. "It is for respect of your

mother that I do not take your head. Speak so again and I shall forget myself."

Moussa spoke scornfully to Attici. "You are surrounded by Senussi then? Is it they who lead you like a lamb? It is they who feed the fires of hatred and treachery?"

"No one leads but I," Attici replied evenly.

"Then there is much blood on your hands. Never have I seen such savagery visited upon a foe by the Ihaggaren," Moussa said.

"Perhaps you have not lived among us long enough to have seen it," Mahdi said. "Perhaps you should return to France as a true *ikufar*, where the sights are more to your liking."

"Was Tadjenout a sight for liking?" Moussa challenged the others standing nearby. "Was Tadjenout a battlefield of honor?"

"Our honor is intact," Mahdi said hotly. "Is deception not a weapon long used between enemies? Is surprise not a weapon, like the sword? Where advantage can be seen, it must be taken. And if our cause were unjust, Allah would not have ensured our victory."

"Through all of history we have warred with the Tebu and the Shamba," Moussa said. "The rules of war are well known among our tribes. But we never spoke of war with the French, who expected peaceful passage. And then the limbs severed, the heads taken at Tadjenout. Is such the noble work we do?"

"I will not argue this with you, Moussa. You are not speaking as Ihaggaren. Your words are soft, like those from a lamb."

"Then tell me this much. What are your intentions now? Those who survived are across the hill, on a parallel course. For what purpose are you following them? Another slaughter?"

"Say nothing," Tamrit said.

"He is of no consequence," Attici said with a contemptuous wave of his hand. "Do I fear the bite of the

French puppy?" He looked at Moussa. "They will continue to be 'discouraged' back to Wargla," he said, enjoying the word. "And from there to France, to carry the message to their countrymen that to mark a place French on the map does not make it so. That the Hoggar is no place for French adventure. Nor even a place to visit."

"They will not make it to Wargla. You have stolen their camels and they have but little food. They will die within a fortnight."

"Camels are the legitimate booty of war," Attici snapped. "Whether the infidels and their Shamba dogs reach Wargla is of no concern to me. Their destiny is in the hands of Allah."

"No," Moussa said. "Not in Allah's hands. In *your* hands just now."

"Where is the difference? My hands move at His pleasure." Attici was losing his patience. "I have said it already—I am not content to debate these matters with you. You should tend the business the amenokal assigned you and remove yourself from matters that trouble you so. Or have you cast your lot with the barbarians?"

For the second time in three days Moussa heard himself saying the same words. "I have cast my lot with no one in this."

"That is a matter within your control," Attici said. "There are many of us who will watch your actions with great interest. Now join with us, or leave the camp."

Moussa turned. A score of Tuareg stood behind him, listening to the exchange.

"Who among you will quit this? Who has had a fill of it? Who has not forgotten how to treat travelers such as those who now walk on the other side of that hill, when they are without food and water? Fight them later if you will, but for now extend to them the hospitality of the desert."

"They are not common travelers," one said. "They are foreign scum. Invaders, not entitled to the desert's just laws."

"*Eoualla*," said another. "Foreigners. Like you." Moussa struck him, and the man dropped like a stone. No one else moved, but Moussa sensed in many of them a hostility he had never felt before. He took the lead of his mehari and led it through the crowd. Taka sat atop the pommel of the saddle, her head turning and nodding. She was nervous.

Attici's voice followed him to the edge of camp.

"Do not interfere in this, Moussa. It will go hard on you."

Taher, his old friend, caught up with him just out of camp.

"You have spoken truly. The French were tricked and then betrayed. It was bloodlust at Tadjenout. I have not seen the like of it. Once begun there was no stopping it. It was as if they were possessed, Moussa. I do not know the answer of it, except that Tamrit has said much to inflame them. I did not help them."

"Nor I," said Moussa. "But the result is the same."

"It is true. Many are not acting themselves in this. I will ride with you, Moussa, if it pleases you."

"No, Taher, but thanks. In this I am alone."

THEY ARRIVED AT THE WELL OF TEMASSINT THE following afternoon. It was situated in a large sandy wadi in the plain. There was a forlorn acacia tree there, flat-topped and twisted from the wind, and a few bushes, but the way the men whooped and cheered it might have been the lush oasis of Wargla.

Most of the men collapsed around the wadi, their leaden limbs heavy and sluggish from the sun. The first four or five fought for position under the acacia, but its shade was hardly worth the effort. Pobeguin detailed some of the others to set about the laborious task of refilling the water skins. Temassint was not a well with solid sides to it, such as at Tadjenout. It was a *tilma,* a seeper. A man could stand on top of it and die of thirst, never knowing it was there. The sand had to be dug out to a level where it became damp, and then deeper, until it got wet. Only two or three bags could be filled before the waiting began again.

Near the well they found evidence of their prior passage, including broken baskets, ashes from campfires, and, to their delight, food. They were grateful for what now appeared to be profligacy on the way south. There were dates that earlier seemed rock hard and had been discarded, but which now looked juicy and perfect. Bits of rice were strewn about, and even little pieces of meat, rejected by complacent men with full bellies. No one was suffering from extreme hunger yet, for they still had a little food. But Pobeguin got a detail working to collect everything. The men chattered excitedly and scooted around on the scorching black rock, salvaging even single grains of rice. When the area had been picked clean Pobeguin divided everything as equally as he could. Each man received a small handful.

Djemel, the chief camel driver, had been desolate on the return trip without his charges, and busied himself collecting their dung for the fires. Djemel's father had been a camelman, and his father before him. He was a short, hyperactive coil of a man, all sinew and passion wrapped in a sickly green turban, dyed permanently that color from camel saliva. His most notable features were his temper, which was legendary, and his nose, which was missing. During one of his heated arguments with a camel the beast had bitten it off. It was said that Djemel had bitten the camel first, but he never talked about the incident and had long since learned to put up with the jests of his fellow drivers and impolite stares on the street. He rarely talked or socialized with human beings, spending all his time among his camels. As the years passed his sounds and mannerisms took on those of the camels he tended. When he growled his missing nose produced a sucking sound not unlike the camels themselves. His looks of arrogance or disdain matched those of any mehari.

That he was miserable without them was evident as he walked around the area picking up pellets and dropping them into the bag. Every so often he would stick his nose, or that part of his face where his nose had been, into the bag and take a deep breath. He seemed to get almost drunk from what to him was the desert's most intoxicating aroma, short of the animals who'd made it. He even talked to the bag's contents, much as he did to the animals themselves, snorting and growling and mumbling as he stooped and grabbed. When others tried to help with the gathering he chased them away. The camels were *his* responsibility.

While the water bags were being filled El Madani had rounded up a hunting party and set off up a wadi searching for game. He took the two Salukis, who had returned to the caravan after Tadjenout. They were marvelous hunting dogs of the Shamba with pedigrees that spanned a thousand years, companions to the great sultans and sheikhs of the north country. It was not their sense of smell but their keen sight that helped them find their quarry. With phenomenal speed and endurance, they would chase their prey until finally it dropped of exhaustion.

But there was no game and El Madani and the Salukis returned empty-handed. The Salukis set about working on the bones of a long-dead camel, snarling when Floop came near. Floop set off on his own. Before long he returned with a lizard in his mouth, its tail, as always, dangling in place of his tongue. Paul thought he walked rather haughtily past the Salukis. Paul greeted the find with such uncharacteristic enthusiasm that before long Floop was back with another, and then another. Each time he trotted up to Paul, Floop would nearly let him have the lizard but then dash off at the last instant. He'd drop it on the ground and paw at it for a while, or crunch around its head a bit if the lizard was too perky and tried to run. Eventually he'd give them up. Floop kept at it until he'd caught six, when he plopped down and refused to part with the last one, preferring to keep it for his own dinner.

To the Shamba, Floop was a hero. Lizards were a much-favored delicacy among them. They quickly built a dung fire and cut the lizards' throats to the ritual prayers. Then they gutted and skewered them with the branches of the acacia tree, and roasted them over the fire. Each man took a tiny bite, then passed the skewer along. The Algerians refused them. Paul didn't mind the taste, remembering the lizard Moussa had cooked him in the cave, but the other Frenchmen declared the delicacy bitter, and settled for the last of the dried meat.

Spirits were high that night in the camp. Nearly everyone had found something to do, some encouragement in the face of the overwhelming challenge that lay before them. The afternoon's events were the subject of much discussion and laughter.

Paul took a cup of rice to Sandeau, who sat propped against the acacia tree. "Bless you, Lieutenant," he nodded gratefully. "I didn't have the energy to get it myself." Paul was dismayed by the engineer's appearance. His face was flushed with the first stirrings of fever. His eyelids were red and swollen.

Sandeau was going downhill quickly.

CHAPTER 27

THE FIRES GLOWED AT A DIFFERENT CAMP ON THE plain, red-hot embers of acacia branches and camel dung smoldering in soft beds of sand. White ash danced through red coals to the rhythm of a cold uncertain wind. The rich sweet odor of bread baking in the sand mingled with the pungent aroma of the camels.

Attici, Mahdi, and Tamrit squatted at one of the fires on the edge of the encampment, talking together as a slave prepared their tea. Their great swords lay on the ground beside them, next to their Gras rifles.

With bare hands the slave quickly pushed aside the bed of glowing coals. He brushed away a layer of sand and felt the bread underneath. It was the shape of a fat pancake. Deftly he flipped it over, covered it with more sand, and moved the coals back onto the fire.

"I tire of waiting," Mahdi said in a strident voice. "We should finish them now."

"It would be foolish," Attici said patiently. "They are too strong. There is no sense in hurry. Let time and the infinite desert wear them down. We have no need to sacrifice a single warrior."

Mahdi lifted the bottom of his litham and spat. "When has a caravan with ten times their number deterred us before? They cannot slay us all."

"When was another caravan armed as theirs? They carry too many of these." Attici nudged his rifle. He was very respectful of its performance. "We do not have enough ammunition or the marksmen to use them."

"What is lost in fighting the infidel is not life," said

Tamrit. "To be slain in the way of Allah is to live eternally. We are His right arm and cannot die. He has made special provision for us in paradise."

Attici sighed. Did he not have enough trouble without taming wild dogs who panted the Koran? Attici cared nothing for Allah or the Koran. It was only the Ihaggaren he cared about, nothing else—nothing except becoming amenokal one day. But Tamrit and his Senussi brethren were gathering strength. Each day there were more among the Sons of the Desert who embraced the way of Islam, enough that Attici could not dismiss them, nor did he wish to. He merely needed to tame them for a short while, to fulfill the amenokal's orders. "It is clear the French cannot understand a message written in ink," Ahitagel had told him the last night at In Salah. "You will write them for me once again, nephew. In blood."

He had been hugely successful. More than two hundred and fifty camels taken, and the insolent French were taught that the master race of Ihaggaren would not be so easily tamed as the peasant farmers of the north. The intruders had been dealt a mighty blow and would not soon return for more. But for others carefully watching—Turks and Italians, Shamba and Tebu, the sultan of Morocco, the amenokal himself—Attici needed complete victory, resounding victory, victory that left no one confused about supremacy in the central Sahara. Victory that left no one confused as to the identity of the next amenokal. Toward that end Attici had struck a devastating first blow at Tadjenout. Now it was time to let the Sahara do its work.

"Even Allah moves His right arm only when the time is right," he replied.

"His right arm moved at Tadjenout," Mahdi said. "He would have us finish it."

"You are as impatient as a camel in heat." Attici chuckled. "I see no gain in risking our success with unseemly haste. We will wait, Mahdi."

"How do you know they will not arrive at Wargla still strong?" Tamrit asked.

"They are not people of the veil." Attici shrugged

matter-of-factly, sipping the hot sweet tea. "It is not possible."

"I agree it is unlikely. But what if they do?" Tamrit picked up his Gras and examined it in the firelight, holding its barrel close to Attici's face. He turned the gun over and over, admiring its lines, and then held it up as if to fire. "Even though we are four to their one," he said, sighting down the barrel, "size is not the only thing that matters. A tiny scorpion can kill a full-grown man with a stinger much less powerful than this." The barrel of the Gras caught the firelight and threw its reflection to Attici's eyes. "The French scorpion is trained in the use of this weapon. We are not."

"It is true," Attici agreed.

"And so I have been thinking," Tamrit said. "Perhaps there is a way to satisfy both needs. A way to attack the French now without attacking them at all."

"I do not take your meaning."

"*Efeleleh.*" Tamrit said it quietly.

Mahdi's blood rushed at the thought.

Attici shook his head. "They would never let us near enough."

"Of course not. We must toy with them first so that they will," Tamrit said. He outlined his plan while they ate bread hot from the coals.

Mahdi and Attici listened carefully.

"I am glad you are not my enemy," Attici said when Tamrit had finished. *This dog of Islam might be rabid,* he thought, *but he is very, very much in control of his senses.* "It is a good plan. A path neither too winding nor too direct. It shall be done." He turned to Mahdi. "Leave tonight, with two others. Then find us at Aïn El Kerma."

Before leaving Mahdi threw an extra blanket over his shoulder and picked up some bread and a freshly brewed pot of tea and walked to where the miserable figures of the prisoners lay huddled on the ground, freezing. He heard them whimpering and crying beneath their hoods. Their feet were bound, so that none could run. Twice each day they were given half an hour outside the hoods while they ate and drank. Experience had taught that they could be kept on a fine edge between life and death for weeks.

Mahdi set down the bread and tea and knelt at the side of the silent one, the one who never cried out, and removed his hood. The man had thick eyebrows, a trim mustache and beard; he was hawk-nosed. He looked haggard and weak. He stared silently at his captor.

Mahdi cut his bonds and helped him sit up. As the man rubbed his wrists to restore the circulation Mahdi threw the blanket over his shoulders, drawing it around the neck that was red and raw from the ropes. He poured a cup of tea and held it out to the *mokkadem*. "Drink this, holy one," he said in Arabic. The man closed his eyes and said a prayer, then downed it quickly. Mahdi poured another.

"I did not choose to treat you this way," he said as the man drank. "You chose this path yourself, by giving aid to the unbelievers." He ripped apart a piece of bread and held it out. It was eaten as quickly as it was proffered. The *mokkadem* ate noisily but said nothing.

"Yes, eat, eat," Mahdi cooed, holding out more. "You must not die, holy one. You must live, for we have need of you now." The man devoured the rest of the bread and finished the tea.

When the *mokkadem* had finished Mahdi retied his hands behind his back, more loosely than before. He left off the hood. He stared at the man through the slit in his shesh. *He suffers in silence,* Mahdi thought. *He is strong because his faith is solid. He is a worthy man.*

He turned and strode back to camp. He told one of the slaves to see that the other prisoners were fed and covered up. He chose two others to come with him, telling them to get the camels ready. One of them asked where they were going.

Mahdi smiled. "To harvest a crop," he said.

THE HAWK GAINED ALTITUDE QUICKLY THROUGH the superheated air, her powerful wings pushing gracefully as she climbed. When she was high enough she leveled off and cut a great slow circle in the sky, floating easily on the currents, dipping her wingtips now and then to steady herself. Taka played with the air, testing it, teasing it, getting her bearings. She hovered for a moment, then dropped her tail and let the drafts push her upward, where she caught another current and swooped down, head dropped, wings back. She reversed quickly on an updraft, bringing her wings slightly forward, feathers rustling, tail twisting ever so slightly, almost imperceptibly, as she balanced herself. She could float for hours without effort.

She flew over the mountains on the west end of the plain, her eyes scanning the desert. Four camels looked for food in a basin in the rocks below. Far to the east, barely visible even to Taka's sharp eyes, a tiny column of men trudged northward on the plain. The bird soared on the wind until it was over the camels, cut tight circles over their grazing figures, and then moved back over the rocks to hunt.

She studied the mountains below, her eyes ranging over the sun-drenched rocks and the shadows between in search of prey. A pair of sand thrushes flew among the trees in a wadi, their wings flapping in short bursts, then resting, then flapping again as they darted through the branches of one tree and raced to the next, perching momentarily and chattering, then descending to the sandy ground below. Taka watched with interest, the double foveas in her eyes rendering the thrushes sharply, as if they were much closer. Then she spotted a lizard sunbathing atop a rock. She had a choice and preferred the reptile.

The lizard sat perfectly still, its stubby legs splayed out on the hot rock, its dark scales soaking up the warmth of the sun. Only its bulbous eyes moved, blinking languorously. Taka swept back her wings, dropped her head and dived almost vertically, her speed increasing quickly, the wind rushing through her feathers. She carefully choreographed her lightning descent, judging wind speed and direction, watching the lizard for any movement. Just when it seemed she must crash she opened her wings and dropped her tail, legs stretching at the instant her wings spread, slowing her approach, her feet opening, stretching forward, six razor-sharp talons in front, two opposing in the rear, poised for the kill. Just before striking, she twisted her tail to adjust her path. The lizard sensed the danger but saw the shadow too late. Taka's talons pierced its head and neck and soft fleshy sides, killing it instantly. She flapped her wings and rose quickly with her kill, her flight barely interrupted, the lizard hanging limply in her grasp.

She flew for a moment until she spotted Moussa waiting near his camel. There was a moment of choice when she could return to him or leave. Screeching loudly, proudly, she flew just past him and descended in a flurry of wings. She settled herself and hopped backward to wait.

Moussa strode forward, quickly drawing his wrist knife from its sheath. With deft motions he severed the legs, head, and tail. He ripped out the viscera and tossed it along with the head to Taka. Her beak ripped eagerly at the flesh, breaking through bone and devouring the brain.

He put the rest of the meat into a leather bag and wiped his hands and knife clean in the sand. He mounted his mehari, which rose awkwardly, tipping him backward, then forward, then backward, then forward once again as its long legs went through the complex motions of standing up. He whistled. Finished with her meal and preening, Taka rose to his outstretched arm with two easy strokes of her wings and accepted the hood. She took her place on the pommel of his saddle.

They moved in the direction where Moussa had seen Taka's tight circles in the air. There would be men or animals there. He had to know. When he drew near the place, he slipped off his mehari and climbed quickly up the rocks. There were no humans in sight. Four wild camels pulled at the leaves in the tops of the acacia trees. He returned to his mehari for rope and set off to catch the camels.

P AUL'S AIDE, HAKEEM, WINCED IN PAIN. HE couldn't remember ever being quite so miserable. He dropped out of the column and sat down. The stream of men passed him by, laboring against the wind and their own problems, many of which were worse than his. A trail of blood marked his path, his imprint sizzling on the rock and sand.

He removed the remnants of his sandals. All that remained of the soles were the edges, which tapered down into holes cut there by sharp rock that shredded them like paper. Now the gravelly shards were tearing at his feet, ripping through thick calluses to make bloody holes in the balls and arches. He unwrapped the sticky strip of material, wincing as the cloth pulled away clotted blood. He threw it away. It caught on the wind and disappeared into the distance, a ragged crimson sail tumbling south over the plain. With grimy fingers he brushed the dirt away from his wounds, picking out the threads left behind by the cloth. He daubed at the shredded skin with the end of his turban. Blood oozed from the deepest wounds. As soon as time and heat sealed the vessels, his walking stretched the skin and reopened them. The holes became packed with sand, which was then ground in by other rocks, leaving his feet excruciating and raw. He tried picking his way carefully through the gravel but it was impossible. His calf muscles were cramped from walking on the edges of his feet. He was fighting a losing battle. He needed goat's butter and new sandals. The thought struck him funny and he laughed to himself, not quite sure where he might find either one in the immediate neighborhood.

The wind lashed his face with stinging bits of silica. Hakeem drew the bloodied end of his turban around his nose and mouth and tucked it into place in back. He hated the wind. Sometimes the air in the desert was quite still. He liked it that way, especially at night when the silence covered him with a blanket so thick it seemed that the only noise was made by the stars passing overhead. But normally the wind blew to one degree or another. This one had begun the night before last, coming from the north, first a steady breeze fluffed by little gusts, then little gusts alternating with bigger ones, the bigger ones then blending together until they were long incessant blasts, whistling over the top of the gravel, flinging stinging bits of sand at eyes and tender skin. The sand coated his teeth and saturated his clothing, which grew stiff with the mixture of sweat and grit.

The noise grated his nerves like the sand did his body, scratching furiously at his sanity. After a few hours it was worse than the wind itself, its mournful howl invading those rare places where the sand couldn't reach until it seemed there was no part of his body left unviolated.

The wind had grown in velocity since that morning, whipping through the ranks of the column and slowing progress to little more than a crawl. It was no sand-storm, but all day they fought to make a meter at a time, the men leaning into the wind at exaggerated angles, pressing hard against the invisible hand trying to push them back.

Hakeem's slight frame and light weight made it difficult to walk. The wind caught his *gandourah* and filled it like a kite. It was all he could do to stay on his feet; and because he had to take care to walk only on their edges, it was awkward going. He was quite certain he looked preposterous. He kept a hostile eye out for anyone laughing at him, but no one seemed to notice. They were all fighting their own battles.

To add to his problems the wind was frigid, an icy reminder of the Atlas Mountains to the north, or perhaps coming from as far as the great sea beyond. It cut through his robe like the rocks through his feet, raising gooseflesh in front, while his back, facing the sun, sweltered in the heat. He tried walking backward for a while until his front warmed up, then turned around to try it the other way until his back got so cold he had to turn again. It was the kind of thing that would have entertained him greatly as a child. To add to his misery, his eyelids were encrusted with sand. Blinking rubbed the particles deeper into his eyes, which were already filigreed with an irritated network of angry veins.

His mouth was parched, his tongue thick with dust, his throat tight. The wind sucked out the water faster than he could put it in, and with Sergeant Pobeguin around it didn't go in very fast. His nose was raw and bleeding. The droplets gathered on the tip of his nose where the wind sprayed them back onto his robe, staining it until it looked like his eyes. He wondered how much blood there was inside his body and whether it would ever all leak out this way, bit by bit from his nose and feet. He would have to ask the patron.

He pulled out his dagger to cut a strip off the bottom of his robe. It was the third time he'd done it, the width increasing each time so he could get more protection. He wound the cloth around his feet. When new holes appeared he would shift the material, tying it in a new position until that wore out as well. So it would continue until the strip was a ragged wisp of bloody cotton and he had to cut another. He wondered whether his blood or his robe would run out first. *Malish*, he thought. He still had his shirt, and then his pants. With Allah's help he would make Wargla before he was stark naked and all emptied out. Of course, he reasoned, that presumed he wouldn't starve to death first. They'd run out of food. His good spirits, tested sorely by everything else, were being slowly strangled by the knots in his stomach. Skinny as he was, he was accustomed to eating several times during the day, but there was nothing to be done. He finished wrapping his feet, slipped on his sandals, and hobbled painfully into the wind.

The procession wore the wind's burden like a yoke, made heavier by the need to wait on stragglers. In ten hours they'd come less than ten kilometers, when they should have made twenty. They were forever stopping, tending to wounds and sores and cramping muscles. The stronger men walked in little circles or stamped their feet while they waited, trying to avoid the spasms that would overcome them if they stopped moving.

"We should leave them," complained one of the

Shamba. "They can catch up tonight." There were murmurs of agreement.

El Madani scowled at them. "Any of you who think you can deal with the desert and the Tuareg alone are welcome to move out in front," he growled. "The rest of us will stay together."

The Shamba who had spoken gave him a scornful look. "Die alone or die with company—what difference does it make?"

"A great deal, when you're alone. If you'd like to try, get on with it. The *tirailleurs* will stay together. We'll bury you on the way past."

The Shamba's gaze fell. He kept trudging.

Paul walked with Sandeau. The engineer's low fever remained, slowly sapping his strength. His green eyes were lost in dark circles. The knees of his trousers were torn and stained with blood where he'd fallen. As soon as the wounds were cleaned and wrapped, Sandeau would fall again. He walked in a stoop, his knuckles white around the Tuareg lance he'd been given as a walking stick. He knew he was the slowest of the slow, yet he plodded on and tried to remain cheerful.

"God's blessings everywhere," he said as they walked.

"What?" Paul hadn't heard him over the wind.

Sandeau raised his voice. "The wind! For the first time in a week I don't have flies all over my face!" He smiled and wiped the sandy film off his teeth. As he did so, his hand slipped on the lance and he fell hard to one knee. He didn't cry out, but the pain brought tears to his eyes. Gasping, he struggled back to his feet. Paul bent down to look at his knees. "You've torn it open again. We'll have to rewrap it."

Sandeau slipped down the lance and sagged to a sitting position. Paul unwound the cloth and exposed his ragged flesh. "It's hard watching your body fail," Sandeau said.

"No failure here," Paul replied as he wiped away the blood. He could see the bone of the engineer's kneecap and tried to shield it with his hand. "Your knees are just getting a little knobbier, Sandeau, that's all. I'm told Arab women fancy that. You'll be swamped in Wargla."

Sandeau laughed through his pain as Paul cleaned out the wound.

"Kind of you to say so, but I'm afraid I can feel everything just giving up. A humbling experience. Your mind can be good as ever, but it's only baggage on dying transport. A pity it can't be made of something stronger." He raised his eyebrows and looked upward. "Not that it isn't the most remarkable creation," he said quickly. "I wish I'd come up with something half as good. But like all structures it eventually fails."

"I wish you had more faith in yourself. Wargla isn't that far."

Sandeau snorted. "I said my body's going, Lieutenant. Not my brain."

A T DUSK THE WIND DIED. THE SUN WENT DOWN and just as suddenly, dead quiet settled over the camp. There were no fires. There was nothing to cook, nothing to eat. No one wanted to talk. Men fell asleep where they sat. Pobeguin and his troopers Marjolet and Brame took turns walking the perimeter, peering into the night. There was no sign of the Tuareg.

Before dawn El Madani took four men out to search for game, as was his custom. They followed a wadi for more than an hour, finding nothing. But then one of the men gave a great whoop. There were four wild camels, grazing on weeds and tufts of dry grass.

El Madani noticed the extra set of camel prints in the soft sand. He squatted to examine them. They were fresh and deep, heavier than the tracks of the wild animals. A mehari had made them, bearing a man. The tracks disappeared up the wadi. He followed them a short distance, Gras at the ready, but they led up over an embankment and disappeared in gravel. El Madani shook his head. It was as if someone had left the camels where he could find them.

He returned to camp a hero. Even the reserved *tirailleurs* jumped up and down and danced in ecstasy.

"*Hamdullilah!* Allah has heard our prayer!" It was an omen; the Almighty would lead them from this wilderness on the backs of four wild camels. Packs were lifted from the shoulders of the weakest of the men and loaded on the animals. Sandeau went atop another, his frail form slumping. Djemel was beside himself, snorting and coughing and spitting, slapping the animals affectionately, lining them up in proper form, then growling and snarling at them as they all began to move.

Jubilation carried the morning, but heat and hunger ruled the afternoon. By dusk Dianous was staggering. Paul was doing better but felt light-headed. Three times the column halted while men who passed out were revived. They pushed on until nearly midnight. Again they built no fires.

In the middle of the night a single shot rang out. Pandemonium broke out in camp as men scrambled awake and clutched cold weapons, peering into the blackness. El Madani had been awake and had seen the flash of the muzzle. He was there in an instant, pistol drawn. Quickly he saw what had happened. He knelt next to the dim form on the ground. It was one of the Algerian *tirailleurs*.

Dianous came up behind him. "What is it, Madani?"

"Abdel Krim, Lieutenant. He has shot himself."

"Is he dead?"

"No sir. He is a poor shot."

Abdel Krim had passed out. The bullet had only torn a bloody crease in his skull. El Madani bandaged his head. "Take away his weapons," El Madani told another *tirailleur*, "and tie his hands."

Slowly the camp slipped back into uneasy exhaustion. Few men slept. The mood the next morning was somber. The omen of the camels had been surpassed by the omen of suicide. The unfortunate man marched alone with his failure, a pariah. Men looked at Abdel Krim with varying degrees of pity for him and fear for themselves. He had been the first to crack, the first to give up. They told themselves they were stronger than he. But no one really knew for sure. "It is a mortal sin, to steal destiny from the hand of Allah," nervous men reminded each other. They missed the *mokkadem*. He would know the things to say, the things to do.

Two men collapsed in the afternoon and were heaped onto the camels like more baggage. Dianous called an early halt that night, his men unable to take another step. He walked slowly through the ranks of exhaustion, past gaunt faces and haunted eyes. He stopped here and there to check supplies of water. At the edge of camp Djemel was settling his babies down for the night. Beyond him, near a low escarpment, Dianous noticed the Salukis. Having had no luck on their own, the dogs were prowling nervously back and forth in front of Floop, who was munching on a lizard and ignoring them. The mighty Salukis were useless at catching reptiles, yet there was no other game on the Amadror. Dianous studied the dogs and made a decision.

"Pobeguin!" he called.

"Sir?"

"Kill the Salukis."

"Yes sir."

Hakeem heard the order and with horror in his eyes limped quickly to Paul. "Patrón," he gasped, "you must stop him!"

Paul shook his head. He'd heard the order and agreed with it, but his heart was pounding all the same. "The men are weak. We need the meat."

"You do not understand, Patrón. The Salukis are allies of the Shamba. Their history is our history, their blood our blood. It is wrong to kill them."

"They can give us life, Hakeem, and we must take it. There is no other way."

For the first time since Paul had met him the aide's eyes were furious. "It is wrong, Patrón," he repeated. "You are ignorant of the ways of the desert. You should kill a camel first."

"It is not yet time for that. We need the camels for transport."

Hakeem glared at him bitterly. He started to say something but then just hobbled off.

"Why not the other dog?" demanded another Shamba. "You spare him because he belongs to the lieutenant?"

"I spare him because he catches lizards," said Dianous. "If he stops or there are no more lizards, and that is all we have to eat—"

"—then the same order will be given." It was Paul who said it.

Two shots rang out in rapid succession. Paul flinched at each one and cringed inside. Floop wagged his tail.

Everyone ate but the Shamba.

D AIA WAS GLAD FOR A DIVERSION. MOVING THE camp required all her attention. There were disputes over property to resolve, sheep to identify, goats to chase, pastures to scout, wells to check, packing to supervise for seven tents, bags to be mended, bags to be made. A dozen slaves asked questions and tended to the children underfoot and added good-natured cheer to the bedlam. Daia was good at moving. Like all Tuareg, Mano Biska moved his *douar* of tents and relatives and slaves and animals several times a year, depending on the pasturage. When his wife was away, the job was Daia's. All the slaves looked to her for guidance and order, and when she stayed busy she didn't have time to think.

She had not been able to sleep of late, or to eat much. Her stomach was sour. Anna, the slave who knew her like a daughter, had spoken the truth of it before Daia herself. She beamed. "A child grows within you," she said.

"No," Daia said, but it was a lie and they both knew it. She had never been late before. "Yes, Anna, it is true."

"It is goo—" Anna spoke before thinking, then caught herself. It was *not* good. It was terrible. There was great shame in bearing a child out of wedlock. A stain on the child, dishonor on the mother. She worried for Daia.

"You must get married quickly, then," she said.

Daia only nodded. Anna didn't know the worst of it. She assumed Mahdi was the father.

Daia went to the *guelta* to think. She sat alone atop the rocks overlooking the water. She watched the sun set and was still awake when it rose again, but the long night in between brought no answers. She struggled with the burden. How could she have been so foolish? How could she have fallen so easily? Her own honor was in ruins for her lies to Mahdi. Never in her life had she been a liar or felt a cheat. Never before had she hurt another person. Now she had to decide what to do. She felt lost and weak.

There was an old woman of the Dag Rali who could end the problem before it grew, but Daia didn't know if she could do that.

Or she could go away now before her stomach grew. She could have the baby and then leave it among the rocks for the animals to kill. Other women did that; often it was the lesser shame. She could return to her life then, and begin again.

Or she could kill herself. But there was time to think about that too.

Must someone die for my weakness?

She thought of Moussa. It made her ache that he was not interested in her. *Damn* him anyway! So polite and solicitous of her feelings. So proper! He sent a book, a beautiful book of stories, with a note that hurt deeply. It had not been his intent, to hurt. He had simply wished her happiness. Of course he had. He was *supposed* to say that. But it wasn't what she wanted him to say. She had admitted it to herself the eighth or tenth or twentieth time she had read his note, her fingers tracing every line of his writing, her mind envisioning his hand on the paper, wishing she could touch it, then lifting the paper to her nose, hoping that she might catch his scent there. She wanted him to say something much different, to say he wanted her, that he wanted them to be together. But he hadn't and never would. Was she so undesirable to him? Why didn't he care for her? She knew the answer;

she had accepted Mahdi too hastily. She regretted ever saying yes to him, and now it was too late to back out, yet she had to back out because Mahdi—

Oh, Mahdi! She could not lie to him again. Once was more than she had lied to any man. She could tell him the truth and call off the marriage. It was her right, the right of a woman to say. Yet Mahdi had done nothing to deserve that. Would she now compound her lie with rejection?

Most of all she feared the truth for what it would do to Moussa. It was a death sentence. She, not Moussa, had been the one to make it happen. Yet when Mahdi learned the truth Moussa would pay with his life, and it would be her doing. She could only hope that Mahdi would kill her as well, and finish it all.

Must someone die for my weakness? Oh, devil Iblis, *when did you enter my heart?*

Honor ruined, a man dead, a child born without a father, or not born at all. The wretched fruits of her desire. She hated what she had done.

And knew she would do it again.

When the sun rose she counted five rays shining up from the horizon like the vanes of a fan. On her journey with Moussa she had seen the same sunrise. "The sunrise of good fortune," she had told him then. "Five rays make the sunrise of a lucky day."

She wept.

SHE IMMERSED HERSELF IN THE DETAILS OF MOVing, her mind needing a rest from her trouble, when she saw him approach the camp on his mehari. She gasped.

"Mahdi! I thought you were in the north!"

"I had to come for—things," he said. "I was near and could not resist stopping here to see you. I brought this."

He leaned down from his mehari and handed her a sand rose.

It was beautiful, a delicate blossom of sandstone

sculpted over the eons. Such roses were much prized. She accepted it guiltily, her misery now complete. "Come walk with me, away from camp," she said.

They walked past the place where the camels were being loaded and into a ravine beyond, heading toward her *guelta*. When they were out of earshot of the camp she blurted it out.

"I am pregnant."

She needed him to know. She could not tell him more lies. She could not let him find out by seeing her swell. She had to be the one to do it, and waiting would help nothing.

Mahdi stared at her. He said nothing, as if he hadn't heard or didn't understand, his brain reeling. His mind ranged back over the nightmares and suspicions, the ones he had forced with such effort from his thoughts—the ones that were true. He felt as if he'd been kicked in the stomach.

"You have lied to me most horribly."

"Yes. I thought it best then, Mahdi. It had already happened when we spoke. I thought I had put him behind me, Mahdi, this much is true. I was wrong to lie to you. I am sorry." Her eyes welled with tears.

He stood rigid and erect, fighting for control. His hands flexed, gripping the handle of his sword. It was all he could do not to draw it, but there was nothing against which to turn it. Rage could not be slain with a blade, nor sorrow. He wanted to kill Moussa, to kill her, to kill himself, to kill everything in sight. But even if honor demanded, he would never turn the blade on her. Another man would do it. Any man. For the thousandth time he wondered how she could have such an effect on him, how she could render him so helpless. For the thousandth time he found no answer. As for Moussa—well, he had already decided what to do about Moussa. Only the opportunity had been lacking, and that would come soon enough.

"You are *sorry*, Daia? Is that anything at all? Should the word ease my heart or take away the wrong? Should the word make me content?"

"There is no way to make anyone content in this, Mahdi, that I know."

"I must confess, Daia, that I did not expect this of you. Ever."

"I did not expect it of myself."

"To cheat and lie and then leave me only words—I never thought you so cruel."

She shook her head and bit her lip. "I did not intend cruelty."

"Does anyone else know?"

"No one but Anna."

"Anna! Then the world will soon know. That woman is a toad of gossip."

"She thinks you are the father. She will say nothing. She wishes to protect me."

Mahdi brooded about that. His self-respect was everything to him. No, not everything, not anymore. This woman before him—*she* was everything. Next to her, his self-respect meant nothing.

"That is my wish as well, Daia."

"I have brought us both dishonor. Of course there can be no marriage. I will go away."

His heart pounded. "*No!* Daia, you cannot do this! Do not say this! You promised marriage after the French matter had been dealt with. It will be finished in a fortnight, no more than two. You would pierce me first with a lance of lies, then strike me again with broken promises? Even the scorpion stings only once. Is there no limit to the loathing in your heart for me?"

"There is no loathing, Mahdi, except for myself. But I cannot ask you to go forward with this."

"Please, Daia, do not speak for me. You have pledged yourself to me and I am willing."

"I cannot ask it." She hated herself, hated what she was doing to the proud man before her.

"My heart is with you, Daia. I have said it before. I would be—I would be willing even to call the child my own. For you would I do this."

She was astounded. It was the last thing she expected him to say.

"I could not ask for that. It would not be right for you."

"*Right?* What about this wears the cloak of rightness? If you would have me, that is the important thing." His eyes were filled with hurt, his voice with longing. "That is, if—answer me this, Daia. Is it finished, then, with Moussa? Truly finished?"

She knew the importance of her answer. "He has made it clear he is finished with me, Mahdi. He sent a gift, for the wedding. A book. And a note to wish me happiness."

"My question is unanswered. I asked your feelings, not his."

She bit her lip to keep it from trembling. "Do not force me this way, Mahdi. Have I not said it was finished?" She turned away. She could not lie again, and she could not say what he wanted her to say. Mahdi looked down, defeated. But then he began to understand. This was her weakness. There was, at last, an advantage to be had.

"Your answer is clear enough. It does not make it easier for me to kill him, knowing that he holds such a place in your heart."

It was what she feared most, and as he said it she knew instantly what she must do. She could not ruin other lives for her own selfishness. She would make the bargain for the life of Moussa, and to make a place for the child.

"I will marry you, Mahdi, if it truly remains your wish. But first I must know that Moussa is safe from your wrath. That you will do nothing to harm him for this. It is not a thing that he did. It was my doing."

"Do I look a fool, Daia? Such things are not done alone."

"He did nothing to encourage it. This you must believe, Mahdi. He kept his honor; it was I who lost mine. You must leave him be. I must have your promise."

"When I am the one wronged, is it for you to make terms?"

"This I must have, Mahdi."

It was more than a reasonable person could ask, that

he leave this stain uncleansed. But the thought of losing her was a price greater than he was willing to pay. He would make the promise. And when something happened to Moussa—and as Allah was his witness, it would—well, *malish, mektoub*. It was the way of things. The desert was a dangerous place.

"Then I promise it."

CHAPTER 28

Prayer is better than sleep, than sleep!
Prayer is better than sleep!
Allah is great! Great is Allah!
There is no God but one God,
and Mohammed is His Prophet!

THE SINGSONG VOICE FLOATED OVER THE CAMP. It belonged to a *tirailleur* who had taken the place of the hostage *mokkadem*. Exhausted men and camels stirred themselves from sleep and groaned a chorus of collective agony. The Muslims in the camp performed their ablutions with sand instead of water, and drew themselves up onto their mats for the morning prayer, to face the east and find God. The sun would be up soon, time to order spent muscles and used-up flesh to move again.

Paul stared at the sky and rubbed Floop's belly. He listened to the prayers. Like the Flatters mission, his own prayers had started dying at Tadjenout. The words he had used all his life seemed as useless here as his muscles. He didn't miss them, really. They didn't seem to affect things one way or another. And Allah wasn't doing much better than God.

He chewed absently on a piece of leather from an old water bag. Hakeem said it would help the thirst. It didn't, but it did help keep his mind off it. There was never enough water. They could only wet their mouths three or four times a day. His lips were deeply cracked, too dry almost to bleed. His throat was choked with volcanic ash kicked up by plodding feet. The water he sipped was gone before it reached his throat, sucked into the parched places of his mouth. His head pounded fiercely from dehydration. As tired as he was, sleep came only fleetingly. He was running on will.

Two days earlier Dianous had ordered one of the precious camels killed. The Muslims cut its throat and said the ritual prayers. Belkasem wielded the colonel's ceremonial sword to do the cutting afterward. Some of the men ate the meat raw, unable to wait for it to be cooked. Most of them doubled over and vomited from the rich meat after so long without. There had been liquid in the camel's stomach, but it was nauseating green muck. Paul hadn't been able to drink it. He chewed his meat and looked away while others choked it down.

The meat was gone too quickly. He could barely remember now what it tasted like. A camel didn't go far among fifty starving men.

"TUAREG!"
The cry sent a ripple of fear through the column. In the distance, just out of rifle range, two tall figures sat atop their meharis, watching. Apparently they wanted to talk.

"I can make the shot, Lieutenant." The *tirailleur* was eager to try. They all were.

"No. Let's see what they want. DeVries, stay here. El Madani, come with me."

Dianous and El Madani walked alone across the plain. The Tuareg didn't move. Paul watched through the field glasses. His throat tightened. *Arrogant bastards,* he thought. *So bold, coming so close.* He wanted to shoot them himself. He could see Dianous and El Madani talking to them. The lieutenant was agitated, shaking his head and gesturing with his arms. El Madani said something, first to Dianous and then to the Tuareg. Then they both turned and trudged back to camp.

"They say they have two camels to sell. And dates and biscuits."

"It's a trick," El Madani grumbled. "I don't trust them."

"What trick? They either have what they say or they don't. If they don't we don't pay. If they do we take it."

"Why don't we just shoot them?" one of the *tirailleurs* grumbled. "Take the camels they're riding."

"What good would that do? We need more than that. Maybe they'll sell us more, later."

"We don't have much choice." Paul shrugged when Dianous looked at him for his opinion. There was little to debate. Dianous still had the expedition's silver. He counted it out. Paul whistled as the pile grew.

"That's a lot of money for two camels and some food."

Dianous shrugged. "It was their price. Do you have something better to do with it just now?"

Dianous sent Pobeguin and El Madani back with the money. One of the Tuareg disappeared behind a low hill in the distance and quickly returned leading two animals laden with packs. Pobeguin and El Madani returned with the camels.

Pobeguin opened the bags eagerly. As promised, there were dates and biscuits, all as tightly wrapped as the day they'd been packed in Wargla.

El Madani laughed bitterly when he saw. "Just like the blue devils," he said. "They've sold us our own food." The irony was lost on empty stomachs. The men began to eat. Even Floop nosed into the dates.

In the distance the two Tuareg watched as the starving men attacked the food.

"They have acted as Tamrit predicted," said one. "One foot in the trap. Attici will be pleased."

THEY WERE PASSING IN THE SHADOW OF THE Garet el Djenoum, the Peak of the Devil, when Floop's howl soared over the rocks and low hills, a terrible howl rising to the shrill excited frenzy of a mad dog. There was another sound, an animal sound that Paul couldn't make out. He rushed forward, followed at some distance by El Madani and four *tirailleurs*. Desperately he looked around, trying to find the source of the noise; the terrain played tricks with the sounds. He rounded a corner expecting the worst when he saw Floop nose-to-nose with a wild ass, the ass braying, Floop running around in front of it, darting from side to side. Floop had never seen such an apparition and concealed his terror behind a curtain of noise. When Floop saw Paul the dog raced to get behind his master, his bravery rising with his bark.

El Madani arrived and with the other *tirailleurs* quickly got a rope around the animal's neck. Paul calmed Floop and scratched him behind the ears, pleased. "Much better than a lizard, even if he caught you."

El Madani scouted the area, studying the ground. He knelt, his fingers on the gravel and sand. "Again they appear," he said, almost to himself.

"Madani?"

"The prints of a mehari, out of place," the old *tirailleur* said. "I saw them the first time the night we found you. Then again near the four wild camels." He shook his head, puzzled. "Why would someone help us?"

On the way back to camp Paul watched the terrain for him, but saw nothing. He knew he wouldn't. *So you're still there. It doesn't matter. Men are dying and you're trying to buy your way out of it with food. Damn you, Moussa! It isn't as easy as that!*

They cooked the ass for dinner.

THERE HAD BEEN NO WATER FOR TWO DAYS. ONE of the scouts found a small field of edible cactus and they collapsed in it, cutting it into pieces and eagerly sucking the bitter liquid. Paul tried to give some to Sandeau but he was nearly unconscious, tied to the camel now to keep him from falling off. He mumbled something and weakly squeezed Paul's hand. The cloth covering his head and neck had fallen away. The motion of the camel had worked his shirt down off one shoulder and he had ridden for hours exposed to the sun. Angry blisters bubbled on skin that was a field of fire. Paul tried to fix the shirt and tuck the cloth into Sandeau's collar. His hand accidentally brushed the skin. A patch of it came off and exposed the muscle beneath. Sandeau seemed not to notice.

When men could talk, they talked of Amguid and little else. They had passed through it on their way south, and were drawing near to it again. Paul recalled a large gorge there with a little stream and wells with good water. But others remembered much more: cool breezes and birds that flitted over date palms, or dikes and the refreshing noise of the water, irrigating gardens filled with sweet fruits and vegetables. It was all a mirage, Paul knew. They were putting the name of Amguid to their memories of Wargla. Even Hakeem had done it.

"We should go fishing in Amguid, Patron. The fish were fat there."

"I don't remember fish at Amguid."

"Oh yes, Patron, fine fish and a lovely stream. It ran through the oasis. There were palms and a little souk where they sold fruit. Allah left a thousand blessings on Amguid. Were you paying so little attention? We bought apricots there, and peaches."

"No. I remember the stream, but none of the rest in Amguid."

"Your memory is weak then, Patron. It is quite clear to me."

Paul shook his head patiently. "There are no apricots in Amguid, Hakeem. And no fish. You've had too much sun."

Hakeem laughed without humor. "That is wonderfully funny, Patron. Too much sun, indeed." His face turned hard. "You mock me now. You were a good patron once, but you have changed and gone cruel. First you took the Salukis from us. Now you take the fish. I am ashamed for you."

Paul thought he saw the little man's eyes mist, but Hakeem turned away. He limped off on bloody feet to find someone who would listen about the fish.

Paul felt shabby after that. He hadn't meant to steal a dream.

In the afternoon the officers had a different notion about Amguid. They sat paralyzed with heat, waiting through the worst of it.

"The sentry said the Tuareg are still there, matching our pace," Dianous said. "Nearly two hundred of them. What do you think they're up to?"

"Planning something," said El Madani. "They're too quiet."

"Maybe they're just making certain we leave." Pobeguin said it hopefully.

"Don't be stupid," El Madani snapped. "What else would we do? That is not their way. I'll tell you their plan. They are waiting for Amguid. Waiting until we are at our weakest from thirst and hunger. That's where they'll make their stand. They'll force us to fight when we have no strength left."

"*Merde.* We're nearly finished now."

"That's what they're counting on."

"I think we should mount a raiding party. Hit them at night," Paul said, dredging it up again.

"Shut up," said Dianous.

The next morning three Tuareg appeared again in the distance, waiting to talk.

"Are they the same ones?" asked Pobeguin.

"How would I know?" Dianous snapped at the sergeant. "All the devils look alike. Take Madani. See what they want."

Pobeguin and Madani set off across the open space. Presently they stood before the three men. Pobeguin didn't like looking up at such an angle but had no choice. The sun was behind the Tuareg, making them even more difficult to see. He had to squint and shield his eyes.

"We are not of the Kel Rela tribe that torments you," one of the Tuareg said. "We have heard of your

treatment at their hands. It is inexcusable. They are vile
men. We have often fought them ourselves. We want no
part of what they have done. We will help you."

"In what way?" asked El Madani, his manner
hostile.

"We have dates to sell. We can arrange for camels
and sheep as well. For a price, of course. We are but
poor nomads. Such treasures are not easy to find in this
place." '

"And your price?"

The man named an amount that was somewhat less
exorbitant than the one they had already paid. "I will
speak with our commander," said Madani. He translated for Pobeguin.

"Tell him we need a sign of good faith," the sergeant
said.

Madani did. The Tuareg talked quietly among themselves. From the rear of a mehari one of them produced
a heavy bag. He threw it at the *tirailleur*'s feet.

"We give you this as a sign of our own fidelity,
knowing you are men of honor and that you will pay
our price. Tomorrow morning you will arrive at the
wells of Aïn El Kerma. We will meet you there with
more."

El Madani and Pobeguin hoisted the sack and returned with it toward the column. The three Tuareg
watched them go.

"They dance flawlessly to your tune," said Mahdi.

"To him who puts a rope around his neck, Allah will
always give someone to pull it," said Tamrit.

Attici laughed. "Tomorrow we will pull."

A swarm of starving men fell on the dates without
waiting for Pobeguin to distribute them. Hunger had
destroyed any semblance of order. Shouted commands
fell on deaf ears. Sticky gobs of dates were snatched
from the bag. Men pushed other men out of the way.
Belkasem's elbow smashed teeth and flattened noses as
he savagely sought the greatest share. There weren't
enough to go around. Paul managed to grab a handful
for Sandeau, but went without himself. He hoped Floop

would hunt well that night, but Floop was tired of lizards and squirmed eagerly into the chaos to snap up his own share.

Pobeguin watched the mayhem with the bitter realization that they were at the mercy of the Tuareg. "I have never seen such greed," he said. "Now they won't be satisfied until they've gotten all our money by selling us our own provisions. It's humiliating."

"As long as we eat, why do you care?" asked Dianous.

MOUSSA PUSHED EAST ACROSS THE DESERT, HURRYing his little caravan as fast as he dared. The camels were loaded with food and skins of water. He had ridden furiously to In Salah to get them, stopping only long enough to rest his mehari. He had arrived long after dark when the oil lamps had gone out and the town slept behind closed gates. He couldn't rouse the guard so he scaled the wall next to the gate. The man was fast asleep and didn't notice his passage. Immediately he began pounding on doors, rousting men from their beds and purchasing what he needed without taking the time to bargain. The traders there knew him well and cheated him only a little. He was gone again before dawn, letting himself out of the gate past the stillsleeping guard. The journey had taken only eight nights. It was record time. Still, he hoped he hadn't been too long. Men died quickly here.

He intended to pick up the French track just to the north of Amguid. He would stay in front of them and leave the camels and supplies a little at a time where they could be found. He would lay a trail of survival to Wargla.

He reached a low plateau and led his camels up a difficult path. They groaned and stalled and complained. He had to dismount four times to adjust their loads to keep them from falling. It was hard going. He regretted sending Lufti back to Abalessa. He could have used his help.

He arrived at the top and began threading his way through a series of wadis. He turned to berate the animal in the rear, a stubborn beast that was more donkey than camel, and didn't immediately see the riders who moved silently out to block his way.

"You have become a trader then, Moussa?"

Moussa drew up sharply. A dozen Ihaggaren were behind Attici.

"If it were your affair I would answer, Attici," Moussa said curtly. "As it is not, kindly move. You are blocking my path."

"My affair is the French," Attici replied, unmoving. "I warned you to return to the south, to stay clear of those things that are not your domain. I believe you have forgotten yourself, if those camels pack supplies for the French. I say again—it is I who carry the *tobol*."

"It is I who remember our honor."

"Zatab, Mastan! Take his animals." Two of the Tuareg moved to respond. Moussa drew his great sword. "Stop there. I have no quarrel with you." They hesitated, then pressed ahead, closing around on both sides of Moussa. It was a classic maneuver he'd seen many times. He couldn't go forward, couldn't back up. He cursed himself for letting it happen, although there was nothing he could do to stop it short of killing. He was quickly penned in. He stared at them, sword ready, but they were all around.

One stopped just behind him, separating him from the pack animals. With both hands he swung his lance like a club. Moussa heard it coming and raised his sword, but too late. He tumbled from his mehari. Taka screeched furiously beneath her hood.

They stepped their meharis back gently, taking care not to let them tread on the unconscious man. They all knew Moussa. Even though he had lost himself in the matter of the French, no one wished him harm.

Attici calculated how best to keep Moussa from his meddling. "Leave only his mehari and enough water for two nights. No food at all. Leave the hawk in shade, with water. Take everything else."

By the time Moussa could return with new supplies, all the French would be dead.

THEY ARRIVED AT THE WELL OF AÏN EL KERMA IN the middle of the night, half-walking, half-dragging themselves to the pit. Worn fingers scrabbled at reluctant soil, trying to reach water. Men argued for their share and *guerbas* filled slowly. The camels were ignored. They would have to wait until later. It took hours to give everyone a drink.

Before dawn the familiar cry of the *tirailleur* summoned the Muslims to prayer. Paul felt Floop nuzzling him, wanting to be petted. He rolled over and opened his eyes. As they adjusted to the dim light he froze. In the distance he saw lances and turbans and meharis and a malevolent long line of Tuareg, watching the sleeping camp.

"*Tuareg!*" he cried, leaping to his feet.

The camp roared to life as men gripped their guns and orders were shouted. The line of Tuareg did not stir.

"Dianous, this is our chance," Paul cried. He pointed excitedly. "Look where they are! They've left themselves vulnerable. If we move quickly we can gain the high ground, there, by that rise! Fifteen men there, another fifteen over there, the rest here! We can get them in a crossfire. If we can't take them, at least we can do some damage, and get them on the run for a change! We've got to hurry!"

Dianous acted as though he hadn't heard a word. He pushed Paul aside. "Pobeguin! Order the men into defensive positions. Form firing lines."

As Pobeguin worked to establish the lines the Tuareg quietly began to move, abandoning their position and riding toward the north. Soon they were out of sight completely.

"You see?" said Dianous, pointing. "We couldn't have done anything anyway. It was too late. They don't want to face our guns. They want no battle here." He said it with a mixture of triumph and uncertainty. He looked around to see if others might agree. El Madani looked away. Pobeguin was busy. Brame and Marjolet looked noncommittal.

"Of course they don't want to face our guns," Paul said. "That is exactly why we must make them." He was angry, struggling with what he ought to do. He thought of the words of the *tirailleur* Mustafa ben Jardi. *We are willing to go with you, to fight like men. We are ready to obey your commands.*

It would be mutiny. But it might be the only way to survive. He was convinced now that Dianous would never fight. He would only run.

At that moment three meharis appeared from the southeast.

"The same ones from yesterday," Dianous said as he watched their approach. "I can't tell about the men for sure, but I recognize their camels." The Tuareg were carrying heavy bags and approached the well. The bags thumped onto the ground, stirring up a cloud of dust.

"El Madani!" Dianous called out. "Pay them! Ask about the sheep!"

El Madani and Pobeguin trudged out to meet them.

"What of the sheep and camels you promised?" Madani asked as Pobeguin counted out the money for the dates.

"The Kel Rela Tuareg are too near just now," one of them said. "Their numbers are too strong for us. We will return this afternoon, after they have gone." They took their money and rode away.

The ranks of *tirailleurs* broke as men scrambled for the bags of dates. Again they were ripped open, frenzied hands plunging into the dark sweet mess. There were enough dates this time, plenty for everyone, but that didn't stop hoarding and quarrels. Again Belkasem blackened eyes and bloodied noses as he stuffed his pack. Floop was everywhere among busy feet, picking up pieces that fell to the ground, wolfing them down.

Paul looked at the teeming mass of greed and decided to wait for his share. His stomach was so shrunken a few more minutes wouldn't matter. He decided to walk the perimeter of the camp to make certain the Tuareg had planned no treachery. El Madani had the same thought and went the other way. Many of the Shamba cameleers sat unmoving, staring sullenly at the wild pack of men fighting over the food. Dianous, Brame, and Marjolet shared a fire, boiling their dates to soften them. Pobeguin was trying to get Sandeau to eat.

Paul and El Madani completed their circuit and met at the far end of the camp, between the well and the place where the Tuareg force had stood. They sat down together in the shadow of a rock that sheltered them from behind.

"It's bizarre," Paul said. "Tuareg just over the hill trying to kill us. Others selling us food. I don't understand it."

"This is not a place for understanding," El Madani said.

Paul considered what he ought to say. El Madani was the most experienced of the *tirailleurs,* the most respected. He himself trusted the man. He had to know how El Madani would act if Paul attempted to relieve Dianous of command. The others would follow him.

"Mustafa ben Jardi came to me," Paul began. El Madani raised his eyebrows but said nothing. "He said some things that I thought out of order at the time, about our failure to fight the Tuareg. He said—"

Paul never had a chance to finish. Shots rang out. Men shouted. Paul and El Madani were up in an instant, weapons at the ready. They looked toward camp, expecting to see an attack under way. But there were no Tuareg in sight. Instead, it was as if the camp had gone suddenly insane. Men were screaming and dancing, scratching at their faces and eyes, ripping off their shirts, fighting each other. Paul watched incredulously as Dianous ran crazily around the fire, shooting his rifle into the air.

"What in God's name—?" Paul looked uncertainly at El Madani.

El Madani began to run, slowly at first, then faster as

it dawned on him. "I should have known, *w'allahi!* The Tuareg have attacked us after all. It is a plant they call *efeleleh*. Nightshade. They've poisoned the dates."

Together they ran into the nightmare.

Hakeem was shrieking and thrashing wildly. He didn't recognize Paul and pushed him away with superhuman strength. He threw himself onto the coals of a fire, bellowing and tearing at his hair. Desperately Paul pulled him off, stamping at the smoldering cloth. Hakeem was a smoking flurry of arms and legs, struggling to get up. "The devil!" he choked, his voice thick and barely intelligible. "There! In there! I must touch him!" He lunged again for the fire. Paul knocked him unconscious. He tore rope from a pack and quickly bound his ankles and feet.

Some of the *tirailleurs* were disappearing into the open desert, stripping off their clothes as they ran, trying to cool the fires inside. Paul was able to stop one, and then another, but there was no reasoning with them. They were delirious and hysterical. They sobbed and moaned. He hit them until they stopped. El Madani had fallen on top of Dianous and had gotten his weapon away. Pobeguin was stuffing his mouth with sand. Both officers had to be tied up.

Brame, the colonel's batman, was walking in a lopsided circle, his gait clumsy. He tried to say something to Paul but only gagged. Then he laughed madly, flecks of foam at the corners of his mouth. Paul shook him by the shoulders, trying to calm him. Brame's face lit with terror. His eyes went wild, filled with fiends and desert dragons. Paul slapped him. He sat heavily and started to sob. Paul turned to get rope and the next instant Brame was all over him. He screamed something unintelligible and bashed Paul on the back with a rock. El Madani materialized and held Brame's arms while Paul got him tied.

Paul was a dervish swirling through camp, trying to douse the flames of a world gone mad. He looked desperately for help. Healthy men who had not eaten any dates sat cringing in dread. He yelled at them, and then hit one of the men viciously, trying to snap the paralysis. It seemed to shake them from their fright and at last they began to move. He dispatched four to act as sentries in case the Tuareg attacked. Others ran off to get more water from the well. A few began tearing cloth into strips that could be used to bind the poisoned men. The rest plunged in to help subdue the raving victims, who staggered and danced crazily through the camp.

One of the *tirailleurs* tried to club another to death and then turned the gun on himself. Men lay sobbing on the ground, hugging their rifles or curled up into tight balls. One of the Shamba tumbled head-first into the well and drowned. Paul had no time to think, only to react as he gave orders and tried to restore sanity. Within the first half hour the worst of those stricken had been tightly trussed and laid out next to each other on the ground, a retching line of tormented humanity. They struggled against their restraints and yelled at demons only they could see. Stomachs heaved and chests labored for breath. Their skin was hot and flushed, their pupils dilated. Only Sandeau was quiet. His breathing was shallow, his stare vacant. His limbs jerked gently every now and then.

When Hakeem regained consciousness he was burning up. His head thrashed from side to side. Paul tried to soothe him, but Hakeem still didn't know him. An angry rash covered his face and neck. His belly was swollen. Paul tried to give him water but he couldn't swallow. He choked on it. He opened his eyes and panicked. "I'm blind, I'm blind!" he cried. He struggled fiercely to get loose. Paul could do nothing for him.

The sounds in the camp haunted Paul as he worked. Men whimpered, others cried. "I want to die," Mustafa ben Jardi pleaded through clenched teeth. "Kill me, kill me, oh merciful Allah take me now. Don't let me be. Death to me. Please! Death now!" Paul tried to shut his ears to it. He moved away to help another man. A few moments later Mustafa fell silent. Paul looked over. One of the *tirailleurs* hadn't been able to stand it, either. He had hit Mustafa with his rifle until the noise stopped.

When Paul had done everything he could do he collapsed onto the ground, exhausted. And then he had an awful thought. He pulled himself to his feet and moved quickly through the camp, past the trussed victims, past healthy men who talked in low voices, their eyes spooked. Paul's eyes darted everywhere, looking, hoping, searching.

"Floop!"

He tried to keep the panic from his voice. There was no response. There was a pit in his stomach, a terrible knot of fear.

"Floop!" *Merde,* where was he?

He looked beseechingly at the men. They shrugged or shook their heads. He ran faster, to the well and to the rocks just beyond. Nothing.

"*Floop!*"

And then he saw.

Floop had made it just out onto the flat. He had been trying to find shade, perhaps, to cool himself. He had not gone far when he collapsed. He had crawled then, dragging his rear legs and leaving a wide trail on the ground. Then his front legs had given out. He had stopped moving when Paul got to him. His eyes were open but their life was gone.

Paul fell to his knees and gently cradled Floop's head in his lap. He rocked back and forth, talking softly and rubbing the dog's golden coat. And then his wrenching cry rose up over the well of Aïn El Kerma.

FROM THE DISTANCE ATOP THE HILL THE TUAREG watched silently as the *efeleleh* did its work and the French column disintegrated into hell. By order of Attici there was no move to attack. The time would soon be right, but for the moment he intended to let his broth of poison simmer in the desert.

Many of the Tuareg were deeply troubled. Taher made for his mehari, to return to the south. "Poison is not the manner of the Ihaggaren," he said. "Moussa was right. There is no honor in this."

"Go, then," said Attici, shrugging. He could not order Taher to stay, nor the dozen others who followed him. It was their right to object. There would be plenty of men of courage left to complete the task at hand.

Attici moved to the side of the hill closest to Aïn El Kerma. He stood with Tamrit and Mahdi. "The second blow falls upon the barbarian," he said. "The world will soon come to know the strength of the people of the veil. Ahitagel will be pleased."

Mahdi wasn't listening. His eyes were on the still form of the dog and the man kneeling over it.

Mahdi was truly moved.

It was a pity, about the dog.

PAUL STUMBLED AND FELL TO HIS KNEES. HIS MUScles quivered painfully. They were making a forced night march, trying to make Amguid. There was no room on the camels, already overloaded with other men, so Paul was carrying Hakeem on his back.

Sandeau had died. No one noticed until he slipped from the ropes and dangled below the belly of the camel. There had been no time or tools or energy to make a proper grave. Paul scooped heaps of sand over him until his hands were bloody. He was too numb to find tears.

"*Je suis désolée*," he whispered. "I wish, Sandeau, that I could have done more. I am sorry that I have no prayers."

Dianous and Pobeguin were barely coherent, just able to walk by themselves. Brame and Marjolet held each other up, clutching their rifles and staggering in a daze. "The *efeleleh* works long," El Madani said. "They will not fully recover for some days."

The column was in wretched condition, devastated and demoralized. There had not been enough time to rest before moving. Five men were missing or dead. More than thirty were desperately ill. Even after two days the poison left them babbling and half-mad. They had to be pushed or dragged in the right direction.

More than once Paul found *tirailleurs* dropping their rifles to the ground, leaving themselves defenseless as they marched forward. Some did it stupidly from the *efeleleh*, simply forgetting what the guns were for. Others did it because they were beginning to give up.

"What does it matter?" asked one when Paul berated him. "What good is a gun against the devil? How can you shoot what you cannot see? How can you kill what will not die?"

Paul was enraged. He drew his pistol and waved it in the *tirailleur*'s face. "You would leave your weapons for the enemy to use against us?" His voice carried into the distance. He fired his gun into the air. The column was shocked to a halt. No one had ever seen Lieutenant deVries that way. He seemed quite as mad as the rest of them.

"It is not the devil we face! These men have no supernatural powers! They are primitive savages, do you hear me? *Bullets will kill them!* I will shoot the next man who abandons his weapon! *Do you understand?*" Meekly, the *tirailleur* nodded and picked up his rifle.

THE BATTLE CAME WHERE EL MADANI SAID IT would, at Amguid.

They saw the dunes first, a high range that skirted the western approaches to the well. Beyond were the heights of the Tassili, a plateau of bizarre shapes and sandstone mysteries. It was a rugged and beautiful place. The column reached the top of a long ridge that dropped steeply away into a deep gorge. At the bottom of the gorge was the stream they had all dreamed of reaching. And between the column and the stream, arrayed in a long line, sat the Tuareg on their meharis, barring the way.

Paul eased Hakeem to the ground. He groaned but remained unconscious. Paul studied the Tuareg through his field glasses. He felt his chest tightening. They had become more than the enemy. They had become an object of loathing. He wanted to jump up and take them all by himself, to give each of them a death, an execution as terrible as the deaths they had dealt. He fought to still his heart.

"They have carbines," he said to Dianous as the lieutenant sagged down next to him. "But not many. They're in a terrible position for defense. We can take them."

"There are too many," whispered Dianous, too weak to talk. "It would be suicide."

Paul blew up. "For God's sake, when will you stop cringing before them? You're no better than the *tirailleurs* who have been throwing down their weapons! Why not just walk down there and surrender? Why wait to die, if you won't fight? What kind of man are you? You're a coward!"

Dianous reddened and lashed out, trying to strike Paul, but he missed and fell weakly to the ground. "You have no right," he gasped. "You will obey orders, Lieutenant deVries. *Look behind you.* These men are in no condition to fight. They're already half-dead. They haven't anything left."

Paul stared at the men arrayed behind them down the slope. Only twenty remained healthy; of those only twelve were riflemen. Yet Paul saw no other option.

"We have no choice now, Dianous. We have to fight here or we're going to die for sure."

Dianous shook his head again. "Wait, I tell you. See what they do."

Paul made up his mind. "I'm through waiting," he said, and he started to crawl backward.

"I'm through arguing," said Dianous. His hand was not steady, but his pistol was leveled at Paul's head. "If you do anything except what I order, I'll shoot you down right here."

ATTICI MOTIONED AND THE FIRST WAVE OF Ihaggaren roared forward in attack, fifty screaming warriors waving their swords and hefting their shields, their meharis bellowing, the noise shattering the silence that had enveloped the gorge. Even armed only with medieval weapons, they were terrifying.

All up and down the French line the *tirailleurs* struggled to get organized, to focus their fire. El Madani ran back and forth shouting orders. The men fired wildly at first, then with more precision and discipline as their training kicked in. Their guns roared in the gorge. Paul and Dianous began firing at the onrushing mass of warriors, their quarrel forgotten. Paul hit a Targui and felt a surge of excitement as the man tumbled from his mehari. He shot again and missed, then again, and another fell. His blood rushed with the fever of it all, his arms steady, his fatigue forgotten.

The charging Tuareg succumbed quickly to the deadly onslaught of the Gras rifles. A dozen had fallen when the others hastily retreated. Dust and noise choked the gorge as the Tuareg reorganized quickly, then charged once again. They swooped down in another frontal assault, while others mounted silent attacks on the flanks as their warriors crawled in to attack unwary *tirailleurs* with spears and knives. Men shouted and died. For hours it went on, violent bursts of terror and death interspersed with quiet anticipation.

Through it all the Tuareg rifles were noticeably silent. "They must have no ammunition," Dianous said.

I N ONE OF THE SILENCES ATTICI MOTIONED AGAIN. Atop a cliff on the other side of the gorge a prisoner was marched forward by a warrior. Everyone on both lines was watching, mesmerized by the scene.

"The *mokkadem*," one of the *tirailleurs* gasped. "He is still alive."

The prisoner was made to kneel. The leather hood was removed from his head. He blinked in the bright light and looked around, taking in the scene. He seemed to understand what was going to happen, and his serene voice of prayer could be heard over the distance. Behind him the Targui raised his great sword in the air, holding it with both hands above the *mokkadem*'s head, then crashing it down in a massive blow. The holy man tumbled forward into the gorge. The other prisoners taken at Tadjenout were brought forward and forced to shout their names. They cried and shook their heads and cringed at the sword. They had suffered through hell, to get to this. One by one they were beheaded and pitched forward into the abyss.

"My God," said Dianous dumbly, finally aroused. He stood up and stepped forward, and turned to beckon to the men behind him. Others had also risen, horrified at the sight, the whole of the French force now stirred to attack. It was what Attici had been waiting for. From various places hidden among the rocks the Tuareg rifles that had been silent all day opened fire. Dianous fell, shot through the head. Brame died, and then Marjolet, trying to help him. Up and down the line Shamba fell, and some of the *tirailleurs*. The remaining French rifles returned fire furiously, with little effect. The Tuareg warriors were well hidden, and shrilled their success.

Attici gloated, his final surprise complete.

T HE SUN WAS SETTING BEHIND DUNES THAT SHONE like hills of gold. Rose-colored clouds filled the western sky, light wisps of cotton lit on fire by the sun. They were luminescent, bathing Amguid in an eerie dreamlike glow. It was the most beautiful sunset Paul had ever seen.

He sat slumped over, drained. They had finished burying the dead in shallow graves. He had done Hakeem's by himself, lifting the little body of his aide and setting it gently inside the rim of stones, taking care to face his head to the east in the way of Islam, then scooping on sand and dirt, and finally packing stones on top. Hakeem had been alive when the battle started, but sometime during the afternoon fever or poison had taken him unnoticed. Paul hadn't known until he had come to give him water.

After the battle he had crawled through the French

positions, assessing their condition. In all, eighteen men had died, leaving thirty-three who were half-dead themselves. Paul felt intensely alone. Among the French only he and Pobeguin had survived, and Pobeguin was raving.

It was all up to him now.

Amguid had been quiet for hours. The Tuareg were still there, but refused to show themselves. They were scattered, waiting. Paul studied their positions, calculating distances and odds. Reluctantly he kept coming to the same conclusion. Their opportunity had passed, lost in cowardice and incompetence, in poison and the awful cunning of their opponents.

"We cannot reach the well," he dejectedly told El Madani.

The old rifleman nodded. "I agree. I counted nearly fifty of the devils dead, but they are still five times our number. They have water and food. They can wait forever. We have to go around. We have to move on."

"What do you think they'll do next?"

El Madani thought about that. "I may be wrong, but I think they are finished with us, Lieutenant. They may send a few men after us to harass us, but this is the northern end of their country. They have no need to go farther. They have shown us the door. They are counting on the desert to continue their work. If some of us survive to see Wargla and tell the world what happened, so much the better for their cause."

"I expect they're right about the desert." Paul had no illusions about what they faced. It had been only three weeks since the massacre at Tadjenout, three weeks that seemed a lifetime, and they were not yet halfway to Wargla.

"It is a shame to miss Amguid, *w'allahi,*" El Madani said wistfully. "I was looking forward to eating some of the fish."

Paul looked at him sharply. "There are no fish at Amguid, El Madani. Hakeem ranted that nonsense with me. Don't you start now." Paul knew he was lost if El Madani's head started going.

"Of course there are, Lieutenant. Why would I make

up such a thing? I saw them myself on the way south. I thought everyone did. I can't believe you missed them."

Paul stared hard into the *tirailleur*'s eyes. El Madani was telling the truth.

Paul's gaze shifted to Hakeem's grave. It had been a little thing, perhaps, but he felt even worse than ever. *You've changed and gone cruel,* Hakeem had told him. He'd died angry at him, over some damned fish in the middle of the Sahara.

THEY LEFT IN THE MIDDLE OF THE NIGHT, PUTTING the weakest men on top of the remaining camels, everyone else struggling behind. They walked all through the night and the next day without food or water or a single stop. Every so often they saw the Tuareg, following, but the blue men stayed well out of range and left them alone. The second night they rested for an hour and then moved on. There was desperation in their pace, a race between their weak bodies and time and the desert.

Paul tried to remember how far it was to Wargla. He couldn't. Everything about the journey south ran together in his mind. He tried to talk whenever he could to El Madani, but talking stole moisture and energy. Pretty soon he contented himself with grunts, and then grunts seemed to cost too much and he could only shrug or nod.

They found water after two days, or was it three, ghastly remnants of men crowding around a dirty little hole where in their hurry they took in as much sand as water. In the middle of the night four *tirailleurs* stole two of the camels and deserted, their tracks disappearing off to the north. Paul wanted to chase them, but there was no way. In frustration he fired his rifle in their direction, the bullet soaring off into sandy oblivion.

They had one camel left. They killed and butchered it quickly. After that Pobeguin had to walk. His eyes were lost in dark circles. His body trembled, his muscles giving up. He was confused all the time, asking nonsensical questions. He was dying in bits.

They dared not stop, for to stop was to die. To stop was to delay Wargla. Wargla was an obsession; Wargla was life. Hour after hour they walked, day after burning day on sand and gravel and granite. Each day bent their backs and shredded their feet a little more. They stumbled beneath the stars and the moon, past mountains and plateaus. They went two whole days through a stretch of desert where there was not the smallest trace of life—not a fly or a blade of grass, not a lizard or a bird.

Paul found discipline almost impossible to maintain. There was nothing to say to lift the men's spirits. Threats made no difference. The backs of his men had bent at Aïn El Kerma, and broken at Amguid. Now each man was engaged in a private struggle to survive the death march. There wasn't enough food or water for them all. Inexorably, each man began fending for himself.

Paul saw a lizard at the same time as two other men. It was sunning itself on a wide flat rock and seemed oblivious to their presence. They all charged at once, only to find that the little reptile had disappeared.

"Idiots!" Paul shrieked at them. "If you'd let me catch it we'd have had something to eat!"

"And which of us would have eaten?" It was a question without an answer.

Paul rebuked himself for letting things slip but didn't know how to fix them.

Men died. They would slow and then drop, or, after a rest, not get up again. Sometimes no one noticed.

They found grass on the lee side of a large dune. It was stiff and brittle but they ate it anyway, breaking it into little pieces that tore at raw throats like tiny spears. They ate belts and sandals, cutting the leather into little bits just big enough to chew. Their jaw muscles cramped and stopped working.

El Madani caught a jerboa, a skimpy little mouse that hopped right in front of him while he was resting. The old *tirailleur* got his hands around it and squeezed until it moved no more. He skinned it carefully and ate it raw. Another man found a snake just at dawn, a viper curled into a little ball beneath the sand, and had its head off before the cold sluggish thing could move. Flies swirled incessantly around faces and eyes. One landed on Paul's tongue. He recoiled and began to spit it out, but then closed his mouth and swallowed. It stuck in his dry throat, where for long minutes he felt it moving before it went down. After that he tried to catch them with his hands.

One morning a gazelle wandered into view. It was upwind and hadn't picked up their scent. A dozen rifles slipped from a dozen shoulders and a hail of fire shattered the quiet. When the smoke cleared they could see the gazelle bounding off, frightened but unhurt.

Late one day angry clouds gathered overhead, dark and violent and laced with lightning, but the storm they prayed for never came. The clouds thinned and passed into memory. They found a well that had sweet water. They stayed a whole day, unwilling to leave the precious liquid behind. Other wells along the way were sometimes dry, or yielded only brackish muck that served for water and filled their bags.

Paul hurt everywhere, his body a collection of blisters and burns and scrapes that ran together in seamless agony. Each step aggravated something on his foot or inside his thighs or under his arms or in his crotch. His feet were raw, the leather of his soles finally gone. Only the thoughts of revenge that consumed him made it possible to keep putting one foot in front of another.

They came upon the body of a camel, mummified by the desert air. Its skin was dried and stretched tight over its gaunt frame, its eye sockets frozen in a timeless stare of death. They fell to their knees and cut it into strips, knives hacking and sawing through the desiccated body as if it were shoe leather. What had been flesh was now powder. They mixed it with water into a paste and drank it eagerly. With bare hands they pulled the skeleton apart, the bones snapping like dry twigs, and ground them with rocks and boot heels until they had more powder to mix with the water, and they drank that too. They grunted while they worked and ate, like animals.

The wind picked up and blew at them from the north. It was stronger than before, and they struggled against it. El Madani watched the sky and waved at Paul to look.

"We need to keep together," he whispered hoarsely, each word painful. "Storm. Big."

For an afternoon the wind stayed steady, throwing a river of sand at them that rose only a few feet off the ground. Above that level the air was clear. On camels they would have been above it, but as it was it assaulted them, finding eyes and ears and noses and throats and cuts, burning and blasting and sucking away what precious little sanity they could cling to. They covered themselves with bits of cloth. The wind grew stronger, shrieking, the sand rising like a fog until it blocked the sun, the storm gathering strength until they had to stop because they could walk no more, could not see their way or fight the wind.

Without shelter, they collapsed where they stood and huddled alone under the raging storm, the sand pouring like liquid over their backs and collecting in great drifts like driven snow. Paul tried to shout at El Madani but his voice was lost in the noise. He couldn't see anyone or anything but the wall of sand. He took off his shirt and lay flat on his belly and tried to make a tent for his head, a little space where he could breathe. It was dark and suffocating beneath it. For the first time since the Hoggar he was desperately afraid. He thought of the stories he'd heard of the great storms of the Sahara, storms in which entire caravans, even armies had been lost, swallowed whole by the desert. Suffocated and buried and forgotten.

The storm raged through the night and all the next day and that night as well. It was hard to tell night from day; it was always dark. Whenever he thought the gale could grow no stronger it would, the wind shrieking at him like a thousand *djenoums,* making him frantic for its end. He had lost his water bag and had nothing to drink. He had not slept for two days and nights and knew he could take it no more. He called out for Floop and cried for his mother. He talked to his father. He had never done that, but now he mumbled and groaned and babbled at his dead father, berating him for leaving, begging him to come back, to help.

Twice his hand felt for the pistol at his belt, his fingers closing over the handle. The first time he pulled his hand away, empty. The second time the gun came up next to his head. Laboriously he turned it around in the cramped space until it faced him. He put the barrel in his mouth, until he could taste the promise of its sweet release. So close, so close now. His finger closed over the trigger and he shut his eyes and his nose flared and he took a deep breath.

He cried out in pain. He couldn't do it.

Oh God please let it end, please please, if you'll just let it end I will believe again, I will recant the blasphemies and the doubts and the heresies and be a good Catholic until the day I die.

But there was no end, not for long hours, not until the early morning of the third day when the winds began to subside. He refused to believe it at first, thinking the desert was playing another of its cruel tricks, but gradually the noise abated and the air cleared, and the dawn came pink and glorious to a new day.

The men roused themselves slowly, stirring from their beds of sand. Not everyone got up. Some had died in the storm, suffocated or claimed by madness or thirst or hunger or by their own hand. Legs and arms and ends of turbans poked up through the sand to mark their places. No one had the desire to dig them up to find out how they'd died. They were already buried.

FOR TWO MORE DAYS THEY WALKED, WITHERED sticks of men whose steps grew increasingly unsteady. A flock of crows appeared and followed them like a black shadow of death. The birds were big and hideous. They cawed and danced on the sand, taunting the men through beaks drawn back as if they were smiling. The *tirailleurs* tried to shoot them but the crows just hopped back.

Djemel, the noseless camel driver, died beside the

well of Gassi Touil. He had seemed all right the night before, but in the morning he had just not gotten up. His little body was curled up around the sack he used for collecting camel dung. They threw some sand over him and placed a few stones. Another tomb in a ritual that had become routine.

Paul noticed more conversation than usual that morning. Normally when the men weren't walking they collapsed in silence where they stopped, too spent to talk. When they walked they ranged out over large areas, looking for something to eat. Now, getting ready to leave, some huddled together in little groups. He noticed a few of them staring, but they looked away quickly. If he came near they stopped talking. Something was going on. He would ask El Madani about it.

Before they had walked very far Belkasem dropped back. Paul saw him away in the distance. He had turned and was walking back to the well, his sword draped over his shoulders like a harness, as usual.

He walked over to join El Madani. "Where is Belkasem going?"

El Madani shrugged. "To perdition."

"We are already there," Paul whispered hoarsely, glad for what he thought was levity from the old *tirailleur*. "Why would he want more?"

"Maybe he's hunting. I don't know." He didn't want to talk. He avoided Paul's eyes.

They had stopped to rest at midday before Belkasem caught up with them. He struggled under a heavy load wrapped in dirty rags. He walked up to where Paul sat and dropped a bundle of meat. Paul looked at him in amazement.

"Take some, Lieutenant," Belkasem said eagerly. "I thought I saw it, back by the well. That is why I returned, to see. *Hamdullilah,* I was right! Allah has blessed us at last with good fortune. A great mountain sheep!"

Paul blinked, staring at what was on the ground. His brain stirred slowly in the heat. It took him a long time to comprehend. The realization swept over him at last. It was no mountain sheep. He recoiled in horror and rolled away in fear. He needed to vomit but there was nothing in his stomach. He got to his knees. He coughed and choked and tried to spit.

He rose and staggered toward Belkasem. The cook regarded him warily, the colonel's sword still in his hand. He would use it on the lieutenant. His eyes promised he would.

"What have you done? How could you? Oh sweet Jesus, Belkasem. If you touch another man, dead or alive, I will kill you. Oh God, oh God, forgive him, forgive us all. Bury it, Belkasem. Bury it now."

The butcher shook his head. He bent over to pick it up. "If you will not eat, others will." Paul's boot lashed out and caught Belkasem in the temple. He collapsed next to the flesh.

"Bury it, I said! Bury it!" He was looking at the other *tirailleurs,* but no one moved to obey. Paul fired his pistol in the air. Men flinched but remained in their places.

El Madani walked up to him. Paul looked at him through eyes wild with horror. El Madani gently touched his shoulder.

"It is not the best thing now, Lieutenant, to bury it. It is the best thing now, to eat it. What has been done is done, and will not be changed. He was already dead."

"No! I cannot allow it! I will not!" Paul pushed him, but El Madani stood firm and caught him by the arm. Paul would have shot him, but he had been through much with this man. El Madani was not the enemy. El Madani was a rock.

"We will die if we do not eat, Lieutenant. Where is the wisdom in that? Have we come so far, only to die here?"

"Not this way, Madani, not this way!" Paul collapsed to his knees, his voice a choked sob. He tried to push sand over the meat, to cover it up, but two of the *tirailleurs* stood and dragged it back out of the way. He looked from one set of eyes to another, and saw their resolve. They were against him in this, all of them.

Even El Madani.

Paul looked to Pobeguin for support. The Breton was

shaken. The poison had never cleared from his brain. He was physically exhausted, near death himself. His expression was vacant, giving only the faintest hint that he understood what was happening. He looked at Paul and at El Madani and at the pile of meat on the ground. A tear formed in his eye and rolled down his dusty cheek. Then he nodded slowly.

"Eat," he whispered.

Paul sat alone as the others ate, his head in his hands. Storms raged in his brain. *To live off the dead!* It was appalling, immoral, bestial.

But what frightened him most was the sure knowledge that the day was coming when he too would take his share.

THE SHAMBA WAS BESIDE HIMSELF WITH EXCITEment. "I think we are near the camp of one of our early guides," he insisted. "I can find it. Allah himself will guide me. That dune with a stone near the top, in the shape of a sword. I remember it clearly. If I am right, there will be a wadi just beyond with a bed of green stone. There, just there." He pointed eagerly. He spoke in a ragged whisper. He was sure of himself. "If it is true I will come back immediately. I will not be gone long."

Paul thought about it. "All right." The Shamba wobbled off, hurrying as much as he could.

Pobeguin fell. Paul went to help him. The Shamba disappeared behind a hill when suddenly Belkasem and another *tirailleur* broke away from the group and followed him. Paul might not have seen, but caught the movement out of the corner of his eye. None of the other men appeared to have noticed. A few moments later he heard a shot.

Now he looked wildly at the others. They shrugged and shook their heads. No one seemed to know what was going on.

For once, Paul did.

It had gone to murder then.

It had gone too far.

If they all turned on him now, if they killed him, it didn't matter. He drew his pistol. "No!" he shouted. "This will not be!" As quickly as he could he raced after them, his body straining with the extra effort, his motions exaggerated as his muscles alternately cramped and failed. He fell twice on his way up the hill, his strength gone. At the top he saw only rocks and more hills. He walked farther and saw the *tirailleur*, who hadn't seen him. Then he saw Belkasem, bending over the Shamba's body.

"*Arrêtez!*" Paul shouted. Surprised, the *tirailleur* lunged and clubbed him hard. Paul fell to the ground. The *tirailleur* stepped over him. He looked at Belkasem, questioning. The butcher nodded. If the rest of them were to live, the lieutenant had to die.

"Kill him."

The *tirailleur* raised his gun casually, not needing to aim. At the instant he fired he was jarred by an impact that shook his entire body. It took his breath away. Dumbly, he looked down at the stain spreading on his shirt, around the shaft of the lance that had been driven through his chest. He had no idea what had happened. He fell backward, dead.

Belkasem looked up in terror at the towering apparition. The Targui stood above him, a vision from hell. He had made no sound at all. His eyes held Belkasem's through the slit of his veil. They were blue and quite cold with purpose. Behind the devil, atop the pommel of his mehari's saddle, a hawk watched too, a white one with a patch of gray on the chest. The Targui drew his great sword and stepped forward. As surely as Belkasem had ever known anything, he knew the specter of death. He was a butcher, not a fighter. He backed away and dropped the colonel's sword. He turned and fled, stumbling over the rocks and bellowing the alarm at the new Tuareg raid.

CHAPTER 29

FATHER JEAN MOREAU RAN THE MISSION OF THE White Fathers near Wargla. He had snow white hair and kindly eyes and weighed little more than a leaf. His mission consisted of an orphanage, an infirmary, and a chapel, all in a compound nestled in the shade of a large grove of palms outside the oasis. The mission was poor. The chapel had a single crucifix on the wall above an altar made of mud bricks. The orphanage had a straw mat for each child and woolen blankets for cold nights. The infirmary was a small room with two cots and a table, and a chest where Father Jean kept medicine. The mission was surrounded by an earthen wall with a large wooden gate that never closed. On one side of the compound there were vegetable gardens and pens for sheep and goats and chickens.

Father Jean pleaded regularly for supplies from Cardinal Lavigerie, the archbishop of Algiers and the founder of the White Fathers. The cardinal invariably responded with abundant blessings and no supplies. Father Jean pestered old friends in France, who sent medicines and tins of food.

The orphanage and infirmary were always filled to overflowing. The chapel was always empty. The people of Wargla were glad to have the White Father's goodwill and medicine, but not his religion. In twenty years in Africa he counted just one convert. But Father Jean was a patient man. "The souls will follow if we tend their bodies and minds," he said. He worked tirelessly from sunup to well after dark. The people of Wargla trusted him.

His one convert was Melika, a young woman who had been abandoned as an infant. Children normally left the orphanage as soon as they were eight, to make room for younger ones, but Melika stayed. She was a quick study. By the time she was ten she was helping teach the other children. At eighteen she knew almost as much about medicine as Father Jean. She had a wonderful manner with the patients. She was indispensable, looking after the animals and tending to the children. She taught them French and geography and sums. She cooked for them and tended to their lumps and bumps and infected eyes.

Melika worshiped Father Jean. She wasn't a convert, really, for she had been raised by the priest. She didn't believe in the White Father's God nearly as much as she believed in him.

I T WAS TO THIS MISSION THAT MOUSSA BROUGHT Paul in the middle of the night. Paul was unconscious, tied atop the mehari. Father Jean had called for Melika and the three of them got Paul settled into Melika's room. The infirmary was full and there was nowhere else to put him. Melika didn't mind. It happened often. She could sleep in the orphanage on one of the mats.

Father Jean worked through the night. In his first life, before his vows, he had been a doctor. War in Europe had killed his wife and children and had turned his hair white before he was twenty-five. He had treated every injury imaginable. He had amputated limbs and patched mangled bodies. He knew as much about medicine as any man in the south of Algeria. So it was with some certainty that he was able to give the prognosis to the Targui waiting in the courtyard.

"The Frenchman will die. He is too far gone. Even without the bullet, I think the desert has killed him."

"He will not die, Father. He is strong and a good man. The desert didn't kill him when it had the best chance. He is one of your God's miracles."

Father Jean smiled. "I forget myself. I have been a doctor too long. You say the words to me I should be saying to you. Of course I pray that you are right. I will do everything I can."

Melika settled in to take the first turn with the patient. Near dawn the Targui left.

T HE WOUND FESTERED AND ROTTED AROUND THE edges. It smelled horrible. Father Jean shook his head.

"If he'd been shot in the arm or leg I could cut it off and stop the poison," he told Melika. "But there's nothing to do when it's in his shoulder."

He clipped away the skin and washed the wound with carbolic acid. He prayed. She cleaned it every few hours and changed the bandages. Sometimes Paul cried out when she did it. The skin came away in bits. There was a big hole where the bullet had gone in, and a bigger one where it had come out. When she turned him over he bled. She shooed away the flies.

In his delirium he talked a lot, mumbling of Moussa and St. Paul's, of Flatters and Floop and Remy. She came to know that name well. Remy, Remy. An arm. His arm. Once the soldier jumped up, clutching his arm, shrieking that it had been cut off. She had said it, over and over. "Your arm is all right. Your arm is still there. *Shhhh.* . . ."

She wiped his head and bathed him with a sponge to cool the fevers. She put goat's butter on his swollen lips and rubbed it into his feet where they had cracked and bled. She read to him even though she didn't think he could hear. She read from Father Jean's Bible, and from a medical text he had. She read him names of places off the maps they used to teach the children, and from anything else she could find.

She was fascinated by him. She had never seen such a handsome man. His hair was thick and nearly white and ran to his shoulders, while his beard was full and the color of honey. As she took care of him she imagined who he was, imagined things about him. She knew he was a soldier, that his name was Paul. The Targui who brought him had said it. But she knew little else.

He shrieked at night, his forehead drenched with sweat. She held him and rocked him back and forth, whispering softly to calm him. She didn't know what he'd been through. The Targui hadn't said.

She fed him goat's milk, nudging his lips with a spoon. He swallowed it without waking, his mouth moving for more. He was all ribs, and she gave him a lot. She sang to him, hymns she'd learned when she was the only one there for the services in the little mud chapel. She knew some Shamba legends and put them to verse, and put the verse to music, just for something to do. It was awful, she was sure, but the soldier was unconscious, after all, and didn't seem to mind. Sometimes it seemed to her that a smile appeared on his face. Father Jean heard her singing too. He nodded and smiled himself.

She looked at his face and imagined the things he'd seen, the things he'd done. So much trouble there, so much terror in his cries. She couldn't imagine. Life with the White Father was quite safe. She was glad of it, when she comforted him. She stroked his cheek with the back of her fingers. She touched the hair on his chest. It was as fine as silk and golden. She drew back the cover and looked at his arms, at his muscles, at his hands. She washed him, lifting his arms one after another, bathing them in cool water. Father Jean said it was good to keep him clean. She knew by the way it felt, that it was good.

She also knew that wasn't what Father Jean meant.

She ran the sponge down his stomach and along his legs. She had never seen a man before, at least not like this one. She felt herself on fire when she did that. She flushed with shame. She was taking extraordinary liberties with an unconscious man. No one had ever taught her about any of this. Certainly not Father Jean.

ON THE FIFTH DAY HE FLOATED UP TOWARD THE surface. There were voices there, and beauty. Music. A woman's voice, soft and soothing. Pretty. He wanted to see.

"Who are you?" His eyes were wide and full of fear.

"Melika."

"Melika . . . beautiful . . . welcome," he said, and he drifted back down to where the mists swirled.

He awoke again the next day.

"Who are you?" His eyes were wide and full of fear.

"Melika," she said again. She took his hand.

"Melika." The fear passed. He smiled and squeezed her fingers. He drifted again through the mists.

The next day his eyes were wide but there was no fear. "Melika," he said. "Have I died? Are you from God?"

She laughed. "You are not dead, Monsieur Paul. Close enough, perhaps, but not dead. You are near Wargla. You are safe."

"*Wargla.*" He said it in wonder. Through his fog he saw soft brown eyes and dark hair and a warm smile in a round face. It was a lovely vision, perfect. He slept. His breathing became deeper, more relaxed.

She combed his hair. She trimmed it where it fell into his eyes, snipping at it with Father Jean's surgical scissors. It hadn't been cut in months. She hoped he wouldn't mind.

She left the room only briefly, to pray for him in the chapel.

He drifted in and out. He remembered bits and pieces. He thought of his name. "Paul," he said to her. "I am Paul." "Yes." She nodded and touched his forehead. It made him cool when she did that, and it made him smile. He learned to smile often, so that she would keep touching him.

A storm came. Rain lashed at her room and ran down the mud walls. He awoke to the flash of lightning and heard the thunder and it took him to some frenzied place. He shouted and cried and she held him to her breast, helpless to offer him anything but her warmth and the comfort of her body. He clung to her desperately. His terrors passed with the storm and once again he drifted off, at peace. She watched him sleep and brushed away the hair from his forehead.

For two weeks he was half-in, half-out of consciousness. His fever would not leave, and it troubled Father Jean greatly. For two weeks she sat with him, whispering, singing, talking, telling stories, cleaning his wound, bathing away the heat with cool cloths. Each day she drew closer to him.

One night she leaned over him for a cloth that had fallen from his forehead. Her breast brushed his cheek. She felt a rush inside, a tingling surge of beauty and longing that hardened her nipples and left her breathless and afraid. Embarrassed, she looked to see if he had awakened. He was quite deeply under, in the world between sleep and unconsciousness where he spent so much time.

She looked at the door. It was late at night. The compound slept. No one would be coming.

Heart pounding, she moved to sit close to him on the bed. Impulsively, without knowing exactly what she was doing, yet compelled to yield to her feelings, she raised her blouse, then the shift beneath it. She shivered, the air caressing her breasts. Once more she felt the fire inside, warm, delicious, and forbidden. She couldn't believe what she was doing, but she was beyond caring, wanting only to follow her need. Trembling, she leaned forward and softly touched the tip of her breast to his lips, closing her eyes and drawing in her breath as the currents of pleasure coursed around her. Paul stirred at her touch, his mouth and tongue instinctively seeking her nipple, gently pulling, circling, exploring, but still he slept. Her nipple tightened and she let out a soft moan of pleasure. She was terrified he would wake up, and yet she wanted him to. She moved against him, and again he responded.

A noise outside the room brought her back. She bolted upright, hurriedly fixing her clothing.

Only a night sound. Nothing at all, but the moment had passed.

She looked at his face, bathed in the light of the candle. He was almost smiling, she thought. She wondered if he knew.

HIS CONSCIOUSNESS GRADUALLY RETURNED. A FEver remained, and his shoulder still festered, but each day he gained strength. Each day he ate more, drank more. Each day the color returned to his cheeks. Now she knew he would live.

"Who are you?" he asked, long after he knew the answer. He liked to hear her say it.

"Melika," she replied patiently every time.

"Melika, Melika, like a poem," he said. If he remembered what had happened he gave no sign.

He sat up and was awake for an hour. Then two. Then five.

"You are back among the living," she said as he ate. She gave him pieces of bread soaked in goat's milk, and bits of fruit cut into little pieces. He couldn't chew yet. He sucked on them.

"This is a wonderful place to be alive," he said. He didn't know for certain how he had come to be in this place, but he knew he was in no rush to change it. It was all coming slowly. He didn't want to hurry. She was perfect. She was beautiful. He didn't have to move, didn't have to do anything. She did it all for him, unbidden, and he wanted it never to stop. She seemed to sense what he needed before he knew it himself. He heard her voice when he slept. He saw her face when he awoke. Saw her in his dreams. It was enough. More than enough. All the rest was behind him now. The others had died. He had lived. Somehow.

"What has happened to the others?" he asked in panic, when he could finally think of the question at all.

"What others?" she said. "You were brought here alone."

"Brought here? Who brought me?"

"A Targui."

A shadow passed over his face. It frightened her.

"I must speak to the commandant of the garrison at Wargla."

"Of course, when you are well enough."

"Now. There are others. They may still be alive. I have to tell them."

"All right. I will ask Father Jean."

The captain of the garrison came with other men. They trooped in on loud rude boots and filled the room. Father Jean made Melika leave. She was afraid they would take him away. But they only talked, until Father Jean made them leave too. They were quieter when they left. Their faces were grim.

H E SLEPT A GREAT DEAL. SOMETIMES WHEN HE awoke and felt well he took the book from her, and read to her instead. She loved it. She sat back in the hard wooden chair and closed her eyes. He read to her about Pasteur and general surgery. "Wonderful stuff," he said wryly, but she loved it.

"When it is you saying it, even anthrax and rabies sound appealing," she said, and he laughed. She loved the rich sound of his voice. He read until he nodded off. She asked Father Jean for more books.

"More books! Is he the only patient left in the infirmary?" Father Jean grumped, but there was no hardness in him. He had never seen Melika so happy. He watched her and thought of his dead wife. His eyes misted and he busied himself looking after the things she had always tended. He could make his own supper and handle the infirmary alone. Just for a while, he told himself.

Paul got up. She held him while he draped his arm over her shoulder. He made five steps and fell hard to the floor. His shoulder opened and poured dark blood. She cried out and Father Jean ran to help. Together they got him back in bed. When she looked at his face, drained of color, she was sure she'd killed him. "Please live," she whispered. "Please, please." The wound got ugly and his body shook with fever. She dared not leave the room. She knelt by the bed and clutched her rosary and prayed.

On the second day his fever broke for good. Melika laughed and cried when he woke up.

"You," she said happily, tears on her cheeks.

"You." He smiled back.

His recovery quickened then. He began to eat by himself. He could hold the spoon, but they both pretended he still needed help.

He asked for a cup of tea. She brewed it carefully, borrowing the leaves from the White Father's own sacred preserve. She would find a way to replace it.

He asked for an orange. She walked all the way to the central market of Wargla so she could pick it out herself. She got a whole box. The juice ran down into his beard and she knew the long trip had been worthwhile. He smiled at her, and touched her cheek. "I need a shave," he said. She helped him with water and scissors and she wielded Father Jean's razor. The result was bloody, "but not nearly as bad as getting shot," she told him.

Next it was an apricot. "Hakeem loved them," he said. He started to tell her about Hakeem, but his voice broke and he began to cry. She held his hand and he looked away, embarrassed by his weakness. She thought he was wonderful.

"Fish," he said, and she panicked. There were no fish to be had within a hundred leagues. She bribed the second cousin to the first servant of the agha of Wargla, who produced a packet of dried sardines caught off the Barbary coast. She thought it awful but he clearly loved it.

"*Tu es un ange*," he told her. *You are an angel*. No one had ever said that to her before.

He watched her coming and going and cherished each moment. She laughed often and each time it brightened his soul.

"I know nothing about you," he said one afternoon. "Tell me of Melika."

"There is little to say," she smiled. "My life is this mission. It is what I know. It is what I do. I am happy here. I do not wear a veil like the women in Wargla. The marabouts leave me alone, and the White Father lets me do as I can. As I wish. Father Jean says he is going to send me to France someday to study, but I don't think he will. There is more to do here in a day than there are hours. There are always too many children without families, too many illnesses. It was so yesterday, and it will not change tomorrow. I will stay and help." She shrugged. "That is Melika."

"Where are you from?"

"Not far from here. My mother was Shamba. She died when I was very young. She was said to be very beautiful."

"It is true. I know it by looking upon her daughter," he said, and she blushed.

Well after he felt strong enough to get up by himself, he didn't. He preferred to sit in the little room and let her tend to him. He wondered how to make it last forever. She fed him couscous, lifting the spoon to his lips. He intentionally spilled it so that she would have to clean him. She was happy for the excuse. She longed to do it.

He learned to moan, to emulate pain.

She was there instantly.

He loved her smell. He loved her smile. He saw the concern in her eyes. For the briefest moment it made him feel guilty.

But mostly it made him feel wonderful.

When he was strong enough she took him for walks, little ones at first. She packed a small basket of goat cheese and bread and fruit and they sat in the mission gardens. In the distance he could see the richness of Wargla, with its flowers and date palms and gardens. He had wanted for so long to see that sight, and now had no desire to go the rest of the way. He picked a palm frond and presented it to her. She laughed in delight and hugged him.

"Thank you," she whispered, and she clung to him, and he to her. She was his escape from the terror. She had brought him back from the abyss, and given him back his life. She was beautiful.

He was falling in love with her.

The walks grew longer. "I have a place to show you," he said.

He took her to the top of a dune, a lovely place. "I stood here once, with a friend," he said.

"You were here?"

"A lifetime ago," he said, "with a man named Remy."

"You spoke of him often, when you were unconscious."

He changed the subject, and talked of another companion. She laughed when he told her about rolling down the dune with the dog. But he didn't say what had become of the dog, either. His story came out only in fragments. She still knew very little. She let him talk when he wanted to talk, and left him in silence when he needed that.

Paul knew the time was coming when he should report to the garrison. It was already past time. He was well enough, really, or soon would be. He had much to do, in the matter of the Tuareg. But he couldn't bring himself to think about all that just yet.

ONE DAY A VISITOR CAME. MELIKA GREETED HIM in the courtyard, near the garden, and thought at first he was a new patient for the infirmary. He was a gaunt old man with graying hair. He could not walk unassisted. Two men supported him, lifting him by his arms. He was a light load for them; he looked to Melika as if a gust of wind might carry him away. He was sun blackened and his body was spent but there was great strength in his face. He was polite and his eyes were kind and she liked him immediately.

"*Istanna*," she said, indicating a seat by the garden. "Rest there, please. I will get the lieutenant."

He shook his head. "I have come too far to rest. I will accompany you, if it is all right."

"Of course." She led him to the little room and showed them inside. Paul looked up and for a moment was too overcome with emotion to react. His eyes brimmed with tears.

"El Madani."

"Lieutenant."

Paul rose to greet him. El Madani let go of the two

men and stood alone on unsteady legs. Gently, trembling, they hugged, the old Algerian and the young Frenchman, and for a long time neither man could speak. They patted each other on the shoulders and held each other's eyes, and just nodded and smiled. Paul helped him sit, while Melika and the two *tirailleurs* slipped from the room.

Paul scolded him. "You should not have come yourself. You are not strong enough. You should have sent word. I would have come to you."

"When I heard you were alive I could not resist. I had to bring you the news myself."

"How did you—"

"A shepherd found us."

"Us? How many—"

"Twelve."

Paul closed his eyes. "*Twelve*," he whispered. Twelve out of ninety-eight.

"Thirteen counting you, Lieutenant. This is the second time you've come back from the dead."

"Pobeguin?"

Madani shook his head.

Paul bit his lip and looked away, overwhelmed. He was the only Frenchman to have survived.

"I went looking for you, Lieutenant, after you ran off and Belkasem started yelling about a Tuareg raid. He said there were six of them, that they'd killed you. I found the body of the *tirailleur*, with a Tuareg spear in his chest. You were gone by then. All I found where you'd been was your blood. I guessed it was yours, anyway. And I found what I'd found before—one set of camel prints, out of place."

He waited, but the lieutenant volunteered nothing.

"I've gone weak in the head, I suppose. It took me a long time before I figured it out. The camel prints were never out of place at all. They were there, Lieutenant, for you." El Madani looked at Paul, searching his eyes.

Paul didn't know what to say. "I'll explain it to you one day, Madani," he said, "when I understand it myself."

CAPTAIN CHIRAC, THE NEW COMMANDANT FOR THE Wargla garrison, arrived from Paris, and immediately paid a visit to Lieutenant deVries.

"You are a hero," Chirac told him. "All France knows your name. There is certain to be a promotion."

"A promotion." Paul was incredulous and laughed bitterly. "For not getting killed?"

Chirac shrugged. "Better than a medal for dying. Most men would be content at the distinction."

Paul knew he deserved nothing of the sort, but his mind was on retribution. "What is France going to do?"

"Do?"

"To the Tuareg, of course. I assume an offensive is being planned. I want to be involved, sir."

"Unlikely, Lieutenant. I have received no official word, of course, but a friend of mine in the ministry has sent me accounts of the debate in the National Assembly. People are outraged about *le mission Flatters,*" he said. "It is a national scandal, a disgrace. But there is fear over outside reaction to an invasion of the Hoggar in force. The Turks, the Italians—it's all very ticklish. And, frankly, there is considerable doubt that it can be done at all. Our garrisons are too far to the north."

"Send *me.*" Paul's eyes were intense. "*I* can do it."

"As much as I would like to, it is not within my province to send a renegade force into the Hoggar. I cannot act without orders."

"So there is to be no reaction then. None at all."

Chirac handed him a paper. "*The foreign ministry condemns in the strongest possible terms the cowardly attack. . . .*"

Paul threw the paper to the floor, furious. "To hell with that," he said. "We need to do something that *matters.*"

Chirac sympathized with the young officer, but in Paris he had seen all the grand talk of railway and empire collapse as completely as the failed mission. All the indignation was simply rouge for an embarrassing blemish on French pride. There would be no military response to the massacre, no response at all. France would soon forget the ugliness of Flatters and find a pretty bauble to occupy her attention.

"Be patient," Chirac told him. "I know how you feel. Time will do nothing to make you forget, but it will take the edge off your bitterness."

"Nothing but defeating the Tuareg will do that, Captain."

"For now that is out of the question. Perhaps later. Sentiment may build as you hope. Who knows how the winds in the assembly may blow in six months? But never mind that. I am sending you home now. You can recover your health in Paris."

"I don't want to go home."

"I am not giving you a choice, Lieutenant. As soon as you have recovered sufficiently to travel, you are to depart for Algiers. The governor wants to hold a reception for you. After that you are to go home, to France." Chirac looked at the dejected officer. "Look, I sympathize with you," he said truthfully. "The lack of response has been a blow to the morale of all the men here."

"The lack of response is an insult to the men who died, Captain. I do not intend to forget them. I do not intend to forget the Tuareg."

Afterward Paul brooded for days. "Is there something the matter?" Melika asked. "Have I done something wrong?"

"Of course not," he said. "I'm sorry." But his mind was in turmoil. He believed in his heart that he had been a poor officer on the march north. He had failed the men who had relied on him. So many things he could have done, that he had not done. To leave them unavenged would be to fail those men twice. He needed to go to Algiers, to see the governor, but not for a party. He needed to stir opinion, to buy back the honor of France with the blood of the blue men.

THE RAINS HAD DISINTEGRATED A SECTION OF THE mission's wall, and Father Jean was laboring in the hot sun to rebuild it. One of the children brought lime and sand and they mixed it on a big piece of canvas. Father Jean laid bricks and troweled on the mortar. Paul watched him working, and volunteered to help.

"Let me help you," Paul said.

"Thank you, Lieutenant, but you are better off saving your strength."

"I haven't done anything for weeks now. I need to do something." He began handing bricks to the priest, and lifted water. The exercise felt good.

Across the garden he saw Melika leaving to go into Wargla for supplies for Father Jean. The priest watched him watching.

"She is a special woman," Father Jean said.

"Yes, she is. She adores you, you know."

"She has little choice," the priest smiled. "I'm the only family she's ever known."

"Where is she from?"

"Shebaba. Southwest of here, in the desert."

"She told me her mother was Shamba."

"Yes. She was raped during a raid. She died giving birth to Melika. After the mother died no one wanted the child. Melika might have been left outside to die, but she was lucky. A trader brought her here."

"They would leave a baby to die?"

"A baby like her, yes," Father Jean nodded. "The people of Wargla don't care much for this orphanage. They need the infirmary, all right, but they don't like barbarians raising their children. Sometimes we have no children at all here, even when there are many in need. Yet Melika was the child of a Tuareg raid. After she was brought to Wargla no one cared enough to take her, and she ended up here."

Paul set down the bucket of water he was lifting and looked at the priest. "A Tuareg raid?"

"Yes, it was the Kel Ajjer. The Tuareg of the Tassili. Hand me that trowel, would you?"

Paul stood dumbly, not responding. Father Jean saw the color had gone from his face. "Are you all right, Lieutenant? Have you taken ill?" Paul stood mute, breathing heavily, struggling to comprehend what the priest had just told him.

"Melika is the child of Tuareg?" His voice was a whisper.

"Yes," Father Jean said. "But more than that, she is the child of God."

A *Tuareg!* Oh sweet Jesus!

Feeling suddenly dizzy, he stumbled against the new wall. He knocked part of it down, and a heavy palate of mortar fell to the ground.

The priest helped him up. "Here, here, sit—" he started to say.

Paul waved him off. "I'm all right, Father. I need to be alone."

In shock he made his way into the garden, walking beneath the palms, blind to the beauty there. A cold wind had blown across his soul, and the flowers they had so enjoyed looking at together might as well have been dead. The air that had smelled so sweet now carried the scent of the Sahara, all the dark stench of his life.

God, how he hated the Tuareg! *How could she be one of them?*

He walked blindly and did not hear the birds or see the butterflies. His insides knotted and his head pounded with it all. He could not let her interfere with his duty. He did not trust himself with her, did not trust what she would make him do, did not trust his own feelings. His first duty, his only duty, was to avenge the men of the expedition. Honor demanded it. After that— there was no *after that.*

He could not bring himself to see her. He didn't think he could tell her good-bye. He knew he couldn't explain. When he found himself at the mission gate he just kept going.

CHAPTER 30

THE HAWK RESTED EASILY ON HIS ARM. SHE WAS at home there. He stroked the feathers behind her neck and she arched in pleasure. "Taka, Taka," he cooed. "I shall miss you."

Moussa undid the knots that held the short leather jesses to her legs. The straps fell away. She flexed her talons, unaccustomed to the feel of freedom.

He stood and pulled away her hood. Taka looked for game. She saw nothing. He launched her. She rose on strong wings that flashed in the sun, gaining altitude quickly, seeking the updrafts that would carry her for hours without effort. She looked below, to Moussa and his mehari. Instinctively she knew she was not to come back. She didn't remember flying without jesses. She circled, testing the currents, soaring higher and higher.

Moussa watched her with pride and sadness. He would miss her company. She was the best he'd had. She was special and he had kept her long past the normal time. Summer was near. She would have to hurry to find a mate. She needed to breed. He knew she would be fine, though; Taka would always be fine. He would catch her daughter, or her granddaughter, and they would fly together again.

She circled a long time. Her seeming uncertainty reflected his own mood. He sat alone in his camp outside In Salah. He'd been there four days, trying to decide where to go, what to do. He was restless and torn.

The horrors of the past weeks had left him drained and uncertain. He felt as if there was nothing for him in the camps of the Ihaggaren. There was always his mother, of course, and Lufti. He still had the affairs of his vassals to mind, and their *douars* to patrol. No matter what had happened at Tadjenout or Aïn El Kerma, life went on with them as before. They depended on him. Yes, even needed him. But it didn't feel like home just now. Had it ever? Had he ever belonged? He had long ago accepted the fact that he was different. But was he forever doomed to be on the lonely side, the other side, the outside?

A part of him wanted to go away, to leave it all behind. He thought of traveling to France. He was curious about his native land. He wondered if its reality would resemble his memory. Yet it was a foreign place, just as foreign now as if he'd never been there. He knew no one but his aunt Elisabeth and Gascon, and after what had happened to Paul he didn't think he could face them. Besides, he'd forgotten the customs. He would be coarse cloth in a silk world. Paris would think him a buffoon. By itself that didn't matter, but it was another place he would be looking at from the outside, the lonely side.

A part of him wanted to demand justice from the amenokal, to bring him to account for lying, to make him repudiate the actions of Attici and Tamrit. Yet his own objections counted for little. His desperate protests had been ignored. He knew that most Ihaggaren would be offended by the initial false offer of safe passage and the poison. The rest of it, as awful as it seemed to Moussa, was nothing more than desert warfare. It had been done properly. It was the way of things. And it did not really matter now how others viewed it. It was already done.

He could stay alone in the desert. It was perhaps the most appealing of his choices, and yet there was something about such solitude just now that left him longing.

No, not "something" that left him longing.

It was Daia, he knew it.

It had been almost three months since he had seen her, and she weighed more heavily on his mind than ever. He had tried to put her out of his mind, honestly tried, but he couldn't. He wanted to see her again,

before she married. He knew it was wrong, that such a
visit could only be awkward for her, or for himself. It
would upset matters that had been settled. And then,
too, he had no idea what he intended to say, or how he
would say it. As he thought of all the reasons not to see
her, he thought of his mother's words as well. *I knew
from the moment I met Henri that I would listen to my
heart. Do I have to tell you which was right?*

He knew he was not being logical, or rational. For
the first time in his life he didn't want to be those things.
He didn't care. It was his heart that needed to see her.
His heart had never been in control before. Always his
head.

He watched Taka, who was but a speck now. At last
she decided. She stopped circling and flew to the south,
toward the Hoggar. He watched until she was gone.

He would go see Daia. He would talk to her, and tell
her at least of his feelings for her. And then he would let
her go, like Taka. At least he would have done it. The
decision flushed him with pleasure.

And he would call a *djemaa*. It was his right; he
would not be denied. There would be an accounting,
before the assembled nobility of the Ihaggaren.

He knew the danger that lay down both roads. Perhaps his own death was at the end of each one. But he
felt no fear. The agony of indecision was behind him.
He knew what to do.

He would ride to In Salah for provisions, and then go
south. He put the saddle on his mehari. For the first
time in months he didn't need to prepare Taka's place.

IN SALAH WAS BUSTLING WITH COMMERCE. A GREAT
caravan had arrived from the southlands, with more
than a thousand camels and five times that many slaves,
all jostling for water and shade. Children played and
explored the mysteries of the caravan. Brochettes of
meat cooked over open fires. Traders slurped tea and
haggled for goods and exchanged preposterous stories.
Moussa moved through the noisy souk buying dates

and flour and tea, greeting his friends among the merchants.

Mahdi and Tamrit were engaged in earnest discussion. Mahdi looked up and saw Moussa and his blood ran cold with hatred. He couldn't kill him just yet, certainly not in the souk, but he couldn't resist taunting him. Mahdi called to him. Moussa stopped and turned. He offered no greeting. Tamrit regarded him sullenly.

"So, Cousin," Mahdi said. "I heard Attici found a Frenchman leading a small caravan of supplies to the dogs of Sheikh Flatters," he laughed. "He was dressed as we dress, to escape detection, but Attici was not fooled."

"I am certain the tale gave you great amusement," Moussa replied, "as did the treachery that followed."

"I draw satisfaction in Allah's wrath in the matter of the infidel, if that is your meaning."

"Does Allah countenance poison?"

"The blade of His vengeance is long and convoluted."

"Much as your tongue. And the Shamba, and the Algerians? Did they too have to suffer Allah's long blade? Were they not believers, like yourself?"

"Walk with the jackal," Mahdi shrugged, "and you shall likely die with the jackal. It is a common enough outcome. And I see Attici was not wrong—it is truly a soft French heart that still beats in your chest."

Moussa would not be aroused. "I have no interest in discussing this now. I will raise the matter with the amenokal and all the Ihaggaren, in *djemaa*. This is not finished for you, or for your jackal-killer Tamrit, or for Attici. There will be honor yet in this."

He turned to leave.

Mahdi caught him gently by the shoulder. He spoke in a low voice.

"There is another thing," he said. "Whatever our differences over the infidel, we are still cousins, after all. There is something you must know."

Moussa waited.

"It is most indelicate, of course. I know I can count

on your discretion, for her honor." Mahdi waited a moment, drawing it out. "Daia is pregnant." It struck Moussa like a blow.

"She and I should have been—well, more careful," Mahdi went on. "We will be marrying quickly now, so that our child will be born within the bounds of marriage. I tell you this because Daia thinks highly of you. She would want you in Abalessa for the wedding."

Moussa fought not to show his shock. He looked into the eyes that had despised him from boyhood. They were cold and unreadable. "Of course," he mumbled.

Devastated, he turned away.

It WAS ALL A GREAT LIE, INCREDIBLE EFFRONTERY, a breach of etiquette—a perfect blow. Mahdi gloated over it. He saw its effect, which Moussa could not hide, and for delicious moments Mahdi savored the thrust. Moussa must never think it was his child inside her. Mahdi would not permit him that thought.

But then he began to brood. It was not enough. He had intended only to place the proper thoughts in Moussa's mind, to remove her from his reach. He didn't want Moussa anywhere near the wedding, anywhere near Daia. Yet he had promised Daia he would not raise his hand against him.

It was an hour later that it came to him, a master stroke that solved many problems at once. He was having tea with Tamrit.

"Moussa will be trouble, in the *djemaa*," Mahdi was saying. "Already I have heard Attici say that the amenokal was furious about the *efeleleh*."

"Bah! The amenokal means nothing. His spine wobbles like a stream of camel piss. His teeth have gone soft. What can he do, anyway? He will complain about Attici, and write to the Turks for help against the French. Attici's time will come, and the French will not."

"Still, it would be well if Moussa were out of the way."

Tamrit shrugged, indifferent to the matter. "Perhaps.

But we must concern ourselves with more important issues. Bou Amama expects us both in Timimoun. We are to meet with the pasha. He is nearly prepared to raise the *jihad* against the French in the north. He proposes small raids against their settlements in the tell. We will raise another force farther east and do the same. In this we will be joined by Arabs and Shamba alike. This will spread like the *simoom* over the whole of the Sahara. The infidel will be swept away in a storm of blood."

"We will need money for a *jihad*," Mahdi said.

"We need nothing but willing men."

"Willing men need weapons."

"Willing men *are* weapons."

"Of course. But armed with the new French rifles they can acquit themselves even better in the holy war."

"It is true. But there is no money. Bou Amama has nothing. Jubar Pasha has promised to support me, but the only real wealth he possesses is a silver tongue, which he uses to spin lies and empty promises. He begs the sultan of Morocco for crumbs from his table and the sultan gives him nothing. It is one thing to dream of *jihad,* another to pay for it. I do not need their money. I am ready to begin without it."

As Tamrit spoke, Mahdi was watching Babouche, the caravan master who was taking tea across the courtyard. Babouche was well known on the caravan routes. He was a ruthless man, corrupt and wealthy.

And that was when it came to Mahdi.

"But there is a way to pay," he said slowly.

"I'm listening."

"Moussa is the way."

"What about him? He has nothing but corrupt blood."

"Ah, yes, corrupt blood. Precisely. The blood of his family. His father was a French nobleman whose wealth was said to be uncountable. The family still lives there. I have heard my aunt Serena speak of it."

Tamrit nodded grimly. "I know only too well of Serena and the family deVries. So?"

Mahdi indicated the caravan master. "Babouche is

always glad for more cargo. We could give him a slave for transport to the north. Babouche could sell him in Timimoun. Jubar Pasha pays well for healthy men, if not for *jihads*. His foggaras devour them like so many insects." The foggaras were a massive system of subterranean irrigation tunnels, dug by slaves.

Tamrit grunted. "So we sell him for a pittance to die in the water works. What has that to do with France? How does it pay for *jihad*?"

"Has not Jubar Pasha agreed to support you?"

"Yes, as if feathers might support a stone."

"It is in our power to give him the means. He is well connected, we are not. He has dealings with the devil in Algiers. He can arrange to ransom Moussa to his French family. Certainly they will pay. It is a backward French custom that the son holds the father's rank. Moussa is thus entitled to the wealth of his father. The family will have no choice. After they send the ransom we will kill him, if the foggaras haven't claimed him already. Think of it, Tamrit! Jubar Pasha fills his treasury. We have our *jihad*. Moussa provides no trouble in the *djemaa*. He will never know of our involvement. Besides, after he is dead, it will not matter what he knows." And, Mahdi did not add, Moussa is forever removed from Daia.

Tamrit mulled it over. A smile grew beneath his litham.

"To use the infidel's own money against the infidel." He liked it. "There is merit in the plan, Mahdi. You are truly worthy of the Senussi."

BABOUCHE HAD BEEN WARNED TO SEND SIX MEN or more to take him. The very idea was beneath contempt. The caravan master respected the Tuareg for their arrogance but not their strength. His men were Ouled Sidi Sheikh. Even a crippled one could subdue a lone Targui.

But just to be safe he sent four. They surprised Moussa in the darkest part of the night, but he hadn't been asleep. Two of them died quickly, the third more slowly. But the fourth presented his prisoner to Babouche as ordered. The caravan was well to the north of In Salah by then. Babouche had no desire to be seen transporting a Tuareg captive near his own country. The devils were hard enough on his trade as it was.

The Targui had been beaten severely but he was not bowed. He stood defiantly before the caravan master, his hands bound behind his back.

"I am told you are the demon himself with a blade," Babouche said. "Let us see what madness lurks beneath the veil." With the tip of his dagger he raised the blood-encrusted cloth. Moussa spat in his face.

Babouche struggled to control himself. He had been warned that this cargo held special value to Jubar Pasha. His own reward depended on delivery in reasonable shape, and money was more precious than vengeance. Nevertheless, he could brook no trouble on the road.

"We must suck the venom from this Targui scorpion. Beat him again."

Later Moussa was dragged to the rear of the caravan and awakened with blows to his feet. The prisoner would walk alone, behind the camels and the Negroes from the southlands.

"Let him walk in the honored place of the Tuareg, deep in the dung of thousands," Babouche ordered. "Chain him neck and foot. Tightly, so the movement of the feet pulls the neck. No water for a day, no food for two. He is not to sleep or sit down. We will see how his spirit fares."

BEFORE LEAVING IN SALAH, MAHDI SAT WITH PEN and paper. There was a piece of unfinished business. He started the letter several times, then crumpled it up and threw it away. The fourth draft satisfied him.

> *Beautiful Daia—*
> *Much as it pains me I cannot yet return to you.*
> *I have urgent business to attend with Tamrit in the*
> *north. I will make the greatest haste possible, and*

*will return as quickly as Allah permits. Thoughts
of our wedding fill my heart.*

*I have grievous news. I did not want you to
hear it from a traveler, or a stranger. Moussa has
been slain. Brigands from the Ouled Sidi Sheikh
fell upon him as he traveled near In Salah. We
were not near enough to help him. He fought well
but they were many. I saw his body with my own
eyes, and buried him after we sent the Ouled Sidi
Sheikh to their maker.*

*It is true Moussa and I were not close. Yet I
share your sorrow because I know your grief.*

My heart is with you.
Mahdi

A productive day. First he had taken her from
Moussa. Then he had taken Moussa from them all.

He gave the note to Attici, who promised to deliver it
personally.

J UBAR, PASHA OF TIMIMOUN, LORD OF LORDS,
Defender of the Faith, Keeper of the Seal, Lion of
Tuat, sat in his reception hall surrounded by his court.
His world was one of considerable comfort. His clothing was silk and bright cotton and richly embroidered,
his turban laced with gold thread. His boots were of the
softest Moroccan leather, rich and red and finely
brushed. He wore a belt of silver from which jeweled
weapons hung in ornate scabbards. Servants poured tea
for his guests from a rich silver service.

Jubar Pasha regarded the Targui standing in chains at
the other end of the Great Hall. Babouche sat next to
the pasha. On the other side sat Tamrit, wearing the
robes and turban of the Ouled Sidi Sheikh. As he moved
through the murky world of the Senussi, Tamrit had
learned to wear many guises. Moussa had never seen his
face, which had always been covered by the veil of the
Tuareg. So long as he kept his voice low Tamrit knew
Serena's son would never realize he was there.

"What manner of man is this, then? Is he French or Tuareg?" asked the pasha.

"He is neither, Great One. Or should I say he is both? He is but a half-breed."

"You are safe despising him in either event," Babouche said. "Or in killing him. His insolence knows no bounds. It was very costly to me to bring him to you."

"The incompetence of your agents is of no concern to me," the pasha replied. "If his life has been costly to you, his death would be costly to me. I trust you do not prefer such an outcome?"

"Of course not," Babouche said quickly. "I only meant—"

"You only meant to wring more money from your trouble."

"I seek only a fair price, Great One."

"It is said you are a devout Muslim," Jubar Pasha said.

"All men will swear it who know me, Lord."

"Then your gift of this man to me shall be a fitting symbol of your devotion. This prisoner is beyond commerce. The price he fetches will further a holy cause. Surely you would not seek personal gain in the face of such a prospect?"

"But sire, I am a merchant—"

"Second, you are a merchant. First, you are a Muslim," Jubar Pasha interrupted. "I am certain your generosity will be as well remembered in paradise as it will be by my own treasurer," he said. He waved his hand dismissively.

Babouche could only scowl. Jubar Pasha was a valued client.

The pasha turned to Tamrit.

"I desire no trouble with the Hoggar Tuareg over this man," he said. "I have had enough trouble with the savages." He seemed indifferent to Tamrit's own identity as a Targui. "They rarely venture this far north, but they have plagued my caravans going to and from the southlands. If only I could count the riches they have cost me. . . ." He waved his hand in exasperation.

"He is noble among them, you say. They can be disagreeable about such things."

"There will be no trouble," Tamrit assured him in a low voice. "He is not well loved among them, and they think him dead."

"As undoubtedly he will be, soon enough."

"Quite so, Great One, when it suits our purpose. But for now we must use him as another lance in the French boil."

Jubar Pasha nodded. "I have given thought to your proposal. There is a man who could do this. Only one. El Hussein. He too is a half-breed. He speaks French. He has traveled to their coastal cities. He has that priceless trader's gift of cutting a person's throat while making his victim feel only pleasure." The pasha smiled thinly. "He has the added qualification of being my brother-in-law. He can be trusted."

"An excellent choice."

"Alas, at the moment he is my ambassador in the court of the sultan in Marrakech. I have made a formal request that the sultan annex all the oases of the Tuat, including this one. I do not expect his return for some months."

"But Lord, delay is not beneficial to either of us. Surely there is another—?"

"It is your own adventure with Sheikh Flatters that has made such an overture necessary. Would you have me delay while the French lion awakens to eat us whole?"

"Of course not. But the *jihad*—"

"Is a part of the greater whole, but only a part. Your holy war can only harass them and make martyrs. Only the power of the sultan is sufficient to stop them. I cannot stand against them alone. There are no alliances among the oases of the Tuat, only raids and counterraids among men who should be brothers, while the French lion picks us off one by one, like lambs."

"You underestimate the power of the *jihad*," Tamrit said darkly.

"I underestimate nothing. Your treatment of Sheikh

Flatters is both a blessing and a curse. A blessing because it might help to raise the one great sword of Islam against the French, and divert us from fighting among ourselves. A curse because it will hurry the French beast, who will be eager for vengeance. We must act in concert across a broad front. Your *jihad* must continue, as the sultan must take us under his wing. The one man to bring about both is El Hussein. He will be required to handle delicate negotiations. He will then be entrusted—if you are correct as to the value of our hostage—with vast sums of money. I would not place such confidence in many men." Jubar Pasha was under no illusion about El Hussein. His brother-in-law would, of course, steal part of the ransom. But El Hussein had always been able to control his greed and had the good sense to steal only part. Another man might steal it all, just as he himself might decide to keep it for himself rather than share it with the Senussi.

"Very well, if it is your wish then so shall it be. It is important that the prisoner be kept alive, Great One. Proof that he lives may be necessary before a ransom is paid."

"There is a fine line between life and death. The master of the foggaras can keep him just this side of that line. I will give the instruction. He will be worked in the upper fields, where death is not such a close companion."

"It is also important that he not escape."

Jubar Pasha laughed heartily at that. "Escape? What man leaves perdition to find hell? We are surrounded by the great desert. No prisoner of the foggaras has ever escaped for long. Now enough talk," the pasha said. More tea was poured and served with biscuits laced with honey. At length the pasha waved the prisoner forward. Moussa's chains dragged on the stone floor.

"Shame, Babouche! What gift for a pasha should be hidden beneath a Tuareg rag? I would see him laid bare." He flicked a finger at one of the household guards.

"Strip him."

Moussa heard the command. Mortified, he struggled

fiercely but he was still chained and weak from the journey. They subdued him quickly. Two men held him as
another removed his robe, then his pants. Finally they
unwound the cloth covering his head, removing meter
after meter of soft cotton until Moussa stood naked before them. He was bruised and cut where the guards
had beaten him. The back of his neck was raw from the
collar they'd made him wear. The metal had rubbed
through his shesh. But he looked strong and stared defiantly at his captors. He recognized only Babouche, the
slaver and caravan master. The big soft one in the middle was certainly the pasha. The eyes of the third man
seemed familiar. They were disturbing and intense, but
Moussa couldn't place them.

Jubar Pasha appraised him with a practiced eye and a
certain hunger. The devil's body was lean and hard.
Muscles rippled gracefully in his arms and legs. There
was a certain elegance in his carriage. The man stood
like a king. He considered for a moment. A beautiful
man, truly. Yet as inviting as he looked, this one was
not for the bed. He was too old and too strong. The
pasha sighed. It was a pity.

This one was for ransom.

"Take him to the foggaras."

IT WAS DUSK WHEN THEY LED HIM OUT OF THE FOR-
tress and through a maze of covered streets of the
walled city. The mud walls were a deep reddish brown
in color. The streets were narrow, choked with people
who ignored his passage. Another slave aroused no interest, not even a light-skinned one.

Moussa had no sense of direction. The streets
twisted and turned and curved back on each other in a
web of confusion. They led him out through the gate,
up a hill, and into a walled compound. It seemed to be
one of several like it that stretched away toward the
open desert. In the courtyard was a large group of
black slaves from the southlands. They roamed freely,
chattering and cooking over open fires. There were
hundreds of them. They shared living quarters in

stable-like enclosures whose roofs and walls were made of matted palms. At the rear of the compound was a door that opened onto a passageway with a guard at each end. On either side of it stood a row of squat mud huts with wooden doors and slits for windows. He was led to one of these and shoved inside. The door closed behind him.

He blinked to adjust to the sudden darkness. It was a small room with a ceiling so low he could only sit or rest on his knees in the dirt. There were no furnishings. He could make out the dim forms of other men sitting along the walls. They stared at him without speaking. He could see a man in the corner, his face barely illuminated by the dying light from the small window. He wore a dirty turban and a loincloth and nothing else. He was a small man, a tight bundle of muscles. His eyes were dark and cheerful. He had been studying Moussa. "Allah's blessings on you, tall one. You will forgive us for not standing." He laughed. "You will get used to small quarters. It is the highest ceiling you'll see here. Soon you will think of this ceiling as you once thought of the sky."

Moussa sat in the opposite corner, trying to gather his thoughts. The little man began to scurry toward the door, which opened suddenly. Moussa hadn't heard anyone outside. His companion accepted the bowls that were handed in and set them quickly on the floor. The door closed.

He passed them around, giving the last one to Moussa. Moussa looked into his bowl without interest. In the low light he could see it was a nondescript blob of something on a rock-hard lump of couscous. It looked unappetizing. He wasn't hungry.

"It is said you are Tuareg," the little man said, greedily eating his own food with his fingers. "Is this so?"

"How did you know that already? I only just arrived."

"News sometimes arrives here before the event. There is nothing to do but talk and gossip. Everyone talks. Even the guards, and caravan drivers. A Targui raises much interest."

"I am part Tuareg, yes."

"You do not look clothed enough to be Tuareg. What is your name?"

"Moussa."

"I once had an ass called Moussa. A good one too. I will not dishonor him by so calling a Targui. I will call you Sidi." There was only good humor in his voice.

"They took my clothes."

"They take everything here, Sidi. What does it matter? We are all naked before Allah," the man said. "I am Abdulahi. I am of the tribe of the Ouled Nail. That"—he pointed—"is Monjo. He is a Hausa man." Monjo was stretched out on his back. He was bulky and looked strong. He was coal black. His eyes were intense but seemed friendly. He nodded, but remained silent. "The other is Mahmoud. He is a Moor. A Berber like yourself, but from the High Atlas."

"*Ma'-tt-uli*, Tuareg dog," Mahmoud said amiably, brushing Moussa's hand with his own and touching it to his chest. "How do you fare?"

"*El Kheir 'Ras*, Moorish pig." Moussa grinned, touching his own heart in kind. He liked the man immediately. Abdulahi laughed delightedly at the exchange.

"It is always thus in here, Sidi. Tuareg, Moor, Hausa, Ouled Nail. Outside these walls we would cut each other's throats. Yet in here we are all brothers. Only the throat of Jubar Pasha is at risk. Like the devil, we are all dwellers of the darkness. All equal. It is a good thing, yes? We need each other to survive."

"Speak for yourself," Mahmoud said. "I am nothing to do with the devil."

"Ah, but you are a darkness dweller."

"How do you come to be here?" Moussa asked.

"Monjo is a slave." Abdulahi said it as if that was the beginning, the middle, and the end of Monjo. "I was taken prisoner in a *razzia*. Mahmoud is being held for ransom. He has been held a long time, and is not worth as much, I think, as a camel. Even Berbers would have paid for a camel by now—at least for a good one. But Mahmoud sits here unbought. Yet he is not such bad company for a Moor. All of us have made trouble in one way or another. It is why they keep us here instead of letting us outside with the Negroes from the south-lands. You saw them?"

"Yes."

"They have the run of the place. They never give trouble, never seek to escape. Only the difficult prison-ers live in these rooms. But there are worse places than this, Sidi. There is another area of confinement for the hardest of the prisoners. They are nothing more than holes cut in the ground, covered by heavy doors. They have no windows. There is no one to keep you com-pany. You are chained inside except when you work, and when you work they put you in the worst tunnels where the sand is soft and your death is sure. I spent time in one of those pits, Sidi. Two months they kept me there. I was quite mad when I got out."

"You were quite mad when you went in," said Mahmoud.

"True enough. But I cannot recommend it even so. You would be wise to avoid giving trouble, Sidi."

"You have been here a long time?"

"Four years. I am expert in the foggaras, Sidi. You are lucky to have found me. I am a good teacher." He eyed Moussa's bowl. It hadn't been touched. "Is it your intention to eat that, Sidi?"

"No," said Moussa, handing it over.

"Blessings," Abdulahi said, attacking it with zeal. With a rock he broke the couscous into two smaller pieces. He gulped them down without trying to chew. "It is the first lesson, by the way."

"Yes?"

"Give no one your food. You will need every bit to survive. It is why I have lived four years here. And why I will live four more."

He grinned and licked his lips.

TELL ME ABOUT THE FOGGARAS. I HAVE SEEN THEM but know little of their workings."

"There is much water here, Sidi, even though we are surrounded by the dunes. It comes from"—he shrugged—"from Allah knows where. Some say it comes from the mountains near the Great Water, that it comes the whole way underground, beneath the sea of dunes. The problem is that like salvation, the water will not come to us. We must go to find it. It runs deep. We must lead it out. This is our work, Sidi, the work of the foggaras. We find the water in the darkness and lead it to the light."

"They are wells, then?"

"No. A well in Timimoun would give little and take forever to fill. The foggaras are tunnels. First we make a deep shaft from the surface. Some shafts, in the lowlands near the oasis and the palms, are quite shallow. A man can nearly stand in them. Others, closer to the open desert, are much deeper—a hundred paces deep at least. We dig down until we find water, much like a common well. That is where we begin the tunnels. We dig them at the level of the water, and slope them down toward the oasis. The water flows inside the tunnels. The longer the tunnels, the more water they bring. Some are many leagues long, Sidi. If you should one day visit the oasis itself you will see rich streams of water, flowing to the gardens and the palms. The pasha sells his water to the *harratin* who till the soil and pay him tribute. It is a beautiful oasis, Timimoun. It could not exist without the foggaras. It would die without them, and be covered with dunes. With the foggaras—only we will die, and be covered with dunes."

"How many slaves are there?"

"Only Allah and Jubar Pasha know, and they do not say. There are five compounds such as this one that can be seen from here. Others are located on the far side of the fortress. How many is that? It takes a multitude to keep the foggaras. The foggaras are like a great underground dragon that eats men. There are cave-ins. Men drown, men disappear. The caravans are always welcome in Timimoun because the caravans feed the dragon. It is a different world down there, a world without light. You must learn to use all your senses, Sidi."

They heard the low jabber of slaves in the courtyard, still socializing by their fires. A baby cried. In the gloom of their little room there was nothing to see. Nothing to do. The men settled down to sleep. There was barely enough room for the four of them. Moussa felt a knee in his back, and his head rested near a foot. Abdulahi took the best place, on the wall opposite the door where he could stretch out. He yawned.

"You will live long if you can out-think the dragon, Sidi. If you cannot you will die."

THEY WERE AWAKENED BEFORE DAWN. ANOTHER bowl of food was passed through the door. Moussa crunched through it this time. They were allowed to visit a common latrine. Men squatted with no privacy. Even in the darkness Moussa felt his nakedness. He tried to cover himself but it was no use. Abdulahi saw him. "There is too much naked man for the hand to cover, Sidi," he laughed. But as they were passing through the courtyard Abdulahi paused to talk with one of the Negroes. Apparently they knew each other well, and the man trotted to his enclosure. He reappeared a moment later with a length of cloth and presented it to Abdulahi amid smiles and chatter.

Abdulahi gave it to Moussa. "For your modesty, Sidi," he beamed. As they walked Moussa tore it into strips. He made himself a loincloth and a skimpy turban for his head. There was not enough to cover his face. He felt better, but still quite naked. It gave him no comfort that everyone else was dressed in the same manner.

They passed through a gate where a slave issued them tools from a wicker basket. Moussa was given a mattock for digging, a length of rope, and a stiff goatskin bag. He watched Abdulahi and copied the way he tied the rope around his waist, then attached the handle of the mattock to the end. He hung the goatskin around his neck. "Take care of these things," Abdulahi said. "If you do not return them tonight you will not eat."

Another man gave them each a handful of dates. Ten each as they passed by. Again Moussa copied what he saw the others doing. As he walked he unwound his turban and tied the dates into a little knot at the end, and then replaced the cloth on his head. Ten dates. Not much, even by Tuareg standards.

Their guard was Atagoom, a burly man with sun-blackened skin. "He is strong as a mule, Sidi," Abdulahi whispered, "and he knows how to use the sword. Yet even more than the sword you should fear the palm. He will use it without hesitation. It will rip your flesh like the beak of a crow."

Moussa studied the switch in Atagoom's hand. It was a large palm branch. Wicked-looking spines ran down each side like a row of needles. They had been cut to stand away from the branch, then lashed into place with twine. They would be effective.

Atagoom walked off to the side and eyed Moussa with a look between hostility and curiosity. "Like everyone, he wonders about the Tuareg devil," Abdulahi explained. "It was to everyone's relief to learn in the latrine this morning that you do not possess two penises, Sidi."

"Yes?"

"But of course. It is a thing I myself have wondered about you devils since I was a child."

ATAGOOM LED THEM OUT OF THE COMPOUND AND away from the town toward the open desert. They walked for half an hour, climbing a slope that rose gently toward a distant plateau. They could see the sun rising bright over orange dunes. Timimoun was coming to life. They heard the faint cry of the muezzin. Donkeys and camels and men stirred beyond the walls. There were two casbahs, or fortresses, one on either side of the town. A long wall stretched between them. On the far side of the town was the oasis, a lush sea of green against the gold. Beyond the oasis Moussa could see a *sebkha*, a blinding white saltwater flat that filled every few years in savage floods.

Low mounds dotted the ground where they walked, stretching away in straight lines up the slope toward the plateau. They were spaced twenty or thirty meters apart, the area around them built up with dirt and rock.

"Foggara shafts," Abdulahi told him. "We will work there today." He indicated an area about halfway up the slope. Groups of men gathered around each opening. Moussa could see them disappearing over the edges, swallowed by the earth.

He tried to imagine the subterranean world described by Abdulahi, the tunnels and the darkness. He was a man of open air, a son of the desert. It made him shudder. It made him afraid.

H E   S A T   O N   T H E   E D G E   O F   T H E   S H A F T   A N D   G R A S P E D the rope. He looked down into the hole. It dissolved into blackness. His heart pounded. Abdulahi, Mahmoud, and Monjo were waiting, along with two other men Moussa didn't know.

Abdulahi put his hand on Moussa's shoulder and spoke quickly.

"Hold to the knots tightly, Sidi," he said. "You must learn to use your toes. Grasp the rope between them, and ease yourself down from knot to knot. This is a deep shaft, I am sorry to say. Three times you will have to change ropes before the bottom. It will seem a long way before you stop. If the wall around you collapses hold tight to the rope and wait. We will try to get to you from the top. If you let go of the rope you will die, Sidi. Do not let go."

Moussa nodded. He clutched the rope tightly.

"Enough talk," said Atagoom. "Down." The palm frond was raised threateningly over Moussa's back.

"Blessings, Sidi. May Allah preserve you. I will join you soon."

Moussa slipped over the edge and into the hole. The rope dangled loosely below him. He could hear it hitting against the sides of the shaft. He knocked some pebbles from the side. He listened as they fell. He didn't hear them hit bottom.

He lowered himself hand over hand, trying to hold the rope with his toes as Abdulahi had told him, but it kept slipping out. He supported himself with his hands. "Do not try to support yourself with only your hands,"

Abdulahi had warned him. "They will tire and then you will have an interesting time." He had no choice. His toes were useless. He was taller than the others, though, and found he could rest by propping his legs against the opposite side of the shaft, so that his back and feet operated as a brake. He was breathing hard by the end of the first rope. His arms ached already. He switched ropes and continued downward.

He descended to the bottom of the second rope and found the anchor where the third was attached. As he let go of one and transferred his weight to the other he slipped. He yelped and grabbed the rope with all the strength in his hands. He slid down almost ten meters before he was able to catch himself. The rope burned his palms, the knots racing by, one by one, as he plunged downward, each one shaking his grasp, threatening to let him plummet to the bottom of the shaft.

"Sidi! Are you all right?" The disembodied voice followed him down.

Moussa gasped with pain. "All right," he called up.

"Do not let go, Sidi."

THE SHAFT WAS NOT PERFECTLY STRAIGHT, SO HE could no longer see the top. It was dark, past dark. The blackness was so complete that it seemed like a wall, like a presence. He couldn't see his own hand. He shuddered. It was cool, much cooler than at the surface, and damp. When his back touched the side it felt almost slimy. He should have worn something. He didn't know what. They'd taken his clothes. He had to get them back. He thought he would freeze to death before the day was over.

As he rested near the end of the rope he heard something different.

Water. The trickle of water. In the open desert the sound was wonderful, the sound of life. In the shaft it was a sound of mystery, ominous and intimidating, a trickle of fear. He was nearing the bottom. Again he tried to make his toes work. Again he failed. Knot to knot to knot he descended with aching arms.

At last he felt the ground. His feet were in the water. He let go of the rope and rubbed his arms. He heard a noise and looked up. Bits of rock and sand fell into his eyes. Someone was climbing down after him. He jerked his head and blinked painfully, trying to clear away the grit. Another lesson.

"Do not look up, Sidi," Abdulahi had warned him. "You will always regret it."

There wasn't room to do anything but kneel. He had arrived at an intersection of tunnels that departed from the shaft. There was a small chamber at the junction. The tunnels were just large enough to crawl through on hands and knees. Even then he could feel the top rubbing against his back. Foggaras were made by men smaller than he. He moved out of the way of the shaft and waited for Abdulahi to descend. He felt his way slowly, his fingers groping in the blackness. He had lived in a world of endless sky and no walls, and now the tunnel and the blackness pressed in around him. He could feel its presence even if he couldn't see. He could hear himself breathing, and he could hear the trickle of water. The sounds nearby were amplified; the more distant one of Abdulahi descending the shaft was muffled. It was all suffocating. He fought to control the beginnings of panic.

A man landed nearby. He moved quickly in the darkness. Easily, like a cat.

"Abdulahi?" His own voice bounced back at him.

"No."

Moussa couldn't make out who it was by the voice. He smelled garlic. The mystery moved past him and disappeared into a tunnel. He listened until the sound was gone. Another man dropped.

"Abdulahi?"

"No. Mahmoud. Fare well today, Tuareg dog." He too scurried past Moussa and followed the other man into the darkness. Moussa couldn't imagine how they knew where to go. Like rats, they vanished into the underworld.

Another body dropped.

"You are all right, Sidi?"

"Yes, but I can't see."

"You will learn to see with your fingers, Sidi, and with an eye in your mind you do not yet know you have. Be patient. Worry will not make it light. Keep your head down and follow me."

He scurried down one of the tunnels. Moussa started after him and immediately banged his head. He rubbed it and moved as fast as he could but couldn't keep up. His hands and knees were in the water, which was freezing. His knees were already sore but he moved quickly. He was deathly afraid of being left behind. He would never find his way out again. He thought he should be unrolling his rope to leave as a marker. There wasn't time, and he didn't know how far they were going. Damn! Abdulahi had already shoveled a thousand instructions at him. How hard could it be to work in the foggaras? Yet for all he had learned he felt he knew nothing at all.

He stopped to listen. He heard something. Straight ahead? To the right? The noise was clear, but not the direction. Crawling on one hand, groping the wall with his other, he finally came to an opening. He listened, then turned and headed into a tunnel that departed from the first at a right angle. He wondered how he would turn around. He didn't want to back all the way out. He crawled for a few moments. The noise seemed closer, and then his face smacked into Abdulahi's rear end.

"Not so fast, Sidi. We are here. It is the end of the tunnel." He spoke in a normal tone yet his voice sounded overloud. Sound played tricks in the tunnels. Moussa wished he could see.

"This is a finger off the main tunnel," Abdulahi said. "A short extension, dug to increase the water flow. We will dig another meter or two. We must also lower the floor. I will work here first. You are not used to it. You will work the shaft."

"What do I do?"

"Untie your rope." Moussa complied as Abdulahi talked. "Tie one end to the handle of the goatskin bag. Here, feel it? Tie the other end to your waist. Crawl back to the shaft where we came down. I will dig until I fill the bag. When I tug on the rope like this, pull the bag out. My own rope will be tied to the other handle. Untie both ropes and attach the full goatskin to the rope hanging from the surface. There is a man standing at the top. Pull on the rope. He will lift it and empty it, and then lower it back to you. While he does that, take your own bag and attach both our ropes to it again. Tug when you are ready. I will pull it back, and the whole process will begin again. You keep changing bags and ropes. Do you understand?"

"Yes." Moussa was thinking of having to crawl back and find the shaft alone.

"As you will discover, it is an amusing way to spend the day, Sidi. And it has its advantages."

"Oh?"

"You never get hot, and there is always plenty to drink." He laughed.

"It is time to work, Sidi. There is another thing. You must listen carefully. Always, with all your senses, listen and feel. There may be a cave-in. A ceiling may collapse, or a wall. You may not hear it. You may only feel it. After a time here you will know the feel. And sometimes water builds in hidden caverns and breaks through. It can flood the tunnel for a time. In all of these things I need you to remember your good friend Abdulahi at the far end of the rope, and to move quickly. Use your own mattock, and save him as you would save yourself."

"Of course. But what do I do if there is a flood?"

"Can you swim, Sidi?"

"Yes."

He giggled. "It doesn't matter here. If the tunnel floods you can't swim anyway. You will probably drown." He was delighted at the humor in it. "Turn on your back and try to keep your nose to the top of the tunnel so that you can breathe. Try to brace yourself on the sides of the tunnel with your arms and legs, to keep the flow from carrying you away. You are a large man and should be able to do it easily. If you feel me floating by, stop me. If you can't, *mektoub*. Someday even I might not out-think the dragon, or Allah may one day tire of my inattention to prayer."

Moussa was feeling overwhelmed. His blood raced at the thought of a raging underground flood.

"We are darkness dwellers, Sidi. We need each other. We live together. We must not die together."

"I understand."

Abdulahi clapped him on the shoulder. "Go with God, Sidi, but trust only your senses." Moussa was surprised that he knew where his shoulder was in the pitch-darkness. He shuddered at the touch. He was not used to being touched on naked skin. He would have to get used to a lot here, it was clear. He felt the terrible burden of responsibility—for Abdulahi, for himself. He clenched his teeth and backed down the tunnel, playing out his rope that was still attached to the bag. When he arrived at the intersection he backed around the corner. He crawled forward, touching the sides, feeling everything, his heart pounding. He was on his own. He was no more than a few meters away from his companion, yet he felt as if he were the only man on earth.

He panicked as he wondered how to find the shaft. He felt the top of the tunnel with the back of his head as he crawled, knowing that he would run into the shaft somewhere along the way. How would he know if it was the right shaft? How many were there? What if he chose the wrong one, and no one was at the top? Would he stand there for hours, waiting for the imaginary man above ground to answer his tug? Or what if he had gotten mixed up and was crawling the wrong way? There was no sense of direction here. None at all. Memory had to serve, and what if memory failed? How far should he go before he went back to begin again? There was the comfort that Abdulahi was at the other end of the rope. But what if the end of the rope slid away from him and he didn't notice? What if he tugged and the other end was lying somewhere out of Abdulahi's reach?

The top of the tunnel was not getting higher. His head scraped along it, his new turban absorbing the abuse. He didn't know how far he'd come. He couldn't tell distances, not at all. On his hands and knees it seemed like a very long way. Then he felt a breeze. It was so gentle he almost missed it. But yes, it *was* a breeze, whispering at his cheeks.

Use all your senses, Sidi.

With a wave of relief he came to the shaft, and felt the dangling rope. Of course, the rope. That would have told him too. There were signs. He must find the signs.

He stood on shaky legs, giddy to be upright again with his head in the shaft. Immediately he felt a tug on the rope at his side. He knelt down and started to pull. The rope curled at his feet as the bag scooted along the ground. Then he felt it, and fumbled at the knot. He tied it to the rope dangling from the surface and tugged. The bag didn't move. He tugged again. Nothing. Had the fool on top fallen asleep? While he waited he decided to attach his own bag to Abdulahi's rope. In the darkness he realized he didn't know which rope was which. It was all a jumbled mess. His fingers played along it. He worried there would be knots now when it stretched out again, knots that might get caught on corners, knots that might prevent him from pulling if he needed to rescue someone. Or if he needed to be rescued.

Suddenly the simple task was too much. He was not doing his job! He got to his knees again and crawled back into the tunnel. He got hold of the single rope that led back to Abdulahi, and kept his hands on it as he felt for the end. When he had it he quickly tied it to the bag, and tugged. Immediately it scooted away. He stood again, to see about the other bag. He felt for it. It was still there. He tugged again angrily. Bits of earth struck the top of his head.

And then he knew. He'd tied the bag to the wrong rope. He'd put it on the end of the descent rope, which was thicker and shorter. There had been three of them in the shaft. He could tug till eternity and no one would respond.

He found the right rope, re-tied it, and yanked. Instantly the bag rose. He kept his eyes closed. He felt humiliated. This wasn't as easy as it seemed. Then he remembered to sink down again. Abdulahi was counting on him to listen, and he wasn't. He was fumbling around like an idiot, trying to make bags of dirt go where he wanted them to go, all the while failing to pay attention.

Floods. Cave-ins.

He was a darkness dweller. He had to listen.

H E WORKED THE ROPES. IT GOT EASIER WITH PRACtice. He began to interpret sounds. Empty bag, coming down the shaft. Full bag, dragging through the water. Empty bag, dragging through the water. Arm over arm, hand over hand, the motions became smoother, more automatic. He found a way to store the rope so it curled neatly at his feet.

Once he failed to tie the bag to the rope properly. It moved toward the surface, rubbing along the sides of the shaft. Then he heard it come loose. He raised his arms to protect his head but jammed his elbows on the side of the shaft. Had the bag hit him it would have knocked him out, or worse. But it plunged right past him and crashed at his feet. He could feel where it spilled. With his hands he tried to pack it back in, but the water carried most of it away, washing it down where someone else would have to pick it up.

After that he paid more attention to his knots.

Hour after hour, bag after bag, the dirt went out. He thought of the thousand other men in the netherworld of the great foggaras, laboring to keep the pasha's water flowing. Bile rose in his throat as he thought of his predicament. *A prisoner!* Such a common fate in the desert, yet he never dreamed it would happen to him. But there was not time now to think of that. There would be time tonight, or tomorrow. Now he must think only of knots and tugs and bags dropping through the blackness, and floods waiting to kill him. Now he wanted only to get through the day.

Hunger gnawed at his stomach. He felt for the end of his turban where he'd tied the dates. He found the lump and carefully unwrapped it. He ate only two. He wanted to space them out so that they would last the whole day, but realized he had as little conception of time as he did of distance. It might be midmorning, or afternoon, or the middle of the night. Summer or winter. No way to tell for the darkness dwellers.

He knelt and drank water directly from the bottom of the tunnel. It was sweet but too cold. The cold wouldn't leave him. He longed to return to the warmth of the surface. After less than a day he could hardly remember what the heat felt like. All he knew was the cold. The air was cold, the water was cold. Coldest of all was the darkness. He rubbed his shoulders and stomped his feet. He shivered and waited and worked.

He was pulling a bag from Abdulahi when he heard a different noise. Instantly he was attentive, concentrating. He stopped pulling.

"What are you doing, Sidi? Why do you stop?"

Abdulahi's voice was close. He had crawled behind the bag to the shaft. Moussa relaxed and crouched down.

"I didn't recognize the new noise. I thought it might be a cave-in."

Abdulahi laughed. "You have far to go, Sidi, if you do not know the difference between Abdulahi and a cave-in."

Moussa nodded in the darkness. "Yes, far to go. Are we finished for the day?"

"No. Halfway. In the darkness time plays cruel tricks. It is only time for you to take your turn digging. My arms have had enough. Can you find your way back?"

"I think so." Moussa wasn't at all certain of it. The thought that he had made it through only half a day was depressing.

"Listen carefully when you dig. If you are working on a piece of rock that hides water the sound of your mattock will change. That should not happen this high in the foggaras, but the dragon is full of surprises."

"How will I know when to come back?"

"Count the strokes of your mattock. When you cannot lift it even one more time, Sidi, then dig twice that many again. That will be the time to stop."

"That is too long. Why don't we just sit without digging?"

"A wonderful idea, but it won't work. They send slaves to check on us every week. They are men who have been freed from heavy labor through long service. They no longer have to dig if they do their job well, so you can imagine how well they do it. They know every inch of the dragon. They measure it. They crawl it from one end to the other. They know how many men have worked an area, and how much should have been done. They look to see there are no secret tunnels or rooms.

"If we have not done well in a week's time they cut our rations. If we continue to go slowly—well, there was a group of slaves who decided not to dig. There were twelve of them. It was just after I arrived in Timimoun. Jubar Pasha knew what to do. He closed off the ends of the tunnels where they worked that day and pulled up the rope of their shaft. Then he summoned the rest of us. Pulled us out of the foggaras, just to see it. Work came to a halt in the entire oasis. There were men twenty deep standing around the shaft. We could hear the men below howling. It was a terrible sound. And then we were each made to drop a bag of earth into the shaft, until the howling stopped." He spat. "After that there was no more talk of slow work."

Moussa shivered.

He found his way back easily enough, and knew he would never get used to the tunnels. His skin was soaked and irritated. His hands and knees were raw. Sand and sharp rocks tore at his flesh. The cold continued its relentless assault on his body. He found his way to where he would dig. He rested a moment, then used his hands to feel the surface he was about to work. The tunnel was oval-shaped but flat across the bottom. He had to lie down to work, his belly and legs in the cold water that trickled from the stone.

Digging was awkward. He couldn't raise the mattock high enough to get a good swing. All he could manage was to hack away at the surface of the soft stone. At first he did it with his eyes open, but quickly learned to close them to protect them from flying pieces. The mattock took only small bits with each blow. When he'd worked awhile he scraped up the dirt with his hands and fumbled to get it into the bag. It seemed to take forever to fill. When he tugged on the rope the bag slithered away instantly. He rested for a moment, surprised at how quickly he felt the corresponding tug that meant an empty bag was ready for him to pull back. No rest yet, he thought.

It was awful work. His hands took the worst of it. They were unused to physical labor, and scraping the dirt up was abrasive. They were too cold for him to be certain, but he thought he could feel his skin shredded and bleeding by the time he was working on his fourth bag. At this rate he'd have nothing left but stumps by the end of the day. He turned his mattock around and used the handle to pick up bits of the earth instead of doing it with his hands. It took longer, but it was the only way. In camp he would try to find something to use as a scoop.

No! He cursed himself for the thought. He was only trying to get through the day, but he must not let that become a habit.

I must not find ways to make things easy. I must find ways to escape.

The day dragged forever. The work savaged his body. His muscles ached. Blisters formed and broke and formed again. Bag after bag slithered away. Bag after bag came back. The dragon was always ravenous for more. He worked until he knew he could not fill another bag, when lifting the mattock through the air was more than he could bear. Then he thought of Abdulahi's words, that he needed to do twice that much. He rested his head on his forearm and willed himself to go on. It occurred to him that like other noblemen of the Ihaggaren, he had never done physical labor. Slaves did it for them. Now he was the slave. It was a startling thought.

Gritting his teeth, he went back to work.

He was moving automatically, his mind blanked to all but the steady repetition of his task, when he felt the first dribble of rock. It fell onto the back of his legs from the ceiling behind him as he swung the mattock. He cried out in terror.

Cave-in!

Frantically he backed up, abandoning his mattock and bag. His heart pounded in panic, his throat tight. At the intersection with the main tunnel he stopped to listen.

There was nothing. Nothing but the sound of his own lungs, rasping in damp fear.

There had been no cave-in. Only a little loose dirt had fallen, along with his courage. He calmed himself. Every instinct told him to leave then, to slither back to the shaft and get out. He'd done more than a man could reasonably do. But he knew it wasn't time, and if he left his mattock and bag behind there would be no food tonight. He had to eat. To eat he must work.

Reluctantly he crawled forward again, into the mouth of the dragon.

H E STRETCHED OUT ON HIS BACK IN THE LITTLE hut, exhausted. It was a relief to be out of the fog-garas, but his body had paid an awful price. Every muscle ached. His hands and knees were flayed, the rest of his skin blistered and torn. He was still shivering from the cold. The dirt on the floor of the hut still held the day's heat. He wriggled in it, trying to dig down into it, to surround himself with its warmth.

He couldn't imagine going through another day of this. Abdulahi had been there four years. Others had been there even longer.

Four years! He would sooner die.

Abdulahi smiled sympathetically at his discomfort. "You will get used to the work, Sidi. Your body will adjust to the cold, and your skin will toughen. Soon you will get to the end of the day and not feel it as you do now."

"No," Moussa said, determined. "Never. I will never

get used to it, because I will be gone first." He started to say more, but the door opened suddenly and the food bowls were handed through. He had to force himself to get up. He needed to eat, to keep up his strength. He sat up. It was nearly dusk. He started on the rock-hard couscous and then remembered the dates still in his turban. He'd forgotten to eat the rest of them during the day. He mixed everything together and ate with his fingers. He noticed his hands were shaking. He wolfed the food down. There wasn't enough—not nearly enough.

"How can I escape?" He said it in a low voice so the sound would not be heard outside the room.

Abdulahi chuckled. "Can you fly, Sidi? It will help greatly if you can."

"I am serious."

"As am I. There is no escape without wings. Do you think I would sit here if it were possible to leave? Few men try it. All of them die. A man cannot get past the desert that surrounds us."

"Then go toward the west. There are other oases there."

Monjo nodded as he licked his fingers. It was the first time he'd spoken. "The man who occupied this room before you was the last to try that. Ammoun was his name. He stored his food, date by date, until he had a bag full. We gave him our own rations when he was ready. He stole a blanket to cover himself from the sun. He made a water bag from used goatskins of the foggaras. It took him six moons to have everything ready. He waited until a day when the regular guard was ill. He hid in the latrine that morning and slipped over the wall after the work parties were gone. The new guard didn't notice. Ammoun made for Timoudi."

"It is a nearby oasis," Abdulahi explained, "along the Saoura, the river that sometimes flows in the west. Well out of the pasha's district." Moussa nodded. He knew of the river.

"By day Ammoun hid so that he would not be seen by travelers. By night he walked. After twelve nights he made the oasis. He was nearly dead, but he thought himself a free man. He pretended to be a pilgrim making his way to Fez. Then he was seized by agents of the agha of Adrar. He was taken to the slave market there and was eventually sold to a passing caravan. After two months he ended up in the Great Hall of none other than Jubar Pasha, his former master. You can imagine the pasha's displeasure when he realized that the man being sold to him was already his property. He purchased Ammoun a second time, and hung him by his ankles over the gate to our compound. The crows left a leg bone. It is still there if you look."

Moussa shrugged. "It was a bad plan. He didn't go far enough. He should have taken a camel."

"A camel, indeed!" scoffed Mahmoud. "There's a fine trick for a Tuareg dog! But there are no camels here, as you have seen. They are all kept behind the wall of Timimoun. You would have to sneak *into* Timimoun to steal one, then slip out again. It is not a large oasis. Men know the business of other men. The guards know the identity of those who pass through the gates. It is not possible to do such a thing unnoticed."

"Unlikely perhaps. Not impossible." Moussa was thinking of the guard at In Salah, the one who had slept through his visit to the town in search of supplies for the French mission. "Guards are the same everywhere. They sleep. They take bribes."

Mahmoud shrugged. "If it is Allah's will you might succeed," he said. "So far Allah has not willed it for any man."

"I do not wait for Allah to will a thing," Moussa replied. "I must will it myself, and do it."

"We have all heard that Tuaregs know no God," Mahmoud said. "You may doubt the power of the Almighty, but do not rub our noses in your blasphemy."

"Then do not rub mine in your surrender," Moussa replied. "There is a way out of here. If you do not seek it, it will remain unknown to you. I intend to find it."

Mahmoud gestured in frustration. The Targui was insane.

"It is not such a bad life when you grow accustomed

to it," Monjo said. "If you work there is food. They are not cruel to us. They do not beat us, unless we give them cause."

Moussa could not understand waiting to die. "Can I walk in the oasis?"

"No."

"Can I eat the fruits grown there?"

"No."

"Can I leave when I wish?"

"Of course not."

"Then I will never grow accustomed to it."

"So you will die."

"Then let it be so." Moussa looked at the others. "When I find a way to escape, do you mean to say you will not come with me? That you will not help? You would stay here forever?"

"I would go, of course," said Abdulahi, "but you will not find a way."

Monjo shook his head. "I came from nothing and to nothing I shall return, Sidi. There is nowhere for me to go that is better than this," he said. "I can never make it back to the southlands. Better a slave here in a hell I know than a slave somewhere else, in one I don't. I can die here as well as anywhere."

Mahmoud sighed. The Targui was mad. But he just might be the will of Allah, waiting to be worked. "I have no wish to die in the dragon's belly. Better to die with you outside. I will go."

CHAPTER 31

THE STORM STRUCK FIRST ON THE SLOPES OF THE Djebel Amour, the Mountains of Love, killing a French farmer and his family. The farmer had immigrated two years earlier and scratched a hard living from land that had been confiscated from an Algerian. He had improved the well and added irrigation ditches, but the soil was poor and his figs and olives withered under the sun. He was clearing rocks for a new vegetable garden while his young son played nearby. His wife and infant daughter were inside their farmhouse.

He saw them coming, a dozen men on camels who descended from a ridge. At first he was not alarmed. There had never been trouble. He saw they were an odd lot of men of different tribes. They rode quickly. He saw one was a Targui, and only then suspected something was not right. The Tuareg did not often venture so far north. When he saw their weapons unsheathed the farmer snatched up his son and started to run toward the house. Mahdi overtook him easily and struck him down. The farmer was dead before he hit the ground, falling on top of the little boy in a futile attempt to save him. It didn't help. The boy died next. Then the raiders swarmed around the house where their swords flashed again. A torch finished the work. It was all done quickly.

The smoke could be seen from a neighboring farm. That farmer, a paroled Sicilian convict, grabbed a rifle and mounted his donkey and rode quickly to help. On the way he encountered the men of the *jihad*. He was able to get off one shot before he was overwhelmed. His own farm was next.

There were four more raids before the first alarm reached the French garrison in Laghouat. The commandant was not overly concerned; there had been sporadic but ineffective uprisings for years. He sent out a party of ten *tirailleurs* under the command of Lieutenant Lebeque, a supremely confident Parisian. His troops rode magnificent Arabian horses. Mules pulled a supply wagon that carried his tent and a casket of wine and the other necessities of life in the wretched regions in which he traveled. He was contemptuous of the filthy lot of ruffians he was chasing. His scouts picked up their trail and followed them into a wadi that ran into the open desert. His wagon became stuck. The horses struggled against the deep sand. His men were busy trying to free it when the lightning of the *jihad* struck again. This time there were more of them, thirty men now, and they used rifles and swords. There was a great shrilling as the warriors of Islam dispatched the French force. Lieutenant Lebeque was the last to die. The life of one *tirailleur* was spared. The rebel leader spoke to him as he was being released. "Tell them my name is Tamrit," he said, "and that my cause is holy. Tell them I will not stop until they are all gone from this place. Tell your brother *tirailleurs* that those who help the French shall also die, even the Muslims among them."

To drive home the point, two Algerians who administered land for the French were murdered that same day in broad daylight in their town squares.

Tamrit's name was made. He was terrorizing a huge area, while hundreds of miles to the west, Bou Amama was mounting a similar insurrection. The settlers were growing panicked. Deputies began making speeches in Paris, decrying the intolerable lack of security. More patrols, stronger in number, were sent from Laghouat. The garrison in Wargla was alerted.

MONTHS BEFORE THE RAIDS BEGAN, PAUL HAD journeyed toward home, as ordered by Captain Chirac, the commandant at Wargla. In Algiers, as Chirac had promised, Paul was greeted by the governor

himself, who insisted on feting him. The lords and ladies of Algiers gathered around him, chattering gaily
and fawning over him like a hero, the lone French survivor of a martyred expedition. A young woman in a
breathtaking dress tried to seduce him. Paul was
shocked by the adulation, which only intensified his
feelings that he was a low failure rather than the hero
they sought to worship. *Where is their anger? They
ought to hold me in contempt.* But the governor was a
gifted orator and the audience was receptive. During a
speech at dinner Paul listened, incredulous, as the politi-
cian managed to turn the Flatters expedition into a triumph of French will. He suffered through it until he
could take no more. Then he rose abruptly and left the
room, retiring to the quiet of the governor's study. He
found brandy there and got roaring drunk.

He couldn't stomach the thought of enduring more
of the same in Paris. He could not return home without
honor. He did not take the boat for Marseilles. "I don't
want to go," he told the governor the next day. "I want
to return to Wargla. I want to kill the enemies of
France."

"That is a lot of killing." The governor smiled gently.
"A matter for a nation, not for one man."

"The nation will not do it," Paul said. "So I must."

As glib as the governor was before an audience, he
sensed what the young officer had been through, and
was deeply troubled by what he saw in his eyes. "Give
yourself some time. Return to Paris, at least for a while.
Find yourself a girl and have a good time. In a few
months all this will fade. Then you can decide what you
must do."

But Paul knew what he wanted. He pulled family
strings he had never tested in order to get it done. It was
far easier than he'd ever imagined. The minister of war
himself overturned the order for his return to France
and granted his request for a posting to the garrison at
Wargla. If redemption was ever going to be possible, the
opportunity would come there.

But he miscalculated. Nothing was happening in
Wargla, and inactivity sharpened his sense of failure.

His hatred for the Tuareg simmered, while his guilt over the cowardly way he left Melika tortured him. He didn't know himself, or understand what he was going through. He was too young to know what to do with his hatred. He seethed inside, slowly disintegrating in the acid of his obsession.

He sat in the dark and thought of Melika and drank himself into a stupor. He ate little. He stopped shaving and didn't bathe. There was no joy in him, no spark of life. There was nothing left of the naïve but enthusiastic officer who had once found treasure in the smallest discoveries of the desert. He wouldn't talk to the other men about what had happened. They began to avoid him, averting their eyes when he walked past, muttering about *le cafard,* the profound depression that carried so many desert soldiers to the very brink of sanity, or beyond.

He did practice with his rifle, and cleaned and polished his weapons. The soft sounds were repeated each day in his room—the stroke of the sharpening stone along the blade of the sword, the soft whisper of the oil cloth against the guns, the cork returning to the neck of the bottle.

He thought of his father, sitting drunk and alone in his room at the château after the court-martial, sharpening his sword and sending everyone away. Both father and son had come to a bitter end. What surprised him was that the son had gotten to the end so much more quickly than the father.

One day a sentry arrived to tell him that a woman was at the gate of the garrison, asking for him. "She says she knows you, sir. Says her name is Melika. She's quite good-looking for a local—" He almost said *whore,* but thought better of it. He envied the lieutenant his wench.

Paul looked away. He took a deep breath.

"Send her away," he said quietly.

A few days later she came again. "Send her away," Paul said. From a window he watched her leave.

The next time she came the sentry didn't bother to

ask. He invited her inside the watch house and unbuttoned his trousers. She turned away angrily. He caught her by the arm and offered her money, pressing the coins into her hand. She slapped him hard and he let go. "Only good enough for an officer's prick, are you?" he sneered.

Father Jean came to the garrison. Paul was disheveled and smelled of rum. But there was no escape from the priest, who had been shown directly to his quarters. Paul stared at him through dull eyes.

"I came to ask if you are well," Father Jean said. His eyes registered disapproval but he said nothing of it.

Paul shrugged, embarrassed by his own condition. "I know you saved my life," he said after an awkward silence. "I should have thanked you for that. I'm sorry I left without saying good-bye."

"As am I, my son," the priest said, his voice on edge. It was the real reason for his visit. Melika was a daughter to him. She had been shattered by the lieutenant's abrupt departure. He permitted himself only a trace of scorn.

"You could have at least said good-bye to her. She cared for you." The words turned inside Paul like a knife.

"I couldn't," Paul whispered. "You wouldn't understand."

"Then help me understand. I will listen." The priest's eyes filled with compassion. He could see Paul's agony.

"I can't, Father."

"Then let us pray together. Ask the Lord for what you need. He will listen."

"I don't believe in God, Father. I only believe in the devil. I've seen the devil. I've seen who he is. I've seen where he lives. But I've never seen God. If He's there He doesn't listen. I won't pray to the deaf, not anymore." Father Jean started to say something but Paul waved him off. "I don't want to argue this. Leave me alone. Mind your own business."

"Of course. I didn't mean to intrude." He turned to go, then hesitated. "Is there any message I can take her?"

Paul shook his head, but as the priest's hand touched the door he changed his mind.

"Yes there is, Father. Tell her . . . tell her Paul deVries is dead." He fought to control his voice as he said it, but it broke anyway.

"I cannot lie to her."

"It isn't a lie, Father."

WHEN CAPTAIN CHIRAC RECEIVED WORD ABOUT Tamrit's raids he summoned three of his officers and ordered each to assemble patrols to hunt and kill the rebel. The captain was concerned about making Lieutenant deVries one of those officers. Like the governor, he worried about Paul's look. Yet he knew the assignment might be the very thing deVries needed to regain his confidence and control. The lieutenant was just near enough to madness that his passion in the pursuit of Tamrit would also serve the interests of France. Indeed, Paul accepted his orders with enthusiasm the captain hadn't seen in months. He pulled himself from his lethargy and didn't touch another drop of alcohol. He was ready to depart a full day before the other patrols.

Paul took twenty men, a third the number the captain suggested. Paul persuaded him that too large a force would be a hindrance, not a help. He chose as his deputy Messaoud ben Sheikh, a crusty NCO who reminded Paul of El Madani. Messaoud was from Algiers, a half-breed whose father was a French seaman and whose mother was Algerian. He hated the Shamba and the Mzabites and the Tuareg and every other tribe whose blood he considered inferior to his own. Even though France would never make him a citizen or allow him to advance past his current rank, he was fiercely devoted to everything French. He was a disciplined soldier who followed orders. He suited Paul perfectly and saw to the details of arming and provisioning the detail.

They passed through the gate of the garrison just after dawn. From the shadows near a well Melika watched them go. He passed only a few feet from her. She called out but he didn't hear. And then he was gone.

TAMRIT MOVED THROUGH THE DESERT LIKE A phantom. He was seen and then he was not. He moved quickly and at night. His force was small but created fear everywhere. He struck without warning and then vanished, only to strike again a great distance away. No one knew for sure what he looked like. It was said he wore the veil of a Tuareg, or that he wore no veil and was dressed like a merchant of the Mzab, or that he wore the rags of a beggar. Still others swore they'd seen him and that he was of the Ouled Sidi Sheikh. His eyes were brown; his eyes were blue; his eyes were gray. There was a scar on his cheek; his face was unblemished; one could not see his face at all.

Paul knew the man he was chasing, if not his face. He had heard the name during his long night in the cave with Moussa. He remembered all the names: Attici, Mahdi—and oh yes, Tamrit. Ahitagel's inner council of treachery. *Tamrit*. He had been there, at Tadjenout. Paul knew it. He had been one of those watching as the poison did its work at Aïn El Kerma and the men of Flatters died one by one. Only Attici bore more guilt, but Attici was for later. Tamrit was for now.

Lieutenant deVries pushed his men to their limit, crisscrossing the desert, traveling vast distances in pursuit of shadows and rumors. He slept little and never permitted his men to grow comfortable in camp. He posted sentries and tested them himself, determined not to be caught by surprise. His men struggled with their horses, which were ill-suited for the desert fringes but always used by the French for patrols. The captain had refused his suggestion that they use camels. "Too undignified," he said, "and far too slow." Paul didn't think so. It was the horses of the hunters that failed on long marches, not the camels of the hunted. Yet he obeyed the captain, at least in the beginning.

Paul looked for patterns in the raids so that he might anticipate where Tamrit would strike next. There were none. If he thought Tamrit was going to move west, he moved east. If he thought he would strike a farm next, he attacked a village. In one thing only did he prove predictable.

He killed without mercy.

Even the most callous of the *tirailleurs* looked away from the grisly scenes they encountered. Only Paul was able to stare at the bodies without flinching. Nothing he saw compared to what he had already seen.

"We will catch them," he said with absolute conviction to Messaoud. "And we will kill them all."

The chase went on for months, ranging from Wargla to the fringes of the Grand Erg Occidental, and south almost to the Tademait Plateau—farther into the desert than any other French patrols had ventured, and well beyond the range approved by Captain Chirac. As hard as they pushed, they were always days or weeks behind Tamrit, who seemed to mock them by the very ease with which he moved.

They nearly caught him once, at an encampment of a few tents that belonged to nomads journeying to the souk in Wargla with a flock of sheep. It was clear that the nomads had fed Tamrit's men, who had stayed the night. They had been gone for some time, but evidence of their presence was everywhere.

Messaoud interrogated the patriarch of the clan, who nervously regarded the waiting French column behind him as he explained what had happened. "He says yes, they fed Tamrit, but only on pain of death. He says they were forced to provide them food," Messaoud said.

Paul nodded. "Then he must pay," he said evenly. Paul didn't know whether the nomad was telling the truth about being coerced. It didn't matter. It was time for an example to be made. "Burn their tents. Kill all the sheep. Butcher one and bring the meat for us."

Messaoud snapped the order. The patriarch watched with horror as he realized what was going to happen. Pleading for leniency, he began wailing and pulling at Paul's pant leg. Unmoved, Paul sat in his saddle.

"What is he saying?"

Messaoud snorted. "That our action is too extreme, sir. That this is all they have in the world."

"No. Their *life* is everything. I am not taking that—not this time. Tell him to be thankful for that. Tell him to spread the word that men caught helping Tamrit will be treated without mercy. They must be prepared to pay a great price."

The women of the camp raised a shrill cry as their belongings went up in smoke. One tried to snatch a leather bag from the flames, a bag of cheap jewelry and sewing utensils. A *tirailleur* pushed her roughly and she collapsed to her knees in tears. Paul watched without sympathy.

The sheep were slaughtered without the ritual ceremony that would have at least permitted their use as food. They were shot where they stood by a soldier who moved quickly through the flock with his pistol. Each shot raised a fresh cry from the nomads, who were beating their breasts and crying.

In addition to the sheep the nomads had eight camels. They grazed next to the camp, oblivious to everything. Paul called out, "Messaoud! Bring the headman's mehari!"

Messaoud cut the camel's hobbles and led the beast to Paul. It was a strong fawn-colored female. Fearing the worst, the patriarch followed along, clasping his hands and whimpering. He looked up at the French lieutenant, whose stare was stone.

"Tell him I want to know of Tamrit—where he is going, how he is dressed, how many men he has, what arms they carry," Paul said.

The headman gave quick answers, shaking his head. The NCO barked at him, clearly dissatisfied. "We might as well ask the camel, Lieutenant. He says he doesn't know which of them was Tamrit. There were several men who seemed to be giving orders. All their faces were veiled. He doesn't know where they were going. He didn't count how many there were."

Paul pulled his pistol from its holster and without a word shot the man's camel. The beast sagged to its knees and rolled over on its side. A fresh wail arose from the members of the clan.

"Bring another mehari," Paul said coldly. "Then ask him again."

It was done. The headman just shook his head, caught in a deadly game he knew he could not win. Whatever the French or the warriors of the *jihad* might do to him, he could not afford the loss of his camels. He began talking. He pointed off toward the eastern end of a low range of barren hills. He drew a map in the sand. Messaoud asked a few questions, nodding at the responses. When he was finished the *tirailleur* looked at Paul with a gleam of satisfaction in his eyes.

"His memory has improved, sir. There are twenty, maybe twenty-five, moving toward El Gassi. They have old muskets and two new carbines, he thinks of Italian manufacture. Tamrit is dressed like a Targui. He swears he could only see his eyes, and that they were as green as emeralds. He thought the man unusual because he wore no amulets, no ornaments of any kind. All Tuareg wear amulets."

Paul was satisfied, knowing the man was telling the truth at last. He watched from his saddle as his men butchered the sheep. The nomads began picking through the smoking ruin of their camp. The soldiers finished quickly and they set out at once. Paul brushed off Messaoud's cautions that they should not travel in the heat of the day. "The heat does not stop Tamrit. It will not stop me."

As they departed, the air was still as only the desert can make it, thick with the smell of blood and smoke.

Paul did not look back.

PAUL RETREATED INTO HIS THOUGHTS AS THEY rode toward El Gassi. He was vaguely troubled that it had been so easy to shoot the camel. Certainly it had been harder than giving the order to torch the camp. Yet he had done both without hesitation and felt no remorse. He knew that had he run out of camels he would have shot one of the men.

You've changed and gone cruel. He remembered Hakeem's words, spoken a lifetime ago. He knew it was true. He felt himself growing cold inside, indifferent to people. At first he had focused on Tamrit as the symbol of everything he hated. But hatred, having taken root, fought to blossom inside him, nurtured in his mind by the death he saw and the death he delivered. He felt some part of himself withering inside. Soon the other men traveling with Tamrit, men of different tribes, became as evil to him as Tamrit himself. The line between Tuareg and all men of the Sahara, all men of Africa, was becoming blurred. The desert faces began to look alike to him, the victims as well as the criminals. Retribution wore no veil.

It was an awful state he'd gotten to, he knew. Yet the demons of Tadjenout were stronger than he was, nipping away at his soul.

He also knew that in his neat mosaic of loathing, there were two parts that didn't fit.

He wanted to hate Moussa the way he hated the others. Moussa had made it difficult, by interfering during the march. He had intentionally ignored Paul's orders to stay away. Now Paul didn't know what he might be capable of doing if he saw his cousin again. How many times had Moussa saved his life on that march? He loved his cousin and he hated him too, and he hated the world that had torn them apart.

Then at night when all was silent in camp and sleep wouldn't come he let himself think of Melika. He saw her face clearly, and felt her touch on his cheek, and heard her soft laughter. He knew he had been falling in love with her, yet when he walked away from her he had crossed an invisible bridge. Could he ever cross back? Would she ever let him, if he could? He was afraid of the answers. His duty was so clear to him, until he thought of her—and so he tried not to let himself think. But Melika never left him.

He still drank no alcohol. He ate little and slept less. He was growing as lean as the desert itself. He learned a great deal about tracks and the telltale signs of the passage of men and animals. He watched the sky and the shifting sands, but only for the hunt. He did not see the beauty of the land, or of the stars at night. Delicate desert wildflowers perished unnoticed beneath the hooves of his horse.

The chase went on.

ELISABETH WAS CONSUMED WITH THOUGHTS OF her son. Of course she knew of the outcome of the Flatters expedition. All France knew and shared a common humiliation. It was all too awful to bear, that her own son had been part of such a debacle. She was cursed by military failure. First Jules and now Paul. The newspaper articles were horrid. Slaughter, retreat, cannibalism. Shame at the hands of savages. Everywhere accounts of the survivor Lieutenant deVries. Some called him a hero. Others—well, others used words she could not repeat. Her friends looked at her with a dreadful mixture of pity and condescension.

Well. Enough was enough. Even Paul would have to see that now. She would get him out of the loathsome military and into his proper civilian role as the Count deVries. She was deliciously close to a resolution in the courts and expected to hear any day. But now, just when she could taste victory, Paul had fallen mute. She knew he was safe, yet he had not even bothered to write her. She had a letter about him from the governor in Algiers, and another from Captain Chirac, but she had heard nothing at all from Paul himself. She had written back demanding the officials *order* him to write her. She had enclosed letters to him, letters in which she made it quite clear what was in his best interest. Still he had not responded. How could he be so unfeeling? She assumed he was chastened by the fiasco, but that was no reason not to write his own mother. And now he was off in the insufferable desert somewhere, chasing some Arab thug.

"There is a . . . someone to see you, *madame la comtesse,*" the butler announced, interrupting her thoughts. "A—foreign . . . gentleman." The distaste was evident on his face as he struggled for the proper word to describe the man. Besides, civilized people did not call before three-thirty and it was not yet noon. "He has no calling card or letter of introduction. He is quite persistent. He says he has news of Count deVries. He insists on seeing you personally."

"*Le comte?* Why did you not say so immediately? I will receive him in the study," she said.

A few moments later the visitor was ushered in and stood before her. "Madame, it is kind of you to receive me. I am called El Hussein. It humbles me to be at your service." The speaker bowed deeply. He was tall and dark skinned and resplendent in the flowing robes of a Bedouin, woven of silk as fine as could be bought in France. A jewel adorned his turban. His face had the sharp lines of a hawk above a neatly trimmed goatee. He had long fingers with lacquered nails and wore rings on both hands. She saw there was a certain elegance about the man, for a desert ruffian.

Elisabeth was fascinated by him, at once repelled and attracted. Were it not for his birth she knew he would have been a gentleman of distinction, a man as comfortable in a French parlor as in a desert tent. His failing, apart from his race, was that his teeth were long and pointed, and he sucked at them quietly. It annoyed her, as did his eyes, which were sharply penetrating, too bold. As he took her hand and bent to kiss it they rested for just a moment on her breasts, and she felt his gaze almost as if he had touched her there. Certainly he was mentally undressing her. His attention turned subtly to the diamonds she wore, clearly assessing their value rather than appreciating their beauty. Next his eyes roamed the rich contents of the study, from the crystal to the silver candelabra to the rich boxes inlaid with mother-of-pearl, to the priceless Gobelin tapestries on the walls. It was all done in an instant, his gaze practiced and smooth. Most people would not even have noticed, but Elisabeth did. She had always been an excellent judge of people, men in particular, and there was something unsettling about this man, something that filled her with a profound unease. She couldn't pinpoint it. He was a cobra with its hood withdrawn—no immediate peril, yet no mistaking the danger.

If El Hussein noticed her discomfort he gave no sign. He turned to business. "Perhaps your manservant has informed you already, madame. I have come about the Count deVries."

"*Oui*. My son. You have seen him? I am anxious for news."

El Hussein gave her a blank look. "He is your son, madame? Perhaps I have made an error. I had been led to believe the count was your nephew."

Elisabeth's blood ran cold. *Moussa.* She recovered quickly.

"Ah, my nephew. There are some, *oui*, who call— *called* him count. He died with his father years ago. A balloon crash. Now it is my own son Paul who—"

"But madame, pardon," he interrupted her excitedly. "It is that very matter about which I have come to see you!" His eyes were alight with triumph, that he could share such glad tidings. "I am delighted to be able to bring you the joyous news that he is *not* dead." He expected a cry of relief, or a gasp, or something more than a mouth turned down in displeasure, but that was all Elisabeth could manage.

"Indeed."

Her reaction puzzled El Hussein. His news had made her tense, alert. *There is something here I do not understand,* he thought. *She said he was dead, yet she knew already he was not. Strange.*

"It is quite so, madame. However, I regret my news is not all good. He is in great peril, being held . . . ah, how should I say it?—captive in a remote desert village. He has been taken prisoner by a powerful sheikh. It is a most unpleasant matter. A question of tribal rivalries. Ordinarily nothing could be done about it, nothing at all. But I was pleased to learn of his family here. It opened the possibility that he need not suffer a most unpleasant fate at the hands of his captors. It is within my power to . . . to intervene with the sheikh. To assist you, and the family of the Count deVries, in obtaining his release."

Elisabeth's anger flared. "You presume much, coming here to me. Your offer to help is nothing more than a bald attempt at ransom. I should call the prefect of police. He knows what to do with brigands."

"I presume nothing, madame, and assure you I am no brigand. Besides, what would your prefect say of me? That I am guilty of attempting to help? I have traveled far, madame, at considerable expense and difficulty, in an effort to render some small assistance to you. I gain nothing from this personally. I have come in the spirit of the Koran. And forgive me, madame, but what could your prefect do while the count suffers in another land? He is deep in the desert, well beyond the realm of French influence. Not even your military can help him. I assure you—there is only one way to the count's salvation."

El Hussein opened his arms in supplication. "I must confess I do not understand your anger, madame. Frankly I had assumed you would be glad of my news, and thankful for my humble effort."

"Of course I am . . . interested," she said. She regarded him warily. She would have to be careful. This was a clever man.

Elisabeth sat down. She rang the bell for the butler, who appeared immediately. He had been waiting just outside the door, as if he expected the foreigner to attack the mistress.

"Countess?"

"Brandy." She looked inquiringly at her visitor. El Hussein started to decline. "It is not permit—" he started to say, but then relented. He was in France, after all. "Of course, you are too kind," and his glass was filled. He raised the glass to Elisabeth, who ignored him. The liquor burned his throat. As he drank he cursed Jubar Pasha for giving him insufficient information. The butler had addressed the woman as "countess." If her nephew Moussa was the count, this woman could not be *la comtesse deVries.* Inwardly he shrugged. There was much about France he didn't understand. Its few customs that weren't odd were backward. And too, there was much about this woman he didn't understand. He sensed a very resourceful woman. He did not like being ignorant of either.

"You say Moussa is alive. You have seen him yourself?"

"But of course, madame." Jubar Pasha had summoned Moussa to stand naked before them, his hands bound behind his back. El Hussein had walked slowly around the prisoner, touching, probing, memorizing every detail for precisely this moment. Even though tightly bound, Moussa had lashed out at him, kneeing him in the groin. A most unpleasant man. El Hussein had beaten him until the pasha would allow no more.

"Describe him to me."

El Hussein complied. Elisabeth didn't know what Moussa looked like anymore. She had no idea whether the description fit. The blue eyes, the dark hair, the noble features all sounded like a man who could have grown from the boy she remembered. There was something of Henri in the description. Yet there was no way to be certain. A thousand men might have similar features.

"That is all? It is hardly proof."

"There is a scar, madame."

"A scar?"

"*Oui.* I saw it myself. In his side. Just here, below his rib cage." He indicated the spot at his own side, drawing a line with his finger. "It appears to be quite old."

Elisabeth closed her eyes. *The boar.* She struggled to maintain her composure.

"And his mother? You know who she is? Where she is?"

"*Certainement,* madame, although I have not met her myself. She is called Serena. She is of the Tuareg. She lives in their tents in the Hoggar Mountains. Deep in the southern desert."

"I know where the mountains are," she snapped.

El Hussein gave her a thin smile. "Of course. Please forgive me. You are convinced, then, that I speak the truth? That it is truly the count in captivity?"

Elisabeth waved her hand. She would not quibble with this man over the identity of the true count. "I believe you have Moussa in captivity, yes."

"I can, of course, guarantee his safety. Arrange a

meeting where an exchange can be made. In Algiers, perhaps. Any place to your liking."

"And tell me, just how much ransom will it take to pry the—my nephew from the grip of this sheikh?"

El Hussein looked pained. "I prefer not to call it 'ransom,' madame," he said. "Such a coarse term for a transaction that is nothing more than commonplace in the desert."

"And what term *is* commonplace enough for you?"

" 'Tribute,' madame. And but a modest one at that. Five million francs." He had discussed the amount carefully with Jubar Pasha. Together they had settled on four. El Hussein had increased the amount upon seeing the château. The pasha would not miss the extra million any more than the deVries family would. Such a fortune in the desert, yet a pittance against such wealth.

"Five million—!" Elisabeth nearly choked on her brandy. "You call this 'modest'? Evidently, monsieur, modesty costs more in your country than in mine."

"Forgive me, madame, but we are talking about a member of the nobility, are we not? Your own nephew, the lord of this great estate? It seems a small price to pay for his safety. Surely the furnishings in this room alone are enough—"

"You presume far too much," Elisabeth snapped. She seethed in quiet turmoil. How hard she had labored toward her object! How many sacrifices she had made! She deserved the estate as much as Paul deserved the title! And now this smelly little thief brought her news of her wretched nephew, who could ruin everything. It was all at risk. Why now, when things were so close to being finished? *Not now!* And ransom? Out of the question. She would let him languish in captivity. If he died everyone would be better off.

But what if he didn't die? How clever could any desert sheikh be? They were ignorant, all of their sort. Everyone knew it. What if Moussa escaped? Then what? As long as he lived he was a threat to her.

It was maddening. She couldn't leave him where he was. She certainly wasn't going to pay this ruffian a fortune to see to his safe return. What was left? She took a drink.

And then it came to her, and it warmed her inside like the brandy.

It always came to her, when she needed it most.

She looked at El Hussein. His eyes had narrowed. She hoped she had not misjudged him. She needed a man as contemptible as she was certain he was.

"You say you can intervene with the sheikh on behalf of my nephew. That does not suggest the level of influence that I require. I need a man with more than influence. I need a man with control."

"I can do whatever is necessary, madame, in the circumstances."

"Do not play games with me. I must know how far your influence reaches with this sheikh. If you persist in being coy I shall terminate this discussion immediately and you can return to the filth from which you crawled." She set her glass on the table and moved as if to stand, indicating it was time for El Hussein to leave. Quickly he relented.

"I assure you, madame, my influence is more than extensive. I have control."

"Very well," she said, nodding. "I thought as much. You are a relation of this sheikh, I suspect, if not the sheikh himself."

El Hussein smiled. "His brother-in-law, madame. You are—"

"I am prepared to pay your price. All of it."

"Allah be praised! A wise decision, madame. It is clear you have the best interests of your nephew at heart."

"As a good-faith measure I will pay you five hundred thousand francs. Today, before you leave."

El Hussein was astonished. It was more than he had expected. More than he had dreamed possible. He changed his mind about her. She was not so clever as she seemed. "That is quite generous, madame. Very wise indeed."

She held up a hand. "I will pay you the balance in full when our business is successfully concluded."

"Of course. You can see him for yourself if you wish."

Elisabeth appraised him coldly. "You misunderstand me, sir. I have no wish to see him. The balance is payable only when you can prove to me that my nephew is dead."

As El Hussein was leaving the château in his coach his mind raced with it all.

A beautiful woman. And she was dangerous. It made her all the more attractive. He had had an erection throughout their meeting. Most distracting.

He wondered what had made her reach such an extraordinary decision. Of course he would complete his end of the bargain. With pleasure. The Count deVries— or whatever he was—would be dead within a fortnight.

It was what happened just before he left that still had his heart pounding. She had told him to wait and had gone into the next room. As he savored the forbidden brandy he had noticed her reflection in a pane of glass in the hallway. She had moved to the far wall and removed a painting. There was a box mounted in the wall. She opened it and withdrew a large bundle of paper. It had taken him a moment to realize what he was seeing. He watched intently as she took the money she needed and put the rest back. She had made no attempt to hide, but then she hadn't known he was watching. His breath came more quickly. The deVries family was richer by far than he had imagined. It was beyond rich. His mind was in turmoil with all the possibilities.

His coachman drove him through the Bois de Boulogne toward the heart of the city. He decided to rent a more expensive room for the night than the one he currently occupied—a *much* more expensive one. At the Hôtel du Louvre.

Paris was such a beautiful city.

Where the devil is deVries?" thundered Captain Chirac to his adjutant. "He was supposed to report three weeks ago!"

"I don't know, *mon capitaine*. I heard he was near El Goléa."

"El Goléa!" The captain's face raged red with anger. "That is far beyond his orders!"

"*Oui, capitaine.* So it is."

"*Merde!* I've unleashed a rogue officer! The commandant in Touggourt will have my head!"

The adjutant smiled inside. French officers in these parts were not known for restraint or the overly careful reading of orders. Chirac was making theater. Practicing, perhaps, for his appearance before the colonel. He cleared his throat. "I understand, sir, that he has given up his horses as well."

"What?"

"Yes, sir. He traded them for camels."

"*Mon Dieu*, a French officer upon a camel in *my* command? It is unspeakable! Against all orders! Has the man no shame?" At this news the captain was truly aghast.

"Apparently not, sir. But he seems to have lit a fire under Tamrit. There are reports everywhere."

Chirac nodded. Secretly he was delighted. The lieutenant's legend was growing as rapidly as that of the man he chased. There were unconfirmed reports of "excesses," reports of civilians—even some women and children—killed in unfortunate incidents. But such incidents were the price one paid for order. Besides, they were followed by reports that local support for the rebel Tamrit was drying up, that he was spending more time running than killing. The gun of France was proving mightier than the sword of Islam.

The captain dismissed the adjutant. "I only hope he reports in sometime this year," he sighed. "I will be embarrassed to say I have no idea where he is. And when he does I hope he isn't riding a *camel*."

CHAPTER 32

THUNK THUNK. SCRAPE.

Sweat. Shiver. Freeze.

Thunk thunk. Scrape.

The mattock chipped at the soft stone in the blackness as the tunnel progressed.

Moussa labored with a practiced swing. His arms had grown accustomed to the work, his muscles rippling with the motion. His skin had grown used to the constant trickle of moisture in which he lay as he worked. But he would never get used to the dark, or to the cold, or to the damp walls pressing in on him. Instead he lost himself in the slow steady rhythm of his work, finding that in its repetition he could forget everything else. Abdulahi was at the other end of the rope. They worked well together, he and the little Ouled Nail, as they fed the hungry dragon. They moved more earth than any other two men.

Thunk thunk. Scrape.

Thunk thwack—

He heard and felt it at the same time, the danger telescoping itself through his mattock into his arms, his brain registering the peril as he scooted back instinctively.

Water!

First a spurt, up in the air where it shouldn't have been, water mixed with bits of earth and sand that stung his face, then stronger, a spout that slammed into him with incredible pressure. Then it burst through with all its fury, driven by a hidden reservoir on the other side of the rock. How many thousands or millions of liters backed up behind it no one knew. Water waiting for release, waiting to overwhelm him, waiting to flood the tunnels.

Abdulahi had promised he would have plenty of warning. There had been only one stroke of the mattock. Abdulahi was wrong.

He screamed at the top of his voice, trying to warn his companion, but his voice was lost in the roar of the rushing torrent. He tried again and took a mouthful of water and gagged. He coughed and managed to suck a lungful of air.

The water rushed to fill the tunnel, sweeping away the precious pockets of air that would give him life. Instinctively he tried to rise above it, but there was nowhere to go. The water hurled him back, banging him like a toy against the walls. He slipped back down onto his stomach, and the water propelled him furiously backward, feet first, down the side shaft toward the main tunnel, the torrent raging through the blackness. All the way he tried to catch hold of the sides, to brace himself as Abdulahi had told him to do, but it was useless. He wasn't strong enough.

Don't try to fight. Ride with it!

He fought the desperate impulse to take another breath. There was only water. *How far to the end? How far to the main tunnel? Twenty meters? Thirty?* He held his breath, lungs raging, arms groping, as he tried both to go with it and to gain some semblance of control. It was impossible. The water's force banged him against the sides of the tunnel, shredding his skin as it scraped along. He felt himself beginning to panic.

I can't breathe! I can't breathe!

He fought back the terror, forcing himself to think.

Float to the main tunnel. Maybe there you can find air.

He was moving fast now, still facedown, feet first, when he hit the main tunnel. His feet smashed against the wall, his knees buckling as the torrent turned the corner and raged violently down the main shaft. The impact stunned him, nearly knocking what little breath he had out of his tormented lungs. Still completely submerged, he fought the impulse to draw a breath. The burning was awful.

He thought about the tunnel. There was a slight elevation in the ceiling, midway between the area where he'd been working and the shaft to the surface. Part of the ceiling at that point had collapsed in a minor cave-in. He thought there might be an air pocket there. It was his only chance.

Get on your back. Your back!

He used his arms with the current and turned over, trying to judge the distance. He would be close now. He spread his arms and legs and tried to stop himself. The little toe of his right foot caught something. The toe snapped and he went on. There was no pain; he pushed harder. Little by little he slowed, and then stopped. The water raged around him, but he had gotten some control. He edged himself upward, his nose searching for air.

There!

It was tiny, precious. He spit and gasped and drew a sweet breath, his face in a space not much bigger than the breadth of a man's hand. Another gasp, and another. His lungs ached deeply. He knew he had little time to decide what to do. Wait? Perhaps the flood would recede quickly. He'd heard they often did. But some went on for hours, depending upon the size of the underground reservoirs waiting for release. If he waited he would run out of air. If he let go he might not find more.

The decision was taken from him. He felt his grip slipping and before he could stop himself the current wrenched him away once again and propelled him into the black hole. He had time to draw more air before he went under. Now on his back, he felt the water going in his nose. Again he forced himself not to give in to the instinct to blow air out. He needed every bit. He had a fleeting thought of Abdulahi. Had he drowned? He would have been standing at the shaft when the rock gave way. Perhaps he had pulled himself up in time, or perhaps he had stayed down, trying to pull on Moussa's rope, to help save him. It wouldn't matter if he had. Moussa had lost his end of the rope.

His mind focused on the shaft. He would be there in an instant. He kept his hands up, running his fingers along the top of the tunnel, planning to act the instant he arrived. The rope from the surface hung down there. He would have less than a second, but maybe he could grab hold of the rope and pull himself up into the shaft, where he could climb to the safety of the surface.

It came and went too quickly. He felt the rope but it slipped past his hand before he could catch it. He caught the edge of the shaft, his fingers clinging to the sandstone, but then it crumbled and gave way, and he was gone again, but not before he took a mouthful of water. There had been no sign of Abdulahi.

Once more he slowed himself, turning his heels outward, trying to find purchase on the sides, stiffening his knees so they wouldn't collapse on him. He knew he was running out of air, that he had only a few seconds before he would let go, let his lungs do what they were desperate to do, take a deep breath, and then the blackness would come, and death would take him.

Suddenly he banged into something softer than a rock. His bare foot felt a shoulder. Another man had jammed the tunnel. *Abdulahi?*

He hadn't meant to push on the shoulder, didn't want to knock the man loose, a man who had probably found his own small pocket of air and was gasping in the blackness as he himself was trying to do.

But it was too late. He felt a hand on his ankle and then the current won and the hand slipped away and the man just disappeared. By then Moussa himself had slowed just enough to stop. There *was* another pocket of air. Once again, thankfully, he took quick deep breaths, trying to store up whatever oxygen he could before the mad ride began again. His muscles strained against the current that still pulled violently at him. He was exhausted. He didn't know how much longer he could do it. The air was glorious, but each breath brought relief mixed with guilt, for each breath was taken at the expense of another man's life.

He knew how Abdulahi feared the water, feared this disaster above all others, that he would drown in the belly of the dragon. The little man couldn't swim. At least death would take him quickly.

I am sorry, Abdulahi.

And then, almost as suddenly as the flood had begun, it finished. He felt the force of the water subsiding, the level dropping a bit and easing the pressure on his arms and legs. Then the level dropped more, and soon he was lying on his back on hard ground, completely spent, listening as the flood still roared below him, making its way to the oasis. He wondered how many men had been caught in its path, how many slaves had died this day. And the danger was far from over. Cave-ins would follow. For another week the tunnel would be a hole of death.

But I am alive.

He shuddered, the tremor starting deep inside as his body reacted to the cold and the fear. He had to get moving. With difficulty he turned so that he could crawl down the tunnel to try to find whoever it was, to see if he could help. Each movement required an immense effort. He forced himself forward.

"Abdulahi?" he called out. There was only silence. He scooted down the tunnel as fast as he could move. He found him near the next shaft. Moussa banged into him, jamming a knee into his head as he crawled.

"Abdulahi?"

Nothing. He leaned forward and bent over, holding his cheek to the man's mouth, trying to feel a breath.

Suddenly the man coughed, sputtering and spitting into Moussa's face.

"Sidi?"

"Yes," Moussa said, so relieved he wanted to hug the little man. "Yes."

Abdulahi gasped for air. "A pity. If it is you then I know this is not paradise." He rested, gathering his strength in the dripping blackness. "We have beaten the dragon this day," he sputtered.

"We have. We have at that. Come, turn over now. Let's get to the shaft before he spits again." He helped Abdulahi turn onto his stomach.

"I *thought* that was you on my shoulder, Sidi. You were trying to ride me, perhaps?" He coughed again. "I thought we had agreed. In a flood, I was to ride *you*."

In spite of their pain and fear they collapsed together in laughter.

FOR THE FIRST TIME IN NEARLY SIX MONTHS OF captivity, Moussa allowed himself to feel despair. The flood had driven it home. He was trapped. There was no way out. At first he had refused to believe it. But he was beginning to see now.

Slaves lived in Timimoun until they died.

In all, six men had died that morning, men drowned beneath a harsh desert. They were the only ones free.

It wasn't that he hadn't kept alert. Each morning on his way up the hill to the foggaras he watched and listened. Each evening on his way down the hill he did the same. But life in the oasis was timeless and predictable. Caravans came and went. Guards patrolled with their swords and their spiked palm branches. Slaves worked and ate and slept and reproduced and died. The muezzin called five times each day, and five times each day men set down their tools and humbled themselves before their merciful God. The sun rose and set and rose again, and the waters flowed in the red oasis of Timimoun, fed by the great dragon.

Moussa thought of organizing a rebellion, but for the most part he found the slaves resigned, exchanging their bodies for the guarantee of food and shelter. Only a few, like himself, were confined to a hut at night. Even if they wanted to fight, the men had little strength for it, or for flight after. They lived on next to nothing. They managed from day to day; there was nothing more in them. They fed the dragon, waiting each day for it to turn on them. And even if they could fight, what would be gained in an uprising? If they killed every guard in the compound, they would be left holding one compound and nothing more. Sooner or later the pasha's main guard would have its way. Men would die to win nothing.

Other choices were equally bleak. The only animals on which to escape were hidden behind forbidden walls. If one tried to sneak out to a departing caravan, its master would instantly find out and return him to Jubar Pasha, the valued client whose favor they all curried. There was no money for bribery. He thought about getting word out to the Tuareg. It seemed his best hope. But how? Who would treat with the Tuareg? Who would carry his message into the forbidden heart of the desert?

It was hopeless.

Yet each day he had repeated it, *I will find a way. I will never give up*. He said it between strokes of his mattock. He said it when he slid on his belly in the cold muck. He said it because he was afraid he would become like the others, from whom all hope had been drained like water from the sands. He fought the routine, trying not to get comfortable with the patterns of Timimoun. But inexorably he found himself caught in it—looking forward to his meals, or to the peace of the evenings, to the chatter of the courtyard, to the glow of the sunrise as each day began. One could learn to live with such cadence. One could say this is all there is, all there ever will be. Other men did, good men. Some even became obsessed with the foggaras, impressed with their own coerced achievements.

But not I! I will find a way! I will never give up!

Until now. Until the flood. In its wake the waves of despair lapped too close. The others were right. There was no escape from Timimoun. He closed his eyes and lost himself in thoughts of his other life, his life with Daia. She would be married by now, a mother perhaps. He imagined what they might have been like together, what their life might have been. The color of their tent, the texture of it, and how it would be inside. What their children might look like.

He constructed whole days with her, thinking out

every detail, having complete conversations. She traveled with him as he patrolled the camps of his vassals. At night they sat before their tent and watched the sun set. They moved camp with the seasons and followed the grasslands in the timeless ritual of the Tuareg. He presented her with a great white horse, a magnificent Arabian, and she rode it like the wind.

It wasn't torture, thinking of those things. It was wonderful. It kept him sane.

"Targui! *Yal-la!* Wake up! Come!"

He awoke slowly, holding on to his dream, but the foot lashed him savagely in the side. He opened his eyes and sat up, blinking. Was it night or day? He didn't know for sure. He had been dreaming.

It was Atagoom, the guard.

"What?"

"Come, I say. Be quick."

Monjo, Mahmoud, and Abdulahi all stirred. It was night, then.

"Fee 'eyh!" Abdulahi groaned. "What is it?"

"None of your affair," Atagoom snapped. Moussa got up. His toe was throbbing, his skin raw. They left the hut and walked through the compound. Slaves sat in small groups around their night fires, chattering and laughing and talking in low voices. They hardly noticed his passage. Atagoom prodded him with the palm branch, his sword sheathed at his side. He carried a torch in one hand. Atagoom was a big man. Unlike most guards he was strong and alert. He never left prisoners an opportunity to break away, never let his guard down.

They left the compound and walked down the long path toward the gates of the oasis. Cookfires flickered in other compounds. The walls were lit at large intervals with torches. Guards opened the gates at the command of Atagoom and passed them through into the town. Moussa's eyes darted everywhere, looking for details that might help one day. He was led through a bewildering maze of streets, some covered, others open to the sky, and he quickly lost his bearings. He would never find his way out, not without help. Presently they arrived at the northernmost casbah, the fortress where the pasha's quarters were located. They went up a wide stairway and onto a veranda. Sleepy guards stood before the doors, armed with swords. Atagoom said something and one disappeared inside.

Vines covered one side of the veranda, which overlooked a large garden that sloped gently down toward the oasis. He heard water trickling somewhere below, beneath the trees—water from the foggaras, water that brought life and pleasure to people who lived here, water bought with the lives of slaves. A warm breeze brought the smells of the oasis to him. He closed his eyes and breathed deeply, savoring the scent of lilacs and violets, of apricot and peach blossoms. Behind the flowers and fruits there were other smells. Something cooking, something with spices he didn't recognize but that made his stomach begin to stir. And then—perfume, the lovely fragrance of a woman. Through the leaves of the palms he saw the stars overhead. It was wonderful to be outside his hut. Wonderful to be aboveground, to smell the evening.

The guard reappeared. "Enter." Atagoom prodded him and they stepped inside. Moussa blinked. He was in the pasha's reception hall. The lights were dim. Music played from some unseen place, a stringed instrument he couldn't identify. Across the hall in the shadows he saw the vague forms of veiled women. They were leaving the hall through a door in the back, laughing and chattering. Evidently a banquet had just ended. Trays of unfinished food sat on the floor, more food than the slaves' compound saw in a week. Moussa eyed the trays. He never had enough.

The pasha sat on plush cushions, laughing at something the man sitting next to him had said. Moussa recognized the man, remembering the beating he'd suffered at his hands. *El Hussein. The ambassador.* A carafe of liquor sat near them, brandy brought from France by El Hussein for the pleasure of his brother-in-law. The devout fires of Islam had been dimmed for the evening by the forbidden liquor of the infidel. Both men were slightly drunk. At first they ignored him. He stood there with Atagoom behind him. After a time the pasha looked at him and saw his eyes on the food.

"The dog would have a bone from our table?" he said. He waved expansively. "Tonight is a night of generosity, a time to share Allah's bounty with the very man who makes it possible. Don't you agree, Hussein?"

El Hussein was the more cautious of the two. Even half-drunk, he preferred this man in chains. He remembered the knee in his groin. "He needs nothing, lord, only an end. It is better to let him stand."

"Nonsense! Is it not written, that generosity is the path to Allah's grace? Let him eat! Atagoom!"

"Lord?"

"Release his hands so that he may enjoy the scraps. Stand close to him. If he moves other than to eat kill him quickly."

Atagoom untied the prisoner's hands. Moussa rubbed his wrists. He looked at the food and stepped forward, then stopped. Jubar Pasha looked at him quizzically.

"You are not hungry? You eat so well, in your quarters? I must have the rations cut then, for all the men."

"I have no interest in eating with you."

Jubar Pasha laughed delightedly. "How I enjoy impertinence from a noble slave! Such excellent breeding in a half-breed! You wear the mantle of arrogance so well. It becomes you!"

"You did not bring me here to feed me."

The pasha's eyes sparkled with brandy and well-laid plans. "No, Moussa deVries. Or Count deVries, should I say? You are quite right. I did not bring you here to feed you. I brought you here to kill you."

Moussa stiffened. *Count deVries!* No one had ever called him that. How would this man know? All this time he had thought himself a common prisoner, the chance casualty of a desert ambush. Obviously he had been naïve. There was more at work here, much more. He felt Atagoom's hand on his shoulder. The guard had noticed his slight movement. He was alert and would tolerate nothing.

The pasha also noted his instinctive reaction. "You need fear nothing, Count. It will be done quickly, I assure you. I am a humane man—even to an infidel. And such an infidel! Twice over, I believe. The French infidel—Christian, I suppose?" There was no response from Moussa. "And the Tuareg infidel. Such a pity, that two halves should add up to less than nothing. If only you were a believer you would stand this night at the side of the Prophet himself, in paradise. Such a noble thing you do for the house of Islam, without doing a thing at all."

El Hussein was disturbed. The pasha was saying too much, his tongue loosened by the unfamiliar liquor. He raised the voice of caution. "I do not think it wise, lord, to tell him—"

"What difference does it make?" The pasha waved him off. "What does a man remember from the grave? That he has been betrayed?"

"You speak in riddles," Moussa said.

The pasha looked at Moussa triumphantly. "There is no riddle, Targui. Yes, you have been betrayed. Not once, like a common man, but many times, like a king! Such disloyalty, from one's own! It does pain me, to see a man treated so poorly by his own kind." He corrected himself. "*Kinds*. I forget myself with a half-breed." He took a long drink straight from the carafe, then wiped his mouth on his sleeve.

"A man should know before he dies just how much he matters, or how little. Evidently you matter not at all. So many people who wish you ill, and so much money to pay for it! I do not agree, of course, in the senseless disposal of a man. Even half a man. I could use you in my foggaras."

A thought occurred to the pasha that seemed to amuse him. "There is such irony here! Only this afternoon the master of the foggaras was flogged for allowing you to come so near death. It was contrary to his instructions and would have been most unfortunate." Moussa's eyes betrayed his surprise. "Ah yes, I know of the flood. I know of all things that happen to you. I have kept you alive, Moussa deVries, and quite carefully so. But I am only a simple desert man. Now I must bow to the winds of persuasion."

"Lord," El Hussein said again impatiently. "Forgive me, but please, this is enough."

Jubar Pasha sighed and took another drink. "Yes, I suppose." He waved at the food. "A pity you will not eat. The food is really quite good. The goats will enjoy it, as the crows will enjoy you. The time has come. Atagoom, tie him."

The big guard moved instantly to obey. He stepped behind Moussa and took his right arm.

Moussa moved without thinking. Like lightning he spun and struck the big man on the ear, a glancing blow that stunned Atagoom but did him no harm. Atagoom swung the palm branch that he still held in his hand. Moussa jumped back, but the branch caught him on the shoulder, the wicked spines ripping his flesh. He grabbed the branch, the spines now tearing his hand, and yanked. Atagoom lost his balance for an instant and tumbled forward. Moussa's knee met the guard's face with a vicious crack. Atagoom bellowed and fell heavily to the floor. Moussa whirled to face the pasha, who was tugging furiously at his belt for his dagger, his mouth open in disbelief. El Hussein was struggling to his feet, reaching for his own weapon. The guards at the far end of the room yelled and started running toward them. Behind them the door opened and another guard ran in. Outside there was more yelling and commotion. Moussa leapt over the plates of food and smashed into El Hussein, knocking him sprawling backward. The pasha was no fighter, his pudgy hand lost in the folds of his robe as he desperately clawed for his knife. Moussa was behind him in an instant, snatching the jeweled dagger from the pasha's hand. He held the pasha around the neck with one arm, holding the knife to his throat with the other. It was all over in a few seconds.

"Move another step and he dies," he barked at the guards, who were nearly upon them, their swords drawn. Jubar Pasha gasped in fright, barely able to breathe. The guards stepped back uncertainly. "Set your swords on the ground," Moussa snapped. They complied quickly.

Moussa looked at El Hussein. "I will take the pistol in your sash," he said. He had seen its handle when the man had beaten him. El Hussein scowled but made no move. "Now!" Still El Hussein hesitated. Moussa's blade pressed into the fleshy neck of the pasha, drawing blood.

"Give it to him, you fool!" Jubar Pasha squeaked. El Hussein drew back his robe and withdrew the weapon. He handed it over. "You will get nowhere—" he started to say.

"Quiet!" Moussa knew he would have to move fast, before they could organize against him. He leaned close to the pasha's ear. "Tell the guard to bring fifteen camels. Well rested, fat humps. And food. Water enough for twenty days. Weapons. Rifles and pistols, with ammunition. They will have everything ready within thirty—twenty—minutes, at the gate. Tell him well, Jubar Pasha. Your life depends on it."

The pasha whimpered.

"Tell him!"

"Do as he says," the pasha gasped, snapping out a stream of orders. The captain of the guard said a silent prayer for himself and his family. His own head would fall from his shoulders this day. He ran from the hall to obey.

Moussa looked at El Hussein. "Take off your clothes."

"What!?"

"Now, quickly. Give them to me." El Hussein's face was dark with humiliation. He was wobbly from the brandy. He took off his rich robes, and his silk shirt, and stopped when he had only his baggy pants left. He looked scrawny and quite pathetic without his rich clothing. He shivered in the cool air of the evening.

"All of them!"

Reluctantly El Hussein complied. At last he stood naked before them. Moussa released the pasha for an instant and held the gun with one hand while he quickly donned the clothes. "The turban," Moussa said. Slowly El Hussein unwound the cloth, which he handed over.

Moussa wrapped it hurriedly over his own head. For the first time in Timimoun he felt whole again, his skin covered and his veins surging with hope. He couldn't help smiling at the sight of El Hussein cringing naked. Moussa looked him up and down, and then laughed. "You are clearly a man of modesty, Ambassador," he said. "And for good reason."

He pulled the pasha to his feet, keeping the pistol jammed to his neck. "Move!" he commanded, and shoved his prisoner forward. They stepped over the food. Moussa stopped and kicked Atagoom. "Get up! Come!"

Atagoom struggled to his feet. He groaned, his mouth a bloody mess. "Leave your sword," Moussa commanded, and it clattered to the ground. "Take us back to my compound," Moussa said. "Do not miss a turn or your master will die. Do it quickly." Atagoom looked at the pasha's frightened eyes, at the barrel of the pistol at his neck. He nodded.

"You go behind him," Moussa said to El Hussein.

The ambassador was mortified. "I will not walk naked through the streets of the town like a common slave—" Moussa lashed out with the barrel of the pistol, opening a small wound on his cheek. El Hussein gasped but began to move.

The guards stood aside as they passed quickly through the doors of the Great Hall and down the stairway. Another small knot of guards stood at the entry to one of the passageways leading to the oasis. Some had flintlocks, all had swords. They watched the procession, uncertain what to do. Moussa spoke to the pasha. "Tell them to stay back. If any man fires, I too will fire. They might miss. I will not."

The pasha cried out at them. "Get away, you fools! Stay back, do you hear?" They melted back into the passageways, helpless, letting Moussa and his captives pass. Atagoom led them back through the maze. Curious people looked at the group, some dropping baskets they carried or gasping as they saw the pasha. Moussa moved them quickly at a half-trot, using the pasha's big body as a shield. He smelled the stench of alcohol and fear mingled in the man's sweat. They arrived at the gate, which opened at a command from Atagoom, and the little party hurried up the path toward Moussa's compound. Jubar Pasha was gasping for breath. The exertion was far more than he was used to. "Please," he said. "I must rest—" Moussa pushed him harder.

They stopped at the gate of the compound, just beneath a torch that was fixed to the gatepost. Moussa spoke to Atagoom. "Fetch the others in my hut," he said. "If you are not back within three minutes your master will die." Atagoom moved to obey, disappearing through the gate into the shadows. Several guards stood inside the compound, unaware of what was happening.

Presently Atagoom reappeared. In the gloom Moussa could barely make out the faces he sought. "What is it?" Abdulahi said, still rubbing the sleep from his eyes. "What is this?" With Monjo and Mahmoud at his side, he moved where Atagoom pointed, to the two men standing by the post. His eyes grew wide as saucers when he saw the pasha, standing like a common man in the darkness. His mouth opened when he realized there was a pistol at the pasha's throat. Next to him stood a naked man, scrawny and shivering in the night. Abdulahi didn't recognize him. He peered carefully at the man with the weapon. In the dim light he still couldn't see his face.

"Our time has come," Moussa said from behind his new shesh. "The pasha himself has been good enough to escort us. Are you ready to leave?"

Abdulahi nearly collapsed in sheer astonishment. "*Sidi?*"

Mahmoud laughed out loud. "Well done, Tuareg dog!" He strode to the pasha and spat in his face.

"Not now," Moussa said. "We must be quick. There is no time to lose." He turned and started back down toward the gate to Timimoun. Without hesitation, Abdulahi and Mahmoud followed. Abdulahi stopped and turned.

"Monjo! What are you waiting for?" The Hausa man had not moved.

Moussa stopped and called to him. "Monjo! You will have no other chance."

"I told you once. I have nowhere to go. Nowhere better than this. Plenty of places worse."

"Stay with me. I will protect you. Don't be a fool. You can't stay anyway. They'll kill you now for sure. *Come on!*"

Monjo wavered uncertainly for another moment. Then he shook his head and muttered a short curse. He fell in behind them.

The camels were waiting. "Monjo, Mahmoud. Check their condition," Moussa said. "Abdulahi, make sure of the food and water. There should be weapons as well." The three men hurried to check, opening packs, feeling pads and humps. They took their weapons from the waiting guards. It was all as arranged.

The pasha caught his breath at last. "You will never escape. My men will find you before this night has passed."

"Then they will find you too, Jubar Pasha. You don't think I would miss a chance to show you Tuareg hospitality on a journey?"

"You cannot do this!" the pasha sputtered. "I will not go!"

"You will." Moussa picked out the captain of the guard. The man's look of misery made clear that he knew he would pay with his life for his failure to protect his master. Moussa cocked his pistol and held it to the pasha's temple. His words were sharp and loud enough for the rest of the guard to hear. "The pasha has decided to travel with us. We will watch carefully. If anyone follows, even ten leagues behind, I will know it and he will die. Do you understand?"

The captain nodded. "I understand."

Moussa looked at El Hussein. "You should put something on. You look like a fool." The naked ambassador stared at him coldly.

The others mounted and their camels rose. Moussa took the reins of the lead camel in one hand and, with his gun at his prisoner's neck, led the procession away from the walls, up the hill past the compounds and into the darkness. He looked back several times. Men were milling everywhere near the walls, but none followed. When he knew a rifleman could no longer see them to attempt a shot, he stopped and put his pistol in his belt. He tied the pasha's hands and got him into a saddle. It was awkward going. Jubar Pasha was fat and out of shape. A man for a litter, not a camel.

When it was done Moussa mounted his own mehari. He looked up into the heavens. The skies sparkled with the promise of a billion stars. The open desert lay before them. He wanted to laugh out loud.

We are free.

He allowed himself a moment to enjoy the new sensation. Then he nudged his mehari forward and led his little caravan into the night.

It took all of Moussa's persuasion to keep his companions from killing Jubar Pasha prematurely. During their imprisonment they had each filled endless hours devising tortures for the very man who was now their prisoner. Greatly tempted, they tormented him with their talk.

They passed a well. Abdulahi dropped a rock down its blackness. They all heard the faint splash. "You will make more noise, much more," he said happily to the pasha, poking at his ample belly. "Can you swim?"

"Drowning is too quick," said Mahmoud, drawing his knife. "There is a more interesting way. Let us feed him to the crows, one piece at a time. He can watch himself disappearing."

Abdulahi laughed enthusiastically. "As much of him as there is, that will be many hours of watching. It is a good plan, Sidi."

Moussa shook his head. "We might yet need him. He is no use to us dead."

"We have no need of a hostage," Mahmoud spat. "No one could follow us the way you have pushed us! It is no wonder people say the Tuareg are mad." They had ridden nearly forty hours straight before their first rest, changing camels frequently. Mahmoud's own backside was sore. He had underestimated his Berber cousins to the south; they were a formidable race indeed. Even by Tuareg standards their march had been extraordinary. Moussa never seemed to tire as he led them across a plateau that ran to the southeast of Timimoun. It was not the easiest path, but Moussa thought it safest. The heights were stony and they would not easily be followed. He intended to skirt In Salah, which would soon be crawling with the pasha's agents, and make directly for the safety of Arak, where there would be Tuareg establishing autumn camps.

But for all their progress Moussa did not relax. "I take more pleasure in freedom than revenge," he said. "I must be certain we are not pursued before giving him up."

"There is nothing barren in revenge," Mahmoud growled, but he let it pass.

It was Monjo who worried the pasha the most. The Hausa rarely said a word, staring for long hours at the captive. His expression was blank, his eyes dark and impenetrable. The pasha split his time worrying about the Hausa and groaning from the effects of the journey upon his aching body.

When they ate it was Moussa who brought food to the pasha. No one else would do it.

"I would know my betrayers," Moussa said to him.

"I will tell you nothing."

"Very well. You heard the Moor. If you do not speak now I will let him have his way with you."

The pasha eyed him fearfully. "And if I tell you?"

"I will let you go—when the time is right."

"How can I trust you?"

Moussa laughed. "An amusing question, just now. You have no choice. But I am a man of my word."

Jubar Pasha decided quickly. He began talking.

THREE DAYS LATER MOUSSA KNEW IT WAS TIME. HE stopped the little caravan. From one of the pack camels he retrieved a *guerba* of water and a small bag of dates. He untied the pasha's hands and gave him the supplies. The pasha looked at him uncertainly.

"You are free to go," Moussa said.

Mahmoud exploded. "*You release this pig?* You cannot be serious! Give him to me!"

"No. He is my prisoner. It is my right to deal with him."

"It is so," Abdulahi agreed, seeing what Moussa had in mind. Monjo just nodded.

At first Jubar Pasha was euphoric. He turned his mehari to the north. And then he hesitated. There was no track to follow. The nearest well was forty leagues distant and he had no illusions about his ability to find it. He wasn't sure of his bearings. "But you must be mad," he sputtered. "This is a mistake. I need more supplies, more water and food. I cannot survive here. Where will I go? What will I do?"

Moussa shrugged. "You are welcome to stay with us, but from now on I will have nothing to do with you. The others will see to your comfort. As it is, I am giving you your freedom. It is all you will get, and more than you deserve."

Moussa's mehari rose to its feet. The four men and their supply animals began to move. Jubar Pasha sat atop his mount, lost and afraid. He watched until they were gone.

"You are too soft, Tuareg," Mahmoud growled, as they pressed toward Arak.

"Probably," Moussa agreed.

"Soft?" said Abdulahi, snorting. "He will have much time to face death. He will perish out there as surely as if you'd fed him to the crows."

"Yes," said Monjo. "Only more slowly."

CHAPTER 33

PAUL LISTENED TO THE MUFFLED SHRIEKS COM-ing from within the cave, where Messaoud was in-terrogating the prisoner.

He had known they were close to Tamrit. He had felt his presence. Tamrit had grown careless. The tracks of his animals were fresh. Instead of running he had re-laxed the previous evening. He had taken tea, assuming his pursuers were soft and lazy like all infidels.

Tamrit had misjudged him.

Darkness had been falling and the attackers couldn't see well, with all the smoke and confusion and shoot-ing. There had been two entrances to the cave. Luck had been with Tamrit and his men and most had gotten out the back. All but the one whose cries filled the air.

The patrol had gone into the cave when the shooting stopped. They counted eight rebel bodies, men with swords or guns.

But they had found other bodies too. Six women and four children, huddled together in a dark corner of the cave. Fire or smoke or bullets—anything might have killed them. He hadn't looked closely. It was enough, that they were dead. They had been inside, with the warriors of the *jihad*. They had waved no flag of surren-der, nor appealed for mercy, nor made their presence known. Instead they had hidden. And then they had died.

Paul noticed his hand was shaking. He took hold of his rifle to still the tremors. He needed to eat something but couldn't. Fatigue clawed at him but there would be no rest. He was close to the breaking point, his insides trembling as badly as his hands. His eyes were glazed, almost wild. He closed them to the vision of the huddled dead in the cave.

Were they the wives and children of the rebels? Nomads? There was no way to know. They could say nothing now. There was no one left to claim them. No one left to tell.

Did it matter, really? There had been so much chaos, so much madness. No one could have known.

He told himself that, over and over. *No one could have known.*

There had been other instances. Once in a village, the next time a caravan. A few guilty men dead, a few innocents gone.

I am at war. War has done it.

It was growing harder to sleep for more than an hour or two at a time. He paced a great deal. He drove himself to extremes. Sometimes he felt himself unraveling inside, but he could not relent. He would show no weakness to his men. He would ask no quarter, and he would give none.

The desert is harsh. Ask the Tuareg about killing. Ask the Tuareg about mercy.

The prisoner's shrieks grew fainter. After a time they stopped altogether.

Messaoud appeared at the entrance to the cave. His face was bloody and caked with grime. He made his way to the rocks where Paul was waiting.

"He is dead, Lieutenant."

Paul nodded without expression.

"He said Tamrit and his men are going to Arak. I think he was telling the truth. He was beyond lying."

"Arak?" Paul had not heard of the place.

"In the Muydir Mountains. The Hoggar, sir. Some of the Tuareg make their winter camp there. It is good news, sir. Arak is quite distant. Tamrit must have tired of our pursuit and seeks safety there."

Paul looked out over the hills. *The Hoggar Tuareg.* "Arak."

"*Oui*, Lieutenant. It is a shame to lose them so, but our mission has been a success. We have driven them away from the French settlements. The threat is ended. The captain will be pleased."

Paul shook his head. "*I* am not finished, Messaoud. It is *not* done."

"But sir, what more is there? They have escaped. We cannot follow them. Not to Arak. It is too far south. *Malish, mektoub.*" He shrugged. It was unthinkable.

Paul watched the smoke rising from the mouth of the cave. A gentle wind carried it away to the south, toward the open desert where it disappeared. He could almost touch it. *How like the smoke is my quarry. How close I am to touching it!*

He could do it. He knew he could. His men were tough and well armed. They would not be caught off-guard; they would not be out-gunned. And if he was wrong? If he failed, if death waited in Arak—yes, even if death there were certain? Well, that was all right. In death he might find release from his madness. In death he might find honor. He would die doing what he must.

"Prepare the men, Messaoud. Tamrit will be traveling more slowly now. He will never expect us to chase him into the Hoggar."

Messaoud looked at the lieutenant as if he had gone completely over the edge. The Algerian relished killing Tuareg and the Senussi and all their lot, but had no wish to die foolishly in the pursuit of such pleasure. "Forgive me, sir, but of course they wouldn't expect it, because they know we would be insane to try. None of us has ever gone that far. I don't know if the men will follow, sir. We have no orders, no maps—"

"You have your orders, Messaoud, and I have no need of maps. Tell the men I will give them each a ten-thousand-franc bonus. From my own pocket. Those who are not man enough have my permission to return to Wargla."

Messaoud passed the word and soon returned.

"Only four men want the money, sir. The rest want to go home."

Paul stared into the smoke, his eyes unfocused. "A hundred thousand."

This time only six men out of twenty chose to return

to Wargla. Messaoud himself was one of the six. As they separated Paul issued final orders about those who had died in the cave.

"Burn their bodies."

"But sir, they are Muslim. To burn their bodies will keep them from their heaven."

"I said burn them, Messaoud. Let other Muslims follow them in peril of their souls."

Lieutenant deVries, Messaoud decided, had indeed gone beyond cruel. But orders were orders and the bodies were burned.

ARAK MADE HER THINK OF HENRI. Every year when the meager rains brought them there with their camels and goats and tents, Serena relived their first journey together through the magical lands near Arak. She could still see it all so clearly: the balloon rising over the dunes, the crash, her instant love for him, his danger at the hand of Tamrit, the night they made love for the first time. All her memories of Henri were sweet, but none sweeter than Arak.

Her little procession passed beneath the towering rock walls of a deep gorge, the early morning light streaming down to bathe the sand floor of the dry riverbed in soft pools of light. The sounds of their animals echoed softly against the cliffs as they moved. She watched the walls for *aoudad,* the wild sheep with curved horns and scraggly beards. If there were many it would mean the rains had been good, and they would be hunted with lances and the Tuareg would want for nothing. If there were few, the coming winter would be difficult, and the Tuareg would have to spread themselves far apart into many camps as they sought pasture for their animals.

Serena was coming early to Arak because Daia's child was due, and she wanted to see her settled before the baby came. With eight children and a dozen slaves Serena had set out from their camp near Abalessa, while the noblemen concluded their affairs with their far-flung vassals and slaves who would remain behind. The men of her own *douar* would not arrive for a week or more, but it was no matter. Generally men got in the way when camps were to be made.

Serena watched for Lufti. He had ridden his mehari ahead, scouting for the best place. *He is a good man,* she thought. Moussa had done well by him. Lufti had come to her immediately upon hearing of Moussa's death. She knew he had worshiped her son. "If it pleases I will serve you and your household as I served my master," he said. "He would have wished me at your side."

At first she had refused to believe the news in Mahdi's letter, certain it was all a mistake. In the evenings she climbed to the rocks overlooking their camp and watched the northern horizon, thinking she would see his familiar figure atop his mehari, returning to camp as always. She could not allow herself to accept the fact of his death, and if she let Lufti into her household it meant a betrayal of her faith in Moussa's survival. If she allowed him in it meant Moussa was dead. So she had declined his offer of service.

But the months had passed and he had not come, and there was no news of him from caravans or travelers. None of his vassals had seen him. Then Mahdi had given her more details when she had seen him at his wedding to Daia—not many details, but enough to dash her hopes, and as she sank into the desolation of grief her optimism had finally died. A mother wanted to die before her children, a wife before her husband. She had managed to outlive both husband and son. It was not the way of things. It was not right. She had lost everyone who was precious to her, first Henri, then her brother the amenokal, and now Moussa. Her nights were long and lonely and filled with private tears.

Serena was a strong woman; her grief would never pass, but she would not be paralyzed by it. She finally accepted Lufti's offer. He brought Chaddy, the bride Moussa had bought for him, and their infant son, Rhissa, and all of Moussa's animals, and overnight Serena's *ehen* was transformed. She was thankful for the many distractions and took enormous delight in playing with Rhissa.

In those months she grew to love Daia as well. Serena had always wondered just how close her son and Daia had been. Daia had seemed as distraught about Moussa's death as she herself had been. Serena knew that Daia wept for him, but if her tears seemed more than those for a friend, Serena never asked for details. It was none of her affair. It was enough that Daia said tender things about Moussa; they sat together at the fire and laughed and wept at shared memories of his mannerisms and humor. They became close friends. As Daia's child grew larger within her Serena took a personal interest in her welfare, keeping her company while Mahdi was away, working leather with her and telling her stories about life in France. Daia always prompted her for more, even when she'd heard the stories a hundred times.

Serena did not envy Daia when it came to the man she had wed. Serena knew all the hard edges of her nephew. She knew he would be gone much from their tent, that he was destined to die violently. The tempests that raged inside him could not be stilled—not by Daia, not by anyone. His hatred for Moussa had always torn at her, but it didn't matter anymore. Moussa was dead.

There were other things that concerned her for Daia's sake. There had been disturbing reports about the Flatters expedition, stories of treachery and poison, and in all the accounts Mahdi had played a major role. There had been a great outcry among the Ihaggaren, but events of the year had kept the nobles scattered throughout the Hoggar, and there had been no reckoning. Moussa's friend Taher had told her what he knew of Moussa's efforts to preserve the honor of the Ihaggaren, and she treasured the knowledge but knew it could only have further alienated her nephew from her son.

Her reverie was interrupted by a piercing cry. Daia was on the mehari just behind her. The journey had been difficult for her. Lufti had rigged two saddles together so that she could ride nearly prone, but it had still been a long ordeal. Daia had not complained. Now Serena could see that her face had gone suddenly white.

"Daia! Are you all right?"

"The water . . . it—it is time," Daia gasped, clutching the pommel of her saddle, leaning sideways as a contraction gripped her. "Ahhh!" She nearly slipped off. Serena quickly moved her mehari alongside Daia's to give her support, while Anna, the old slave who had raised Daia, came up from behind on the other side. What she saw in Daia's face made her worry. Like most Tuareg, Daia was stoic about pain, but her breathing was sharp and shallow. She was suffering a great deal. The women knelt their meharis and helped Daia down onto a pile of blankets. Anna stayed with her a few moments. "All is not well, Mistress Serena," she said gravely. She had been through many deliveries. Outwardly she was calm, but Serena heard the edge to her voice. "There is difficulty. A breech, perhaps."

"Lufti!" Serena yelled up into the rocks, her voice echoing back. Where was he? She couldn't wait. One of their old camps lay just ahead. It was normally a good one, located in an amphitheater surrounded by rocks that provided shelter from the cold north wind. She would get them settled there. They could move later if need be. She gave instructions quickly. "Abdou, Chaddy! Quickly! Make the tents ready, there in the shade!" They hurried off to comply. The youngest of the children, excited to be stopping so soon in the day, scampered off to explore and play in the rocks. The older children pitched in to help the slaves set up camp.

In a few short moments a tent had been prepared for Daia. They lifted her inside, atop skins pulled tight like a litter. Serena and Anna helped get her settled on a soft bed of skins. Already her cheeks were flushed red and she was wet with perspiration. Serena stood aside and let Anna take over. She looked outside and saw Lufti in the distance. He waved when he saw the camp. Behind him rode another man, a Targui she recognized immediately. It was Mahdi.

Serena greeted her nephew as he dismounted. "*Ma'-tt-uli*," she said without warmth. She looked behind him. "Where are the others, Mahdi? Tamrit and the rest? Surely you are not alone?"

"No. They have camped near the gorge. They did not wish to . . . intrude."

"They are wise. Tamrit will never find welcome among those he dishonored. The rest would not find a warm reception here, either."

"Speak for yourself, Aunt Serena. There are others who will not be so cold as you."

"Perhaps. We shall see."

Mahdi looked around, puzzled. He had expected a full camp, but saw only children and slaves. "Where are the others? The amenokal? And Attici?"

"We came ahead. Daia will deliver soon. We wished to make her comfortable."

Mahdi nodded. "For that I thank you." He paused a moment. He knew he had to tell her.

"There is danger for you, Serena. I fear I have brought the French to Arak."

"Danger? What do you mean?"

Mahdi was genuinely worried now, knowing the Tuareg men had not yet arrived. He worried not for himself, but for Daia, for Serena, for all of them. Only that morning he and Tamrit had spotted their pursuers. For weeks they had seen no trace, certain that the French had stayed in the north, where the *ikufar* always remained.

But this Frenchman was different. He did not stop, did not rest. He had abandoned his Arabians for fast Shamba meharis and he traveled light, like a Targui himself. He traveled as if possessed, riding into forbidden land, indifferent to the fact that his life might well be forfeit as a result. It was puzzling. *Ikufar* did not give up their lives so easily.

"This Frenchman is the demon himself." Tamrit had chuckled in amazement when he saw the column of *tirailleurs,* still specks on the horizon when the light of dawn was just bright enough to make them out. He was surprised and delighted. "Into the arms of Islam they ride," he said.

Mahdi had initially shared his enthusiasm. He feared no man—not this officer, nor any *ikufar,* nor any Arab or Tuareg. He looked forward to the battle. But Mahdi had expected all the warriors of the Ihaggaren to be in Arak by now, along with their women and children and slaves. He knew Daia would be in one of the camps, waiting for him. They had talked of it after the wedding. He had come to see her and their new child, if it had been born. He had longed for the day. Now he realized he had brought peril to her very tent.

"You will have to move quickly," Mahdi told Serena. "Without the men of the Ihaggaren you are in grave peril."

Serena shook her head. "Daia is in labor. She is having difficulty. She cannot move, not now. Not for some time."

"Hear me! There is no choice!" He calmed himself. He knew his aunt did not respond to orders. He had to persuade her. "There is a French officer. It will not trouble him to kill everyone in this camp. The women, even the children. No one is safe."

Serena scoffed at that. "Have you forgotten my own past? The French are not demons, Mahdi. I know them well. Spare me, Nephew. Spread your lies among those who know no better."

"This one is not like the others you have known, Serena. I have seen his rage. He *is* a demon. He is a pig."

There was something he wasn't telling her, she knew. "From whence springs such rage? Why has he come here? Why would such a man wish us ill?" And then it dawned on her. "Ah. Sheikh Flatters. This man seeks vengeance for your treatment of his men. Poison for poison?"

Mahdi's disgusted grunt told her she was right. "There is no time for this. Listen to me well," he said. "You must leave immediately. If you will not move Daia then I shall do it myself."

"Then you will have her death on your hands. Perhaps that of the baby as well."

Mahdi cursed. Angrily he pushed past her and went inside the tent.

He could see for himself that Daia was in great difficulty. A spasm made her go rigid, and she arched her back until it passed. Anna held her hand and wiped sweat from her brow. "Get out, woman," Mahdi said.

Anna glared at him, but obeyed quickly.

He knelt near Daia. His face softened beneath his veil. He took her hand in his own. His voice was strong, reassuring.

"It is I, Daia. I am with you now."

"Mahdi," she said, trying to smile but gritting her teeth as the pain swept over her.

"It wounds me to see you suffer so."

"It is not so bad. Like being trampled by mad camels, I think," but at that she gave out a gasp.

"Anna!" Mahdi called out nervously. Men with mortal wounds did not worry him like a woman in labor. Anna returned at once and knelt beside her. Mahdi held Daia's hand while the old woman worked.

"There are no *inad* with you, sire?" Anna asked him. The *inad* were smiths and surgeons, mysterious vagrants generally despised by the Tuareg but quite useful as they moved among their camps. Anna wished for one now. The baby was turned wrong. She was sure of it.

"No."

Anna shook her head, hoping for a miracle. "Then she shall need much *baraka*."

Mistress Serena! Men approach!" Lufti called from his post atop an outcropping from which he could observe the passage that led out to the gorge. Mindful of Mahdi's warning, Serena had sent him there to stand watch. She ran across the clearing and climbed to where he stood.

"Is it the French?"

Lufti peered at them. "No, mistress. I think not. I cannot tell. Travelers, not soldiers. I don't know their tribe. Four men and twice as many meharis."

She watched the little band of men. The one in front wore robes of white. His turban was oddly tied, a cross between a litham and a turban of Morocco. There was a slave behind him leading a few of the camels, followed by two men carrying rifles. *Perhaps a rich merchant,* she thought. It was a rare traveler, bold indeed, who entered a Tuareg camp uninvited, yet this one approached as if without a doubt as to his welcome.

He halted his mehari twenty meters from where she stood. He saw the woman and the slave and watched them without saying a word. Lufti fiddled with his knife in its sheath, uncertain and afraid and all but useless. Serena waited for a sign of the man's intentions. At length he made a soft sound and the camel sank to its knees. Dismounting, he strode directly toward them, his bearing strong and sure. It was then that she knew, even before she could see him more closely. Lufti had seen it at the same instant. They knew his walk as surely as they knew his eyes, that strong, purposeful stride so like his father's, yet so much his own.

"*Master?*" Lufti said it tentatively, in disbelief. His knife fell to the ground and he clutched the amulets around his neck, pumping them as if to summon the protection of their *baraka*. "Oh-oh-oh, is it you truly, or the *djenoum* come to take me?" At last he knew it was not a spirit. He jumped and spun and gave a great whoop. "*Hamdullilah,* sire, you are alive!"

Moussa broke into a run toward his mother, who stood overwhelmed. He swept her into his arms, lifting her easily. He felt her trembling, and heard the cry of delight that rose from her heart.

Then she whispered, the words pouring out in a torrent of French, the language of his childhood. "*Est-ce possible*—Is it—oh, *mon Dieu,* my son, I thought you dead! How can this be? How can this be?"

"Maman, Maman, how beautiful you look! *Que tu es belle!* How I have missed you!" He spun her around, hugging her tightly. She could see his face and she took it between her hands as she spun, crying as she did, tears of joy mingled with those of disbelief. She felt weak with happiness. "Come, come inside, sit, tell me, tell us all—" and then she hesitated, suddenly confused, everything crashing together in her mind, and with growing purpose she led him by the hand across the clearing and into the tent, where Mahdi was absorbed with Daia.

"*Mahdi!*" Serena said, her voice imperious and cold. "A most curious thing. The dead man lives!"

Mahdi stiffened. He turned, his eyes taking in the white robes, the odd jeweled turban, the partially exposed face—and he gasped when he realized who it was. He stood quickly, his hand on the hilt of his sword.

"Cousin." His voice was low with menace.

Daia's eyes opened. Mahdi had only one cousin. "*Moussa?*"

Moussa ignored Mahdi. His eyes brimmed with tears as he saw her. For a moment he couldn't speak. So many thoughts he had had of her, so many dreams of this moment. Finally he managed to nod. "*Eoualla.* Yes."

"How is it possible? I thought you dead! All of us— Mahdi said—I don't underst—" Her eyes went to Mahdi, and she bucked suddenly in pain and cried out. Anna bent over her. "Mahdi," Daia gasped. "Your letter! I have it still! You wrote that he was dead—"

"And that you saw it with your own eyes," Serena finished for her. "And tried to help him. All this time, on your word, we thought my son dead." The pain in her voice was terrible. "I cannot believe such cruelty, Mahdi. Not even from you."

Mahdi said nothing, his hand squeezing, then releasing the hilt of his sword. This was the thing he had feared least, for no man could escape Timimoun. *No man!* His fury was enormous. He wanted to throttle Tamrit and the fool Jubar Pasha with his own hands. He cursed himself for permitting the notion of ransom to override his own instincts. He should have killed Moussa long ago. Now he was tangled in deception before the very woman for whom it had all been done. His head pounded with rage.

"I was mistaken! I did not know! I thought it was you who had fallen—"

"You said in your letter . . . you . . . buried . . . him . . . *yourself!*" Every word was an effort, but Daia forced them out. Inwardly Mahdi cringed at her tone. He knew this damage could not be undone.

"He wrote such things?" Moussa stared at his cousin, shaking his head as the monstrous picture grew clear in his mind. There were so many things he had not understood after hearing Jubar Pasha's rambling story, so many gaps he could not explain. Not until now. There was more sadness than anger in him as the extent of Mahdi's treachery became clear. The long months in the foggaras had been the work of his own cousin. "How can a man despise another so? What have I ever done to you, to earn such treachery?"

Mahdi started to protest again but Moussa cut him off.

"It is time to stop the lies, Mahdi. I had a long conversation with Jubar Pasha himself, only a fortnight ago. He told me a wild tale, a tale of Tamrit and ransom. I thought him mad. By himself Tamrit would never have known enough. I see that now. The pasha didn't know about you—*he just didn't know.*"

"Ransom? Tamrit? What is this?" Serena asked. She was even more confused than before, and was becoming alarmed as she sensed the deadly tension growing between the two men.

There was no time to answer. Daia cried out again, whether from anguish or pain no one could tell. The sound drove Mahdi to action. Without warning he sprang forward and knocked Moussa hard to the ground. They rolled outside, carrying with them one of the posts that held up a corner of the tent. Part of the tent collapsed. Anna leaned over Daia to shield her as the post crashed down. Struggling against shock and labor and fear, Daia yelled past her. "Mahdi! Stop it! Do not harm him!" Her voice was lost in the bedlam.

Mahdi's stabbing knife materialized in his hand. Instinctively Moussa reached for his own, only to realize it wasn't strapped to his forearm. It hadn't been there for months. His sword and pistol were with his mehari. He was unarmed. Mahdi's blade flashed near his neck, but caught nothing except cloth. Moussa grabbed for Mahdi's hand, pinning it to the ground. Their eyes locked as the deadly struggle wore on. "I should have killed you long ago, Cousin!" Mahdi hissed. Hatred burned hot in eyes that already sensed triumph. *I have you now*, the eyes said. *You are mine.*

Mahdi managed to push Moussa back as he sprang up to a crouch, slashing savagely but missing each time.

Monjo, Mahmoud, and Abdulahi had been waiting atop their mounts, expecting Moussa to beckon them inside, when suddenly they saw the two men explode out of the tent. Of the three only Mahmoud was a fighter; he responded quickly when he saw the knife in Mahdi's hand.

"Take this!" he shouted. He drew the pasha's jeweled sword from its scabbard and flung it to his friend. Moussa caught it deftly and spun to face Mahdi. Mahdi turned and ducked. His blade flashed again, this time at Moussa's knee. He caught flesh through the robe. Moussa gasped and staggered back, falling heavily. With incredible speed Mahdi sheathed his knife beneath his sleeve and in the same motion drew his great sword. He lunged but Moussa turned aside and the blade pinged against rock, sparks flying from the cold Spanish steel. Instantly Mahdi struck again, and a second time the blade missed Moussa's head by a millimeter. Moussa rolled to his feet and backed away.

The fight went on that way, Mahdi the stronger and faster of the two, always on the attack, a magnificent warrior swirling and slashing, Moussa on the defensive, rolling and twisting out of the way, the light blade of the pasha's sword no match for the heavier steel of Mahdi's great sword. The two men moved constantly, their blades clashing with frightening speed and power.

Mahdi was a patient fighter, his breathing labored but steady as he moved in for the kill. He stroked and slashed overhead, time and again bringing the heavy steel down, Moussa parrying and blocking and stepping backward, unable to strike a blow in return, Mahdi wearing him down with strength rather than cunning or speed. The mismatch was beginning to show when Moussa, desperate, spun and dropped suddenly to a crouch, clutching his sword to his side so that it came around like a scythe. It caught Mahdi in the thigh, drawing blood. Instantly Moussa spun the other way, unable to get his sword up for another strike but managing a powerful blow with his hand to Mahdi's head.

Mahdi shook it off, wavering only a second before springing forward to attack once again, more determined than ever. But he swung and missed, and Moussa caught his hand this time in a powerful grip strengthened by months wielding a mattock in the foggaras. Mahdi pulled away sharply, but his balance was off and he had no chance. Moussa plunged his sword to the hilt. As quickly as it had begun the deadly struggle ceased. With a long gasp Mahdi sank to the ground.

Mahdi's last thoughts were not for himself or for his soul, or for the *jihad,* or of his loathing for Moussa, who even now stood above him with a pathetic and tortured look on his face. Mahdi worked hard to form the words. Moussa saw his struggle and knelt to listen.

"Get Daia to safety, Cousin," he whispered. "The Frenchman. Tamrit will not hold him long. He will kill her. He will kill you all."

With that he died.

THE FRENCH COLUMN GREW EVER LARGER AS Tamrit made last-minute preparations. It was perfect; they were riding directly into his trap. He could see their meharis plodding along in a line, one after the other, unwary lambs riding to slaughter. They were better armed, but his men outnumbered them three to one and had the advantage of surprise. His men waited on either side of the entrance to the gorge, hiding behind massive boulders. The two with carbines overlooked the approaches, while the four with muskets crouched close to the canyon floor, ready to fire their ancient weapons at his command. After the first volley the fearful wrath of Allah would descend upon the invaders as the rest of his men fell upon them with swords and lances and knives.

Tamrit was impressed with the French officer. It would be an honor to kill such an earnest man.

PAUL'S COLUMN HAD DONE THE UNTHINKABLE, crossing uncharted desert straight to the lair of the enemy. He was proud of the *tirailleurs* who followed him, but found satisfaction not in the feat itself but in knowing that his long tortured road was nearing an end.

He looked at the gorge of Arak, at the massive cliffs rising from the desert floor, and knew instantly it was there they would be waiting. Once before he had felt Tamrit's presence, and had nearly caught him. He felt it again now, a peculiar tingling in his belly. He looked up at the soaring walls of the natural fortress. *A spectacular place*, he thought. *A good place to die.*

His men were somber but alert as they entered the forbidden country of the Tuareg. They were edgy, weapons at the ready, all eyes probing the long shadows for danger. Paul halted them and drew a *tirailleur* aside. He pointed to a massive granite pillar that stood like a sentinel at the entrance to the gorge. Its base was littered with boulders the size of houses, massive rocks that had broken off the walls. The pillar was reflected in a large pool of water, its image dancing through sunlight that gleamed on the surface.

"They are watching us now. Waiting for us just there, I think."

"*Oui,* it is a good place, sir. But I am not so certain they even know we are following. For weeks they have given no sign."

"They know." Paul knew it without doubt. "Besides, you wish to take a chance?"

The *tirailleur* shook his head firmly. "No, sir."

Together they climbed to a place where they had a commanding view of the entrance to the gorge. Paul carefully studied the approaches and the rock walls with his field glasses, following the ledges and contours of the granite. When his plan was formulated he spoke earnestly with the *tirailleur,* giving instructions, pointing to ledges and boulders. Afterward they returned to the waiting patrol and ordered the men into action. Some dismounted, waiting, while others formed into what appeared to be two small scouting patrols. Before they left the lieutenant spoke briefly.

"There will be no prisoners today," he said. "On either side."

Grimly they disappeared in opposite directions, and were soon lost to view in the rocks.

Tamrit watched them coming.

TAMRIT KNEW NOTHING OF THE TACTICS OF WAR. He was accustomed to night attack or frontal assault. His men were out-maneuvered within moments of Paul's attack, flanked on both sides and from above by *tirailleurs* who had climbed into position and rained murderous fire down on them, killing three of his riflemen before they'd had a chance to fire a single shot. The fourth musket misfired, and the two men with carbines had to scramble to safety when they saw they themselves were in exposed positions.

Nothing happened the way Tamrit thought it would. He watched his surprise evaporate, and then saw the Frenchman with a half-dozen men, surging furiously atop their meharis through the gorge toward his position. Tamrit screamed orders at his men, who fell yelling on the attacking force, the wild warriors of Islam swinging their swords as the grim *tirailleurs* fired at them point-blank. Some of Tamrit's men had pistols, which they fired with little effect. The noise was deafening and the still air of the gorge filled with smoke and screams and the panicked cries of the camels. The two forces surged through each other's ranks, and the firing all but stopped as men grew afraid to hit their own companions. The battle became a ferocious hand-to-hand struggle.

It was a thicket of death and Paul was in the middle, sword in hand, the sweat and dirt mingling in muddy streaks that poured down his brow and into his eyes as he attacked and parried and attacked again. It had all happened with furious speed, precisely as he had hoped. He was wounded twice, each time more blood than substance. The wounds seemed only to fuel his intensity as he pressed forward with a ferocity unmatched by any man there. He saw two of his *tirailleurs* killed in the howling crush of swordsmen, a third mortally wounded. But the rest of his men were fighting well, taking a heavy toll of their own.

Finally he saw the man he sought. His back was toward him, but Paul knew him at once by his air of command. The man was shouting orders.

Tamrit.

Paul drove his mehari through the melee, knocking down one of his own men but too intent to notice. Tamrit turned and saw him coming, his litham covering all his face except for his eyes, eyes that Paul could at last see were cobalt, eyes that were unwavering as he drew his own pistol, an ancient weapon. The two men moved toward each other, the rest of the battle forgotten, a noisy abstraction, their attention riveted on each other. Their mounts moved together and Paul was upon him, sword raised. At that instant Tamrit fired straight at his adversary's face.

With a searing flash the powder detonated, but the old gun misfired. The ball glanced off Paul's forehead, ripping a gash in his skin. The impact knocked him from his mehari to the ground. Paul lay stunned, burned and nearly blinded by the powder. Tamrit drove his mount forward, trying to trample him, but Paul's own camel was in the way and in the confusion would not move. Tamrit pounded at the beast with his empty pistol, cursing, and drew his sword to strike it. Paul recovered his breath sufficiently to roll out of the way. He found his sword. Eyes burning, blinking furiously, everything a fog, he struggled unsteadily to his feet, rising up just next to Tamrit's leg. Tamrit saw him too late. Paul drove his sword up with all his force, straight up through Tamrit's midsection.

Tamrit took the blade with a contentment no European would ever understand. Death in the name of Allah was victory, not defeat. With a cry he toppled over, falling directly on top of Paul. On the way down Tamrit tried to stab him but missed. He could not yell, but Paul heard him choke out the words as they both went down. "*Allah akbar!*" Allah is great!

Staggering but fiercely determined, Paul forced himself back to his feet. He stared through burning eyes at the hated creature at his feet, a creature still alive and mumbling devotions to his God and clutching at a belly that was on fire. Paul picked up Tamrit's greatsword and lifted it high on the memory of Remy, on the memory of them all. His head pounding with the passion of his vengeance, he brought it down with all the force he could summon. He brought it down once more and Tamrit went still. *That couldn't be all,* Paul raged. *It wasn't enough.* Long after there was nothing left to kill, he brought it down again and yet again, an awful sound rising in his throat as blind frenzy wielded the heavy blade.

Seeing their leader fall, three of Tamrit's men broke free from the battle and ran up the gorge, intending to regroup in the Tuareg camps where they might find help. Still holding Tamrit's sword, Paul looked up and saw them fleeing. It was only a moment before he was after them, chasing them up the gorge on foot, following as they disappeared into a ravine. He tugged at his belt to get his pistol. He fired once wildly, his vision blurred, eyes caked with blood and sweat and dirt, and heard the roar of battle fade behind him as he entered the ravine. The men he chased were nowhere to be seen; they had disappeared into the rocks.

I have been here before, he told himself, remembering Tadjenout. *Only then they were chasing me.*

He tripped and fell hard. Dazed, he staggered to his feet. Blood streamed from the wound on his head. He wiped at it with his sleeve and moved through the rocks, firing at shadows and voices and anything that moved. Were they firing back, or was that his own gun, splintering rocks and roaring in his ears? He heard a shrill scream and found a man cowering between two rocks. The man looked at him terrified, pleading. He dropped his sword and held his hands out in front of him, as if they might shield him. Paul fired and a neat hole appeared in the man's head, and he fell.

Paul's hands were shaking and it was hard to see. He was dizzy, so terribly dizzy. He looked around through the smoke and saw that he had come near to a camp. He saw tents with red roofs, and the bloodlust rose in his throat. The red roofs meant he was among them at last, among the hated Tuareg, and he knew he would kill them all.

He moved as if through a dream, through the smoke and the smells and the frenzy, everything slowed down, everything eerie and quiet except his own heart, his heart sounding in his head like a cannon. And then a flash, a movement. Someone running? Small—a child? He couldn't risk waiting to find out. He fired. He missed. He moved forward, his step unsteady. A knife flew through the air and hit him in the stomach, hilt-first, and fell harmlessly to the ground. A lance clattered next to him. He saw his assailant and fired again. The man fell. Paul saw he was dressed in Arab robes and his fury rose. *Where are the Tuareg? They cannot hide!* He could not wait for his men, whose guns he heard dimly, firing behind him. *I will kill them. I will kill them all.*

He began running in a crouch, making for the tent. Suddenly a man blocked his way, a man in a white robe who carried a sword. Paul straightened to meet him, but the man deflected his charge and knocked him down. The enemy—yet he didn't strike out with his blade.

"Paul! Stop it!" Moussa yelled, but made no move to protect himself, no move to fight.

"*You.* Get out of my way, damn you," Paul rasped, out of breath. "I'll kill you too, if you don't."

Exhausted, Paul pulled himself to his feet. His gun had fallen somewhere. He couldn't see it. He wanted to raise Tamrit's sword to strike, only his strength was failing him and the heavy blade barely moved. Again Moussa knocked him down with a ringing blow. "Stop it! Enough!"

"It is not enough! Not until everyone . . ." Frantically he felt for the gun, one hand sweeping across the ground, the other wiping away the salt and sweat and blood that was blinding him. And then he had it. He raised it, his eyes pulsing with hatred. Moussa stood there, just waiting to die, and Paul knew he could purge himself if only he could finish, if only he could kill them all, if only he could get his balance. The world was spinning, everything moving and bouncing and out of focus. He wiped again at his eyes and tried to steady his shaking hand, the barrel of his pistol wavering wildly. Again a blow knocked him to the ground, only this time it was not Moussa who had struck it. Paul couldn't tell who it was, only that the blood was too thick in his eyes and he couldn't see and he heard himself moaning like a bull, hurt and angry and ready to kill, but he couldn't kill, he was half-blind and wounded and rolling on the ground.

And he knew his own death was at hand, that they had him now. A feeling of peace swept over him and he wasn't afraid, not at all, but even if it was finished he wasn't going to let them take him so easily. With a huge effort he pulled himself up, raising his gun once more.

Another figure stood before him.

He blinked and tried to clear his vision. He tried to fire but his hand wouldn't move. Someone had it, someone was holding it. He cried out in fury, squeezing his finger. "*Why won't it work? Why can't I kill you?*" Tears welled in his eyes, tears of fury and frustration.

"Paul!"

A woman's voice.

He hesitated, weaving, crying.

"Stop it! Paul! Do you know me?" He looked into her face, and it was swirling, everything was swirling, he was so dizzy. He struggled with his pistol, his hand shaking violently as he fought to understand. A woman. A Tuareg. Yes, he could kill her too.

"Get out of my way," he croaked, his voice choked. "Stop hiding the murderers."

"Paul! I know you, and you know me."

He blinked, still trying to see the face. The voice was soothing, soothing and so familiar.

"Paul deVries, it is Serena. Your aunt, do you hear me? Stop it, do you hear? Do you kill so easily? Have you become such an animal?"

He surged against her, trying to get past, but she was strong and he was weak and she held firm.

"Must kill," he whispered hoarsely. "All."

She slapped him, trying to bring him to his senses. She let go of his pistol and he raised it again, but she ignored it now. "*I* am Targui, Paul. I was Targui when you knew me as a child, in Paris. I am Targui today. I am what you loathe. Do you hear me? *I am what you hate!*"

He shook his head, dazed and uncertain. It was all too much, all too confusing.

"Serena?" *A Targui? Yes, of course. Does it matter?* He tried to stay still, to think, but his hand was wavering and he couldn't think.

"Moussa told me what happened to you. I am ashamed for it. But you have let it ruin you. You have become what you hate. You have become the very thing you set out to destroy!"

Still he struggled with it. He shook his head. She slapped him again, so hard he nearly lost his balance. "Paul! Do you see me? Do you hear?"

He tried to roar at her, but it was only a husky rasp. "Get away!"

Then she took his hand in hers and guided it, until the pistol barrel touched her cheek and he could feel the warmth of her breath on the back of his hand. "If you must hate so much, Paul, then you must shoot me first."

His finger was perilously close to pulling the trigger. He saw the images of his nightmares—Remy, his arm twirling through the air, the butchers at Tadjenout, the poisoned dates and Floop, the flesh of the camel driver Djemel as his companions began to eat him.

And he saw Melika.

His head pounded with it all, and finally the visions all crashed down upon him and he fell to his knees, tears streaming down his cheeks. His pistol fell from his hand to the ground. He buried his face in her robe and cried like a baby.

CHAPTER 34

IT WAS A DELICATE TIME FOR THEM BOTH, THE END of much and the beginning of much. They stayed together in the tent, moving slowly through the sunrises and sunsets, holding each other close while they tried to make their way through all that had happened. Anna did not approve. No Targui noble ever acted in such frontal fashion toward a woman. There were forms to be followed, customs to be observed. But Master Moussa, it was well known, had always been odd.

And besides, he wouldn't leave the tent.

Daia had nearly died in delivery, but after a long afternoon Anna had emerged with a proud smile on her weary face, holding a healthy baby girl.

"She is yours," Daia whispered to Moussa when she could say anything at all. He sat down heavily, dumbstruck, looking in wonder at the tiny face.

"I did not know," he said at last. "I thought the child Mahdi's."

"It was his price for your life. He said he would take the child as his own, if I would marry him. I had no choice, Moussa. He said he would leave you in peace." The thought of her bargain brought tears to her eyes. "It had gone too far then. I did not dare to dream that . . . I did not think it possible that we—" She didn't finish. They both knew.

They named her Tashi. He held her in awe.

Daia grieved for Mahdi at the same time she hated him for his deception. She understood only some of what had moved him, but she knew the heart of it. "He loved me too much."

"That is not possible," Moussa said, "for I love you even more." His own words surprised him, but he was determined to make up for his past reluctance to open his heart to her. In the foggaras, when he thought he might never see her again, his mother's words had haunted him. *I don't know how you can be so quick to show a camel your feeling for it, Moussa, and so slow to show a woman.*

There was much to share and they talked until they were hoarse, trying to recover lost moments and precious thoughts. Sometimes reality mixed with fantasy in Moussa's mind, and he thoroughly confused her with things that had happened only in his foggara dreams. He tested some of those dreams on her to see if they were real, or only his longings. To their delight, many of them were real.

As Daia regained her strength and they found each other once again, sounds of laughter began issuing from their tent, bright sounds that mingled with the voice of Tashi, whose lusty cries rang through the mountains of the Muydir.

One evening Daia pulled an oilcloth wrapping from her pack and took from it the gift he'd sent her from the south. It was the book he'd bought from a trader, the book he couldn't read himself. Moussa's eyes lit up when he saw it, because he saw the pleasure she took from it.

"Let me tell thee a tale," she said, and she read to him, stories of the fisherman and the genie, and Ali the Persian, and Sinbad the seaman, and the other enchantments of Scheherazade. By the light of the candle she read late into the night, Moussa resting on one elbow, watching her face, Tashi sleeping between them. Serena heard it, and thought of another woman reading to another man so many years ago, in the forests near the Château deVries. The sound of Daia's voice was melodic. Serena closed her eyes and listened from her place by the fire, and let herself be carried away. It seemed to her as if something had become complete, as if a broken circle had been mended.

SERENA SAW TO THE CARE OF PAUL'S MEN, ONLY A few of whom had survived the battle with Tamrit. She set up a small camp for them, away from the main Tuareg camp, as she sensed their discomfort. Even though she spoke Arabic and French better than they did and was taking care of their lieutenant, they eyed her with suspicion.

She tended to Paul in a tent of his own. He recovered quickly from the physical effects of his wounds, but for days he lay drained on his mat, his eyes bloodshot and hollow, his spirit sapped. He watched as she moved about the camp, and found her to be the same extraordinary woman he remembered. He thought of how much he had loved her as a child and shuddered at what he had almost done. When she brought him food he accepted it gratefully but with shame. "I don't—" he started to say, but his voice cracked and he couldn't finish. Even looking at her was difficult for him.

She touched his shoulder. "It's all right," she said. "You are with your family now. You need say nothing." Later she heard him sobbing.

She tended him patiently and didn't press him.

ABDULAHI AND MAHMOUD GREW ANXIOUS TO leave for their homes in the north. "You should wait for a caravan," Moussa told them. But Abdulahi snorted at that. "And have them sell us to the sons of Jubar Pasha?" he asked. "We will take the long way around In Salah, Sidi," he said. "Life is lived longer that way."

"And above ground," Moussa said. "Of course, you are right." He gave them fresh camels and supplies. "I owe you my life," he told the little man as they departed.

"Happily, as you are Targui, that means you owe me but little," Abdulahi said. "I will miss you, Sidi." They clasped each other. "There is no dragon so clever as a Tuareg."

"Nor any dog so foul," added Mahmoud, and the two men were gone.

A few days later a large caravan passed near Arak traveling southward, nearly three hundred camels laden with great bolts of cloth and bright beads from Italy, bound for Kano. Moussa sat with its master, an honest man who would not sell Monjo to a slaver, and arranged safe passage. Moussa gave Monjo money, weapons, and clothing for his journey. Monjo found it impossible to believe that after so many years he was going home to Sokoto in Hausaland, a free man. When the time came to leave he couldn't find words. The big man took Moussa by the shoulders and hugged him, and then lifted him completely off the ground as if he weighed nothing at all.

Moussa was haunted with memories of the foggaras, of his own enslavement there. One afternoon he summoned Lufti and Chaddy. Carefully he poured them tea, ceremoniously filling their glasses three times. Chaddy squirmed as the master poured for his slaves. She never grew accustomed to his peculiar habits.

When they had finished the tea Moussa handed Lufti a paper that had been carefully lettered in Tifinar, Arabic, and French. Lufti took it in both hands and looked expectantly at Moussa, awaiting instructions. "Shall I deliver this, sire? To whom?"

"It is already where it belongs," Moussa said.

"A riddle, then? But I cannot read."

"It is your freedom," Moussa said simply. It did not need to be written; it was enough that a nobleman said it. But Moussa wanted to record it, to give Lufti a paper to keep. He remembered trying to do this the day he met him, when the slave boldly cut the ear of his camel, but the old amenokal had forbidden it, telling his nephew he needed to be at least eighteen before tampering with the laws of man.

He had his eighteen years now and more. Freeing slaves was not at all uncommon among the Ihaggaren. Lufti's freedom was long past due.

"But sire, I have no need of this. I have always been fortunate in your household. With you my status has always been more that of free man than slave. Yaya, the others know it well, and envy me for it. And who would feed the spirits for you and keep the evil eye at bay, when you refuse to wear amulets?"

"You are welcome to remain with me always. Nothing need change," Moussa said. "Nothing except that you are a free man, able to own a goat of your own, if that is your wish."

Lufti thought about it and the idea grew in his mind. He looked at Chaddy and there was a broad smile on her face.

To own a goat of their own was a wonderful thing.

ONE MORNING PAUL TOOK UP A WATER BAG AND A lance to use as a staff, and went hiking alone into the mountains. As he reached the top of a path that overlooked the Tuareg camp he saw Moussa next to one of the tents. A woman was with him, and Moussa was holding an infant. His cousin played easily with the child, rocking it in his arms or lifting it into the air and whirling gently around. Paul felt a curious fullness in his chest as he watched. He heard their laughter and it brought a smile to his heart. The sight filled him with longing.

After a while he continued up the path, wandering aimlessly for the entire day. It felt good to walk, to stretch his muscles and breathe the fresh air. It was the first time in months he'd paid attention to his surroundings, and they were lovely. He saw the cone of a volcano, and a gazelle. A butterfly landed on his hand. It always surprised him to see such fragile life in the deep desert. He marveled at the delicate opalescent wings that changed color as they fluttered in the soft light. When he waved gently to let it fly away it didn't want to leave. It was a little thing, but it made him smile.

The next morning as he was leaving camp to repeat the hike, Moussa appeared at his side. "Do you mind if I come along?"

Paul stared awkwardly at the ground. "No. Not if you want."

Moussa didn't try to talk, preferring to let Paul pick his own time. Paul, to his surprise, found that the silence was not uncomfortable. Their strides were uncannily alike, and when one of them wanted to turn or to stop or to climb or to descend they both seemed to do it at the same time, each somehow sensing the other's intent. At midmorning they sat in the shade of a tamarisk tree and Moussa produced goat's milk and cheese. While they ate they watched some mountain sheep moving as if by magic up an impossible rock wall.

In the afternoon Moussa's slingshot materialized and he shot a hare that Paul hadn't even seen, in a motion so quick it was a blur. Paul smiled and gave a low whistle. Moussa skinned it quickly and started a fire. Paul stuck the hare on the end of his lance and began roasting it. He sat back by the fire and lost himself watching the sky.

Suddenly he felt a little nudge. "That's getting a bit crisp," Moussa said.

Paul looked at the smoking ruin and laughed at himself. "I'm not much at cooking, I guess." He cut the blackest part off for himself and gave the rest to Moussa.

As the day passed Paul felt himself letting some of the grimness and the shame slip away, losing himself in the easy company of his cousin, who pointed out landmarks and made little jokes and seemed completely at ease. Paul realized that Moussa hadn't really changed very much. And there was something else. For months Paul had felt like an old man inside. With Moussa he felt like a boy again.

In the afternoon they stopped at a *guelta*. "The first time I came here there was a little crocodile living in this pool," Moussa said. "I don't know how it got here, or what happened to it. I haven't seen it since."

Paul looked at him skeptically. He knelt by the water and put his hand in. "Jesus," he whispered. "It's cold."

Moussa harrumphed. "There's a *guelta* where I swim near Abalessa. When I jump in my head breaks the ice. *That's* cold." He began removing his clothes, dropping his robe, then his pants, and finally, in long stretches, his blue veil, until he stood naked before his cousin. Paul saw the old scar, still prominent, and noticed something that surprised him. "Your face looks blue," he said.

"It's the dye in the cloth," Moussa nodded. "It rubs off. It's why they call us the blue men, idiot. Are you coming?" And he climbed up onto a rock and dove in, making barely a splash. Paul stripped quickly and followed him in, the water slamming his system like an ice hammer.

He came to the surface and sputtered. "Ten minutes in here and I'll bet that's not the only part of you that's blue." Moussa laughed and they swam and splashed and dove off an even higher rock, turning flips in the air before they hit the water.

After they were both shivering to the core they lay down next to each other on the rocks to let the sun warm their backs. Paul nestled his face in the crook of his arm. He closed his eyes and felt the healing warmth on his skin, and he willed the day never to end.

"I'm sorry, Moussa," he said simply.

"As am I. For everything. But it's over now."

THAT NIGHT PAUL JOINED MOUSSA AND SERENA AT the fire.

"I don't know what to say to you," Paul said to Serena as Moussa poured them all tea. "I think I really might have shot you."

She shook her head. "But you didn't. You couldn't, even after all you had been through."

"There was a time when I too would have said I couldn't. But I wasn't *me* anymore. I knew it, but I didn't seem to be able to stop it." He stared into the fire, and when he continued his voice was a whisper. "The things that happened to me weren't as bad as the things I did. No one knows the worst parts. No one but me. I keep imagining—hoping—I was only watching it all happen, instead of doing it myself, but I know it isn't true. Things got all twisted somehow. I found out there's a monster inside me. I don't know if I can ever forgive myself."

"I saw what happened at Tadjenout," Moussa said, "and I know about Aïn El Kerma. I don't know if I would have reacted any differently than you did."

"I wonder. I found myself standing over Tamrit, holding his sword and doing the same thing to him he had done to us. The whole time I kept telling myself I was doing it for honor. *For honor!* The thought frightens me more than anything in my life. And now Tamrit and Mahdi are dead. But others will rise to take their place, just as someone will rise to take mine. So after all the killing, nothing will have been accomplished."

They talked for hours, trying to find sense in any of it, and as they talked Paul felt the terrible weight beginning to lift from his soul. He was awakening at last from his long nightmare.

After Paul had said good night Serena sat talking alone with her son. She worried for Moussa. "It will be difficult for you when the amenokal arrives with Attici," she said. "There are many who are angry with you for the way you tried to help Flatters."

"I didn't try to help him so much as I tried to keep us from hurting ourselves."

"Few will understand the difference."

He shrugged. "All my life people have hated me—for my birth, or for something else. I've been too much of one thing and not enough of another. Too noble or too common, too Tuareg or too French, or not enough of either. Not Catholic, not Muslim. Always an infidel." He saw her eyes mist at that, and reached to take her hand.

"It is not something to fault, Maman. I have always been stuck between worlds. I don't remember it being any better in France than here. It was worse in some ways." He smiled ruefully. "Sister Godrick gave me as much pain as any son of the desert. More, really. I've always been an outsider, on the wrong side of things. I don't suppose that will ever change."

He watched as a cinder rose from the fire to the sky, and lost himself there in the blanket of stars. He saw

Orion's sword and thought of Taka. It was the season to find another hawk, a young one to nurture and train.

"Daia wants to see other places," he said finally. "You've been talking to her while I was away, I see. She is more than a nomad; I think she has my father's need to travel. I've wondered what it would be like to see France again. I think I might take her and Tashi and show her what little I know of it, although now we'll all be strangers there. I loved the château and the woods were beautiful, but I wouldn't want to live there. I wouldn't know what to do with a roof over my head. I had a roof in Timimoun. I didn't like it."

"What will you tell Paul about his mother?" Moussa had told her about Jubar Pasha's confession, that Mahdi and Tamrit had engineered his ransom while Elisabeth had paid El Hussein for his death.

"Nothing, I think. There is no point. He knows her as well as anyone, and this would only hurt him. He will find out what he needs to find out. And he will make a good count, if he wants it."

"Do *you* want it, at all?"

He shrugged. "The title means nothing to me, any more than the money. Better to leave it to Elisabeth and her little schemes, if she wants it so much."

"I think you're wrong about that. And about telling Paul. He knows his mother, certainly, but he doesn't know this. This is more than one of her little schemes, Moussa. She tried to have you killed. It is something he must know. Something he must hear from you."

"After everything that's happened, I worry it will only make him hate me again. I don't want that."

"Nor do I. But you have no choice."

THE NEXT NIGHT MOUSSA COOKED BROCHETTES OF goat over the fire and told Paul the story. Paul was stunned by the accusation. At first he stalked angrily away from the fire, pacing in the shadows at the edge of camp, denying it to himself and to Moussa. But then, as he thought about it, he knew it was true. Under the circumstances Jubar Pasha would not have lied to

Moussa. More important, he'd watched his mother for a lifetime, and knew her obsession with wealth and position. As much as the thought devastated him, he knew in his heart that she was quite capable of striking such a bargain.

He stopped pacing and slumped to a sitting position by the fire. He stared into the flames. "I feel more lost than ever now," he said. "My God, the thought of it. I want to strangle her, Moussa."

"The thought had occurred to me as well."

"Short of that, I don't know what to do. Maybe we should turn her over to the police."

"Which police? African? If Jubar Pasha survived, he *is* the police. I'm certain he didn't, but we're not going to accomplish anything in Timimoun. And in France they'd never be able to prove anything."

"Well, then, maybe we could ransom *her* somehow," Paul said. "Teach her a lesson."

Moussa laughed grimly. "You'd only have to buy her back."

"There's got to be something."

"Do you even want what she's been plotting to have? The estate, or the title?"

"I never really allowed myself to consider it. It was always yours, by right. I don't know that it matters to me, really. At the moment it certainly seems unimportant."

"I don't know much about the law in these things. I suppose if nothing else happens, everything will pass to you anyway."

"More likely to Mother, if I know her," Paul mused. "She's been maneuvering in court for years. I have no idea what she's done. She sent me a letter a few months ago. I read it in Wargla but never wrote back. If I remember she said everything would be final in December." Paul brooded for a while. "I know you don't want it, and I don't either. Certainly not everything that's there. But after what Mother has done it would be wrong to simply leave things the way they are. We have to do *something*. She must be held accountable."

"I'm out of ideas," Moussa said.

"You didn't *have* any ideas," Paul reminded him.

"I guess not."

Paul stood and warmed his back on the fire and then turned around. He was staring absently into the flames, watching the meat roasting on skewers, when a notion came to him. As he thought of it a slow grin spread on his face. "Moussa!" Excitedly he began talking, at first just thinking out loud. Moussa asked a lot of questions and his enthusiasm began to grow. Inevitably, Moussa added a few refinements, and soon the two men were chattering like mad, planning and drinking sweet tea. They sat under the stars and the hours flew by and the night passed to dawn.

CHAPTER 35

AT LONG LAST, THE OLD COUNT AND HIS HEIRS were legally dead.

Long live the new count!

Elisabeth had planned a grand afternoon reception, at which she intended to make the formal announcement. She regretted that Paul would not be there, that he was still playing soldier in Africa. In fact she had had no word at all from Paul, although a month earlier the commandant of the garrison in Wargla had written to assure her that the lieutenant who was fast becoming a desert legend was still very much among the living, but that regrettably, he did not know where. She had known that much from the newspapers, which had reported enthusiastically about the second lieutenant crushing the Saharan uprising, the man who had repeatedly refused promotion and lived and traveled like a native. The story was captivating the press, and the fickle winds of public opinion had begun to shift in a favorable direction. To her delight her son was becoming famous.

She regretted his absence, but the reception would not wait a moment longer. Paul would understand. It was, after all, for him.

And then two telegrams brought glorious word. The first, delivered on a silver tray by the butler, made it seem to her as if God Himself had orchestrated the timing. It said simply:

I have resigned my commission. I am coming home.

Her heart raced at the wondrous omen. At last he had come to his senses! Elisabeth had never been happier. Yet less than an hour later her joy found new heights when the butler gave her a second telegram.

> *It is my sad burden to report to you the unfortunate death of Moussa, the Count deVries. I will soon present myself to you to express my most sincere condolences.*
> El Hussein

PAUL'S CARRIAGE TURNED DOWN THE LONG TREE-lined drive to the Château deVries. He listened to the *clip-clop* of the horse's hooves on the cobblestone and reveled in the familiar sights. The air was crisp and the trees had lost their leaves. He smelled wood smoke from the chimney of the château. It was glorious to be in France.

He saw that the grounds and château were teeming with extra staff, and he permitted himself a little smile. Of course, his mother had planned a party; he should have guessed. It gave him an idea. He looked at his watch. There was still plenty of time. He would make his mother squirm a little before the real party began.

Elisabeth greeted him with her usual breathless cheer, as if he'd been gone but a week and written every day. She regarded his clothing with disdain, turning up her nose at the unsavory appearance of the new count, still dressed in his flannel desert wardrobe. "You really must freshen yourself," she said. "Your guests are due to begin arriving."

"My guests?"

"Of course! A celebration! Now come along for a moment, so that I can tell you why." She drew him into the study and pulled the door closed. "Paul, it is the most *wonderful* thing," she said. "A present for your homecoming. The court has declared you the new count. The papers are on their way here now."

"Really," he said.

"Is that all you can say? '*Really*'? I thought you'd be happy. In your telegram you said you were ready."

"It's difficult to be happy if it means Uncle Henri and Moussa are really dead." He watched her face carefully for any reaction, but she was as smooth as ever.

"Of *course* it is, dearest. But we *must* accept it, and move along."

"I wanted to talk to you about that," he said. "On the train I was thinking."

"Can't it wait?" she asked. "Our guests will begin arriving any moment. You must change into something more appropriate."

"Certainly it can wait, Mother," he said obediently.

"Good," she nodded, "we can discuss it later. Now if you don't mind I—"

"It's just that I don't want to be count," he said. "I'm going to renounce the title. Everything."

She gasped, mortified. "You cannot! It is too late! And what of my friends? They are all coming for this!"

"I'm sorry, Mother, but I didn't ask you to have a party. I don't want it. If the title's mine as you say I'll give it away." He thought his voice was masterfully indifferent, and hoped he wouldn't give himself away by appearing to enjoy her obvious discomfort. He would let her panic for a while. He knew it was cruel, but he enjoyed it.

"This is utter nonsense. You've been too long in the sun! This is not the sort of thing one gives away. It is your duty to accept your station in life. Do that now, Paul. Afterward you will be free to do whatever you wish. Don't you see?" Her eyes were wide with alarm.

"Too much happened in Africa. I've come to realize it means nothing to me."

"Well, it means something to me!"

"Then be my guest, Mother. You take it."

"You know I can't!"

"I'm sorry, Mother. Neither can I."

She was becoming truly alarmed. "You must! Your father would expect you to do it. He would tell you to do it for the honor of the deVrieses."

"What would he care about this? He walked out on his family."

"No, he didn't!" Elisabeth railed. "His letter proved—!" She caught herself, knowing she'd made a terrible error, but she recovered with grace and there was barely an interruption in the flow of her words. "His career, his entire life, proved that he cared about honor. There was nothing more important to him than that."

Paul looked sharply at her. "*Letter?* What letter? And what do you mean he didn't walk out? You always told me he did."

"Did I say letter? I was mistaken. You have me upset, that's all. There was no letter. I meant—"

"You don't make mistakes like that, Mother. You meant exactly what you said." Her expression told him it was true. Paul hadn't expected this, but wasn't about to let go. "Show it to me now, or I'll leave this instant and I'll never come back."

"I didn't show it to you because you were too young then," she sniffed. "It was just a note, that's all. *Rien.*"

He started for the door. "Good-bye, Mother."

"No, wait! Very well." She went to the desk. She lifted the chain from around her neck and opened the drawer. He could see her rummaging through some papers, and then she withdrew an envelope. "As I said it is nothing, really. Read it if you wish. And then you'll see—if you won't do this for me, do it for your father. *He* would have wanted you to do it, for the family. Perhaps I should have—"

"Just give it to me." She handed it to him. She could hear talking and laughter outside. The guests were beginning to arrive. She cursed the timing of this wretched confrontation.

Paul trembled as he stared at the envelope. He recognized the distinctive hand of his father in the word *Paul* written in large script on the front. The envelope showed signs of age and wear. Obviously his mother had read the letter more than once. He looked up at her, trying to control himself.

"How *dare* you keep this from me?"

Elisabeth had never before heard menace in her son's quiet voice. For a brief moment she was almost afraid. But then she took the offensive. "Save your outrage for someone who hasn't spent a lifetime protecting you," she said huffily. "You have never appreciated the lengths to which I've gone in your interests."

"Like hiding this?"

"Yes. *Exactly* like that. It was for your own good. You idolize your father but he was a miserable failure. I was protecting you from him. I was protecting you from his disgrace. After you're through sniveling and you come to your senses you'll see that. If you don't like the disagreeable things that must happen in this world to make your way in it, you had better prepare yourself for a rude awakening. What seems painful today will be worth it tomorrow. The sooner you learn that—"

"Just leave, Mother." Paul sat down at the desk and waved her away. "I want to be alone."

She almost said something, but caught herself. Shaken, she was nonetheless recovering her aplomb. What could he do, after all? Jules had been dead ten years. Paul would be angry with her for a week, and then he would get over it. Life would go on, and someday he *would* appreciate her—for all of it.

"Very well," she said, straightening herself. "When you are finished, kindly come into the party and start acting like the count you are. The guests are coming to see *you.*"

30 November 1870
My Dear Son—
I feel all of the world's weight upon me this night, and I am not strong enough to hold it up. I cannot keep fighting. I have lost my honor. It wasn't stolen from me, as you might someday be tempted to believe. I will not have you harboring false notions about your father. The truth is I let them take it; I surrendered it.
I have felt the hatred of my accuser, and of Paris and all France since the trial. I pride myself

that I did not earn it, but that has not kept the poison from my blood. In my lifetime I have faced enemies whose weapons were deadly, but I have never faced an enemy like hatred. It was stronger than I am, and I yielded to it. And only when I yielded—not before—did I lose my honor. I realize now that the only place to find it again, and take it back, is on the Prussian lines outside the city.

I have fallen short in many things in my life, but I regret nothing more than that I have failed you as a father. My desire to serve my country, to do my duty, has always been paramount. Only tonight do I realize the magnitude of that error. I will never fully understand, and do not ask you to forgive, my treatment of you these past weeks. Such extremes are inexplicable to me, when no one on earth means more to me than you. It was never my intention to do you harm, yet I have done so horribly. I can never express my sorrow to you in such a way that you will feel it as deeply as I mean it.

I have no lesson to leave you, because I have lost my way and no longer know how to guide you. But you have excellent teachers in Henri and Serena. Be good to them, as they have been good to you.

Be strong for the family name.

You have always made me proud.

Your loving father,
Jules deVries

Paul felt his throat burning. A tear streaked down his cheek. He wiped it away and looked out the window through unseeing eyes. *Forgive me, Father. It wasn't the way I thought. All these years, I thought you had left because of me.*

He found himself staring at the drawer where she'd gotten the letter. He wondered what else she might have hidden there—in his best interests. For a moment he couldn't decide. He pulled on the handle, but the drawer was locked. He yanked harder but the desk was old and sturdy and the drawer didn't budge. He crossed to the fireplace and picked up an iron ash shovel. He pried gently at the corner of the drawer, trying not to damage it, but then he didn't care anymore and put his force behind it. With a cracking sound the drawer front splintered and the lock gave way.

There were two bundles of letters inside. He flipped through one. Numbly, he realized they were his own letters to Moussa, dozens of them written over the years. They had all been opened. He set them down and slowly picked up the other bundle, knowing what he would find. He pulled one from the middle of the stack. September 1875. Moussa had been fifteen. Paul smiled as he read it, the letter full of a boy's enthusiasm about a journey with a caravan. He laughed out loud over a passage about a goat, but then his laughter dissolved into anger and his expression went hard.

He thought he had seen the worst of her, in her plot against Moussa. But his mother was a woman of great depth when it came to deception. The memories surged back: he saw her cheating on his father, that night in the pantry. He heard her voice, telling him his father had walked out on them, that he didn't care. He heard her saying Moussa and Serena were dead, when she knew they weren't. A lifetime of lies.

He didn't know which hurt more: the extent of her deceit, or the magnitude of his loss.

He lost track of time as he sat at the desk, reading the letters and thinking. There was a knock at the door and the butler stepped into the room. "Excuse me, Count, but madame has asked me to remind you. Your guests are waiting."

Paul was startled by the form of address. "Not now," he said, starting to wave him off, but then he looked at the clock on the mantel. There was business to attend to. It was nearly time. "Oh, very well. I'll be along in a moment." He put his father's letter in his coat pocket and the other letters back into the drawer. One by one he opened the other drawers, which weren't locked. There was household correspondence, along with numerous invitations to social functions. Nothing of particular interest. Then he noticed the distinctive gray color of a telegram. He pulled it out and opened it up. There were actually two telegrams. One was his own message to his mother. The other was from El Hussein, announcing Moussa's death. Startled, Paul read it twice. Then he thought he understood, and smiled with grim satisfaction. He put the telegrams back into the drawer and stood up.

He saw his reflection in the mirror. His face was as brown as his flannel and he needed a shave. His hair was long, wild, and nearly white, swept back as if he'd just gotten off a fast horse. He thought his eyes looked just as wild as all the rest. *Much too scruffy to be a count,* he thought, but it was time to join the party.

He opened the door and entered the ballroom. Elisabeth had been anxiously watching for him. When she saw him emerge she smiled grandly, acting as if nothing at all had happened. More guests were arriving and she moved quickly, wanting to show him off. She swept across the room and collected him on her arm. "I am glad you've come to your senses, *Count,*" she said, her face radiant. He didn't reply and his look was cold, but she knew her son and she knew that look. He would glare for a few days, and then he would get over it. His very presence in the room was proof. He was coming along. She had won.

With Paul at her side she greeted a succession of guests, stopping to chat briefly with each one. "Ah, Baron!" she gushed happily. "You remember my son the count, of course?"

"Congratulations!" the old man said. "I understand you caught Tamrit. Well done, well done. Brilliant." Paul said nothing. He was preoccupied and kept watching the door.

"Please," Elisabeth prodded him as they moved away. "Do try to be civil, won't you?"

"Of course, Mother."

"Ah, the hero of Flatters," gushed Baroness de Chabrillan, and Elisabeth beamed.

"There are no heroes of Flatters," Paul replied with a frosty smile. "Most of them were butchered or poisoned. The rest of them ate each other." The baroness blanched.

"*Paul!*" Elisabeth said, horrified. "I'm so terribly sorry, Celestine. He's simply exhausted from traveling. He isn't himself. Now, if you'll please excuse us."

She led him quickly away. "That was quite uncalled for."

"I was just being polite, Mother. Your friend seemed so sensitive. I thought she wanted to talk about what really happened."

"No one wants to do that, Paul. You're making me— ah, Monsieur Jacquard! Paul, let me introduce you to the president of the central bank." As she led him through a succession of guests, Paul marveled at her cool poise. Nothing fazed his mother. Nothing at all.

Waiters were circulating with trays of hors d'oeuvres and drinks. Music floated from the ballroom, and the house was filled to overflowing. At the door, the butler was still announcing guests, reading their names from calling cards presented by their coachmen. And what the butler was reading was a litany of official, noble, glittering Paris. "The minister of finance. Countess Greffuhle. Monsieur Jules Ferry. Monsieur le maire de Montmartre. Monsieur le prefect de police. General Georges Boulanger. The editor of *Le Figaro.* Le duc d'Aumale. Monsieur le maire de Paris."

Elisabeth fairly soared through the room on the wings of her pride. The old days, when her efforts to fill such an affair with the first rank of society were a struggle, were gone forever. During the years in which she had headed the house deVries, she had thrown increasingly successful parties, attracting a succession of political, literary, and artistic guests. She had been lavish with her contributions to the arts. And now, whether they came to celebrate her, or her son, or whether they came merely to see each other and to be seen, they *came.* As even the most exalted of them greeted Elisabeth by her first name and she walked with the new count on her arm, she knew the world was hers.

She left Paul talking with General Boulanger and was going to speak with the chef when she heard another announcement from the entry, delivered not in the reserved and dignified tones of the butler, but by someone else.

"Ladies and gentlemen." The new voice was deep and carried like a thunderclap across the room. She recognized it at once, although she hadn't heard it in years.

Gascon! What on earth would *he* be doing here? Puzzled, she looked at Paul, who was still talking with the general. Paul glanced over the general's shoulder, directly at her. He didn't seem surprised. The voice boomed on.

"Ladies and gentlemen, distinguished guests, it is my great pleasure to present the Count and Countess deVries."

The stunning announcement took an instant to register on her brain. She *knew* she couldn't have heard properly. She quickly made her way through the room.

And then she saw. Her hand flew to her mouth, but not in time to cover her gasp. She nearly lost her balance and only the quick action of a passing waiter kept her from falling. No one noticed. All conversation had stopped. Everyone was staring at the door.

Standing in the entry was a tall man, dressed in the flowing robes of the Sahara. His presence was commanding, extraordinary. No man had so dominated the room since Henri himself had stood in it. Next to him stood a woman holding an infant wrapped in thick cloth. The woman wore a scarf over her hair, and was strikingly beautiful. While no one could see the man's face, her countenance showed grace and dignity. Paul crossed quickly to them and conversation in the room gradually resumed, laughter blending with urgent gossip as speculation ran fast.

Out of breath and quite pale, Elisabeth made her way to a chair. She didn't sit, but supported herself on the arm. She realized that Paul was leading Moussa straight to her, and did her best to regain her composure.

Paul had been watching her from the moment he

heard Gascon's voice, thoroughly enjoying the effect Moussa's entrance had had upon her. Now he smiled broadly. "Isn't it *wonderful*, Mother?" he said. "Moussa is alive!"

She nearly croaked her greeting, instead of pouring it out as she intended.

"Moussa! Is it . . . is that . . . can you . . . under there? I thought you were . . . you look so . . . so *well*," she said, doing her best not to unravel, and trying to read the eyes behind the veil. "What an . . . interesting disguise. So . . . *interesting*. How very practical of you." At first her smile looked as if it had been pasted on her face, but gradually she felt herself recovering. "But I am so *happy* to see you."

"I thought you might say 'surprised.'"

"Yes, of course, but what a *marvelous* surprise! And this?" she said, nodding toward Daia with faint condescension. "This would be your—"

"This would be the *countess*," he said, and Elisabeth flinched at the word. "My wife, Daia, and daughter, Tashi. A pity Daia does not speak French; I know how much she would enjoy a conversation with you." Elisabeth couldn't quite make out his tone: was he mocking her, beneath that silly veil? "I must also apologize," Moussa continued, "that I was unable to have a special guest here today. A friend of yours, I believe. El Hussein, from Timimoun."

Moussa saw the color drain from his aunt's face. She sat down so quickly it was as if she'd been dropped. She was having difficulty breathing. "I . . . I don't believe I know the name, Moussa."

"Really. I must have been misinformed. It's just as well; I was unable to locate him anyway. Now, if you'll pardon me, I have some minor business to attend to."

Elisabeth watched him walk off, her mind in turmoil. *Why didn't Paul tell me? Does he know, too, of El Hussein? What is Moussa planning? If Paul knew Moussa was alive then what is all this about being count?* The questions shrieked at her. She wondered where her lawyer, Oscar Bettencourt, had gotten to. The judge had assured her that the decision would be entered that morning, and Oscar was to have personally brought the papers to her before the party, which the judge himself would be attending. Of course he would; he'd wanted to sleep with her for months, and knew only those papers would turn back the covers of her bed.

Whatever Moussa was up to, she knew all was not lost. If the court had already declared Paul the rightful heir, then she had what she needed for a fight, and a fight there would be. She waved at the butler.

"Madame?"

"Take my calèche, and the fastest horses," she said. "Go to the offices of Oscar Bettencourt, on the rue Madeleine." She would feel better with the papers in her possession.

"At once, madame," the butler said, but before he had even turned to go, Oscar Bettencourt himself appeared in the entryway, carrying a heavy box. Relieved, Elisabeth rushed to meet him. "Oscar!" she said, but to her astonishment he waved her off. "Not now, madame," he said.

"*Madame?*" Elisabeth said. "Oscar, what are you doing? Talk to me this instant!" But he was already across the room, falling in behind Moussa and Paul.

"You didn't tell me we would be doing this at a party before all these people," Moussa whispered to Paul as they worked their way through the crowd.

"I didn't know," Paul said, "but I could have guessed. She's holding it to honor the new count, naturally. We'll have to improvise."

"With pleasure."

As Moussa moved through the crowd he stopped and greeted people politely, exhibiting at least a measure of his father's flair. People shook hands somewhat tentatively, trying to decide what to make of the apparition behind the veil.

When they reached the stairway Moussa showed Daia to a chair, where she sat with Tashi. Moussa had explained what was happening to her, but the lights and the candles and the guests were overwhelming, and she kept her eyes on her husband.

Paul and Moussa ascended a few steps, and turned to overlook the crowded room. The noise subsided as Paul called for their attention. "Ladies and gentlemen, it is with great pleasure that I introduce to you my cousin, Moussa, the Count deVries." There was polite applause, most of the guests still uncertain how to react. Their hostess was no guide. Elisabeth had moved closer to the stairway and sat on an overstuffed divan. Her face was a study in neutrality.

Moussa spoke in a rich voice, the guests riveted by the perfect French coming from beneath the litham of the Targui nobleman. "It is a great pleasure to see you all," he began. "For years I have wondered about many of you, as I know you have wondered about my family. I regret to tell you that my father, the Count Henri deVries, died in 1870."

A shock wave of whispers swept through the room. Many of those present had known Henri, while all had heard the stories.

"I have lived away from France for these many years, and in recent months the thought of returning to this beautiful château and forest—and, of course, to the city of Paris—has occupied my thoughts."

Elisabeth closed her eyes. *A fight then. After all my work, it is still not done.*

"I came here today expecting to discuss matters affecting this noble house with members of its family, in private. I did not know this gathering was being held here today, but when I discovered its purpose—to celebrate the Count deVries—I changed my mind immediately. I can see that I am among old friends, and there could be no better occasion on which to share the happy affairs of this noble house." There was polite applause, the crowd growing expectant. "I am aware that even in a republic—*especially* in a republic—the obligations of a family whose roots are those of France herself, are not insignificant. The estate has grown during my absence and deserves to have its affairs properly administered, for the good of its land and tenants and the nation of which it is part. It is time for the count to take his place at the head of this household."

Elisabeth and her hopes sank deeper into the divan until she was nearly swallowed whole. "Are you all right, my dear?" whispered the Baroness de Chabrillan. "You look so pale!"

"Yes, just . . . yes, I'm fine."

"Today," Moussa continued, "on my way here, I visited with officials of the court. An inventory of the estate's assets had been filed there by my aunt Elisabeth, who has so selflessly managed the affairs of the household since my departure ten years ago. I believe she, too, was seeking to settle these complicated matters through the courts, thinking me dead." He raised his hands, palms upward. "Happily, as you can see, I am not."

Elisabeth squirmed inside at the words, but managed the appearance of laughter along with the guests.

"She had made several errors, but all with the best of intentions, I'm sure; and with the assistance of Monsieur Oscar Bettencourt I trust I have corrected them." Elisabeth stiffened. *Oscar! Meeting with Moussa! Then Moussa knew of everything, even the properties acquired after Henri died. Why didn't Oscar—*

Moussa indicated the box in the lawyer's arms. "Monsieur Bettencourt was kind enough to assemble certain papers for me, including the very document declaring me deceased." Oscar handed him the paper, and Moussa tore it up with a flourish. "*Voilà.* Moussa deVries breathes again," he said. There was more laughter. "And now, having reviewed the affairs of the estate and satisfied that they are in order, I must say that I do not feel that my place is here any longer. My wife and I have decided not to make our home in France."

Elisabeth exhaled in relief.

"Therefore, I am pleased to present to you the very man you came to celebrate today. Ladies and gentlemen, my cousin, Paul, Count deVries, to whom I have this day relinquished all right and title to the entire estate." Oscar produced another paper, which Moussa presented to Paul amid applause and congratulations.

Elisabeth ripped herself from her reverie as Moussa's words penetrated her brain. His announcement was as shocking as his surprise appearance had been. *The fool himself has made Paul the count! It doesn't matter what he knows! El Hussein doesn't matter! The courts don't matter! There will be no fight!* In her entire life things had never been laid quite so neatly at her feet, and the wretched little heir himself had done it!

It was Paul's turn to speak, and Elisabeth thought he had never looked more noble, his shabby road clothing notwithstanding. No man, no court, would ever undo what Moussa had done. She was still feeling bewildered; events were moving much too quickly for her to absorb them all. But she found herself able to stand then, and to join in the applause, and she moved closer to where her son stood, to bask in the moment.

"It is with great humility that I accept my cousin's confidence and the deVries estate. I must confess that I am nothing but a simple lieutenant—no, a former lieutenant—in the army. I am afraid that the deVries estate is far too extensive for such a simple man to manage. Consequently I will share with you some decisions I have made, and then I will let you return to the truly important business of this gathering, the fine vintages of Bordeaux."

To more laughter Paul accepted another paper from the lawyer. Paul flashed his mother a brief smile, ignoring her quizzical look. "Ah yes, here it is. First, all of the property belonging to the estate in the city proper, I am placing into a perpetual trust. The proceeds from their sale and administration shall be used for the establishment of a university which shall be named after my uncle, Henri deVries, and which shall specialize, as he would have wished, in the furtherance of geographical and scientific knowledge."

There was enthusiastic applause. "Bravo! *Magnifique!*" Elisabeth nodded blankly at the congratulations people were showering on her, her face frozen in a vacant smile as she ran the figures in her mind. This was preposterous! Out of the question. Her son had no idea! The *Paris* properties! He was talking about millions of francs, tens of millions. She would have to undo this folly later, in private with her son.

But then he went on.

"And I wish to announce the grant of twelve million francs to the Société Géographique . . . two and one-half to the national theater . . . two million to the ballet . . . three million to the Louvre, for the restoration of works damaged during the war. . . ." At each new figure the crowd gasped, while at each new height Elisabeth came closer to crumpling altogether. The amounts were staggering.

But he went on.

"There are twenty valiant men who fought with me in the Sahara, when we chased the rebels Tamrit and Mahdi. Most of them died in that effort. To each of their families I had promised a hundred thousand francs. . . ."

And he went on. The vineyards in Burgundy, the holdings in Provence, the lands in the Midi, the securities in the Bourse . . . And on . . . "And I must not forget the farms that have belonged to the house deVries for hundreds of years. Those farms, and their animals and tools, are all granted to the families who have worked them. . . ." For ten minutes the guests stood absorbing news of the most prodigious shower of wealth that had rained on charities and causes and individuals in the memory of anyone present.

As Paul read from the paper Oscar Bettencourt studiously avoided meeting Elisabeth's gaze. Paul and Moussa had arrived in Paris several days earlier and had appeared unannounced in his offices. It was a great shock to Oscar when he realized it was Moussa himself, the rightful Count deVries, who stood in his foyer. Even so he refused to cooperate at first, telling the two men somewhat pedantically that Elisabeth was his client, not the estate.

"You're quite correct," Moussa had said. "I suppose the first thing I'll need to do once I've retained a new lawyer is to examine your conduct of the affairs of my estate during my absence." Oscar had instantly seized the opportunity to become more helpful.

The results were breathtaking, and now as Paul summarized their efforts there was disbelief and awe at the scale of it all, at the extraordinary generosity—the sheer lunacy, many thought—of the new count. The editor of *Le Figaro* was busily scribbling notes like a novice reporter, trying to capture details for the huge story that would stun all France the next morning.

"What remains of the estate," Paul concluded, "besides the château and its forests, which I intend to retain, are the seven farms granted to Comte Auguste deVries by Louis IX for services rendered to the king during the seventh Crusade. These farms have always represented the foundation of the strength of the estate." Paul heard his mother give a little moan at his mention of the last of the holdings. "I give them in free title to a man who served Count Henri deVries with equal distinction, Gascon Villiers."

Gascon stood anonymously and proudly in the back of the room, eyes glistening.

Paul smiled at Moussa. Their work was nearly complete. They had dismantled it all. As much as Elisabeth sought to mask her feelings, the look on her face bore clear witness to what a devastating stroke it had been. But Paul needed to finish it. There was something left, something he hadn't discussed with Moussa. Something just for her.

"In closing, I have saved the most important announcement for last." The crowd hushed, wondering what could possibly be more momentous than what had already transpired. "I cannot overlook my mother, a woman well known to you all." Elisabeth forced a brave smile to acknowledge the polite applause, wondering what pittance he'd left for her, after his charitable insanity.

"I announce that Elisabeth deVries is disinherited from the estate and its remaining assets. She is banned from its grounds. She may take whatever clothing and personal effects she can carry in a calèche, and nothing more. She is never to return." Paul's face showed no emotion as he said the words.

There were gasps of disbelief as the astonished guests looked from son to mother and back to son again, to see if this had been some enormous joke. But the face of the Count deVries was set like stone, and Elisabeth's had lost all color. Slowly the whispers faded into a dead silence. Elisabeth took a few unsteady steps toward her son.

"Paul!" Her voice fluttered weakly. Her self-assurance had vanished along with her dreams. "Stop this! You must stop this horrid little charade at once! It isn't amusing, not at all! Tell them—tell everyone this is just—" But as she tried to touch him, he drew back from her, his eyes cold.

"If you do not leave now," replied the voice of ice, "I myself will call upon the prefect to remove you."

He could not have stricken a deadlier blow with a weapon.

Moussa remembered a time when, as a boy, he had left a man to die in the desert, a Shamba raider who had tried to harm his mother. He remembered the man's cry as he understood his fate. He thought it was nothing compared to what he heard then, from his own aunt.

H ALF AN HOUR LATER MOST OF THE GUESTS HAD departed, embarrassed, thrilled, and titillated by the afternoon's events. Drinks were abandoned, food left untouched. Paul and Moussa were in the study, with the last of the guests.

Elisabeth walked in. She seemed to have aged years. Her hair was disheveled, her eyes vacant from shock. She was surprised to see guests, and dreaded approaching Paul while they remained in the house. But she felt she had no choice; she had to try once more.

When she saw that Paul was talking to the editor of *Le Figaro,* their heads bowed in earnest conversation, she knew that the whole sordid story was going to come out. And Moussa was talking with the prefect of police. Moussa looked her way and said something to the prefect, who stared at her coldly. She felt herself dying inside. Was that to be next, then? The police? She could not believe the treachery of her own flesh and blood.

Paul glanced up at her. "You are not welcome here,

Mother," he said, and the cruelty in him stunned her anew.

"We must talk, Paul," she said, and for the first time in his life he heard utter defeat in her voice. He almost felt sorry for her. "Please," she whispered. "You owe me that much."

"I owe you nothing," he said. "There is nothing to discuss."

"But one simply doesn't—"

At that moment Moussa approached. "Paul," he said in a voice just loud enough that she heard, "the prefect wishes to know whether we want to press charges." Paul drew him away a few steps, and they turned so that their words couldn't be overheard.

"Of course not," Paul said. "I just want her to stew a little."

"He didn't ask me that at all," Moussa said. "It was the best I could think of for your mother's benefit." He nodded toward the editor of *Le Figaro*. "What's he want?"

"To talk about Africa."

"Your mother thinks you're talking about her."

"Good. I probably should be."

Certain that the morning's headlines would scream scandal, convinced that her own arrest was imminent, Elisabeth turned and did her best to make a dignified exit from the room.

IT WAS NEAR DUSK WHEN GASCON BROUGHT A CAR-riage to the front of the château. Elisabeth watched from her bedroom window. She saw Moussa and Daia, with the baby, climb into the carriage, followed a few moments later by Paul, who was carrying a travel bag. The butler had told her that Paul was going to the train station. He was leaving immediately, but the butler didn't know where.

Now the château was empty except for herself and the butler, who had been instructed by Paul to see her out of the château and to then escort her wherever she wished to go in the city. Elisabeth had delayed her departure with one excuse or another, as she waited for everyone to leave. There was an unfinished piece of business. She hoped she would encounter no trouble from the butler, who had reported the count's instructions with what she thought was thinly disguised enthusiasm. Whatever his orders, she knew she could bribe him if need be.

When she saw the carriage pull away and disappear at the end of the drive, she hurried down the back stairs, carrying a large leather bag. She hesitated, listening for the butler. She heard him in the kitchen. *No doubt stealing the wine.*

She entered the drawing room next to the study and crossed to the wall safe. She fumbled twice, but managed to get it open, and began stuffing its contents into the bag. There were securities and cash and jewelry, and even a few deeds. As she hurried to pack it all in, she felt a glimmer of bitter satisfaction. He might throw her out, but he had not succeeded in stealing *everything* that belonged to her. There was more than enough in the safe to enable her to leave Paris and avoid poverty.

It wasn't what she deserved, but it was something.

THEY STOOD ON THE PLATFORM IN THE GARE, waiting for the train to depart for Marseilles. Paul's bag was slung over his shoulder. Other passengers were gawking at Moussa in his flowing robes, and at Daia, radiant with her sleeping baby.

"Where are you going next?" Paul asked.

"Austria," Moussa said. "We'll stay in Paris a few days, and then I promised Daia the mountains. After that I must have my *djemaa*." A locomotive shrilled its steam whistle, startling Daia, whose eyes went wide, and waking Tashi, who screeched like a hawk. Moussa took her gently into his arms and shielded her face with his cloak. He rocked her back and forth, and soon she was quiet. "I still think you ought to stay a few days," Moussa said, "to put things in order. Your mother will be up to no good if no one's there to watch."

Paul shrugged, feeling an odd mixture of elation and depression at the events of the day. He had enjoyed himself and hated himself at the same time. Now he was drained, and didn't care what his mother did. "I have no doubt she will. But it doesn't really matter now. Almost everything is done. And Gascon will be there. He's going to pick up his things tonight and he's moving back into the château until I return. Besides, Wargla won't wait. I've been away too long already." Paul had watched Moussa with Daia for a month. He saw the tenderness between them, and it had fueled his longing.

Moussa nodded. "I understand. Until September, then."

"I'll be there." They had agreed to meet in Algiers in nine months. Paul turned to Daia and took her hands in his own. "*Ehentaúded*," he said. "Good-bye. When I see you again I'll know enough Tamashek and you'll know enough French that we can both laugh at Moussa in the same language for a change." Moussa translated and Daia smiled. "*Ar essaret*," she said, kissing him on both cheeks. "One needs no language for such laughter. Fare well in Wargla."

Moussa carefully handed Tashi to her. He shook hands with his cousin, and they embraced. Paul was stepping up onto the platform when he had a thought. He turned. "That telegram was a nice touch, by the way."

"Telegram?"

"From El Hussein, telling Mother you were dead. It doubled her shock when she saw you. That wasn't part of our plan. You forgot to tell me you did that."

Moussa stared at him blankly. "But I didn't."

EL HUSSEIN BENT OVER THE MUSIC BOX, A PORCE-lain treasure from the palace of the czar in St. Petersburg, and turned the little handle. The figure on top, a Cossack mounted on a white horse standing on hind legs, spun around to the music of Tchaikovsky tinkling from within the base. It was magic! He clapped his hands with pleasure. The house was filled with such treasures, tapestries and jewels and silks, more riches than he could imagine. He put the music box carefully into the carton with the other things, on the floor next to the bag in which pile after pile of new franc notes were stacked. He hadn't taken the time to count. It was well over a million francs: he knew it without counting. Enough to keep him quite well for a considerable period of time.

He turned and stepped over the body. He had not wished to do her harm, not at all. She was far too beautiful, a treasure as exquisite as the objects that filled the château. It was most unfortunate. But alas, what was one to do? Upon arriving in Paris he had come directly there, intending to deceive the countess into thinking that her nephew was dead. To accomplish his end he had brought a piece of skin from the leg of an unfortunate slave whose coloring was similar to Moussa's. The skin bore an old scar. El Hussein doubted the woman would know the difference.

He had seen the carriages assembled for the grand party, and had hidden in the woods, watching and waiting for his opportunity. Then had come the great shock of seeing Moussa himself leaving the château. He had never expected that; he thought the Targui would have stayed in the deep desert after escaping from Timimoun. Of course, his plan to deceive Elisabeth was ruined now. The only thing left was to steal what he could from the house.

He stayed hidden until the carriage was gone. The house appeared deserted. He broke in through a garden window where he could not be seen from the drive. He had found her there, emptying the safe. She had screamed when she saw him, and the fireplace poker had been the only weapon at hand. Now it lay between Elisabeth and her manservant, who had rushed into the room upon hearing her cries. The poker was matted with blood and hair. It was all most unpleasant. El Hussein was not a violent man.

When he finished he led a horse from the stables and harnessed it to a calèche in the carriage house. It took four trips to load everything. There had been more, much more, but he didn't want to be greedy. Greed was a sin.

El Hussein climbed into the carriage, and set off down the drive.

SHE WAS STANDING IN THE GARDEN, HELPING FATHER Jean to right a small peach tree that had leaned too far in the wind. She was tying a cord around the trunk when she saw him. He stood on the far side of the wall, watching, just distant enough that she couldn't see his face clearly, but close enough that there was no question who he was. She recognized his posture and the color of his hair in the sun. She felt an awful sick feeling in her stomach, and her knees sagged. She had to steady herself against the tree. Father Jean saw him then. He looked at Melika and excused himself quickly and disappeared into the chapel.

Melika did not move to greet Paul. She turned away from him, kneeling to clear one of the little channels that carried water through the gardens. While she worked all the anger and the hurt welled up, and she told herself that she must not weaken. She prayed that he would just leave.

But he didn't leave, and soon he stood behind her. "Melika," he said, his voice barely above a whisper. It sent a shiver through her and she dug more deeply in the channel.

"Go away," she said without looking at him. She wiped her cheek. "I didn't want you to come back. I have nothing to say to you."

"I know—" Before he could finish she stood and hurried down the path, and disappeared inside the mission.

He returned the next day, forlorn but determined. She had thought it over through a long sleepless night, and this time when she saw him her anger flared. "How could you come back now? How could you? Just go away," she said. "I do not want to feel that way again."

"Melika, please, if you'll just let me explain. I am sorry I hurt you before. I'm not here to hurt you now. I want all the hurt to be gone."

"So easily as that! It will never be gone, Lieutenant deVries." She fled again, leaving him standing alone in the garden.

He made a little camp outside of town, in the garden of a palmerie where he could sit in the shade and listen to the birds and ruin simple meals on a fire. He avoided the garrison and wandered the souks of the town, where he looked for gifts. He bought a *djellaba* from Morocco and a silver necklace from Tunis. He wrote a note and left it with the gifts on the low stone wall near her room. The next day he saw the gifts were still there. The note had fallen into one of the water channels and all the ink had run. She hadn't read it.

Every day he came back to the mission. Once he thought he saw her looking at him through a window, but then she was gone. The next day he rode a horse into the compound, leading another behind him, wanting to take her for a ride. She loved horses. She sent him away.

Paul had expected her to be angry, but he had expected her to soften. Now his own pain was just beginning to teach him how deeply he had hurt her. He went to see Father Jean. "I know I have no right to ask," he said to the priest. "But I must. Please talk to her for me, Father. Please help her. Please help me."

Father Jean agreed to try. But she waved him away too.

"Perhaps with more time," Father Jean told Paul. "Pray, my son."

Paul felt his desperation mounting. He waited a few days without visiting the mission, trying to give her time. Finally when he could stand it no longer he tried once more. He brought a picnic basket and knocked at the gate. The look on his face tore at Melika's heart. His eyes beseeched her. But she could not bring herself to relent. Her memory of the ache was too strong, and the ache had come from allowing herself to feel something for the man who now stood before her. She wanted him to go.

"*Please,*" she said, looking into his eyes. "Do you care for me, at all?"

"Yes," he whispered.

"Then you will honor my wish and leave me alone. Go back to France, Paul deVries."

Her words crushed him. There was nothing left to do. Defeated, dejected, he left the mission. He opened a bottle of brandy, intending to drink it all. But he poured it into the sand.

He started another note that soon became a letter.

> *Melika—*
> *I cannot hurt you further and will honor your wish. I am leaving in the morning. Nothing in my life has been as hard as this. But I cannot leave without telling you the whole of what happened, why I had to leave when I did. I am not certain I know how to explain, but I must try.*

He dipped his pen into the ink reservoir and poured himself into his words, holding nothing back. He had brought only six sheets of paper and soon filled both sides. He went to the souk to find a letter writer's stall, where he bought more. When he finished it was late afternoon and he delivered his letter to the mission. She wasn't there. He found Father Jean, and put the letter into his hands. "I haven't sealed it, Father. If it's already open maybe she'll feel more inclined to read it. Give it to her for me."

"I'll place it in her hands myself," he promised.

Paul turned to leave when he stopped. "I almost forgot, Father," he said, taking a thick envelope from his pack. "I won't be back again. After I'm gone, open this."

The priest took the envelope, a look of curiosity on his face. "What is it?"

"Something for the mission from someone who didn't need it anymore." Father Jean would never again want for supplies or medicine.

Paul took a blanket from his camp and spent the night on the dune that overlooked the vast desert beyond Wargla. The December wind blew cold off the Sahara. As he drew the blanket around his shoulders he realized it had been a year since he had first stood there, with Remy and Floop. Nearly six months had passed since he had stood there again, with Melika. Now they had all gone from his life and he stood there alone, defeated.

How the world has changed in a year.

He burrowed a niche into the dune where he could sit and rest his back and spend the night watching the stars. The cold deepened with the darkness and he heard the sand sighing softly in the wind. He didn't sleep. When the dawn light was bright enough he pulled his father's letter from his pocket. He opened it carefully. The paper was already beginning to tear along the creases, and the corners were fraying. He read it through and his eyes lingered on the same haunting lines that they always did. *I have never faced an enemy like hatred. It was stronger than I am, and I yielded to it. And only when I yielded—not before—did I lose my honor.*

He had met the same enemy, and like his father he had yielded. They had both paid an awful price.

He could stand it no more. Prolonging things only made the hurt worse. It was time to go. He didn't know where, or to what. For now he would return to the north, and decide when he reached the sea.

He stood and shook the sand from his clothes and the cold from his soul. He took one long last look at the desert. He picked up his blanket and turned to begin the long journey home.

And he saw her, walking up the dune to meet him.

AFTERWORD

THIS IS A WORK OF FICTION, BUT MANY OF THE events depicted occurred much as I have described them.

There are many more accounts of the Flatters expedition than there were survivors. Where conflicting historical accounts exist—as they inevitably do—I have reserved the right of the novelist to make matters suit the story. The fate of the expedition shocked the French nation and managed to accomplish precisely what the Tuareg had hoped: foreign intrusion into the area was halted for more than twenty years. But it was not halted forever, and inevitably the blue men of the Sahara were overwhelmed. In battle after battle they were brutally slain, bravely but vainly using swords and spears and shields of hide against the modern weapons of war. Sporadic revolts against the French continued through World War I, fueled by the Turks and Senussi intrigue. The uprisings were met with stunning cruelty as the French "subdued" the desert.

Ahitagel remained amenokal until his death in 1900. He was succeeded by Attici, whose role in the poisoning of the Flatters expedition was for years a source of shame to those Tuareg who considered such an act beneath the dignity of desert warriors. Attici was amenokal at the time of the final military defeat of the Hoggar Tuareg by the French.

During the twentieth century, successive governments—first French, later Algerian, Nigerian, Libyan, and Malian—have taken from the Tuareg the very things that once made them kings: their land, their freedom to move, their slaves, the caravans they once controlled. Frontier lines were arbitrarily drawn, and borders closed where once no borders existed. The Tuareg were doomed, in part, by their own medieval civilization, destined to see their way of life perish before the relentless onslaught of colonialization and nationalism.

Their life, like the desert in which they dwell, retains a terrible and stark beauty. They remain unbowed, among the more noble and spirited people of the earth. But if their women are still strong and their men still proud, if they are still a race of poets and romantics, they now cast but a small shadow of their former magnificence. Their existence is one of poverty and drought, their heritage lost dreams. To this day, isolated rebellions occur, but the ancient Tuareg ways have passed forever into history.

The trans-Saharan railroad was never built.

The foggaras, a system for water collection of Persian origin, are still in evidence in many parts of the Sahara, although they are no longer maintained by slave labor. For centuries, however, countless slaves lived and labored and died clawing precious water from beneath the oases of the northern desert. The Algerian Sahara at the foot of the Tademait Plateau has huge subterranean stores of water, making a particularly productive area for this system.

DURING THE SIEGE OF PARIS MORE THAN SIXTY balloons were launched over the Prussian lines. Five fell into Prussian hands, while two were lost at sea. Little of military value was accomplished with the flights. Nonetheless they were, after the humiliations of the battlefield, a stirring symbol of French bravery, determination, and ingenuity that inspired the world.

The labyrinth of catacombs, sewers, tunnels, and old quarryways beneath the city of Paris remains today, a haunt of old skeletons and the rats that were hunted and cooked when food ran short in the winter of

1870–71. During the civil war after the siege, a number of National Guardsmen sought sanctuary there and managed to escape from opposing forces by fleeing through the tunnels.

The diocese of Boulogne-Billancourt and St. Paul's Cathedral are fictitious.

In matters of spelling and vocabulary I have taken certain liberties in the interest of clarity. There are multiple spellings for every name, Arabic and Tuareg alike. Belkasem can be Belcaçem or Bel Kassim; Attici is seen as Tissi or Tichi; Ahitagel as Aitarel. I used Wargla instead of the more common Ouargla.

There are a score of Tuareg names for camel, from *akhelkhali* (a simple pack camel) to *amekkalu* (a pack camel walking in a caravan) to *taletmot* (a very fast riding camel). They are all impossible for the Western ear. I have settled on *mehari,* which is, in fact, an Arabic word, used widely throughout the desert.

The name Algeria, as it is used in this novel, applies to only a relatively small area along the north coast of Africa and does not, as it does today, encompass great parts of the Sahara.

ABOUT THE AUTHOR

DAVID BALL has traveled in thirty-two countries on five continents. He has lived and worked in various parts of Africa. He has crossed the Sahara Desert four times, and been lost there only once.

He is a former sarcophagus maker, pilot, and businessman. He has driven a taxi in New York City and built a road in West Africa. He has installed telecommunications equipment in Cameroun and explored the Andes in a Volkswagen bus. He has renovated old Victorian houses in Denver and pumped gasoline in the Grand Tetons.

Mr. Ball lives with his wife, Melinda, and their children, Ben and Li, in the Rocky Mountains.